In the Presence of Mine Enemies

HARRY TURTLEDOVE

NEW AMERICAN LIBRARY

New American Library
Published by New American Library, a division of
Penguin Group (USA) Inc., 375 Hudson Street,
New York, New York 10014, U.S.A.
Penguin Books Ltd, 80 Strand,
London WC2R 0RL, England
Penguin Books Australia Ltd, 250 Camberwell Road,
Camberwell, Victoria 3124, Australia
Penguin Books Canada Ltd, 10 Alcorn Avenue,
Toronto, Ontario, Canada M4V 3B2
Penguin Books (N.Z.) Ltd, Cnr Rosedale and Airborne Roads,
Albany, Auckland 1310, New Zealand

Penguin Books Ltd, Registered Offices:
80 Strand, London WC2R 0RL, England

First published by New American Library,
a division of Penguin Group (USA) Inc.

First Printing, November 2003
10 9 8 7 6 5 4 3 2 1

Part of Chapter I appeared in different form in the January 1992
issue of *Isaac Asimov's Science Fiction Magazine*

LIBRARY OF CONGRESS CATALOGING IN PUBLICATION DATA
Turtledove, Harry.
In the presence of mine enemies / Harry Turtledove.
p. cm.
ISBN 0-451-52902-2 (alk. paper)
1. World War, 1939–1945—Fiction. 2. Germany. Oberkommando der
Wehrmacht—Fiction. 3. Mothers and daughters—Fiction. 4. Berlin
(Germany)—Fiction. I. Title.
PS3570.U76I54 2003
813'.54—dc21 2003008122

Set in Minion
Designed by Ginger Legato
Printed in the United States of America

PUBLISHER'S NOTE
This is a work of fiction. Names, characters, places, and incidents either are the product of the author's imagination or are used fictitiously, and any resemblance to actual persons, living or dead, business establishments, events, or locales is entirely coincidental.

To Ernest Turtledove, Herman Appelman, Bernard Appelman,
Harry L. Turtledove, David R. Friesner, and Ralph Shwartz,
all of whom, along with so many others, helped ensure
that this is alternate history.

I

HEINRICH GIMPEL GLANCED AT THE REPORT ON HIS DESK TO MAKE SURE HOW many Reichsmarks the United States was being assessed for the *Wehrmacht* bases by New York, Chicago, and St. Louis. As he'd thought, the numbers were up from those of 2009. Well, the Americans might grumble, but they'd cough up what they owed—and in hard currency, too; none of their inflated dollars. If they didn't, the panzer divisions might roll out of those bases and take what was owed the Germanic Empire this year. And if they collected some blood along with their pound of flesh, the USA might complain, but it was hardly in a position to fight back.

Heinrich entered the new figures on his computer, then saved the study he'd been working on for the past couple of days. The Zeiss hard disk purred smoothly as it swallowed the data. He made two backups—he was a meticulously careful man—before shutting down the machine. When he got up from his desk, he put on his uniform greatcoat: in Berlin's early March, winter still outblustered spring.

Willi Dorsch, who shared the office with Heinrich, got up, too. "Let's call it a day, Heinrich," he said, and shook his head as he donned his own greatcoat. "How long have you been here at *Oberkommando der Wehrmacht* now?"

"Going on twelve years," Heinrich answered, buttoning buttons. "Why?"

His friend cheerfully sank the barb: "All that time at the high command, and a fancy uniform to go with it, and you still don't look like a soldier."

"I can't help it," Heinrich said with a sigh. He knew too well that Willi was right. A tall, thin, balding man in his early forties, he had a tendency to shamble instead of parading. He wore his greatcoat as if it were cut from the English tweeds professors still affected. Setting his high-crowned cap at a rakish angle, he raised an eyebrow to get Willi's reaction. Willi shook his head. Heinrich shrugged and spread his hands.

"I'll just have to be martial for both of us," Willi said. *His* cap gave him a fine dashing air. "Doing anything for dinner tonight?" The two men lived not far from each other.

"As a matter of fact, we are. I'm sorry. Lise invited some friends over," Heinrich said. "We'll get together soon, though."

"We'd better," Willi said. "Erika's going on again about how she misses you. Me, I'm getting jealous."

"Oh, *Quatsch,*" Heinrich said, using the pungent Berliner word for rubbish. "Maybe she needs her glasses checked." Willi was blond and ruddy and muscular, none of which desirable adjectives applied to Heinrich. "Or maybe it's just my bridge game."

Willi winced. "You know how to hurt a guy, don't you? Come on. Let's go."

The wind outside the military headquarters had a bite to it. Heinrich shivered inside his greatcoat. He pointed off to the left, toward the Great Hall. "The old-timers say the bulk of that thing has messed up our weather."

"Old-timers always complain. That's what makes them old-timers." But Willi's gaze followed Heinrich's finger. They both saw the Great Hall every day, but seldom really looked at it. "It's big, all right, but is it big enough for that? I doubt it." His voice, though, was doubtful, too.

"You ask me, it's big enough for damn near anything," Heinrich said. The Great Hall had gone up sixty years before, in the great flush of triumph after Britain and Russia fell before the planes and panzers of the Third *Reich*. It boasted a dome that reached two hundred twenty meters into the sky and was more than two hundred fifty meters across: sixteen St. Peter's cathedrals might have fit within the enormous monument to the grandeur of the Aryan race. The riches of a conquered continent had paid for the construction.

The dome itself, sheathed in weathered copper, caught the fading light like a tall green hill. At the top, in place of a cross, stood a gilded Germanic eagle with a swastika in its claws. Atop the eagle, a red light blinked on and off to warn away low-flying planes.

Willi Dorsch's shiver had only a little to do with the chilly weather. "It makes me feel tiny."

"It's a temple to the *Reich* and the *Volk*. It's supposed to make you feel tiny," Heinrich answered. "Set against the needs of the German race and the state, any one man *is* tiny."

"We serve them. They don't serve us," Willi agreed. He pointed across the Adolf Hitler Platz toward the *Führer*'s palace on the far side of the immense square next to the Great Hall. "When Speer ran the palace up, he was worried the size of it would dwarf even our Leader himself." And, indeed, the balcony above the tall entranceway to the *Führer*'s residence looked like an architectural afterthought.

Heinrich's short laugh came out as a puff of steam. "Not even Speer could look ahead to see what technology might do for him."

"Better not let the Security Police hear you talk that way about a *Reichsvater*." Willi tried to laugh, too, but the chuckle rang hollow. The Security Police were no laughing matter.

Still, Heinrich was right. When the *Führer*'s palace went up, another huge eagle had surmounted the balcony from which the Germanic Empire's ruler might address his citizens. The eagle had been moved to the roof when Heinrich was a boy. In its place went an enormous televisor screen. Adolf Hitler Platz held a million people. When the *Führer* spoke to a crowd these days, even the ones at the back got a good view.

A bus purred up to the *Oberkommando der Wehrmacht* building. Heinrich and Willi got on with the rest of the officials who greased the wheels of the mightiest military machine the world had known. One by one, the commuters stuck their account cards into the fare slot. The bus's computer debited each rider eighty-five pfennigs.

The bus rolled down the broad boulevard toward South Station. Berlin's myriad bureaucrats made up the majority of the passengers, but not all. A fair number were tourists, come from all over the world to view the most wonderful and terrible avenue that world boasted. Blasé as any native, Heinrich usually paid scant attention to the marvels of his home town. Today being what it was, though, the oohs and ahhs of people seeing them for the first time made him notice them, too.

Sentries from the *Grossdeutschland* division in ceremonial uniform goose-stepped outside their barracks. Tourists on the sidewalk, many of them Japanese, photographed the *Führer*'s guards. Inside the barracks hall, where tourists wouldn't see them, were other troops in businesslike camouflage smocks. They had assault rifles, not the ceremonial force's old-fashioned *Gewehr* 98s, and enough armored fighting vehicles to blast Berlin to rubble. Visitors from afar were not encouraged to think about them. Neither were most Berliners. But Heinrich reckoned up *Grossdeutschland*'s budget every spring. He knew exactly what the barracks held.

Neon lights came on in front of theaters and restaurants as darkness deepened. Dark or light, people swarmed in and out of the huge Roman-style building that held a heated swimming pool the size of a young lake. It was open twenty-four hours a day for those who wanted to exercise, to relax, or just to ogle attractive members of the opposite sex. Its Berlin nickname was the *Heiratbad,* the marriage bath, sometimes amended by the cynical to the *Heiratbett,* the marriage bed.

Past the pool, the Soldiers' Hall and the Air and Space Ministry faced each other across the street. The Soldiers' Hall was a monument to the triumph of German arms. Among the exhibits it lovingly preserved were the railroad car in which Germany had yielded to France in 1918 and France to Germany in 1940; the first Panzer IV to enter the Kremlin compound; one of the gliders that had landed troops in southern England; and, behind thick leaded glass, the twisted, radioactive remains of the Liberty Bell, excavated by expendable prisoners from the ruins of Philadelphia.

Old people still called the Air and Space Ministry the *Reichsmarschall*'s Office, in memory of Hermann Göring, the only man ever to hold that exalted rank. Willi Dorsch used its more common name when he nudged Heinrich and said, "I wonder what's happening in the Jungle these days."

"Could be anything," Heinrich answered. They both laughed. The roof of the ministry had been covered with four meters of earth, partly as a protection against bombs from the air, and then lavishly planted, partly to please Göring's fancy (his private apartment was on the top floor). The

Reichsmarschall was almost fifty years dead, but the orgies he'd put on amidst the greenery remained a Berlin legend.

Willi said, "We aren't the men our grandfathers were. In those days, they thought big and weren't ashamed to be flamboyant." He sighed the sigh of a man denied great deeds by the time in which he chanced to live.

"Poor us, doomed to get by on matter-of-fact competence," Heinrich said. "The skills we need to run the Empire are different from the ones Hitler's generation used to conquer it."

"I suppose so." Willi clicked his tongue between his teeth. "I envy you your contentment here and now. I almost joined the *Wehrmacht* when I was just out of the *Hitler Jugend*. Sometimes I still think I should have. There's a difference between this uniform"—he ran a hand down the front of his double-breasted greatcoat—"and the ones real soldiers wear."

"Is that your heart talking, or did you just remember you're not eighteen years old any more?" Heinrich said. His friend winced, acknowledging the hit. He went on, "Me, I'd fight if the *Vaterland* needed me, but I'm just as glad I don't have to carry a gun."

"We're all probably safer because you don't," Willi said.

"This is also true." Heinrich took off his thick, gold-framed glasses. The street outside, the interior of the bus, and even Willi next to him turned blurry and indistinct. He blinked a couple of times, then set the glasses back on the bridge of his nose. The world regained its sharp edges.

The neon brilliance of the street outside dimmed as the bus went past the shops and theaters and started picking up passengers from the Ministries of the Interior, Transportation, Economics, and Food. *More uniforms that don't have soldiers in them,* Heinrich thought. The buildings from which the new riders came were shutting down for the day.

Two ministries, though, like the *Oberkommando der Wehrmacht,* never slept. A new shift went into the Justice Ministry to replace the workers who left for home. German justice could not close its eyes, and woe betide the criminal or racial mongrel upon whom its all-seeing gaze settled. Himself a thoroughly law-abiding man, Heinrich still shivered a little whenever he passed that marble-fronted hall.

The Colonial Ministry stayed busy, too. Much of the world fell under its purview: the farming villages in the Ukraine, the mining colonies in central Africa, the Indian tea plantations, the cattle herders on the plains of North America. As if picking that last thought from Heinrich's mind, Willi Dorsch said, "How many Americans does it take to screw in a lightbulb?"

"The Americans have always been in the dark." Heinrich clucked sadly. "Your father was telling that one, Willi."

"If he was, he sounded more relieved than I do. The Yankees might have been tough."

"Might-have-beens don't count, fortunately." Isolation and neutrality had kept the United States from paying heed as potential allies in Europe went down one after another. It faced the Germanic Empire and Japan alone a generation later—and the oceans weren't wide enough to shield it from robot bombs. Now it was trying to get back on its feet, but the *Reich* didn't intend to let it.

Just ahead lay another monument to German victory: Hitler's Arch of Triumph. Heinrich had been to Paris on holiday and seen the Arc d'Triomphe at the end of the Champs-Elysées. It served as a model for Berlin's arch, and was a model in scale as well. The Arc d'Triomphe was only—only!—about fifty meters tall, less than half the height of its titanic successor. The Berlin arch was almost a hundred seventy meters wide and also a hundred seventeen meters deep, so that the bus spent a good long while under it, as if traversing a tunnel through a hillside.

When at last it emerged, South Station lay not far ahead. The station building made an interesting contrast to the monumental stone piles that filled the rest of the avenue. Its exterior was copper sheeting and glass, giving the traveler a glimpse of the steel ribs that formed its skeleton.

The bus stopped at the edge of the station plaza. Along with everyone else, Heinrich and Willi filed off and hurried across the square toward the waiting banks of elevators and escalators. They walked between more displays of weapons from Germany's fallen foes: the wreckage of a British fighter shown inside a lucite cube, a formidable-looking Russian panzer, the conning tower of an American U-boat.

"Into the bowels of the earth," Willi murmured as he reached out to grab the escalator handrail. The train to Stahnsdorf boarded on the lowest of the station's four levels.

Signs and arrows and endless announcements over the loudspeaker system should have made getting lost inside the railway station impossible.

Heinrich and Willi found their way to the commuter train without conscious thought. So did most Berliners. But the swarms of tourists were grit in the smooth machine. Uniformed boys from the *Hitler Jugend* and girls from the *Bund deutscher Mädel* helped those for whom even the clearest instructions were not clear enough.

All the same, the natives grumbled when foreigners got in the way. Dodging around an excited Italian who'd dropped his cheap suitcase so he could use both hands to gesture at a Hitler Youth in brown shirt, swastika armband, and *Lederhosen,* Willi growled, "People like that deserve to be sent to the showers."

"Oh, come on, Willi, let him live," Heinrich answered mildly.

"You're too soft," his friend said. But they rounded the last corner and came to their waiting area. Willi looked at the schedule display on the wall, then at his watch. "Five minutes till the next one. Not bad."

"No," Heinrich said. The train pulled into the station within thirty seconds of the appointed time. Heinrich thought nothing of it as he followed Willi into a car. He noticed only the very rare instances when the train was late. As the two men had done on the bus, they put their account cards into the fare slot and sat down. As soon as the computer's count of fares matched the car's capacity, the doors hissed shut. Three more cars filled behind them. Then the train began to move. Acceleration pressed Heinrich back against the synthetic fabric of his seat.

Twenty minutes later, an electronic voice rang tinnily from the roof-mounted speakers: "Stahnsdorf! This stop is Stahnsdorf! All out for Stahnsdorf!"

Heinrich and Willi were standing in front of the doors when they hissed open again. The two commuters hopped off and hurried through the little suburban station to the bus stop outside. Another five minutes and Willi got up from the local bus. "See you tomorrow, Heinrich."

"Say hello to Erika for me."

"I'm not sure I ought to," Willi said. Both men laughed. Dorsch got off the bus and trotted toward his house, which stood three doors down from the corner.

Heinrich Gimpel rode on for another few stops. Then he got off, too. His own house lay at the end of a cul-de-sac, so he had to walk for a whole block. *It's healthy for me,* he told himself, a consolation easier to enjoy in spring and summer than in winter.

The *snick* of his key going into the lock brought shouts of, "Daddy!" from inside the house. He smiled, opened the door, and picked up each of his three girls in turn for a hug and a kiss. They ranged down in age from ten by two-year steps.

Then he lifted his wife as well. Lise Gimpel squawked; that wasn't part of the evening ritual. The girls giggled. "Put me down!" Lise said indignantly.

"Not till I get my kiss."

She made as if to bite his nose instead, but then let him kiss her. He set her feet back on the carpet and held her a little longer before letting her go. She made a pleasant armful: a green-eyed brunette several years younger than he who'd kept her figure very well. When he released her, she hurried back toward the kitchen. "I want to finish cooking before everyone gets here."

"All right." He smiled as he watched her retreat. While he hung up his greatcoat and took off his tie, his daughters regaled him with tales out of school. He listened to three simultaneous stories as best he could. Lise came out again long enough to hand him a goblet of liebfraumilch, then started away.

The chimes rang before she got out of the front room. She whirled and stared at the door. "I am going to boot Susanna right into the net," she declared.

Heinrich looked at his watch. "She's only ten minutes early tonight. And you know she's always early, so you should have been ready."

"Hmp," Lise said while he went in to let in their friend. Meanwhile, the girls started chorusing, "Susanna is a football! Aunt Susanna is a football!"

"Heinrich, why are they calling me a football?" Susanna Weiss demanded. She craned her neck to look up at him. "I'm short, yes, and I'm not emaciated like you, but I'm not round, either." She shrugged out of a mink jacket and thrust it into his hands. "Here, see to this."

Chuckling, he clicked his heels. "*Jawohl, meine Dame.*"

She accepted the deference as no less than her due. "*Fräulein Doktor* Professor will suffice, thank you." She taught medieval English literature at Friedrich Wilhelm University. Suddenly abandoning her imperial manner, she started to laugh, too. "Now that you've hung that up, how about a hug?"

"Lise's not watching. I suppose I can get away with it." Heinrich put his arms around her. She barely came up to his shoulder, but her vitality more than made up for lack of size. When he let go, he said, "Why don't you go into the kitchen? You can pretend to help Lise while you soak up our Glenfiddich."

"Scotch almost justifies the existence of Scotland," Susanna said. "It's a cold, gloomy, rocky place, so they had to make something nice to keep themselves warm."

"If that's why people drink it, your boyfriend is lucky he didn't set himself on fire here a couple of years ago."

"My *former* boyfriend, *danken Gott dafür*." All the same, Susanna blushed to the roots of her hair. Her skin was very fine and fair, which let Heinrich watch the flush advance from her throat. "I hadn't found out he was a drunk yet, Heinrich."

"I know," he said gently. If he teased her too hard, she'd lose her temper, and nothing and nobody was safe if that happened. "Go on. Lise's trying that recipe you sent her."

The girls waylaid Susanna before she got to the kitchen. Though she'd never been married, she made an excellent ersatz aunt. She took children seriously, listened to what they had to say, and treated them like small adults. Heinrich smiled. Come to that, she was a small adult herself. He knew better than to say so out loud.

Walther and Esther Stutzman arrived a few minutes later, along with their son, Gottlieb, and daughter, Anna. Anna promptly went off with the Gimpel girls; she was a year older than Alicia, the eldest of the three. Heinrich Gimpel stared at Gottlieb. "Good heavens, is that a mustache?"

The younger male Stutzman touched a finger to the space between his nose and upper lip. "It's going to be one, I hope." At the moment, the growth was hard to see. For one thing, he'd only just turned sixteen. For another, his hair was even fairer than his father's. And, for a third, he'd chosen to keep untrimmed only a toothbrush mustache; the first *Führer*'s style was newly popular again.

Walther Stutzman differed from his son in appearance only by the presence of twenty-odd years and the absence of even the vestiges of a mustache. As he handed Heinrich his topcoat, he asked quietly, "Tonight?"

"Yes, I think Alicia's ready," Heinrich answered, as quietly. "I told her she could stay up late. How has Anna done, the past year?"

"Well enough," her father said.

"We're still here, after all," Esther Stutzman put in. A slim woman with light brown hair, she peered at Heinrich through glasses thicker than his own. Somehow, in spite of everything, her laugh held real mirth. "And if she hadn't done well, we wouldn't be, would we?"

"Wouldn't be what, Aunt Esther?" Alicia Gimpel asked, a doll under one arm.

"Wouldn't be standing out here in the hall if we expected the curly-haired *Gestapo* to listen in." Esther's grin took all sting from the words.

Imitating her father, Alicia said, "Oh, *Quatsch!*" Anna Stutzman tried to sneak up behind her, but she whirled before she got tickled. Both girls squealed. They ran off together, Alicia's brown curls bobbing beside Anna's blond ones. They were very much of a height; though Anna was older, Alicia was tall for her age.

"Dinner!" Lise called from the kitchen. "Dinner, dinner, dinner!" Everyone trooped into the dining room. Heinrich Gimpel and Gottlieb Stutzman dropped the leaves on the table to accommodate the unusual crowd. Walther, meanwhile, fetched in a couple of extra chairs, and Susanna Weiss placed them around the table.

They all paused to admire the fragrantly steaming pork roast before Heinrich attacked it with fork and carving knife. With onions, potatoes, and boiled parsnips, it made a feast to fight the chill outside and leave everyone happily replete. Most of the talk that punctuated the music of knife and fork was praise for Lise's cooking.

Smooth wheat beer mixed with raspberry syrup went with the meal. The two younger Gimpel girls usually got only small glasses. Tonight, they found grownup-sized mugs in front of them. Francesca and Roxane proudly drained them dry, and were nodding by the time their mother brought out dessert. They munched their way through the little cakes stuffed with prunes or apricots or mildly sweet chocolate, but the filling sweets only made them sleepier. The food and beer slowed Alicia down, too, but she was buoyed by the prospect of sitting up and talking with the adults.

Seeing her daughter's excitement, Lise said, "She doesn't know yet how boring we can be, with our chatter of children and taxes and work and who's going to bed with whom."

"Who *is* going to bed with whom?" Esther asked. "It's more interesting than taxes and work, that's for sure."

Susanna parodied a *Hitler Jugend* song:

"In the fields and on the heath,
We lose strength through joy."

Gottlieb Stutzman blushed almost as red as she had before. She teased him: "Why, Gottlieb, don't you hope to meet a friendly maiden when you go to work your year in the fields?"

"It is not . . . not practical, not for me," he answered stiffly, rubbing a finger over his peach-fuzz mustache.

"It is not practical for any of us, as Susanna knows." Walther Stutzman gave her a severe look. "It is also not practical for us to sing that song anywhere but among ourselves. If the Security Police hear it—"

"It's wiser not to draw the attention of the Security Police, anyway," Lise Gimpel said with her usual solid good sense. "Even children know that." She looked at her own two younger children, who were valiantly trying not to yawn. "After I get the table cleared away, time for the little ones to go to bed."

Heinrich nodded to Walther and Gottlieb Stutzman. "Nice to have some other men in the house for a change," he remarked.

"You are outnumbered, aren't you?" Walther said. "I kept the numbers even. But then, that's what they pay me for." He held a moderately important post with the computer-design team at Zeiss.

Everyone, even the men, pitched in to help Lise cart dirty dishes and leftovers (not that there were many of those) back to the kitchen. The two younger Gimpel girls exchanged their party dresses for long cotton nightgowns. Francesca and Roxane collected kisses from the grownups, then went off to the bedroom they shared—not without a couple of sleepily jealous glances at Alicia, who got to stay up.

Despite being sleepy, Alicia Gimpel felt about to burst from curiosity and excitement. She sat on the edge of the couch. Her eyes flew from her parents to Aunt Susanna or Aunt Esther or Uncle Walther or Gottlieb. As her mother had said, Alicia didn't know what the grownups talked about after she went to sleep, and she could hardly wait to learn.

Her gaze swung to Anna. She stuck out an accusing forefinger. "You've found out what this secret is."

"Yes, I have." Anna sounded serious enough to startle Alicia. She looked back to her father. Behind his glasses, he was blinking quickly, as if fighting back tears. Alicia saw that, but had trouble believing it. She couldn't imagine her father crying. And she couldn't imagine Anna keeping a secret from her. Her mouth twisted down. Her eyes narrowed. It was what her family called her Angry Face. Her father started to raise a hand. Before he could say anything, Anna, who also recognized it, hastily went on, "After tonight, you'll know, too."

"All right," Alicia said, partway mollified. But it wasn't all right. She could tell. "Why are you all staring at me like that? I don't like it!" She twisted around to press her face against a sofa cushion.

"It's an important secret, sweetheart," her mother said. "Come out, please. It's such an important secret, you can't even tell your sisters."

That got through to Alicia. She did pull away from the pillow and stared at her mother, her eyes wide. Her father said, "You can't tell anyone. Not anyone at all, not ever. We've waited till you got old enough so we could tell you, because we wanted to be sure, or as sure as we could be"—sometimes he was maddeningly precise—"you wouldn't give us away by telling somebody you shouldn't."

"I've known for a year now, and I didn't even tell *you,*" Anna said. "See how important it is?" She sounded proud of herself. Alicia looked over to Aunt Esther and Uncle Walther. They looked proud of Anna, too. And they also looked frightened. Alicia had never seen them frightened before, but she couldn't mistake it. Seeing that frightened her, too.

"What's going on, then?" she asked. "You're right, Anna—I never knew you had a secret, and we're best friends." She still sounded hurt, but only a little now: whatever it was, her time to learn it had come. She repeated, "What's going on?"

Her father and mother didn't answer, not right away. They looked frightened, too, which alarmed Alicia far more than the fear on the Stutzmans' faces. Whatever this was, it had more weight than anything she could have imagined. At last, after a deep breath, Susanna Weiss spoke one blunt sentence: "You are a Jew, Alicia."

Alicia stared. She shook her head, as if at a joke. "Don't be silly, Aunt Susanna. There are no more Jews, not anywhere. They're *kaputt*—finished." She spoke with the assurance of one reciting a lesson well learned in school.

But her father shook his head, too, to contradict her. "You *are* a Jew, Alicia. Your sisters are Jews, too. So is Susanna. So are Esther and Walther and Gottlieb and Anna. And so are your mother and I."

He means it. He's not kidding, Alicia realized. Her ears and cheeks felt cold. That meant she was turning pale, all the blood going away from her face. "But—But . . ." She didn't know how to go on, so she stopped. After a moment, she rallied: "But Jews were filthy and wicked and diseased and racially impure." Perhaps trying to convince herself, she went on, "That's why the wise *Reich* got rid of them. That's what my teachers say."

"All the textbook lessons." Her father let out a long, long sigh. "I learned them, too."

Walther Stutzman said, "One of the hardest lessons anybody learns is that not everything your teachers tell you is true. For us, it's twice as hard."

"Is Anna filthy?" Alicia's mother asked.

"Of course not." Alicia got angry at the very idea. She looked over at her friend, still wanting Anna to tell her this was all just a game. But Anna looked back with impressively grown-up solemnity. She'd had a year to think about what rode on holding this secret close.

"Are your father and I wicked?" Alicia's mother persisted. "Is Susanna diseased?"

"I can get to feel that way, the morning after too much Scotch," Susanna said.

"Hush, Susanna," Lise Gimpel said impatiently.

"But—what happens if anyone finds out I'm—I'm a Jew?" Alicia pronounced the name with difficulty; it was too strong a curse to fit in the mouth of a well-brought-up ten-year-old. "If my friends at school know, they won't like me any more."

"If your friends at school find out, dear, it will be worse than that," her father said. "If anyone learns you're a Jew, the *Einsatzkommandos* will come for you, and for your sisters, and for your mother and me, and for the

Stutzmans, and for Susanna—and, after that, probably for other people, too." His voice was usually soft and gentle. Now he made it hard as armor plate, sharp as a Solingen dagger.

Alicia couldn't doubt he meant exactly what he said. She'd learned about the *Einsatzkommandos* in school, too. In the lessons, they were heroes, cleaning up the conquered east and then the ghettos of New York and Los Angeles. But if they came to clean up her family . . .

Her mother tried to soothe her: "Nobody has to find out, my little one. Nobody will, unless you give yourself away, and us with you. We're well hidden these days, the few of us who are left. We have to be." But worry clouded even her sunny face. *She must have learned the same lessons I did,* Alicia thought, remembering what her father had said moments before. *She's scared of the* Einsatzkommandos, *too.* Her mother repeated, "We're well hidden."

But Alicia wildly shook her head. She knew about the millions who had died in Europe and then, a generation later, in the United States. Every schoolchild knew. The *Reich* made sure of that. *And now they'll come for me! Oh, God, they'll come for me!*

"My father helped keep us hidden," Uncle Walther said. "He altered the *Reichs* genealogical database to show that our families are all of pure Aryan blood. No one looks for us any more, not here at the heart of the Germanic Empire. No one thinks there's any reason *to* look. We're safe enough, unless we give ourselves away. Maybe one day, not in our time but when your children or grandchildren have grown up, Alicia, we can be safe living openly as what we are. Maybe. Till then, we go on."

His soft words about changing databases had begun to reassure Alicia. What he didn't know about computers, nobody did. But when he spoke of living openly as Jews, she only stared at him. She felt like an animal caught in a trap. "It will never be safe! Never!" she said shrilly. "The *Reich* will last a thousand years, and how can there be room in it for Jews?"

"Maybe the *Reich* will last a thousand years, the way Hitler promised," her father said. "No one can know that till it happens, if it does. But, dear, there have been Jews for three thousand years already. Even if the Germanic Empire lives out all the time Hitler said it would, it will still be a baby beside us. Uncle Walther was right: one way or another, we go on. It's hard to pretend not to be what we really are—"

"I hate it," Susanna Weiss broke in. "I've always hated it, ever since I found out."

Alicia's father nodded. "We all hate it. But when times are dangerous for Jews, the way they are now, what other choice have we got?"

"This isn't the first time Jews have had to be what they are only in secret," Esther Stutzman said. "In Spain a long time ago, we pretended to be good Catholics. Now we have to pretend to be good Aryans and National Socialists. But underneath, we still are what we've always been."

The grownups all sounded so cool, so collected. As far as they were concerned, everything was fine, and everything would stay fine no matter what. That wasn't how it felt to Alicia. "I don't want to be a Jew!" she shouted.

Her father's head whipped toward the windows. Sudden stark fright filled his face, and everyone else's. Alicia understood that. She clapped her hands to her mouth. If one of the neighbors heard, the Security Police were only a phone call away.

After a deep breath, her father said, "You have a way out, Alicia."

"What is it?" She stared at him, tears and questions in her eyes.

"You can just pretend this night never happened," he told her. "You know we'll never betray you, no matter what you decide. If you choose not to tell your husband one day, if he's not one of us, and if you choose not to tell your children, they'll never know you—and they—are Jewish. They'll be just like everybody else in the Germanic Empire. But one more piece of something old and precious will have disappeared from the world forever."

"I don't know what to do," Alicia said.

To her surprise, her father got up, came over, and kissed her on top of the head. "You may not realize it, but that's the most grownup thing you've ever said."

Alicia didn't want to sound like a grownup, any more than she wanted to be a Jew. She didn't seem to have much choice about either. Figuring that out was another grownup thing to do, not that she knew it at the time.

"It's not so bad, Alicia," Anna said. "I cried, too, when I found out—"

"So did I," Gottlieb added, which made Alicia's eyes widen. He was so much older than she that she thought of him as practically a grownup.

Anna went on, "But it's special in a way, like being part of a club that won't take just anybody. And it's not like what we are is written on our foreheads or anything like that, even though it does feel like it at first. But if we keep the secret, no one will find out what we are. We even have our own special holidays—today is one."

"What's today?" Alicia asked, intrigued in spite of herself.

"Today is the festival of Purim," her father answered. "The Germans and the Spaniards Aunt Esther was talking about weren't the first people who wanted to get rid of the Jews. We've always stood out a little because we're different from the other people in a country. And a long time ago, in the Persian Empire . . ."

He got out a Bible to help tell Alicia the story. Not every family had one in its house or flat these days. Still, the National Socialists mostly tolerated quiet Christianity. Alicia's teachers sometimes made scornful noises about a religion better fit for slaves than for heroes, but she'd never heard of the Security Police paying a call on anybody who believed in Jesus. She didn't know what would happen if somebody made a fuss about Jesus, but people knew better than to make fusses about such things. Christianity that wasn't quiet was dangerous, too.

"And so," her father finished, "King Ahasuerus hanged Haman on the very gallows he'd built for Mordechai, and Mordechai and Queen Esther lived long, happy, rich lives afterwards." Caught up in the ancient tale even though she hadn't really wanted to be, Alicia laughed and clapped her hands.

Very softly, Susanna Weiss said, "I wish someone had built a gallows for Hitler and Himmler. So many of our people gone . . ." She stared down into her snifter of Scotch.

Alicia stared, too—at Aunt Susanna. The first *Führer* and the first *Reichsführer*-SS, who'd later followed Hitler as ruler of the Germanic Empire, were saints nowadays, or as close to saints as made no difference. Even with what Alicia had learned tonight, hearing someone wish they'd been hanged was a jolt. And Susanna . . . Susanna sounded as if she felt guilty for living on where so many of her people—*so many of my people, too,* Alicia thought wonderingly—had died.

"I wish I could tell my sisters," Alicia said.

Her father and Walther Stutzman smiled at each other. A moment later, Alicia discovered why, for Anna said, "When I found out last year, I said, 'I wish I could tell Alicia.' "

Uncle Walther said, "It's new, little one. It's a shock. I remember how confused finding out what I was made me."

"But you can't say anything to Francesca and Roxane, you know—not anything at all," Alicia's father told her. "They're too little. It would be very dangerous. They'll learn when the time comes, the way you have now. If this secret gets to the wrong ears, we're all dead. Just because there aren't many Jews left doesn't mean people won't start hunting us. We're still fair game."

"Are we—the people in this room—all the Jews who are left?" Alicia asked.

"No," her father said. "There are others, all through Greater Germany and the rest of the Empire. Sooner or later, you'll meet more, and some of them will surprise you. But for now, the fewer Jews you know, the fewer you can give away if the worst happens."

Who? Alicia wondered. Her eyes went far away. *Which of our friends are really Jews?* She never would have guessed about the Stutzmans, who with their blond good looks seemed perfect Aryans, not in a million years. Her teachers went on and on about how ugly Jews had been, with fat, flabby lips and grotesque hooked noses and almost kinky hair. It didn't seem to be true. What else had they told her that wasn't true?

Her mother said, "Even though we have our own holidays, sweetheart, we can only celebrate them among ourselves. The little three-cornered cakes we had tonight are special for Purim—they're called *Hamantaschen*."

" 'Haman's hats,' " Alicia echoed. "I like that. Serves him right."

"Yes," her mother said, "but that's why you won't be taking any of them to school for lunch. People who aren't Jewish might recognize them. We can't afford to take any chances at all, do you see?"

"Not even with something as little as cakes?" Alicia said.

"Not even," her mother said firmly. "Not with anything, not ever."

"All right, Mama." The warning impressed Alicia with the depth of the precautions she would have to take to survive.

"*Is* it all right, Alicia?" Her father sounded anxious. "I know this is a lot to put on a little girl, but we have to, you see, or there won't be any Jews any more."

"It really is," Alicia answered. "It . . . surprised me. I don't know if I like it yet, but it's all right." She nodded in a slow, hesitant way. She thought she meant what she said, but she wasn't quite sure.

She and Anna yawned together, then giggled at each other. Aunt Susanna got up, grabbed her handbag, walked over to Alicia, and kissed her on the cheek. "Welcome to your bigger family, dear. We're glad to have you."

My bigger family, Alicia thought. That, she did like. Aunt Susanna and the Stutzmans had always been like family to her. Finding out they really *were* a family of sorts—or at least part of the same conspiracy of survival—was reassuring, in a way.

Susanna turned to Alicia's father. "I'd better get home. I have to teach an early class tomorrow."

"We ought to go, too," Esther Stutzman said. "Either that or we'll wait till Anna falls asleep—which shouldn't be more than another thirty seconds—bundle her into the broom closet, and leave without her." Her daughter let out an irate sniff.

Alicia's mother and father passed out coats. The friends stood gossiping on the front porch for a last couple of minutes. As they chattered, a brightly lit police van turned the corner and rolled up the street toward the end of the cul-de-sac. "They know!" Alicia gasped in horror. "They know!" She tried to bolt inside, away from the eagle and swastika that had suddenly gone from national emblem to symbol of terror.

Her father seized her arm. Alicia had never thought of him as particularly strong, but he held on tight and made sure she couldn't move. The van turned around and went back up the street. It turned the corner. It was gone.

"There. You see?" her father said. "Everything's fine, little one. They can only find out about us if we give ourselves away. Do you understand?"

"I—think so, Father," Alicia said.

"Good." Her father let go of her. "*Now* you can go on in and get ready for bed."

Alicia had never been so glad to go into the house in all her life.

Susanna and the Stutzmans walked off toward the bus stop. Heinrich and Lise Gimpel went back inside the house. Once he closed the door, he allowed himself the luxury of a long sigh of mingled relief and fear. "That damned police van!" he said. "I thought poor Alicia would jump right out of her skin—and if she had, it might have ruined everything."

"Well, she didn't. You stopped her." His wife gave him a quick kiss. "I'm going to make sure she's all right now."

"Good idea," Heinrich said. "I'll start on the dishes." He rolled up his sleeves, turned on the water, and waited for it to get hot. When it did, he rinsed off the plates and silverware and glasses and loaded them into the dishwasher. The manufacturers kept saying the new models would be able to handle dishes that hadn't been rinsed. So far, they'd lied every time.

Heinrich was still busy when Alicia came out for a goodnight kiss. Usually, that was just part of nighttime routine. It felt special tonight.

He said, "You don't have to be frightened every second, darling. If you show you're afraid, people will start wondering what you have to be afraid of. Keep on being your own sweet self, and no one will ever suspect a thing."

"I'll try, Papa." When Alicia hugged him, she clung for a few extra seconds. He squeezed her and ran his hand through her hair. "Good night," she said, and hurried away.

He let out another sigh, even longer than the first. Finding out you were a Jew in the heart of the National Socialist Germanic Empire was not something anyone, child or adult, could fully take in at a moment's notice. A beginning of acceptance was as much as he could hope for. That much, Alicia had given him.

His own father had shown him photographs smuggled out of the *Ostlands* and other, newer, ones from the USA to warn him how necessary silence was. He still had nightmares about those pictures after more than thirty years. But he still had the photos, too, hidden in a file cabinet. If he thought he had to, he would show them to Alicia. He hoped the need would never come, for her sake and his own.

Lise walked into the kitchen a couple of minutes later. She dragged in a chair from the dining room, sat down, and waited till the sink was empty and the washer full. Then, as the machine started to churn, she got up and gave him a long, slow hug. "And so the tale gets told once more," she said.

As he had with his daughter, Heinrich hung on to his wife. "And so we try to go on for another generation," he said. "We've outlasted so much. God willing, we'll outlast the Nazis, too. No matter what they teach in school, I don't believe the *Reich* can last a thousand years."

"*Alevai* it doesn't." Lise used a word from a murdered language, a word that hung on among surviving Jews like the ghost of Hamlet's murdered father. "But, of course, now that the tale is told, the risk that we'll get caught also goes up. You did just right there, keeping her from running when the police van came by."

"Couldn't have that," Heinrich said gravely. "But she'll be nervous for a while now, and she's so young. . . ." He shook his head. "Strange how the worst danger comes from making sure we go on. No one would ever suspect you or me—"

"Why else buy pork?" Lise broke in. "Why else have a Bible with the New Testament in it, too? Because we'd have to want to commit suicide if we used one that didn't, that's why."

"I know." Heinrich knew more intimately than that: he still had his foreskin. He took off his glasses, wiped his forehead with his sleeve, and set the spectacles back on his nose. "We do everything we can to seem like perfect Germans. I can quote from *Mein Kampf* more easily than from Scripture. But it's not so easy for a child. I remember."

Lise nodded. "So do I."

"And we still have two more to go." Heinrich let out yet another sigh. He hugged her again. "I'm so tired."

"I know," she said. "It must be easier for me, staying home with the *Kinder* like a proper *Hausfrau*. But you have to wear the mask at the office every day."

"Either I pretend to others I'm not a Jew or I pack it in and pretend the same thing to myself. I can't do that, dammit. I know too much." He thought again of the hidden, yellowing black-and-white photographs from the east, and of the color prints from North America. "We *will* go on, in spite of everything."

His wife yawned. "Right now, I'm going on to bed."

"I'm right behind you. Oh—speaking of the office, on the way home today Willi said he admired how content I was here and now."

"Did he? Good," Lise said at once. "If you must wear the mask, wear it well."

"I suppose so. He also asked if we were busy tonight. I said yes, since we were, but we'll be going over there one evening soon."

"I'll arrange for my sister to stay with the girls," Lise said. "Let's give Alicia a little more time to get over her shock before we take her out. And she'll realize Katarina's one of us, too, and maybe talking with her will help."

"Sensible. You usually are."

"Ha!" Lise said darkly. "I'd better be. So had you."

"I know." Heinrich chuckled. "Besides, with the girls at home we'll be able to play more bridge—we won't have to ride herd on them."

"That's true." Lise also laughed. Both of them, by now, were long used to the strangeness of having good friends who, if they learned the truth, might well want to send them to an extermination camp. Heinrich *was* looking forward to getting together with Willi and Erika Dorsch for an evening of talk and bridge. Within the limits of his upbringing, Willi was a good fellow.

Heinrich pondered the limits of his own upbringing, which were a good deal narrower than Willi Dorsch's. In one way, telling Alicia of her heritage was transcending those limits. In another, it was forcing them on her as well. In still another . . . He gave up the regress before he got lost in it. "Didn't you say something about bed?"

"You're the one who's been standing here talking," Lise said.

"Let's go."

When her mother shook her awake, Alicia had to swallow a scream. Evil dreams had filled her night, dreams of being a monster in a world full of ordinary people, dreams of being taken from her parents, dreams of being taken from her parents to a place from which she would surely never return, dreams of. . . . She didn't remember all of them. She hoped she would forget the ones she did remember.

In the instant when her eyes came open, she thought the hand on her shoulder belonged to a man from the Security Police. The scream turned to a gasp of relief as she recognized her mother. "Oh," she said. "It's you."

"Did you think it would be anyone else?"

"Yes," Alicia said.

The one flat, stark word wiped the smile from her mother's face. "Oh, little one," she said, and hugged Alicia. "Now get up and go eat your breakfast—and remember, your sisters don't know, and they mustn't know."

"How am I supposed to hide it?" Alicia asked.

"You have to, that's all," her mother said, which was no help at all. "Now get up and wash your face and eat breakfast and brush your teeth. You've got to be ready when the school bus gets to the stop."

That scream wanted to come out again. Alicia couldn't imagine how she'd get through the day without revealing herself to her teacher and, even more appallingly, to her friends. But she had to try. She'd learned to swim when her father tossed her into a stream and she had to claw her way back to him or drown. So she'd thought at the time, anyhow, though of course he would have saved her if she'd got in trouble.

But if she got in trouble here, no one would save her. No one could save her. She didn't know much about being a Jew, but that seemed all too clear.

She wanted to stay in bed. She wanted to stay in bed forever, in fact. She couldn't, and she knew it. Her mother had already gone down the hall to wake Francesca and Roxane. And there was Francesca, mumbling and grumbling. She hated to get up in the morning. Given half a chance, she would have slept till noon every day.

Alicia got out of bed a moment before her mother reappeared in the doorway and said, "Get moving," and then, "Oh. You are."

"Yes, Mama." Being a Jew meant trouble. Alicia could see that. But being late to school meant trouble, too, trouble of a sort she'd known about for years. That trouble she could stay out of. The other . . . ? To Alicia, they both seemed about the same size just then. She was ferociously bright, but she was only ten.

She ducked into the bathroom as her sisters came out of the bedroom they shared. They would camp in the hall waiting for her, so she hurried. When she opened the door again, she pushed past them and back into her room to get dressed. That meant she didn't have to say anything much to them for a little while longer.

Like any ten-year-old girl, she put on the tan blouse and skirt that were the uniform of the *Bund deutscher Mädel*. She remembered how proud she'd been when she turned ten the summer before and could join the League of German Maidens like Anna and her other older friends. Putting on the uniform, with its swastika armband, was a sign she was growing up.

As she pulled up her white socks and tied her stout brown shoes, though, the uniform suddenly seemed a lie, a betrayal. *I'm not a German maiden,* she thought unhappily. *I'm a Jewish maiden.* She shivered, though a steam radiator kept her room cozy and warm.

On her bookshelves stood a children's classic from the early days of the *Reich*, Julius Streicher's *Trust No Fox in the Green Meadow and No Jew on His Oath.* Like millions of German youngsters across three generations, she'd learned the difference between Aryans and Jews from the slim little volume. The blond, handsome, muscular Aryan could work and fight. The pudgy, swarthy, hook-nosed, flashily dressed Jew was the greatest scoundrel in the *Reich*. Alicia had believed that with all her heart. It was in a book—in every book. How could it be wrong?

Aryan children with blond or light brown hair jeered as homely, black-haired Jewish children and a Jewish teacher were ousted from their school. A few pages later, an Aryan boy grinned and played a concertina while more ugly Jews with big noses and fleshy lips trudged into exile past a sign that said ONE-WAY STREET. The colorful pictures were so bright and cheerful, they commanded belief. Alicia had the companion volume, *The Poison Mushroom*, too.

She stared at the caricatures of the Jews. She didn't look like that, nor did her sisters and parents. The Stutzmans and Susanna Weiss didn't, either. Realizing that helped steady her. If *Trust No Fox* had one lie in it, maybe it had lots of lies in it. With all her heart, she hoped so.

"Alicia!" her mother called. "Hurry up! It's breakfast!"

"Coming!" she said, and put the book away.

"Slowpoke," said Roxane, who with Francesca was already digging in to sausages and eggs. She was the teaser in the family, always looking for ways to get under her older sisters' skins and usually finding one.

Francesca asked the question Alicia had been dreading: "Well, what did you do when you got to stay up late last night?"

Behind Alicia, her mother suddenly stopped bustling about the kitchen. She stood still and quiet, waiting to hear what her oldest daughter would say—and maybe to jump in and help if she had to. "It wasn't very exciting," Alicia answered, as casually as she could. "Just a lot of talk. Grownups." She rolled her eyes. If she exaggerated, it wouldn't hurt, not here. Francesca already knew what she thought of grownups.

Her sister accepted what she said. Her mother started moving again, as if she'd only just noticed she'd stopped. And Alicia . . . Alicia was sunk in misery. She couldn't ever remember lying to Francesca before.

The girls got their books and went to the bus stop on the corner. Older girls in tan uniforms like Alicia's, older boys in brown Hitler Youth togs, and younger children dressed every which way waited for the school bus.

"Hello, Alicia," said Emma Handrick, who lived a few doors away. "Did you get the math homework?"

"Sure," Alicia said, surprised Emma needed to ask; she almost always got the homework.

"Can I copy it from you on the way to school?" Emma asked eagerly. "Please? My mother said she'd clobber me if I got another lousy grade."

She'd asked before. Alicia had always said no. Her father and mother had taught her only to do her own work. They said anything else was dishonest. She'd gone along with that; it fit the way she thought. But today everything seemed up in the air. If she said no, would the neighbor girl denounce her as a Jew? Whatever else happened, that couldn't. Not just her safety rode on it. So did her sisters' and her parents'. She nodded and smiled. "All right."

Emma's rather doughy face lit up in surprised delight. Francesca and Roxane looked horrified. Roxane had an I'm-going-to-tell expression on her face. Most of the time, that would have worried Alicia. Now she had bigger things to worry about. She felt like Atlas (her class had done Greek mythology the year before), with the weight of the heavens on her shoulders.

The school bus stopped at the corner. The doors hissed open. The children got on. A couple of Alicia's friends waved to her. She waved back, but found a seat with Emma. Her sisters perched together on another pair of seats. Their backs were stiff with disapproval at first, but then they started talking with friends of their own and forgot Alicia's scandalous behavior—for the time being, anyhow.

"You're a lifesaver," Emma said, her pencil racing over the paper. She finished the last problem—they were multiplying fractions—as the bus pulled into the schoolyard. "I even think I see how to do them myself."

"That's good," Alicia said. She wasn't sure she believed it. She was pretty sure she *didn't* believe it, in fact. Emma would never be one of the smartest people in the class, which was putting it mildly. But hearing it salved Alicia's conscience.

She put the homework back in her folder and got off the bus. Francesca and Roxane waved as they hurried to the lines in front of their classrooms.

Maybe they'd forgiven her sin. Maybe. She took her own place in line—right in front of Emma, in alphabetical order.

At precisely eight o'clock, the classroom door opened. "Come in, children," the teacher boomed.

"*Jawohl, Herr* Kessler," Alicia and the rest of the class chorused. All over the schoolyard, other classes were greeting their teachers the same way. They all marched into the classrooms in perfect step—well, not quite so perfect in the younger grades.

Again with the others, Alicia set her books and papers on her desk and stood at attention behind her chair. She faced the swastika flag that hung by the door, but her eyes were on *Herr* Kessler. He stood so stiff, he might have turned to stone. (Alicia thought of Perseus and the Gorgon.)

Suddenly, the teacher's right arm shot up and out. "*Heil!*" he barked.

Alicia and her classmates also honored the flag with the German salute. "*Heil!*" they said. Till this morning, she'd been proud to salute the flag. Why not? Till this morning, she'd been an Aryan among Aryans, one who deserved that privilege. Now? Now everything seemed different. No one else knew what she was, but she did, and the knowledge ate at her. Hadn't Hitler himself called Jews parasites on the nation? Alicia felt like an enormous cockroach. For a wild, frightening moment, she wondered if anyone else could see her metamorphosis.

Evidently not. *Herr* Kessler got to work on grammar: which prepositions took the dative, which the accusative, and which both and with what changes of meaning. Alicia had no trouble with any of that. But some people did—Emma, for instance. Alicia knew the Handricks had the televisor on all the time; she'd heard her mother talk about it. Even so, if you listened to how educated people talked, if you paid any attention at all, how could you make mistakes? Emma did, and she wasn't the only one. *Herr* Kessler made notations in the roll book in red ink. Emma's mother was liable to clobber her in spite of the arithmetic homework she'd got from Alicia.

History and geography came next. The teacher pulled down a big map of the world that hung above the blackboard. The Germanic Empire, shown in the blood-red of the flag, stretched from England deep into Siberia and India. Paler red showed lands occupied but not formally annexed: France, the United States, Canada. In the Empire's shadow were the little realms of the allied nations: Sweden's gold, Finland's pale blue, the greens of Hungary and Portugal, Romania's dark blue, purple for Spain and Bulgaria, and the yellow of the Italian Empire around the Mediterranean. Africa was mostly red, too, though Portugal, Spain, and Italy kept their colonies on the dark continent and the Aryan-dominated Union of South Africa was another ally, not a conquest.

Only the Empire of Japan, with Southeast Asia, China, the islands of the Pacific and Indian Oceans, and Australia all shown in yellow, came anywhere close to matching the Germanic Empire in size. The Japanese were strong enough to survive for the time being, not strong enough to make serious rivals for the *Reich*.

"And the Japanese, of course, are not Aryans," *Herr* Kessler said. "Because of this, they have no true creativity of their own. Already they have fallen behind us in technology, and they will fall further behind with each passing year. Our triumph may not come soon, but it is sure." The children nodded solemnly. They knew how important being an Aryan was. Alicia did—all the more so now that she realized she wasn't one.

Math came next. They passed in their homework and did problems on the blackboard. Alicia got hers right. Emma botched hers. *Herr* Kessler frowned. He flipped through papers. "You were correct on your homework," he rumbled ominously. "Why do you fall down here?"

"I don't know, *Herr* Kessler," Emma said. "I'm sorry, *Herr* Kessler." She sounded sorry, too—sorry about what would happen to her when her mother found out she wasn't doing so well.

"Your paper from last night is as good as Alicia Gimpel's," the teacher said, and Alicia's heart leaped into her mouth. Had he realized Emma was copying? But he only set the homework down and went on, "Now you must learn to follow through, as Alicia has done."

"*Jawohl, Herr* Kessler!" Emma didn't seem worried about cheating. How many times had she copied work before, and from how many different students? Enough to take it for granted—that was plain.

Oddly, Emma's matter-of-factness helped Alicia at lunch. If Emma could keep the teacher from suspecting she was a cheater, why couldn't Alicia keep anyone from suspecting she was a Jew? Emma left evidence, if only *Herr* Kessler had looked more closely. Alicia didn't: no *Hamantaschen* in her lunch pail, no mark of Cain on her forehead. *Father was right,* she thought with enormous relief. *If I don't make a silly mistake, no one will think I'm anything but what I've always seemed to be.* And one of the things she'd always been was somebody who despised mistakes of any kind, and especially silly ones.

The afternoon turned out to be a snap. She was good in science, and good enough at the computer keyboard—like her father, she was less than graceful, and couldn't type as fast as some of her classmates, but she was accurate. No one gave her any trouble going home, either. Her first day knowing she was a Jew, and she'd got away with it.

A three no-trump contract. Three tricks to play. Heinrich Gimpel needed to take all three to make it. No help in the dummy. Lise sat across the table from him, but they'd got where they were largely out of his hand. He didn't need *much* help; he held the ace and queen of spades and the ace of diamonds. But the king of spades remained unaccounted for. Did Willi Dorsch have it on his right, or did Erika on his left?

Willi had taken the last trick, so it was his lead. He grinned at Heinrich, who smiled back. They both knew what was what. Grinning still, Willi flipped out the jack of spades.

Heinrich kept smiling, too, as much by main force as anything else. Now he had to choose. If he played the queen and Erika had the king, he'd go down. If he played the ace and the king didn't drop, he'd also go down, because he'd have to lead the queen for the last trick, and the king would clobber it.

He glanced at Willi, who chuckled, enjoying his perplexity. Then he looked at Erika. She was worth looking at: heart-shaped face; blue, blue eyes; a wide, generous mouth; gilt hair that hung to her shoulders. However much he enjoyed the excuse to study—hell, to ogle—his friend's wife, though, all the study told him nothing about her hand. Erika took bridge seriously.

The ace or the queen? The lady or the tiger? The devil or the deep blue sea? Heinrich looked back at Willi Dorsch. "You like to lead away from kings," he remarked, and played the queen.

Erika sluffed a heart.

"Ha!" Heinrich said in triumph. He laid down the last two aces. "Made it!"

"Dammit!" Willi said. He laid down the king of spades and the king of diamonds.

"That's the rubber," Erika said sadly. She wrote in the scorebook.

Lise said, "Willi, if you'd led the diamond we would have gone down. Heinrich would have had to take. Then he would have led the ace of spades, and you would have dropped the jack—and had the king waiting for the queen."

Willi thought for a couple of seconds, then said, "Dammit," again, on a different note this time.

"I've spent the last fifteen years trying to teach him not to do things like that, and I haven't had any luck," Erika said. "I don't think you will, either."

"I'm a stubborn goose," Willi remarked, with a certain amount of pride. He gathered up the cards and swept them into a neat pile. "Have we got time for another rubber?"

"What time *is* it?" Heinrich looked at his watch. "A quarter past twelve." He raised his eyes to Lise. "What will your sister say?"

"That we're pushing it," she answered. She turned to Erika Dorsch and spread her hands. "You know how it is. You don't want to get your best babysitter mad at you, because if you do you'll never get out of the house again."

"Oh, yes." Erika nodded. The Dorsches' son and daughter were asleep in their bedrooms. *They* hadn't had to worry about babysitters tonight. And Heinrich hadn't had to worry about bringing Alicia along. *Maybe she'll talk to Katarina about things, if her sisters give her the chance,* he thought. *That will help. She thinks Aunt Käthe's interesting. Lise and I are just—Mama and Papa.*

Willi got to his feet. "Don't disappear quite yet. I'll fix one for the road." He headed off into the kitchen.

"Oh, good heavens. My back teeth are already floating." Lise headed off, too, in the direction of the bathroom.

That left Heinrich briefly alone with Erika Dorsch. In a film, he would have run a finger around the inside of his collar. He'd never quite figured out whether she knew how provocative she was. Had things been otherwise, he might have been tempted to find out. As they were . . . every once in a while, he was tempted to find out anyhow. He'd never yielded to temptation. Too much rode on it.

All she said was, "You played that well," which hardly encouraged fantasies.

Heinrich shrugged. "I thought it was the best chance I had to make. And the four of us have been playing bridge a long time. I know how Willi's beady little mind works." He grinned to make sure Erika didn't take him seriously.

She smiled, too, but only for a moment. "You think about things," she said in musing tones. "And you think other people—even women—can think about things, too." She paused, then added, "I wonder if Lise has any idea how lucky she is." She eyed him speculatively.

Not knowing what to say to that, he didn't say anything. *And does Willi have reason to worry about me?* he wondered. The mere idea made him nervous for all sorts of reasons, of which temptation was among the least important. When he was tempted by a woman like Erika Dorsch, that showed how urgent the other reasons were.

Not saying anything proved a good idea on general principles, for Lise and Willi both came back into the dining room at the same time. Willi carried a tray with four glasses of Kirsch on it. He couldn't resist doing a little routine with the tray, as if he were one of the English butlers in such demand among wealthy German families. Lise laughed. Erika rolled her eyes up to the ceiling. Plainly, she found her husband less than amusing tonight.

Willi handed everyone a glass of cherry brandy, then raised his own in salute. "*Sieg heil!*" he said.

"*Sieg heil!*" The others echoed the words. Erika sounded subdued. Heinrich made sure he seemed enthusiastic. So did Lise. If they were the good National Socialists and Aryans they pretended to be, they had to sound that way when they hailed victory... didn't they? All at once, Heinrich wondered. Erika really was an Aryan and, he presumed, a good Nazi. She didn't worry about sounding indifferent. But, being who and what she was, she could afford to slack off on small things. The Gimpels couldn't afford to slack off at all. Like Caesar's wife, they had to be above suspicion, for suspicion meant disaster.

"That's quite a nightcap," Heinrich said, and mimed being hit over the head with a club.

"You can sleep late tomorrow," Willi Dorsch said, knocking back his own Kirsch.

Lise snorted. "You know our children too well to say anything silly like that. Francesca likes to sleep in, but Alicia and Roxane will be up at the crack of dawn."

"Ghastly habit," Willi said. "Our two like to lie in bed, the lazy good-for-nothings." He stuck out a finger in Heinrich's direction. "Meant to ask you: *are* the Americans going to make their assessment this fiscal year?"

"I'm . . . not sure," Heinrich answered cautiously. He knew the Americans were unlikely to, but didn't want to say so in front of Lise and Erika, neither of whom had the security clearance to hear such things.

Willi's wave said he understood why his friend was being so cagey. It also said he thought Heinrich was being a wet blanket. He asked, "Are we gearing up to wallop the Americans if they don't meet the assessment?"

"Not that I've heard," Heinrich said, which combined caution and truth.

"I haven't, either," Willi said. "You know how I was complaining a while ago about not living in glorious times?" He waited for Heinrich to nod, then went on, "I didn't think we were getting *this* soft when I grumbled, I'll tell you that."

"I don't think we're soft," Heinrich said. "Germany rules the biggest empire the world has ever seen. Ruling and conquering are different businesses. A ruler can forgive things a conqueror would have to step on."

"Not if he wants to keep on ruling, he can't," Willi said, going red in the face.

"No, Heinrich's right," Erika said, which made Lise raise an eyebrow and made Willi turn even redder. Erika went on, "If you want to hold a country down without a rebellion every other year, you—"

"Kill the first two or three batches of rebels and everybody who's related to them," Willi broke in. "After a while, the people who are left—if there are any—get the idea and settle down. That's what finally worked for us in England."

In a way, he was right; England hadn't risen against the *Reich* since the mid-1970s. Even so . . . Heinrich said, " 'Finally' is a word with a lot of bodies behind it. When we can, we ought to run things more . . . more efficiently. That's the word I want." It was, he hoped, a word that wouldn't rouse the interest, let alone the anger, of the Security Police.

"We ought to run, period," Lise said. "Käthe's going to be impatient with us." She didn't want any sort of political argument, even with friends. In that, she was undoubtedly wise. When she rose to her feet, Heinrich followed suit as automatically as he would have in the bridge game.

"I'll get your coats out of the closet," Erika said, which meant she thought the evening was at an end. Willi walked out to the front hall with them, but he didn't say anything. Heinrich hoped his friend wasn't fuming about being contradicted. It wouldn't have been so bad had Heinrich been the only one to disagree with him. But when Erika did, too, that must have felt like a stab in the back. Willi managed a smile and a bad joke when the Gimpels headed for the bus stop. That eased Heinrich's mind. But, after the door closed behind Lise and him, Willi's voice rose angrily—and so did Erika's.

"What's that all about?" Lise pointed back toward the Dorsches' house.

"I think Willi thinks he ought to be jealous of me," Heinrich said unhappily.

"Jealous? Jealous how?" his wife asked. He didn't answer. His wife walked on for a couple of paces before stopping short. "Jealous like *that*?" Even more unhappily, Heinrich nodded. "And does he have reason to be jealous like that?" Lise inquired ominously.

"Not on account of me," Heinrich said. That covered the most important part of the question. Not quite all of it, though; he felt he had to add, "I'm not so sure about Erika."

They got to the brightly lit bus stop. Lise tapped her toe on the cement of the sidewalk. "I can't fault her taste, but I did see you first, you know. Kindly remember it."

"I will. For all sorts of reasons, I will," Heinrich said.

"She's pretty. You'd better," Lise said. The bus rolled up just then, which saved him from having to answer: a small mercy, but he took what he could get.

II

FRANZ OPPENHOFF LOOKED AT SUSANNA WEISS THROUGH SPECTACLES THAT grotesquely magnified his bloodshot blue eyes. "I fail to see the necessity for this journey," he said, and scratched at the bottom edge of a white muttonchop sideburn.

Susanna looked back at the department chairman with a loathing she tried to conceal. "But, *Herr Doktor* Professor, it is the annual meeting of the Medieval English Association—and only the third time it's met *in* England since the war."

Oppenhoff paused to light a cigar. It was a fine Havana, but the smoke still put Susanna, who didn't use tobacco, in mind of burning long johns. She coughed, not too ostentatiously. After a puff, he said, "Many—even most—of these meetings are a waste of time, a waste of effort, and a waste of our travel budget."

"Oh?" Somehow, Susanna made one syllable sound dangerous. "Is that what you said when Professor Lutze asked to attend?"

"I didn't. . . ." Professor Oppenhoff paused, evidently deciding he couldn't get away with the lie direct. He tried again: "I thought the conference would enhance his professional development, he being—"

"A man?" Susanna finished for him.

"That is not what I was going to say." The chairman sounded offended.

Susanna Weiss *was* offended. "What were you going to say, then, *Herr*

Doktor Professor? That Professor Lutze is junior to me? He is. That he has published less than half of what I have? He has. That what he *has* published is superficial compared to my work? It is, as any specialist will tell you." She smiled with poisonous sweetness. "There. You see? We agree completely."

Professor Oppenhoff tried to draw on the cigar again, but choked on the smoke. Susanna held the poisoned smile till his coughs subsided into wheezes. He wagged a shaky forefinger at her. "You have not the attitude of a proper National Socialist woman," he said severely.

"Do I have the attitude of a proper National Socialist scholar?" No matter how offended, no matter how angry, Susanna was, she took care to throw back the Party's name as if she were returning a lob in a game of tennis. "Don't you think that is how you ought to judge me?"

"You should be turning out babies, not articles," Oppenhoff said.

That she remained unwed, that she had no children, was a private grief for Susanna. Her back stiffened. Her private griefs were none of Oppenhoff's damned business. "If Professor Lutze's work is good enough to let him deserve to go to London for the Medieval English Association meeting, what part of mine disqualifies me from going, too?" She didn't say Lutze didn't deserve to go, no matter what she thought. That would have got her another enemy. Academic politics were nasty enough without trying to make them worse.

"The travel budget . . ." the chairman said portentously.

This time, Susanna's smile was pure carnivore. "I've spoken with the accountants. We have plenty. In fact, they recommend that we spend more before the end of the fiscal year in June. If we have unexpended funds, people are liable to decide we don't need so much next year."

Franz Oppenhoff went gray with horror. A budget cut was every department chairman's nightmare. He threw his hands in the air. Cigar ash fluttered down onto his desk like snow. "Go to London, *Fräulein Doktor* Professor Weiss! Go! Uphold the reputation of the university!" Not quite inaudibly, he added, "And get the devil out of my hair."

Susanna pretended not to hear that. Having got what she wanted, she could afford to be gracious. "Thank you very much, Professor Oppenhoff. I'll make my travel arrangements right away." In fact, she'd already made them. If she hadn't been able to browbeat Oppenhoff into letting her go, she would have had to cancel. She could easily have afforded the plane ticket and hotel, but she couldn't have gone during the semester without leave from on high. Now she had it.

"Is there anything else?" Professor Oppenhoff inquired.

She was tempted to complain that her office was smaller and had a worse view than those of male professors less senior than she—she seldom did things by half. Here, though, she judged she'd pushed the chairman about as far as she could. "Not today, thanks," she said grandly, like a snooty shopper declining a salesgirl's assistance. Small, straight nose tilted high, she strode out of Oppenhoff's office.

Spring was in the air when she left the east wing of the university complex and walked out into the chestnut grove that lay between the wings. The chestnuts were still bare-branched, but the first leaf buds had begun to appear. Soon the trees would be gloriously green, with birds singing and nesting in them. For now, Susanna could see down to the garden and the bronze statues of the great scholars there: Wilhelm von Humboldt, the founder of the university; his brother, Alexander; Helmholtz; Treitschke; Mommsen; and Hegel.

Towering above all the other statues was a colossal bronze of Werner Heisenberg. Arno Breker, Hitler's favorite sculptor, had commemorated the physicist at the first *Führer*'s personal request. Susanna had seen photos of Heisenberg. He was tall, yes, but on the scrawny side, almost as much so as Heinrich Gimpel. Breker had turned him into one of his countless Aryan supermen: broad-shouldered, deep-chested, with a narrow waist and thighs like a draft horse's. The usual heroic Breker nude struggled to burst forth from the suit in which the sculptor had reluctantly had to drape his subject.

Susanna sighed. If Heisenberg and the other German scientists hadn't been so quick to see the implications of atomic fission . . . She sighed again. The world would be different, but who could guess how? One of the things she'd seen was that different didn't necessarily mean better.

A swarthy young man who wore a neat black beard and had a turban wrapped around his head hurried past Susanna. "Please to excuse me," he said in musically accented German.

"*Aber natürlich,*" she replied with regal politeness. The beturbaned young man went up the stairs two at a time and into the east wing of the university building. The Department of Germanic Languages shared the wing with the German Institute for Foreigners, which since 1922 had been instructing those from abroad on the German language and German culture, and the more recent Institute for Racial Studies, which helped decide which foreigners deserved to survive and be instructed about the blessings of German culture.

The fellow who'd gone past Susanna in such a rush had to be from Persia or India, probably the latter. Despite their complexions, folk from those lands got credit for being Aryans, and so lived on as subjects—sometimes even privileged subjects—within the Germanic Empire.

Had the young man been born farther west, had he been an Arab rather than an Aryan . . . As far as the Institute for Racial Studies was concerned, anti-Semitism extended to Arabs as well as Jews. Some of the things the *Reich* had done, and had browbeaten the Italians into doing, in the Middle East were on a scale to rival the destruction of the Slavic *Untermenschen* in Eastern Europe.

We aren't the only ones, Susanna thought with a shudder. *We remember better than most of the others, though. That is one thing we have always done: we remember. But so do the Nazis. Can we really hope to outlast them? Heinrich and Walther think so, or say they do, but do they believe it when a noise outside wakes them up in the middle of the night?*

She didn't know how they kept from screaming when they heard a noise like that. She had no idea at all how *she* kept from screaming when she heard a noise like that. Even fourth-generation Nazis who'd never had an ideologically impure thought in their lives started sweating at noises in the night. *They* might know their thoughts were unsullied, their bloodlines uncontaminated. Yes, they might know, but did the Security Police? You never could tell.

And if you really had something to hide . . .

So far, though, all the noises Susanna had heard in and around her block of flats were those of everyday life: neighbors trying to go in and out quietly or sometimes too drunk to bother, a tree branch scraping on her window, traffic swishing by outside, once in a great while the trashcan-rattle of an accident. No men in high-crowned caps and black trenchcoats pounding on the door and roaring, *"Jüdin, heraus!"*

Not yet. Never yet. But the fear never went away, either.

With another shiver, Susanna hurried down toward the garden, down toward the statues of the men who had advanced German scholarship. And if she tried not to look at Breker's bronze of Heisenberg, well, even the Security Police weren't going to notice that.

Heinrich Gimpel kissed Lise and went up the street to the bus stop. He got there five minutes before the bus did. As it stopped, the door hissed open in front of him. He fed his account card into the fare slot, then withdrew it and stuck it back in his wallet as he looked up the aisle for a seat. He found one. At the next stop, a plump blond woman sat down next to him. When Willi Dorsch got on a couple of stops later, he and Heinrich nodded to each other, but that was all.

Not sitting with Willi didn't break Heinrich's heart. His friend had been cooler than usual since the awkward end to their evening of bridge. *Does he worry that I'm looking for an affair with Erika?* Heinrich shook his head as Willi sank into a seat near the back of the bus. He enjoyed looking at Erika Dorsch, but that wasn't the same thing at all. Even Lise, who wasn't inclined to be objective about such things, understood the difference.

But then a new, troubling thought crossed Heinrich's mind. *Or does Willi think Erika's looking for an affair with me?* Even if Willi didn't think Heinrich wanted the affair, he might not be so happy about seeing him every morning. And Heinrich hadn't the faintest idea what he could do about that.

The bus made its last few stops and pulled into the train station. Everyone got off. Almost everyone went to the platform for the Berlin-bound commuter train. As people queued up, Heinrich and Willi weren't particularly close. Heinrich sighed. More often than not, the two of them had chatted and gossiped like a couple of *Hausfrau*s all the way in to the city. It hadn't happened the past few days, and it didn't look as if it would today, either.

It didn't. When the train came into the the Stahnsdorf station, Willi sat down on the aisle next to a taken window seat. The seat on the other side of the aisle was taken, too. Whatever Willi Dorsch wanted, Heinrich's company wasn't it. Willi pulled a couple of the *Völkischer Beobachter* out of his briefcase and started to read.

Heinrich also read the Nazi Party newspaper: one more bit of protective coloration. He found a seat halfway down the car from Willi, got out his own copy, and looked it over. He did find it professionally useful every now and then. What the Party decided could dictate what *Oberkommando der Wehrmacht* did next. Reading the paper carefully—especially reading between the lines—gave clues about which way the wind was blowing at levels of the Party more exalted than those in which Heinrich traveled.

Today he went to the imperial-affairs section first. It still looked as if the United States was going to fall short on its occupation assessment. Heinrich kept waiting for someone in the Foreign Ministry or the *Führer*'s office to comment. So far, no one had. That in itself was interesting. When he first started at *Oberkommando der Wehrmacht,* the Americans wouldn't have got a warning if they were late or came up short on what they owed. They would simply have been punished. Things *were* more easygoing these days.

Some things were, anyhow. A small story announced the execution of a dozen Serbs for rebellion against the *Reich*. Serbs had touched off the First World War, almost a hundred years ago now. They'd been nuisances ever since. And another story told of the jailing of an SS man who'd been caught taking bribes in a French town near the English Channel.

Such shameless corruption, the *Völkischer Beobachter* declared, *cannot be tolerated in an orderly, well-run state*. Heinrich nodded to himself. He'd seen three or four anticorruption drives since his university days. That the *Reich* needed a new one every few years told how well they worked.

This one, though, gave signs of being more serious than some of its predecessors. An SS man, behind bars? That was news of the man-bites-dog sort. Heinrich wondered which German bigwigs the Frenchmen who'd been shaken down happened to know. Odds were they'd known somebody. SS men seldom got into trouble for what they did even inside Germany, let alone in occupied territory.

When the train pulled into the station in Berlin, Heinrich and Willi naturally went the same way, for they had to catch the same bus to the same office. The story about the SS man intrigued Heinrich enough to make him wave the *Völkischer Beobachter* under Willi Dorsch's nose and ask, "Did you see this?"

"Which?" Willi asked. He sounded more distant than usual, but not actively unfriendly. Heinrich pointed to the story. "Oh, that," Willi said. "Yes, I saw it. Politics. Has to be."

"Politics?" Heinrich said it with such surprise, he might never have heard the word before.

Willi gave back an impatient nod. "I don't see what else could be going on."

"I just figured somebody knew somebody," Heinrich said. "You know what I mean."

"Oh, sure." Willi nodded again, with a little more animation this time. "It's possible, I suppose, but how likely is it? Who could a bunch of froggies know who's got the clout to land somebody with SS runes on his collar tabs in hot water? Pigs will fly before we see that." He started walking faster. "Come on—there's the bus, just waiting for us."

It did wait. They even found seats, which they didn't manage every day during the morning rush. "Politics," Heinrich repeated. "Well, I suppose you're right."

"You bet I am," Willi said as the bus pulled out of the station. He patted Heinrich on the knee. "You have any other problems you can't see your way around, you come to your Uncle Willi, and he'll set you right."

He smiled a superior smile. If Erika admired Heinrich for anything, it was his brains—it couldn't very well have been his body or his looks, as he was ruefully aware. And if Willi felt smarter than he was, then all of a sudden he didn't seem such a threat. He hoped that was how things were working inside his friend's head, anyhow. He didn't want to be a threat to anybody or anything. Threats were visible. He couldn't afford that kind of visibility.

And maybe Willi was right, too. To most of the Germanic Empire's subjects, politics had to seem simple. The Germans gave orders, and the subjects obeyed. Subjects who didn't obey paid for it, often with their lives. (Sometimes subjects who did obey paid with their lives, too, but they seldom knew that ahead of time.)

But, seen from within the ruling bureaucracy, things weren't so simple. *Wehrmacht* and SS officials warily watched one another. The *Wehrmacht* and civilian administrators didn't always see eye-to-eye, either. And the administrators and the SS quarreled over who really represented the National Socialist Party. It wasn't just a factional split, either. Personalities in each camp further complicated things. The *Führer,* Kurt Haldweim, was supposed to keep everyone going in the same direction, but Haldweim had celebrated his ninety-first birthday just before last Christmas. For his age, he was said—frequently and loudly said—to be vigorous and alert, but how much did that prove?

When the bus stopped in front of *Oberkommando der Wehrmacht* headquarters, Willi Dorsch had to nudge Heinrich. "We get off here, you know," he said, enjoying the tiny triumph. "No matter what great thoughts you think, they won't do you any good if you can't find the place where you're supposed to use them."

"You're right, of course." Heinrich stood up, feeling foolish. As he hurried to get off the bus, he noted that Willi sounded much more like his usual self. *And why? Because I'm acting like an idiot. I've never heard of the power of positive stupidity, but this must be it.*

The guards at the front of the building saw the two of them five mornings a week. Nonetheless, they held out their hands for identity cards. They not only matched photos, they also fed the cards, one after the other, into a machine reader. Only after a light on it glowed green twice in a row did they stand aside.

"Nice to know I'm me," Willi said, sticking his card into his wallet again. He pointed at Heinrich. "Or maybe I'm you today, and you're me. The machine didn't say anything about that." He laughed.

So did Heinrich, relieved to see Willi acting like his usual silly self. But one of the guards scowled suspiciously at Willi. The other eyed the card reader, as if wondering if it could change a man's true identity. Sometimes Heinrich worried about the younger generation's brains, if any. But he knew people had been doing that since the days of the Pyramids, so he kept quiet about it.

"Pass on!" the second guard barked, still sending the machine a fishy stare.

Once inside the building with Willi, Heinrich said, "He's not going to trust that gadget for the next week. You're a subversive, you know."

Willi drew himself up in mingled alarm and hauteur. "That's a fine thing to call me in this place." But he was joking again, and kept right on doing it: "Did you lay down the trail of bread crumbs last night? No? How the devil are we going to find the way to our desks, then?"

Oberkommando der Wehrmacht was something of a maze, but not so bad as Willi made it out to be. Old-timers who remembered how things were before central Berlin got rebuilt said the old headquarters building really had been a nightmare to navigate. This one was just big, with lots of corridors and lots of rooms along each one. Even strangers—strangers with security clearances—found their way without too much trouble. Heinrich and Willi were in their places in a couple of minutes.

As soon as Heinrich sat down, he turned on his computer and entered the password that gave him access to his files. He tapped the keyboard and looked over his shoulder at Willi, saying, "These things are the biggest change since I came to work here. Used to be only a few specialists had them. Now they're everywhere, like toadstools after a rain."

"They're handy, all right." Willi had his computer up and running, too. "Sometimes I wonder who's in charge, though, us or the machines."

"I have a friend"—Heinrich didn't name Walther Stutzman—"who says they could all be connected into one giant linked system."

"There's a hell of a difference between 'could' and 'will,' " Willi said. "I don't believe it'll happen, not in a million years. Can you imagine the security nightmare with that kind of system? Anybody could put anything on it. Anybody could *find* anything on it. The Party's got too much sense to let that sort of nonsense get started. You couldn't stop it once it did; it'd be like unscrambling an egg."

"You're right," Heinrich said. "It only stands to reason." He knew he had more book smarts than Willi. But his friend was plenty shrewd, and understood the way the world—especially the part through which he moved—worked.

"You bet I'm right," Willi said now. "Once security starts to slip, everything's in trouble."

"*Ja,*" Heinrich said absently. He was busy typing in another password, the one that gave him access to the *Wehrmacht*'s information links. Thanks to Walther, he knew a lot more passwords than he was supposed to. He carried them in his memory; he wasn't mad enough to write any of them down. He wasn't mad enough to use any of them, either, except in direst emergency. The one he entered he'd acquired legitimately, in the course of his job. "I want to find out what's going on with the United States."

"Yes, that will be interesting," Willi Dorsch agreed. "If they're going to fall short of their assessment, that will put *our* budget in the red."

"Further in the red," Heinrich said.

Willi nodded. "Further in the red, true. The powers that be won't like it."

"The Americans will scream that we're trying to get blood from a turnip," Heinrich predicted.

"They've been screaming that ever since we beat them," Willi said. "So far, blood's come out every time we've squeezed."

"True, but I don't suppose it can go on forever," Heinrich said. "Look at France. Look at Denmark. They don't pay their way any more—we spend more both places than we take out. We would in Britain and Norway, too, if they hadn't struck oil in the North Sea." He waited to see if Willi would argue with him. He could call up the budget numbers with a couple of keystrokes and use them as a club to beat his friend over the head.

But Willi didn't argue. He knew Heinrich always had facts and figures at his fingertips. Instead, Willi poked through a different part of the *Wehrmacht* network. He cherished oddities the way Heinrich cherished precision. He got more attention—and certainly more laughs—with them than Heinrich did with tribute assessments, too. That was fine with Heinrich, who didn't want attention anyhow.

Willi scrolled down, scrolled down, then all at once stopped short. "Well, I'll be damned," he said, and let out a low whistle of astonishment.

"*Was ist los?*" Heinrich asked, as he was surely supposed to.

"They just found three families of Jews in some backwoods village in the Serbian mountains," Willi answered. "Probably hadn't seen German soldiers more than three or four times since the war ended. Can you believe it? Real live Jews, in this day and age? Men had their cocks clipped and everything. The damned Serb headman says he didn't know he was doing anything wrong harboring them. Likely story, eh? You can't trust Serbs, either—look at those bandits in the news today—and that's the God's truth."

His rant let Heinrich pull his face straight. "What happened to them?" he asked, his voice steady, mildly curious, as if it had nothing to do with him. Willi drew a thumb across his throat. Heinrich nodded. "Just what they deserved," he said. *Yisgadal v'yiskadash sh'may rabo:* the opening words of the Mourner's Kaddish, lovingly taught him by his father, echoed in his mind. So did another thought. *If I show my grief, I am dead. My family is dead. My friends are dead.* He showed not a thing.

Herr Kessler leaned forward. To Alicia, as to every other student in the class, he seemed to be leaning straight toward her. He took a deep breath.

His usually sallow cheeks turned red. He let out the breath in a great shout: "*Jews!*"

Everybody jumped. Half a dozen girls squealed. Alicia's own start, her own squeal—nearly a shriek—hadn't betrayed her after all. In fact, no one paid any attention to her. All eyes were riveted on the teacher.

And *Herr* Kessler was wrapped up in his own performance. "*Jews!*" he roared again, even louder than the first time. "Our brave *Wehrmacht* soldiers caught up with more than a dozen filthy, stinking Jews in the mountains of Serbia. Otto Schachtman!" His forefinger stabbed out at a boy.

Otto sprang to his feet. "*Jawohl, Herr* Kessler!"

"Show me immediately the location of Serbia on the map. Immediately!"

Otto couldn't do it, though the occupied country was plainly labeled. The teacher paddled his backside. He took the swat in stoic silence. Showing pain would have earned him another one. He didn't get in trouble for sitting down with great care, though. Alicia had only so much sympathy for him. She could have found Serbia without the label; she'd always been good at geography. But why couldn't poor Otto just *read*?

Herr Kessler pointed out Serbia himself. Then he went back to his tirade: "You see now, dear children, why we must stay ever on our guard. The hateful enemy still lurks within the borders of the Germanic Empire. Like a serpent, the Jew waits until our attention is turned elsewhere. He waits, and then he *strikes*! We must track him down and hunt him out wherever he may hide. Do you understand?"

"*Ja, Herr* Kessler," the children chorused. Alicia made sure her voice rang as loud as any of the others. She was still frightened at the idea of being a Jew, but it didn't throw her into blind panic any more. She'd had a little while to get used to it, a little while even to develop an odd sort of pride in it.

But then the teacher pointed at her. "Alicia Gimpel!"

She was out of her chair and at attention behind it in a heartbeat. "*Jawohl, Herr* Kessler!"

"What is a Jew?"

All she had to do was point at her own chest and say, *I am a Jew,* to ruin herself and everyone she loved. She knew that. Knowing it came close to bringing the blind panic back. It came close, but didn't quite manage—not least because the familiar fear at being unexpectedly called on left little room for the other.

She knew her lessons well. No one in the class knew them better. "The Jew is the opposite of the Aryan, *Herr* Kessler," she recited. "He is and remains the typical parasite, a sponger who like a noxious bacillus keeps spreading as soon as a favorable medium invites him. Wherever he appears, the host people dies out after a shorter or longer period. Existence impels the Jew to lie, and to lie perpetually. He lacks idealism in any form. His development has always and at all times been the same, just as that of the peoples corroded by him has also been the same."

She stopped. She knew she had the textbook definition straight. Up until a little while before, she'd believed every word of it. Part of her still did. The rest . . . The rest seemed to stand outside of the self she'd had before the night that turned out to be Purim. She felt somehow bigger than she had before that night. Her new self enclosed the old—and who could say how much else besides?

Herr Kessler drummed the fingers of his right hand against the side of his thigh. "This is correct," he said, as if he didn't care to admit it. "Now—you will tell me the meaning of the word *noxious*." He spoke with a certain gloating anticipation. If she were parroting the definition without grasping what went into it, he would make her pay for that.

But she wasn't. "*Jawohl*," she said again, still at attention. "*Noxious* means disgusting or nasty or poisonous."

Kessler's fingers drummed on his thigh for another few seconds. Then he gestured peremptorily. Alicia sat down. From the desk beside hers, Emma whispered, "Smartypants."

That whisper wasn't quite quiet enough. "Emma Handrick!" the teacher thundered.

Emma almost knocked over her chair jumping out of it. "*Jawohl, Herr* Kessler!"

"Since you enjoy talking so much, you will now tell the class from what source we have the proper definition of the Jew."

Alicia could have answered. Emma stuttered and stammered and looked up at the ceiling. Paddle in hand, the teacher bore down on her. "*Mein Kampf!*" she blurted in desperation. "It must be *Mein Kampf!*"

Kessler had already begun to swing back the paddle. Ever so slowly, he lowered it. Emma might have made a lucky guess, but she hadn't been wrong. "*Ja,*" the teacher said. "Be seated, and do not speak out of turn any more."

"*Jawohl, Herr* Kessler. *Danke schön, Herr* Kessler." Emma sat down in a hurry, as if glad to put the nice, solid chair seat between her bottom and the paddle.

Balked of his prey, Kessler lobbed an easy question to the whole class: "And who wrote *Mein Kampf,* children?"

"Our beloved first *Führer,* Adolf Hitler!" everyone said together.

"That's right. Very good." The teacher nodded. "If it weren't for Adolf Hitler, the Jews would still be running the world and exploiting the Aryans." His finger shot out. "Hans Natzmer!" The boy leaped to his feet. Kessler said, "Tell me what *exploiting* means."

Hans had red hair and freckles that showed ever more plainly as he went pale. Licking his lips, he said, "I am very sorry, *Herr* Kessler, but I do not know."

Whap! The paddle struck home, and Hans was sorrier yet. Kessler said, "*Exploiting* means *taking advantage of.* Remember it. You must not merely bleat out your lessons like so many sheep. You must understand them, must understand the fundamental truth in them, down to the depths of your souls."

Fundamental truth? Alicia wondered about that. Till she'd learned what she really was, she'd accepted everything her teachers taught her. They all said the same things. Her books all said the same things. Didn't that mean they were all true? She'd thought so.

Where she'd believed everything, now suddenly she doubted everything. If what her teachers and the books said about Jews was a lie (and it had to be, because they said Jews were evil, and she refused to believe that about her family and its friends—she knew better), did they lie about everything else, too? Was anything they taught her the truth, anything at all? Did the Earth really go around the sun? Were four and four really eight?

She could find out about that last one. She looked down at her hands. Four fingers on each, her thumbs hidden beneath her palms. Yes, four and four really did make eight. She sighed, a little regretfully. She would have to keep all the arithmetic they'd rammed down her throat. *Too bad,* she thought. It wasn't her favorite subject. Everything else, though . . . Everything else remained up for grabs.

She had to make another surrender a few minutes later, when *Herr* Kessler went through the day's grammar lesson. She didn't suppose he was lying about that. People did talk the way he said they did, and they did look down their noses at what he said were mistakes.

What she felt after that was a strange mix of exaltation and terror. From now on, she was going to have to figure things out for herself if she wanted to know what was so and what wasn't. She would have to weigh and judge and decide. She would have to try to see what her teachers weren't telling her from what they did say. It wouldn't be easy. She realized that, too.

Beside her, Emma was humming to herself. Alicia didn't think the other girl even knew she was doing it. Would Emma be able to handle something like this? Alicia laughed at the very idea. Emma had the imagination of a potato. She had to believe everything the teachers said, because she couldn't think for herself. Tell her one thing was true but she had to behave as if another were, and she'd go to pieces like a broken mechanical toy.

Alicia laughed again, perhaps a little cruelly, imagining gears and springs popping out of Emma's nose and ears. That was funny, all right—too funny. "Alicia Gimpel!" the teacher shouted.

Out of the chair. At attention. "*Jawohl, Herr* Kessler!"

"Perhaps you would care to tell the whole class what you find so amusing?"

"Nothing, *Herr* Kessler. Please excuse me, *Herr* Kessler." If he swatted her . . . Well, if she got punished for small things, maybe no one would notice she deserved to be punished for something enormous.

"Be seated. Keep quiet."

"*Ja, Herr* Kessler. *Danke schön, Herr* Kessler."

"Lucky," Emma whispered as Alicia sat down. Alicia nodded without a word. Most of her mind was far away. *If being a Jew* isn't *bad, why do I deserve to be punished for it?* The more she looked at it, the more complicated it got.

Lise Gimpel was chopping cabbage when Francesca came into the kitchen and waited to be noticed. She didn't have to wait long. Her mother put down the knife and said, "Hello, little one. What can I do for you?"

"Can I ask you something, Mommy?" Francesca said seriously.

"Of course you can, dear. What is it?" Lise was especially fond of her middle daughter, though she tried hard not to show it to her children or her husband. Alicia had a clear, cool intelligence very much like Heinrich's. Roxane . . . Lise smiled. Roxane was a law unto herself. But Francesca reminded Lise of what she'd been like when she was a little girl.

With eight-year-old solemnity, Francesca asked, "What's wrong with Alicia? She's sure been acting funny lately."

"Has she?" Lise said. "I hadn't noticed." She didn't like lying to her children. She didn't like it, but she didn't hesitate, either.

"Well, she has." Francesca rolled her eyes at adult blindness. She looked more like Lise than either of the other girls, too. Her face was broader than theirs, and her hazel eyes were a compromise between Lise's green and the brown Heinrich had passed on undiluted to Alicia and Roxane.

"Acting funny how?" Lise asked, though she had a pretty good idea.

"She doesn't want to play so much," Francesca said. "And she just stays in her room looking at books and thinking about things."

"Well, you know Alicia." Lise tried to pass it off lightly. "She gets that way sometimes." That much was true. The oldest Gimpel daughter had developed a series of enthusiasms—collecting seashells was the latest—that consumed her for days or weeks or sometimes months and then vanished as if they'd never been.

But Francesca shook her head. "It's not like that this time. Usually when she gets that way, she wants Roxane and me to get that way, too. She *expects* us to get that way, too, and she gets mad when we don't."

Lise hid a smile. Francesca wasn't wrong—Alicia did act like that. Another way Francesca was like her mother was that she noticed the way people behaved. Alicia was all too often blind to it. Now Lise did smile, a little sourly. That also came straight from Heinrich. Since Francesca did notice, Lise would have to answer her. She tried another question: "But not this time?"

"Not this time," Francesca agreed. "I asked her what it was, and she looked at me and she said, 'Nothing.' " Her mouth twisted. "I don't know what it is, but it's not nothing. I hope she's . . . I hope she's not in trouble at school and trying to hide it."

That was the worst thing she could think of. Lise's heart went out to her because it was the worst thing she could think of. "I'm pretty sure you don't need to worry about that," Lise said. "*Herr* Kessler would let me know if anything were wrong. He's very diligent." He reminded her at least as much of a policeman as of a teacher, but that was a different story.

She'd succeeded in distracting her daughter, anyhow. "What does diligent mean?"

"It means he takes care of everything that needs taking care of."

"Oh." Francesca spread her hands, a gesture of pure frustration. "Well, what *is* wrong with Alicia, then?"

"I don't know. Whatever it is, she'll probably get over it pretty soon," Lise said. *She'd better get over it pretty soon. If she doesn't, more people than Francesca will notice.* No doubt her own parents had had the same worries, the same fears, over her. And no doubt they'd had good reason to.

Roxane bustled into the kitchen. She greeted Francesca: "Oh, there you are. What are you doing?"

"Talking with Mommy." Francesca looked down her nose at her little sister.

"What are you talking about?" Roxane wouldn't have recognized a snub if it bit her in the ankle.

"What a nuisance you are," Francesca said.

"We were not!" Lise said. "You apologize this instant."

"Sorry." Francesca sounded anything but.

"Well, what *were* you talking about, then?" Roxane persisted.

"About Alicia," Francesca said reluctantly.

"Oh." Roxane nodded. Her hair, even curlier than Alicia's, bounced up and down. "She's been peculiar lately, all right." She fixed Francesca with a baleful stare. "*Aber natürlich,* you're pretty peculiar yourself."

"Roxane, you stop that, too." Not for the first time, Lise Gimpel had the feeling of being in no-man's-land between forces that were going to keep sniping at each other no matter what she did. Sometimes the squabbles among her children were three-sided, which only made her feel completely surrounded. She did her best to sound severe: "Now you say you're sorry."

"Sorry." Roxane outdid Francesca in insincerity. Then, happily, she went back to talking about Alicia, who wasn't there to defend herself: "She's been reading those funny Jew books again, and just a little while ago she was talking about how they were still in her room even though they're too easy for her."

Those funny Jew books. Streicher's poison had a candy coating that had made it seem tasty to German children for almost eighty years. Lise remembered thinking the same thing about his books before finding out what she was. Carefully, she said, "Sometimes you most want to look back at something just when you're getting too big for it."

To her relief, Francesca nodded in agreement to that. "I think the kindergarten rooms are a lot cuter now than I did when I was in them."

"They aren't cute," said Roxane, who was in kindergarten now. "They're just . . . schoolrooms." She laced the word with scorn.

"But they have all those tiny little desks and chairs and things," Francesca said. "They're so *sweet.*" She was the sentimental one in the family, another way she took after Lise. Roxane made a horrible face. Francesca made one back at her—she wasn't too sentimental for that.

"Cut it out, both of you," Lise said. "You're behaving like a couple of Hottentots." She had no idea how Hottentots behaved, or even if the *Reich* had left any of them alive, but she liked the sound of the name.

Instead of cutting it out, Francesca and Roxane egged each other on. That gave Lise the excuse to shoo them out of the kitchen. If they wanted to drive each other crazy somewhere else, she didn't mind. If they were driving each other crazy, they weren't wondering why Alicia was acting strange.

Lise hoped they weren't, anyway. She also hoped no one outside the family had noticed anything out of the ordinary. Alicia was a bright child and, more than either of her sisters, a solitary child. That ought to make any odd behavior from her stand out less and be more likely to get forgiven. It ought to. Lise hoped it would.

She wondered if there was any point to praying it would. Did God listen to a Jew's prayers these days? If He did, why had He let the Nazis do what they'd done? *What did we do—what could we have done—to deserve that?* The question had haunted Lise ever since she learned she was a Jew. She'd never come close to finding an answer that satisfied her.

And how long till Alicia asked the same thing? Not very, not if Lise was any judge. Alicia was too clever—too clever by half—not to wonder about that. There were times when Lise wished her eldest daughter were a little less clever, or at least had a little more in the way of sense to go with her precocious intelligence. She laughed. *As well wish for the moon while I'm at it.*

She went back to getting supper ready. *And then, in a couple of years, we'll have to tell Francesca, and after that Roxane. How long can we hope to get away with it? How long can we keep being what we are?* She was chopping an onion. She told herself the tears in her eyes came from that. Maybe she was right. Maybe.

Heinrich Gimpel poked a button on the remote control. The televisor in the living room came to life. It was seven o'clock, time for the evening news. The news reader, Horst Witzleben, looked like a cross between an SS man and a film star. "Come on, Lise," Heinrich called. "Let's see what's gone on today."

"I'll be there in a second," she answered from the kitchen. "Dishes are nearly done. Turn up the sound so I can hear it."

"All right." He did.

That made Witzleben's booming greeting—"Good day, *Volk* of the Greater German *Reich*"—sound even more impressive than it would have otherwise. He owned an almost operatic baritone. Heinrich wouldn't have been surprised if technicians in the studio pumped it up electronically to make it sound more impressive, more believable, still. The Ministry of Propaganda didn't miss a trick. "And now the news."

And now what they want people to hear, Heinrich thought. He had excellent good reasons not to rely completely on the Propaganda Ministry's trained seal. It wasn't just that he was a Jew and the Nazis had been thundering lies about his kind since before they came to power. He also worked in the *Oberkommando der Wehrmacht;* things he found out about professionally sometimes showed up on the news. When they did, they were often distorted past recognition.

Ordinary people, though—butchers, bakers, candlestick makers, *goyim*—had no way to know that, no reason to believe it. As far as they were concerned, Witzleben might have been spouting Holy Writ. *I heard it from Horst* was a synonym for *You can take it to the bank*. Heinrich had a sneaking suspicion the Ministry of Propaganda had set out to make it one.

"Our beloved Leader, Kurt Haldweim, is reported to be resting comfortably in the *Führer*'s palace, recovering from what his physicians describe as a stubborn cold," Horst Witzleben intoned. "Routine matters proceed normally. Should anything extraordinary arise, the *Führer* is fully capable of attending to it on the instant."

The picture of the *Führer* on the screen behind Witzleben had to be at least fifteen years old. Like Hitler himself, Kurt Haldweim had been born in the Ostmark when it was still Austria, and separate from Germany. He'd been a young officer in the Second World War. He was perhaps the last of that generation still in the saddle—if he *was* still in the saddle. Over the past few years, he'd had a long series of "stubborn colds" and "minor illnesses" that kept him out of the public eye for weeks at a time. Everything went on in his name. How much that meant . . . was not the sort of thing Horst Witzleben discussed on the air.

Even working where he did, Heinrich didn't know the full answer there. Along with everyone else in the Germanic Empire, he could only wait and see if the *Führer* rallied, as he had several times before.

Lise came in then. Heinrich turned down the sound and slipped an arm around her as she sat down on the sofa beside him. She rested her head on his shoulder. "You didn't miss a thing," he told her. "Horst was just going on about the *Führer*'s 'cold.' " He put a certain ironic twist on the word.

"He says everything with Haldweim is fine, then?" Lise asked. Heinrich nodded. She sighed. "And one of these days before too long he'll be dead—but he'll still be fine."

Heinrich automatically turned his head to make sure nobody, not even the children, could hear such a thing. Only when he was sure it was safe did he laugh. "That's how it was with Himmler, all right," he agreed. Only dialysis had kept the second *Führer* going the last five years of his life, but not a word of that had ever got into the news. Some people claimed Himmler had really died in 1983, not 1985, and that a junta of SS men and generals had run the Empire till they finally agreed on Haldweim as a successor. Heinrich had never spoken with anyone in a position to know who was willing to talk about that, though.

The televisor screen suddenly cut away from Horst Witzleben's Aryan good looks to a shot of a city rising from a prairie of almost Russian immensity: Omaha, the capital of the United States since the destruction of Washington. A tight shot of German jet fighters circling overhead. Another shot of uniformed German officials conferring with dumpy Americans who looked all the dumpier because they wore business suits.

"Discussion of payment of remaining American debts for the current fiscal year continues in a frank and forthright manner," Witzleben said. "A solution satisfactory to the *Reich* is anticipated."

A stock clip showed a company of panzers rolling through the American countryside. Another one, older, showed a city disappearing in atomic fire. Lise shivered. "Would the *Reich* really do that again?" she whispered.

"It can," Heinrich answered. "Because it can, it probably won't have to. The real questions are, how much of what they owe will the Americans pay, and how loud will the *Reich* have to yell before they do?" He nodded to himself. Those were the questions that counted, all right. Who persuaded—or browbeat—the Americans into coughing up how much could have a good deal to do with who followed Kurt Haldweim into the *Führer*'s palace.

Another camera cut, this one to London. Like Paris, the town was more a monument to what had been than to what was nowadays. Parts of it remained in ruins more than sixty years after its fall to German panzers and dive-bombers. Horst Witzleben said, "The British Union of Fascists will be convening for their annual congress next week. Their full support for all Germanic programs is anticipated."

Heinrich and Lise both snorted at that. The British fascists had always followed Berlin's line. They'd always had to, or the *Reich* would clamp down on them even harder than usual. But no sooner had that thought crossed Heinrich's mind than a beefy, red-faced Englishman in BUF regalia appeared on the televisor screen. In Cockney-accented German, he said, "We're good fascists, too, we are. We think we've got a proper notion of what's right for Britain."

Dryly, Witzleben commented, "Whether the British Union of Fascists will endorse this position remains to be seen."

The next story was on the state visit of the *Poglavnik* of Croatia to the King of Bulgaria. Heinrich thought he knew what they would be talking about: hunting down the Serb terrorists who kept the Balkans bubbling. He was still amazed the Englishman had had the nerve to say what he'd said, and that the news had shown it. Someone in the Ministry of Propaganda had gone out on a limb there. And the Englishman had gone out on a bigger one. Were the Security Police looking for him even now?

Lise had a different thought: "Susanna will be in London for this, *nicht wahr?*"

"For it? No." Heinrich shook his head. "But yes, at the same time."

His wife sent him a severe look. "There are times, sweetheart, when you're too precise for your own good. You—"

He waved her to silence. There on the screen were the *Poglavnik* and the King, each in a different fancy uniform, shaking hands. And the correspondent from Sofia was saying, "—lating each other on the discovery and elimination of a nest of Jews deep in the Serbian mountains. Back to you, Horst."

"Danke," Witzleben said as his image reappeared on the screen. He looked out at his vast audience. "The menace of world Jewry never goes away, *meine Damen und Herren*. It is as true now as it was when our *Führer* served in Salonica during the Second World War."

Lise shivered. "They don't give up, do they?"

"Not likely." Heinrich made a fist and pounded it down on his knee. "No, not likely, dammit."

"We thought things would be easier when Himmler finally kicked the bucket," Lise said in a soft voice no one but Heinrich could possibly hear. "And then what did we get instead? Kurt Haldweim!" She didn't try to hide her bitterness.

Heinrich stroked her hair. "Maybe it will be better this time. The SS isn't so strong now—at least, I hope it isn't."

"I'll believe it when I see it," Lise said, and he had no answer for that.

The next story was about a riot at a football match in Milan, when the home team's goal against visiting Leipzig was disallowed on a questionable offside call. The crowd did more than question it. They bombarded the field with rocks and bottles, so that both teams and the officials had to flee for their lives. One German football player was slightly injured; one official—not the one who'd made the dubious call—ended up with a broken collarbone.

"Leaders of the German Federation of Sport have called upon their Italian counterparts for explanation and apology," Witzleben said in tones of stern disapproval. "Thus far, none has been forthcoming. These disgraceful scenes have grown all too common at matches on Italian pitches. The German Federation of Sport has declared it reserves the right to withdraw from further competition with teams from the Italian Empire unless and until the situation is corrected."

That would hurt the Italians a lot worse than it did their German foes. They depended on revenue from matches against visiting German powerhouses to keep themselves in the black. And if they couldn't tour in the Germanic Empire . . . Some of their teams would probably have to fold.

Heinrich tried to look at things philosophically: "What can you expect from Italians? They get too excited about what's only a game."

And then Lise brought him down to earth, saying, "And who was it who whooped like a wild Indian when we won the World Cup four years ago?"

"I don't know what you're talking about," Heinrich said, whereupon Lise made a face at him. He poked her in the ribs and found a ticklish spot. She squeaked.

"What's that funny noise?" Francesca called from upstairs.

"That funny noise is your mother," Heinrich answered.

"Why are you a funny noise, Mommy?" their middle daughter asked.

"Because your father is tickling me, which he's *not* supposed to do," Lise said. She tried to tickle him back, but he wasn't ticklish. "Unfair," she muttered. "Very unfair."

"And why is this night different from all other nights?" Heinrich murmured. The first of the Four Questions from the Passover service reminded Lise that life wasn't fair for Jews, never had been, and probably never would be. *But we—somehow—go on anyway,* Heinrich thought. His wife didn't answer him. He did stop tickling her.

Esther Stutzman worked a couple of mornings a week as a receptionist at a pediatrician's office. It wasn't so much that the family needed the money; they didn't. But she was a gregarious soul, and she'd wanted to see people after Gottlieb and Anna started going to school and didn't need to be looked after all the time.

The doctor was a short, plump man named Martin Dambach. He wasn't a Jew. Several of his patients were, but he didn't know that. "Good morning, *Frau* Stutzman," he said when Esther came in.

"Good morning, Doctor," she answered. "How are you today?"

"Tired," he said, and rubbed his eyes. "There was a traffic accident outside the house in the middle of the night—one of the drivers reeked like a brewery—and I gave what help I could. Then the police wanted to talk with me, which cost me *another* hour of sleep. Would you please get the coffeemaker going?"

"How awful! Of course I will," Esther said. Dr. Dambach was a skilled and knowledgeable physician, but when he tangled with the percolator he turned out either hot water faintly tinged with brown or unpalatable mud. As she got the coffee started, she asked, "Was anyone badly hurt?"

"Not the drunk," he said sourly. "He was so limp and relaxed, you could have dropped him from the top of the Great Hall and he wouldn't have got hurt when he hit the ground. A woman in the other car broke her leg, and I'm afraid the man with her had internal injuries. They took him away in an ambulance."

"What will they do to the drunk?" Esther asked.

Dr. Dambach looked less happy still. "That I cannot tell you. He kept blithering on about what an important fellow he was in the Party. If he was lying, he'll be sorry. But if he was telling the truth . . . You know how these things go."

Being an Aryan, the pediatrician could afford to grumble about the way the world worked. Esther Stutzman nodded, but she never would have complained herself. Even nodding made her feel as if she was taking a chance.

"What appointments do we have this morning?" Dambach asked.

"Let me look." She went to the register. "There are . . . three immunizations, and the Fischers will be bringing in their seven-year-old for you to check his scoliosis, and—" The telephone rang, interrupting her. She picked it up. "Dr. Dambach's office. How may I help you? . . . Yes . . . Can you bring her in at ten-thirty? . . . All right. Thank you." She turned back to the doctor. "And Lotte Friedl has a sore throat."

"Probably the first of several," Dambach said, in which he was probably right. "Anything else?"

"Yes, Doctor. The Kleins are bringing in their little boy for another checkup," Esther answered. She tried not to change her tone of voice. Richard and Maria Klein and their son, Paul, were Jews—though Paul, who was only eight months old, had no idea that he was.

Dr. Dambach frowned. "Paul Klein, *ja*. That baby is not thriving as he should, and I do not know why." He sounded personally affronted at not knowing, too. He was a good doctor; he had that relentless itch to find out.

"Maybe you'll see something this time that you didn't notice before," Esther said. She paused and sniffed. "And the coffee's just about ready."

"Good," Dambach said. "Pour me a big cup, please. I have to get my brains from somewhere today."

The outer door to the waiting room opened. In came the first patient and her mother. Esther started to say hello, then got interrupted when the telephone rang again. Sure enough, it was a woman whose son had a sore throat. Feeling harried, Esther made an appointment for her. As if by magic, a cup of coffee appeared at her elbow. Dr. Dambach had not only poured one for himself, he'd poured one for her, too, and laced it with cream and sugar.

"*I'm* supposed to do that," she said indignantly.

He shrugged. "You were busier than I was just then. I suspect it will even out as the day goes along."

Esther had her doubts about that, though she kept quiet about them. Dr. Dambach's work was more specialized than hers; she knew that. But the phones, the patients and parents in the waiting room, the billing, and the medical records often made her feel like a juggler with a stream of plates and knives and balls in the air. If she didn't pay attention every moment, everything would come crashing down.

On the other hand, she'd felt that way ever since she found out what she was. At worst, an office disaster could get her fired. A disaster of a different sort . . . She resolutely declined to think about that. Staying busy helped drive worry away. Busy she was.

But she was reminded of her heritage when the Kleins brought in little Paul. *Something* was wrong with him; she could see as much. He seemed listless and unhappy and somehow less well assembled than he should have been. He didn't hold his head up the way a baby his age should have, nor did he act fascinated with his hands and feet like most eight-month-olds. His parents, especially his mother, looked drawn and worried.

They were the last appointment before lunch. Dr. Dambach stayed in the examining room with them for a long time. Paul cried once. He didn't sound quite right, either, though Esther had trouble putting her finger on why. It wasn't a *strong* cry; that was as close as she could come. Working here, she'd heard plenty of unhappy babies. Paul Klein should have raised a bigger fuss.

At last, the Kleins came out of the examining room, the baby in Maria's arms. "Thank you, Doctor," Richard Klein said. "Maybe this means something important."

"I will have to do more investigating myself before I can say for certain," Dr. Dambach replied. "Make an appointment with *Frau* Stutzman, please—I'll want to see him again in another two weeks." He sounded brisk and businesslike. The Kleins probably wouldn't know he used that demeanor to mask alarm.

Having worked with him for two years, Esther did. After she'd made the appointment, after the Kleins had left, she turned to the doctor and asked, "What's wrong with him?"

"His muscular development is not as it should be," Dambach said. "He seemed normal up until a couple of months ago, but since then. . . ." He shook his head. "If anything, he has gone backwards, when he should be moving ahead. And I saw something peculiar when I looked in his eyes: a red spot on each retina."

"What does that mean?" Esther asked.

"I'm not sure. I don't believe I've ever seen anything like it before," the pediatrician said. "I don't know if it is connected to the other problem, either. Can you order some food brought here, please? I was going to go out for lunch, but I believe I will stay here and go through my books instead."

"Of course, Doctor," Esther Stutzman said. "Will one of those Italian cheese pies do? The shop is close, and they deliver."

Dambach nodded. "That will be fine. I know the place you mean. They promise to get it where it should go in under half an hour, which is all to the good today."

"I'll take care of it." Esther made the call. The cheese pie arrived twenty-seven minutes later. She'd heard the owner had fired delivery boys for being late, so she was glad this one showed up on time. She paid for it from the cash drawer, then brought it in to Dr. Dambach.

"Just set it on the desk, please," he said without looking up from the medical book he was going through. Only his left hand and his mouth gave the food any notice; the rest of his attention was riveted on the book. Esther thought she could have substituted a coffee cake or plain bread without his knowing the difference.

She was eating her own lunch, ready to go home as soon as the afternoon receptionist came in, when Dambach exclaimed in what might as easily have been dismay as triumph. "What is it, Doctor?" she called.

"I know what Paul Klein has," Dr. Dambach said.

Esther still couldn't tell how he felt about knowing. She asked, "Well, what is it, then?"

He came out of the office, a half forgotten slice of the cheese pie still in his left hand. His face said more than his voice had; he looked thoroughly grim. "It's an obscure syndrome called Tay-Sachs disease, I'm afraid," he answered. "Along with the rest of his condition, the red spots on his retinas nail down the diagnosis."

"I never heard of it," Esther said.

"I wish I hadn't." Now the pediatrician sounded as unhappy as he looked.

"Why?" she asked. "What is it? What does it do?"

"There is an enzyme called Hexosaminidase A. Babies with Tay-Sachs disease are born without the ability to form it. Without it, lipids accumulate abnormally in the cells, and especially in the nerve cells of the brain. The disease destroys brain function a little at a time. I will not speak of symptoms, but eventually the child is blind, mentally retarded, paralyzed, and unresponsive to anything around it."

"Oh, my God! How horrible!" Esther's stomach did a slow lurch. She wished she hadn't eaten. "What can you do? Is there a cure?"

"I can do nothing. No one can do anything." Dr. Dambach's voice was hard and flat. "There is no cure. All children who have Tay-Sachs disease will die, usually before they turn five. I intend to recommend to the Kleins that they take the baby to a *Reichs* Mercy Center, to spare it this inevitable suffering. Then I intend to go out and get drunk."

He couldn't bring himself to come right out and talk about killing a baby, though that was what he meant. The Germans who'd slaughtered Jews hadn't talked straight out about what they were doing, either, though people weren't so shy about it any more. Here, Esther had more sympathy. "How awful for you," she said. "And how much worse for the Kleins! What causes this horrible disease? Could they have done anything to keep the baby from getting it?"

Dr. Dambach shook his head. "No. Nothing. It's genetic. If both parents carry the recessive, and if the two recessives come together . . ." He spread his hands. Even that gesture didn't remind him of the cheese pie he was holding. Intent on his own thoughts, he went on, "We don't see the disease very often these days. I have never seen it before, thank heaven, and I hope I never see it again. The books say it used to be fairly common among the Jews, though, before we cleaned them out. . . . Are you all right, *Frau* Stutzman?"

"Yes, I think so. This is all just so—so dreadful." Esther made herself nod. Dambach nodded back, accepting what she'd said. He couldn't know why her heart had skipped a beat. A good thing, too. He couldn't come out and talk about killing a baby, but he took the extermination of the Jews for granted. Why not? He hadn't even been born when it happened.

"Dreadful, *ja*. A very unfortunate coincidence. Even among the Jews it was not common, you understand, but it was up to a hundred times *more* common among them than it is among Aryans." Dambach thoughtfully rubbed his chin. "Did you happen to see on the news a few days ago the story about the Jews found in that village in backwoods Serbia?"

How to answer? Esther saw only one way: casually. "I sure did. Who would have imagined such a thing, in this day and age?" What she wanted to do was get up and run from the doctor's office. That that would be the worst thing she could possibly do didn't matter. Reason held her in her chair, held a polite smile on her face. Behind the façade, instinct screamed.

Still thoughtful, Dr. Dambach went on, "Tay-Sachs disease is so rare among Aryans, it almost makes one wonder. . . ."

Ice lived in Esther. "Don't be silly, Doctor," she said, keeping up the casual front. "None of *them* left any more, not in a civilized country." Pretending she wasn't a Jew was second nature to her; she'd done it almost automatically ever since she learned what she was. But mocking, scorning her true heritage wasn't so easy. She didn't have to do that very often, simply because Jews were so nearly extinct.

"I suppose you're right," the pediatrician said, and relief flowered like springtime in her. But then he added, "Still . . ."

The door to the waiting room opened. In came Irma Ritter, who would work in the afternoon. She was even rounder than Dr. Dambach. Pointing to the slice of cheese pie in his hand, she asked, "Any more of that left?"

He looked down in surprise. "I don't know," he said, sounding foolish. "Let me go look." While he did, Esther made her escape—and that was exactly what it felt like.

* * *

Alicia Gimpel and her sisters were playing an elaborate game with dolls. Part of it came from an adventure film they'd seen a few weeks before, but that was only the springboard; more came straight from their imaginations. "Here." Roxane picked up one of the few male dolls they had. "He can be the nasty Jew who's trying to cheat the dragons out of their cave."

"No!" Alicia exclaimed before remembering she wasn't supposed to say anything like that no matter what.

"Why not?" Roxane clouded up. "You never like any of my ideas. It's not fair."

"I think Alicia's right this time," Francesca said. "He's not ugly enough to be a Jew."

That wasn't why Alicia had said no, of course. She seized on it gratefully all the same. "Yes, that is what I meant," she said. She still didn't like lying to her sisters, but she didn't see what she could do about it, either. She couldn't tell the truth. She could see that. *They'll find out soon enough,* she thought from the height of her own ten years.

Roxane examined the doll, who was indeed plastic perfection. "Well, we can *pretend* he's ugly," she declared, and made him advance on the cardboard box doing duty for a cave. In a high, squeaky, unnatural voice, she said, "Here, dragons, I'll give you these beans if you'll move away from here and never come back. They may be magic beans." She laughed shrilly and whispered, "And they may not, too."

Francesca reached into the box and pulled out a stuffed dragon. "You nasty old Jew, you're trying to fool us. You'd better get out of here or I'll burn your ears off."

Roxane made the doll retreat. "I'll figure out another way to get your gold, then—you see if I don't."

"Oh, no, you won't," Francesca retorted. "I'm an Aryan dragon, and I'm too tough for you."

Alicia got to her feet. "I don't think I want to play any more."

"Why not?" Roxane said. "Things are just getting good." She looked down at the doll. "Aren't they?" It responded—she made it respond—with a thoroughly evil chuckle and a, "That's right," in the high, squeaky voice she'd used before.

"She's a wet blanket, that's why," Francesca said. "She's been a wet blanket for weeks now, and I'm tired of it."

"Wet blanket! Wet blanket!" Roxane sang, now in her own voice, now in the one she'd invented for the Jew doll.

"I am not!" Alicia said angrily. "This is a stupid game, that's all."

Roxane got angry, too. "You're just saying it's stupid because I'm doing something I thought up all by myself." She wheeled out the heavy artillery: "I'm going to tell. Mommy says you can't do things like that."

And Francesca was also angry, in a quieter way. "How can you say it's a stupid game when you thought up half of it?"

"Because—" But Alicia couldn't say what she couldn't say. Knowing what she knew and not being able to talk about it threatened to choke her. "Because it is, that's all."

"I'm going to tell," Roxane said again. "*Mommy!*"

"You and your big mouth," Alicia said, whereupon her little sister opened it as wide as she could and stuck out her tongue. Alicia was tempted to grab that tongue and give it a good yank, but it was too slimy for her to do it.

"What's going on?" came from the ground floor. Ominous footsteps on the stairs followed, each one louder than the one before. Their mother appeared at the doorway to Francesca and Roxane's room. "Can't the three of you play together nicely?"

"I didn't want to play any more, that's all," Alicia said.

"That's not all. You didn't like my ideas, that's what it is," Roxane said, and proceeded to explain in great detail what her ideas were.

Understanding kindled in their mother's eyes. She started to say something, then closed her mouth again. Awe trickled through Alicia. *She can't tell, either,* she thought. *She's a grownup, and* she *can't tell.* That spoke more clearly than anything else of how important the secret was. It was important enough to constrain a grownup, and grownups by the very nature of things were beyond constraint.

Their mother tried again. This time, she succeeded. "Play the game, Alicia," she said gently. "Go ahead and play the game. It's all right. That's what we have to do."

"See?" Triumph filled Roxane. "Mommy told you to."

And so she had. But she'd told Alicia something else, too, something that had gone by Roxane and Francesca. *That's what we have to do*. People who weren't Jews were going to say things about them. They were going to mock them. They couldn't help it. They believed all the things they'd learned in school. (Alicia still half believed them herself, which sometimes left her half-sick with confusion.) If you couldn't get used to that, if you couldn't pretend it wasn't anything, you'd give yourself away.

"All right," Alicia said. "I'll play the game."

By the way their mother smiled, she'd also sneaked a message past her sisters. "Good, Alicia," Lise Gimpel said. "In that case, I'll get back to what I was doing." She went down the hall. She went down the stairs.

Roxane eyed Alicia expectantly. Francesca eyed her suspiciously, as if to say, *You can't just start and stop like that.* But Alicia could. At first, she felt as if she were in one of the little plays students sometimes had to put on at school, as if this weren't happening to her but to the person she was pretending to be. The longer she did it, though, the more natural it got.

She and her sisters foiled the doll that was being a Jew. Another doll brought an—imaginary—sack of gold, so the dragons, who'd been tricked out of theirs, got to keep their cave. Then, while the Jew was gloating over his ill-gotten gains, more dolls, these proper Aryans, swooped down on him. They took him away to another box.

Roxane closed the lid. "And that'll be the end of him," she chortled. Then, in a more practical frame of mind, she added, "Till we need him for another game, anyhow."

"See, Alicia?" Francesca said. "That was pretty good."

"I suppose so," Alicia said: for her, no small admission, and more than enough to satisfy her sister. *But it's not all a game,* she thought. Some of the things her father had said made that very plain. *If you put a real person in a box and close the lid and go, that'll be the end of him. He won't come out again for the next game*. Roxane wouldn't understand. She was too little. Alicia had trouble understanding it herself. One of the teachers at her school, though, had had the misfortune to step in front of a bus. And *Frau* Zoglmann would never be back again.

Death was permanent, no matter what Roxane thought. Yes, death was permanent. And so was fear.

III

"AREN'T YOU GOING TO LUNCH?" ASKED WALTHER STUTZMAN'S BOSS, A BIG, beefy fellow named Gustav Priepke.

Walther shook his head. "Not today. I'm swamped."

"You?" Priepke scratched his head. "Maybe we need more system designers. If you've got as much as you can handle, everybody else is bound to be drowning. You're the one who keeps the whole section afloat."

"Thanks." Just at that moment, Stutzman would have preferred a less enviable efficiency record. He said, "If I get a chance, I'll grab something at the office canteen later on."

His boss made a face. "Make sure you tell your wife you may never see her again first. I'm going down the street to a real restaurant instead." Off he went. The belly that hung over his belt said he liked good food, or at least lots of food.

Alone in the cubicle, Walther typed in a security code he wasn't supposed to use. Because of what he did, he had unusual access to the *Reich*'s electronic networks. He could have wreaked untold havoc if that were what he wanted. It wasn't. Staying invisible, and helping other people stay invisible, counted for much more.

Nobody at Zeiss Computing should have been able to access the official genealogical records of the Germanic Empire. But Walther's father had helped transfer those records from paper to computers. He'd left a few highly unofficial ways to get into them. Those wouldn't stay safe if anyone used them too often. Here, though . . . Here, Stutzman judged the risk worth taking.

Richard Klein's ancestry appeared on the monitor in front of him. His own father had given Richard's grandfather a perfect Aryan pedigree, at least in the database. In those terror-filled days, no one had taken the least chance with blight on a family tree. Now, though, if someone suddenly suspicious because of the dreadful misfortune that had befallen Richard's baby should compare electronic records with whatever lingered in a dusty file drawer somewhere . . .

"That would not be good," Walther murmured.

He went back seven generations in Klein's family and changed the entry under *Religion* for one of his multiple-great-grandmothers from LUTHERAN to UNKNOWN. Then he did the same thing with two of Maria Klein's even more distant ancestors. After studying his handiwork, he nodded to himself and left the genealogical records.

That should take care of it, he thought. Possible Jews so far back in the woodpile were safe. Anyone applying for the SS had to show his ancestors had been *Judenfrei* for longer than that, but Richard Klein, who made a good living playing the trombone, was never going to apply for that service. And finding distant ancestors who might have been Jews in his family tree and his wife's would keep the Security Police from wondering if the Kleins themselves carried their blood and their faith down through the generations. *It had better, anyhow.*

One more danger remained. A program on a machine somewhere in the Zeiss works recorded every keystroke every employee made. If anyone ever started wondering about one Walther Stutzman, he could go through the record and see that Walther had done things he wasn't authorized to do. He could . . . till Walther keyed in the phrase RED CHALK AND GREEN CHEESE. A dialog box appeared on his monitor. He entered the time he'd begun fiddling with the genealogical records and the time he'd left them. The hidden override on the keystroke monitor would substitute a copy of what he'd been doing yesterday during that period for what he'd actually done today.

He muttered to himself. This was only the third time he could remember using the override. It carried risks of its own. Those, though, were smaller than the risk of showing he was mucking about with anything connected to Jews. He couldn't think of any risk bigger than that one.

After he got back from the canteen—where lunch, Gustav Priepke notwithstanding, wasn't half bad—he called Esther. "I've taken care of the shopping," he said.

"Oh, good," his wife answered. "You'll bring home something nice for me, won't you?"

Walther laughed. "Of course. What else have I got to spend my money on?"

"That's why I love you: you have the right attitude," Esther said. They chatted for a couple of minutes. Then he hung up. He assumed any line out from the office could be tapped at any time. Esther had understood what he was telling her, though, and he didn't think anyone from the Security Police could have.

His boss stuck his head into Stutzman's cubicle. Priepke was smoking a pipe apparently charged with stinkweed. "Everything under control?" he asked.

"Everything except that." Walther pointed at the pipe. "I thought they outlawed poison gas a long time ago."

"Ha!" Priepke took it out of his mouth and blew a smoke ring. "If you ask me, it's all to the good."

"How's that?" Walther asked. He'd been kidding on the square; the pipe really was vile.

"How? I'll tell you how." Another smoke ring polluted the air. "If there are any Jews around, I'll gas 'em out." Priepke threw back his head and guffawed.

Walther laughed, too, a little more than dutifully. How many times had he heard jokes like that? More than he could count. What could he do but laugh?

The Lufthansa airliner taxied toward the terminal at Heathrow Airport. First in German and then in English, the chief steward said, "Baggage claim and customs are to your left as you leave the aircraft. You must have your baggage with you when you clear customs. All bags are subject to search. Obey all commands from customs officials. Have a pleasant stay in London."

Obey all commands. Have a pleasant stay. Susanna Weiss snorted. The steward saw no irony there. Neither did the hack who'd written his script. And neither did the hack's bosses, who'd told him what to write.

"Purpose of your visit to the United Kingdom?" a British customs man asked in accented German.

"I am here for the meeting of the Medieval English Association," Susanna replied in English. She was more fluent in his tongue than he was in hers.

Maybe she was *too* fluent, fluent enough to get taken for a fellow national despite her German passport. Whatever the reason, the customs man went through her baggage with painstaking care while other passengers headed out to the cab stand. She fumed quietly. Arguing with a petty functionary while he did his job was likely to make him more thorough, to cost more time. At last, finding nothing more incriminating than copies of *Anglo-Saxon Prose* and *One Hundred Middle English Lyrics,* the customs man stamped her passport and said, "Pass on"—still in German.

"Thank you so much," Susanna said—still in English. The sarcasm rolled off him like water off oilcoth.

She let out a sigh of relief when she saw black British taxis still waiting at the cab stand. A cabby touched the brim of his cap. "Where to, ma'am?"

"To the Silver Eagle Hotel, please," Susanna answered.

"Right y'are," he said cheerfully, and tossed her bags into what the British called the boot. He held the door open for her, closed it after her, and got behind the wheel. The cab pulled away from the curb. Susanna had a momentary qualm, as she did whenever she came to Britain. Then she remembered they *did* drive on the left here, and the cabby wasn't drunk or insane—or, if he was, she couldn't prove it by that.

London's sprawl was even more vast than Berlin's. The British capital also had a far more modern look than the centerpiece of the Germanic Empire. After the fight Churchill's backers had put up trying to hold the *Wehrmacht* out of London, not much from the old days was left standing. Susanna had seen pictures of the old Parliament building, Big Ben, and St. Paul's cathedral. Pictures were all that remained. And after the war, London had taken a generation to start rebuilding, and still hadn't finished the job. German urban planners often came here to see how their British counterparts were doing what they needed to do. Whizzing past one newish block of flats or industrial park after another, Susanna wondered why. The British had worked here with a clean slate, which no one ever would with a German city.

A graffito, gone before she could read it. Then she saw another one, painted in big blue letters on the side of a wall. LET US CHOOSE! it said. A moment later, the same message appeared again.

"What's that all about?" she asked the taxi driver.

"What's what, ma'am?"

" 'Let us choose.' "

"Oh." He drove on for a few seconds, then asked, "You're . . . not a Brit?"

She'd fooled him into thinking she was a native speaker. This time, unlike going through customs, that pleased her enormously. What praise could be higher for someone who'd learned a foreign language? But she had to answer: "No, I just got here from Berlin."

"Oh," he said again, more portentously this time. "There's . . . well, there's some talk of 'ow to run the British Union of Fascists." He nodded to himself. "Yes, that's what it is, all right."

That might have been some of what it was, but not all. Having lived so much of her life hiding things from others, Susanna recognized when somebody wasn't saying everything he might have. She didn't push the cabby. If she had, he would have decided she worked for the *Gestapo* or some other German security outfit, and would have clammed up altogether.

Even now, almost the Biblical threescore and ten after the conquest, people on the streets here were thinner and shabbier than their German counterparts. Their gaze had a certain furtive quality to it. It wouldn't rest on any one thing for long, but flicked now here, now there. Seldom did anyone meet anyone else's eye. In Germany, people were careful about the Security Police, but most of them knew they were unlikely to draw suspicion unless they stepped out of line. Here, security agencies assumed anybody could be the enemy, and everybody knew it.

" 'Ere you are, ma'am," the cabby said, pulling up in front of a glass-and-steel pile decorated, if that was the word, with an enormous eagle of polished aluminum. It wasn't quite the Germanic eagle that so often bore a swastika in its talons, but it certainly made anyone who saw it think of that eagle at first glance. " 'Ope you 'ave a pleasant stay at the Silver Eagle. Your fare's four and tuppence."

Susanna handed him a crown. He pocketed the big aluminum coin stamped with the image of Henry IX on one side and the lightning bolts of the British Union of Fascists on the other. "I don't need any change," she said, "but I would like a receipt."

"Right you are. I thank you very much." He wrote one for the five shillings she'd given him, then got her bags out of the boot and set them on the sidewalk.

He was about to drive off when she pointed across the street to the even bigger and more garish hotel there. A lot of the people—almost all of them men—going in and out of that hotel were in uniforms of one sort or another. "Is that where the British Union of Fascists is holding its meeting?"

"Yes, ma'am," the taximan said. "They always gather at the Crown, they do." A crown of aluminum anodized in gold outdid even the silver eagle on Susanna's hotel for gaudiness. Before she could find any more questions, he put the cab in gear and whizzed away.

WELCOME, MEDIEVAL ENGLISH ASSOCIATION! The banner in the lobby of the Silver Eagle greeted newcomers in English, German, and French. Not all the people queuing up in front of the registration desk were tweedy professorial types, though. Close to half were hard-faced men in those not-quite-military uniforms. *Overflow from the Crown,* Susanna realized. This might prove a very . . . interesting meeting. She remembered the convention in Düsseldorf a few years before, when the medievalists had shared the hotel with a group of mushroom fanciers. She'd had the best omelette she'd ever eaten, but several of her colleagues and even more of the mushroom lovers came down sick at a feast she'd missed. Luckily, no one died, but she knew two or three professors who'd sworn off mushrooms for good.

Two British fascists in front of her talked as if they were alone in the hotel lobby. One said, "Nationalism and autonomy aren't just catchphrases to trot out on the wireless whenever morale needs a bit of pumping up."

"They'd bloody well better not be," his friend agreed. "We can run our own show here, by God. We don't need someone from the Continent to tell us how to handle the job."

The first man nodded so vehemently, his cap almost flew off his head. "That's right. Sir Oswald started banging heads almost as soon as Adolf did. If the Germans let *us* choose, we'll do fine. If they don't . . ."

Susanna didn't find out what he thought would happen then, because the pair of uniformed men reached the head of the queue and advanced on the desk clerk. A moment later, another clerk waved to Susanna.

To her relief, the hotel hadn't lost her reservation. She'd feared the fascist contingent might have had enough clout to oust the medievalists, but evidently not. "You are a German national?" the clerk asked.

"Yes, that is correct," Susanna answered. To the outside world, it was. How a Jew could feel like a German national after everything the Third *Reich* had done was a different question, but one each survivor wrestled with silently and alone, not in front of a registration clerk.

"Your passport, please," the man said. He was years younger than Susanna, but had shiny white teeth of perfect evenness and alarmingly pink gums: dentures. A lot of Englishmen and -women needed false teeth. Even before it was conquered, Britain hadn't been able to raise all the food it needed, and the people often preferred things like sweets and potato crisps to more nourishing food. They paid the price in dentistry.

"Here." Susanna handed him the document. He opened the red leatherette cover with the swastika-carrying eagle embossed in gold, compared her photograph to her face, and wrote the passport number in the registration book. Then he gave the passport back to her. She put it in her purse. Things were looser here than they were in France—looser here than they were for foreigners in Germany, too, for that matter. She didn't have to surrender the passport to the clerk for the duration of her stay.

He turned the registration book toward her and held out a pen. "Your signature, please. This also acknowledges your responsibility for payment. You will be in Room 1065. The bank of lifts is around the corner to your left. Here is the key." He handed it to her. "Enjoy your stay."

"Thank you," she said. As if by magic, a bellman appeared with a wheeled cart to take charge of her bags. He was a scrawny little man with—almost inevitably—bad teeth and a servile smile that put them on display. She gave him a Reichsmark when they got up to the room. The swastika-bedizened banknote brought out another smile, this one broad, genuine, and greedy. A Reichsmark wasn't much to her, but it was worth more than a pound here; ever since the war, Germany had pegged the exchange rate artificially high. The bellman did everything but tug his forelock before bowing his way out of the room.

After unpacking, Susanna took the lift back downstairs to the lobby. She shared the little car with a professor from the Sorbonne whom she knew, and with two hulking, uniformed British fascists. Professor Drumont read, wrote, and understood modern English perfectly well, but did not speak it fluently. Susanna enjoyed the chance to practice her own rusty French.

The fascists' disapproval stuck out like spines. "Bloody foreigners," one of them growled.

He was at least thirty centimeters taller than Susanna. Since she couldn't look down her nose at him, she looked up it instead. "*Was sagen Sie?*" she inquired with icy hauteur.

Hearing her speak German as opposed to French—a losers' language—took the wind from his sails, as she'd thought it might. "Ah . . . nothing," he said. "I didn't mean anything by it."

She switched languages again, this time to English: "Let me see your identity card."

He didn't ask what right she had to see it. He just handed it over. She acted as if she had the right. As far as he was concerned, that put her above doubt. She studied the card, nodded coldly, pulled a notebook and pen from her handbag, and wrote something down (actually, it was "Whan that Aprill with his shoures soote," but the fascist would never know—and surely wouldn't have been able to read her scrawl anyhow). Only then did she return the identity document. Trembling, the Englishman put it back in his wallet.

"*Vous avez cran,*" Professor Drumont remarked as both fascists dashed from the lift and hurried away.

"Guts? Me? Give me leave to doubt." Susanna shook her head. "What I have is a—how would you say it in French?—a low tolerance for being pushed around. I think that would be it."

Drumont shrugged a very Gallic shrug. "It amounts to the same thing in the end. Now, where do we register for the meeting?"

To Susanna's annoyance, they had to walk up a flight of stairs to find registration. "If I had known that, we could have got out sooner," she grumbled. "We would not have had to spend so much time in the car with those *salauds*."

"It could be that you were too hard on them," Professor Drumont said gently. "You are, after all, a German. You may not always understand the . . . the strains upon other folk in the Germanic Empire."

That was a brave thing for him to say, or possibly a foolish one. Somebody from one security organization or another was bound to be keeping an eye on the Medieval English Association. Susanna could have been that person, or one of those people, as easily as not. The Frenchman's words were also funny, in an agonizing way. *I don't know about the strains on other folk in the Germanic Empire, eh? Well, Professor, have you ever contemplated the strains on Jews in the Empire?* She doubted that. Oh, yes. She doubted it very much indeed.

And yet . . . Her gaze flicked over to Professor Drumont. What did he look like? A gray-haired Frenchman, nothing else. But suppose he were a Jew. How could she tell? He would no more dare reveal himself to a near-stranger than would she. Sudden tears stung her eyes. She blinked angrily as she waited to get her name badge. *We might be ships passing in the night. We might be, but neither of us would ever know. And not knowing is the worst thing of all.*

Heinrich Gimpel leaned back in his swivel chair. "Lunch?" he asked.

"Sounds good to me." Willi Dorsch nodded. "Where do you feel like eating today?"

"I've got kind of a yen for Japanese food," Heinrich answered. Willi made a horrible face. Heinrich needed a moment to realize what he'd said. He held up a hasty hand. "I didn't do that on purpose."

"For one thing, I don't believe you," Willi said. "For another, if you're telling the truth, that just makes it worse. Unconscious punning? If that's not enough to send you up before a People's Court, what would be?"

In spite of himself, Heinrich shivered. Few who appeared before the judges of a People's Court ever appeared anywhere else again. He pushed the dark thought out of his mind, or at least out of the front part of it. "Well, *does* Japanese food suit you?" he asked.

"I was going to suggest it myself, till you made me lose my appetite," Willi said. "Admiral Yamamoto's is only a couple of blocks from here. How's that sound?"

Heinrich rose—all but leaped—from his chair. "Let's go."

The Japanese who ran Admiral Yamamoto's had come to Germany ten or fifteen years earlier, to study engineering. He'd got his degree, but he'd never gone home to Tokyo. Some of the sushi he served would have got him odd looks if he had. What he called a Berlin roll, for instance, had seaweed and rice wrapped around thinly cut, spicy white radish and a piece of raw Baltic herring. It might not have been authentic, but it was good, especially washed down with beer. Heinrich ordered half a dozen, and some sashimi as well.

"I don't quite feel like raw fish today," Willi Dorsch said, and chose shrimp tempura instead. The batter in which the shrimp were fried wasn't what it would have been on the other side of the world, either, but it was tasty. In place of tempura sauce, Willi slathered the shrimp with wasabi. "It's green, not white, but it cleans out your sinuses just like any other horseradish."

"You put that much on and it'll blow off the top of your head." Heinrich used wasabi mixed with soy sauce for his sushi and sashimi, too, but not nearly so much.

"Ah, well, what difference does it make? No brains in there anyhow." Willi took a big bite, and found out what difference it made. He grabbed for his own stein to try to put out the fire. When he could speak again, he said, "I'm *not* going to tell Erika about this."

"Mm," Heinrich said—the most noncommittal noise he could find. Anything that had anything to do with Erika Dorsch made him nervous. He didn't want Willi thinking he had designs on her. He didn't want her having designs on him. He didn't want . . . He shook his head. He couldn't say he didn't want Erika. He didn't want her enough to throw away what he was for her, and to endanger his family and friends.

When I found out I was a Jew, I knew it meant I had to watch a lot of things. I never imagined then that it would rob me of adultery, too. Such irony appealed to him.

But when he laughed, Willi asked, "What's so funny?"

He couldn't tell the truth. One thing he'd soon learned about being a Jew was always to have a cover story handy. He said, "The look on your face after you took that mouthful, that's what."

"Oh. Well, you can't really blame me," Willi Dorsch said. "If you ask me, wasabi's the first step toward what goes into atomic bombs."

That made Heinrich laugh without needing any cover story. "I wouldn't be surprised," he said, and then, looking out the window, "What's going on? Everybody's stopping. Is there a traffic accident down the street?"

"We would have heard it, wouldn't we?" Willi sent the wasabi paste a suspicious glance. "Unless this stuff made my ears ring, too."

The owner of Admiral Yamamoto's came out from the kitchen. In his accented German, he said, "*Meine Damen und Herren,* please excuse me for disturbing your meals, but I have just heard important news on the radio. The *Führer* of the Germanic Empire, Kurt Haldweim, has passed away. Please accept my deepest sympathies and condolences." He bowed stiffly, from the waist, arms at his sides, and then disappeared again.

Heinrich Gimpel stared down at his half-eaten lunch. He'd known this day might be coming, yes, but he hadn't thought it would come quite so soon.

Willi took a last big bite of tempura. If the wasabi bothered him this time, he didn't let it show. He got to his feet, took out his wallet, and pulled out enough money to cover his lunch and Heinrich's. "Come on," he said, suddenly all business. "We'd better get back to the office."

"You're right." Heinrich rose, too.

Half the diners in Admiral Yamamoto's were finishing up in a hurry and getting out. That surprised Heinrich not at all. Given where the restaurant was, most of the people who lunched here would work for the *Wehrmacht* or the SS or the Party. Haldweim had no obvious successor. Intrigue and jockeying for position had begun years earlier, when he started having "colds." Now things would come out into the open.

"Who will it be?" Willi murmured as they hurried up the street. The same thought was uppermost in Heinrich's mind, too.

When they got back to Adolf Hitler Platz, they saw Horst Witzleben's perfect image on the huge televisor screen on the front wall of the *Führer*'s palace. The square was filling up fast as people got the news. Already, the large swastika flag above the palace had been lowered to half-staff. Witzleben's almost operatic voice blared from powerful speakers: "Even so soon, messages of sorrow and mourning have begun pouring in from around the world. In a moving joint tribute, the King and the *Duce* of the Italian Empire spoke of Kurt Haldweim as a man of power and a man of peace. The Emperor of Japan has expressed his sympathy with the German people on their loss, in which the Emperor of Manchukuo joins. The

Caudillo of Spain described our beloved *Führer* as a man of world-historical proportions, while the *Perón* of Argentina termed him a model for all rulers aspiring to greatness." Someone's arm slid a paper onto Witzleben's desk. The news reader glanced down at it. "And this just in: the *Poglavnik* of Croatia has declared a day of mourning in his country, while stating that the *Führer*'s memory will live in the hearts of men forever."

"Nice," Willi remarked. "All that sympathy and a Reichsmark will buy me a glass of beer."

"Well, what do you expect them to say?" Heinrich asked. He knew what he would say if he had the chance. *One more murderer in a line of murderers. A little smoother than the last two, but a murderer all the same.* Except with Lise, he wouldn't get that chance. Even thinking such things was dangerous.

"Oh, just what they are saying," Willi answered, turning his back on the televisor. "But how many of them mean it?"

"If you had to mean what you said, we'd have an awful lot of diplomats who never opened their mouths—and the world might be a better place," Heinrich said. His friend laughed, supposing he'd been joking.

He and Willi went up the broad stairway to the entrance of the *Oberkommando der Wehrmacht* building. "Identification cards," a guard snapped. Heinrich dug out his wallet and produced the card. The guard carefully compared the photo to his face before running the card through the machine reader. Only when the light glowed green did he nod for Heinrich to proceed. Willi got the same treatment.

"They aren't usually so jumpy during the lunch break," he said once they were safely inside and out of earshot of the guards.

"Did you think they wouldn't be?" Heinrich asked. "Nobody's going to trust anybody till we have a new *Führer*. Suppose the SS tried to sneak somebody in here to find out which way the *Wehrmacht* will go."

"They'd be fools if they did. They'd be bigger fools if they didn't have spies in place here years ago. And we'd be fools if we didn't have spies planted over there. And the Party's watching us and the SS both. The Air and Space Ministry's likely got fingers in a few different pies, too. Maybe even the Navy—who knows?" Willi took to intrigue like a duck to water. He eyed a secretary walking past as if he thought she was spying for the SS and the Navy and the Japanese all at once: or he might have looked at her that way because she was a cute redhead in a skirt that rose almost to her knees.

Just because he was melodramatic, that didn't mean he was wrong. The *Wehrmacht,* the SS, and the Party surely were all spying on one another. Air and Space and the Navy were smaller players, but they could get big in a hurry if they managed to put one of their people in the *Führer*'s palace.

Once Heinrich got back to his desk, he checked to see what was coming over the *Wehrmacht* computer network. Most of it was what he'd expected. The United States sent a message of condolence. So did the British Union of Fascists—with one intriguing difference. Their spokesman added that he hoped the new *Führer* would be chosen "according to the principles set forth in the first edition of *Mein Kampf.*"

Heinrich scratched his head. "Why is the first edition different from all other editions?" he asked Willi Dorsch. The question eerily reminded him of the one he'd asked Lise a few days earlier. *Why is this night different from all other nights?* Only a few people in the Germanic Empire—a handful of hidden Jews, and another handful of scholars who studied dead things—had any idea what that question meant and how it should be answered.

Willi didn't know how Heinrich's question should be answered, either. "What are you talking about?" he said.

"See for yourself." Heinrich pointed to his monitor.

Willi came around to his desk to look. "Isn't that interesting?" he said when he'd read the British message. "I don't know what the difference between the first edition and the others is, either. I didn't think there was much difference, except for cleaning up typographical errors and such."

"Neither did I," Heinrich said. The powers that be had never forbidden any edition of *Mein Kampf.* That strongly argued the differences between editions weren't large. But they had to be there. Otherwise, the British Union of Fascists wouldn't have specifically cited the first edition.

Like everyone else at *Oberkommando der Wehrmacht,* he had a copy of *Mein Kampf* on his desk. His was, of course, the fourth edition, revised by Hitler after Britain and Russia went under. As always when he opened the book, he found his way to one passage near the end. *If at the beginning of the War and during the War twelve or fifteen thousand of these Hebrew corrupters of the people had been held under poison gas, as happened to hun-*

dreds of thousands of our very best German workers in the field, the sacrifice of millions at the front would not have been in vain. On the contrary: twelve thousand scoundrels eliminated in time might have saved the lives of millions of real Germans, valuable for the future. But that passage was plainly old, for by *the War* there Hitler had to mean World War I. *Damn him,* Heinrich thought wearily. He'd known what he wanted to do, what he intended to do, long before he got the chance to do it.

But what did he say about choosing a new *Führer?* Finding out took some poking through the index. In this edition, it was exactly what anyone would have expected. *The young movement is in its nature and inner organization anti-parliamentarian; that is, it rejects in general and in its own inner structure a principle of majority rule in which the leader is degraded to the level of a mere executant of other people's will and opinion. In little as well as big things, the movement advocates the principle of unconditional authority of the leader, coupled with the highest responsibility.*

That was the way things had worked in the *Reich* for as long as Heinrich could remember, and for years before. How was the first edition of *Mein Kampf* different? Willi Dorsch had his copy open, too. He read aloud the passage Heinrich had just found.

"It can't be the same in the first edition," Heinrich said. "If it were—"

"But how could it be different?" Willi asked. "What other way to do things is there?" He'd said Heinrich was more content living in the world as it was, but he was the one for whom that world was water to a fish. He couldn't see beyond what was to what might be.

"There has to be something," Heinrich answered. He didn't know what it was, either, but he could see the possibility. As a Jew, he necessarily perceived the *Reich* from an outsider's viewpoint. Sometimes, as now, that proved useful. But he found himself longing for Willi's simple certainties at least as often.

"I think the British are just out to make trouble," Willi said now. "They're probably plotting with the Americans. The damned Anglo-Saxons have always been jealous of Germany. For years, they tried to keep the *Reich* from taking its rightful place in the sun. Now they're paying for it, and I say it serves them right."

He'd learned those lessons in school. So had Heinrich Gimpel. But Heinrich, for reasons of his own, had found he needed to doubt a lot of what his teachers said. As far as he could tell, Willi never doubted. *Does that make him a fool, or the luckiest man I know?*

"They've spent a long time paying for it," Heinrich said.

"Good," Willi Dorsch declared. "So did we."

"Well, yes." Heinrich couldn't—didn't dare—disagree with that. "Still, I do wonder what's in the first edition."

From his herringbone jacket to his long, narrow, bony face to his decaying teeth, Professor Horace Buckingham might have been a stage Englishman. Even his own countrymen had trouble following his Oxonian accent. It had made the panel discussion on Chaucer's "Wife of Bath's Tale" an ordeal for Susanna Weiss, who'd had to respond again and again to points she wasn't sure she understood.

When the panel ended, the audience applauded politely. Buckingham turned to Susanna. "I thought that went off rather well," he said. His breath was formidable, no doubt because of those mottled teeth.

"Not bad." Susanna still thought his interpretation naive, but she wasn't inclined to argue—not at close range, anyhow. A paper in a learned journal would offer her a more impersonal way to stick a knife in his scholarship, and would also give her something she could show her department chairman.

"Would you care to discuss things further over a drink?" he asked. The way he smiled said scholarship wasn't the only thing on his mind.

I don't want to be within three meters of you, let alone closer. The retort hovered on the tip of Susanna's tongue. Not without regret, she let it die there. She said, "Not now, thanks. I have no more discussions until the evening session, and nothing on the program really draws me, so I am going to go across the street. The British Union of Fascists' meeting has turned out to be fascinating, don't you think?"

"Fascinating. Indeed." Professor Buckingham departed with marked haste. At first Susanna thought that meant he had no use for fascists, which got him a point in her book despite his bad breath. Then she realized another explanation was more likely. To him, she was a German, nothing else. She knew otherwise, but he didn't. And what did a German interested in the congress of the British Union of Fascists add up to? Someone with connections to a security bureau.

Under different circumstances, that might have been funny. As things were . . . Susanna sighed. Buckingham would talk—what else did academics do? If the other professors at the Medieval English Association didn't start sidling away from her, it would be a miracle, and God was depressingly stingy with miracles these days.

She went across the street to the Crown Hotel anyhow. She'd never been able to resist political drama. This was the genuine article—what Americans called, for no reason she could fathom, *the real McCoy*. On the surface, everything seemed exactly as it should have. Union Jacks and BUF flags with lightning bolts that resembled the SS runes flew at half-staff in commemoration of Kurt Haldweim. English and Scottish fascists had praised the departed *Führer* to the skies. They'd also spent at least as much time patting one another on the back as the scholars of the MEA had done.

That was the surface. Underneath, and sometimes not so far underneath, things were different. Susanna hadn't even got into the Crown when a parade came up the street toward her. Nothing out of the ordinary there; British fascists were no less enamored of public display than their German counterparts.

But these tough-looking men in uniforms and shiny jackboots carried signs that said, REMEMBER THE FIRST EDITION! The mere idea was enough to make Susanna want to hug herself with glee. Political action mixed with textual analysis? The earnest academics at the Medieval English Association didn't know what they were missing.

To make sure their British colleagues and, more to the point, the National Socialists in Germany *did* remember, other paraders carried banners that stretched from one side of the street to the other, with the relevant passages spelled out in English and *auf Deutsch*. The English read, IN LITTLE AS WELL AS BIG THINGS, THE MOVEMENT ADVOCATES THE PRINCIPLE OF A GERMANIC DEMOCRACY: THE LEADER IS ELECTED, BUT THEN ENJOYS UNCONDITIONAL AUTHORITY. Other banners declared, THE FIRST CHAIRMAN OF A LOCAL GROUP IS ELECTED, BUT THEN HE IS THE RESPONSIBLE LEADER OF THE LOCAL GROUP and THE FIRST PRINCIPLE APPLIES TO THE NEXT HIGHER ORGANIZATION—THE LEADER IS ALWAYS ELECTED and AND FINALLY, THE SAME APPLIES TO THE LEADERSHIP OF THE WHOLE PARTY. THE CHAIRMAN IS ELECTED, BUT HE IS THE EXCLUSIVE LEADER OF THE MOVEMENT. And, at the very tail of the procession, another big banner proclaimed, MEMBERS OF THE MOVEMENT ARE FREE TO CALL HIM TO ACCOUNT BEFORE THE FORUM OF A NEW ELECTION, TO DIVEST HIM OF HIS OFFICE IN SO FAR AS HE HAS INFRINGED ON THE PRINCIPLES OF THE MOVEMENT OR SERVED ITS INTERESTS BADLY.

British policemen in their blue uniforms and tall helmets stood on the sidewalk watching the fascists' procession. They didn't seem to know what to make of it. Neither did the German occupation authorities. If *they* had decided to come out and quash it, they would have used panzers and rocket-firing fighter jets. They'd done that more than a few times in the earlier years of the occupation, though not so often lately.

As for Susanna, she marveled that the British Union of Fascists, or at least one wing of the party, had managed to find a way to call for democracy without immediately getting lined up in front of a wall and shot. How could you give a man a cigarette and a blindfold for quoting Adolf Hitler, whose words were close to Holy Writ all through the Germanic Empire? You couldn't possibly.

Susanna rapidly discovered the marchers represented one wing of the BUF, not the entire organization. More men in uniform swarmed out of a side street and attacked the men in the parade with clubs and brass knuckles. The marchers fought back with similar weapons. Other fascists rushed out of the Crown to join in the mêlée, on whose side Susanna wasn't sure. She had all she could do to keep from getting bowled over.

Whistles shrilling, the British bobbies waded into the fray. They flailed away with their truncheons, whacking brawlers on both sides with fine impartiality. "Break it up!" they bawled. "Break it up, you bloody sods!" But nobody on either side seemed to want to break it up.

Even as the men who extolled the first edition fought, they raised a chant in English: "The whole world is watching! The whole world is watching!"

Odd sort of battle cry, Susanna thought. But maybe it wasn't. Sure as the devil, televisor cameras from the BBC and the German RRG were filming the clash. The marchers must have known the cameras would be there; otherwise, they wouldn't have quoted from *Mein Kampf* in both English and German.

Police cars raced up, sirens screeching. The men inside them wore pig-snouted gas masks. They shot tear-gas canisters into the riot. Where nothing else had worked, that did. Fascists for and against the first edition fled.

So did Susanna, not quite soon enough. Her eyes were streaming and her stomach twisting with nausea when she made it back into the lobby of the Silver Eagle. The academics in there were fleeing, too, for fresh wisps of gas came in every time the doors opened.

Susanna repaired to the bar, which seemed a popular port in the storm. Of course, the bar was a popular port in the storm at every academic conference she'd ever attended. She took off her glasses and dabbed at her eyes with a tissue. It didn't help much. The single-malt Scotch she ordered didn't help her eyes much, either, but it made the rest of her feel better.

"Dear God in heaven," said a British professor who also staggered in weeping like a fountain, "what *is* going on out there?"

Susanna eyed him—blurrily. "Literary criticism," she said.

"*Achtung!* Form your lines!" *Herr* Kessler shouted as the schoolchildren got off the bus to one side of the Great Hall. He sounded more like a *Wehrmacht* drill sergeant than a teacher—but then, that was true a lot of the time. "Take your partner's hand! Hold your flag in your free hand! Now—forward to the end of the queue!"

Alicia Gimpel took Emma Handrick's hand. The alphabet made them line partners, as it made them sit close together. Alicia wished she were paired with someone else. Emma had cold, sweaty palms. Nothing Alicia could do about it. She imagined complaining to *Herr* Kessler. Imagining the paddling she would get for trying it immediately squelched the idea.

The swastika flag she held in her left hand was bordered in black, a token of mourning for the departed *Führer*. Kurt Haldweim lay in state under the monstrous dome of the Great Hall. Along with other children from all over Berlin—from all over Germany—Alicia and her schoolmates would file past his body and then line the parade route as his funeral procession went past.

"This way!" *Herr* Kessler shouted.

"No—over here," a uniformed attendant said, pointing in the opposite direction. "Your group is to take its place behind those bigger children." Fuming, his face beet red, the teacher led them to the right place.

"He doesn't know everything," Emma whispered, and smiled maliciously. For that, Alicia forgave her her sweaty palm.

The line moved forward with what the world had learned to call Germanic efficiency. Not even *Herr* Kessler could find anything to complain about there. Within twenty minutes, Alicia and her classmates had entered the Great Hall. The space under that unbelievable dome seemed even vaster within than without. The interior appointments had a simple grandeur to them. A recess clad in gold mosaic opposite the entrance broke a circle of a hundred marble columns, each twenty-five meters tall. In front of the recess, on a marble pedestal fourteen meters high, stood a German eagle with a swastika in its claws. And in front of the pedestal lay the mortal remains of Kurt Haldweim.

Floral decorations and shrubbery surrounded the casket of gilded bronze in which the *Führer* lay in state. SS guards stood on either side of the coffin, displaying the many decorations Haldweim had won in his long, illustrious career as a soldier and National Socialists administrator. Yet try as they would, the wizards of ceremony who had staged this scene could not overcome one basic difficulty: the Great Hall altogether dwarfed the pale, still remains of the hawk-faced man who had ruled the Germanic Empire for a quarter of a century.

Haldweim had been *Führer* far longer than Alicia had been alive; to her, then, he was as one with the Pyramids of Egypt. But the Pyramids remained, and now he was gone. If anything, his last surroundings stressed how transitory any mere man was. To make any sort of show at all, he would have had to be the size of a *Brachiosaurus*. Alicia had always imagined the *Führer* as being more than a man, but here she saw at first hand it wasn't so.

Young mourners went by in a steady stream, almost close enough to touch the nearest wreaths. With a ten-year-old's instinctive love of horror, Alicia wondered what would happen if anybody did. She supposed one of those SS men—each as still now as if himself carved from stone—would suddenly spring to life and shoot the miscreant. Or maybe even that wouldn't be enough. Maybe they would drag him away to SS headquarters and take their time disposing of him.

Then she was past the display, past the coffin, past the wizened corpse inside, and walking quickly towards a door of simply human proportions that led out to Adolf Hitler Platz. The square was already filling with people either in uniform—military, Party, and SS—or in civilian mourning attire. "We won't be able to see," Emma whispered in dismay.

"Yes, we will," Alicia whispered back. "They wouldn't bring us all the way here and then hide us. Besides, they'll want people to see we're here." Televisor cameras on platforms stood out from the throng like islands in the sea. More cameras on the Great Hall, on the *Führer*'s palace to the left, and on the *Oberkommando der Wehrmacht* building across the street gave broader views. The building where Alicia's father worked seemed like an old friend.

She proved right, too, which always made her feel good. Officials in particularly fancy uniforms shepherded the schoolchildren into reserved spaces right next to the route of the funeral procession, which was marked off by red-and-black tape imprinted with swastikas. There the officials arranged them roughly in order of height, shortest in front, so they could all be seen to best advantage.

"Told you so," Alicia whispered. Emma stuck out her tongue. *Herr* Kessler coughed and glared. Emma turned pale. He wouldn't whack her in public, not on this somber occasion, but he wouldn't forget, either. When the bus took them back to Stahnsdorf . . .

"I have to go to the bathroom!" exclaimed a little redheaded boy who couldn't have been much older than Roxane. One of the officials took him by the hand, led him to a portable toilet, and then brought him back. Alicia giggled—but first she made sure *Herr* Kessler was looking the other way.

Buses and commuter trains brought more and more mourners into the Adolf Hitler Platz, until the entire immense square was full. Most of the people there wouldn't be able to see much, although the televisor screen mounted on the front of the *Führer*'s palace showed them what they were missing. A lot of them had doubtless been ordered to come, as Alicia had, but what about the others? Did they want to be a part of history, if only a tiny part?

Alicia looked down at the German flag with the mourning border in her hand. Suddenly she wondered why *she* was supposed to be sorry Kurt Haldweim had died. He'd been *Führer* of the Germanic Empire, yes. If she'd been all German, that would have made reason enough. A few weeks earlier, she would have thought it did. Now . . . Now she knew what the Germans had done to *her* folk.

She still felt like a German. She also felt like a Jew—and wouldn't a Jew be glad, not sorry, the German *Führer* was dead? Not for the first time lately, she felt very confused.

Funereal music poured from speakers mounted at the edge of the square. "Everyone keep quiet and look sad," *Herr* Kessler hissed.

Next to Alicia, Emma had a good reason for frowning. She just needed to think about what would happen to her when she got back to school. Alicia had to work hard to make the corners of her mouth turn down. She finally managed it the way she had in the game with her sisters: by pretending she was in a play and had to act a part.

Pallbearers wearing Army field-gray, *Luftwaffe* light blue, Navy dark blue, SS black, and National Socialist brown bore Kurt Haldweim's coffin out of the Great Hall and set it on a wheeled bier drawn by eight black horses that had pulled up in front of the entrance. Every one of the men was blond and handsome and close to two meters tall—and every one of them was made to seem taller still by a high-crowned cap. The pallbearers looked magnificent in closeup shots on the televisor screen at the front of the *Führer*'s palace. Seen live, they might have been ants in front of the inhuman, overwhelming immensity of the Great Hall.

The bier set out across the Adolf Hitler Platz towards Alicia at a slow walk. It was draped in black velvet, against which the red in the German national flag stood out like blood. The pallbearers goose-stepped behind the bier. Their somber faces might have been stamped from the same mold.

Behind them came visiting heads of state, some in uniform, others wearing dark civilian garb. German military and Party functionaries followed, all in their distinctive costumes. Next came foreign ambassadors, and after them elite units from the military and *Waffen*-SS, from the National Socialist Party hierarchy, and from the *Hitler Jugend*.

When the bier was almost directly in front of Alicia, one of the horses did what horses do. Half the sorrowful schoolchildren suddenly snorted and squealed. Half the teachers hastily hissed in horror. The goose-stepping pallbearers couldn't alter their paces, not without looking bad. One of them stepped in it. He marched on past, his expression unchanged no matter what clung to the sole of his gleaming boot.

Most of the heads of states and other dignitaries evaded the unfortunate substance. By the time the soldiers and fliers and sailors and SS men and brownshirts and Hitler Youths had gone by, though, it was quite thoroughly trodden into the concrete of the square.

By then, the teachers had stopped hissing. Once Haldweim's coffin had passed, the cameras turned away from the schoolchildren. They'd served their purpose. *Herr* Kessler and another teacher started talking in low voices. "I wonder when we'll have a new *Führer,*" the other man said.

"I hope it's soon," Alicia's teacher answered. "It wasn't like this when Himmler died. I remember that. Back then, everybody knew we'd stay on a steady course. Nowadays?" He shook his head. Disapproval radiated from him.

"They'll make a good choice, whoever it finally is," the other teacher said.

Herr Kessler seemed to realize he might have gone too far. "Oh, I'm sure they will," he said quickly. You never could tell who might be listening. Alicia had learned that long before she found out she was a Jew.

I could report him, she thought. The news always ran stories about heroic children who turned in evildoers they'd discovered—sometimes even their own parents. Getting rid of her bad-tempered teacher was tempting, too.

But the idea died before it was fully formed, for Alicia's next thought was, *If I denounce him, they'll probably investigate me, too.* She shook her head in horror of her own. How did the handful of Jews at the heart of the Germanic Empire survive? By never drawing any special notice to themselves. Perhaps someone else would report *Herr* Kessler, but she wouldn't. She couldn't. She didn't dare.

The last unit of brownshirts left the Adolf Hitler Platz. It began to empty, and did so almost as quickly and efficiently as it had filled. People streamed away to the buses and trains that had brought them to the square. The lines were long, but they were orderly, and they moved fast. There was next to no pushing and shoving and shouting, as Alicia's schoolbooks said there was in less enlightened parts of the world.

Again, she wondered, *Are my books telling the truth?* If they lied about Jews—and she had to believe they did—what else did they lie about? Had there ever been a Roman Emperor named Augustus? Was Mt. Everest really the tallest mountain in the world? Had Horst Wessel been a hero and a martyr? Were two and two truly four?

She muttered in annoyance. She'd checked her arithmetic lessons before, and they held good. But how could she test what the books said about Mt. Everest, which was far away and hard to get to, or about Horst Wessel and Augustus, who'd lived in the altogether irretrievable past? She saw no simple way.

Maybe Daddy knows, she thought as she scrambled aboard her school bus. Her father knew all sorts of strange things, many of them useless but most of them interesting or entertaining. If he didn't know these, she couldn't think of anyone who would.

Herr Kessler got on the bus. He counted the students to make sure nobody had been left behind, then grunted in satisfaction. "Everyone present and accounted for," he told the driver before returning his attention to the class. "Out of respect for the memory of our beloved *Führer,* you will be silent—completely silent—on the return journey to Stahnsdorf. If you are not silent, you will be very, very sorry. Do you understand me?" He sounded as if he looked forward to making someone, or several someones, very, very sorry.

Alicia didn't expect anyone to respond to what was obviously a rhetorical question, but a boy held up his hand and said, "*Herr* Kessler!"

"*Ja?*" The teacher was taken aback, too.

"*Herr* Kessler, when will we have a new beloved *Führer*?"

Kessler blinked. "Why, when we do, of course," he answered. Alicia had no trouble figuring out what that meant. It meant he didn't know, either.

Heinrich Gimpel suspected the highest authorities in the *Reich* would have suppressed the first edition of *Mein Kampf* if they'd thought they could get away with it. But plenty of old copies were still floating around, and word of the first *Führer*'s startlingly subversive statements spread too wide and too fast for suppression to have any hope of success. That being so, those in high places simply sat tight, hoping the fuss would die down of its own accord.

"Who would have imagined Hitler wrote such a thing?" Heinrich said at work one morning. He didn't like talking about Hitler at all, but the first edition, despite official silence—maybe because of official silence—was so much on people's minds that not talking about it would have seemed odd. He didn't want to seem odd in any way.

"I know what it must have been," Willi Dorsch said.

"Tell me, O sage of the age," Heinrich said.

"He must have written the first edition before he got the Party fully into his hands," Willi responded. "As soon as he did, then the *Führerprinzip* took over, and everything ran from the top down, the way it does now."

"That . . . makes a certain amount of sense," Heinrich said. In fact, it made more than a certain amount. Willi was shrewd, no doubt about it.

He was also smug. "You bet it does," he said. "And, if you look at things the right way, it makes the first edition an antique, too, something that's not worth getting excited about."

"Do you think that's the line they'll take?" Heinrich asked.

"I think they'll try," Willi replied. "Interesting to find out whether they can get away with it."

"What do you think?"

Willi's grin wasn't quite pleasant. "I could ask you the same question, but you've never much cared for sticking out your neck, have you?"

"Well, no." Heinrich tried to sound sheepish, not cowardly. Feeling he needed to add something to his confession, he said, "You don't have to answer if you don't want to."

"Oh, I will. I can always run my mouth, or stick my foot in it, or stick my neck out for the chopper." Willi sounded happy, almost gay. He could talk about sticking his neck out because he didn't really believe the chopper would come down on it. Heinrich knew full well the chopper would descend if *he* were discovered. Willi, meanwhile, went on, "Sure, I'll tell you what I think. I think they have a pretty good chance of getting away with it. That's how things always work."

"You're probably right." Heinrich made sure he didn't sigh. He wouldn't have sworn his office was bugged, but he wouldn't have sworn it wasn't, either. If anyone was listening to him, he didn't want to do or say anything that could possibly be construed as disloyal to the *Reich*.

"If you bet that tomorrow will be just like today, you'll win more often than you lose," Willi said. "But you won't *always* win, and you'll look more like a chump when you lose. We wouldn't have gone to Mars a few years ago if we'd thought things would stay the same all the time."

"That's true." Heinrich had been no less impressed than anyone else by live televisor pictures from another world. Men had been flying back and forth to the moon since he was a boy, and the observatory there had been a going concern for fifteen years. But Mars *felt* different, even if there'd been not the slightest hint of Martians. The Ministry of Air and Space was talking about a manned mission to the moons of Jupiter. That would be something, if it ever got past the talking stage.

"So anyway," Willi said, "the people who go on about the first edition are the ones who don't have power, and the people who do have power don't give a damn about the first edition. That's the way it looks to me."

"Seems reasonable," Heinrich said, and so it did. Again, he refused to show he didn't like it, no matter how reasonable it seemed. Instead, he looked at his watch. "Shall we head for the canteen and see what sort of experiment the cooks are serving for lunch?" Nobody ever got in trouble for complaining about the food here. Not even the Security Police could afford to arrest that many people.

Today's special included tongue sausage and a cabbage salad with chopped apples, oranges, and grapes in a mayonnaise-based dressing. The sausage wasn't half bad. The menu called the salad Swedish. After a couple of bites, Heinrich called it peculiar.

Willi looked down at his foam plate. His verdict was, "I didn't know the Swedes hated us that much."

Heinrich took another forkful. After crunching away, he said, "It's probably very nutritious."

"It would be," Willi said.

Despite grumbles, they both kept eating. Heinrich sipped coffee from a foam cup. It wasn't especially good, either, but it was strong. He could feel his eyes opening wider. He wouldn't doze off at his desk this afternoon. He'd done that once or twice when he had a new baby in the house. He hadn't got in trouble. He mustn't have been the only one.

As he ate, he listened to the lunchroom chatter. Now it was official: the Americans would fall short on this year's assessment. Plenty of people at *Oberkommando der Wehrmacht* wondered what the *Reich* would do about it. Heinrich wondered himself. Someone a couple of tables over said, "The Yankees are lucky bastards. If we had a *Führer* in place, he'd have made them knuckle under, you bet."

Willi Dorsch heard that, too. "He's right," he said, and got up to pour himself some more coffee. Heinrich nodded, though he couldn't help thinking that getting devastated by nuclear weapons and then spending the next forty years under German occupation wasn't precisely the kind of luck he most wanted to have.

On the other hand, most of the Americans remained alive. Aside from the war casualties, the conquerors had worked their usual horrors on Jews and Negroes. Even so, the population of the USA was only about a third lower than it had been before the war. Maybe the Americans as a whole *were* lucky—if you compared them to such *Untermenschen*.

At another table not far from the one where Heinrich and Willi were sitting, a colonel growled, "To hell with the first edition! This is all a bunch of claptrap, if anybody wants to know the truth."

Heinrich took a bite of tongue sausage. Who would presume to argue with such an august personage? Willi looked smug as he came back with his refill. He must have heard the officer, too. He wagged a finger at Heinrich, as if to say, *You see?*

But two colonels sat at that table. The second one, a younger man, shook his head and said, "I'm not so sure, Dietrich. I've been a good Party man for more than twenty years now. If there's a way to stay in the rules and let me help choose the new *Führer*, I'm for it."

"That's the leadership's job," the first colonel—Dietrich—said.

"Well, yes," the other colonel answered. "But how do leaders get to be leaders? If the people under them don't want to follow, what have you got? A mess, that's what. Look at France in 1940."

Dietrich snorted. "Oh, go on, Paul. If the *Reich* ever comes to that, we can all stick our heads in the showers, because we'll be done for anyway."

"I didn't say it would be that bad—we're not Frenchmen, after all," Paul replied. "But the principle is the same."

Another snort from the first colonel. "Principle? What's principle? Something losers talk about to explain why they've lost."

"Oh, really? Are you saying the Party has no principles?" Paul's voice was silky with danger.

But Dietrich wouldn't fall into that trap. "I'm saying victory is the first principle, and none of the others matters much." He had a fat cigar smoking in an ashtray. Now he picked it up and thrust it at his friend. "If I'm wrong, how come we shout, '*Sieg heil!*'? Explain that to me."

A captain who'd been siting at another table came over and said, "Excuse me, sir, but how does following the Party's original rules make victory any less likely?" He would never have had the nerve to do anything like that if Paul hadn't spoken up in favor of the first edition, not when Dietrich outranked him by three grades. As things were, he had a protector.

The table with the two colonels quickly became the day's focal point for that particular argument. *Wehrmacht* officers and civilian experts gathered around it. Things got more heated by the moment. Willi's face lit up. "Shall we join them?" he asked.

"Go ahead, if you want to," Heinrich answered. "But what we say won't matter a pfennig's worth either way." *And that's been true everywhere in the* Reich *ever since Hitler took over.* One more good line he added to the long, long list of things he couldn't say no matter how true they were.

Sometimes a pounding on the door didn't make Lise Gimpel panic. When it came just after half past three, it made her smile. It meant the children were home from school. She hurried to the door and opened it. "Hello, girls," she said. "What did you learn today?"

"Klaus Frick eats bugs," Francesca announced.

Alicia and Roxane both made disgusted noises, but not big disgusted noises. From this, Lise concluded her middle daughter was going on with things she'd said on the school bus. The other two girls must have had the chance to start getting used to that lovely piece of news. "How do you know he eats bugs?" Lise asked, remembering how schoolyard rumors could claim anybody did anything.

But Francesca answered, "Because I saw him do it. He caught one and put it in his mouth, and it went crunch."

"And he's in your class, isn't he?" Lise said unhappily. Francesca nodded. Lise shuddered. "That's . . . pretty bad." Eight-year-old boys frequently were disgusting creatures, but this Klaus Frick went overboard.

Roxane giggled. "Tell her the rest!"

"The rest? There's more?" Lise said. "Do I want to know?"

"No," Alicia said quickly.

From that, Lise got a hint about what *more* might be. But Roxane was still snickering, and Francesca was laughing, too. At their age, what was disgusting was also funny. The potty jokes that had made the rounds when Lise was in the lower grades still circulated. Alicia also laughed at a lot of them; ten wasn't too old. Not today, though. Francesca said, "Klaus said—he said he was eating just like a Jew. He said Jews ate bugs all the time."

Hearing it again sent Roxane into gales of laughter. Francesca thought it was pretty funny, too. Alicia gave her verdict in one word: "Revolting."

"He's probably right, though. Jews *were* revolting," Francesca said. "Everybody knows that." Her little sister nodded. Alicia started to say something, then very obviously didn't.

Lise Gimpel spoke up before her oldest daughter could slip: "Jews may have been revolting, but how does Klaus Frick know what they ate? How could he? Nobody your age has ever seen one—and I'm sure they don't teach you about bugs in school. I'm with Alicia here: Jews may have been revolting, but your classmate certainly is."

Alicia stuck out her tongue at Francesca. That was a good, healthy, normal reaction. But Roxane, always an agitator, pointed and exclaimed, "Eww! It's got a bug's leg on it!"

"Enough!" Lise said. "All three of you, go in the kitchen right now and have your snacks." She held up a warning hand. "I'm not done. The first one who says anything—*anything*—about bugs or Jews or anything else disgusting while you're eating is in big trouble. *Big* trouble, you hear me?"

They all nodded. The two younger ones hurried to the kitchen. Alicia hung back for a moment. "Jews or anything *else* disgusting?" she asked softly.

"That's how you've got to say it," Lise whispered back, biting her lip. "You have to wear a mask, remember?" Alicia nodded, though the mask had slipped. Lise gave her a little push. "Go on. Eat your snack. This was just foolishness. Don't let it worry you." Nodding again, and looking a tiny bit happier, Alicia went.

Lise Gimpel's sigh sounded amazingly like Heinrich's. You needed to have a hide like an elephant's to hope to survive. Children didn't naturally come equipped with that kind of hide. They had to acquire it, one painful scar after another. Lise remembered how many tears she'd shed when she was younger.

Jokes about Jews and gibes about Jews went on and on. Lise couldn't remember the last time she'd heard anything about *live* Jews before those few luckless families were found in the Serbian hinterlands.

Everyone needed someone to hate. Americans hadn't hated Jews the way Europeans had, but they'd had Negroes to hate instead. Now there were hardly any Jews or Negroes in the USA. Did people on the other side of the Atlantic still tell jokes about the Negroes who weren't there any more? Lise wouldn't have been surprised. People were like that, however much you wished they weren't.

Back in the ancient days, after David slew Goliath and the Hebrews triumphed in Palestine, had they told jokes about the Philistines? That wouldn't have surprised Lise, either. She didn't think Jews were the *Herrenvolk,* the master race, the way Germans thought about themselves. She just thought they were people like any others, with all the faults and foibles of any other folk. Was it too much to ask for other people to see them the same way?

Evidently.

She sighed again. The survivors remaining in the *Reich* were well hidden. Ferreting them out wouldn't be easy, even for the Nazis. For a few years, Lise hadn't worried much about it. She hadn't even thought much about it. She'd just felt like—*been*—one more person living out her life like anybody else.

But then Gottlieb Stutzman got old enough to tell, and then Anna, and now Alicia. And half of Lise felt like the terrified child she'd been when she first found out the truth. Children made mistakes. Making mistakes and learning from them helped children grow up. But if a Jewish child made the wrong kind of mistake, she wouldn't grow up, and what would she learn from that?

Not to be born a Jew, of course.

"Mommy!" Francesca screamed. Roxane echoed her, even higher and shriller.

Lise raced for the kitchen, her heart in her mouth. What had Alicia done? Had she told her sisters? If she couldn't keep her mouth shut, how could she think they'd be able to?

Alicia stood in the middle of the floor, her face stricken. Francesca and Roxane both dramatically pointed at her. "I'm sorry, Mommy," she whispered, her face pale as milk—pale as the milk that had been in her tumbler and now splashed all over the floor, along with the tumbler's shards.

Once Lise started to laugh, she had to work to stop. All three of her daughters stared at her. She took a deep breath, held it, let it out. "What did you think I was going to do?" she said. "*Cry* over spilt milk?" The girls made horrible faces. Lise didn't care about that. Relief left her giddy. "Come on. Let's clean up the mess."

She did most of the work, but she made the girls help. As she mopped up milk and swept up broken glass, she also marveled. *I didn't hear the crash at all. Was I that lost in my own worries? I guess I was.*

"I'm sorry," Alicia said again. No, she didn't like making any mistakes, no matter how small.

"It's all right, dear," Lise said. And, compared to what might have been, it was.

IV

HEINRICH AND LISE GIMPEL WERE DEFENDING AGAINST A SMALL SLAM IN SPADES, doubled, that Willi Dorsch was playing. Heinrich was the one who'd doubled. With the ace of hearts in his hand, why not? One more trick after that, he thought, ought to come from somewhere. That ace had been his opening lead—whereupon he'd discovered, painfully, that Erika had a void in hearts. Willi had grinned like the Cheshire Cat when he trumped the beautiful, lost ace.

One trick for the defenders had materialized, when the clubs split evenly and Heinrich's queen survived. He couldn't see where they would come up with a second one, the one that would set the contract. His two meager trumps were gone, pulled, and Lise had had only one.

Willi led the queen of diamonds. Heinrich glumly tossed out the seven. The ace lay face-up on the table in the dummy's hand. Willi confidently didn't play it, instead choosing the three. Lise didn't even smile as she ruined the finesse by laying her king on top of the queen. "Down one," she said sweetly.

"Oh, for God's sake!" Willi said. He might have added something more pungent than that, but the three Gimpel girls had gone to bed only a few minutes before and could have heard if he did. He sent Heinrich an accusing stare. "You were the one who doubled. I was sure you had that . . . miserable king."

"I doubled on the strength of the ace," Heinrich said. "When you ruffed it, I thought we were doomed. Let's finish the hand—maybe we'll come up with another trick, too."

Lise led. Willi handily took the rest of the tricks, but he and Erika still went down one. His wife sighed mournfully.

"I would have played that one the same way." Heinrich came to Willi's defense.

"Would you?" Erika didn't sound as if she believed it.

"Sure I would," he said. "Lise didn't bid at all during the auction. You have to figure what strength we've got is in my hand."

"Maybe." Erika still seemed dubious—and annoyed at her husband. "If *you'd* tried that finesse, Heinrich, it probably would have worked."

Willi Dorsch didn't say anything. He did turn red, though, as he gathered up the cards. Heinrich tried to defuse things, saying, "Ha! Don't I wish? I've had more finesses go down in flames than the Russians lost planes the first day we hit them."

"But you don't run them unless you need to," Erika said. "Willi tried that one for the sake of being cute. We could have made without it."

She spoke as if her husband weren't there. Willi noticed, too, and turned redder than ever. "We were in trouble if I *didn't* try that finesse," he insisted.

"I don't think so," Erika said.

"Whose deal is it?" Lise asked. That might not have been the wisdom of Solomon, but it sufficed to forestall the argument. The next hand was unexciting; the Gimpels bid two hearts and made three. The hand after that, Erika Dorsch made four spades and chopped off the Gimpels' leg.

She didn't say anything to Willi. She made such a point of not saying anything to him, he turned red all over again. "Yes, you're a genius," he growled. "There. I admit it. Are you happy now?"

"I just played it sensibly," Erika said. "It's not that you haven't got brains, sweetheart. It's just that you don't always bother using them. If you ask me, that's worse, because you could." Things would have been bad enough if she'd left it there, but she added, "Heinrich, now, he gets the most from what he's got between his ears."

Lise Gimpel sent her husband a hooded look. He didn't need it to know this was several different flavors of trouble. The most immediate one was between Willi and Erika. Willi took a deep breath. By the nasty glint in his eyes, Heinrich knew with sudden, appalled certainty just what he was going to say. It would have been crude in a locker room. At the bridge table, it would have been a disaster. Heinrich got there first, saying, "If I'm as smart as all that, why aren't I rich? If I'm as smart as all that, why wasn't I smart enough to pick a better-looking face, too?"

He hoped that would help calm Willi, who was by anybody's standards better-looking than he was. And it might have, if Erika hadn't poured gasoline on the fire: "Some things, we can't choose. Some things . . . we can." She was looking straight at her husband.

Willi had managed to get some grip on his temper. His voice was thick with anger when he said, "We'll talk about this later," but at least he seemed willing to talk about it later instead of having a row right there on the spot.

"Why don't I bring out the coffee and cake?" Lise said. "I think maybe we've had enough bridge for the night."

Heinrich hoped Erika would hop up and help, but she didn't. She was, he slowly realized, as angry at Willi as he was at her. She might have realized what her husband had almost said, too—or maybe she was angry for reasons that had nothing to do with bridge but came out over the game. Sitting there with them, waiting for Lise to come back, Heinrich felt like a man in the middle of a minefield.

When the minefield went up, though, it went up from an unexpected direction. Erika Dorsch turned her blue gaze on him and asked, "What do you think of the whole business about the first edition of *Mein Kampf*?"

Few residents of the *Reich* would have been comfortable answering that question. It horrified Heinrich for all sorts of reasons, most of which Erika knew nothing about. He tried to pass it off lightly: "What I think doesn't matter. What the powers that be think will be what counts."

"It's what I told Heinrich at the office: that whole business is nothing but a lot of garbage," Willi said. "Nobody who counts will pay any attention to it."

The blue glare Erika turned on him might have come from twin acetylene torches. "I already know what you think. I ought to—I've heard it often enough. I'm trying to find out what Heinrich thinks."

Wherever that anger came from, it was genuine. Heinrich wondered whether Erika really had her sights set on him, or whether she was only using him to make Willi angry and jealous. Either way, it worked. Willi visibly steamed. Heinrich said, "Like I told you, I don't know what to think. How about you, Erika?" He regretted the last question as soon as the words were out of his mouth, which was, of course, too late.

"Me? I think it's about time somebody brought this up," she said. "Who is the *Reich* for, if it's not for the people in it? And if it's for us, shouldn't we have some say about who runs it?"

Heinrich agreed with that, to the extent that he could. He would never have dared to say it out loud, though. Willi Dorsch sneered. "My wife, the democrat. This is *why* Hitler changed things after the first edition. Look what that kind of nonsense got the French. Look what it got the Americans. If you go around electing politicians, they'll kiss the backsides of the people who voted them in. You need men who can *lead,* not follow."

At long last, Lise brought in the cakes and coffee. She set plate and cup in front of Willi. "Here. Why don't you lead off on this?"

"Thanks, Lise," Willi said as he cut himself a slice of cake. "I don't hear you going on about how wonderful the stupid first edition is. You've got the sense to know it's rubbish."

His wife said, "I'm with Heinrich. I can't do anything much about it one way or the other. What's the point of fussing over something like that?"

"There *is* a point," Erika Dorsch insisted. "If the Party *Bonzen* know the people are looking over their shoulder and just waiting to throw them out if they do something stupid or feather their own nests, maybe they'll watch themselves."

Heinrich had the same hope. Wouldn't leaders responsible to the people they ruled be milder than leaders responsible to no one but their courtiers? They could hardly be harsher. No matter what he hoped, though, he'd had keeping quiet and staying noncommittal inalterably drummed into him. Silence meant more than security. Silence meant survival.

And that held true for others besides the last few hidden Jews, as Willi pointed out: "When all this is over, when we've got ourselves a new *Führer,* the Security Police are going to take a good, long look at everybody who babbled about the first edition and how wonderful it is. They may figure some people are just fools, and let them off the hook. But some people, the agitators, will win themselves noodles for their big mouths." The camp slang for a bullet in the back of the neck had become part of the ordinary German language.

All he succeeded in doing was getting his wife angry again. "So what shall we do, then?" Erika snapped. "Sit on our hands and keep quiet because we're afraid? Pretend we're nothing but a bunch of Mussulmen?" That was camp slang, too, slang for prisoners who'd given up and were waiting to die.

Her question prompted only one answer from Heinrich. *Yes,* he thought. *What else is there? Don't you realize what you're up against?*

Maybe Erika didn't. She'd lived a life of comfort and privilege, confident she was one of the *Herrenvolk.* So had most Germans in the forty years since the United States went down. They were top dogs, and seldom had to think about how they stayed on top.

Sure enough, Erika stuck out her chin and said, "I'm just as good an Aryan as any of the Party big shots. I'm just as good an Aryan as Kurt Haldweim was—and so are you, Willi, and Heinrich and Lise, if you'd just stand up on your hind legs about it."

Could sheer Aryan arrogance pave the way for the measures the first edition of *Mein Kampf* outlined? There was a notion that hadn't occurred to Heinrich up till now. *We're all set about everyone else, so we must be equal to one another*. It made a very Germanic kind of sense. But just because Erika thought it was true, would anyone else? That was liable to be a different story.

Willi said, "I think we'd better head for home. Some nights there's just no reasoning with some people." Though he did his best to sound cheerful, Heinrich thought he was fuming underneath.

Erika didn't help when she said, "I've been telling you that for years, and you never paid any attention to me."

They were still sniping at each other when they left the Gimpel house and headed up the street toward the bus stop. Heinrich closed the door behind them. "Whew!" he said—a long whoosh of air.

"Yes." Lise stretched the word to three times its usual length. "That was a fascinating evening, wasn't it?"

"There's a good word for it." Heinrich could imagine several other words he might have used. *Fascinating* was the safest one he could come up with.

"I don't think you're part of the problem between Willi and Erika," his wife said.

"That's good," he answered, most sincerely.

"I don't think you're part of the problem," Lise repeated, "but I think Erika thinks you're part of the solution."

"You . . . may be right." Heinrich didn't want to admit even that much. It felt dangerous: not dangerous in the hauled-off-to-an-extermination-camp sense, but dangerous in the simpler, more normal, this-complicates-my-life sense. He was not the sort of man who cared for danger of any sort.

Lise tapped her foot on the tile of the entry hall. "And if I am right, what are you going to do about it?"

"Me? Nothing!" he exclaimed.

The alarm in his voice must have got through to her, because she relaxed—a little. "Good," she said. "That's the right answer." She paused pensively. "Erika's a very good-looking woman, isn't she?"

Heinrich couldn't even say no. She would have known he was lying. "I suppose so," he mumbled.

"Maybe it's not such a bad thing you have more on your mind than most husbands." Lise tried to eye him severely, but a smile curled up the corners of her mouth in spite of herself.

The same thing had occurred to Heinrich not so long before. He was not about to admit that to Lise. He told himself Security Police torturers couldn't have torn it from him, but he knew he was liable to be wrong. Those people were very good at what they did, and got a lot of practice doing it.

He realized he had to say something. He couldn't just keep standing there. Otherwise, Lise was liable to think he thought it was too bad he had more on his mind than most husbands, which was the last thing he wanted. "I know when I'm well off," he told her.

That turned the tentative, reluctant smile wide and happy. "Good," she said. "You'd better." She paused. "Do you know when you're well off well enough to help me clean up?"

"I suppose so," he said once more, as halfheartedly as he had when admitting Erika Dorsch was pretty.

Lise sent him a sharp look. Then she figured out why he'd sounded the way he had. She made as if to throw something at him. "It's a good thing I've known you for a long time," she said.

"Yes, I think so, too," Heinrich said, and that, for once, turned out to be just the right answer.

Esther Stutzman turned the key to get into Dr. Dambach's outer office. "Good morning, *Frau* Stutzman," the pediatrician called from his inner sanctum.

"Good morning, Doctor," she answered. "Have you been here long?"

"A while," Dambach said. "Would you please see to the coffeemaker? It's turning out nothing but sludge."

"Of course." When Esther did, she discovered he'd put three times as much coffee on the filter as he should have. She didn't point that out to him; experience had taught her that pointing such things out did no good. With children, he knew what he was doing. With the coffeemaker . . . no. She just set things to rights and brought him a proper cup of coffee.

"*Danke schön,*" he said. "I don't know what goes wrong when I put my hands on that machine, but something always does. I can't understand it. I follow the instructions. . . ."

"Yes, Doctor," Esther replied. From what Irma, the afternoon receptionist, said, she wasn't the only one who'd given up arguing with Dambach about the coffeemaker.

He sipped from the cup Esther had brought him. "This is much better," he told her. "I don't know how you make that miserable thing behave, but you always manage to." Esther only smiled. If the pediatrician wanted to think she was a genius when it came to coffee, she wouldn't complain. He tapped at the papers on his desk. "I've found something interesting—something peculiar, even."

Was he trying to show that he was good for something even if he couldn't make coffee worth a damn? Esther already knew that. She also knew she had to ask, "What is it, Dr. Dambach?" and sound interested when she did.

And then, all of a sudden, she *was* interested, vitally and painfully interested, for he said, "Do you remember the case of Paul Klein a few days ago?"

"The poor baby with that horrible disease?" Esther said, doing her best not to think, *The poor baby who's a Jew.*

"Yes, that's right. I have found a fascinating discrepancy on his parents' genealogical records."

Dear God! Did Walther make a mistake? None of the fear Esther felt showed on her face. If she'd shown fear whenever she felt it, she would have gone around looking panic-stricken all the time. When she said, "Really?" she sounded intrigued, but no more than a good secretary should have.

Dr. Dambach nodded. "I don't know what to make of it, either," he said. "In the records I got from the *Reichs* Genealogical Office, both Richard and Maria Klein are shown to have distant ancestors who may possibly have been . . . well, Jews."

"Good heavens!" Esther had had a lot of practice simulating that kind of shock.

"As I say, these were distant ancestors," Dambach went on hastily. "Nothing to involve the Security Police, believe me. I don't care for that business any more than you do." *I doubt that,* Esther thought. *I doubt that very much.* The pediatrician, fortunately oblivious, continued. "But the slight Jewish taint would help account for the presence of the Tay-Sachs gene on both sides of the family."

"I see," Esther said. What she didn't see was where the problem lay in that case.

Dambach proceeded to spell it out for her: "While I was going through the Kleins' records, I happened to come across another copy of their family tree, one they'd given me when Paul's older brother, Eduard, was born. *Those* pedigrees show unquestioned Aryan ancestry on both sides of the family, as far back as can be traced."

"How . . . very strange," Esther said through lips suddenly stiff with dread. Changing a computer record threw any future hounds off the scent, yes. But compare the change to a printout from before it was made . . . *I should have pulled those records from Eduard's chart,* Esther thought. But it had never crossed her mind. Eduard had been born before she came to work at Dambach's office, and she'd forgotten about his files. Guilt made her want to sink through the floor.

"Strange indeed. I've never seen another case like it," Dr. Dambach said. "And what's even stranger is, I called the *Reichs* Genealogical Office yesterday afternoon, and they said their records show no signs of tampering."

Thank heaven for that, Esther thought. *Walther's safe.* But were Richard and Maria Klein? "Maybe . . . I hate to say this of people, but maybe they tried to hide their Jews in the woodpile, and used altered documents to do it," Esther suggested, doing her best for them. "Even if you're not enough of a *Mischling* to be disposed of, a lot of folks don't care to have anything to do with you if you've got even a trace of Jew blood."

"Altering official documents is illegal," Dambach said severely. But then he paused, a thoughtful expression on his round face. "Still, I suppose it could be. It makes more sense than anything I thought of. I would have hoped, though, that the Kleins might have trusted their children's physician. I am, after all, a man with some experience of the world. I know that a small taint of Jewish ancestry may be forgiven. It's not as if they were half breeds or full bloods, for heaven's sake—as if there were such folk at the heart of the *Reich* in this day and age."

"Of course not, Doctor. What a ridiculous idea." Esther Stutzman clamped down hard on a scream. Dr. Dambach thought of himself as a man of the world, but he thought—he'd been trained to think—of Jews as different from other people. He thought of himself as tolerant for being willing to ignore some distant trace of Jewish ancestry. And so, for the Greater German *Reich,* he was. . . .

The pediatrician arranged papers in a neat stack. "As I say, I am a man with some experience of the world. I have seen forged genealogical papers before. You would be surprised how many people want to claim a grander ancestry than they really own. Most of them are crude jobs, though—altered photocopies and such. But what the Kleins gave me with Eduard seems perfectly authentic."

That's because it is *perfectly authentic, at least as far as the* Reichs *Genealogical Office knows.* "As long as you have the proper information now, is there really any point to making a fuss?" Esther said. If Dambach said no, she could go out to her receptionist's station and breathe a sigh of relief when he wasn't looking.

But Dambach didn't say anything at all. He just sat there eyeing the different sets of genealogical records. Esther knew she'd pushed things as far as she could. If she said another word, her boss would start wondering why she was sticking up for the Kleins so much. *Don't let anyone start wondering about you* might have been the eleventh commandment for Jews in the *Reich.* A smile on her face, she walked out of Dr. Dambach's private office.

She had plenty with which to busy herself out front: filing, billing, preparing dunning letters for people whose payments were late. She bit her lip when the pediatrician used the telephone, even though she couldn't make out whom he was calling. *His wife, his brother, his mother,* she thought hopefully.

The telephone she was in charge of—not Dambach's personal line—began to ring, too. Patients and their parents—mostly their mothers—started coming in. She scheduled appointments and led children and the grownups with them back to examination rooms. Once, she made a followup appointment with a specialist for a boy whose broken arm wasn't healing as straight as Dambach would have liked.

As noon approached, the flood of people coming in slowed down and the flood of people going out picked up. Dr. Dambach sometimes worked straight through lunch, but this didn't look like a day where he would have to. Esther relaxed a little. She got the chance to look around for things she could take care of before she went home. That way, Irma wouldn't have to worry about them this afternoon, and Esther herself wouldn't have to worry about them tomorrow morning.

The last patient had just left when the door to the waiting room opened again. Esther looked up in annoyance—was someone trying to bring in a child without first making an appointment? Unless it was an emergency, she intended to send anyone that foolish away with a flea in his ear.

But the tall man in the unfamiliar dark brown uniform was not carrying a baby or holding a child by the hand. He nodded to her. "This is the office of Dr. Martin Dambach?" he inquired, his accent Bavarian.

"Yes, that's right," Esther answered. "And you are . . . ?"

"Maximilian Ebert, *Reichs* Genealogical Office, at your service." He actually clicked his heels. Esther tried to remember the last time she'd seen anyone outside of the cinema do that—tried and failed. The man from the Genealogical Office went on, "Dr. Dambach is in?"

Esther wanted to tell him no. Had she thought that would make him go away and never come back, she would have. As things were, she had to hide alarm and reluctance when she nodded. "Yes, he is. One moment, please." She went back to Dr. Dambach's office. The pediatrician was eating a liverwurst sandwich. "Excuse me, Doctor, but a *Herr* Ebert from the *Reichs* Genealogical Office is here to see you."

"Is he?" Dr. Dambach said with his mouth full. He swallowed heroically; Esther thought of an anaconda engulfing a tapir. When Dambach spoke again, his voice was clear: "I didn't expect him so soon. Please tell him he can come in." He stuck the remains of the sandwich in a desk drawer.

"*Danke schön, gnädige Frau,*" Ebert said when Esther delivered the message, and he clicked his heels again. *Dear lady?* Esther wondered. That took politeness a long way when talking to a receptionist. Did he like her looks? It wasn't mutual. He was dark and jowly, and she thought he'd have a nasty temper if he weren't trying to be charming. She was careful to stand well away from him when she led him to the doctor's private office.

They didn't bother closing the door. Esther heard bits of conversation floating out: ". . . obviously genuine . . ." ". . . *also* obviously genuine . . ." ". . . don't know what to make of . . ." ". . . wouldn't bother but for the Jewish aspect . . ." ". . . a puzzlement, without a doubt . . ."

After twenty minutes or so, Dr. Dambach and Maximilian Ebert emerged together. The man from the Genealogical Office asked Esther, "What do you know of this business about the Kleins?"

"Should we be talking about this with her?" Dambach asked.

"I don't see why not," Ebert said. "She's obviously of impeccable Aryan stock. Well, *Frau*"—his eye picked up the little name badge at her station—"ah, *Frau* Stutzman?"

"Only what Dr. Dambach has told me," Esther answered. *Obviously of impeccable Aryan stock.* She couldn't shriek laughter, however much she might want to. Cautiously, she went on, "I do know the Kleins a little away from the office." If she didn't say that, they could find out. Better to admit it. "They've always seemed like good enough people. I'm sorry their child has this horrible disease." Every word of that was true—more true than Maximilian Ebert could know.

"Have you any idea how they could have got two different sets of genealogical records, each one plainly authentic?" Ebert asked.

"No. I don't see how it's possible," she answered, which was anything but the truth.

"Are you really sure they *are* both authentic?" Dr. Dambach asked.

"As certain as I can be without the laboratory work to prove it," Ebert said. "I'll take both of them with me to get that. And then, if they do both turn out to be genuine, we'll have to figure out what that means. At the moment, Doctor, I have no more idea than you do. And now I must be off. A pleasure to meet you, *Frau* Stutzman. *Guten Tag*." He touched the brim of his cap and strode out of the office.

"Now we'll get to the bottom of this." Dr. Dambach sounded as if he looked forward to the prospect.

"So we will." Esther hoped she sounded the same way, even if it was another lie. No—especially if it was another lie.

The Medieval English Association meeting was winding down. In another couple of days, Susanna Weiss would have to fly back to Berlin. The conference hadn't been the most exciting she'd ever attended. She was bringing home material for at least two articles. That would keep Professor Oppenhoff happy. But there hadn't been any really spectacular papers and there hadn't been any really juicy scandals. Without the one or the other, the conclave itself would go down as less than memorable.

Still, there were compensations. First and foremost, there was London itself. Along with her ideas for articles, Susanna was also bringing home enough new books—used books, actually—to make excess baggage charges all but certain. Her campaign against the bookstores of London would have made General Guderian sit up and take notes. She always shopped as if she were a big-game hunter organizing a safari. All she lacked were beaters to drive the books off the shelves and into the range of her high-powered account card. She had to find the volumes and pick them out herself—but that was part of the sport.

Along with the books, she was bringing back several pairs of shoes. She'd gone after them with the same effective bravado she'd used on her bookstore campaign. She was particularly proud of one pair, which were covered all over with multicolored sequins. If she wore them to a faculty meeting, she might give the department chairman heart failure—and if that wasn't worth trying, she didn't know what would be.

She had one more reason for hating to leave London, too: no matter how stodgy the MEA had been this year, the British Union of Fascists across the street had more than made up for it. Susanna thought she might have spent more time at the Crown than she had at the Silver Eagle. She'd got to know several BUF men who thought she was a delegate to *their* gathering: not the sort of compliment she most wanted, perhaps, but a compliment all the same.

" 'Ere's the little lydy!" they would roar when they spotted her, and other endearments in dialects never heard among the scholars of medieval English. They pressed buttons and badges and stickers on her, and bought her pints till her back teeth floated. She would rather have had Scotch, but the rank-and-file fascists were a beer-drinking crowd.

They were also a crowd overwhelmingly in favor of doing business the way the first edition of *Mein Kampf* outlined. "Only stands to reason, don't it, dearie?" said a bald-headed, broken-nosed bruiser named Nick, breathing beer fumes into Susanna's face. "It's the buggers 'oove already got it made 'oo don't want ordinary blokes to 'ave their say."

"That certainly seems reasonable to me," Susanna said. Her precise, well-educated tones sent Nick and his pals into gales of laughter. She couldn't help liking them. If there was any hope for changing the way things worked, it rested on their shoulders. But the way they kept laughing while they bragged of brawls and brutalities past chilled her. *If they knew I was a Jew, they would laugh like that while they stomped me to death.*

She forgave, or at least forgot, their hypothetical sins when they smuggled her onto the floor for the climactic session of their assembly. They didn't think of it as smuggling, of course, and she wore enough BUF ornaments that no one, not her companions and not the even nastier thugs at the doors, even noticed that a membership badge was not among the gewgaws.

Things were undoubtedly livelier here than they were at the Medieval English Association meeting. People roared out songs in raucous choruses. The tunes came from British popular music. Some of the words were fierce, some were funny, some were obscene. Most were either for or against the first edition. Here and there, people for the older rules brawled with people opposing them. BUF guards tried without too much luck to keep the two sides apart.

A beer bottle smashed on the floor a couple of meters from Susanna's feet. "Someone will get killed!" she exclaimed.

"Some of these bastards deserve killing," Nick answered.

The brute simplicity of fascism had always fascinated and repelled Susanna at the same time. Somebody doesn't like the way you're going? Get rid of him, and then keep on going that way anyhow. If you're strong enough, you can, and it proves you were right all along.

There was, of course, a certain problem. . . . "Suppose they decide you are the ones who need killing?" Susanna asked.

"Only goes to show they're a pack of bloody sods, eh?" Nick said.

One of the ruffian's pals, though, saw what Susanna was driving at. "If they let counting 'ands stand for banging 'eads, I expect we will, too," he said. "That's what this business is about, right?" Susanna nodded. After a moment, reluctantly, so did Nick.

Another bottle shattered, this time on somebody's head. Friends led the bleeding man out of the hall. Susanna shivered, feeling as if she'd been swept back through time. This was how the Nazis had started ninety years earlier: gathering in taverns for what were as much brawls as meetings. No Communists would come to try to break up this conclave, though. Another shiver. If any Communists were left alive, they were as much in hiding as the *Reich*'s handful of Jews.

Bang! Bang! Bang! To her relief, that wasn't gunfire. It was the chairman plying his gavel in front of the microphone on the podium. "That will be enough of that," Charlie Lynton called, his amplified voice booming through the hall. *Bang! Bang! Bang!* "Settle down!" Lynton was in his mid-fifties, with an upper-class English accent that belied his birth in Edinburgh. He was smooth and smart. He had to be smart; he'd headed the British Union of Fascists since the mid-nineties, and steered as independent a line as he could without rousing German wrath.

"Which way will he go, do you think?" Susanna asked.

"Oh, 'e's with us," Nick said, and the men around him nodded. " 'E can win a show of 'ands, and 'e knows it."

His friends' heads bobbed up and down. One of them, a fellow everybody called Blinky Bill because of his squint, said, "It's them other old fools on the platform we've got to worry about."

Sure enough, a good many of the uniformed men up there looked as if they'd been chewing lemons. Things had run the same way for almost seventy years, ever since Britain fell to the *Wehrmacht*. As old guards will, the old guard here had expected them to keep on running the same way forever. But whatever else Charlie Lynton was, he was a breath of fresh air in a party that hadn't seen much for a long time.

He plied the gavel again. *Bang! Bang! Bang!* "Come on, lads, settle down," he called once more. "Let's have some order here." No call could have been better calculated to appeal to fascists. Putting things in order—their notion of order—was fascists' *raison d'être.*

But even that precious call didn't work here. At the same time as Nick was bellowing, "Huzzah for the first edition!" another fascist with an even more impressive set of lungs roared, "To hell with the bloody first edition!" Chaos broke out anew.

Bang! Bang! Bang! Lynton pounded so hard, he might have used a gun if he'd had one. "Enough!" he shouted, and he had the microphone working for him. By the way the word resounded through the hall, that might have been God shouting up there—on the assumption, which Susanna found unlikely, that God took an interest in the internal squabbles of the British Union of Fascists.

"First edition! First edition!" This time, it was an organized chant, deep and rolling and thunderous. The British had learned their lessons well; similar shouts of, *"Sieg heil!"* resounded through Nazi rallies in Berlin and Munich and Nuremberg.

The first edition's foes weren't so well disciplined. They had no counterchant prepared. Shouting out their protests as individuals, they couldn't drown the cries of those who favored change.

"First edition! First edition!" Susanna shouted with her comrades—her friends, she supposed she had to call them for the moment. The endless chant was intoxicating. It beat in her brain. It beat in her blood. Back home, she had as little to do with National Socialism as she could without drawing suspicion to herself. She hadn't really appreciated the power of mass rallies. Now that she found herself in the middle of one, she understood. She felt caught up in something greater than herself. It wasn't a feeling she was used to having. She distrusted it, but oh, it was heady!

Charlie Lynton let the chant build for two or three minutes, then used the gavel once more. "Enough!" he boomed for a second time. "We've got a lot to get through, and we won't do it if we spend all our bloody time shouting at each other." He took a piece of paper from the breast pocket of his black uniform tunic. Most BUF men put Susanna in mind of brigands. A few reminded her of Army officers. Charlie Lynton somehow contrived to look like a corporate executive, epaulets notwithstanding. "I have here," he said, "a message from his Majesty, King Henry IX."

Where nothing else had, that won him silence and complete attention.

Henry was like King Umberto in Italy: he had no real power, but enormous prestige. The *Duce* and the Italian Fascist Party didn't have to listen to Umberto, but they did if they were smart—and most of them wanted to. The same held true here for Charlie Lynton and the BUF with respect to King Henry.

"'My loyal, brave, and faithful subjects,' " Lynton read, " 'I am pleased and proud that so many of you should wish to return to the earliest and, in my view, the best traditions of the party so closely affiliated with your own. Wishing you wisdom in your debate, I remain, Henry, *Deo gratia* King of England and Defender of the Faith.' "

Beside Susanna, Nick erupted volcanically, with a great roar of glee and delight. Susanna clapped her hands and whooped, too. Like the British Union of Fascists, King Henry had found a way to praise democracy and the National Socialists at the same time. That wasn't easy. Susanna hadn't even imagined it was possible. But they'd done it here.

And will we? she wondered wistfully. *How* are *we going to go about choosing the next* Führer? No one on the RRG or the BBC had said much about that. Deliberations were proceeding: that was as much as anybody would admit. It sounded more like a criminal case than anything else. Susanna grimaced. *It probably is.*

Up on the platform, someone from the old guard was inveighing against the first edition and everything it stood for. The longer he talked, the more loudly the rank and file booed and jeered and mocked him. Seeing as much, Charlie Lynton let him go on and on and on. He hurt his own cause worse than Lynton could have.

When the old man finally stumped back to his seat on the rostrum, the BUF leader smiled out at the rank and file and said, "Well, I think that tells us a good deal about where we all stand, doesn't it?"

A few stubborn souls booed and hooted at Lynton. But their outcry seemed almost lost in the big hall, for most of the foes of the first edition sat in embarrassed silence, as if ashamed to admit they agreed with the disastrous speaker and disagreed with both their chairman and their King.

"That's done it, by God!" Nick boomed, and planted a beery kiss on Susanna's cheek. Part of her wanted to haul off and slap him. The rest was too excited at being here even to mind very much.

"We have a quorum," Charlie Lynton said. "Time to call the question.

Shall we change our rules to give back to the members of the British Union of Fascists the powers that are rightfully theirs, as outlined in the first edition of *Mein Kampf,* or shall we go on as we have been for so long, with the few dictating to the many?"

One of the advantages of being chairman was that Lynton not only got to guide the debate but also to frame its terms. Had he opposed the change, he might have called it destroying tradition and giving in to mob rule. Since he didn't . . .

Reform passed overwhelmingly, by better than three to one. This time, Susanna kissed Nick on his bristly cheek. To her astonishment, the hard-bitten British fascist blushed a brighter red than she ever had.

"Thank you, friends," Lynton said when the tally was complete. "You've done the right thing, and you've done a brave thing. And now let us hope our German colleagues may profit by our example."

Herr Kessler's forefinger shot out like a striking serpent. "Alicia Gimpel!"

Alicia leaped to her feet. She stood at stiff attention. "*Jawohl, Herr* Kessler!"

"What is the principle upon which the National Socialist Party and all fascist parties are founded?"

"The *Führerprinzip, Herr* Kessler," Alicia answered. "The principle that the leader of the party knows best the direction in which it should go." She'd learned that the year before. She didn't forget her lessons.

"Correct," her teacher growled. "Be seated." Kessler prowled in front of the blackboard. That was the only word Alicia could find for the way he moved. He might have been a lion or a leopard hunting for something to tear to pieces. She wondered what had put him in such a dreadful temper. He glared at the class. "Does anyone have any business telling the National Socialist Party of the Greater German *Reich* how to run its affairs? Anyone at all?"

"No, *Herr* Kessler," the children chorused—that was obviously the answer he wanted.

He nodded, his face still intent and angry. "No is correct. So what should we do when the Englishmen have the nerve to tell us such things? What should we do?" A boy's hand flew up in the air. Kessler pointed at him. "Wolfgang Priller!"

The boy leaped to his feet. "Punish them, *Herr* Kessler!" His voice was loud and shrill.

Kessler nodded again, and scribbled in the roll book. "You have the proper German spirit, Priller," he said. "I also think this would be the best course for the *Reich* to take. But what we *will* do . . ." He looked most unhappy. "Without a *Führer,* who can say what we will do? And if we do nothing, if we allow the English to get away with their insolence, is this not a sign of weakness?"

"*Ja, Herr* Kessler," the class said dutifully.

"What about the first edition, *Herr* Kessler?" a girl asked.

"Trudi Krebs," the teacher murmured. "Do your father and mother speak of the first edition? Do they?" he asked sharply. The girl nodded. He wrote in the roll book again, then slammed the book shut with a dreadful finality. He did not answer Trudi's question.

Silence—a particular kind of silence—filled the classroom. *She's in trouble,* Alicia thought, and then, *and her mother and father are liable to be in trouble, too.* Even before she'd found out she was a Jew, her parents had taught her not to say too much to other grownups. Most children in the Germanic Empire got similar lessons. The less you showed the outside world, the safer you stayed.

But Trudi had slipped. Children sometimes did. Alicia knew that was why she couldn't tell Francesca and Roxane what they really were, why she had to go on listening to them say horrible things about Jews when they were Jews themselves, why she'd said horrible things about Jews herself till not very long before . . . and why she had to go on saying horrible things about Jews now, just to make sure no one ever suspected.

Herr Kessler breathed out hard through his nose. He knew what sort of silence that was, too. "The first edition of *Mein Kampf,*" he said heavily, "is full of Adolf Hitler's earliest thoughts about the way the National Socialist Party should work. Most of these were wonderful thoughts, marvelous thoughts. *Aber natürlich*—our beloved first *Führer* was a wonderful man, a marvelous man, a brilliant man. But sometimes, when he looked back at what he had written, he found later that he had better ideas yet."

Wolfgang Priller raised his hand again. "Question, *Herr* Kessler!" The teacher nodded. Wolf said, "Is it like when you have us revise a theme?"

"Yes. Exactly!" *Herr* Kessler's smile, for once, was broad and pleased and genuine. "That is exactly what it is like. And if even Adolf Hitler saw that he could improve his work by revision, I trust you will see you can do the same."

The children nodded, Alicia among them. She was playing the chameleon again, though, for inside she sniffed scornfully. She hated revising more than anything else she did at school. It struck her as a waste of time. If you thought a little before you settled in to work, so you did it right the first time, why did you need to fiddle around with it afterwards?

"So you see," the teacher went on, "if the great and wise first *Führer* changed *Mein Kampf,* as he did, the first edition must be of smaller worth than those that came later. Anyone who would argue otherwise must surely suffer from a lack of proper understanding."

When the children went out to the schoolyard to play at lunchtime, no one had anything to do with Trudi Krebs. Most of her classmates pretended she wasn't there. Some of them—mostly boys—talked about her as if she weren't there. "Boy, is she going to get it," Wolfgang Priller predicted with a certain gloomy relish. "They'll knock on her door in the middle of the night, and then. . . ." He didn't say what would happen then, but he didn't have to. The other children shuddered in delicious horror. Everybody knew the kinds of things that happened when they knocked on your door in the middle of the night.

Trudi sat all alone on a bench, fighting back tears. Alicia wanted to go over and try to give her what comfort she could. Before finding out she was a Jew, she would have. Now she didn't dare. Being what she was made a coward of her. She hated that, hated herself for hanging back. But she didn't move. She wasn't afraid of getting in trouble herself. She'd been in trouble plenty of times. Putting her family and friends in trouble, though, was a different story. She couldn't do that. And so, biting her lip, she stayed where she was.

Alicia wondered if Trudi would even show up at school the next day. But she did, and the day after that, too, and on through the rest of the week. *Herr* Kessler seemed surprised. Alicia knew she was surprised. If the knock on the door in the middle of the night hadn't come . . . well, who could say what that meant?

Esther Stutzman liked to shop, though she didn't treat expeditions to the department store like hunting trips across the veldt the way Susanna Weiss did. For a Berliner who enjoyed seeing what there was to see and spending some money, there was only one place to go: the Kurfürstendamm. Back before the Second World War, lots of rich Jews had lived there—lived there openly, which made Esther marvel. They'd got away with it for years, too, till *Kristallnacht,* when the broad street turned into a glittering ocean of broken glass.

Nowadays, the Kurfürstendamm still glittered, but with multicolored neon signs and the reflections of the sun off plate-glass windows. People came from all over the Germanic Empire—and from the Empire of Japan and the South American countries as well—to part with their Reichsmarks in style.

Fashions on dummies in the plate-glass windows ranged from coquettish to outrageous, while some were both at once. *Before long,* Esther thought, *Anna will want to wear clothes like that.* Her sigh was part horror and part mere sadness at the passage of time.

Last year's turbans, she saw, were out of favor. Hats this year looked like nothing so much as the high-crowned, shiny-visored caps Party and SS bigwigs wore, decorated with brightly dyed plumes sprouting from improbable places. Esther eyed them dubiously. She didn't know if she cared to look like a *Sturmbannführer* who'd just mugged a peacock.

She paused in front of a telephone booth. The man inside might well have come from South America. He was certainly too swarthy to live comfortably within the Greater German *Reich.* He hung up, came out of the booth, and tipped his fedora to Esther as he hurried into the milliner's shop.

Fumbling in her handbag, she pulled out a fifty-pfennig coin and went into the telephone booth. A man who'd started towards it turned away in disappointment. He would have to find another place from which to call, not that there weren't plenty of public telephones along the Kurfürstendamm. Esther fed the coin into the slot and dialed the number she needed. The phone rang once, twice. . . .

"*Bitte?*" a woman said in Esther's ear.

"*Guten Tag, Frau* Klein," Esther answered. "I have an important message for you."

"I'm sorry, but I'm not inter—" Maria Klein broke off, perhaps recognizing Esther's voice. Esther hoped that was why she stopped, anyhow.

After a moment, the other woman said, "Well, go ahead, as long as you've got me on the line."

She had the sense not to name names, just as Esther had had the sense not to call from her own home or from Dr. Dambach's office. If the Kleins' phone was tapped (as it might well be, after Dambach had discovered the two versions of their family tree), technicians could trace the call here—but how much would they gain if they did? Precious little, because Esther intended to leave as soon as she hung up.

"Thank you," she said now. "I just wanted to let you know that there are people who know there are two sets. Isn't that interesting?" She tried to sound bright and cheerful, as a telephone solicitor should.

"This, too?" Maria said. "This, too, on top of everything with the baby?"

"I'm afraid so." In the face of the other woman's bitterness, Esther's good cheer collapsed like a burst balloon. *And it's my fault,* she thought miserably. *Mine—nobody else's.* She didn't know how she was going to live with that.

"What are we supposed to do now?" Maria Klein demanded. "*Gott im Himmel,* what are we supposed to do now?"

She wasn't really asking Esther. And if she was asking God, He'd had few answers for Jews these past seventy-five years. "I'm sorry. I'm sorry for everything," Esther whispered, and hung up. As soon as she left the booth, another woman went in. She hoped the other woman had happier business. She also hoped the other woman, and whoever used the booth afterwards, would cover up all of her own fingerprints.

Esther wanted to find another phone booth and call Walther, to let him know she'd warned the Kleins. She wanted to, but she didn't. Calls into and out of Zeiss were too likely to be monitored. She could have worked out some sort of code phrase to tell him what she'd done, but she didn't want to take the chance today. Such phrases were fine if nobody was likely to be paying close attention. If, on the other hand, someone was trying to build a case . . .

With a shiver, Esther shook her head. "No," she murmured.

A man gave her a curious look. Susanna would have frozen him with a glare. Heinrich would have walked past him without even noticing the curious look, which would have confounded him just as well. Esther's way was to smile sweetly at him. He turned red, embarrassed at wondering about such an obviously normal person.

If only you knew, Esther thought. But the truth, no matter how little the Nazis wanted to admit it, was that Jews were, or could be, normal people, some good, some bad, some indifferent. Shylock's words from *The Merchant of Venice* echoed in Esther's mind. *If you prick us, do we not bleed? if you tickle us, do we not laugh? if you poison us, do we not die?*

Esther tried to imagine an SS man tickling a Jew. The picture was enough to set her laughing without the deed—but only for a moment. The Nazis had poisoned Jews, poisoned them by the millions, and the Jews had died.

Shylock went on, *and if you wrong us, shall we not revenge?* She doubted a Jew was left alive who didn't dream of revenge at least once a day. But dreams were only dreams.

Survival is a kind of revenge, Esther thought. *Just by living on, by passing our heritage to our children, we beat the Nazis.* She smiled. Now Alicia Gimpel knew what she was, too. Pretty soon, her sisters would also know.

And if all went well—and Esther, with her sunny disposition, still hoped it would—Eduard Klein would find out one of these days, too. But then that smile disappeared. No matter how sunny Esther was, she couldn't keep it. The Kleins had passed on some of their heritage to little Paul, too, and he would never live to find out what he was.

Heinrich Gimpel was starting to get used to seeing long black limousines pull up to *Oberkommando der Wehrmacht* about the time he and Willi got off their bus in front of the building. He was getting used to watching Party and SS *Bonzen* he'd seen on the televisor and read about in newspapers and magazines climbing the steps he climbed every day.

And he was beginning to gauge how the generals in charge of the *Wehrmacht* liked their high-ranking visitors by the way the guards treated the newcomers at the entrance. If they came to attention and waved the politicking bigwigs through, those officials were in good odor with his bosses. If they made the muckymucks wait, checked identity cards against faces, and fed the cards through the machine reader to get a green light, those men weren't so well liked.

One morning, the machine reader showed a red light. "This is an outrage!" an SS *Obergruppenführer* shouted. "Let me pass!"

"Sorry," a guard replied, obviously enjoying being rude to the SS equivalent of a lieutenant general. "No green light, you don't come in." He turned to Heinrich and Willi. "Next!"

"You have not heard the last of this!" the *Obergruppenführer* warned. He stormed off, his face as red as the stripe on a General Staff officer's trousers.

Heinrich wondered if his identity card would pass muster, but it did. So did Willi's. Once they got inside, Willi said, "The generals really didn't want to see that fellow, if they programmed the reader to reject his card."

"People are starting to show where they stand," Heinrich replied.

"I'd say so," Willi Dorsch agreed. "And if that SS man's faction wins, I'd say we'll see our budget cut."

Heinrich shrugged. "The *Waffen*-SS has always thought it could do the *Wehrmacht*'s job. The next time it's right will be the first."

"Not to hear its officers tell the story." Willi shrugged, too. "Ah, well. Ours is not to wonder why. Ours is but to do or die."

"You so relieve my mind," Heinrich said. Willi laughed. He could talk blithely about dying—he didn't have to worry about it very much. Heinrich, on the other hand, had days when he felt he was living on borrowed time, and that it was about to run out. The feeling would have been bad enough had he worried about himself alone. Worrying about the rest of his folk left in the *Reich* seemed twenty times worse.

As they sat down at their desks, Willi said, "You see, though? It's just like I said. Nobody cares what the limeys did, and nobody's calling a Party congress to pick the next *Führer*. So much for the precious first edition. The big shots will do the choosing, same as always."

"It does look that way," Heinrich agreed, and did his best not to sound too unhappy in case the room was bugged. "They're taking their time, too."

"They've got to find somebody they can all at least stand," Willi said, which was doubtless true. "That weeds out the zanies and the men who only have a following in one faction."

"So it does." If Heinrich thought, *A Party congress would do better still, because then everything would be out in the open*, he kept it to himself. Willi was right: no Party congress would choose Kurt Haldweim's successor. That being so, to go on talking about the first edition might mark a man as a dangerous dissident.

He settled in to work. No matter what the *Waffen*-SS thought, the

Wehrmacht was the strong right arm of the Greater German *Reich*. And no matter who became *Führer*—even if it turned out to be that belligerent *Obergruppenführer*'s candidate—the *Wehrmacht* had to go on. It had to—and it would. Plenty of people like Heinrich Gimpel (though not many of them *just* like Heinrich Gimpel) made sure it kept running smoothly.

Willi asked, "Are we on for tonight?"

"The brains of the outfit hasn't told me anything different," Heinrich said, by which he meant Lise. Willi grinned; he sometimes called Erika the High Command in the same way. Carefully, Heinrich added, "We might do better if we don't talk politics too much, though."

Willi's grin slipped. "You know that, and I know that, but whether Erika knows that. . . . Well, we'll find out."

That was what Heinrich was afraid of, but he made himself smile and nod. The date for dinner and bridge alarmed him, so that part of him wished he'd backed out. If Willi and Erika's marriage was blowing up, he didn't want it to blow up in his face. But what would Erika do if he made that too obvious? He didn't want to find out. Getting back to work was something of a relief.

Willi didn't joke any more about Erika being the one who wanted Heinrich over. Heinrich wished he would have. If he was joking about it, he probably wasn't brooding over what it meant. If he wasn't joking . . . Well, who could say?

They got through the day's work. Canteen rumor was full of talk about the rejected *Obergruppenführer*. Since Heinrich and Willi had seen that happen, they scored points for eyewitness accounts. Another analyst sighed enviously, saying, "I'd've paid money to watch one of those arrogant so-and-sos head off with a flea in his ear." Several other people nodded.

Rumor also spoke of *Bonzen* from the Party and from the Navy who had been admitted to *Oberkommando der Wehrmacht*. Heinrich tried to read tea leaves from that. All he could see was that the Navy, like the *Wehrmacht*, was a conservative service. If they were joining with one section of the Party, maybe with an SS faction different from that *Obergruppenführer*'s . . . They might be trying to promote a candidate, or they might be trying to block one. Only time would tell.

Heinrich and Willi rode home together. "See you a little before seven,"

Willi said as he got off the bus. "We can all watch Horst and then get down to cards."

"All right." Heinrich hoped it would be.

Katarina came over to babysit the girls. Käthe was a kid sister, closer in age to Alicia than to Lise. Heinrich suspected she'd been a surprise to her parents. He wished he could ask them even such a nosy question; a drunken truck driver had broadsided their little VW a few years before, and they hadn't survived the wreck. A People's Court gave the truck driver summary justice, but that didn't bring back the Franks.

Tante Käthe fascinated the children. She dyed her brown hair a yellow as artificial as oleomargarine, and sometimes wore styles that looked like what SS uniforms would have been if they were designed to titillate rather than terrify. *In my day, you'd have done a stretch in a camp for clothes like that,* Heinrich thought. He laughed at himself. *And if going on about "In my day . . ." doesn't make me an old fogy, I don't know what would.*

Tonight Katarina had on dungarees of blue American denim, which were almost as scandalous as some of her other clothes. She refused to be ordinary. That was dangerous for a Jew. On the other hand, a fair number of young men and women dressed the way she did, so she had a crowd into which she could blend in.

"Have fun with your bridge," she told Heinrich and Lise. She might have been saying, *Have fun with your warm milk and slippers.* Käthe's eyes sparkled as she turned to the girls. "While they're gone, we'll have *real* fun, won't we?"

"Ja!" Alicia, Francesca, and Roxane chorused, entranced. Every so often, Heinrich wondered what *real* fun consisted of. He'd never found the girls' heads spinning with hashish after *Tante* Käthe watched them, so he didn't lose sleep over it, but he did wonder.

Getting out of the house felt good, even if it was only for the short jaunt over to the Dorsches'. As Heinrich and Lise got off the bus, she said, "Willi and Erika are lucky to live so close to their bus stop."

Heinrich nodded. "I've thought the same thing." Thinking along with your wife was supposed to be another mark of fogydom. He didn't care. He liked thinking along with Lise.

When he rang the bell, Erika opened the door. She smiled at the Gimpels. "Come on in," she said. "Horst will be on in a minute, and Willi wouldn't miss him for the world." Erika made watching the news sound like a vice. *First danger sign,* Heinrich thought.

From the front room, Willi's voice rose in excitement: "Come quick, everybody! I think we've got a new *Führer!*" That sent Heinrich and Lise—and Erika—hurrying to join him.

"Germany, awake!" Horst Witzleben spoke in millions of homes as if he were a close friend. "After long and serious discussions, senior Party, SS, and military leaders have chosen the present minister of heavy industry, Heinz Buckliger, to guide the future of the Greater German *Reich* and the Germanic Empire. I am proud to be among the first to say, '*Heil* Buckliger!' " His arm shot out in the Nazi salute.

Behind him, a new picture appeared on the screen. Heinrich wouldn't have known Heinz Buckliger from the man in the moon. He proved to be a ruddy-faced man of about fifty, with a thick shock of graying blond hair and a toothy smile. "He's so young!" Erika Dorsch said. A moment later, she added, "And handsome, too."

Heinrich didn't know about handsome. Young the new *Führer* certainly was: younger by far than Kurt Haldweim had been when he began to lead the *Reich.* "They passed over a lot of senior people to put him in place," Willi said. "The new generation's here at last."

"The new head of the *Reich* was born in Breslau in 1959," Horst Witzleben said. That made Buckliger more than forty years younger than Haldweim—closer to two generations than one. The newsreader went on, "He studied economics in Munich, graduating with highest honors from the university there. Before joining the Ministry of Heavy Industry, he served for seven years in the *Allgemeine*-SS, rising to the rank of *Hauptsturmführer.*" *Captain,* Heinrich thought, automatically translating to what he thought of as a real rank. Not bad. Not spectacular, but not bad.

"Once in the Ministry, *Herr* Buckliger rapidly became known as an efficiency expert," Witzleben said. "He has promised to bring that passion for efficiency to the *Reich* as a whole. Here is his first statement after his selection."

Heinz Buckliger sat at his desk in the *Führer*'s palace in what was obviously a piece of videotape. "*Volk* of the Greater German *Reich,* I accept the role of *Führer* with pride, but also with great humility," he said in a pleasant if not ringing baritone. "Mindful of the triumphs of the past, I shall do all I can to lead you to a still more glorious future. Many things have grown slack in recent years. I hope to tighten them, and to make the *Reich* and the Germanic Empire run more smoothly. With your help, I know I shall succeed."

"He sounds all right," Willi said as Horst Witzleben reappeared and began talking about the congratulations pouring into the *Reich* on Buckliger's rise to supreme power.

"So he does," Heinrich agreed. "But he's plainly someone's fair-haired boy. I wonder whose." His first guess for the new *Führer*'s patron was Lothar Prützmann, head of the SS: once an SS man, always an SS man. That wasn't a sure thing, but it was the way to bet.

"All right, now we know," Erika said. "After that, the rest of the news will be small potatoes. Shall we play some cards?"

"Good idea," Lise said. Heinrich nodded. Willi's sigh said he would have liked to stay in front of the televisor, but democracy was alive and well in the Dorsch household, even if the big wheels in the German government had been able to ignore it in choosing Heinz Buckliger.

The very first hand they played, Willi bid and made a small slam in clubs. Heinrich and Lise couldn't do a thing about it. If you didn't have the cards, you were stuck. Willi chortled. Heinrich said, "I wonder what's on the news."

On the next hand, Erika Dorsch made three no-trump: as quick and one-sided a rubber as possible. Lise said, "Heinrich's right. Watching the news seems better and better." Their hosts laughed at them.

They played steadily, with a couple of pauses when Erika helped the Dorsches' son and daughter with their homework and one when Willi broke up a squabble between the children. "This all looks and sounds familiar," Heinrich said.

"Life goes on," Erika said, "one way or another." If that wasn't a hooded glance she sent toward Willi, Heinrich had never seen one.

Willi himself affected not to notice. Or maybe he really didn't notice; you never could tell with Willi. He said, "Whose deal is it?"

"Mine, I think," Lise answered. She gather up the cards and started shuffling. "It is now, anyway."

Heinrich got the contract when everybody passed at two hearts. Playing it was routine, so much so that things got sidetracked halfway through when Lise and Willi started arguing about a newspaper story on Babylonian archaeology that they'd both seen and Heinrich and Erika had somehow missed. Willi insisted the find proved Hammurabi's code was 250 years older than everyone had thought up till now; Lise was just as sure it proved no such thing. As people will when disagreeing about something of such monumental unimportance, they both got more and more certain they were right. As they pointed fingers at each other, they might have forgotten anyone else was in the room—or, for that matter, on the planet.

Heinrich set his cards on the table, face down. Lise hardly ever got so excited when she argued with him, and he was glad she didn't. If Willi raised his voice and turned red—well, Willi was in the habit of doing such things. "A good thing they're friends, or they'd murder each other," Heinrich remarked to Erika.

With all the noise Lise and Willi were making, he wasn't sure she even heard him. But she nodded. "Willi's as bad as the children," she said, like Heinrich talking under the noise of the argument. "You, now, you have too much sense to waste your time with such foolishness."

"I don't know," he said. "Lise's doing it, and she's got more sense than I do."

"Maybe." Erika waved her hand. "But I don't want to go to bed with Lise."

What Heinrich wanted to say was, *Are you out of your mind?* Even if she did want to sleep with him (which struck him as strange enough when she was married to the much handsomer Willi), to say so in front of her husband and his wife? Maybe she'd known what she was doing, though, because neither Willi nor Lise leaped from a chair with a cry of fury. They were too busy quarreling over cuneiform styles and tree-ring chronology and other things about which neither of them knew a great deal.

Which left Heinrich the question of how to respond. Part of him knew exactly how he would like to respond. The rest of him told that part to shut up and forget about it. If he hadn't been happy with Lise, or maybe if he'd just been a few years younger, a few years randier, a few years stupider (assuming those last two weren't one and the same), that one part might have won the argument, especially since he got the idea he could have taken Erika right there on the card table without making either Willi or Lise notice.

But, things being as they were, yielding to temptation wasn't practical. And so he answered, "I'm sorry, but with all the racket these two are making, I didn't hear a word you said."

Erika Dorsch's sour smile told him she didn't believe a word of it. What *did* she believe? That he didn't want to go to bed with her? Or just that he didn't want to do anything about it then and there? *Isn't that an interesting question?*

Deciding he didn't want to know the answer, Heinrich reached out and waved his hand up and down between Willi and Lise. "Can we get back to bridge, please?" he asked loudly.

His wife and Erika's husband both blinked, as if they were coming back to the real world. Willi said, "I don't know why you're so impatient. We just started talking—"

"And talking, and talking," Erika broke in, her voice acid-edged.

"It *was* fifteen minutes ago," Heinrich said.

"Oh, *Quatsch,*" Willi said. Then he looked at his watch and blinked again. He grinned a rather sickly grin. "Oh. Well, maybe it was." Lise seemed almost as surprised as he did.

"It's your lead, Willi, if you can think of anything besides ancient history," Erika said.

"Let me look at the last trick, please," Willi said, which went a long way toward proving he couldn't. He examined it, muttered to himself, and threw out a low diamond. As far as Heinrich could see, the lead might have come at random as readily as from reflection on what had gone before.

Heinrich made the contract. He and Lise went on to win the rubber, though not by nearly so much as they'd lost the first one. Shuffling for the first hand of the next rubber, Willi said, "We'll really hammer you this time."

"Tell me a new story," Heinrich answered. "I've heard this one before, and I don't believe a word of it."

"You'll see." Willi picked up his hand, arranged it in suits, and said, as casually as if he were asking the time, "Three no-trump."

"What?" Heinrich stared. His own hand didn't have opening strength, but he hadn't imagined Willi owned that kind of powerhouse. He hadn't seen a three-no opening in at least five years. He passed. So did Erika. Willi yelped and sent her a wounded look. Visions of another slam must have danced in his head. Lise passed, too. Heinrich led. Erika laid out her hand as dummy. It was ten-high—no wonder she'd passed.

Willi didn't even make the three he'd bid. With no strength on the board, he had to play everything out of his own hand, and came up one trick short. The honors bonus for all four aces more than made up for that. Even so, he let out a sorrowful sigh. "Twenty-eight high-card points I was looking at, and down one! I'll never see another hand like that."

The rest of the evening's bridge was less dramatic. The Gimpels and Dorsches ended up about even. As Heinrich and Lise walked to the bus stop, she asked, "What did you and Erika talk about while Willi and I were wrangling over Babylonians?"

"Oh, nothing much," Heinrich answered. He knew he would probably end up in trouble for not telling his wife what Erika had said. But if he did tell her, he'd end up in trouble, too. *Sometimes you can't win,* he thought, and kept walking.

V

AFTER GIVING THE FLAG THE NATIONAL SOCIALIST SALUTE, *HERR* KESSLER LED Alicia Gimpel's class in singing "*Deutschland über Alles*" and the "Horst Wessel Song": the German and Party anthems. That wasn't part of the usual morning routine, but he explained, "This is a special day, children, because the *Reich* has a new *Führer*." His right arm shot out again. "*Heil* Buckliger!"

"*Heil* Buckliger!" Alicia and her classmates echoed dutifully. She hadn't known about the new *Führer* till breakfast this morning, when her mother and father talked about him. Aunt Käthe hadn't watched Horst Witzleben, the way her parents did. Instead, she'd played with Alicia and her sisters, and sung silly songs, and told stories that were not only funny but also a good deal sassier than the ones the Gimpel girls heard from anybody else in the family.

Herr Kessler said, "The new *Führer* will do wonderful things for the *Reich* and for the Germanic Empire. He is very wise and very good and very strong. He must be all those things, or he never would have been chosen *Führer*."

He sounded very sure. Almost all the pupils in the classroom nodded without a moment's hesitation. Alicia nodded, too. She was learning to be a chameleon. But she couldn't help wondering, *How does he know?*

"Will things be any different now, *Herr* Kessler?" asked a boy—Alicia didn't see who.

The teacher frowned. The question was good enough that he had to answer it, but for a moment he seemed unable to find a way. *Maybe nobody told him what to say,* Alicia thought. *He doesn't seem very good at figuring things out for himself.* At last, Kessler said, "I think things will be better. The new *Führer* is a young man—not too much older than I am—and he is active and vigorous. The old *Führer* was very old indeed. He was sickly and feeble. Some of you may have grandparents or great-grandparents who are like that."

Several children nodded. Behind Alicia, Emma Handrick raised her hand. When *Herr* Kessler called on her, she said, "When my great-granddad got that way, my folks took him to a *Reichs* Mercy Center. Is that what they did with the old *Führer*?"

"No. *Gott im Himmel,* no!" The teacher turned very red. The question must have rocked him. Alicia couldn't remember him ever saying anything about God before. She couldn't remember any of her teachers saying anything about God. She'd always had the idea that they weren't supposed to. *Herr* Kessler needed a moment to gather himself. Then he said, "Kurt Haldweim lived out his whole life. He had to, you see, because he was serving the *Reich*. Do you understand?"

"*Ja, Herr* Kessler," Emma answered. She wasn't going to argue with him.

Alicia wanted to. Before she found out she was a Jew, she might have. She didn't dare stick out her neck now. Not being able to say what she thought sometimes made her feel as if she were choking. She wanted to cheer when a boy stuck up his hand. When the teacher pointed his way, he asked, "Excuse me, *Herr* Kessler, but if the old *Führer* was all feeble, why *didn't* they take him to a *Reichs* Mercy Center? Isn't that what you're supposed to do, before he becomes a burden?"

"The *Führer* is not a burden," Kessler said stiffly. "The *Führer* cannot be a burden. The *Führer* is the *Führer*."

By the way he spoke, that was supposed to settle things. Nobody in the class asked any more questions about the *Reichs* Mercy Centers, so maybe it did. Or maybe all the children realized asking more questions like that would only land them in trouble.

And maybe *Herr* Kessler realized he hadn't satisfied everybody with his answers, for he quickly changed the subject and plunged into the day's usual lessons. No one could challenge him on those. He went back to being the classroom *Führer,* lord of all he surveyed.

For the history lesson, he rolled up the usual map of the world as it was now and rolled down a different map, one that showed the way things had been before the Second and Third World Wars. "Do you see how tiny the *Reich* was in those days, and how big our enemies were?" he said. "And yet we beat them, because we were Aryans and they were full of Jews. France, England, Russia, the United States—all full of Jews. And they fell into our hands one after another. What does this tell you? Alicia Gimpel!"

She sprang to her feet. "That Aryans are superior to Jews, *Herr* Kessler."

"Very good. Be seated."

She knew her lessons. She could recite them without fail. Reciting them when she didn't believe them, though, made her feel all slimy inside. She wanted to know what was true. She wanted to say what was true. She knew she would get in trouble if she did. That made going on with what she learned in school necessary. It didn't make it palatable.

Herr Kessler asked the next question of someone else. It was also anti-Semitic. Alicia didn't like hearing it, either. She wondered how *Herr* Kessler would like listening to anti-Aryan questions all day. She suspected he would get sick of it in a hurry.

She sighed. Things had been a lot simpler before she knew what she was.

When Lise Gimpel was a girl, she'd grated cabbage by hand. As often as not, that had involved grating some fingertip or knuckle in with the cabbage. Her father, an engineer, had always found that funny—they weren't *his* fingertips or knuckles, after all. When she yelped, he would say, "Adds protein," and puff on his pipe.

These days, Lise used a plastic rod to guide quartered chunks of cabbage into the maw of the food processor. The push of a button, a whir, and the job was done—not even a tenth the time, and never any need to reach for the Mercurochrome. But every time she did it, she imagined she smelled pipe tobacco.

She bit her lip. She'd been pregnant with Francesca when the damned drunk cut short her parents' lives. Alicia had been only a toddler then. She didn't remember her grandparents, and they'd never got to know their other grandchildren. Sometimes life seemed dreadfully unfair.

Lise laughed, not that it was funny. *As if a Jew in the Third* Reich *should look for fairness*. But somehow God seemed extra malicious in piling a personal disaster on top of the one she'd been born with.

Alicia came into the kitchen. She liked to help cook. So did Roxane. Francesca didn't care one way or the other. Lise was glad to see her daughter. "Hello, sweetheart," she said. "How did it go today?" Talking with Alicia would help ease her out of her gloom.

So she thought, anyway, till Alicia blurted, "Mommy, do I have to be a Jew? I don't think I want to."

Before Lise answered, she automatically looked around. "Where are your sisters?"

"Upstairs doing homework. I finished mine."

"All right. Good. You have to be careful even saying that word." Lise put her hands on Alicia's shoulders. "Now—why don't you? What happened today that made you think you don't?"

"It's not just today," Alicia answered. "It's everything that's happened since I found out. People just keep saying mean things—horrible things—about Jews—and everybody *believes* them. It's like they're calling *me* names all the time."

"Oh, my dear." Lise gave Alicia a squeeze. Her daughter's head already came up past her shoulder. "I remember that, and I remember how much it hurt, too. They don't know any better, that's all."

"But if I weren't a Jew, then it wouldn't matter any more." Alicia could be as painfully logical as her father, though at ten she didn't always see as far as she needed to.

Lise cocked her head to one side to make sure she didn't hear one of Alicia's sisters charging downstairs at the worst possible moment. Even after she'd satisfied herself that they were busy, she needed a few seconds to marshal her thoughts. "If you decide that's what you end up wanting, pumpkin, you can do it. You can always pretend what we told you isn't real. We said so, remember?"

Alicia nodded. "I want to do that."

"You can. But I have to tell you, it may not be quite so simple. If you beat eggs together to scramble them, can you separate the whites out again afterwards to make meringue?"

"Of course not," Alicia said.

"Well, you can always live as though you're not a Jew, pretend you're not a Jew," Lise said. "But you'll know even so. You'll have to know. You can't very well forget, can you?"

"I can try." Alicia screwed up her face. Lise could tell she was doing her best to pretend that that evening with the Stutzmans and Susanna had never happened. Lise could also tell, by her daughter's despairing expression, that she was having no more luck than anyone else would have. Alicia pointed an accusing finger at her. "You and Daddy didn't tell me anything about that."

"No, we didn't," Lise admitted. "We thought it would be pretty obvious—and we didn't know you wouldn't want to be a Jew."

"I haven't got much choice, have I?" Alicia asked bleakly.

"You have a choice in the way you live." Lise picked her words with great care. "You haven't got a choice about what you *are,* not any more. When you have children, you'll have a choice about telling them what they are."

"Why would I ever want to put anybody else through this?" Alicia said.

Were there any Jews left in the *Reich* who hadn't asked themselves that question at least once? Were there any who hadn't asked it a thousand times? Quietly, Lise answered, "Because if you don't, then the Nazis win. They say we don't deserve to live, we don't deserve to be here at all. And if you don't tell your children what they are, who they are, aren't you saying you think the Nazis were right all along?"

"Weren't they?" Pain filled Alicia's voice. "If they thought Jews were horrible, if *everybody* thought Jews were horrible, if nobody tried to stop the SS from doing what it did, maybe Jews—maybe *we* really were horrible. Maybe we *deserved* what happened."

That was another thought that had probably crossed every surviving Jew's mind. People saw themselves, at least in part, in the mirror their neighbors held up to them. If the mirror showed a twisted image, wouldn't they start to believe that was the way they really seemed? How could they help it?

"Some people did try to stop the SS. Not enough, though, and most of them got killed. But I don't think anybody deserves to be killed for what he is," Lise said. "You can't help that. If you *do* something bad enough, maybe you deserve to die. That's a whole different argument, though. For just trying to live, and to get along as best you can?" She shook her head. "No, sweetheart."

Her daughter looked haunted. That was fair enough, too. How many millions of ghosts crowded the Germanic Empire? Better, maybe, not to try to count them all. That way lay despair. Alicia said, "I sure hope you're right."

So do I, Lise thought. *But how can I know? How can anybody know?* One thing she did know was that she had to conceal her doubts from her daughter. She said, "Of course I am."

"What am I going to do?" Alicia said, more to herself than to Lise.

But Lise answered her, with forced briskness: "What are you going to do? Since you've finished your homework and your sisters haven't, you're going to take a bath. And make sure you rinse all the shampoo out of your hair and wash behind your ears. Sometimes you leave enough dirt to grow potatoes in."

"Potatoes." Alicia thought that was funny. She was a child; she couldn't stay gloomy for long. She went up the stairs singing, "I'm my own vegetable garden."

Lise envied her that ability to swing away from sadness so fast. *I used to be able to do that,* she thought. *I wonder where it went.* Wherever it went, it was gone for good now. She went to the cupboard and poured herself a glass of schnapps. She hardly ever drank when she wasn't with other people who were drinking, but today she made an exception.

When Heinrich came through the door a few minutes later, Alicia—who hadn't yet started getting rid of the potatoes—Francesca, and Roxane all swarmed downstairs to give him hugs and kisses. He needed a couple of minutes to wade through them and make his way into the kitchen. He hugged Lise and kissed her, then noticed the glass of schnapps on the counter near the sink. "Tough day?" he asked. Lise nodded. Her husband pointed to the glass. "Must have been. You don't usually do that. What happened?"

"Later." Lise nodded in the direction of the children.

"Oh." Heinrich nodded, too. He went to the cabinet for a glass of his own and also filled it full of schnapps. "Well, here's to us."

"To us," Lise agreed. They both drank. Their daughters wandered into the kitchen. Roxane wanted to help. Francesca wanted to tell her father about something that had happened at school. Lise couldn't tell what Alicia wanted—maybe just to remind herself that they were a family. Alicia kept eyeing her little sisters with an expression that said, *I know something you don't know.*

By what she'd said to Lise a little while before, she wished she didn't.

After a while, the girls went back upstairs. "Make sure you get clean," Lise reminded Roxane—she'd sometimes skip a bath if she saw the chance.

"Well?" Heinrich asked.

Lise sighed. In a low, weary voice, she said, "Alicia said she didn't want to be a Jew. She said maybe the *Einsatzkommandos* knew what they were doing when they got rid of us."

"Oh. Oh, hell." Heinrich reached for his glass of schnapps and gulped at it. The laugh that burst from him was an ugly sound, one that had nothing to do with mirth. "Well, God knows she's not the first one of us to feel that way."

"I understand that," Lise said. "But still . . ."

"Yes. But still." Another swig and her husband's glass was empty. He poured it down like that about as often as Lise drank alone. With another ugly laugh, he said, "Did I ever tell you I wanted to be an SS man when I was a little boy? Before I knew, I mean."

"No." Lise shook her head in astonishment. They'd been married almost fifteen years, but startling things still surfaced, like rocks working their way up through thin soil. "No, you never said a word about that."

"Well, I did. I thought the black uniform was the most wonderful thing in the world, and of course this wasn't too long after we beat the United States, so SS men were heroes in all the movies and televisor shows where *Wehrmacht* men weren't. When my father told me, I didn't want to believe him. For a long time after that—a *long* time, I'm telling you—I thought we had it coming to us."

"You never said anything about that. Never," Lise said.

Instead of answering right away, Heinrich poured himself another glass of schnapps. His back was to her as he said, "It's not exactly something I'm proud of, you know."

"I think we all go through it," Lise said. "You sound like you had it worse than most of us, though."

"I probably did." Her husband shook his head, still not looking at her. "No, I certainly did. Even now, there are days when working at *Oberkom-*

mando der Wehrmacht seems like a poor second best, and I ought to have the SS runes on my collar tabs."

"Could you have kept up the masquerade if you did?" Lise asked.

"Some people do," Heinrich said, and she nodded. He sighed. "I'm glad—most of me is glad—I didn't have to try, though. Do you want me to talk with Alicia? Is she all right?"

"Maybe don't push it too hard right now," Lise said after a little thought. "You know how, how—overwhelming it can be. I think she'll settle down. She just realized she'll always *know* what she is, no matter what she decides to do about it."

"Ah, yes," Heinrich said. "That's another moment we all have, sure enough. The curse of knowledge . . ."

"Alicia thinks it's a curse right now," Lise said.

"I don't know what to do about it." Heinrich set about emptying that second glass of schnapps. "I wish I did, but I don't think anybody who's . . . in our boat does."

"We ought to have the Stutzmans over again," Lise said. "Anna's been coping with it for more than a year now. Maybe she can help Alicia—and even if she can't, they can play together. And I was on the phone with Esther this afternoon, and she says Susanna's back from London with all sorts of wild stories."

"Sounds good to me," Heinrich said. "I'm going to have lunch with Walther in the Tiergarten tomorrow. I'll set something up then, and you can call Susanna."

"All right." Lise nodded. "What does Walther want to talk about?" She assumed he wanted to talk about something. People met in Berlin's greatest park to get out in the open air—and also to get away from the possibility of talking where microphones might overhear.

Her husband answered with a shrug. "Don't know yet. I'll find out."

"Fair enough," Lise said. "What's new at work?"

"Not much. We're all waiting to see what sort of *Führer* Heinz Buckliger makes, same as everybody else." Heinrich held up a hand. "Wait. I take it back. There is one other interesting thing. These past few days, Willi's been very friendly with Ilse, for whatever that may be worth."

"The secretary?" Lise asked. Heinrich nodded. Her next question was obvious: "Is she worth being friendly to?"

"Well, she doesn't do anything for me," he answered. "Of course, I'm not Willi, and I'm not squabbling with my wife. I hope I'm not, anyway." He leaned over and kissed her.

"You'd better not be," Lise said. "How does Ilse compare to Erika?"

"As far as looks go, she doesn't," Heinrich said. "But she's not telling Willi all the different kinds of fool he is every time he turns around, either. That's got to count for something, wouldn't you think?"

"It would with me," Lise agreed. "But with a man, who can say?" Heinrich made a face at that, but he didn't try to argue with her.

Walther Stutzman liked the Tiergarten. He enjoyed eating lunch there, regardless of whether he needed to talk with someone in something approaching privacy. If he brought a sandwich and some fruit and a vacuum flask of coffee to the large park west of the Brandenburg Gate, he could imagine himself in the country—if the country in which he imagined himself included plenty of other people eating, watching birds, strolling hand in hand, walking or running for exercise, or lying around in the sun in any clothing or next to none. The Berlin police did frown on complete public nudity, but more as a matter of excessive zeal than one of criminal intent. And what might go on under cover of the bushes . . . neither Walther nor the police were in the habit of investigating too closely.

Today he made a point of getting to the Tiergarten early, so he could stake out a bench before the noontime crowd made looking for one a hopeless chore. The grass was long and green. Come fall, a snorting harvester would mow it down and turn it into hay for animal fodder. In the meantime, it grew as it would.

He found a place to sit near the Hubertus fountain and the bronze foxhunting group at the center of the park. He smiled, pleased with himself; he'd told Heinrich to start looking for him by the fountain. And here came his friend. Heinrich's gangly height and ungainly walk made him impossible to miss. Walther stood up and waved. A couple of beats slower than he should have, Heinrich waved back and came toward him.

"Hello," Walther said. "Nice day, isn't it?"

"Why, so it is," Heinrich said in mild surprise, as if he'd only just realized it. Maybe he had; there were times when Walther wondered how much that went on outside his own head his friend noticed. Heinrich sat down beside him. "*Was ist los?*"

"You know about the Kleins?" Walther said.

"Oh, yes." Heinrich nodded, his long face set in unhappy lines. "I do know about that. What's up with them?"

"I changed their genealogy, to give them a couple of possibly Jewish ancestors," Walther said. Heinrich nodded again. With a sigh, Walther went on, "Their pediatrician is too damned efficient, though. He compared the revised chart with one he had from when their first son was born, and he noticed the changes. He not only noticed, he called in the genealogical authorities."

"Yes, I've heard all this," Heinrich said. "Esther told Lise, and Lise told me. It's a mess. One more thing for the Kleins—and for all of us—to worry about. Robert and Maria are still free, aren't they? That would be all we need, if they hauled them in for questioning—that on top of the poor baby."

"We're probably lucky we haven't seen more Tay-Sachs cases," Walther said. "So few of us left these days, and we marry among ourselves so much. . . . But that's not what I wanted to talk about."

"What, then?" Heinrich asked.

"I made a mistake when I altered the Kleins' charts," Walther said. "Anything that gets us noticed for any reason at all is a mistake. The question is, how do I fix it?"

"How *can* you fix it? It's done," Heinrich said. A very pretty blond girl in a short sun dress walked by, leading a dachshund on a leash. Heinrich noticed her—and the ridiculous little dog.

Walther knew a certain amount of relief that some of the real world did impinge on his friend. He said, "Well, that's what I wanted to ask you about. I could go back into the *Reichs* database again, and change the Kleins' records back to the way they were before I meddled the first time. Or I could just leave them alone and hope the storm blows over. Which do you think is the better bet?"

Heinrich's eyes got a faraway expression. Walther wasn't the avid bridge player some of Heinrich's *goyishe* friends were, but he'd sat down at the card table with him a few times. He wore this look when he was figuring out whether to run a finesse. He said, "If you leave things alone, they may decide the system hiccuped, or they may bring in the Kleins to try to find out what they know."

"That's how I see it," Walther agreed.

He wondered if Heinrich even heard him. His friend went on without even a pause for breath: "But if you change things a second time, they may decide the system hiccuped once but now it's back to normal, or they may decide somebody who isn't supposed to has access to it and can fiddle with it whenever he pleases."

Walther Stutzman nodded again. "I see it like that, too."

"All right, then," Heinrich said. "Both ways, if they think it's a hiccup, everything is fine. So which is more likely and more dangerous—them questioning the Kleins or them questioning the software in the database system? With the Kleins, it goes from no Jews in the woodpile to a few possible Jews in the woodpile a long time ago."

"On paper," Walther said. The Kleins were as Jewish as the Stutzmans or the Gimpels. He needed to make sure Heinrich remembered that. "If they have a baby with Tay-Sachs disease, that's a red flag about what they really are."

"It's a red flag, but it's not proof. This disease *can* happen to gentiles, too," Heinrich said.

"If the genealogical authorities want to snoop, they're liable to find enough proof to satisfy them," Walther said. "And there's no law that says they can't question the Kleins *and* check the database programming."

Heinrich looked astonished. Maybe he'd been so caught up in *either-or* that that hadn't occurred to him. Walther wished it hadn't occurred to him, too. Unfortunately, it was all too likely to occur to the authorities. He said, "This isn't damned if I do or damned if I don't. It's liable to be damned if I do *and* damned if I don't."

"I'm afraid you're right," Heinrich said.

"I'm afraid I'm right, too," Walther said. "And I'm afraid, period."

"You'd better be afraid. We'd all better be afraid," Heinrich said somberly. "If we're not afraid, we're dead. I think our best chance is sitting tight now, though. There's nothing to show the Kleins had any way to fiddle with the genealogical records, is there? He's a musician, and she's a *Hausfrau*. They can't lean on them too hard, not when the changes are so small."

He sounded as if he was trying to convince himself as well as Walther.

"They *can* do anything they want," Walther said bluntly, and his friend winced and nodded, for that was undoubtedly true. He went on, "What they choose to do . . . may be a different story. I hope you're right about that. So you think we ought to wait and see what happens, then?"

"Don't you think that's our best bet?" Heinrich asked.

Walther Stutzman sighed. "Overall, probably," he said. "But it's liable to be rough as hell on the Kleins. They're already trying to deal with what their baby has. If the genealogical authorities or the Security Police land on them, too—well, how much can one family take?"

Heinrich didn't answer. Walther hadn't expected him to. No one could answer that question for himself till the time of testing came, let alone for anyone else. Instead, Heinrich came back with a question of his own: "If you change the Kleins' records again, don't you think the genealogical authorities and the Security Police are liable to land on *you*? How much can you take, Walther?"

And that was the other side of the coin. "I don't know," Walther said. "Here's hoping I don't have to find out, and the Kleins don't, either."

"That's interesting." Heinrich Gimpel tapped his copy of the *Völkischer Beobachter* to show Willi Dorsch what was interesting.

Willi shifted on the commuter-train seat beside Heinrich. "Which?" he said. "Oh, the story about the budget? Well, what to you expect Buckliger to say? Easy enough to promise to bring things under control. Doing it?" He shook his head. "Don't hold your breath."

"He sounds like he means it, though." Heinrich read out loud: " 'For too long, the Greater German *Reich* has balanced its budget only with the aid of tribute from other lands within the Germanic Empire. If we are the greatest nation the world has known, should we not be able to pay our own way?' "

"Hell with that," Willi said. "Make the other bastards pay instead. They're the ones who lost. You wait and see. He's got it off his chest now: the new *Führer* can talk tough. But nothing's going to change."

Willi usually had good political sense. Heinrich reminded himself of that. Still, he couldn't help adding, "He's going on about high labor costs, too, and how we need to be honestly competitive and not just dictate favorable exchange rates to the rest of the world. We can't quite dictate to the Japanese, and look how their electronics have come on the past ten years."

"Are you going to tell me they stack up to Zeiss?" Willi snorted. "Don't make me laugh."

"A friend of mine works for Zeiss, and he's not laughing," Heinrich said. "You're right—what the Japanese make isn't as good as our stuff. But it's good enough to work, and it's a lot cheaper. For people who haven't got a whole lot of Reichsmarks to spend—"

"People who think like Jews," Willi broke in.

Heinrich shrugged. "Joke all you please." To Willi, it was just a joke, too. Heinrich knew he should be used to gibes like that. He *was* used to them, in the sense that his face didn't show what he thought. But they still burned. He went on, "No matter how you joke, though, plenty of people who can't afford our electronics can afford to buy from the Japs."

Willi twirled his finger in a gesture that had meant *so what?* for the past two generations. "That hasn't really got much to do with the budget, you know."

Although Heinrich didn't know any such thing, he didn't argue. He'd been taught since childhood not to disagree too strongly with anyone. Instead, he rustled the *Völkischer Beobachter* and changed the subject a little, saying, "What do you make of this? The *Führer* says, 'As part of an ongoing effort to strengthen the state, a thorough examination of its political underpinnings must also be undertaken.' What's that mean?"

"What? Where does he say that?" Willi opened up his own copy of the paper again. "Have to tell you, I missed it."

"Page four, third column, about halfway down."

"Page four . . ." When Willi finally found it, he shook his head. "He couldn't have buried it any deeper in a graveyard, could he?" He rubbed his chin and frowned. "I have to admit, I don't know exactly what that means. I bet nobody else does, either, except maybe Buckliger. It might just be the sort of stuff politicians use to pad out a speech." But he was still frowning. "You wouldn't put padding there, though—not usually. He wanted to say it, and he wanted to say it where not many people would notice he'd said it. I sure didn't. You notice everything, don't you?"

"Me? Only thing I notice is, we're coming into the Berlin station." Heinrich folded his newspaper and stuck it in his briefcase. Easier to carry just one thing when they hurried up the escalators to the level where they caught the bus to *Oberkommando der Wehrmacht* headquarters. Willi did the same.

A three-car accident snarled traffic to a fare-thee-well. Ambulances, police vehicles, and rubberneckers meant nothing could get through at a busy intersection. The police were slower setting up detours than they should have been, too. Everyone in the bus grumbled and complained. That did no one any good. Heinrich and Willi got to work half an hour late.

The guards at the entrance clucked sympathetically as the two of them hurried up the steps. "Came from South Station, didn't you?" one guard said when Heinrich held out his identity card. "Things are buggered up good and proper between there and here."

"Don't I know it!" Heinrich said. "I thought I'd be on that damned bus forever." The card went through the reader. The light flashed green. The guard returned the card and waved him through.

Willi joined him a moment later. "At least we're not the only ones," he said. "Misery loves company."

"Misery doesn't love anything," Heinrich said. "That's what makes it misery."

"*Jawohl, Herr Doktor* Professor!" Willi came to attention and saluted. "Thank you so much for clearing that up for me."

"When we work in the same room, I can't even tell you to go away," Heinrich said sadly.

They navigated the maze of corridors to get to the room they shared with several other budget analysts, secretaries, and clerks. Willi promptly disappeared from his desk. Heinrich knew he was heading to the canteen for coffee, and didn't think anything of it. Willi came back with two foam cups. He kept one and, with a flourish, handed the other to the secretary he and Heinrich shared. Ilse stammered out thanks, simpering like a starstruck teenager. Willi preened. Heinrich fought not to gag.

He had plenty to keep him busy. He always did. His fingers flashed across the keys of his adding machine. The number and function keys had grown smooth and shiny from long use. Some of the more senior men in the department were getting new adding machines, half as big and half as noisy as the old ones. The new machines came from Japan. Heinrich wondered if Willi knew. As for himself, he didn't want to give up the one he'd used for so long. In a lot of ways, he was intensely conservative. Change made him suspicious; it might lead to exposure. As long as things went on as they had up till now, his family and he stayed safe.

The phone on Willi's desk rang. Heinrich noticed it only peripherally. He was trying to unravel by exactly how much the Americans were pretending to be poorer than they really were. He might not have noticed the phone on his own desk. The Americans used numbers the way a cuttlefish used ink: to obscure, to conceal, to confuse. Figuring out what lay behind their smokescreen took not only patience but imagination.

But in spite of his best effort to focus on the columns of numbers in front of him, Willi's loud, angry voice eventually pierced his concentration: "Dammit, Erika, don't call me here for crap like that! I haven't got time to worry about it, and I sure as hell haven't got time to deal with it."

Heinrich looked up. He couldn't help himself. He saw he wasn't the only one. Nor, of course, was Willi the only one who'd ever had his personal life intrude on work. But he was the one with problems at the moment, which meant he was the one everybody else was pretending not to listen to now. That he was one of the more flamboyant men in the office only made his troubles more fascinating.

Erika said something. Heinrich couldn't make out what it was, but she sounded angry, too. He wouldn't have wanted to talk to her the way Willi just had. Whatever she said, it struck a nerve. Willi went red from the base of his neck all the way up to his forehead and ears. "That's a lie, too," he growled. "I'm just being friendly. You wouldn't know about friendly, would you?"

Someone must have told Erika about Ilse—or maybe Willi was being friendly, or more than friendly, with some woman Heinrich knew nothing about. He looked back to the numbers the Americans had submitted to the *Reich*. Before he could do anything but look, Erika said something else.

"Me?" Willi exclaimed. "*Me?* You've got your nerve! What about you and—" He didn't go on. Instead, he slammed the receiver into its cradle hard enough to start a young earthquake.

Had be been about to say, *What about you and Heinrich?* Erika hadn't been subtle. She'd done everything but send up a flare, in fact. Up till now, Willi hadn't paid much attention—or so it seemed. But maybe he could see what was right under his nose after all.

Or, then again, maybe he couldn't. His color faded as quickly as it had risen. He managed a smile of sorts as he swung his swivel chair toward Heinrich. "Women are strange creatures—you know that?" He might have been imparting some great philosophical truth. "We can't live with them, and we can't live without them, either."

Fourteen placid, happy years of marriage with Lise looked better and better to Heinrich. "I hope everything turns out all right for you," he said.

"So do I," Willi said. "Sometimes, though, what can you do?" He sounded as happy-go-lucky as usual. He meant, *You can't do anything—things will either work out or else they won't.* If Heinrich's marriage were in trouble when he wanted to keep it going, he would have tried everything under the sun—and looked in the dark, too, in case it was hiding something the sun didn't show. Did that mean Willi didn't want to keep his marriage going, or did it mean he didn't want to try? Heinrich didn't know. He couldn't tell. He wondered if Willi knew.

When lunchtime came, Heinrich said, "Shall we go to Admiral Yamamoto's?"

Willi nodded. "Why not? We haven't been there since the day old Haldweim kicked the bucket."

"Uh, right." True, the old *Führer* was dead. Even so, Heinrich couldn't have made himself talk about the ruler of the Germanic Empire so casually—so callously, even. Willi, confident in his perfect Aryanness, could be more expansive. *Or maybe he doesn't think about it at all. Maybe he just says the first thing that comes out of his mouth.*

Heinrich found that hard to imagine, let alone believe. But Willi was a law unto himself. He had been for as long as Heinrich had known him, and no doubt for years before that.

Sitting in the Japanese restaurant, eating Berlin rolls and sashimi and rice and washing them down with a seidel of beer (German beer, not Japanese—Japanese electronics were fine, but Japanese beer couldn't measure up to the *Reinheitsgebot*, the medieval purity law, and was barred from the Greater German *Reich*), Heinrich tried not to worry about anything except the havoc the wasabi was playing with his sinuses. But Admiral Yamamoto's got customers from a lot of ministries, and the SS men at the next table were too loud to ignore.

"Did you read the *Völkischer Beobachter* this morning?" one of them demanded of his pals. "*Did* you?"

"*Can* SS men read?" Willi said—in Heinrich's opinion, not nearly quietly enough.

"I saw it, all right," another blackshirt—a bruiser—answered. "That goddamn son of a bitch."

"Takes one to know one," Willi said—again, much too loud.

"*Oh,* Willi," Heinrich murmured. The other table held five SS men. If they got mad, it wouldn't even be a brawl. It would be a slaughter. But getting Willi to pay attention . . . was like getting him not to lead away from kings. You could wish, and much good wishing would do you.

Then the first SS man, a *Sturmbannführer,* said, "He's going to bring it in by the back door. You wait and see if he doesn't."

Before Willi could make yet another rude comment—and Heinrich knew just what sort of rude comment he would make about that—the bruiser nodded and said, "Bet your ass he is. 'A thorough examination of its political underpinnings.' " He made a loud retching noise.

And Willi Dorsch, canny political creature that he was, suddenly became quiet as a mouse. If he could have wiggled his ears, he would have swung them toward the table full of SS men. Heinrich felt the same way. The blackshirts weren't talking about just any goddamn son of a bitch. They were talking about Heinz Buckliger, newly chosen *Führer* and the most powerful man on the planet.

"Sure as hell, we'll hear more crap about the first edition," another SS man predicted gloomily. "If we'd had *our* way, we'd've knocked that stinking nonsense over the head once and for all."

"That's about the size of it," the *Sturmbannführer*—the most senior man at the table—agreed. "But the *Wehrmacht* wouldn't play ball with us, and so we got stuck with this asshole."

A fragment of Latin went through Heinrich's head. *Quis custodiet ipsos custodes?* Who *would* watch the watchmen? The SS was and always had been a law unto itself. Maybe, between them, the rest of the Party and the *Wehrmacht* could keep it in check. And, by all the signs, the SS itself had split on a candidate to replace Kurt Haldweim. That seemed promising. If no one else could, maybe some of the watchmen would keep an eye on the rest.

"He's young, too." The bruiser sounded depressed at the prospect.

"Well, maybe—" But the *Sturmbannführer* broke off. What *had* he been about to say? *Maybe he won't live to get old?* No, that wasn't the sort of thing to blurt out in a crowded restaurant. Had Heinrich wanted to say it, he couldn't imagine anyone but Lise whom he trusted enough to hear it. Even as things were, the blackshirts had run their mouths far more than he thought wise.

He looked at his watch. "Getting on towards one o'clock," he said. "We'd better head back to the office." Willi looked at him as if he'd lost his mind, or possibly started speaking Chinese. He wanted to hang around and listen to the SS men. That was exactly why Heinrich wanted to leave. He kicked his friend in the ankle under the table. Reluctantly, Willi left his chair. Heinrich paid the bill. They left the restaurant together.

Once out on the sidewalk, Willi practically exploded with excitement. "Did you hear them?" he demanded. "Did you *hear* them? Practically talking treason, right there in Admiral Yamamoto's!"

"Don't be silly. How can SS men talk treason?" Heinrich said. "What they want is what the state wants. And if you don't believe me, just ask them."

"Ha!" Willi said. "I didn't know you were such a funny fellow."

"I wasn't joking."

"I know. That only makes it funnier, but you have to look at it the right way to see it." Willi walked along for a while, whistling a tune from the new show about a theater owner who wanted an excuse to close down his firetrap of a house, booked a dreadful play about the evil machinations of Churchill and Stalin, and found to his horror that it was bad enough to become a comedy smash. The show itself was a comedy smash in Berlin, too, and had already spawned several companies touring the rest of the *Reich*. After a block or so, Willi stopped whistling—a mercy, because he was flat. He said, "Well, I hate to admit it, but you were right."

"About what? Getting out of Yamamoto's? You bet I was."

"No, no, no." Willi impatiently shook his head. "About that piece in the *Beobachter* this morning. If those bastards don't like it, there's got to be more to it than I thought. Buckliger does need to take a good long look at our underpinnings after all." A girl with nice legs came toward them. Willi said not a word about her underpinnings. Heinrich knew then that his friend was serious. After a few more steps, Willi added, "You may have been right about something else, too."

"What, twice in one day?" Heinrich said. "Such compliments you pay me. I've caught up with a stopped clock."

"No, you haven't, because this other one was a while ago." Willi waited to make sure Heinrich was suitably chastened, then went on, "If our lovely luncheon companions don't care for the first edition, it's probably got something going for it, too."

"You never said anything like that before." Heinrich didn't try to hide his surprise.

"That's because I thought it was a load of garbage before," Willi answered. "But if those *Schweinehunde* think the same thing . . . then they're wrong, and that means I must be wrong, too."

Heinrich made as if to feel his forehead. "You must be feverish, is what you must be. Saying I'm right? Saying you're wrong? Delirium, if you ask me."

"Get away from me." Willi sidestepped to escape Heinrich, and almost bumped into a man wearing the light blue of a *Luftwaffe* official. They made mutual apologies. The *Luftwaffe* man kept going up the street, towards Admiral Yamamoto's. Willi looked back over his shoulder. "I *am* in a state. I can't help wondering if that fellow's on his way to plot with the thugs in black shirts."

That hadn't even occurred to Heinrich. "If you see plotters behind every potted plant, they're going to put you in a rubber room, you know."

"Not if the plotters are really there," Willi said. "Was Hitler wrong when he said everybody ganged up on Germany after the First World War? No, because everybody really did. You only get in trouble when you see things that aren't there."

"Right." Heinrich knew when arguing with Willi was more trouble than it was worth. This looked to be one of those times.

When they got back to *Oberkommando der Wehrmacht,* Ilse came up to them and said, "Excuse me, Willi, but you got another call from your wife." She rolled her eyes to show what she thought of that. The secretary was supposed to call Willi *Herr* Dorsch. That she didn't made Heinrich Gimpel want to roll his eyes. She did address Willi as *Sie* rather than using the intimate *du,* but she sounded as if she were using *du* even when she wasn't.

"What did Erika want?" Willi asked. "Do I want to know?"

Ilse pouted. Willi's eyes lit up. The Berlin rolls roiled in Heinrich's stomach. Ilse said, "She wouldn't leave a message—just told me to tell you to call her back. And she said she wondered why I was there when you weren't. That wasn't very nice."

Scowling, Willi said, "I'll call her. I don't know what I'll call her, but I'll call her." Ilse thought that was very funny. Heinrich retreated to his desk. He'd never seen financial statements look so alluring.

But, however much the numbers beckoned, he couldn't avoid hearing Willi's side of the conversation—if a shouting match could be dignified by the term. The longer it went on, the louder and angrier Willi got. At last, he slammed down the phone. "*Scheisse,*" he muttered.

Heinrich felt like saying the same thing. If Willi and Erika were fighting, she'd be looking for a shoulder to cry on, and the first shoulder she was likely to look for was his. His shoulder wouldn't be the only thing she was looking for, either. He stared up to the heavens—or at least to the sound-deadening tiles and fluorescent panels of the ceiling. What red-blooded man wouldn't want a beautiful blonde in hot pursuit of him? Heinrich didn't, and he had one. Most of the men who would have liked nothing better had to do without. If that wasn't unfair, he couldn't imagine what would be.

"*Guten Morgen,* Dr. Dambach," Esther Stutzman called as she walked into the pediatrician's office.

"*Guten Morgen, Frau* Stutzman." Dambach's voice floated out from the back. "How are you today?"

"I'm fine, thanks. How are you?" Esther answered. He didn't ask her to help him set the coffeemaker to rights, which had to mean he hadn't tried messing with it before she got there. She took a look. Sure enough, it wasn't even plugged in. She loaded it with water and ground coffee and put in a filter. "I'm making coffee, Dr. Dambach," she called. "Would you like some when it's ready?"

"*Ja, bitte,*" he said. "Somehow, you always get it just right."

"I'm glad you like it," she said, in lieu of calling him a thumb-fingered idiot. He wasn't an idiot, and she knew it. He was a very sharp man; she could wish he were less so. But, whenever he got near a coffeemaker, thumb-fingered he definitely was. Before long, she brought him a steaming foam cup. "Here you are, Doctor."

"*Danke schön.*" Dambach sipped. "Yes, that's very good. And you know just how much sugar I take, too."

"I should, by now." Esther lingered for a moment, wondering if he felt like making small talk. Sometimes he did; more often he didn't. When he picked up the coffee cup again, she slipped back to her station and looked at the morning's appointments. When she saw Paul Klein's name on the list, she grimaced. If only she'd thought to look in Eduard's chart. . . .

She tried not to think about that as she checked the computer to see whose bills were overdue. She printed out polite dunning letters for those whose first notice this was, sterner ones for people getting a second reminder, and letters threatening legal action for two dedicated deadbeats. She happened to know Dr. Dambach had never sued anybody, but with a little luck the people who hadn't paid him wouldn't.

She took the letters in to him for his signature. She could have made the squiggle that passed for that signature at least as well herself, but that wasn't how things were done. "Oh, the Schmidts," Dambach muttered when he came to one of the strongest letters. "I just heard they bought themselves a new Mercedes—and they paid cash."

"Oh, dear," Esther said. "Maybe you really ought to talk to your lawyer, then."

The pediatrician shook his head. "I don't want to have anything to do with the courts, not if I can help it. Whether you're right or you're wrong, you go into court a pig and you come out a sausage. I'd rather do without the fee. But seeing the Schmidts spend their money on everything but their bills does sometimes tempt me to prescribe ipecac for their brat."

Esther laughed; she knew he was even less likely to do something like that than he was to sue. Take his anger out on a child? Impossible. Unthinkable. But what if he found out a child he treated was a Jew? She had no doubt he would call the authorities, and never lose a moment's sleep afterwards worrying about what happened to it or to its family. He was conscientious, law-abiding—a good German.

She took the signed letters and made envelopes for them. The stamps she used were black-and-white mourning issues for Kurt Haldweim. As she put them on one by one, she wondered about the folk among whom she lived—something else she'd done many times before. Germans were the sort of people who would stay on the path and off the grass in a park even if someone was shooting a machine gun at them.

And yet . . . A lot of the Jews surviving in Berlin were there because Germans had helped their parents or grandparents get false papers during the war. Without the right papers, life in the *Reich* had been impossible even so long ago. They'd been easier to get then, when enemy bombs sent records up in smoke and replacements were issued without many awkward questions. More than a few friends and neighbors had vouched for Jews, and some of them, discovered, had paid for their kindness with years in prison or with life itself.

And some Jews in Nazi hands had kept themselves alive—for a while—by going out onto the streets of Berlin and capturing other Jews still free. Set them in the scales against the brave Germans and it taught you . . . what? Esther sighed. Only what anyone with a gram of sense already knew: that there were good Jews and bad Jews, in proportions not much different from those of any other folk.

The door to the outer office opened. Esther looked at the clock in surprise. Was it nine already? It really was. In came a squat, heavyset woman with jowls and protruding eyes. She looked like nothing so much as a bulldog. And her seven-year-old daughter, poor thing, might have been her in miniature.

"Good morning, *Frau* Bauriedl," Esther said. "And how is Wilhelmina today?"

"Well, that's what I want the doctor to see," *Frau* Bauriedl answered.

She brought Wilhelmina in every couple of weeks regardless of whether anything was really wrong with the little girl. Dr. Dambach tried to discourage her, but he hadn't had much luck. She did pay her bills on time; neither Esther nor any of the other receptionists had ever had to send her even the most polite letter.

The telephone rang. "Excuse me," Esther said, glad for an excuse not to have to talk to *Frau* Bauriedl. She picked up the handset. "Dr. Dambach's office."

"*Frau* Stutzman?" The woman on the other end of the line waited for Esther to agree that she was herself, then went on, "This is Maria Klein, *Frau* Stutzman. I'm . . . I'm afraid I'm going to have to cancel Paul's appointment this morning. You see, we are under investigation for something . . . something of which we are certainly not guilty. Good-bye." She hung up.

She hadn't let on that she knew Esther in any way except as the pediatrician's receptionist. There in the warm, bright, sterile calm of Dambach's office, Esther shivered as if caught in a Lapland blizzard. Was Maximilian Ebert or some other hard-faced Nazi in the uniform of the *Reichs* Genealogical Office or the Security Police standing next to Maria, listening to every word she said and how she said it? Or was she just afraid her line was tapped?

Under investigation. How long had it been since the Germans caught a Jew in Berlin? It must have been some time not long after Esther found out she was one. There had been a great hue and cry then. How much more strident would it be now, when the whole *Reich* was thought to be *Judenfrei* for years? And if the Kleins were found guilty of such a heinous crime, what else would the investigators be able to tear out of them?

When Esther got to her feet, her legs didn't want to hold her up. She held on to the top of the desk for a moment till she steadied. She made the trip back to Dr. Dambach's personal office more by main force of will than any other way. He looked up from a medical journal, a question on his face. "That telephone call was from *Frau* Klein," Esther said carefully. She had to watch every word, too, in case her turn came up next. "She won't be bringing Paul in this morning after all."

"No?" Dambach said. "Have she and her husband decided to take him to the *Reichs* Mercy Center, then? It's the only sensible thing to do, I'm afraid."

Was it? For someone old and in torment from, say, cancer, it might be. For a baby? But, on the other hand, for a baby doomed to a lingering, horrible, certain death? Esther just didn't know. That was beside the point now, though. Shaking her head, she answered, "No, because she and her husband are—under investigation, she said."

"Are they?" Dr. Dambach didn't need to ask why they were being investigated. He was the one to whom the possibility had first occurred. "Well, I'm sure the authorities will get to the bottom of it. If they do turn out to be Jews, who could have imagined such a thing in Berlin in the twenty-first century?"

"Yes, who?" Esther hoped she matched his tone. Feeling spiteful, she added, "And *Frau* Bauriedl is here with Wilhelmina."

"Is she?" The pediatrician scowled. "It's a shame the powers that be aren't investigating her. The Kleins have always seemed like nice people. But appearances can be deceiving. If they're Jews . . ." He shook his head. "We certainly can't let that sort of thing go on, can we?"

Before Esther had to come up with a response to that, the telephone rang again. "Excuse me, Doctor," she said, and hurried out to answer it. A worried mother had a three-year-old who was throwing up. Esther fit her into the slot the Kleins had vacated. Even that made her want to cry.

The worst of it was, she didn't dare call people to warn them. If the Kleins were under suspicion, she and Walther might be, too. Her warnings could turn into betrayals. She wouldn't risk that. Even if she called to say she would be dropping by to pass on some news—even that might be too much. She had to assume she was being watched, being listened to. Maybe she wasn't. She hoped—she prayed—she wasn't. But she couldn't take the chance. She had to act as if she were.

And what's the use of praying to a God Who has made us fair game all over the world for a lifetime? That question and others of the same sort floated to the surface like rotting corpses whenever times turned black. Only one answer had ever occurred to Esther. She fell back on it now. *If I don't believe, if I turn my back and walk away, then aren't I saying the Nazis were right all along, and we shouldn't go on?*

Usually, that was enough to keep her on her course. She could be very stubborn. A Jew who wasn't stubborn these days didn't stay a Jew. When times got uncommonly black, though, she couldn't help wondering, *Did I stay on course for so long—for* this?

If God couldn't forgive her for wondering . . . *Too bad for Him,* she thought.

"Come right in, *Frau* Bauriedl, Wilhelmina," she said. "I'm sure Dr. Dambach will be so glad to see you again." If Dambach couldn't forgive her for lying . . . *Too bad for him.*

A woman brought in a wailing toddler who was tugging at his ear. She looked harried. "I hope the doctor can see me soon," she said. "Rudolf started this at ten last night, and he's been going ever since. My husband and I haven't had much sleep."

"There's only one patient in front of you, *Frau* Stransky," Esther said. "I'm sure it won't be too long. Would you like some coffee while you're waiting?"

"Oh, please!" *Frau* Stransky said, as if Esther had offered her the Holy Grail. Esther gave her a cup. By the way she gulped it down, she wished she had an intravenous caffeine drip hooked up instead. Esther had had mornings like that, too, even if her children hadn't had to go through many earaches.

More women came in with children in tow. In the examination room, *Frau* Bauriedl droned on and on about Wilhelmina's imaginary afflictions. The only thing really wrong with Wilhelmina was that she looked like her mother.

At last, after too long, Dr. Dambach must have got a little more abrupt than he was in the habit of doing. *Frau* Bauriedl's tones grew shriller and more indignant. "The nerve!" she said as she swept her daughter past Esther. "I think we'll see someone else the next time." She'd made that threat before. Esther wished she would do it, but she hadn't yet.

Whenever the door to the waiting room opened, Esther had to fight against a flinch. Would it be someone in the somber uniform of the Security Police? Whenever the phone rang, her hand wanted to shake as she reached for it. Would someone be warning her of a new disaster?

If the Security Police had operatives in Dr. Dambach's office, they were disguised as worried mothers—one of the most effective disguises Esther could imagine, and also one of the most unnecessary. All the phone calls featured more worried mothers except one. That one had a worried father: a cartoonist who worked out of his house. "*Ja, Herr* Wasserstein, you can bring Luther in at half past two this afternoon," Esther told him.

As soon as Irma came in during the lunch hour, Esther left. She had one more anxious moment walking out of the building. Would they bundle her into a car and take her away to God only knew where? They didn't. She walked to the bus stop. No one bothered her at all.

But the fear didn't go away. It never would.

Susanna Weiss had lived in fear ever since she was ten years old. Fear made her angry. It always had. She'd been living with rage since she was ten, too. Most of the time, she lived with it by making everyone around her live with it. That had made her more respected—and certainly more feared—than any of the other handful of female professors in the Department of Germanic Languages. "Don't mess with her—it's more trouble than it's worth" was the watchword these days at Friedrich Wilhelm University, not just in the department but also in the administration.

Some things, though, were too big and too strong to fight.

Jews didn't—couldn't—fight the apparatus of the Nazi Party. That was as much an article of faith these days as *Hear, O Israel, the Lord our God, the Lord is one.* The *Reich* bestrode the world like a colossus. *And we petty Jews walk under its huge legs, and peep about to escape our dishonorable graves.*

Susanna knew that was a misquotation, no matter how true it was. Shakespeare, these days, was more vitally alive in Germany than in his native land. A series of splendid nineteenth-century translations left his words much closer to modern German than his original language was to modern English, which made him easier for people here to follow.

If the *Reichs* Genealogical Office was going to start asking questions of the Kleins . . . Her heart turned to a lump of ice within her. She couldn't help it, any more than a bird was supposed to be able to keep from letting a snake mesmerize it.

"Do you want to talk here?" she asked Esther Stutzman. "Or would you rather go over to the Tiergarten? It's only a couple of blocks."

Her apartment was small and cramped and full of books, and even closer to the university than to the park. It ate up an inordinately large chunk of her salary, but she couldn't think of anything on which she would rather have spent her money.

Esther set a teacup down on a table crowded with ill-informed essays on *The Canterbury Tales.* "Well, that depends," she said carefully, and waited.

It depends on whether you think someone has planted a microphone here. That was what she meant, all right. Susanna looked around the place. She had books in German and English and Dutch and all the Scandinavian languages (including Old Icelandic). Paintings and prints filled the wall space bookshelves didn't. An alarmingly authentic reproduction of the helmet from the Sutton Hoo ship stared from an end table. She was not the neatest of housekeepers. If the Security Police had sneaked in to bug the place, she would never know it till too late.

"Why don't we walk?" she said. "The park is very nice in the afternoon."

"Then let's go." Esther got to her feet.

And the Tiergarten *was* very nice in the afternoon, too. The sun was bright and warm. Sparrows hopped here and there, trying to steal bread crumbs from the pigeons that pensioners fed. *Germans are a strange folk,* Susanna thought. *They're very kind to animals. They save their savagery for people, where it really counts.*

"All right," she said. "Tell me how this happened."

Esther did, flaying herself in the process. To make matters worse, she had to flay herself in a bright, cheerful voice so people walking or cycling past wouldn't wonder what the two women were talking about so intently. "If only I'd found Eduard Klein's old genealogy chart, none of this would have happened," she said, a wide, false smile on her face. "But I didn't think to look, and so the Kleins . . . have a problem." She could say that safely enough. Anyone might have a problem.

The problems goyim *have aren't so likely to be fatal.* Susanna bit her lip. The Kleins would have had a fatal problem even if Esther had purloined the chart. Susanna had never heard of Tay-Sachs disease till a few weeks before, but that kind of problem didn't care whether you'd heard of it. It came right in, introduced itself, and settled down to stay.

"Too late to fret about it now," she told Esther. "It's done. We'll go on."

"Easy for you to say," Esther replied. "You didn't do it. You don't wake up in the middle of the night wishing you had it to do over again."

Susanna shrugged. "If it goes wrong, it goes wrong for me, too. If they squeeze the Kleins tight enough to get them to name you and Walther, do you think they won't name me?"

They walked past a fountain. Esther said, "I want to jump in and drown myself."

"Don't be foolish. If you're foolish, you're liable to give yourself away." Susanna paused to think. Fighting her way up through the male-dominated hierarchies at Friedrich Wilhelm University had taught her one thing: the system was there to be manipulated, if only you could find the lever. She thought she saw one here. "You say Maria told you they were being investigated?"

"That's right." Esther nodded miserably.

"And she was at home?" Susanna persisted.

"Yes." Esther nodded again.

"Then they aren't sure. They can't be sure," Susanna said. "If they were sure, they'd haul her and her husband—and Eduard, too, damn them—off to the Genealogical Office or to the closest police headquarters and go to work on them. Thank God Eduard's too little to know what he is."

Esther remained distraught. "Who says they won't?"

"Nobody says they won't. But if they were *really* suspicious, they would have done it already," Susanna said. "That means they're trying to panic people into doing something foolish so they get more to work with."

"They're doing a pretty good job, too," Esther exclaimed.

But Susanna shook her head. As it did with her, fear began to give way to anger. "Not yet. Not if the Kleins can sit tight and keep saying, 'We have no idea how any of this happened.' They ought to find a lawyer, too, a big, noisy one."

"As if a lawyer will do them any good!" Esther said. "What lawyer in his right mind would want anything to do with somebody who might have Jewish blood? The first case he lost, he'd go to the camp along with his clients."

"You'd think so, wouldn't you? But you'd be wrong. There are lawyers who deal with *Mischlingsrechts*," Susanna said. "One of the games they play in the Party is accusing somebody they don't like of having Jewish blood. Most of the time, it's a big, fat lie, which is why the attorneys who specialize in mixed-blood law *don't* go to camps. It happened at the university a few years ago, too, which is how I happen to know about it." She made a face, as if she'd smelled something foul. "You wouldn't believe how nasty academic politics can get."

"After all the horror stories you've told, maybe I would," Esther said. Susanna had her doubts. Her friend was simply too nice to imagine the depths to which people could sink. And if that wasn't an aid to survival in the Greater German *Reich*, Susanna didn't know what would be.

She said, "They ought to threaten to sue, too."

Behind her glasses, Esther's eyes got big. "Sue the government? They'd get shot for even thinking about it!"

Susanna shook her head again. "No, they'd just lose or have their suit quashed before it ever came to trial. But if they talk big, if they hit back hard, people will think they must be innocent, because nobody who's guilty acts like that."

There was, or had been, a saying in English. *The Hun is either at your throat or at your feet*—that was how it went. It held some truth, too. Germans who thought they had the whip hand acted like it. And those who didn't, groveled.

Esther was a quiet and quietly orderly person herself. Susanna wasn't, and never had been. She hit back whenever she could, sometimes in small ways, sometimes not. Up till now, she'd never had the chance to hit back at the *Reich* itself. She'd imagined it—what Jew didn't? But dreams of vengeance remained only dreams. She wasn't crazy. She knew they'd never be anything else. Still, even the prospect of tying the system up in knots looked good to her.

"Do you really think I ought to tell this to the Kleins?" Esther asked doubtfully. "Won't it just land them in worse trouble?"

Susanna looked around. Nobody was particularly close to the two of them. No one was paying them any special heed, either. She could speak freely, or as freely as anyone could ever speak in the Greater German *Reich*. "They're under suspicion of being Jews," she said. "How can they get in worse trouble than that?"

To her surprise, Esther actually thought it over. "Maybe if they were homosexual Gypsies . . . But then they wouldn't have a baby, would they?"

"No." Susanna fought laughter, though it was only blackly funny. The *Reich* had been at least as thorough about getting rid of Gypsies as it had with Jews. She didn't know whether any survived. If so, they too were in hiding. As for homosexuals, the few high up in the Party hierarchy and those who traveled in certain circles of the SS did as they pleased. Others still faced savage persecution. Unlike Jews and Gypsies, they couldn't be rooted out all at once, for they kept springing up like new weeds every year. If nothing else, they gave the authorities something to do.

"We've come all the way to the zoo," Esther said in amazement. "Shall we go in and look at the animals?"

"No!" Susanna startled even herself with the force of her reaction. She had to stop and think to figure out why she felt the way she did. "I don't want to look at lions and elephants and ostriches in cages, not when I'm in a cage myself."

"Oh." Esther thought that over, too. After a little while, she said, "But people like the animals. Berliners have always liked animals." As if to prove her point, a man perhaps old enough to have served in the Second World

War sat on a park bench scattering torn-up bits of bread for birds and squirrels.

"You're right, but I don't care." Susanna stuck out her chin and looked stubborn. That was the expression *Herr Doktor* Professor Oppenhoff had come to dread. "They're still trapped in there, and I don't want anything to do with them."

Esther didn't argue. She'd known Susanna long enough to know how impractical arguing with her could be. She just shrugged and said, "In that case, let's head back to your apartment."

"All right." Susanna was glad enough to turn around. She sighed. "I never thought I'd wish I were living in England."

"Why would you?" Esther asked. "Over there, they have their own people watching them, and they have us, too."

"But they have a party that's serious about turning over a new leaf," Susanna answered. "We don't. Oh, people say the new *Führer* will be something different, but I'll believe it when I see it."

"I hope it's true," Esther said. "Maybe it'll mean easier times for . . . everybody." She chose the innocuous word because a man in a brown Party uniform came past them. He looked intent on his own business, but Susanna would have used an innocuous word anyplace where he could hear, too.

"Easier times," Susanna said wistfully. "I'll believe that when I see it, too, especially with what's going on now." She wished she hadn't said that as soon as she did; Esther looked on the point of tears. Susanna often talked first and worried about consequences later. When she was younger, she'd thought she would outgrow it. But it seemed to be a part of her. Sometimes that landed her in trouble. Sometimes it proved very valuable. Every so often, it managed both at once. She knew she had to repair the damage here, and did her best: "One way or another, everything will turn out all right."

"I hope so," Esther said, "but I'm sure I don't see how."

"As long as we act the way any other citizens of the *Reich* would if their rights were being violated, I think we'll do all right," Susanna said.

"If we were any other citizens of the *Reich,* our rights wouldn't be violated," Esther said. "Not like this, anyhow."

"Not like this, no," Susanna admitted. "But they still would be. That's what the *Reich* is all about: the government can do whatever it wants, and everybody else has to hold still for it. But people don't. Germans don't, anyway. If it bumps up against them, they bump back."

"Or they get bumped off," Esther said.

Susanna wished she hadn't put it like that, not because she was wrong but because she was right. *Or they get bumped off.* That had always been the *Reich*'s answer for everything—and, judging by the past seventy years, a very effective answer it was, too.

VI

HEINRICH GIMPEL KISSED LISE, GRABBED HIS ATTACHÉ CASE, AND HEADED OUT the door. It was a fine, bright summer morning, the sun already high in the sky. The orbiting weather platforms predicted that this heat wave would last for the rest of the week. A heat wave in Berlin would have been nothing in Algiers, or even in Rome, but it was better than the week of rain and mist that could come even in the middle of July.

Volkswagens and the occasional Mercedes zoomed past Heinrich as he stood at the corner and waited for the commuter bus. He'd never seen much point to owning a motorcar. To him, they were just swank, and more expensive than they were worth. With the buses and trains, you could get anywhere you needed to go.

As if to prove as much, the commuter bus pulled up a minute later. He got on, fed his account card into the slot, reclaimed it, and found a seat. A few stops later, Willi Dorsch got on, too. He plopped himself down beside Heinrich with a grunted, "*Guten Morgen.*"

"*Guten Morgen,*" Heinrich said. "*Wie geht's?*"

"Well, I'll tell you, it could be better," Willi answered. "How's it going with you?"

"I'm doing all right." Heinrich couldn't tell Willi how worried he was about the Kleins. That would have required too much in the way of explanation. But he could sound sympathetic when he asked, "What now?"

Unlike him, Willi wasn't inclined to suffer in silence. When Willi felt wronged, the whole world heard about it. And so, all the way to the train station, Heinrich got a blow-by-blow account of his friend's latest tiff with his wife: who'd said what, who'd thrown what, and how Willi had had to sleep on the sofa in the front room. "Why is it," Willi asked, "that when you have a row with your woman, you're always the one who sleeps on the couch? She stays in bed and she stays comfortable. My back is killing me."

"I don't know. I never really thought about it," Heinrich said. Except when Lise was in the hospital after giving birth to one of their girls, the two of them had never slept apart.

"I never thought about it, either, not till this morning," Willi said. "Erika acts like it's a law of nature—*she* isn't happy, so *I* have to go somewhere else. You call that fair? Do you?"

The bus came up to Stahnsdorf's train station just then. Heinrich didn't need to answer, which was probably just as well. As far as he could remember, he'd never heard of a woman sleeping on the sofa while a man stayed in bed. It didn't seem fair. It wasn't anything he'd ever had to worry about himself, but it didn't.

In the station, he put fifteen pfennigs into a vending machine and pulled out a copy of the *Völkischer Beobachter*. Even in buying a newspaper, he fed the Party's coffers. Were he the good German he pretended to be, he supposed that would have made him feel proud, or at least patriotic. As things were, it left him mildly—perhaps a little more than mildly—irked. He couldn't even find out what was going on in the world without helping to finance his own destruction.

Willi put coins in the machine and got a paper, too. Along with the other people who'd ridden the bus to the station, they went to the platform to wait for the train to downtown Berlin. Heinrich glanced at his watch. They wouldn't have to wait long.

When the train pulled up a very few minutes later, the commuters fed their account cards into the slot one after another. Willi was in front of Heinrich in the queue. He sat down by a window, and thumped the seat next to him to show Heinrich was welcome. They both started reading the papers.

"Buckliger's going to talk to a bunch of big shots in Nuremberg tomorrow," Heinrich remarked. "I wonder what he'll have to say."

"Whatever the *Bonzen* want to hear," Willi predicted. "What other point is there in going to Nuremberg?" He spoke with a Berliner's cynicism and a Berliner's certainty that no other place in the *Reich* really mattered.

"Maybe," Heinrich said. "But maybe not, too. He didn't say what everybody expected him to the last time, you know."

He waited to see what Willi would make of that. Willi started to tell him he didn't know what he was talking about—started to and then, very visibly, stopped. "That's true," his friend said. "He didn't. But why would you go to Nuremberg to say anything that's out of the ordinary? Out of the ordinary isn't what Nuremberg is for."

"Who knows?" Heinrich shrugged. "If we're confused after he makes his speech, Horst will tell us what to think about it."

"Well, of course he will," Willi Dorsch said, with no irony Heinrich could hear. "Telling us what to think is what Horst Witzleben is for."

"He's good at it, too," Heinrich said.

"Not much point to having a Propaganda Ministry where the people aren't good at what they do, is there?" Willi said.

"Oh, I don't know. Look at the Croats," Heinrich said. The Croatian *Ustasha* did their jobs with an enthusiasm even the *Gestapo* found frightening. The German secret police were—mostly—professionals. The Croats were zealots, and proud of being zealots.

But Willi shook his head. "They want to show how frightful they are, and so they do. The national sport down there is hunting Serbs. And if the Serbs had been on the winning side, their national sport would have been hunting Croats. And do you know what else? They would have bragged about it, too. Tell me I'm wrong."

He waited. Heinrich thought it over. "I can't," he said, "not when you're right."

To his surprise, Willi looked angry. "You'd be more fun to argue with if you didn't admit you were wrong when you're wrong," he complained with mock severity.

"No, I wouldn't," Heinrich answered.

"Yes, you—" Willi broke off and sent him a reproachful stare. "Oh, no, you don't. You're a devil, is what you are."

"*Danke schön*. I do appreciate that."

"You would," Willi said. They both laughed. The train pulled into the

Berlin station. Everything seemed the way it had in happier, less nervous times. Then Willi asked, "When are we going to play some more bridge? It's been too long."

Air-raid sirens started howling inside Heinrich's head. He couldn't show them, though, any more than he could show so much of what he felt. He couldn't even show this particular alarm in front of Lise. He'd dug that trap for himself, and now he'd fallen into it. Knowing he had, he said, "Why don't you and Erika come over Friday of next week after work?"

"Sounds good," Willi said.

Did it? Heinrich was anything but sure. He did think—he certainly hoped—Erika was less likely to say or do anything drastic at his house than at hers. If he turned out to be wrong . . . *If I turn out to be wrong, Lise will clout me one, and I'll deserve it.* Still, next to some of the other things that could happen, even a clout from his wife didn't seem too bad.

Then he had no more time for such worries. He stuffed the *Völkischer Beobachter* into his briefcase and performed the elaborate dance that took him from the downstairs train platform to the upstairs bus queue. As with any dance, if you had to think about what you were doing, you didn't do it so well. Willi matched his movements as smoothly as one ballerina in an ensemble conforming to another.

Their reward for such a performance was not an ovation but standing room on the bus that would take them to *Oberkommando der Wehrmacht* headquarters. Someone on the bus hadn't seen soap anywhere near recently enough. Heinrich took in small, shallow sips of air, which might have helped a little. Then Willi muttered, "Who brought along his polecat?" You couldn't take small, shallow sips of air when you were laughing like a loon.

Once they got to the office, Heinrich phoned home and let Lise know about the invitation: he was a well-trained husband. "That sounds like fun," she said, which proved she didn't know everything that was going on. Heinrich couldn't tell her, either, and not just because Willi's desk was only a couple of meters away.

Willi, for that matter, might not have heard a word he said. Willi was busy flirting with Ilse. By the way she laughed and teased him back, his plot was thickening nicely. "Shall we go out to lunch?" he asked her.

"Why not?" she said.

Heinrich could have thought of any number of reasons why not, but nobody'd asked him. He went to lunch at the canteen, by himself. The meatloaf was grayish, with slices of what he hoped was hard-cooked egg scattered through it. He made the mistake of wondering what sort of meat had gone into the loaf. Then he wondered why he was eating it if he couldn't tell.

A couple of tables over, an officer looked at lunch and said, "They don't waste anything at those camps, do they?" After that, Heinrich finished the boiled beans that came on the side, but he didn't touch the meatloaf again. He was sure the officer had to be joking. He was sure, but still. . . .

Willi and Ilse were a long time coming back from lunch. Heinrich wondered what they were eating. Then, hastily, he wondered where they were eating. That seemed safer.

He eyed them when at last they did come back. Willi didn't look particularly smug. Ilse didn't look rumpled. That proved nothing, one way or the other. Heinrich knew as much. He eyed them anyhow. Curiosity—nosiness, to be less polite about it—wouldn't leave him alone.

Would Willi brag on the way back to Stahnsdorf? The answer turned out to be no; if there was anything to brag about, Willi concealed it. Instead, he went on and on about the havoc he intended to wreak at the bridge table. "In your dreams," Heinrich said sweetly.

"Sometimes dreams are better than the way things really work out," Willi said. "Sometimes." And that, oracular in its ambiguity, was as close as he came to saying anything about whatever he had or hadn't done with Ilse—or perhaps about the way things had gone for him and Erika. Heinrich thought about asking him to explain, thought about it and then lost his nerve.

The next day's *Völkischer Beobachter* said not a word about the new *Führer*'s speech in Nuremberg. Neither did the paper from the day after that. Had Buckliger made it? If he had, what had he said? The *Beobachter*, the chief Party newspaper, wasn't talking. Nor was anyone else: no one Heinrich knew, anyhow. He scratched his head, wondering what the devil that meant.

Alicia Gimpel had been helping her younger sisters with their homework ever since Francesca started going to school. Why not? She was bright, she remembered her lessons, and she'd had them only a couple of years before. Sometimes she got impatient when the younger girls didn't catch on right away. That had made Francesca angry more than once. Now Francesca helped Roxane, too—and sometimes got impatient when she didn't catch on right away. For reasons Alicia couldn't quite follow, her father and mother thought that was funny, though they'd yelled at her when she showed impatience.

She was slogging her way through reducing a page of fractions to lowest terms when Francesca came into her bedroom and said, "I'm stuck."

"With what?" Alicia was sick of fractions, and the one she was about to tackle—39/91—didn't look as if it would ever turn into anything reasonable. Whatever Francesca was working on had to be more interesting than arithmetic.

"I'm supposed to write a poem about Jews, and I can't think of anything that rhymes," Francesca said anxiously.

"How long does it have to be?" Alicia asked—the automatic first question when confronting schoolwork.

"Eight lines!" By the way Francesca said it, her teacher was expecting her to turn in both parts of *Faust* tomorrow morning.

"What have you done so far?" Alicia asked. Sometimes her sister got brain cramps and wanted her to do all the work instead of just helping. She didn't like that.

But Francesca had a beginning. "Jews are nasty. Jews are bad./They hurt Aryans and make them sad," she recited in the singsong way children have with rhymes.

"That's a start, all right," Alicia said encouragingly. "Only six lines to go."

"But I can't think of anything else!" Francesca wailed. "Besides, once I've said that, what else do I need to say?"

What would happen if I told you you were writing a poem about yourself? Alicia wondered. Trouble was, she had a pretty good notion of the answer. *You'd have hysterics, that's what.* She'd learned the word not long before, and fallen in love with it. It sounded much grander than pitching a fit.

She took a deep breath, willing herself to forget what she'd found out earlier in the year. If she imagined she still was the way she had been then, helping with assignments like this one came easier. She said, "Maybe you can say the same thing over again in a different way."

"Like how?" Francesca asked, interested but doubtful.

Alicia flogged her muse and came up with a line: "Jews were Germany's bad luck." She eyed her sister. "Now you find something that rhymes."

Francesca screwed up her face as she thought. Her sudden smile was like the sun coming out from behind a cloud. "That's why we made them a dead duck!" she exclaimed.

It wasn't very good poetry; it rhymed, but the rhythm was off. Alicia started to say so, but then, for a wonder, held her tongue. For somebody in Francesca's grade, it would do. And criticizing it would only get Alicia more deeply involved in shaping the poem, which was the last thing she wanted. Pretending she wasn't something she was came hard enough around strangers. It was harder still with her sisters.

Francesca, inevitably, wanted more help. "Give me another line," she said.

"No," Alicia said. "Come on. You can do it yourself."

Her sister hauled out the heavy artillery: "I'll tell Mommy."

It didn't work. "Go ahead," Alicia answered. "You're supposed to do your own homework, and you know it."

"You're mean!" Francesca said.

"I've got my work to do, too," Alicia said. Compared to writing rude verses about Jews, even reducing 39/91 to lowest terms didn't look so bad.

"You're so mean! You lie and cheat!" When Francesca got angry, she didn't care what she said. She just wanted to wound.

But she didn't, not here. "That's good," Alicia said. Her sister gaped at her. "That's good," she repeated. "That will do for another line, if you change 'you' into 'they.' "

"Oh." Francesca thought about it. The sun came out from behind the clouds once more. "You're right. It will." She thought a little more. "They are so mean. They lie and cheat./And take away the food we eat." She looked toward Alicia, who was suddenly a respected literary analyst again, for her reaction.

And Alicia nodded. She didn't think it was wonderful poetry, but she also didn't think Francesca's teacher was expecting wonderful poetry. The lesson was more about hating Jews than about writing poetry, wonderful or not. Alicia stared suspiciously at 39/91. To encourage Francesca—and to encourage her to go away—she said, "See? Just two lines left."

"Uh-huh." Francesca didn't go away, but she didn't nag Alicia any more, either. Now that she'd come up with more than two lines mostly on her own, she could make others. "We're glad they aren't here any longer./Without them, the *Reich* grows ever stronger." She beamed. "I'm done!"

"Write them all down before you forget them," Alicia advised.

Francesca hurried off to do just that. A couple of minutes later, she cried out in despair: "I forgot!"

Alicia remembered the deathless verses. She recited them for her sister—slowly, so Francesca could get them down on paper. Francesca even said thank you, which would do for a miracle till a bigger one came along.

Back to arithmetic. 39/91? Now, 3 went into 39 evenly, but did it go into 91? No—she could see that at a glance. *They're trying to trick me,* she thought. *This is going to be one of those stupid fractions that* doesn't *reduce, that's already in lowest terms.* Then, remembering that 3 × 13 made 39, she idly tried dividing 13 into 91. To her surprise, she discovered she could. 3/7, she wrote on the answer sheet.

Francesca sounded like a stampeding elephant going downstairs (Roxane, who was smaller, somehow contrived to sound like an earthquake). "Listen, Mommy!" she said from down below.

"Listen to what?" the Gimpel girls' mother asked. "I'm fixing supper."

"Listen to this poem I wrote," Francesca said proudly. She didn't mention anything about help from her big sister. In most circumstances, that would have infuriated Alicia, more because of its inaccuracy than for any other reason. Here, she didn't much mind.

Her mother's voice floated up the stairs: "All right. Go ahead."

And Francesca did. Either she'd already memorized it or she had her paper along with her. "What do you think?" she asked when she was done.

If Francesca had written the poem all by herself and then read it to her, Alicia knew she would have been speechless, at least for a moment. Her mother didn't hesitate, even for a heartbeat. "That's very good, dear," she said, and sounded as if she meant it. "Are you playing a game with Alicia and Roxane, or is it for school?"

"For school," Francesca answered.

"Well, I'm sure you'll get a good grade. Now go on back upstairs and let me finish dealing with the tongue here. I want to be sure your father doesn't have to wait too long to eat before he gets home from work."

Francesca thundered up the stairs again. To Alicia's relief, she didn't stop to talk any more, but went straight into her room. That left Alicia alone to wonder about something more complicated than fractions.

She knew she was smarter than most grownups. They sometimes knew more things than she did, but that was only because they'd been around longer, which often struck her as most unfair. Up till now, she'd never had any trouble learning whatever she set out to learn.

But what her mother had just done was beyond her, and she knew it. How had Mommy managed to sound so natural with no warning at all? Alicia knew Jews had to if they wanted to survive. She'd already slipped more times than she could count, though. She hadn't got caught yet, but she knew she'd slipped. As far as she could tell, her mother and father never slipped, not like that.

She sighed. Up till now, she'd been sure adults ruled the roost for no better reason than that they were bigger than children and could shout louder. That had always struck her as most unfair. But now, after listening to her mother perform, she thought she might be willing to admit that maybe, just maybe, there was something to this business of growing up after all.

No word in the *Völkischer Beobachter*. Day followed day, and the Party newspaper said not a thing about Heinz Buckliger's speech to the *Bonzen* in Nuremberg. The longer the silence lasted, the more puzzling it got for Heinrich Gimpel. No matter how much curiosity gnawed at him, though, he couldn't do anything about satisfying it.

He couldn't even show he was curious, not after the first day or two. That curtain of silence had to have fallen for a reason, even if he had no idea what the reason was. Asking too many questions under circumstances like that was dangerous.

Willi Dorsch plainly felt the same way. He kept his head down and his mouth shut. If his ears were open—well, then they were, that was all. Open ears were safe enough, because they didn't show.

But Heinrich was the one who caught the first break. The Friday Willi and Erika were going to come over for bridge in the evening, Willi took Ilse out to lunch again. Heinrich was curious about that, too, and couldn't show he was curious, either. He went to the canteen, ordered the day's special—a chicken stew with heavy gravy and too many onions—and sat down at a small corner table to eat.

He'd got there early; the place wasn't very full. Over the next half hour, more officers and analysts, technicians and clerks, sweepers and secretaries came in, sometimes by themselves, sometimes in pairs, most often in groups. The loners and pairs took the tables at the edges, while the groups mostly used the bigger tables in the middle of the room. Things got loud in a hurry.

Heinrich did his best to listen without seeming to, even if separating signal from noise wasn't easy. When he heard the word "Nuremberg" from the table behind him, he wished he could prick up his ears. As things were, he could only sit there, slowly eat the unappetizing stew, and try to hear what the two officers—he thought two officers had walked past him and sat down at that table, although he wasn't a hundred percent sure—who were also eating lunch were saying.

"He stuck his foot in it, if you ask me," one of the men declared.

The other fellow grunted. "The cook stuck his foot in this stew, if you ask me. Troops in the field would mutiny if it came in a ration tin. For people at headquarters, though, it's plenty good enough."

"Dammit, I'm serious," the first man said.

"So am I," his friend replied. "And if I have to finish this, I'll be critical." He made a gagging noise. Heinrich almost stopped paying attention. Everybody groused about the food at the canteen, which didn't stop people from coming.

But then the first officer said, "He had no business saying things like that to the bigwigs—none, I tell you."

"No?" the second officer said. "For one thing, we don't know just *what* he said, because nobody's talking on the record."

"Oh, we know, all right," the first man said. "And it's because he said that kind of rubbish that nobody *is* talking."

A longish pause followed, as if the second officer was deciding how to respond to that, and whether to respond at all. At last, he said, "I don't know. If what we hear is what really happened, some of what he said at Nuremberg has needed saying for a long time. What did he say that wasn't true? Answer me that, if you please."

"Who cares whether it was true?" the first man retorted. "It was—undignified, that's what it was."

Who cares whether it was true? If that didn't sum up the way things had gone all through the history of the *Reich,* Heinrich couldn't imagine what would. He was in a better position to know than the vast majority of his countrymen. Another pause at the table in back of him. Then, slowly, the second officer said, "Doing things like going in the red when we're the strongest country in the world—*that's* undignified, if you ask me. Telling the truth about lies we told and mistakes we made a long time ago . . . What's undignified about that? How do we get better if we don't even know where we were?"

"What has raking up all that old stuff got to do with whether the budget's balanced or not?" the first officer said.

"If my watch has run two hours slow for weeks, I won't get the right time when I look at it, will I?" the other man said.

"If your watch has run slow for weeks, you're a *Dummkopf,*" the first officer said. "You go out and buy a new battery—or else a new watch."

"That's what the truth is—a new battery. And we've needed one for a lot longer than weeks. It's just that nobody had the nerve to say so."

The first officer came back with something in broad Bavarian dialect. It sounded pungent, but Heinrich couldn't quite make out what it meant—to him, broad Bavarian was hardly German. And he couldn't sit there much longer without making people realize he was eavesdropping. He got to his feet, dumped the foam plate and plastic utensils in the trash, and headed back to his desk. What *had* Heinz Buckliger said down in Nuremberg? Whatever it was, he had a notion why the *Beobachter* hadn't printed it.

He wondered whether Willi had heard anything interesting at lunch. If rumors about whatever had happened in Nuremberg were starting to circulate here at *Oberkommando der Wehrmacht* headquarters, they were bound to be bubbling with SS men and Party officials, too. And people liked to blab.

But when Willi and Ilse got back, it was obvious they hadn't been paying attention to anything but each other. He didn't have lipstick on his collar, but his hair went every which way and his tie was yanked askew. Ilse's blouse was buttoned wrong. When she realized that and fixed it, she got a fit of the giggles.

Well, well—or maybe not so well, Heinrich thought. *Bridge tonight is liable to be even more interesting than it has been lately.*

* * *

Susanna Weiss got her first hint of something out of the ordinary that same afternoon, when the telephone in her office rang. She muttered an unpleasantry. She had neither classes nor students on Friday afternoons. If she couldn't do her research and writing then, when would she ever get the chance? Never, maybe. She picked up the phone. "*Bitte?*"

"*Guten Tag,* Susanna. This is Rosa, *Herr Doktor* Professor Oppenhoff's secretary. The *Herr Doktor* Professor would like to see you in his office immediately."

"Would he?" Susanna muttered. Rosa was a withered old crone; Susanna often thought of her as Grendel's mother, straight out of *Beowulf.* She was also studiedly rude to Susanna. She would never have presumed to call a male professor in the Department of Germanic Literature by his first name: he would have been *Herr Doktor* Professor So-and-So. Susanna, Rosa implied, was no better than hired help herself. But Rosa was Professor Oppenhoff's right hand and two or three fingers of his left. With a sigh, Susanna made herself say, "I'm coming."

Despite that *immediately,* when Susanna got to the department chairman's office, she had to cool her heels for almost fifteen minutes before Rosa ushered her into the exalted presence: another way of putting her in her place. It didn't work. She'd expected nothing else. She'd brought an article with her, and took notes while she waited. Rosa couldn't even complain about that.

At last, Rosa said, "Professor Oppenhoff will see you now."

How did she know? She hadn't gone in to ask. "Thank you so much—dear," Susanna said, and scribbled a last deliberate note before entering the chairman's malodorous sanctum.

Franz Oppenhoff wasn't actually smoking a cigar when she came in, but sour smoke and the stubbed-out corpses of several in the ashtray served as all-too-vivid reminders of his habit. Unlike his secretary, he was scrupulously polite, saying, "And how are you today, *Fräulein Doktor* Professor?"

"Well enough, thank you," Susanna answered. "What can I do for you today, sir?"

"Professor Lutze has had several . . . interesting things to say about the recent meeting of the Medieval English Association in London," Oppenhoff said.

"Oh, yes—the meeting you were reluctant to let me attend." Susanna didn't believe in letting anyone off the hook.

Professor Oppenhoff coughed and scratched at the bottom edge of his left muttonchop. The gesture and the flamboyant whiskers made Susanna think of Emperor Franz Joseph and the dying days of Austria-Hungary. "Hmm . . . ah . . . hmm," Oppenhoff said. He needed to pause and gather himself before he could come out with actual words: "Be that as it may, were you not intimate with the British Union of Fascists during your stay in England?"

"Intimate? I should hope not!"

The department chairman went red. "With their deliberations, I should say."

"Oh, with their deliberations?" Susanna sounded as if that were occurring to her for the first time. Franz Oppenhoff turned redder. She grudged him a nod. "Yes, I suppose so."

"And they had something to do with . . . with matters pertaining to the first edition of *Mein Kampf*?" Professor Oppenhoff chose his words with uncommon care, which only made him more opaque than ever.

Susanna nodded again. "That's right, they did. Excuse me, *Herr Doktor* Professor, but what does this have to do with the Department of Germanic Languages?"

"Perhaps nothing. Perhaps very much indeed." Oppenhoff, who was usually fussy and precise, was fussy and imprecise today. He scratched at his side-whiskers again. "You are not familiar with the *Führer*'s recent remarks in Nuremberg?"

"I'm sorry, Professor, but *Herr* Buckliger is not in the habit of confiding in me."

Oppenhoff stared at her. Irony was a weapon he seldom encountered, and he seemed to have no idea how to cope with it. "Er—yes," he managed.

"What did the *Führer* say?" Susanna asked. "That's important for every German." *And even more important for every Jew.*

"Well . . ." The chairman hesitated. *He doesn't know himself, or doesn't know much,* Susanna realized. *Isn't that interesting?* Oppenhoff as much as confirmed her thought when he broke out of his hesitation: "I do not have this at first hand, but I am given to understand that he addressed the principles underlying National Socialist rule in the *Reich* and the Germanic Empire."

"Did he?" Susanna said—as neutral a remark as she could find. "I'm sorry, but I don't see what that's got to do with anything in the department."

"No?" Professor Oppenhoff looked at her in surprise. "If National Socialist doctrine changes, why then naturally our presentation must also change in accordance with it."

He worried more about what was ideologically appropriate than about what was true. Susanna had known that before, but hadn't had her nose rubbed in it like this up till now. She could add two and two, though. "Did the *Führer* talk about the first edition of *Mein Kampf*?"

"I believe so, and about other matters related to that topic," Oppenhoff answered. "Since you saw developments in England, I thought you would be able to contribute some insight into what is likely to follow here in the *Reich*."

What could *contribute some insight* mean but *tell me how to think?* As far as Susanna could remember, the last original idea Franz Oppenhoff had had was to use staples rather than paper clips to hold multipage documents together. Such things were his province; he made a better bureaucrat than he did an academic. She would have pitied him more if he hadn't been proud of that. "I'm sorry, *Herr Doktor* Professor, but I really couldn't tell you," she said. "We'll have to wait and find out what the people think, won't we?"

"What . . . the people think." By the way the department chairman brought out the phrase, Susanna might have said it in Gothic—it plainly meant nothing to him.

She nodded. "Yes, sir. That's how the British fascists interpret that passage of the first edition, anyhow. *Herr* Lynton put considerable weight on it. What else could our new *Führer* mean?"

"I don't know." Oppenhoff made a production of taking a Havana from his gold-plated cigar case, getting it going, and blowing noxious fumes in Susanna's direction. "Things seemed satisfactory as they were," he said plaintively. "This being so, what point to changing them?"

Had Susanna been only another German, she might have had more sympathy—perhaps even pity—for Franz Oppenhoff. Since she was what she was, though, she didn't think everything had been fine before. "Change comes, *Herr Doktor* Professor," she said, trying to sound gentle and not scornful. "It comes, and we have to be ready for it."

"This is true." But the department chairman still looked like a large, white-haired, wrinkled, cigar-smoking little boy on the edge of a tantrum. "No matter how true it is, I don't like it!" he burst out.

"I'm sorry," said, Susanna, who, if she'd ever prayed for anything in her life, prayed for change now.

The doorbell rang. "There they are," Heinrich Gimpel said.

"Well, let them in," Lise answered. "The house isn't as clean as it ought to be, but no house with children in it is ever as clean as it ought to be. They have two of their own. At least they'll understand."

Heinrich opened the door. Willi Dorsch thrust a big jug of Rhine wine at him. "Here," Willi said. "If I get you drunk enough, maybe you won't remember to count the cards while we're playing."

"Thanks." Heinrich took the wine. "You seem to be forgetting something, though."

"What's that?"

"If we all get drunk—"

"If we all get drunk, who knows what will happen?" Erika Dorsch said from behind Willi. She looked at Heinrich.

Willi didn't see that. He laughed, saying, "If we all get drunk, we won't remember, so whatever happens, it won't count."

Is that how you explained things to Ilse at lunch? Heinrich wondered. One more question he couldn't ask. He hefted the jug, saying, "Come on in. We'll drink some of this, anyhow, and we'll see how bad the bridge gets."

"Not to worry." Willi laughed again. "We can play bad bridge drunk or sober."

"Some of us certainly can," Erika murmured. The smile fell off her husband's face. She pointed to Alicia, who was reading on the sofa. "My goodness, she's getting big, isn't she?"

"They do that," Heinrich said. "Maybe if we stopped feeding her, she wouldn't. We've talked about it, but we haven't done it yet."

Alicia looked up from her book. "I've heard that one before, Daddy." Jab delivered, she went back to reading.

Willi Dorsch winced again. "They get dangerous awfully early, don't they?" He wasn't looking at Alicia, though. He was looking at Erika. This time, luckily, she was the one who didn't notice.

Lise came out to the front room. "Hello, hello," she said, and then caught sight of the jug of wine. "*Gott im Himmel!* If we drink all that, we'll pass out under the table like a bunch of Russians."

"I think that's part of Willi's evil plot," Heinrich said, "except that he was going to pour all of the wine down *my* throat."

"Oh, he was, was he?" Lise sent Willi a mock-ferocious glare. "He doesn't think he needs to get me drunk, too? I'm insulted."

Alicia closed her book. "I'm going upstairs," she announced. "How is a person supposed to hear herself think around here?" Except for the pronoun, she was quoting her father. The indignant flounce, however, was all her own.

"That one's going to be trouble." Erika Dorsch's voice held nothing but admiration.

"That one's already trouble," Heinrich replied. "Well, let's see how the cards go. And let's see what we've got here." He handed Lise the jug of Rhine wine. She made as if to stagger under the weight, but then took the wine back into the kitchen to use the corkscrew. When everybody was at the table with a glass of wine, Heinrich said, "I heard something interesting at lunch today," and told of what the officers had to say about Heinz Buckliger's speech.

The longer he went on, the unhappier Willi looked. Heinrich wondered why. Willi's politics weren't nearly so reactionary as, say, those of the SS men in Admiral Yamamoto's. But then Erika turned to Willi and said, "You didn't tell me anything about this. You said you had lunch with Heinrich today, didn't you?"

"Well, yes," Willi said. *Well, no,* Heinrich thought. *If you tell your wife lies, you can't expect me to know about them.* But Willi recovered brilliantly: "Old man Kallmeyer came over to the table and started bending my ear about depreciation. I couldn't pay any attention to the juicy stuff."

Erika didn't buy that, or not right away. "Why wasn't he bending Heinrich's ear, too?"

"Don't be silly," Willi said. "Heinrich already knows everything there is to know about depreciation."

That wasn't true, but it was plausible. Erika eyed her husband, eyed Heinrich, and slowly nodded. "Well, maybe," she admitted. "But I wish you'd been paying attention to what really matters."

"I was," Willi said. "If Kallmeyer gets mad at me, my job turns into hell on earth."

Erika hardly paid any attention to him. She was thinking about what Heinrich had said. "If the government is going to admit it made mistakes and told lies . . . it's like the end of the world. Who knows where it will end?"

"Not at the bridge table," Lise said. "Shall we play?" With some people, getting together to play bridge was just an excuse to sit around and talk and drink. For the Gimpels and the Dorsches, it was an excuse to sit around and talk and drink, but it wasn't *just* an excuse. They all took the cards seriously (Willi took them as seriously as he took anything, anyhow). The wine and the snacks and the chatter were all very well, but the evenings revolved around the bridge game.

As they cut the cards to see who would deal, Lise glanced at Heinrich for a split second. He answered just as quickly with an eyebrow raised and lowered. He'd already told her what he'd heard in the canteen, and he hadn't said a word about Willi's being there. The eyebrow said there were good reasons why he hadn't.

Willi won the cut and dealt like a machine—a machine that desperately needed repair and oiling. He tossed out cards seemingly at random. He would do that every once in a while, for comic effect. Sometimes he would misdeal doing it, too. When everyone ended up with thirteen cards, Heinrich breathed a silent sigh of relief. He arranged his hand. It was nothing special, but he could open up at one heart and see what Lise had.

"Four diamonds," Willi announced, sounding proud of himself.

"Oh, dear," Heinrich said. He knew what a preempt like that meant—Willi had a diamond suit as long as his arm, and not much else. Seeing that he had a singleton six of diamonds himself, that didn't much surprise Heinrich. *Do I want to jump in at the four level myself?* He looked at his hand again. He knew he couldn't. "Pass."

Erika and Lise also passed. Willi went down two, but he had a hundred honors points in diamonds, so he broke even on the hand. And he'd kept Heinrich and Lise from finding out they could easily have made two hearts, which meant the preempt worked.

"If you'd made that hand, I would have figured you cooked the deal on purpose," Heinrich said as he shuffled for the next one.

"Who, me?" Willi looked innocent: one of his less convincing expressions. "I'm not smart enough to do anything like that."

"How right you are," Erika murmured.

Willi's smile seemed cheerful enough. "You can be replaced," he said. It might have been one of their usual gibes. It might have been . . . if Ilse hadn't come back from lunch with her buttons misaligned. Heinrich looked down at the table till he was sure his face wouldn't give anything away.

He and Lise got to five clubs. She'd bid them first, so she played the hand. She went down one when the trumps split badly against her. "Looks like everything's going to be above the line tonight," Heinrich said.

Nobody went down on the next hand, because nobody had cards good enough for an opening bid. They tossed that one in and tried again. When Erika Dorsch bid three diamonds on the hand after that and not only made the contract but added an overtrick, she got a round of applause.

Erika and Willi won the first rubber, a long, inartistic affair. After the clinching hand, Lise said, "Let's take a break. I'll get a little something to eat." She went into the kitchen.

Willi got up, too. "Rhine wine's revenge," he said, and headed in the other direction.

That left Heinrich alone at the table with Erika, exactly where he didn't want to be. "I'm going to give Lise a hand," he said, and started to rise.

But when Erika said, "Wait," he didn't see what else he could do. She asked, "Was Willi at lunch with you today?"

He didn't want to lie. He didn't want to tell the truth, either. In the end, he didn't say anything. That was also unlikely to help, as he knew only too well.

And it didn't. Erika's eyes narrowed. "Uh-*huh*," she said, packing a world of meaning into two wordless syllables. "Well, where was he, then?"

"I don't know." Heinrich could tell the literal truth there, and did, gladly.

By then, telling the truth didn't help, either. Erika asked the next question he dreaded: "Wherever he was, who was with him?"

"How am I supposed to know that if I don't know where he was?" Heinrich hoped he sounded reasonable, but feared he sounded desperate.

Erika sent him the sort of look he hadn't got since the last time he'd tried explaining to a teacher why he didn't have his homework. But before she could call him a liar to his face or ask another question he didn't want to answer, the toilet down the hall flushed. Out came Willi, whistling. *Saved by—well, no, not the bell,* Heinrich thought.

"*That's* better," Willi said.

Lise brought in a tray of cold cuts and crackers and cheese. "Here," she said. "We don't have to think about this."

"I didn't have to think about what I was doing before," Willi said.

"Are you sure?" Erika asked, in tones that would have given him credit for any disgusting habit. Heinrich built himself a snack. That was probably the safest thing he could do. Even scratching his head struck him as dangerous.

Erika had come right out and propositioned him, or as near as made no difference, and she didn't see anything wrong with that. The only place where she saw anything wrong was with what Willi did. Willi had had some sort of interesting time with Ilse. But if he ever found out what Erika had said to Heinrich . . .

It sounded like one of the televisor dramas that ran on weekday afternoons. Unfortunately, it was real. *If Willi finds out, will he try to knock Erika's block off, or mine?* Heinrich got up and poured himself another glass of wine. That was a more interesting question than he really wanted to contemplate.

In the kitchen, Lise had missed the byplay. "We're all cheerful tonight, aren't we?" she remarked.

"*I* am," Willi said, piling a wobbly mountain of meat and cheese on a cracker. "Why wouldn't I be?" When he devoured his creation, he looked like a hamster stuffing sunflower seeds into its cheek pouches. Heinrich wouldn't have believed all that would fit in a man's mouth, but it did.

"Yes, why wouldn't you be?" Bombers were taking off in Erika's voice. Panzers were rolling for the border. *Why wouldn't you be, when you were out screwing around?* She didn't say it, but it hung in the air.

Somehow, Willi seemed not to hear it. Heinrich didn't know whether to be appalled or jealous. Willi assembled another monster snack. He managed to eat this one, too, and smacked his lips in triumph. *Did you do the same thing after you ate . . . ?* Heinrich made himself stop, not quite soon enough.

Now Lise realized something was wrong. She didn't know what, but she did find a solution of sorts. Reaching for the cards, she asked, "Whose deal is it, anyway?"

"Mine," Willi said with his mouth full. He took the deck from Lise and started shuffling. "I'll deal them off the bottom this time. Only way to make sure I get myself some decent cards."

"Wouldn't you rather have indecent ones?" Erika asked. Again, Willi only gave back a vague smile. He went on dealing.

Heinrich arranged his hand. "This looks like you dealt it off the bottom, all right," he told Willi.

"I told you I was going to." Willi took a look at his own cards. "One heart."

"Pass," Heinrich said gloomily.

"One no-trump," Erika said, which meant she had some help for Willi but not much. Heinrich told himself not to look at bridge bids as a metaphor for life. As often happened, telling himself was easier than making himself listen.

"Two diamonds," Lise said.

That made Heinrich look at his hand in a new way. He had five diamonds to the queen: not really a biddable suit, not with the rest of the junk that accompanied them, but pretty decent support. His singleton heart looked better, too.

"Two hearts," Willi said.

"Three diamonds," Heinrich said.

Erika passed. So did Lise. Willi muttered to himself. "Three hearts," he said. Now Heinrich passed. His wife had the stronger hand. She was the one who'd have to decide whether to go up. After Erika passed, Lise did, too. Willi made gloating noises. "Mine! All mine!"

Heinrich led a diamond. Erika laid out the dummy, which was about what Heinrich had expected: not much. She did have two little diamonds in it. Willi put one of those on the lead. Lise played the ace and took the trick. Then she threw out the king, saying, "Maybe this will go and maybe it won't." Heinrich didn't think it would. He had five diamonds, he figured Lise for five, the dummy showed two—and that left only one for Willi.

But Willi had two after all, which meant Lise had had only four. No wonder she hadn't rebid them. Willi looked disgusted at setting his second and surely last diamond on the trick. Lise led the eight of spades. Willi took the trick with the ace from his hand. He looked put upon. He didn't want to be there, but he didn't have much in the way of entries to the board.

He played the hand about as well as he could, and ended up going down two anyhow. Lise had stronger cards than he did. "I was going to open at one no-trump," she said, "but I couldn't, not when it got to me, and I had even distribution and no rebiddable suit. So"—she shrugged—"I played defense instead."

"And ran over me," Willi said sadly.

"You were the one who overbid the hand," Erika said.

"The hell I did," Willi retorted. That got to him, where the other sneers hadn't.

Heinrich grabbed the cards and started shuffling. "We've all butchered a hand or two—or twenty-two," he said. "And some of us—I'm not sure now, but I think it's just barely possible—some of us may even have made some other mistakes, too." He started to deal.

"You've got good sense, Heinrich," Willi said gratefully. Erika also nodded. Neither Dorsch looked happy about agreeing with the other. Heinrich wasn't happy about having Erika praise him in any way. It might give her more ideas than she had already—ideas about which Heinrich couldn't and wouldn't do anything.

The second rubber turned out even longer and sloppier than the first one had. Heinrich and Lise took two games out of three, but they went set three times while they were vulnerable and the Dorsches had a couple of hands with honors bonuses, so in spite of "winning" the rubber they came out 150 points in the hole.

"Well, no one will send any of those hands to the bridge magazines," Heinrich said ruefully.

"Oh, I don't know," Willi said. "If they're looking for lessons on how not to do it, I think we just wrote the book."

"Another rubber?" Lise asked.

Willi nodded. "Why not? The night is young, and I am beautiful."

Even Erika laughed, and she'd been sniping at her husband all evening. She still had the tricks they'd taken during the last hand in front of her. She tossed them across the table to Willi. "Shut up and deal."

"Always a good idea," he said, and did. When he picked up his hand and arranged it, he solemnly shook his head. "Nothing's going to go right tonight, though. I pass."

Everybody passed. Heinrich took the cards and shuffled them extra hard, trying to get rid of the mediocre hands people had been having. He looked at what he'd dealt himself. No such luck, not as far as he was concerned. "Pass."

They all passed again. "At this rate, we'll be here forever," Willi said, which proved economic planners in the USA weren't the only ones given to extrapolating too far from not enough data.

"Give me the cards," Erika said. As she shuffled, she sent the deck a severe look. "Have to be some playable hands in here somewhere." By the way she said it, the cards would go to bed without supper if there weren't. She nodded briskly once she saw her own hand. "One heart."

She won the contract at four hearts, and made it without much trouble. Even Lise murmured, "About time," as she shuffled for the next deal. She and Heinrich made three diamonds and then made two hearts, so they were vulnerable, too.

That sent the deal to Heinrich. He liked the face cards that looked back at him when he picked up his hand. He put things together, and. . . . "One no-trump." Erika passed. Lise made it two no-trump. Willi opened his mouth and then closed it again, as if he wanted to jump in but couldn't, not at the three level. Heinrich said, "Three no-trump. Let's see if we can steal this rubber." Everyone passed.

Erika led. Lise set out the dummy. Heinrich looked at what she had and added it in his head to what he had. He saw eight sure tricks, one more with a spade finesse—and he knew which way he intended to try it, because of Willi's wiggling—and maybe a couple of overtricks if he could set up her clubs and run them.

Everything turned out the way he thought it would. He ran the spade finesse past Willi the first chance he got, while he still had the other suits stopped—vital in no-trump—and it worked. After that, everything else flew on automatic pilot. He ended up making five.

"Very neat," Willi said. "Nothing we could do about that one."

"I don't know," Erika said. "Why didn't you hold up a sign that said, *I've got the strength*?" Willi bridled. As he had in the auction, he started to say something. This time, Erika forestalled him: "And who did you really have lunch with today?"

"I told you—with Heinrich," Willi answered.

"Yes, you told me. Now try telling the the truth, because I know crap when I hear it," Erika snarled. Lise looked at Heinrich in surprise—she'd known something was going on, all right, but she hadn't realized Willi was out-and-out lying. Heinrich did his best to keep all expression off his face. Anything he did or said now was only liable to throw gasoline on the fire.

Willi got to his feet with ponderous dignity. "I don't have to take these kinds of questions," he declared. "You're not the Security Police, even if you think you are." He left the table and walked down the hall again.

Erika looked daggers at his back. "Bastard," she said, just as the bathroom door closed. She turned back to Heinrich and Lise, her eyes going from one of them to the other and then returning. "I swear, there are times when I'd like to sleep with the first man I happen to see, just to pay him back." She was staring squarely at Heinrich when she said that.

He tried to look at the floor, at the ceiling, out the window—anywhere but at either Willi's wife or his own. He kept waiting for Willi to flush the toilet again. But Willi, this time, was using the bathroom as a bomb shelter, and odds were he wouldn't come out any time soon.

Silence stretched. At last, warily, Lise said, "Don't you think that's a little . . . drastic?"

"Why?" Erika didn't keep her voice down. If anything, she pitched it to carry. "If he's fooling around on me, why shouldn't I fool around on him?"

More silence. Heinrich decided he'd better say something. If he didn't, Lise was liable to get the idea he wanted Erika thinking about him like that. He chose his words with even more caution than Lise had: "If you're going to stay married, it's probably a good idea that neither one of you fool around on the other."

"Ha!" Erika said: a one-syllable demolition of the very idea. Lise had started to nod in agreement with her husband. That scornful laugh froze her for a moment with her chin in the air. She looked as if she needed a distinct effort to bring her head back down to a normal posture.

After what seemed like forever, water ran in the pipes at the far end of the hall. Willi came back to the bridge table looking grim. "We'd better go," he said to Erika. "It's getting late."

"It certainly is—in a lot of ways," she answered. "And we have a few things to talk about, don't we?"

"Yes, just a few," Willi said. The Dorsches headed up the street for the bus stop after the most perfunctory good-byes. They were shouting at each other long before they got there.

"Well!" Lise said. "That was another interesting evening."

"Interesting." Heinrich considered. "Mm, yes, that's one word for it, anyhow."

"It was the politest word I could think of," his wife replied. "What exactly did Erika mean there? And who *was* Willi at lunch with?"

Answering the second question seemed safer, so Heinrich did that first: "Ilse—again—if lunch is where they went." Lise's eyes widened. Her mouth shaped a silent *oh*. But her expression said she hadn't forgotten the other question, either. Unhappily, he told her, "Erika probably meant just what she said. She usually does."

"I know she does. That's why I wondered." Lise frowned. "But she was looking at you when she said it. I didn't much care for that. What did you think about it?"

Now there was a question to make a man want to pretend he'd suddenly gone deaf. "It's a compliment of sorts," said Heinrich, whose ears still worked, however much he wished they didn't. His wife coughed dangerously. "Will you let me finish?" he exclaimed. Lise gave back a pace in surprise; he didn't raise his voice very often. He went on, "It's not *much* of a compliment, not when she would have said the same thing to any man who happened to be in the neighborhood." He didn't mention that Erika had already said the same thing about him in particular. He did add, "And I've told you before—I know when I'm well off."

"Oh, you do, do you?" Lise sent him a challenging stare. "How am I supposed to be sure of that?"

He took her in his arms. He kissed her. His hands wandered. "I'll think of something," he said, before adding the father's usual caveat: "If the children stay quiet, anyhow."

He was lucky. They did.

Children in the United States, Alicia Gimpel had learned, got long summer vacations from school. Her teachers said that scornfully. They offered it as one of the reasons Germany had beaten the USA: Americans didn't study enough, and had been too ignorant to take full advantage of their country's riches. No matter what her teachers said, though, the idea sounded wonderful to Alicia.

Here it was the middle of August, and she remained in school. The only real breaks she got were two weeks around Christmas and New Year's and another week at Easter time. The rest of the year was school, punctuated by much-too-occasional holidays.

Herr Kessler said, "Many important things have happened in our country. The *Führer* is setting us on a new course, and that is the way we shall go. Matthias Walbeck!"

The boy jumped up and came to attention. "*Jawohl, Herr* Kessler!"

"Tell me how the *Führer* is changing the *Reich*."

Poor Matthias couldn't do it. He was a big, strong boy, but good-natured—not a bully at all. Unfortunately, he also was not a scholar at all. He stayed at attention, his face a mask of misery. "I'm very sorry, *Herr* Kessler," he whispered. "Please excuse me."

Kessler took the paddle off the nail where it hung. Matthias turned and bent over. The teacher delivered a swat that made the boy hop forward. But Matthias let out not a peep. Showing weakness would only have earned him more. "You must study, Matthias," the teacher said. "You must pay attention."

"I will, *Herr* Kessler. I promise, *Herr* Kessler," Matthias said. Everyone in the classroom—probably including him—knew the promise would be broken.

The teacher's glower raked the room. Alicia knew the answer. She didn't throw up her hand, though. Volunteering too often got you a reputation as a teacher's pet. She already had more of that reputation than she wanted.

Herr Kessler picked another hapless student, this one a girl. She couldn't answer, either. He swatted her, too. When he was in a bad mood, he would choose children who weren't likely to know what he wanted, just so he could hand out swat after swat. He wasn't the only teacher in the school who did that, either. *Frau* Koch was universally known as "the Beast" to her students, and had been for years—but not a teacher ever heard the nickname.

After dealing out yet another whack on the bottom, *Herr* Kessler put the paddle back in its place. "I don't know what the younger generation is coming to," he said sadly. "When the *Führer* speaks, you must listen. And what is his name, class?"

"Heinz Buckliger, *Herr* Kessler," the children chorused.

"Very good. You've learned that, anyway," the teacher said. "And Heinz Buckliger has said that not everything we did in days gone by was perfect, so some things must change. And why must things change?"

"Because the *Führer* is always right, *Herr* Kessler," the whole class said together.

That was the right answer. Alicia knew it was. Teachers had been drilling it into students since kindergarten. She sang out as confidently as her classmates. So she was amazed when *Herr* Kessler shook his head. "No. What did I just say?"

They were trained to repeat his words back to him. They did now: "And Heinz Buckliger has said that not everything we did in days gone by was perfect, so some things must change."

"Yes." Kessler nodded. "So why must things change, then?"

"Because the *Führer* says so." Again, all the children were sure they had it right. Again, Alicia was as sure as any of the others.

But the teacher shook his head once more. "No. You are wrong. What did the new *Führer* say?"

"That not everything we did in days gone by was perfect, and—"

"Stop!" *Herr* Kessler held up his hand. "There is the answer. We must change because not everything we did in days gone by was perfect."

He paused to let that sink in. The children murmured among themselves. *Herr* Kessler didn't correct them, which was at least as astonishing as the lesson he was teaching. Alicia wanted to ask several questions. She didn't think she ought to ask any of them. But Wolfgang Priller's hand rose. "Question, *Herr* Kessler!"

"Go ahead, Priller." The teacher braced, as if expecting bad news.

Wolf stood up and came to attention. "Sir, if the *Führer* is always right, the way we know he is, how is it that not everything we did in days gone by was perfect?"

Sure enough, that was one of the questions Alicia had wanted to ask. It had occurred to her because of the logical inconsistency. She suspected it had occurred to Wolf Priller because he remained convinced the *Führer* was always right. He took to indoctrination the way a duck took to water.

Herr Kessler said, "Heinz Buckliger is the *Führer* now. If he says not everything we did in days gone by was perfect, is he not right to say so?" Wolfgang Priller frowned as he tried to work that out. Alicia frowned, too. Again, she thought *Herr* Kessler's logic was that of a dog chasing its own tail. The teacher gestured. "Be seated, Priller." Wolf sat down. He looked as if a dog were chasing its tail inside his head, too.

"What did we do in days gone by that wasn't perfect, *Herr* Kessler?" another boy called without raising his hand.

Alicia didn't see who it was. Kessler didn't see who it was, either, which had to be lucky for whoever had spoken out of turn. The teacher growled, "I don't have to respond to questions not put in proper form. I don't have to, and I don't intend to. Let us continue with the lesson."

Does that mean you don't know the answer? Alicia wondered, which would have been unimaginable not so long before, when she thought her teachers knew everything. *Or does it mean the new* Führer *hasn't said what the answer is, so there isn't any answer yet?* She could see Kessler was parroting what Heinz Buckliger had said, the same way students parroted what the teacher said.

At lunch, Wolf Priller declared, "I don't like these changes. I think they're stupid." Nobody disagreed with him, not out loud. He could beat up any of the other boys in the class.

Alicia wondered if anything would really change, if anything could really change, or if everything that was going on was just a lot of talk. Sometimes people said this or that without meaning a word of it. If the men who ran things wanted to do something like that, they could easily enough.

But there was Trudi Krebs, skipping rope with some other girls and as happy as any of them. *Herr* Kessler had taken down her name for speaking well of the first edition of *Mein Kampf*. Wolf Priller had gloated about how the knock on her door would come in the middle of the night. Everybody—including Alicia—had been sure it would happen. It hadn't.

If Kurt Haldweim were still *Führer*, it would have. Alicia remembered the beaky, waxy face she'd seen in the Great Hall when Haldweim lay in state. No man with a face like that would have let anybody get away with anything. But Trudi and her parents *had* got away with it. Therefore, things *had* changed, at least some.

There was logic that didn't chase its own tail. And if Wolf Priller didn't like it, so much the better. Alicia threw her orange peel in the trash and ran to join the girls with the jump rope.

Because of who he was, because of what he did, and because of what he was, Walther Stutzman had access to far more of the *Reich*'s computer records than anyone else knew about. The problem was being able to use the access codes he had. If anyone spotted strange things on his monitor, he would lose his access privileges in a hurry—and also, very likely, his freedom, and also, quite possibly, his life.

Lunch was a good time to poke around. Most people in Walther's office at the Zeiss works went out to eat. That helped. As usual, he kept his monitor turned so it wasn't easy to see unless you came right into his cubicle. That helped, too. All the same, especially after things had gone so badly wrong fixing the Kleins' genealogy, he got extra nervous whenever he went looking where he wasn't supposed to.

He had to keep doing it, even if it was dangerous. He knew that. Finding out more than he could through ordinary channels might help keep him and all the Jews left in the *Reich* safe. And he couldn't help being curious, either.

His boss said, "There's a gang of us going over to this new place that serves American hamburgers and hot dogs and fried chicken. Want to come along? Guaranteed heartburn or your money back."

"Can't do it." Walther pointed to his desk. It was as neat as usual, but did have more stacks of paper on it than people were used to seeing there. "This changeover to the new operating system is tougher than we ever thought it would be. I don't know if we can meet the schedule they've set us."

Gustav Priepke grimaced. "Lord help us if we don't. We've already had three false starts. If we botch it this time, they're liable to throw us out on our ear and hire a bunch of programmers from Japan."

Priepke was kidding on the square, and Walther knew it. The *Reich* had pioneered in electronic computers—and the core operating system still showed as much, for it lacked protected memory and preemptive multitasking. The Japanese had got off to a later start, and had had the advantage of seeing the mistakes German programmers made. Japanese systems were more robust and often more reliable, even if they weren't so elegant.

"I think we can make it happen, but it's going to take a lot of work," Walther said. "And so . . ." He apologetically spread his hands.

His boss nodded. "If you're on the trail of something, keep after it. I'll have an extra hot dog for you." Off he went—and, knowing him, he'd probably have two.

Walther waited till more people went off to lunch, whether at the American place—it was called, for no reason he could see, the Greasy Spoon—or somewhere else. When the big room that held his cubicle had quieted down, he used one of those access codes he wasn't supposed to have. This one took him to an archive of the *Führer*'s speeches. He wanted to—and he was convinced he needed to—find out just what Heinz Buckliger had said at Nuremberg, because it had so many people hopping.

The Nuremberg speech was there in the menu, sure enough. When he tried to call it up, though, it demanded another authorization code from him, one with a much higher security level. He blinked. He'd never seen anything like that before, not for a speech. He knew the second code, but hadn't imagined he would have to use it. What *had* Buckliger been talking about? Nuclear bombs and missile design?

Even after he entered the authorization code, the system hesitated before it coughed up the text of the *Führer*'s speech. He got ready to bail out in a hurry and cover his tracks. But then the speech did come up. If someone—or something electronic—was making special note of his presence, none of his own tools for detecting such things sensed it.

He quickly scrolled through the speech to see how long it was. When he did, he got another surprise. It seemed to go on forever. The *Führer* had the privilege of length, of course. Had any ruler of the Third *Reich* ever used it so extravagantly as Heinz Buckliger had here, though? Maybe the *Völkischer Beobachter* hadn't published it because it would have filled two days' editions.

Walther started to read. He couldn't go through the whole speech in detail, as he'd intended. It was just too damned long; he wouldn't have been halfway through by the time his boss got back from the Greasy Spoon. So he skimmed—and even skimming was plenty to make him sit up and take notice.

Buckliger came right out and said things that everybody knew but that nobody—certainly not the *Führer*—ever talked about. What had Lothar Prützmann and the rest of the leaders of the SS thought when he declared, "For far too long, this state has been founded on one thing and one thing only: terror"? If that didn't infuriate them . . .

If that didn't infuriate them, the speech had plenty of other things to do the job. The new *Führer* said that all his predecessors, from Hitler on, had received reverence as if they were gods, "but they are only men, with all the failings to which men are heir." Walther found himself nodding. That seemed obvious when you came out and said it—but who in the nearly eighty years of the *Reich*'s history *had* come out and said it? Nobody—and a ruling *Führer* least of all.

And Heinz Buckliger had also said, "Force can win victories, but force alone cannot maintain them forever without more expense than Germany can readily afford." If that didn't fly in the face of everything the *Reich* had stood for since the early days, what did?

With each new bombshell, Walther wanted to slow down and read more carefully. He knew he couldn't, not with his boss and his colleagues coming back soon, not if he wanted to see as much of what was there as possible. But he wanted to.

If he had slowed down, he wouldn't have come to the question the new *Führer* asked near the end of the speech: "If everything we say about Aryan descent is true, how do we explain the recent rapid progress of the Japanese, who have not mingled their blood with Aryan stock any time recently?"

How Buckliger answered that question, Walther didn't find out; he had to get the speech off his monitor because the room started filling up again. But that the *Führer* thought to ask it said more than any answer could. No, they couldn't very well publish this speech. The country wasn't ready. And Walther would have bet anything he owned that the Party and SS *Bonzen* who'd listened to it at Nuremberg hadn't been, either.

VII

Heinrich Gimpel had tried the Greasy Spoon before, and hadn't been much impressed. No matter how trendy the American place was, he didn't like the food all that much. But if Richard and Maria Klein wanted to go there to celebrate, he and Lise weren't about to tell them no. The Kleins had reason to celebrate. The Security Police didn't call off an investigation every day, not when they were trying to find out if you were a Jew.

"I wish we could throw a proper party at home," Maria said. She'd been thin and pale to begin with, and the troubles of the past few months had only made her thinner and paler. She had a very nice smile, though, even when she shrugged and said, "You know how things are liable to be."

"Oh, yes." Heinrich nodded. So did Lise. If the authorities were still looking for evidence, what better way to get it than to fill the Kleins' house with microphones and listen to everything they said—and, if they did throw a party, to everything their friends said, too?

Richard took a big bite out of his cheeseburger. He had a musician's hands, all right: long, clever fingers, the tips slightly spatulate from endless hours of practice. He said, "I don't have any idea what finally made them quit. They just said, 'All right, we're done. Go on about your business. Doesn't look like you are what we thought you were.' " He had too much sense to say *Jew* where anyone who wasn't might hear. Grinning with relief, he sipped from a mug of beer.

"Was it your lawyer?" Lise asked. "From what Susanna says, he's a tiger."

The Kleins shrugged in unison. "He made a lot of noise, I'll say that for him," Maria answered. "I don't know how much real good he did, though."

A girl in what was supposed to be an American waitress's outfit from before the Third World War came up to the table. "Hi!" she said—the standard server's greeting at the Greasy Spoon. She returned to German to ask, "Would you like some dessert? Cherry pie, maybe, or brownies?"

"We're not quite ready yet," Heinrich said.

"Okay," she said brightly, doing her best to project old-time American enthusiasm. "I'll come back later, then." Away she went. Heinrich wondered whether waitresses in the United States had really worn clothes like that. Wouldn't the customers have been too distracted to order?

"I think maybe the lawyer helped," Richard said. "It helped that we had the nerve to hire one. That told them that we really hadn't done what they said we had."

"Good," Heinrich said. "*Danken Gott dafür.*" He still wondered what the authorities had been thinking. A lot of times, they arrested people just because they felt like arresting them, not because the people had actually done something. Things did seem looser under Buckliger than they had under Kurt Haldweim, but were they loose enough for the powers that be to let Jews slip through their fingers? Heinrich had his doubts.

But the Kleins were here. Maria nodded. "Thank God for that is right," she said softly. And if she thought about God in a way different from that of most citizens of the *Reich*—well, who could know by the way she looked or what she said when strangers might hear? Nobody. Nobody at all.

Lise also spoke quietly: "How is Paul?"

"He's no better. He's not going to get better." Richard Klein spoke through clenched teeth. "They brought in specialists who know a lot more about this disease than Dr. Dambach does. They all say the same thing. When he gets worse, the Mercy Center will be a—a kindness."

"He's still happy, though," Maria said. "He's not too bad, and he's too little to know something's wrong with him."

"That's the one mercy we have," Richard agreed. "He doesn't know anything is wrong. But we do." He lifted the seidel of beer, drained it, and waved for a refill. The waitress brought it to him, then swayed off to get something for someone else.

Heinrich watched her. He would have needed to be blind not to watch her. Lise watched him watching her. "Come here often for lunch?" she asked.

"Me? No. It's not close enough to where I work." Heinrich enjoyed sounding virtuous. "As a matter of fact, Walther Stutzman told me about this place."

But Lise and Maria Klein stared at him. "Walther?" his wife said in astonishment. He and Lise were happily married. By all appearances, Richard and Maria got on well, too. But the Stutzmans were like two sides of one coin. Lise plainly had trouble imagining Walther coming to a restaurant where the waitresses were as big a part of the attraction as the food.

Taking pity on her, Heinrich said, "His boss has brought him here. Sometimes you can't say no." He ate some french fries. They were hot and salty, and certainly lived up to the name of the place.

"He says that's how he got here, anyway," Richard Klein said, his voice sly. "I bet he was just kicking and screaming when his boss dragged him in." He was waitress-watching, too.

Maria looked at Lise. "What are we going to do with them?"

"Well, we've had them for a while by now," Lise answered. "I don't suppose they'd bring much if we traded them in on new models."

"Mm—maybe not." By the way Maria said it, it was one of those unfortunate, inconvenient facts you just couldn't get around.

Heinrich finished his burger and fries. "If Americans eat like this all the time, why don't they all weigh two hundred kilos?" he said. "I feel like I swallowed a boulder."

Richard nodded. "Me, too," he said. But when the waitress came back and asked about dessert again, they both ordered cherry pie with a scoop of vanilla ice cream slapped on top. So did their wives. Away went the waitress, cheerful as could be.

"*Now* I get it," Lise said. "They wear what they're almost wearing to get the men to order more." Heinrich wouldn't have been surprised if she was right, no matter what he'd thought a little while earlier about distractions. He hadn't been too distracted to lay out some extra Reichsmarks, had he?

He found the only defense he could: "You wanted dessert, too, sweetheart, and I don't suppose the girl's clothes had anything to do with that."

Richard Klein clapped his hands. "That's good. I wish I could come up with snappy comebacks like that."

"Don't," Heinrich told him. "They usually just get you in trouble."

"Listen to him," Maria said. "This is a man who's been married longer than you have. He knows what's what."

The waitress came back with a tray heavy with desserts. The two couples dug in. Sure enough, Heinrich made his pie disappear. Nor was he the only one facing an empty dessert plate with an expression of disbelief. "You don't need to put me on the train tonight," he said. "You can just roll me home."

"Me, too," Lise said. "Did I really do that? Tell me I didn't."

"If you didn't, then we didn't, either," Richard said. "Let's pretend the whole thing never happened."

Everybody laughed. Heinrich put money on the table, including an extra Reichsmark or two in appreciation of the waitress's outfit. As he walked out of the Greasy Spoon, he said, "I'm glad everything turned out all right," from the bottom of his heart. Then, because he was who and what he was, he added, "I wonder why it did."

Lise sent him the sort of look she always did when he came out with something like that, the look that said she wished he had better sense than to open his big mouth that way. But Richard Klein only laughed and clapped him on the back. "Hell, Heinrich," he said, "so do I."

Alicia Gimpel repeated the nonsense-sounding syllables that her father had had her memorize: *"Sh'ma yisroayl adonoi elohaynu adonoi ekhod."*

"That's right. That's just right." Her father nodded. "You've got the *Sh'ma* down very well. And do you remember what the words mean?"

" 'Hear, O Israel, the Lord our God, the Lord is one,' " Alicia said.

"That's right, too," her father said. "That's the most important prayer we have. It should be the last thing you ever say if, God forbid, there's a time when you have to say a last thing. We few are all that's left of Israel these days. We have to keep it going."

"I know." Alicia liked learning things in the secret language, the nearly dead language. It strengthened the feeling of belonging to a special club. "Show me the other thing again," she urged.

Her father frowned, which made him look even more serious than he usually did. "All right," he said, "but you've got to be especially careful with this. You can't let your sisters see it, not ever, and you've always got to scratch over it or tear it up into little pieces before you throw it out. That's because it says just what we are if anybody recognizes it."

"I understand. I promise." Alicia started to cross her heart, but then checked herself with the motion only half done. If she was a Jew, the cross didn't count for anything, did it? So many things to think about . . .

With careful attention, her father drew—wrote—four curious characters on a piece of paper: יהוה. "This says *adonoi*—it's the name of God. Now you do it." He handed her the pen. She started to: וה. He set his hand on hers, stopping her. "No, that's not right. Remember what I told you?"

"What do you mean? They look just like the ones you made." But then Alicia did remember. "Oh. I'm sorry. I started from the wrong end again, didn't I?" Her father lifted up his hand. She began again, writing a י, a ה, a ו, and then another ה. "Why does it go from right to left instead of from left to right, Daddy?"

"I don't know why Hebrew does that," he answered unhappily. "I just know *that* it does. My father knew more about being a Jew than I do, and *his* father knew much more than he did, because his father had grown up in the days when Jews in Germany were free to be what they were. I'll teach you as much as I can, and you need to remember it so you can teach it to your children."

"If we keep learning less and less every time, will a time come when we don't know enough?" Alicia asked.

Her father looked more unhappy still. "I don't know that, either, sweetheart. All I know is that I hope not. We have to try to pass it along, and that's what I'm doing."

Alicia looked down at the curious set of characters she'd written. "Which letter says what? Which one says *ah* and which one says *do* and which one says *noi?*"

"It's not that simple," her father said.

"Why not? What do you mean? This is confusing!" Alicia said.

"Because it doesn't really say *adonoi*. It says *Jahweh,* more or less—it's the word *Jehovah* comes from. But that's the name of God, and Jews aren't supposed to speak the name of God, so we say *adonoi* instead. That means *Lord.*"

"Oh." Alicia eyed those four formidable letters once more. "This *is* confusing. Are there books where I can find out more about it?"

"Yes, there are, and you can't have any of them," her father answered. Alicia stared at him in something close to shock. Their family loved books. The shelves in the front room and in her parents' bedroom held everything from mystery novels to books about the theater to bird-watching guides to studies of ancient Greece. But there were, she realized, no books about Jews except the Streicher children's classics in her own room. Her father went on, "You won't find those books in any Jew's house. It's not safe for us to have them. People might wonder why we do. And the last thing we want is people wondering about us. Not having those books is part of the disguise we wear. Do you see?"

"I suppose so," Alicia said unwillingly. "But it seems a shame that we can't learn more if the books are there."

"One of the things we could learn is what gives the Security Police an excuse to arrest us," her father said. "When you're a grownup, you can decide for yourself what you think is safe. For now, we're not going to take any chances."

He didn't use that tone of voice very often. When he did, it meant his mind was made up and he wouldn't change it no matter what. Alicia sighed. It didn't seem fair. He usually pushed her toward learning as hard as he could. Here, he was pushing her away instead. But when he sounded like this, she would only waste her breath arguing with him.

He picked up the paper where they'd written the name of God, the name too holy to be spoken, and methodically began tearing it into little pieces. "Most of what we know, we have to pass on by word of mouth," he said. "That's not so dangerous. It's there, and then it's gone. Paper, now, paper lasts. Paper is what gets you into trouble, because it stays there. Even if you've forgotten about it, it stays. That's what got the Kleins into trouble—a piece of paper that stayed in a file."

"The Kleins—are Jews?" Alicia asked. Excitement flared in her when her father nodded. The more people she knew who shared this burden with her, the less heavy it seemed and the less alone she felt.

Her father said, "Because of this paper, the *Reichs* Genealogical Office thought they were, too. But nobody could prove anything, and they had to let them go. And one of the reasons nobody could prove anything is that the Kleins are careful about what they keep at home. They didn't have anything where people could point and say, 'Ha! They have that, so they must be Jews!' "

From everything Alicia had heard, people didn't need to be sure to settle with Jews. She said as much to her father, finishing, "Why didn't they take them away and do things to them anyhow?"

That made her father frown. "I don't quite know," he admitted. He sounded grumpy; like her, he was someone with a restless, relentless itch to find things out. "There has to be a reason. I just hope it's not a bad one."

"What do you mean?" Alicia asked.

"Well, they could have let them go so they could help catch other Jews," he said. Her mouth fell open. That hadn't occurred to her. He nodded grimly. "Yes, they do things like that."

"They may, but would the Kleins?" Alicia asked.

Her father let out a long, sad sigh. "Sweetheart, I just don't know. How can you tell what anybody will do when someone says to him, 'Do this or else we'll kill you'? You can't know that about anyone else ahead of time. You can't even know about yourself ahead of time."

"I would never do anything like that," Alicia declared. Her father only sighed again. *He doesn't believe me,* she realized. She started to get angry. Then she wondered what would happen if the Security Police told her they would do something horrible to him or to her mother or to one of her sisters if she didn't do what they told her. Wouldn't she do anything to keep them from hurting people she loved? Maybe she would.

Her thought must have shown on her face, for her father reached out and tousled her hair. "You see?" he asked gently.

Alicia gave back a reluctant nod. "I guess I do." Then a really nasty thought occurred to her, one that made her gasp with fright. "What if the Kleins *are* doing that now? What if they're helping to catch *us*?"

"It's possible," her father admitted. All the terror Alicia had felt when she first found out she was a Jew, terror that had eased a little with the passage of time, came flooding back. But he went on, "It's possible, but I don't think it's true. If they were only pretending everything was all right last night, they could have been movie actors, they were doing such a good job. And besides, if the Security Police squeezed our names out of them, they wouldn't need to play games. They'd just break down the door in the middle of the night and take us away."

"*Ja,*" Alicia said, more than a little relieved. That was what the Security

Police did, all right. Everybody knew it. Her heart stopped thumping quite so hard.

Her father laughed. "Funny, isn't it, that they're always such bastards that knowing they haven't been mean shows they really did let the Kleins go free?"

"That's just what I was thinking!" Alicia exclaimed. "How did you know?"

"Because I was thinking the same thing," he answered, "and I'm just as happy about it as you are, believe me." Alicia did.

Esther Stutzman was trying to juggle three phone calls, two mothers who needed to make return appointments, and another mother who was arguing about her bill when the door to Dr. Dambach's waiting room opened. Instantly, all the women with squalling children in the waiting room tried to shush them. The sight of a stern-faced man in a uniform did that to people, even if the dark brown outfit wasn't one most men and women in the *Reich* recognized at sight. Who wanted to take a chance?

Maximilian Ebert strode up to the receptionist's station. Ignoring mothers and children, the man from the *Reichs* Genealogical Office clicked his heels, as he had the first time he visited the pediatrician's office. "*Guten Tag, Frau* Stutzman," he said. "I need to see Dr. Dambach right away."

Esther wished he hadn't remembered her name. There were several reasons he might have, and she liked none of them. She took what revenge she could by answering, "I'm very sorry, but he's with a patient at the moment. If you care to sit down and wait, I'm sure it won't be too long." By the way she said it, she might have been sure he'd wait for weeks.

But Ebert wasn't about to inconvenience himself like an ordinary person. "Please tell him I am here," he said. "I'm sure he will see me immediately."

"The nerve!" said a woman from behind his back. He stiffened, but did not turn.

"One moment, please," Esther told him; the request was too reasonable for her to refuse outright. When she went back to talk to Dr. Dambach, she found him poised with a hypodermic needle above a baby's round bare bottom. She waited till he gave the shot and the baby yowled. Then she said, "Excuse me, Doctor, but *Herr* Ebert is here. He needs to see you right away, he says."

"*Herr* Ebert?" Dambach looked blank.

"From the *Reichs* Genealogical Office," Esther said, wishing Ebert had never had any reason to visit the pediatrician.

"Oh. Him." Memory jogged, Dr. Dambach nodded. "What the devil does he want now?" Esther only shrugged. Dr. Dambach muttered. Before answering her, Dambach turned to the baby's mother. "Dora may be cranky and run a small fever for a day or two. Acetaminophen syrup should relieve most of the symptoms. If she's in more distress than that—which is very unlikely—bring her back in."

"Thank you, Doctor. I will," the woman said.

Still muttering, Dambach gave his attention back to Esther. "I suppose I'd better see him. Bring him to my private office, and I'll be there in a few minutes. I have another patient to see first."

"All right, Doctor." Esther went out and delivered the word to Maximilian Ebert.

"Thank you very much," he said, and then, once she'd taken him into the office, "Have you got a telephone number, my sweet?"

She'd thought he was unduly attentive the last time he came in. This . . . "What I have, *Herr* Ebert, are two children and a husband."

He stared at her in what looked like honest bewilderment and asked, "What's that got to do with anything?"

"I'm fond of all of them, thank you very much," she said. "And now, if you'll excuse me . . ." She went back out to the receptionist's station, where she announced, "Dr. Dambach has a visitor. He'll be with you as soon as he can, I promise." She nodded to the woman who'd questioned her bill. "I'm sorry for the delay, *Frau* Mommsen. What were you saying?"

Frau Mommsen poured out a history of her troubles, most of which had little to do with the twenty-five Reichsmarks she owed Dr. Dambach. Esther listened with half an ear. Most of her attention was on the pediatrician's private office. She hoped Dambach would tell Maximilian Ebert where to go and how to get there. She knew it was a forlorn hope, but she cherished it just the same.

Dr. Dambach didn't even get in there for another ten minutes. Esther could hear the functionary from the Genealogical Office drumming his fingers on Dambach's desk. "About time," Ebert said when the doctor finally did appear.

"You're the one who's interrupting my work," Dambach replied, his voice chilly. "What do you want?"

Before she could find out what he wanted, someone new to the practice—a woman with a squalling toddler in her arms—came up and had to be guided through Dr. Dambach's paperwork. Because the little boy cried all through the process, Esther caught only brief snatches of conversation from the doctor's office: ". . . got a lot of nerve blaming me for . . ." ". . . put all of us in hot . . ." ". . . my fault, when I was only trying to . . ." ". . . but this is how it turned . . ."

Dr. Dambach said something else in response to that. A moment later, Maximilian Ebert stormed out of his office and out of the waiting room, fury on his face. He tried to slam the door that led to the hall, but the shock-absorbing arm at the top of the door thwarted him. The slowly closing door cut off his curses when at last it did swing shut.

"Goodness!" said the woman with the toddler. "What got under *his* skin?"

"I don't know," Esther answered. "Whatever it is, I hope it's nothing trivial." The woman gave her a strange look, then decided she couldn't have meant what she said and forgot about it.

But Esther had meant every word. She stayed busy till noon dealing with mothers, children, and the occasional father. When the office closed for lunch, she went back to bring Dr. Dambach a fresh cup of coffee in the hopes that he might feel like talking. "Oh, thank you," he said around a mouthful of sandwich. "I was just going to get up and pour myself one."

When he said no more, Esther took the bull by the horns: "Why did that Ebert fellow storm out of here as though he had a Messerschmitt on his tail?"

"Him?" Dambach gave forth with a dismissive grunt. "I think we've seen the last of him, and I can't say I'm sorry, either. What he basically told me was that I had done my job too well. I'm sorry, *Frau* Stutzman, but the only way I know how to do it is as well as I can."

"Well, I should say so," Esther said, still wishing he'd been less conscientious. "What on earth was he talking about?"

"When the Kleins had the Tay-Sachs baby and the altered genealogical chart, they were suspected of being Jews," the pediatrician answered. "You know about that."

"Oh, yes." Esther nodded. "I know about that. What has it got to do with you doing your job too well?"

"Everyone in the *Reichs* Genealogical Office, and, for all I know, the Security Police, too, was all set to make an enormous hue and cry over it, and why not? It's been years since any Jews turned up in Berlin, for heaven's sake."

Esther nodded again. "That's true," she said casually, hiding her fear. "Why didn't they make their big hue and cry, then?"

"Because it turns out that Lothar Prützmann's niece, poor woman, has a baby with Tay-Sachs who's three weeks older than Paul Klein," Dambach said. "If they accused the Kleins of being Jews on account of this, how could they keep from tarring the head of the SS with the same brush? They couldn't, and they knew it, and so they had to drop the charges against the Kleins."

"Good Lord!" Esther didn't care to think about what a narrow and dreadful escape that was. She also couldn't help sympathizing with the SS chief of the Greater German *Reich,* something she hadn't thought she would ever do. She said, "But how does *Reichsführer*-SS Prützmann's misfortune reflect on you?"

"It's simple, for someone with the sort of mind *Herr* Ebert has." Dr. Dambach scowled. "If I hadn't brought the one Tay-Sachs case to his notice, his office wouldn't have got in trouble with Prützmann for pushing too hard. And what does Ebert do as a result of that? He blames me, of course."

"I see." And Esther did, too. "Well, the other choice would be blaming himself, and that's not likely, is it?"

The pediatrician grunted again. "Some miracles demand too much of God. But I gave him a piece of my mind before he left. You may be very sure of that."

"Good for you, Dr. Dambach," Esther said. He was a good doctor—and, within the limits of his education, a pretty good man.

"I'm sick and tired of getting pushed around by little tin gods in fancy uniforms just *because* they wear fancy uniforms," Dambach said. "I think everybody is, don't you? If the new *Führer* is serious about calling some of those people to account, he'll have a lot of folks on his side, I think. How about you?"

"Me? I never worry about politics," Esther lied. She had trouble hiding her amazement. Her boss was solid, reliable, conservative. If he said things like that, a lot of people had to be thinking them.

"I try never to worry about politics, either," he said now. "Who with his head on straight needs to most of the time? But sometimes politics worry about me, the way they did here this morning. And I'll tell you, *Frau* Stutzman, I don't care for it. I don't care for it at all."

"Well, for heaven's sake, Dr. Dambach, who could blame you?" Esther said. Who needed to worry about politics most of the time? People like her, people whom politics constantly affected, did. And the very foundations of Nazi Party politics were built on worrying about Jews. Would Heinz Buckliger think about changing that? Could he think about changing that and hope to survive? Some of the things Walther said he'd talked about in Nuremburg were remarkable. But changing the way Nazis saw Jews would be more than remarkable. It would be miraculous. When Esther saw a miracle, she would believe in it. Till then, no.

"Why don't you go on home, *Frau* Stutzman?" Dambach said. "I don't mind answering the telephone till Irma gets here. It should be only a few more minutes, anyway."

"Thank you very much," Esther said. "Let me start a fresh pot of coffee before I leave, though. That should last the two of you most of the afternoon." If she didn't, he'd fiddle with the coffeemaker while he was in the office by himself. She wanted to do something nice for him in return for his letting her go early—and for the news he'd given her. Keeping him away from the coffeemaker was the nicest thing she could think of.

When Willi Dorsch got on the commuter bus, he wore his uniform as if he'd slept in it. He'd shaved erratically. His hair stuck out from under his cap in all directions, like the hay in a stack made by somebody who didn't know how to stack hay. "Good heavens!" Heinrich Gimpel exclaimed. "What happened to you?"

"Another lovely night on the sofa," Willi answered, plopping his posterior down beside Heinrich. His breath was high-octane. As if to explain that, he went on, "I took a bottle with me for company last night. It was more fun than Erika's been lately, that's for damn sure."

"Will you be able to think straight when we get to headquarters?" Heinrich asked. "Maybe you should have called in sick instead of letting people see you like this."

"Coffee and aspirins will make a new man of me," Willi assured him. "That wouldn't be so bad. I'd say the old one's worth about thirty pfennigs, tops. Besides, if I called in sick I'd have to spend more time with the blond bitch, and I'm not—quite up for that." He belched softly.

Heinrich wondered if he ought to leave it there. But he and Willi had been friends for a long time. He felt he had to ask the next question: "If you're so unhappy, why are you still there?"

"The kids," Willi answered simply. "Joseph and Magda mean everything to me. If I walk out, Erika will fill their heads full of lies about me. Things are bad enough as is." He glanced over at Heinrich. "You're a lucky bastard, you know that? Things go so smooth for you. As far as I can see, you haven't got a single worry in the whole goddamn world."

That would have been funny, if only it were funny. Instead of shrieking mad laughter, which was what he wanted to do, Heinrich answered, "Well, I would have said the same about you and Erika till a few months ago."

"Only goes to show you can't tell from the outside," Willi said. That was truer than he knew, but Heinrich didn't say so. His friend pointed ahead. "We're just about to the station."

"So we are." Heinrich got ready to hurry to the platform where they'd catch the train from Stahnsdorf up to Berlin's South Station.

Willi groaned when he had to get up. "My head's going to fall off," he said. "I almost wish it would."

"You can probably get aspirins in the station, if you need them that badly," Heinrich said.

"Well, so I can. And so I will. And I can get coffee, too, even if it's shitty coffee. I was going to wait till I made it to the office and buy them at the canteen, but to hell with that. I feel too lousy." Willi sounded as haggard as he looked.

When they got to the station, he made a beeline for the little concession stand at the back. Heinrich, meanwhile, bought a *Völkischer Beobachter* from a vending machine. Willi joined him on the platform a couple of minutes later. He too had a paper under his arm. He peeled two aspirin tablets from a foil packet and used a gulp of coffee to wash them down. Heinrich said, "That's got to be hell on your stomach, especially if you drank too much last night."

"Now ask me if I care," Willi answered. "The way my head's banging, I'm not going to worry about anything farther south."

He winced when the train came up, even though it was powered by electricity, and not nearly so noisy or smelly as a steam engine or a diesel locomotive would have been. He let Heinrich sit by the window, and pulled his cap down low on his forehead to keep as much light as he could out of his eyes. When the train got moving, he pretended to read the *Völkischer Beobachter,* but his yawns and his glazed expression said it was just pretense.

Heinrich, by contrast, went through the paper with his usual care. He tapped a story on page three. "The *Führer*'s going to speak on the televisor tomorrow night."

"Be still, my beating heart." Willi was indifference personified. "I've heard a speech or two—thousand—in my time."

"I know, I know. Most of the time, I'd say the same thing." Heinrich tapped the *Beobachter* again. "But don't you think this particular speech might be interesting, after what he said in Nuremburg?"

"Nobody knows what he said in Nuremburg—nobody except the *Bonzen,* and they aren't talking much," Willi replied. But he'd heard the same rumors Heinrich had; he'd heard some of them *from* Heinrich. And maybe the aspirins and coffee were starting to work, for he did perk up a little. "All right, maybe it will be interesting," he admitted. "You never can tell."

"If he's serious about some of the things he said there—"

"The things people say he said there," Willi broke in.

"Yes, the things people say he said there." Heinrich nodded. "If he said them, and if he meant them—"

Willi interrupted again: "Half the people—more than half the people—will watch the football game anyhow, or the cooking show, or the one about the SS man where the American spy's always right on the edge of falling out of her dress. I swear she will one of these days."

Heinrich was damned if he'd let his friend outdo him for cynicism. "She won't when she's on opposite the *Führer*'s speech," he answered. "The programming director's head would roll if she ended up stealing that much of the audience."

"Mm, you've got a point there," Willi said. "Too bad." He managed a bloodshot leer.

"South Station!" came the call as the train glided to a halt. "All out for South Station!" Heinrich hurried up the escalators to catch the bus to *Oberkommando der Wehrmacht* headquarters. Willi shambled along after him like something created in a mad scientist's experiment that hadn't quite worked.

As soon as they got to the office, Willi headed off to the canteen. He returned with a large foam cup of coffee in each hand, and poured them both down in record time. Not surprisingly, he went to the men's room shortly thereafter, and then again a few minutes later. "Vitamin P," he said sheepishly when he came back after the second trip. "And speaking of Vitamin P, why didn't you tell me my eyes looked like two pissholes in the snow?"

"What could you have done if I had?" Heinrich asked.

"Well, nothing, but even so . . ." Willi opened those vein-tracked eyes very wide now. "I'm awake. I may live. I may even decide I want to."

Ilse came up to set some papers on his desk. She started to turn away, then stopped and did one of the better double takes Heinrich had seen. "Good God! What happened to you?" she said, almost exactly echoing his words of an hour earlier.

"Erika and I had a small disagreement last night," Willi answered. "Yes, that's about right. Just a small disagreement."

"You poor dear!" Ilse was the very picture of sympathy, fussing over him, straightening his collar, and generally making him feel three meters tall. He lapped it up like a cat in front of a bowl of cream. Heinrich had to suppress a strong impulse to retch. On the other hand, he wondered how long it had been since Erika buttered Willi up like that. Such artful dodges weren't her style.

Later that morning, Willi said, "I'm going to lunch with Ilse today."

"Why am I not surprised?" The tart retort came out of Heinrich's mouth before he could stop it.

His friend turned red. "I don't know. Why aren't you? You've got things going good for you now, so you get all sanctimonious. If you were the one with troubles, I wouldn't look down my nose at you."

"You wouldn't? What's the fun in having a nose if you don't look down it?" Heinrich replied, even more deadpan than usual.

Willi looked at him, started to say something, and then started to laugh instead. "Dammit, how am I supposed to stay angry at you when you come back with things like that?"

"If you work at it, I expect you'll manage," Heinrich said, again with next to no inflection in his voice. He got another laugh from Willi, too, although he hadn't been joking.

Ilse snuggled up to Willi as they walked toward the door. Willi slipped his arm around her waist. Heinrich went back to his paperwork. *Would I do something like that if I were having trouble with Lise?* he wondered. *Who knows? Maybe I would.* But he had trouble imagining trouble with Lise. *Maybe I don't understand how lucky I am.*

The telephone on Willi's desk rang. Heinrich was going to let it keep ringing till whoever was on the other end got sick of it and hung up. But what if it turned out to be somebody with important business? He picked up his own phone and dialed Willi's extension to transfer the call. "Analysis—this is Heinrich Gimpel."

"Oh, hello, Heinrich—I wanted to talk to Willi." That was Erika Dorsch's voice. Heinrich winced. He wished he'd let the phone ring. When he didn't answer right away, she asked, "Where is he?" in a way he didn't like at all.

He responded with the exact and literal truth: "You missed him by two minutes—he just went to lunch."

"And he didn't go with you, obviously," Erika said. Heinrich *really* wished he hadn't answered the telephone. Willi's wife went on, "Did he go with the lovely and talented Ilse instead?"

"I, ah, didn't see him leave," Heinrich said, which was true in the highly technical sense that he'd looked down at the papers on his desk before Willi actually opened the door.

"Now tell me another one, Heinrich. You aren't much of a liar, you know," Erika said. The way she meant it, that might have been true. In several ways she knew nothing about, it couldn't have been more wrong. That she knew nothing about those several ways proved how wrong it was.

He said, "Erika, I'm not his father. I'm not his watchdog, either. I don't keep an eye on him every minute."

"Somebody ought to," Erika Dorsch said bitterly. "Is something wrong with me, Heinrich? Am I ugly? Am I unattractive?"

"You ought to know better than that," he said, too surprised at the question not to give her an honest answer.

"Should I?" she said. "If something isn't wrong with me, why have we only made love six or seven times this year? Why is Willi going around with that round-heeled little chippie instead of me?"

"I don't know," Heinrich answered, which was also certainly true. If he'd had a choice between . . . But he didn't have choices like that, so what was the point of imagining he did? He said, "Don't you think you'd do better asking Willi? He might actually tell you."

"He'd tell me a load of garbage. That's what he's been telling me all along," Erika said. "What's he been telling you? That's probably more garbage."

Heinrich pretended not to hear her. Bad enough to have to listen to both sides in a dissolving marriage. To tell tales from one to the other . . . He shook his head. No. He didn't know much about such things, but he knew better than that.

"Can you get a little time off?" she asked. "If you come over here, I can tell you how things really are."

What was that supposed to mean? What it sounded like? If it did, would he kick himself for the rest of his days if he said no? Most red-blooded males would. He could arrange things so Lise never knew, and. . . .

"Erika," he said gently, "I don't think that would be a good idea right now."

"No?" She sounded tragic. "You mean you don't want me, either?"

"I—" He stopped. One more question for which there was no safe answer. He did his best: "I'm married to Lise, remember? I like being married to Lise. I want to stay married to her." He looked around to make sure nobody in the big room was paying too much attention to him. He couldn't do anything about anyone who might monitor the call. It wouldn't land him in trouble, anyhow. He consoled himself with that.

A long, long silence followed. At last, Erika said, "I didn't know people talked that way any more. Well." Another silence. "She's luckier than she knows—or else you can't get it up, either." The line went dead.

Heinrich stared at the telephone, then slowly replaced the handset in the cradle. He'd been ready to sympathize with Erika—even if he wasn't ready to go to bed with her—and to think Willi was a louse and a fool for not giving her more of what she obviously wanted. But if she kept making cracks like that, he didn't see how he could sympathize with either one of them—except they were both his friends. He muttered something that didn't help and trudged off to the canteen.

Susanna Weiss loved good food. What she didn't love was cooking. She should have; learning to cook, and to be happy cooking, was drummed into girls in the Greater German *Reich* in school and in the *Bund deutscher Mädel.* With Susanna, it hadn't taken. With Susanna, the more something was drummed into her, the less likely to take it was.

Frozen and freeze-dried food had come a long way since she was a girl. A lot of the advances had been military first; nothing was too good for the *Reich*'s soldiers and sailors. Little by little, things had trickled out to the civilian world as well. A faint stigma still clung to eating such food too often. It said you were lazy, or you didn't care enough about your family to take care of them yourself. Being a Jew, Susanna didn't worry about stigmas that were merely faint. And she was convinced she had better things to do with her time than stand in front of a stove. When she ate in her flat, she had frozen or freeze-dried food most of the time.

She was eating beef stroganoff that had started life in a plastic pouch when Heinz Buckliger came on the televisor screen. The Russians, those who were left alive, had been pushed east far past the Urals. Some of their recipes lingered on in the Germany they couldn't hope to threaten for generations.

Recorded, abridged versions of "*Deutschland über Alles*" and the "Horst Wessel Song" prefaced the *Führer*'s appearance. The screen cut to an image of the Germanic eagle with a swastika in its claws to the *Führer*'s study. Like so much Nazi architecture, the room was on a heroic scale that did its best to dwarf the man who occupied it. The walls of red marble with ebony wainscoting rose nearly ten meters to the cofferwork ceiling of rosewood. The televisor camera panned slowly, lovingly, along those walls. Along with gilded Party symbols, they held portraits of Bismarck, Hitler, Himmler, and a new one—over which the camera lingered—of Kurt Haldweim looking Viennese and aristocratic and more than a little snooty.

The picture cut away to the *Führer*'s desk. The cabinetmakers who'd created insanely ornate inlaid furniture for French noblemen during the

Old Regime would have owned they'd met their match in the craftsmen who made that desk. On the wall behind it hung a genuine Gobelin tapestry from the seventeenth century. Next to the tapestry, a German flag hung limply from a pole. Another gilded swastika-bearing eagle topped that pole.

As the camera shot tightened to the tawny leather chair in which Heinz Buckliger sat, the flag remained at the edge of the picture. Susanna had seen that whenever she watched a speech from the *Führer*. Tonight, she really noticed it, which was not the same thing. She gave a grudging nod of approval. Party propagandists didn't miss a trick. Of course they associated the head of state with the state itself. That they did it so she *didn't* consciously notice most of the time was a testimony to their skill.

Then she noticed something else, and her eyes widened. Heinz Buckliger was wearing a plain gray suit, not a Party uniform. She couldn't remember the last time she'd seen any *Führer* in civilian clothes. She wondered if she ever had. She didn't think so. Buckliger's necktie was of a red that perfectly matched the flag. After a moment, she saw it bore a pattern: small black swastikas. Any men's-wear store might have sold it.

What did that say? What did it mean? Anyone alert who watched the televisor looked for meanings behind meanings, for what was said without a word being spoken. What was Buckliger trying to get across here? All Susanna could think of was, *I'm as patriotic as the next fellow, but I'm transposing the tune into a new key.*

"Good evening, citizens of the Greater German *Reich*," the *Führer* said. "Not long ago, in Nuremberg, I spoke to officials of the National Socialist Party about some of the problems I see facing the *Reich* and the Germanic Empire. You also need to know some of the things I told them."

As who in the *Reich* had not, Susanna had seen films of Hitler. He'd dominated, whether screaming for war or vengeance, pleading for greater effort, or cajoling people into sacrifice. Himmler, who'd led Greater Germany and the Empire when she was a child, had dominated in a different way. His style was flatter than Hitler's, but you could sense the iron underneath. If you caused trouble, you would get it—in the neck. Kurt Haldweim had talked down to people, as if convinced he knew things no one else did. If he happened to be wrong, who was going to tell him? And if he happened to be wrong, would he ever admit it? Not likely.

Heinz Buckliger simply . . . spoke. "For a good many years now, we have been living off the great deeds of our ancestors," he said. "And our ancestors *were* great men who did great things. But we are like a family that lives off an inheritance from Grandpa, doesn't take care of its money very well, and doesn't have enough people in it who have gone out and looked for work on their own. After a while, the inheritance runs dry, and they have to figure out what to do next.

"I want to try to figure out what to do next *before* we run dry. We have plundered much of the world. But how long can that go on? Many of the folk of Western Europe and North America are as Aryan as we are. How long can we justify in racial terms their continued exploitation?"

Charlie Lynton had said things like that at the gathering of the British Union of Fascists. Susanna hadn't expected to hear them from him. Hearing them from the *Führer* was like a thunderclap. Like Lynton, Buckliger was using fascist ideology to cloak doing things that would have appalled his predecessors.

"Further conquest is not an option for us, as it was for Hitler and Himmler," he continued. "Forty years ago, we were lucky the United States didn't do us more damage. We could bring the Empire of Japan to its knees tomorrow—but if we did, Japan would bring us to our knees, too. Both we and the Japanese have too many rockets to make war anything but mutual suicide.

"So what are we to do? Things aren't the way they were in our fathers' time, and they certainly aren't the way they were in our grandfathers' time. Do we go on looking at our troubles in the same old way? This, it seems to me, is foolishness. When Hitler saw the *Reich* with troubles that were new in his time, did he answer them the way his parents and grandparents had? Of course not! He changed with the times. We must always change with the times, or the times will change without us."

"He's doing it again!" Susanna exclaimed, too excited to keep quiet. Fascist ideology didn't lend itself to change. What was fascism, after all, but reaction on the march? But, like Charlie Lynton, Heinz Buckliger had seen that, if he appealed to well-established authority to justify the changes he was making, he might have a chance of getting away with them. The Party *Bonzen*—and the Party rank and file—were surely listening to him along with everybody else. What did they think? Did they understand what they were hearing?

Or am I the one who's wrong? Susanna wondered. *Am I hearing what I want to hear, listening with my heart and not my head?* The last time she'd done that was with the boyfriend who'd turned out to be a lush, the one Heinrich still teased her about every now and then.

She cursed softly. Lost in her own thoughts, she'd missed a few sentences of what Buckliger was saying. ". . . greater responsiveness to the needs and desires of the *Volk* as a whole," was where she started paying attention again. "Of course we cannot and will not challenge the primacy of the Party and of National Socialist ideals, but are we not all Aryans together?"

When he said *of course,* he sometimes meant anything but. How many people would see that? Instead of going into detail, as she'd hoped he would, he continued, "This is a topic I will return to in times to come. Staying on old ground is always safe and certain. That is the reason so many of us like it so well. Finding a new way is harder. We may make mistakes. We probably will. But, if we keep going long enough, we will find ourselves in a place we never could have reached by sticking with the tried and true. Let us make the journey together. Good night."

The *Führer*'s study vanished from Susanna's televisor screen—from televisor screens all over the *Reich.* Horst Witzleben's familiar newsroom replaced it. The broadcaster said, "That was, of course, Heinz Buckliger, *Führer* of the Greater German *Reich* and the Germanic Empire." When Witzleben said *of course,* he meant it. He blinked a couple of times before going on, "An extraordinary address. A memorable address. The *Führer* set his mark on the *Reich.* As he leads us, as he guides us, so we shall go. That is our only proper—indeed, our only possible—course. A new era is upon us, and in times to come, as the *Führer* said, we shall learn exactly what this means. For now, good night, and I return you to your regularly scheduled programming."

Regularly scheduled programming was a vacuous quiz show. To Susanna, the hardest question was why anyone would watch it. People did, though. She heard them talking about it.

What *she* wanted to talk about was Buckliger's speech. She hurried to the telephone. *The Gimpels or the Stutzmans?* she wondered as she picked it up. After a moment's hesitation, though, she replaced the handset in the cradle without calling anyone. After a speech like that, weren't the phone lines too likely to be monitored? And wasn't she likely to be under some suspicion anyhow, as someone who knew the Kleins? Better safe than sorry. That wasn't heroic, but it was probably smart.

No one called her that night, either. Heinz Buckliger talked about abandoning old ground and striking out in new directions. The people living in the Greater German *Reich* were only too familiar with the old ground, and with its minefields. Buckliger might lead. After so long making such careful calculations, could the people follow?

At the bus stop, Emma Handrick sniffed. "I saw a little of the speech last night," she told Alicia Gimpel. "Only a little, though. He didn't look like a *Führer* to me. How could he be a *Führer* if he wasn't wearing a uniform?"

Seeing Heinz Buckliger in an ordinary suit had also startled Alicia. Still, she said, "He's the *Führer,* all right. Who else could he be? He spoke from the *Führer*'s study. We've seen it a million times. Who else could do that? What would they do to somebody who tried?" She didn't quite know who *they* might be, but there was always a *they* for such things. She had no doubt of that.

Emma sniffed. "He didn't look like it." She had a one-track mind. "He looked like a businessman or a salesman." In the regimented *Reich,* there weren't too many groups that didn't wear uniforms of one sort or another.

"He does seem to be something different," Alicia said. Her parents had warned her not to talk too much about Buckliger's speech; people might pay unusual attention to what she said. Since she wasn't sure how much was too much, she changed the subject: "New school year coming up in a couple of weeks."

"Thank heavens!" Emma exclaimed. "I don't care who I get next time. *Herr* Kessler thinks he's a concentration-camp guard, not a teacher."

Emma didn't care what she said, or who heard it. Alicia envied her. "Some of the others are just as bad," she said.

"They're pretty bad, all right. I think you have to be mean to want to be a teacher—look at Beast Koch," Emma said. "I never had her, but still. . . . Kessler's the worst I ever had."

"He's not very good," Alicia agreed. She hadn't had *Frau* Koch, either, and thanked heaven she hadn't. She pointed down the street. "Here comes the bus."

When they got to school, they played in the yard till it was time to line up in front of their classroom. Less than half a minute before the bell rang, Emma let out a gasp of horror. "I was going to ask you for your arithmetic homework," she said in stricken tones. "I couldn't do it last night."

"Too late now," Alicia said. The clang of the bell confirmed her words.

Herr Kessler opened the door. "*Guten Morgen, Herr* Kessler!" the children chorused. "He's going to skin me," Emma whimpered under that chorus. Alicia could only stand there. Her friend was all too likely to be right.

"Good morning, children," the teacher said. "Come in now, and no talking out of turn."

In they filed. If anybody talked, Alicia didn't hear it. Neither did Kessler. He led them in the salute to the flag. Their arms shot out. Alicia remembered how, up till this past spring, she'd been proud to be a German like everybody else. Part of her still was. The rest recoiled in horror from the very idea. There were times when she wondered if she'd been torn in two inside.

But she didn't have time to stay torn in two, not when *Herr* Kessler prowled to the front of the classroom. All of her had to pay attention to him. "How many of you saw the *Führer*'s speech last night?" he asked. Most of the students' hands went up. Kessler pointed to a boy who hadn't raised his. "Hans Dirlewanger!"

"*Jawohl, Herr* Kessler!" Hans jumped from his seat and stood stiff and straight.

"Why didn't you watch that speech?" Menace lurked in the teacher's voice. His eyes went to the paddle on the wall.

"Sir, my father is a captain in the *Wehrmacht*," Hans answered. "He came home on leave from occupation duty in the United States. We all went out to supper, and then to the cinema. We didn't get home till late."

"Oh." *Herr* Kessler considered. Reluctantly, he nodded. "This is acceptable. Be seated." As Hans sat down, Alicia wondered if the teacher would pick on somebody else so he could give out a swat. Not this morning, though. Kessler paused, then found a question: "What is the most important thing the *Führer* said last night?"

Had he asked about arithmetic or history or grammar, Alicia's hand would have shot into the air. Had he asked about this before she knew what she was, she would also have been eager to answer. Now she hesitated. She couldn't help worrying that a mistake would endanger not only her but all the other Jews in Berlin, even the ones of whose existence she was ignorant.

Others weren't so shy—and had less to worry about. The teacher pointed to a girl. "Trudi Krebs!"

That's interesting, Alicia thought. *She probably hasn't had less to worry about than I do.* But now that new ways of doing things seemed important, *Herr* Kessler thought Trudi had the answers. Before, he'd wanted to see her and her family in trouble. Trudi said, "The *Führer* told us the *Reich* needs to change so it can work better."

When she put it like that, it seemed safe enough. The teacher nodded. "*Sehr gut,*" he said. "Yes, that is exactly what the *Führer* said. And so, as he leads us, we shall change, and we shall be better for it. Do you understand?"

"*Ja, Herr* Kessler!" the children sang out.

"*Sehr gut,*" Kessler said again. "Then let us go on with the day's lesson." He spoke with a certain amount of relief, or so it seemed to Alicia. Did he sometimes think, as she did, that too much talk of politics might be dangerous? If students got answers wrong, they got paddled. What happened to teachers who got answers about politics wrong? Maybe *Herr* Kessler didn't want to find out. He nodded. "Arithmetic, then. Pass in your homework. At once. No talking."

Behind Alicia, Emma Handrick let out a soft gasp of dismay. Kessler's head swung toward her. But he couldn't decide who had made the sound. Sometimes he punished everyone in the neighborhood if he didn't know just who had got out of line. Maybe he still felt on unsafe ground today, for he looked away.

But then he said, "We will do some of the problems at the blackboard." He called on Alicia and several children who sat near her. She knew what he was doing. If one of them had no idea what to do, he would decide that was the person who'd made a noise. It wasn't a bad ploy in the unending war between teachers and students—except that he didn't summon Emma to the board.

Alicia got her problem right. She stood in front of the blackboard till Kessler nodded and sent her back to her seat. One boy made a mistake, but it was a careless, obvious kind of mistake: he multiplied seven by four and got thirty-five early in the problem, which naturally made his answer wrong. Other than that, he knew what he was doing. *Herr* Kessler corrected him, but didn't haul out the paddle.

Balked, the teacher went on with the lesson. Alicia hated these problems. If the German fighter plane flew forty kilometers an hour faster than the American one, started from a base sixty kilometers behind it, and took off fifteen minutes later, how far would it have to go to catch up? You had to keep track of everything at once. She was good at that kind of thing, but even she found it hard. She wondered how poor Emma, who wasn't any too bright, was faring.

After arithmetic came grammar. *Herr* Kessler passed out worksheets where the student had to identify parts of speech and the cases of nouns and adjectives. While they slaved away on those, he graded their arithmetic papers.

Alicia was good at arithmetic, but she was very, very good at grammar. She zipped through the paper, and finished well ahead of anybody else. Of course, all that got her was the chance to sit quietly till the other children finished, too. She watched the teacher correcting papers. Every so often, he would look up to see if anyone was getting into mischief, and she would have to look away. But then he would go back to arithmetic, and she would go back to watching him.

She knew when he got to Emma's homework. She'd got a glimpse of it as they passed papers forward, and it was truly hopeless. *Herr* Kessler's head came up. He stared towards Emma. He might have been a cat spotting a juicy mouse.

"Emma Handrick!" he roared.

Emma squeaked in terror. She'd been intent on her worksheet, and hadn't paid attention to what the teacher was doing. "*Jawohl, Herr* Kessler!" she said, springing to her feet.

"What is the meaning of this—this *Dreck* you turned in?" Kessler waved the offending paper for everyone to see.

"I'm very sorry, *Herr* Kessler," Emma babbled. "I tried as hard as I could, but I really didn't understand. Please excuse me. Please."

"A Jew could have done better work than this. Jews were vile and wicked, but they were supposed to be clever. You, on the other hand . . ." The teacher let that hang in the air, then added two more words: "Come here."

He applied the paddle with vigor. Emma came back to her desk biting back the tears that would have landed her in more trouble. She sat down gingerly. No one said anything at all.

At lunchtime, Trudi Krebs sidled up to Alicia and whispered, "When the new *Führer* changes things, do you think he'll change school, too?"

"*Gott im Himmel,* I hope so," Alicia exclaimed. "It's probably too much to ask for, though." She hoped Trudi would argue with her, but the other girl only nodded.

When the bus out of the Stahnsdorf train station pulled up to Willi Dorsch's stop, Heinrich Gimpel got off, too. "What are you doing?" Willi said. "You don't live here—or if you do, Erika hasn't told me."

"Heh." Heinrich smiled what he was sure was a sickly smile. "Lise wanted me to pick up some onions and a head of cabbage at Tinnacher's grocery." He pointed toward the store, which, fortunately, lay in the direction opposite Willi's house.

"A likely story," Willi said, but he didn't sound as if he meant anything by it. With a sour laugh, he went on, "Hell, the way things are, why would I care if you were living there instead of me?" He didn't wait for an answer, but headed up the sidewalk toward his house.

Shaking his head, Heinrich walked over to the corner grocery. He was glad Lise hadn't sent him after potatoes. She inspected every spud he bought, and didn't seem to like about half of them. Harder for him to go wrong with onions and cabbage. *I'd never make a* Hausfrau, *not in a million years,* he thought.

BEST VEGETABLES IN TOWN! boasted the sign in Tinnacher's window. "*Guten Tag, Herr* Gimpel," the grocer said as Heinrich came in. He did have the best vegetables for several kilometers around, and he gave unmatched personal service. Lower prices at bigger stores that sold more kinds of things made staying in business hard for him even so.

With a certain amount of relief, Heinrich skirted the bins of potatoes and headed for the onions. Lise had said she wanted the mild purple ones, not the stronger ones with the yellow-brown outer layer. Intent on the onions, Heinrich almost bumped into Erika Dorsch before he noticed she was there.

If he had noticed her, he might have tried to sneak out of the grocery and buy his vegetables somewhere else. Too late for that now. "Hello, Erika. I didn't mean to run over you there," he said, fearing his smile here was even sicklier than the one he'd given Willi.

Hers, on the other hand, dazzled. She had a stringbag full of mushrooms and garlic and scallions and potatoes and a couple of enormous turnips. "It's all right," she said. "Any attention is better than none."

"Er—yes," he said, feeling as if he were walking into a hornets' nest but unable to escape. He did his best: "Excuse me, please. I need some of those purple onions."

Erika didn't step aside. "Heinrich, why don't you like me?" she asked.

Hornets all around, sure as hell. "I like you fine," he said. "I still need onions, though."

"You don't act like you like me," Erika said.

She said it most pointedly—too pointedly for him to ignore. "I like you fine," he repeated. "I also like your husband. I also like my wife."

"I like your wife, too," Erika said. "So what? As for my husband, you're welcome to him. And if you like him the way you like me, the Security Police will sew a pink triangle on your camp uniform for you."

If he got a camp uniform, it would have a yellow Star of David, not a pink triangle. Would they bother? Or, if they found out what he was, would they just dispose of him like a crumpled-up tissue? He suspected the latter, but he didn't want to find out. He said, "I really do need those onions." He supposed he should have said something about not liking Erika that way, but she would have known he was lying.

"I've never chased a man in my life," Erika said, wonder in her voice. "Up till now, I never had to." Heinrich believed that. She eyed him with genuine curiosity. "What makes you so stubborn?"

I'm a Jew, he thought. *Of course I'm stubborn. I have to be. If I weren't stubborn, would I have clung to this?* He also had to be stubborn about not revealing what he was to anyone who could harm him with the knowledge. No matter how decorative Erika was, she fell into that group. She wanted him now, or thought she did. Odds were the challenge he represented interested her more than his skinny body did. But if she knew and she decided she didn't want him any more . . . In that case, he was one telephone call from disaster.

Since he couldn't tell her his first reason, he fell back on the second one: "I told you—I like Lise. We've been happy together for a long time. Why do I want to complicate my life? Life is complicated enough already."

"You make everything sound so sensible, so logical." Erika shook her head. "It isn't, not really."

Part of him knew she was right. But he clung to rationality anyhow—clung to it all the harder, perhaps, because it offered something of a shield against the horrors the German regime had perpetrated. "I try to make it that way for me, anyhow," he said.

She eyed him for a moment, then shook her head. "You'll find out," she said, and pushed past him to give her money to *Herr* Tinnacher.

Heinrich didn't like the sound of that. He also didn't like her going home with a stringbag full of vegetables. Willi was liable to think they'd arranged a meeting at the grocer's. Heinrich sighed. He couldn't do anything about that. He could get the onions and the cabbage. He took them up to Tinnacher.

The grocer weighed them, told him what they cost, took his five-Reichsmark note, and handed him change. Since Heinrich didn't have a sack of his own, Tinnacher grudgingly pulled one out from under the counter. "Fine-looking woman, *Frau* Dorsch," he remarked as he put the purple onions in on top of the cabbage.

"Can't argue with you there," Heinrich said.

"If she set her sights on me, I wouldn't complain." *Herr* Tinnacher chuckled rheumily. He was in his mid-sixties, and looked like a wizened frog. The chance that Erika would set her sights on him was better than the chance that he would win the state lottery, but it wasn't much better. Of course, without evidence to the contrary Heinrich would have said the same about the chance of her setting her sights on *him*. But he had that evidence, even if he didn't want it.

He also had to answer the grocer. "We're just friends," he said. Tinnacher chuckled again. That knowing little croak was one of the most obscene sounds Heinrich had ever heard. It said Tinnacher didn't believe a word of it. Heinrich got out of the grocery so fast, he almost left the sack with the cabbage and onions on the counter.

When he came home, he thrust the sack at Lise. "Here's your damned vegetables," he snarled.

"I'm sorry," she said in surprise. "If you'd told me it would be a problem, I would have gone and bought them myself."

"It's not the vegetables," he said. "I ran into Erika at the grocer's."

"Oh?" His wife packed a lot of meaning into one word. "And?" She packed a lot of meaning into two words, too.

"She's not happy with Willi. She's not happy with anything," Heinrich said.

"Would she be happy with you?" Lise asked.

"It doesn't matter. I wouldn't be happy with her," he answered. *Not for more than half an hour, anyway*. The animal part of him was harder to extinguish than he wished it were.

"Uh-*huh*." The look in Lise's eye said she knew all about that part. "And would you say the same thing if you were a *goy*?" She dropped her voice at the last word, which was one Jews could safely use only around other Jews.

Heinrich winced. It was a much better question than he wished it were. Instead of answering directly, he took two bottles of beer out of the refrigerator, opened them, and gave Lise one. "Here," he said, raising the bottle he still held. "Here's to us. I know when I'm well off."

"You'd better," she told him. She knew he hadn't really answered her. He could tell. She undoubtedly knew why, too. But she drank with him even so. If that wasn't love, he had no idea what to call it. She said, "I can't be too annoyed at you. She *is* pretty, and you do seem to have some idea where you belong. Some."

"I should hope so!" Heinrich said fervently.

Too fervently? So it seemed, because his wife started to laugh. "You also overact," she told him, and swigged from the beer.

"Who, me?" he said—overacting. Lise laughed louder. Changing the subject looked like a good idea, so he did: "How are the children?" He waited to see if Lise would let him get away with it.

She did, answering, "They're fine. Alicia is *so* glad she's getting out of *Herr* Kessler's class soon. I don't blame her a bit, either. I've talked with the man a few times. He wishes he belonged in the SS. Do you know what I mean?"

"Oh, yes." Heinrich nodded. "I had a couple like that myself. They're the lords of the classroom, and don't they know it?"

"Alicia asked if the new *Führer*'s changes would have anything to do with schools," Lise said. "How do you answer a question like that?"

" 'I don't know' usually works pretty well," he said. She made a face at him. He held up a hand. "I'm serious, sweetheart. Who can tell which way Buckliger's going to go with this stuff? He's already talked more about changing things than anybody who came before him. Will he do more than talk? Can he get away with more?"

His wife shrugged. "Who knows? We'll find out. And how are Erika's children?" She brought the question out casually, which only made it more dangerous.

"I don't know," Heinrich said, which was the truth. "She didn't talk about them."

"Uh-*huh,*" Lise said again: not quite *Mene, mene, tekel upharsin,* but a judgment just the same.

VIII

LIKE THE REST OF THE JEWS IN THE GREATER GERMAN *REICH*, LISE GIMPEL HAD never been to, never even seen, High Holy Days services. She'd heard about going to a synagogue to celebrate the New Year and the Day of Atonement from her grandfather. Being able to worship openly struck her as even more amazing than the holidays themselves.

She couldn't so much as fast on Yom Kippur. *Don't do anything to get yourself noticed* was a Jew's unbreakable rule. If, say, Roxane asked, *Why aren't you eating, Mommy?*—how could she answer? Whatever she said, her daughter might tell a school friend she'd stayed hungry all day long. If that reached the wrong ears . . . Even so small a thing could mean disaster.

And so she ate breakfast with everybody else, and silently apologized to God. Heinrich, no doubt, was doing the same thing. By the somber expression on Alicia's face, so was she. Lise had told her what the holidays were and what they meant and how they were supposed to be celebrated if only that were possible. Francesca and Roxane ate pancakes and sausage without the slightest idea that today was different from any other day.

Heinrich got to his feet and grabbed his attaché case. "I'm off," he said. "I'll see you all tonight." Collecting kisses all around, he hurried out the door. It closed behind him. Lise sighed and smiled at the same time. She didn't worry about him running off with Erika Dorsch or anybody else, even if she teased him. He wasn't the sort to leave unfinished anything he started. If his eyes sometimes wandered—well, he was a man. His hands and, more to the point, his heart didn't.

"Come on, eat up," Lise told the girls. "Then get out of your nightgowns and into school clothes. I know you don't have to leave as early as Daddy does, but you can't lie around eating grapes all day, either."

She got giggles from the younger two girls and a disdainful sniff from Alicia, who said, "You've used that one before, Mommy."

Lise wasn't about to put up with literary criticism before eight in the morning, especially when she hadn't finished her coffee (the biggest advantage she saw to not fasting on Yom Kippur was that she didn't have to miss it). She said, "I don't care whether I have or not. It's still true. Get moving."

Alicia was the one she had to bully, the one a bird or a book or anything else might distract from the business at hand. Francesca could barely grunt before ten, but she did what she had to do on automatic pilot. Roxane liked mornings, probably because her sisters didn't.

Lise got them out the door in good time. She always did, and she always breathed a sigh of relief once they were gone, too. *Especially today,* she thought. The Day of Atonement she wanted to herself. Had things been different, gathering with her fellow Jews would have been sweet. But, though they got together on minor holidays like Purim, they didn't dare meet on the big ones. Someone might be watching, might be listening, might be wondering. You never could tell.

She sat down in front of the televisor. It was off. She left it off, too. She didn't want any distractions, not while she was doing her best to forgive the people who'd troubled her during the past year. In spite of her earlier forgiving thoughts about Heinrich, she wasn't surprised when Erika rose to the top of the list. Lise's smile was slightly sour. Erika couldn't help being what she was, any more than a tiger could.

Things around a tiger had a way of ending up dead. Things around Erika . . .

Methodically, Lise went through the rest of the list, starting with *Herr* Kessler, who'd vexed her because he vexed Alicia, and ending with the cleaner who had returned a linen blouse with a scorch mark and without two buttons. Then she took on the hard one she attempted every Yom Kippur: to forgive the German people.

She'd never done it, not in her heart. She'd never even come close, and she knew it. That wasn't only because their crimes were so enormous, either. Worse, they had no idea they'd committed crimes. They were convinced they walked the path of truth and justice and righteousness. If they didn't see they had anything to atone for, what was the point to forgiving them? Was there any? Not that she'd ever been able to see.

This year . . . This year, for the first time since she was a girl, she wondered. Heinz Buckliger seemed to have some idea that the *Reich* and the *Volk* of the *Reich* didn't come to their dominant position in the world with hands perfectly clean. If the *Führer* thought the German people stood in need of atonement for some things . . . Well, how much did that mean?

Buckliger hadn't said a word about Jews, not in his speech on the televisor and not in anything else Heinrich and Walther had been able to uncover. But he had cast some doubt on the overwhelming importance of Aryan blood. And how much did *that* mean?

"I want to hope," Lise murmured, to herself and possibly to God. "It's been so long. I *want* to hope."

Willi Dorsch glowered in mock severity—Heinrich Gimpel hoped the severity was mock, anyway—as he climbed aboard the bus that would carry Heinrich and him to the Stahnsdorf train station. He sat down next to Heinrich and demanded, "Well, what have you got to say for yourself?"

Did he know? Had Erika been as forthright as she often was? Or had he just added two and two and come up with—surprise!—four? If he did know, he was going to have to come out and say so. "Well, how does 'good morning' sound?" Heinrich answered.

"It'll do." With a grin, Willi thumped him on the back. "Better than a lot of things you could have told me."

"I'm so glad." Heinrich hoped irony would keep Willi from noticing he was telling the exact and literal truth. Having got away with one question, he tried another: "And how are you today?"

"I could be worse. I have been worse. I probably will be worse again before too long," Willi answered. Heinrich concluded he and Erika hadn't fought during the night. The way things had been going with them, that was indeed something. His friend went on, "How about yourself?"

"Me? I just go on from day to day," Heinrich said. That was true enough. Getting through the High Holy Days every year reminded him of just how true it was.

"Just go on from day to day," Willi repeated, and sighed gustily. "Christ, I wish I could say the same. I never know if tomorrow will blow up in my face."

Neither do I, Heinrich thought. *And you're talking about your marriage. I'm talking about my life.* He'd grown very used to thinking things he couldn't say. What he could say was, "I hope everything turns out all right."

"You're a good fellow, you know that?" Willi sounded a little maudlin, or maybe more than a little, as he might have after too much to drink. But this morning he didn't smell like a distillery, and he didn't wince at every noise and every sunbeam like a man with a hangover. Maybe he really was just glad to have a friend. And how glad would he be after a few ill-chosen words from Erika?

Those words evidently hadn't come. Maybe they wouldn't. Heinrich dared hope. In the *Reich,* the mere act of hoping was—had to be—an act of courage for a Jew. With a shrug, Heinrich said, "All I know is, I've got too much work waiting for me at the office."

"Ha! Who doesn't?" Willi said. "Our section could have twice as many people in it, and we'd still be behind. Of course, if the new *Führer* cuts the assessments in the Empire the way he's been talking about, we'll all end up out of work."

"Do you think he will?" Heinrich asked with even more genuine curiosity than he dared show.

"Me? I'm not going to try and guess along with him any more, no, sir," Willi said. "I was wrong a couple of times, and all that proves is, I shouldn't do it."

The bus pulled into the train station. Heinrich and Willi hurried off. They both paused to buy copies of the *Völkischer Beobachter* from a vending machine, then went to the platform to catch the commuter train into Berlin.

They sat side by side, reading the paper. Heinrich, as usual, went through it methodically. Willi was a butterfly, flitting from story to story. He found as many interesting tidbits as Heinrich did, and sometimes found them faster. "Americans question assessment," he said, pointing to a piece on page five.

Heinrich, who hadn't got there on his own yet, flipped to the story. He read it, then shook his head. "They can question, but it won't do them much good," he said. "The occupying authorities will collected their pound of flesh one way or another."

"Ah, a pound of flesh." Willi laughed wistfully. "I remember how much fun that used to be."

Heinrich winced at the pun. Maybe that wince was what made him ask, "What about Ilse?" Normally, he would think such a thing, but he wouldn't say it. The wry joke had made him drop some of his defenses. He didn't like that. He couldn't afford to drop them, even for an instant.

Willi blinked. He hadn't expected the question, any more than Heinrich had expected to ask it. After a pause when Heinrich wondered if he would answer at all, he said, "Ilse's sweet, and she's good in bed, but it's not the same, you know what I mean?"

"I . . . think so," Heinrich said. He thought about making love with a near-stranger after so long with Lise and nobody else. Yes, that would be very odd, especially the first few times. Then he thought about making love with Erika, who was, after all, anything but a stranger. What would *that* be like? *Cut it out,* he told himself sternly. Most of him listened.

"You're lucky, being happy where you are," Willi said, and dove back into the newspaper.

"Yes, I suppose I am," Heinrich said, which was certainly the truth, for he would have been stuck where he was whether he was happy or not. Divorce drew notice to a couple, even these days. Jews mostly stayed married no matter how badly they got along.

A lot of *goyim* did the same thing. Willi said, "If it weren't for the kids, and if it weren't for the way people look at you funny afterwards, Erika and I would have split up by now. Hell, we may yet, in spite of all that stuff."

"I hope not," Heinrich said, which was true for all kinds of reasons his friend didn't understand. He chose one Willi would: "If you guys broke up, we'd have to find somebody else to beat at bridge."

"Ha! What *have* you been smoking?" That touched Willi's pride where a lot of other gibes wouldn't have. And if he thought of Heinrich as a rival at the card table, maybe he wouldn't worry about him any other way.

The train pulled into South Station. Heinrich and Willi rode the escalators to the upper level, where they caught the bus to *Oberkommando der*

Wehrmacht headquarters. Heinrich went to his desk with more than a little apprehension—not only because now he knew Willi was sleeping with Ilse, but also because the Americans were acting up. When they did that, they made his job harder. He had enough other things to worry about without trouble from the far side of the Atlantic.

But sure as hell, four people came up to him in the first hour he was there, all of them with the *Beobachter* in their hands. They all wanted to know what the Yankees would do, and what the *Reich* would do to them after they did it. "We'll have to wait and see," Heinrich said again and again, which satisfied no one.

He said the same thing to two more men on the telephone. One was a lieutenant general, a man who disliked ambiguity of any sort. "Dammit, I need to know if we're going to move or not," the officer growled.

"So do I, sir," Heinrich answered. The general swore and hung up.

When the telephone rang again, Heinrich felt like swearing, too. "Budget analysis—Gimpel speaking," he said.

"Good morning to you, *Herr* Gimpel. This is Charlie Cox, calling from Omaha." The American's German was fluent, but had the flat accent English-speakers gave the language.

"I know your name, *Herr* Cox. You are in the Department of the Treasury, *nicht wahr*? What can I do for you today?"

"You can tell me how serious *Herr* Buckliger is about a new deal for the different parts of the Germanic Empire." Cox didn't beat around the bush. And that, of course, would be *the* question in the eyes of any American administrator.

It was also *the* question, or at least closely related to *the* question, in Heinrich's eyes. It happened to be one he couldn't answer, either for Charlie Cox or for himself. "I'm very sorry, *Herr* Cox," he said, and meant it. "I don't make policy. I just implement it when someone else has made it."

Cox grunted. "Well, I don't suppose I really could have expected you to say anything else. But you've got to have some kind of idea about how things will work out. You're a hell of a lot closer there than we are here."

"If I knew, I would tell you," Heinrich answered, and he might even have meant that. "But I'm afraid I don't. The person who sets policy, whom I mentioned a moment ago, is the *Führer,* no one else. When he decides what he wants to do, we will do it."

"Do it to us," Cox muttered in English. Heinrich was less fluent in that language than, say, Susanna Weiss, but he spoke it well enough. Even though the Empire ran on German, English came in handy for dealing with Americans. Charlie Cox had just put his life in Heinrich's hands.

"Sooner or later, we will all see what the *Führer* has in mind," Heinrich said. While true, that was unlikely to be comforting. "In the meantime, I suggest you pay your assessments promptly. That way, there won't be any unfortunate incidents both sides might regret."

"Incidents we would regret a hell of a lot more than the *Reich* does." Cox dared say that in German.

"Probably," Heinrich agreed. "The losing side does have a way of regretting incidents more than the winners."

"If we didn't know that already, *Herr* Gimpel, the past forty years would have proved it to us," Cox said. "*Auf wiedersehen.*" He hung up.

From his desk a couple of meters away, Willi Dorsch asked, "The Americans?"

Heinrich nodded. "Oh, yes. Did you expect anything else? They want to see how much they can get away with, too."

"Who doesn't, these days?" Willi said. "If we had any Jews left, they'd be trying to persuade us they were good Aryans, too." He laughed at the absurdity of the notion.

Heinrich laughed, too. But the shriek inside didn't go away. One of these days, he would have an ulcer—or a stroke. A stroke had killed his father. Things came back to haunt you one way or another.

Ilse set some envelopes and a small package on his desk. "Morning mail delivery, *Herr* Gimpel," she said.

"Thank you," he answered, hardly looking up.

She went over to Willi's desk and gave him the same sort of stuff. "Here's yours, Willi," she purred in a bedroom voice.

"Thanks, sweetie." He made as if to grab her. Laughing, she spun away.

Heinrich punched keys on his calculator with altogether needless violence. *If you're going to have an office romance, can't you at least pretend you're not?* he wondered. *It makes life easier for everyone around you—especially people who know your wife.*

A moment later, another question crossed his mind. *Am I angry at Willi, or am I just jealous?* He shook his head. He didn't want Ilse. But the idea of having his choice between two women he did want . . . He shook his head again, annoyed at himself for poking beneath the surface. Purely in the abstract—or so most of him insisted—he liked that idea pretty well. *Maybe I am jealous of Willi after all.*

Alicia Gimpel liked the idea of a new year that began around the end of summer, a new year that corresponded to the beginning of the new school year. She liked it so well, she wished she could talk about it with her sisters and her friends. But her mother and father had both warned against that. "You never can tell who might be listening, or what they might know," her father had said. She could see how that made sense, but she didn't like it.

On the day the new school year started, she and everybody else who'd put up with *Herr* Kessler seemed happy enough even without a real New Year's celebration. At the bus stop, Emma Handrick said, "I feel like they just let me out of a camp. Whatever happens now, it can't be worse."

"He was awful, all right," Alicia agreed. She turned to Francesca, who stood close by. With a big-sisterly combination of concern and sadism, she said, "Maybe *you'll* have him next year."

"You're mean!" Francesca said shrilly. "I've got *Frau* Koch this year. Isn't that bad enough?"

"Getting stuck with the Beast is pretty bad, all right." Alicia spoke with sincere but detached sympathy. She hadn't been unlucky enough to have *Frau* Koch herself.

Emma said, "I wonder what this *Herr* Peukert is like. He's new. Nobody knows anything about him yet." The noise of a motor made her look down the street. She nodded to herself—the bus was coming. "Whatever he's like, he can't be worse than Kessler." She spoke with the conviction of someone who'd been paddled more often than she thought she should have.

The schoolyard held more confusion than usual that morning, with students lining up in front of unfamiliar rooms—and with new kindergartners not sure they should line up at all. Their teachers came out early and shouted them into place. Alicia smiled at the little kids from the height of just-turned-eleven. It had, of course, been a million years ago when *she* had so little idea of what to do. Even Roxane was starting first grade now.

"*Guten Morgen, Kinder.*" A man's voice close by made Alicia forget the kindergartners and her little sister, too.

"*Guten Morgen, Herr* Peukert," she said, along with the rest of the fifth-graders in her line. Somebody—she couldn't see who—said, "*Guten Morgen, Herr* Kessler," out of habit. That drew a few giggles from children close by, but the chorus must have drowned it out for the new teacher, since he didn't react.

Alicia sized him up. He was very tall—within a couple of centimeters of two meters. Was he taller than her father? She thought so. The resemblance ended with height. *Herr* Peukert was blond and bronzed and broad-shouldered. He held himself so straight, he might have had a ramrod in place of his spine.

Behind Alicia, Emma breathed, "Oh! Isn't he gorgeous?"

Under the new teacher's ice-blue stare, several of the boys in line tried to stand straighter themselves. Before taking the class inside, Peukert called off names from the roll book he carried. He looked at the students as they answered, matching faces to names. Alicia looked back steadily when he came to hers. She wasn't thinking of herself as a Jew just then, only as somebody wondering what the next year—a very long time for a fifth-grader—would be like.

"Here!" Emma said when *Herr* Peukert called her name next. Her voice held a funny catch Alicia had never heard in it before. She looked back over her shoulder. Emma was gazing at the new teacher with what could only be adoration. Alicia had never before found a recognizable thing to go with the word. Now she did.

When *Herr* Peukert finished calling the roll, he led the class into the room. The children sat down in the same alphabetical order they'd used to take their places in line. Then they rose to give the flag the Party salute and to call out, "*Heil* Buckliger!" Daily rituals accomplished, they sat down again.

Alicia didn't expect much to happen on the first day of the new school year, and she proved right. *Herr* Peukert talked a little about what he expected them to learn in the upcoming term. "Ask questions," he urged them. "Things are changing. What we used to think we were sure of isn't always so clear any more. Some people think this is exciting. It frightens others. However you feel, though, it won't go away any time soon. You'd better get used to it."

He passed out arithmetic books, grammar books, books of stories, and geography books to the students. Alicia filled out a white card and a blue card for each textbook, giving her name, her teacher's name, the title of the book, and the condition of the copy she had. The cards warned her that her parents would have to pay if she damaged the book.

"Question, *Herr* Peukert!" Trudi Krebs raised her hand.

"Go ahead, Trudi," the teacher said. Alicia nodded, impressed in spite of herself. One way students judged teachers was by how fast they learned the names of the children in their class. Peukert was doing well.

"Sir, where are our history books?" Trudi asked.

That flabbergasted Alicia. She'd been so busy filling out cards and sneaking glances at the books she had got, she hadn't noticed one was missing. She made a face—not quite what her parents annoyed her by calling her Angry Face, but close. She didn't like missing things, not one bit.

Herr Peukert took the question in stride. "I told you, things are changing. They're writing a new history book, but it isn't done yet, so I can't give you that one. They've decided the old one isn't so good, so I can't give you that one, either. For a while, we'll make do without one."

How could things in history change? That flummoxed Alicia all over again. Either they'd happened or not, right? So it seemed to her. Or did the teacher mean the new history book would get rid of some lies in the old one? That would be good, if it happened. She didn't suppose she could ask him if the old book was full of lies. Too bad.

"Question, *Herr* Peukert!" That was Emma Handrick. Alicia wanted to poke a finger in her ear. Emma never asked questions. She didn't care enough about school—except when it came to avoiding the paddle—to bother with them. And then Alicia understood. Emma still didn't care about school. She cared about *Herr* Peukert.

"Go ahead," the teacher said. He didn't remember Emma's name right away, as he had with Trudi's.

Emma must have noticed. She was noticing everything about him. But she plowed ahead anyway: "*Herr* Peukert, is the *Führer* always right?"

There was a question to make politically alert people sit up and take notice. Trudi Krebs stared at Emma. So did Wolfgang Priller, who liked the way things always had been much better than Trudi seemed to. Emma was oblivious. All she'd wanted was to make the teacher pay attention to her.

She'd done that. *Herr* Kessler would have said yes and gone about his business. *Herr* Peukert looked thoughtful. By Emma's soft sigh, that made him seem more intriguing. Slowly, he said, "When he speaks as the head of the *Reich* or the head of the Party, he tells us which way we need to go, and we need to follow him. When he's just talking as a man . . . well, any man can be wrong."

Even you? Alicia thought. *Herr* Kessler never would have admitted anything like that, not in a million years. Alicia had always liked school; she soaked up learning the way a sponge soaked up water. But the days ahead looked a lot more interesting than the ones with *Herr* Kessler that she'd just suffered through.

When they went out for lunch, Emma sighed and looked back over her shoulder toward the classroom. "Isn't he wonderful?" she said.

"He's . . . not bad," Alicia answered. The one was higher praise from her than the other was from Emma.

Susanna Weiss had always watched the evening news with interest. If she wanted to know what was going on in the *Reich* and the world (or what the powers that be wanted people to think was going on—not always the same thing, or even close to it), that was the place to start. Since Kurt Haldweim's death, she'd watched the news with fascination, which also wasn't the same thing.

"Good evening," Horst Witzleben said from her televisor screen. The set from which he spoke hadn't changed. Neither had his uniform. But something about him had. Susanna had needed a while to notice it, let alone figure out what it was. Before Heinz Buckliger became *Führer,* Witzleben had talked to the people of the Greater German *Reich*. Now he talked *with* them. The difference was subtle, but she was convinced it was real.

She glanced down at the quiz she was grading. Most of her undergraduates wouldn't have recognized a subtlety if it walked up and bit them in the leg. *Would I, when I was twenty?* she wondered. Without false modesty, she thought she would have done better than they could. Of course, she was a Jew. Spotting subtleties helped keep her alive.

She scrawled *Not necessarily!* in red beside a sweeping generalization, then paused with her pen frozen a couple of centimeters above the page. How did she know none of her students was a Jew? She didn't. All she knew was, none of them came from a family she was acquainted with. Given how secretive Jews had to be, that didn't prove a thing. There could be another little Jewish community in Berlin, parallel to hers but unaware it existed.

If that went on for a few hundred years and then they got to come out into the light of day once more, would one group recognize the other as Jews? Or would their beliefs have changed so much in isolation that one saw the other as nothing but a pack of heretics?

Susanna laughed at herself. Talk about building castles in the air! She'd not only lost the thread of the student's argument, such as it was, she'd also lost track of what Horst was saying. Pretty impressive woolgathering, especially when what she'd wondered about was so completely unprovable—to say nothing of unlikely.

The picture cut away to an advertisement for Volkswagens, and she realized the whole lead story had gone in one ear and out the other. It had been . . . something to do with banditry in the Caucasus, she thought. She wouldn't have sworn to it. In one ear and out the other, all right.

Mercifully, the singing advertisement ended. Horst Witzleben's handsome, regular features returned to the screen. He said, "The *Führer* announced today that a division of occupation troops will soon return to the *Reich* from the United States. *Herr* Buckliger said, 'The situation no longer calls for so large a force in a country nearly as Aryan as our own.' "

Susanna frowned. Not very long before, Buckliger had questioned whether Aryan blood really mattered as much as Party doctrine said it did. Now he was using it as an excuse to pull soldiers back from the USA. What did he really think about it? Did he have any consistent beliefs, or was he just grabbing whatever tools came to hand for a given job?

Before Susanna could decide what she thought about that, Witzleben went on, "In London, Charles Lynton, the recently chosen head of the British Union of Fascists, applauded the *Führer*'s move."

The newsreader's face disappeared again, to be replaced by Charlie Lynton's boyish visage. In pretty good German, Lynton said, "This important step can only lead to better relations between the *Reich* and the states that make up the Germanic Empire. Recognizing the proud history of many of these states, *Herr* Buckliger begins to give them some say in their internal affairs, for which I applaud him."

Instead of returning to Witzleben, the camera cut away to an advertisement for Agfa cameras and film. That gave Susanna a moment to scratch her head and think. Was Buckliger really giving the USA any say in its internal affairs? She'd taken the troop transfer as a cost-cutting measure. There'd been a lot of those lately. But maybe Lynton had a point. With fewer *Wehrmacht* soldiers around to point guns at their heads, the Americans would be able to do more as they pleased, with less fear of having their actions forcibly overruled.

When the advertisement ended, Horst Witzleben came back on camera. "The leaders of France, Denmark, and Finland were also quick to express their unreserved approval for *Herr* Buckliger's order." Their photos came up on the screen, but they didn't get quoted, as Charlie Lynton had. Witzleben continued, "And the King of Italy and the *Duce* both termed the *Führer*'s move a positive step. In other news . . ."

That chorus of approval and applause didn't sound as if it had sprung from nowhere. It sounded as if Heinz Buckliger had carefully orchestrated it ahead of time. While Witzleben showed horrific footage of a train wreck in Hungary, Susanna wondered what that meant if it was true. It struck her that Buckliger was a politician of a sort that no previous *Führer*, except maybe Hitler in his early days, had ever needed to be. She took that for a good sign.

But then she frowned again. Why did Buckliger need to be that kind of politician, where Hitler through most of his career, Himmler, and Haldweim hadn't? The only answer that occurred to her was that Buckliger was facing opposition of a sort his predecessors had never met. They'd ordered and been obeyed. He was ordering, too, but it also seemed he was cajoling and maneuvering in ways they hadn't had to.

Hitler invented Party doctrine, or most of it, Susanna thought. *Himmler and Haldweim believed in it. They didn't rock the boat—though there were long stretches when Haldweim didn't do much of anything. Buckliger's different. Buckliger* is *rocking it, sure as hell. No wonder the old guard's unhappy. And no wonder he has to—what's the English phrase?—to wheel and deal, that's it. If he doesn't, he's in trouble.*

Witzleben's next story was a tribute to the *Gauleiter* of Bavaria, a paunchy, jowly, white-haired man in a gorgeous uniform who was finally retiring after leading the Party organization in his state for more than forty years. And there was Heinz Buckliger, shaking his hand as he stepped down. "*Herr* Strauss' contributions cannot be overestimated," the *Führer* said graciously. "He served the *Reich* and the Party long and well. New blood comes, though. Such is the way of nature."

Buckliger said no more than that. He let pictures do the rest of the work for him. There he stood, strong and vigorous, next to the doddering official who'd been in charge for so long. *Which would you rather see over you?* the image asked without words.

Doing something like that would never have occurred to gray, astringent Kurt Haldweim. For one thing, he'd been even older than Strauss, old enough to have fought in the Second World War. For another, all through his long rule he'd never believed in putting anybody out to pasture. And, for a third, he, like Himmler, had taken the televisor largely for granted. Buckliger didn't. Like Hitler long before him, he understood exactly how much pictures could do.

Susanna wished she hadn't thought of it that way. She wanted to like Buckliger, wanted to trust him, wanted to believe him, wanted to reckon him a new star in the Nazi firmament. He was different from anything she'd ever known. But did that make him *really* different? Did it make him *better*? Hitler, after all, had been dead for years before she was born.

She shook her head. The longer Hitler stayed in charge of things, the more power he'd gathered into his own hands. Buckliger seemed to be going in the opposite direction. He hadn't quashed Charlie Lynton for proclaiming his allegiance to the first edition, the democratic edition, of *Mein Kampf*. He'd even talked about it himself.

And so? Susanna wondered. *The devil can cite Scripture for his purpose.* Shakespeare wasn't quite medieval English. When the quotation occurred to her, she had to look it up to see which play it came from. She shivered when she found it. It was from *The Merchant of Venice.*

When Heinrich Gimpel found something he could sink his teeth into, he worked like a man possessed. His surroundings all but disappeared, leaving nothing but the numbers he was manipulating, his right hand dancing on the calculator or the keypad of the computer keyboard, and the figures going up on the screen.

The only reason he looked up from this particular blitz of calculations was to take another sheet full of raw data out of his in-box. When he did, he saw the office full of SS men in camouflage smocks, assault rifles at the ready. All the guns seemed to point straight at him.

He froze, the sheet of paper still between thumb and forefinger.

Willi Dorsch burst out laughing. A couple of the SS men grinned, too. "What's the matter, Heinrich?" Willi said. "Didn't you even notice them come in?"

"Uh, no," Heinrich said sheepishly.

Willi laughed some more. "I didn't think so. The way you were working there, the world could have ended, and you'd never have known the difference."

What went through Heinrich's mind was, *Oh, thank God. Maybe they haven't come for me, then.* He took another, less horrified, look at the big, blond, hard-faced men. When he didn't see them with eyes full of terror, the muzzles of their assault rifles pointed every which way.

"Uh—" He still couldn't avoid that dismayed stutter. "What *are* they doing here, then?"

Before Willi could answer, Heinz Buckliger strode into the room.

Along with everybody else at a desk, Heinrich sprang to his feet. He drew himself up as straight as he could. His right arm shot out. "*Heil* Buckliger!" he bawled at the top of his lungs. He remained in place, frozen like a statue.

Casually, the *Führer* returned the salute. Even more casually, he waved to the men in the analysis section. "Relax," he said, sounding much more like a human being than an icon. "This isn't anything fancy. I'm here to pick somebody's brain, that's all." He peered down at a piece of paper, then up, then down at the paper again. *It's an office plan,* Heinrich realized. *He's comparing the plan to the room.* And then, to his amazement, Buckliger's eyes met his. "You're Gimpel, *nicht wahr*?" the *Führer* said.

For a mad moment, Heinrich wanted to deny it. Clearly, that wouldn't do. He managed to mumble, "Uh, *ja, mein Führer*."

Heinz Buckliger seemed used to people mumbling and stammering when they spoke to him. "Good," he said. "I want to talk with you about the Americans." He snagged the chair by Heinrich's desk with his ankle, pulled it closer, and sat down in it. "By how much can we reduce their assessment to let their economy breathe a little easier and still keep ours going?" Noticing Heinrich still stood at attention, he waved him to his chair. He also waved to the rest of the people in the office. "Relax, I told you. Go back to work. Pretend I'm not here."

With those trigger-happy SS guards eyeing everybody, that wouldn't be easy. Heinrich dizzily sank into his seat. Of itself, the calculating part of his mind engaged the *Führer*'s question. Even as another part of him wailed, *This can't be happening,* he heard himself saying, "Well, sir, a lot of that depends on how much the Americans think they can get away with not paying if you let up on them. They're looking for signs of weakness."

"I don't want to be weak," Buckliger said. "I do want the *Reich* to be able to stand on its own two feet without being propped up so much from outside. That sets a bad example, and it sets a bad precedent, too, don't you think?"

He cocked his head to one side. Heinrich realized he really was waiting for an answer. *I want the* Reich *to grow like an onion—with its head in the ground.* No, he couldn't very well say that. "*Ja, mein Führer,*" was less truthful but much safer. As for the numbers . . . His right hand, flying on automatic pilot, cleared the figures he'd been working with and started entering the ones that would let him answer Buckliger's question.

"You have the data at your fingertips," the *Führer* said approvingly. "That's good. That's very good. Efficient."

"Thank you, sir. Assuming the Americans will keep on paying the same percentage of a lower assessment as they do of the current one, I would say you could reduce it by. . . ." His voice trailed off as his fingers flew on the keypad. He considered the answer the computer had given him, then passed it to Buckliger: "By about nine percent."

"Those are the figures from the machine, right?" Buckliger said. Heinrich nodded. The *Führer* asked, "What's your personal opinion of them?"

"That if you reduce the proposed assessment by nine percent, you'll get back fifteen to twenty percent less. That's if you don't go out and take the full assessment by force. Give the Americans a centimeter and they'll take a kilometer."

"I want to use less force in America, not more," Buckliger said. Since he was moving a division back to the *Reich,* Heinrich believed him. He went on, "All right, then. To get nine percent less revenue from the Americans, by how much would I have to reduce the assessment?"

That was a genuinely interesting question. "This is only an estimate, you understand," Heinrich warned as he started stroking the keypad again. "The computer is very good with numbers, not so good at figuring out how much people are liable to cheat."

"Aber natürlich." The *Führer* laughed. "We need other people for that."

"Uh, yes, sir," Heinrich said. Then he gave his attention back to the screen. Designing a function on the fly to figure out how much more enthusiastically the Americans would cheat if they saw their risks as diminished was nothing he'd ever tried before, but he did it. He punched ENTER one last time, looked at the answer on the screen, and slowly nodded to himself. "I'd say a formal cut of six percent, *mein Führer,* would give you an actual cut of nine."

Buckliger nodded. "Sounds reasonable. *Danke schön.* Your number's about what I'd figured for myself."

Heinrich wondered how to take that. He didn't think Buckliger could have made these calculations for himself. The new *Führer* had been a bureaucrat, but not that kind of bureaucrat. But Buckliger didn't sound as if he were just trying to make himself sound clever. After a moment, Heinrich realized working out how much the Americans were likely to cheat wasn't only a mathematical calculation. It was also a political calculation. And if anybody could make political calculations, the *Führer* was, or needed to be, the man.

"Happy to help, sir," Heinrich said. His own interior calculations hadn't taken more than a second and a half.

Heinz Buckliger gave him another one of those I'm-just-a-regular-fellow smiles. "Good. I like to have clever people working for me. It keeps the wheels going round." He got to his feet and nodded to the SS troopers. "Come on, boys. Now we go and talk with Field Marshal Tetzlaff." Out they went, some of the guards preceding Buckliger, the rest following.

A considerable silence reigned in the room after the *Führer* left. Heinrich tried to get back to what he'd been doing beforehand, but discovered he couldn't, not when everybody was staring at him. He simply sat there, dazed. The two thoughts that kept going round and round in his head were *Oh, thank God—I got away with it* and *Lise will never believe this, not in a million years.*

"Well, well," Willi said at last. "You and Field Marshal Tetzlaff, is it? And he came to see you first. Not too shabby, *Herr* Gimpel. No, sir, not too shabby." He got to his feet and saluted, as he had a few minutes earlier for the *Führer*.

That roused the Berliner's almost automatic cynicism in Heinrich. "Oh, *Quatsch*," he said. The room exploded in laughter. People came over to pound him on the back and shake his hand. Ilse perched on a corner of his desk, showing a lot of leg. She eyed him with frank calculation. She'd never looked at him *that* way before. He didn't particularly want her looking at him that way now.

I'm supposed to be invisible, dammit, he thought. *How can I be invisible when people keep . . . noticing me?* He felt absurdly indignant.

"Seriously, Heinrich my boy, I'd say your promotion chances just got themselves a kick in the pants." Willi didn't sound serious. He was grinning. To Heinrich's relief, his friend also didn't sound jealous. Willi went on, "I can just see your next performance review. There's the examiner, looking over what you've done. '*Ach, ja,* consulted with the *Führer*.' What can he say about *that*?"

"I don't know. If he's like most performance examiners, he'll find something rude," Heinrich answered. He hadn't meant it for a joke, but everybody laughed. Someone the *Führer* consulted had to be a very funny fellow. Heinrich reached for the telephone. "Excuse me, please. I'm going to call my wife."

Ilse stopped posing. She got down from his desk and stomped back to Willi's. Heinrich thought *that* was funny. He dialed for an outside line. When the dial tone shifted, he called his home number. "*Bitte?*" Lise said.

"Hi, sweetheart. It's me," Heinrich said. "You'll never guess who just came in. . . ."

"The *Führer* came to see a friend of mine last week," Esther Stutzman told her boss with what she hoped was pardonable pride.

Dr. Dambach nodded. He never seemed to get very excited about anything. "Good for your friend," he answered now. "I also know some people who have met him, though I haven't myself."

"Neither have I." Esther had never imagined wanting to meet the ruler of the Greater German *Reich* and the Germanic Empire, either. But maybe Buckliger was different. Maybe. Even wondering felt not only strange but also more than a little unnatural.

"I've been doing something interesting," Dr. Dambach said.

"Oh? What's that?" Esther asked, as she was plainly meant to do. Whatever it was, it didn't involve the coffeemaker. What the pediatrician thought interesting there was liable to seem ghastly to anybody else. Some of the things he'd done trying to fix coffee merited the word. Lately, though, the coffeemaker had been fine.

When he spoke, Esther wished he'd spent his time messing with the machine, for he said, "Do you remember how the Kleins' genealogy charts had two different versions?" He made it a casual question, for he didn't know how important it was to Esther.

"Yes, I do," she answered. *I'm not likely to forget,* went through her head. *You didn't know it, but you were trying to kill me, too.*

And he still was, still in perfect ignorance. "Well, I've been going through some of the other patients' charts, to see if I can find more with the same problem."

"I certainly hope not!" Esther exclaimed. Dr. Dambach would reckon the horror in her voice a horror of disorder and illegality, the sort of horror he had himself. And, indeed, she was acquainted with that horror in her everyday life. But what made her voice go high and shrill now was old and deeper and less . . . less Germanic. It was raw fear, fear of disaster, fear of death. She had to fight to hold it in check as she asked, "Have—have you found any?"

Dr. Dambach paused to sip from the cup of coffee she'd made for him. That only gave her a few more seconds to worry and to try to remember whether Walther had had to change anybody else's pedigree. She didn't think so. No, she didn't *think* so, but doubt tore at her. Maybe she'd forgotten. Maybe he'd done it without bothering to tell her. It wouldn't have seemed that important at the time. Now it loomed as big as the world.

The pediatrician set down the foam cup. "As a matter of fact, yes," he said deliberately, and Esther wanted to sink down through the floor. But then he went on, "Not quite like the Klein baby's case, though."

Esther dared breathe again, if barely. "What's the difference?" she asked. The question was dangerous, but it had to come out. Dr. Dambach wouldn't read too much into it . . . would he? He'd all but invited it . . . hadn't he?

He took another sip of coffee. Was he trying to drive her crazy? If he was, he was doing a bang-up job. He set the cup on his desk again. "The Kleins' charts showed two different family trees, so it made me wonder whether they had more Jews in their ancestry than they were willing to admit," he said, and cocked his head to one side, waiting for her response.

She made herself nod. "I remember." *I'm not likely to forget. I almost got them killed. I almost got more of my friends killed, and my family, and me.* The nod showed only polite agreement. None of the nightmare underneath came out.

"I haven't found any more cases like that," Dambach repeated.

"I hope not!" Esther repeated herself, too. "You'd better not!" Her knees didn't want to hold her up. She felt giddy with relief. "But what have you found? You said you'd found something."

"I have found that people will lie even when there is no good reason for them to lie." The pediatrician looked as disgusted as if he'd discovered maggots on a dressing that was supposed to be sterile. "I have found people inventing inflated ancestries for themselves, people trying to connect themselves with noble families—one family even trying to connect itself to the Hitlers. All of the forgeries are inept. Many of them are pathetic. But they riddle the files. Why?" He looked at Esther as if he really believed she had an answer.

She did the best she could: "There are people who want to seem more important than they really are."

"It's so stupid!" Dr. Dambach said. "And it could be dangerous to them, too. If I think a child's ancestry is different from what it really is, I'm liable to make the wrong diagnosis. Don't people think of *that*?"

"Most of them probably don't," Esther said. Working for the pediatrician had gone a long way toward convincing her most people thought very little—certainly less than she'd believed when she took the job. Then, because she couldn't help herself, she asked, "What are you going to do about these fake pedigrees?"

She knew she probably should have left well enough alone. But her boss had reported the Kleins without a second thought. Would he prove as hard on people he didn't suspect of being Jews?

"I've already done it, as a matter of fact," he said. "I've talked with the *Reichs* Genealogical Office. They want me to forward some of the more serious cases of abuse to them for possible prosecution. And they suggested

I write an article for a medical journal, alerting other physicians to the problem."

Esther eyed him with reluctant respect. He did what he thought was right, no matter whom it involved. She could wish he didn't think getting rid of Jews was right. How many people in the *Reich* didn't, though? Pitifully few. That was probably the hardest part of being a Jew in Berlin these days. Everyone you met was sincerely and honestly convinced you had no right to exist.

Asking any more questions might have made Dambach wonder why she was so curious. Instead, she said, "I'm sure the article will be very interesting."

"Articles in journals are not supposed to be interesting. They are supposed to be informative," Dambach said, a touch of frost in his voice.

"Why not both?" Esther asked.

The pediatrician shook his head. "That would not be good, *Frau* Stutzman. I have occasionally seen an article that is frivolous, and who could hope to learn from such a thing?" He was serious himself, as serious as he wanted medical articles to be. Esther couldn't understand it. She thought she would learn more from an article that was entertaining as well as fact-filled. That anyone could think otherwise hadn't occurred to her. But Dr. Dambach did.

Arguing with the boss when his mind was made up struck her as one of the more pointless things she could do. Instead, she went back out to the receptionist's desk and worked on billing and medical records till patients started coming in. Out of curiosity, she looked at some of the genealogical records in the charts. She soon saw that Dr. Dambach was right. Some of the pedigrees were faked, and pretty obviously faked. *Foolishness,* she thought. The Kleins and her own family had the best of good reasons for tampering with their ancestries: what was more important than survival? But changing a great-grandfather for the sake of vanity? What was that? What could it be but the urge to buy a Mercedes if your neighbor had a new Audi?

She almost didn't notice the outer door to the waiting room open. But the yowl of a baby brought her back to the real world in a hurry. She closed a chart and looked out. "Oh, *guten Morgen, Frau* Baumgartner," she said. "How is little Dietrich today?"

"Teething," *Frau* Baumgartner answered. She would have been a pretty strawberry blond if she hadn't had dark circles under her eyes. "He never wants to sleep any more, and if he doesn't sleep, I can't sleep, either. I hope the doctor can give me something to make him more comfortable."

"I hope so, too," Esther said. "Your appointment isn't till a quarter to ten, though, you know."

Frau Baumgartner nodded. "*Ja*. I do know. But I thought that if I got here early, I might get to see the doctor early, too."

Sometimes things did work out like that. Sometimes they didn't. "I can't promise you anything, not yet," Esther said. "If some of the people with earlier appointments don't show up, though . . ."

Little Dietrich jammed his fingers into his mouth. Somehow, he managed to let out an earsplitting howl despite the obstruction. His mother looked frazzled. "Oh, I hope they don't!" she said fervently.

Another mother came into the waiting room, this one with a two-year-old who was tugging at her ear. The little girl howled even louder than Dietrich Baumgartner. "*Guten Tag, Frau* Abetz," Esther bellowed over the din. "Liselotte's earache isn't any better, is it?"

"What?" said *Frau* Abetz, who couldn't have heard the Trump of Doom through that racket.

Esther repeated herself, louder this time. *Frau* Abetz took the screaming Liselotte into an examination room. She had one of the nine o'clock appointments *Frau* Baumgartner coveted. The move redistributed the noise without making it much softer, at least for Esther. Dr. Dambach emerged from his sanctum. "Going to be one of those quiet mornings, is it?" he said with a wry chuckle, and went into the examination room himself. Moments later, Liselotte screamed louder than ever.

And it was one of those mornings. *Frau* Baumgartner did get to take Dietrich in twenty minutes early, but that did nothing for the general level of peace and quiet, of which Esther saw very little. Every few minutes, another mother would bring in a shrieking baby or toddler. The phone kept ringing at the most inconvenient moments, too.

By the time the lunch break arrived, Esther felt as if she'd worked two whole days, not half of one. As a pediatrician, Dr. Dambach had to have more than an ordinary mortal's share of patience, but he also seemed to be feeling the strain. "I ought to put some brandy in this coffee," he said, pouring himself a fresh cup.

"I was thinking of asking if you could prescribe something stronger than aspirin for a headache," Esther said.

"I will if you like," Dambach answered.

She shook her head. "Thanks, but no. I was only joking—mostly."

When Irma Ritter came in for the afternoon shift, she said, "How are things?"

"Don't ask!" Esther said. "About the only good thing I can think of to tell you is that the office didn't catch on fire."

She thought of one more waiting for the bus that would take her home. Maximilian Ebert hadn't come out from the *Reichs* Genealogical Office to confer with Dr. Dambach—and to bother her. And that, she was convinced, was very good news indeed.

Wolf Priller walked up to Alicia on the playground. He looked at her as if he'd never seen her before. She looked at him with nothing but suspicion. He had no use for girls, and she had no use for him. Now, though, he wouldn't quit staring. "What do you want?" she demanded after half a minute or so.

"Is it true?" he asked.

"Is what true?"

"Did the *Führer* really come and talk with your dad, the way people say?"

"Oh, that. Yes, it's true."

Wolf's blue eyes got wider yet. "Wow," he breathed, as if she'd become important on account of the news. She supposed she had—to him, anyway. Then he asked, "How come *you* aren't more excited about it?"

Alicia shrugged. "I don't know. I'm just not." That wasn't the whole truth, or even very much of it. Wolfgang Priller was the last person to whom she wanted to tell the whole truth. The truth was, she didn't know what to think about Heinz Buckliger's call on her father. Before she found out what she was, the visit would have thrilled her as much as it seemed to thrill everybody else.

Now that she knew she was a Jew, the whole structure of the *Reich*—the structure she had loved—disgusted her. (It disgusted her when she remembered, anyhow. Some of the time, she didn't. Then, for a little while, she *was* the good little German she had been and still pretended to be.) But, from what she'd gathered, the new *Führer* didn't seem to be of the same stripe as the ones who'd come before him. Maybe he wasn't quite so bad after all.

Where did that leave her? In confusion, that was where.

Wolf said, "When I told my dad about it yesterday, he said he'd give this finger"—he solemnly displayed the index finger on his right hand—"to be able to sit down with the *Führer* and talk about things."

"They didn't talk about *things*—not like that," Alicia said. "They talked about stuff that had to do with my father's work."

"Even so," Wolf said. "My dad was *so* jealous. You have no idea how jealous he was. I am, too. I never thought I'd be jealous of a girl, but I am." And then, as if afraid he'd said too much, he rushed off and savagely booted a football.

Why is he jealous of me? Alicia wondered. *I didn't meet the* Führer. *My father did.* She had never run into the phrase *reflected glory,* but she was groping her way toward the idea.

Wolf wasn't the only one who wouldn't let her alone. Emma sidled up to her, whispered, "Lucky," and then scooted off. She'd done that four different times since hearing the news two days earlier. Alicia counted herself lucky to be alive and safe. Past that, she didn't worry about anything.

Even Trudi Krebs eyed her in a different way. It wasn't approval halfway down the road to awe, the look she got from most of her classmates. She couldn't quite make out what it was. Disappointment? That would have been her first guess.

Why would Trudi be disappointed in her if her father had met the *Führer?* Was Trudi a Jew? Could she be? Alicia knew she couldn't ask, in case the other girl said no. *I'll ask my mom,* she thought. *She'll know, or be able to find out.* Alicia thought Trudi just came from a family of political unreliables. That was almost as dangerous as being a Jew.

Herr Peukert knew about what had happened to Alicia's father, too, of course. *Herr* Kessler would have made a big fuss about it, till Alicia couldn't stand it any more. *Herr* Peukert didn't do that. He just seemed . . . interested. Alicia hardly knew what to make of that. It made her want to talk too much. Had her own secrets been less important, she might have.

When she went to wait for the bus that afternoon, she found Francesca there ahead of her, face thunderous with fury. "*Gott im Himmel!*" Alicia exclaimed. "What's the matter?"

"I got a swat from the Beast," her younger sister answered, looking even angrier than she had already.

Alicia wouldn't have believed she could. "What did you do?" she asked. Francesca, to put it mildly, wasn't the sort who usually got paddled.

"I didn't do anything! Not a single thing!" she burst out now. "She called me up to the front of the class and gave me one anyway, just for the fun of it. I hate her! I'll always hate her!" When she got angry, she didn't fool around. "This isn't a camp with a bunch of Jews in it. It's supposed to be school!"

"You already knew *Frau* Koch was like that," Alicia said. "Everybody knows it. Why are you so mad now?"

"Because she did it to *me*!"

Alicia started to laugh. She choked it down before it even began to show. Her sister's outrage was only part of the reason why, and a small part at that. Maybe, at last, she'd found some of the reason people hadn't complained about what the Party did to Jews. Who would complain, when something like that was happening to a small group of other people and not to themselves? That was doubly true because, if they *did* complain, such things *were* all too likely to happen to them.

"It will be all right," she told her sister. "Remember, you're only stuck with the Beast for a year. It's not forever."

"It seems like forever!" Francesca often looked for the cloud, not the silver lining. She added, "And then next year I'll probably get *Herr* Kessler."

She probably would, too. Alicia didn't want to tell her so, especially since that was also when she would find out she was a Jew. How would she react to that? Like Alicia—maybe even more than Alicia—she believed everything she'd learned in school about Jews. She would have to change her mind.

The school bus turned the corner and rumbled toward the stop. Alicia pointed towards it. "Here. We're going home now," she said. Sometimes distracting Francesca worked better than actually answering her.

Heinrich Gimpel had never imagined he could be a celebrity. What occurred to him was a most un-Jewish thought: *O my Father, if it be possible, let this cup pass from me*. Celebrity meant visibility. Visibility, in his mind, was inextricably wed to danger.

He was stuck with it, though. Half the analysts in *Oberkommando der Wehrmacht* headquarters made a point of coming up to him and passing the time of day. Even crusty *Wehrmacht* officers—real soldiers, not just bureaucrats in uniform—unbent around him where they never had before. Some of them—not all, but a surprising number—proved to be pretty good fellows under the crust.

And all because someone stopped at my desk for fifteen or twenty minutes, he thought dazedly. *People do that all the time. It shouldn't be so important.*

He laughed at himself. Other analysts stopped at his desk all the time. Officers stopped there every now and again. The *Führer*? The ruler of the Greater German *Reich* and the Germanic Empire? Well, no. The *Führer* didn't pay a call on an ordinary analyst every day.

Some people didn't try to cozy up to Heinrich. Some people turned green with envy instead, and wanted nothing to do with him. He was glad Willi didn't. Willi, instead, made a joke of it. "Me? I'm going to get rich from knowing you. How much do you suppose I can charge for twenty minutes of your time? Fifty Reichsmarks? A hundred? A hundred and fifty?" He ran his tongue across his lips. "You could get a pretty fancy floozy for that kind of money, but plenty of people would sooner see *you*. What do you think of that?"

"I think they'd have more fun with a girl," Heinrich answered. Willi laughed till he turned red. Heinrich hadn't been kidding.

Willi didn't seem to have noticed the speculative look Ilse had given Heinrich after the *Führer*'s visit. Since Heinrich had pretended not to notice it, too, Ilse's dallying with Willi hadn't paused. They were given to enough long lunches to make other analysts grin and nudge one another—but only when they weren't around.

What irked Heinrich about it at least as much as anything else was that he had to cover Willi's phone during those long lunches. He didn't mind dealing with business. That was what he was there for. Dealing with Erika Dorsch was a different story.

"Analysis section, Heinrich Gimpel speaking," he said after transferring a call from Willi's desk to his own.

"Hello, Heinrich," Erika said. "I was hoping for my husband. Too much to expect, I suppose."

If you really want to talk to Willi, why don't you call him when he's likelier to be here? Heinrich wondered, a little resentfully. He didn't say that out loud. It would only cause trouble. What he did say was as neutral as he could make it: "I'll take a message for you, if you like."

"In a bit," she answered. "Where is he?"

They'd gone around this barn before. "At lunch," Heinrich said.

"He should be back by now, shouldn't he?" Erika said. Heinrich didn't respond to that at all. She asked, "Where did he go?" and then said, "You're going to tell me you don't know. See? I read minds."

"Well, I don't," Heinrich said defensively. "I ate at the canteen today."

"I'm so sorry for you. Wherever he went, did he go there with Ilse?" Erika waited. Again, Heinrich didn't want to answer, either with the truth or with a lie. Her laugh had a bitter ring. "You're too damned honest for your own good, Heinrich."

Was that true? Heinrich didn't think so. He had, after all, been living under an elaborate lie for more than thirty years. Erika didn't know that, of course. As long as nobody who wasn't also living the lie knew, he could go on with it. He realized he would have to respond, though. He said, "I wish you and Willi weren't having troubles, that's all." Not only did he mean it, it sounded like an answer to what she'd just said. He could have done much worse.

He could also have done better. Erika's sour laugh proved that. "Wish for the moon while you're at it."

Heinrich could have laughed even more sourly. When she wished for the moon, the wildest thing she could think of was repairing what had gone wrong between her husband and her. Heinrich's wish would have been not only lunar but lunatic: he would have wished for the chance to live openly as what he was. He knew too well that that wasn't going to happen no matter how hard he wished.

All that went through his mind in what couldn't have been more than a heartbeat. Erika hardly even paused as she went on, "You don't need to wish, do you? You've really got the world by the tail." He did laugh then. He knew he shouldn't, but he couldn't help himself. That made Erika angry. "You do," she insisted.

"Not likely," Heinrich said. He couldn't tell her why, but hoped his voice carried conviction.

Evidently not, for she said, "No? I didn't see the *Führer* paying a call on my dear Willi."

If anybody had called Heinrich *dear* in that tone of voice, he would have run away as fast as he could. He answered, "He might have, but I'm the specialist on the United States, and he wanted to find out something about the Americans." Even that was more than he felt comfortable saying. Along with the God of Abraham, Isaac, and Jacob, he also worshiped Security, a jealous god indeed. But Erika already knew what he did. If she didn't wish Willi would dry up and blow away, she could figure this out for herself.

Slowly, she said, "There are times when you're too damned modest for your own good, too."

She's angry at me *now,* he realized in astonished dismay. *What the devil did I do?* "I told you the truth," he said.

"No, I'll tell you the truth," Erika said. "The truth is, the *Führer* came to see you. You, not anybody else. The truth is, that's important. It could make you important. And the truth is, you don't seem to want to do anything about it or even admit it."

She might have been a wife giving a husband a pep talk. She *was* a wife giving a husband a pep talk. The only trouble was, she wasn't Heinrich's wife, and she didn't know him as well as she thought she did. "I don't want to be important," he said, which was not the smallest understatement he'd ever made. "I don't, Erika, and that's the truth, too."

A long silence followed. Heinrich hoped she would lose her temper, hang up on him, and either leave him alone or just think of him as her husband's friend—somebody who was fun to drink wine with and a decent bridge player, but nothing more than that.

What he hoped for and what he got were two different things. "Well, at least you know your own mind," Erika said at last. "At least you've got a mind to know. You don't do all of your thinking below the belt. I like that. It's different in a man."

Did she realize how much of her own thinking she was doing below the belt? Not as far as Heinrich could see, she didn't. He almost pointed it out to her. At the last minute, he didn't. Talking with her about things below the belt struck him as a very bad idea.

"I'd better go," was what he did say. "Is there a message for Willi?"

"Tell him I hope Ilse gives him the clap," Erika answered promptly. "He won't have the chance to give it to me, and you can tell him that, too." She did hang up then, loudly.

Heinrich hung up, too. Rubbing at his ear, he pulled a message pad from his top desk drawer. *Erika called while you were out,* he wrote. *No need to call her back.* If she wanted to deliver any more forceful message, she could do it himself. He put the small sheet of yellow paper on Willi's desk. It didn't spontaneously combust. As he retreated to his own desk, he wondered why.

Willi came back to the office about half an hour later. He looked almost indecently pleased with himself—and that probably was the word for it, too. Ilse, by contrast, just sat down and started typing. Willi picked up the message. "What's this?" he said. He read it and set it down, then started to laugh. He looked over at Heinrich. "What did she really say?"

"You can ask her yourself and find out," Heinrich answered.

"No, thanks." Willi laughed again. "She thinks the world revolves around her. High time she finds out she's wrong."

Don't you do the same? Heinrich wondered. But he couldn't ask Willi that, any more than he could have asked Erika about the way she thought. Neither one of them would have taken the question seriously, and they both would have got angry at him. He wanted that no more than he wanted any other kind of notice.

Willi said, "You're our fair-haired boy right now. Why don't you fix Erika up with Buckliger? That would make everybody happy."

"You really are out of your mind!" Heinrich exclaimed in horror.

"Thank you," Willi said, which only disconcerted him more. "I thought it was the—what do you call it?—the elegant solution, that's what I'm trying to say."

"Shall I tell you all the things that are wrong with it?" Heinrich asked. "How much time have you got? Have you got all day? Have you got all week?"

"What I've got is a report to write." Willi looked lugubrious. "The boss wants it this afternoon, too. I'm going to have to rush like hell to finish it on time."

"You wouldn't, if—" Heinrich broke off. Telling Willi he'd have less to do now if he hadn't spent a long, long lunchtime screwing his secretary was true. Some true things, though, just weren't helpful.

"Yes, Mommy," Willi said, which proved this was indeed one of those things.

"All right. All right." Nothing annoyed Heinrich like being condescended to. "But if you're going to complain about what you've got to do, you'd better have a look at what you've been doing."

"I did. A nice, close look, too." Willi's expression left no doubt what he meant.

Heinrich found nothing to say to that, which was no doubt exactly what Willi'd had in mind. Shaking his head, he went back to work. Over at the other desk, Willi looked as desperately busy as a man juggling knives and torches. He would type like a man possessed, then shift to the calculator, mutter at the results, and go back to the keyboard.

At five o'clock, Heinrich got up. He put on his coat and his cap. "I'm heading for the bus stop," he said. "Are you coming?"

"No, dammit." Willi shook his head, looking harassed. "I'm still busy."

"Too bad," Heinrich said, and left. Willi stared after him, then plunged back into the report.

IX

WHEN SUSANNA WEISS LISTENED TO THE RADIO IN HER OFFICE, SHE USUALLY hunted for Mozart or Handel or Haydn or Beethoven or Bach. Verdi or Vivaldi would do in a pinch. The Italians were reckoned frivolous, but they were still allies; you couldn't get in trouble for listening to them.

She sometimes let Wagner blare out into the hallway, too. That was protective coloration, pure and simple, and not only because she despised him as an anti-Semite. No matter how the Nazis had slobbered over him for the past eighty years and more, she couldn't take him seriously.

A lone, lorn woman stands upon a stage trying to make herself heard, an Englishman had written at the start of the twentieth century. *One hundred and forty men, all armed with powerful instruments, well-organised, and most of them looking well-fed, combine to make it impossible for a single note of that poor woman's voice to be heard above their din.* She'd seen it that way long before she ran into Jerome K. Jerome. Now she couldn't even listen to Wagner without wanting to giggle.

These days, though, less classical music lilted from the radio. She tuned it to the news station more and more often. A lot of what she heard was the same wretched sort of propaganda she'd avoided for years. A lot of it, but not all. Every so often, startling things came out of the speaker. She listened in the hope of hearing more of them.

Whenever the *Führer* made a speech, she found herself urging him on, thinking, *You can do it. I know you can.* And sometimes Heinz Buckliger would, and sometimes he wouldn't. Sometimes he was flat and pedestrian, praising manufacture or agriculture or the Hitler Youth. Then, as she had with too many boyfriends, she decided she'd been fooling herself. She'd been right about the boyfriends. About Buckliger . . .

The trouble with Buckliger was, he could be astonishing. She was discussing a midterm with a student who had trouble understanding why he'd got only a 73. Susanna knew why—he wasn't too bright and he hadn't studied too hard. However much she wanted to, she couldn't come right out and say that. She had the radio on, not very loud, as she went over the exam with him point by point. It was one of those painful conferences. If the student worked harder, he might get a 76 next time, or even a 78. He would never blossom and get a 92.

Susanna hardly listened to herself as she explained all the myriad ways he'd misunderstood the Old English riddles he'd tried to interpret. More of her attention was on Heinz Buckliger, who was speaking to an audience of German female pharmacists. He'd been blathering on about how pharmacists were vital for the health of the *Reich,* and how the women's group to which he was speaking had a long history of devoted service. It didn't seem one of his more inspired efforts.

But then, with just a few words, everything changed. Buckliger went on, "We must examine the history of the *Reich* in the same way: that which is good, and also that which is not so good. We must not flinch from finding and noting our forefathers' failures."

"*Fräulein Doktor* Professor, I think you should raise my grade because—"

"Wait," Susanna said. The student tried to go on talking. She waved a hand at him. "Hush. I want to hear this." He couldn't very well complain, not when she was listening to the *Führer*. He still looked . . . aggrieved. Susanna didn't care.

"Those who complain about the recent emphasis on the first edition of *Mein Kampf* ignore certain essential facts," Heinz Buckliger went on. "It is perfectly obvious that inadequate representation by the *Volk* was at the root of past illegalities, arbitrariness, and repression—crimes based on abuse of power."

"Professor Weiss—" The student tried again.

"Hush, I told you," Susanna snapped. The female pharmacists were applauding the *Führer,* but hesitantly, as if they weren't sure what they were hearing. Susanna was. She just wasn't sure she could believe her ears. What Buckliger was saying was true—was, in fact, a colossal understatement. But that the *Führer* of the Greater German *Reich* should say even so much . . . !

And Buckliger wasn't done. He said, "The responsibility of past National Socialist leaders"—he didn't name Hitler or Himmler, but whom else could he mean?—"and those close to them for undoubted repressions and illegalities is both difficult to forgive and difficult to admit. But we must. Even now, writers try to ignore important questions in our history. They try to pretend nothing out of the ordinary occurred. This is wrong. It neglects historical reality, of which we all must be aware."

He paused for applause. He got . . . a little. Had Susanna been in the audience, she would have been on her feet whooping and hollering. The student tried to get her to pay attention to his earnest, inept essay again. She silenced him with a glare.

"Everyone's dearest wish," Buckliger went on, "is for the *Reich* and its ideology to stay unchanging for the thousand years Hitler promised us. But history does not work that way, however much we wish it did. We will either find ways to develop or we will stagnate and fail and go under."

Murmurs said the pharmacists didn't know what to make of the hard truths Buckliger was telling them. And even the *Führer* seemed to wonder if he'd gone too far. He quickly added, "Fascism has offered to the world its answers to the fundamental questions of human life, at the center of which stands the *Volk*. The errors we may have made will not, must not, turn us from the path we embarked upon in 1933. We are traveling to the New Order, to the world of the *Reich* and the *Volk*. We shall never leave that road."

There, at last, he gave the earnest women who'd come to hear him something they could get their teeth into. They cheered thunderously. Susanna wanted to yawn. The speech continued, but only in banalities.

"*Fräulein Doktor* Professor—" The student was nothing if not persistent.

"*Ja, ja*." Susanna realized she would have to get rid of him so she could think. She pointed to the essay. "You do understand that the ostensible answer to this riddle here is *a key*. That gets you a passing grade. But you don't see all the double meanings hiding underneath. What else might a man have on his hip that could fill a hole if he hiked up his clothes?"

"Excuse me?" The student stared at her as if she'd suddenly started spouting Hindustani. "I'm very sorry, but—" He broke off. She could tell exactly when he did get it. His stare changed from one sort to another altogether. He blushed like a schoolgirl. Prone to such problems herself, Susanna knew a good blush when she saw one. "But . . . But . . ." He sputtered, then tried again: "But this . . . this is a *text, Fräulein Doktor* Professor!"

"It's a text now," Susanna said. "It's a text to you. But to the man who wrote it, it was a riddle, it was a joke. And if you can't see the joke, well, I'm sorry, but you don't deserve anything more than a bare pass."

He tried to argue some more, but he couldn't, or not very well. He was both demoralized and embarrassed. Had he been a dog, he would have had his tail between his legs as he left her office.

For a wonder, no one else came in right away to complain about the exam. That left Susanna a few minutes to marvel at what she'd just heard. Heinz Buckliger had been careful about what he did. He'd surrounded the meat in his speech with clouds of puffy, obscuring rhetoric. But the meat was there. He'd admitted the Nazi regime had made mistakes. He'd also admitted it had covered them up. And he'd admitted it shouldn't have.

Once he'd done that much, gone that far, what else was left? Only spelling out what the mistakes had been. Would Buckliger have the nerve to do that? Would anyone else, now that the *Führer* had given permission? Maybe so, if people started to see that telling the truth didn't mean a trip to a camp or a bullet in the back of the neck.

Susanna could hardly wait to find out.

Lise Gimpel was sorting laundry—a labor of Sisyphus if ever there was one—when the girls came home from school. Francesca, for once, didn't start complaining about the Beast right away. She and Roxane went into the kitchen to fix themselves snacks. Roxane opened the refrigerator. "Olives! Yum!" she exclaimed. He older sisters made disgusted noises. Except for Heinrich, she was the only one in the family who really liked them.

Alicia hunted up Lise instead of getting a snack. She sat down on the bed beside her and said, "We talked about the *Führer*'s speech in class today."

"Did you?" Lise's mind was still more on socks and underwear than the classroom.

"We sure did." Alicia nodded solemnly. "Did he really say the *Reich* did things that were wrong, things that were against the law?"

"I think he did," Lise answered. "I can't say for certain, though. I didn't hear the speech."

"Well, suppose he did." Alicia waited till Lise nodded to show she was supposing. Her oldest daughter looked out the bedroom door to make sure Francesca and Roxane couldn't hear, then went on in a low voice, "Does that mean he thinks the *Reich* was wrong about what it did to Jews?"

"I don't know," Lise said. "What people did to Jews wasn't against the law, though, because they made laws ahead of time that said they could do those things."

"But it was wrong," Alicia said fiercely.

"Oh, yes. It was wrong. I think so just as much as you do. But—" Lise broke off and put both hands on Alicia's shoulders. "The people who run things probably don't think it was wrong. You have to remember that. And even if they say they do think it was wrong, we can't just come out and go, 'Oh, yes, here we are. Now we can get on with our lives again.' "

"Why not?" Plainly, Alicia wanted to do exactly that.

"Because it might be a trap. They might be trying to lure us out so they can get rid of us once and for all. The Nazis have been killing us for almost eighty years. Why should they stop now?"

Alicia bit her lip. She was, after all, only ten years old. "Would they do such a thing?" she whispered.

"Would they? I don't know," Lise answered. "Could they? You tell me, sweetheart. What do they teach you about Jews in school?"

"Nasty things." Alicia made a face. "Horrible things. You know that."

"Well, yes, I do," Lise said. "I wanted to make sure you did."

"Oh." Alicia thought that over, then nodded. "I'm going to go get a snack before sisters eat everything good in the house." She ran out of the bedroom and started gabbing with Francesca and Roxane. She didn't even tease Roxane about the olives. To her, they weren't part of everything good in the house, and Roxane was welcome to them.

Lise went back to stacking socks and underwear into neat piles, one for each person in the family. She wished there were a laundry fairy to do the job for her, but no such luck. If she didn't do it, nobody would. Heinrich, at least, put away his own clean clothes without being told. The girls . . . Lise wished for a laundry fairy again.

She also wished she could share Alicia's optimism. She wanted to, maybe more than anything else in all the world. She hated living in hiding, hated fearing a knock on the door that could mean the end not just for her but for everybody she loved. Feeling she carried the weight of the world hadn't been easy when she was a child, and hadn't got any easier now that she'd grown up.

But I do, she thought miserably. *We all do, the handful of us who are left. If we let go, if we give up—or if, God forbid, we get caught—a world goes with us.*

"Why have you got yipes stripes, Mommy?" There stood Roxane in the doorway, holding an olive impaled on a toothpick.

"Have I?" Lise was sure she did. She tried to make the frown lines leave her forehead. "There. Is that better?"

"A little," Roxane said dubiously.

"How about this?" Lise stuck out her tongue and crossed her eyes.

Roxane giggled. That suggested some improvement. But then the youngest Gimpel girl said, "You didn't tell me why you had them in the first place." Her stubborn streak was as wide as she was. It would probably help make her a good Jew when she got old enough to find out she was one. In the meantime . . . In the meantime, it made her hard to distract.

"Grown-up stuff," Lise answered. "Nothing for you to worry about." *Not yet. Not for another few years. And when you do find out, you'll be one more who knows—and one more who can give us away.* Letting children know what they were was the hardest part of this secret life. Considering the rest of it, that was no small statement.

Roxane made a face of her own. "What good is being a grownup, if you have to have yipes stripes so much?" She darted away without waiting for an answer.

"What good is being a grownup?" Lise echoed. She thought of the obvious things, the things that appealed to a child—going to bed as late as you wanted to, being able to drive, having all the money you needed, getting out of school forever, not having anybody standing over you waiting to yell "No!" all the time. Then she thought about all the worries that accumulated when you grew up. When you had a family, you worried plenty even if you weren't a Jew. If you were . . . "What good *is* being a grownup?" Lise said again. It was, when you got right down to it, a damned good question.

In the Stahnsdorf train station, Heinrich Gimpel remarked, "Never know what's in the paper these days."

"God knows that's true," Willi Dorsch agreed. "Sometimes you wonder if you want to find out, too."

They threw fifteen pfennigs apiece into the vending machine. Nothing would have stopped them from grabbing two copies of the *Völkischer Beobachter* when Willi opened the machine to take out his copy. Nothing would have stopped them, but it didn't occur to either man. A man had to do all kinds of things to get along in the Third *Reich*. That kind of petty theft, though, was downright un-German. Willi was a good German. In most ways, so was Heinrich.

The train got there almost as soon as they walked out on the platform. They sat down side by side and started going through the newspaper. Some of the fuss over Heinz Buckliger's speech to the pharmacists was starting to die down. Nobody'd said much in public except Rolf Stolle, the *Gauleiter* of Berlin, and he'd been all for it. He'd also thundered fearsome warnings about all the *Bonzen* who hated the very idea of reform. Heinrich thought Stolle at least as much a clown as a politician—with friends like him, who needed enemies? Clown or not, though, he probably hadn't been wrong about the *Bonzen*.

"Nothing too much today, doesn't look like," Willi said.

"No, I don't see anything very exciting, either." Heinrich tried not to sound too disappointed. People might wonder why he was. If the thaw ended—and he knew too well it could, knew too well it was probably going to—someone might remember. Landing in trouble for being on the wrong side of a political squabble would be just as bad for him (though perhaps not for everyone around him) as landing in trouble for being a Jew. He went on working his way through the *Völkischer Beobachter*. When he got to page eight, he stopped. "Hello! What's this?"

"What's what?" Willi hadn't got there yet.

"Two men arrested in Copenhagen for carrying an anti-German banner through the streets," Heinrich answered. "They wanted full independence for Denmark."

"Damn fools," Willi said. "Hell, the Danes have it, or close enough. Those idiots don't know when they're well off. They ought to go to Poland or Serbia for a while. That'd teach 'em."

"It sure would." Heinrich hoped that sounded like agreement. The Danes were better off than the Poles or the Serbs or what was left of the Russians and Ukrainians. Like Dutchmen, Norwegians, and Englishmen, Danes got credit for being Aryans. They weren't Slavic *Untermenschen*. They'd always been pretty peaceful—or at least resigned—under German occupation, too.

But they plainly still remembered they'd been free for hundreds of years before 1940. Heinrich wondered if . . . Before he could even finish the thought, Willi beat him to it: "They probably listened to the *Führer*'s speech the other day and figured anything goes from here on out."

"I wouldn't be surprised," Heinrich said. If he had finished the thought, he would have kept quiet about it. Willi, confident about who and what he was, didn't censor himself so severely.

He didn't waste much sympathy on the Danes, either. "They're lucky they *did* get arrested, not shot down on the spot. We're softer than we were in Hitler's day. I've told you that before." Then, shifting gears, he went on, "You want to have lunch today?"

"Can't," Heinrich answered. "Our goddaughter's birthday is three days from now, and I've got to find her a present." Anna Stutzman wasn't literally a goddaughter—Jews didn't use that custom—but came close enough. Heinrich couldn't resist asking, "Besides, what about Ilse?"

"I'm not eighteen, for God's sake," Willi said. "I can't do it every day any more. And I've got to save *some* for Erika. Otherwise, she'd be even crankier than she is."

"Generous of you," Heinrich murmured. He'd intended that for sarcasm. It didn't quite come out that way. Willi had his own inimitable style, but at least part of his heart seemed to be in the right place.

He grinned now. "Isn't it?" he said complacently. The train rattled on toward South Station in Berlin.

When lunchtime came, Heinrich hopped a cab up to the Kurfürstendamm. He knew—he had detailed instructions from Lise—what he was supposed to get for Anna. Like everyone else who was breathing and halfway conscious, he'd seen advertisements for the Vicki dolls imported from the United States. They had flaxen hair, vacant expressions, improbable figures, and clothes Mata Hari would have envied. They looked perfectly Aryan. Maybe that was why they were so wildly popular in the *Reich*. Or maybe not—you never could tell with kids. With three of his own, Heinrich knew that.

At least people weren't fighting hand to hand these days, the way they had been when the dolls first came out. Heinrich had asked Lise if she was sure he wasn't getting something passé for Anna. She'd shaken her head. "I checked with our girls," she'd answered. "They're still popular. With all the different outfits you can get for them, they'll stay that way for years." If the girls said it, it had to be true.

Heinrich did wonder who made clothes for the swarms of Vickis. They weren't that expensive, and they didn't come from the Empire of Japan with its ocean of cheap labor. Did the doll manufacturer know an official who could pull seamstresses out of a prison camp?—or maybe not pull them out of a camp, but make them work inside? They'd sew as if their lives depended on it. Their lives would, too.

He grimaced. You could ask that kind of question about a lot of things you saw every day. Sometimes—usually—not knowing was better. He shook his head. That wasn't right. You needed to know. Heinz Buckliger was dead on target there. But ignorance could be easier for your peace of mind.

Ducking into Ulbricht's toy store banished such gloomy reflections. If you couldn't be happy in Ulbricht's, you were probably dead. Dolls, stuffed animals, brightly colored children's books, football and basketball and archery sets, toy soldiers and sailors and panzers and U-boats and fighter planes (*Landser* Sepp was the counterpart of Vicki for boys, and came with enough matériel to conquer Belgium), all waited for your money. Loud, cheerful music made you want to smile—and to part with your Reichsmarks.

There. He'd been told to get that one: a New Orleans Vicki, dressed in lace and satin and looking as if she'd just stepped out of *Gone with the Wind*. (That had been one of Hitler's favorite movies. It still got rereleased every few years. Susanna loved to go to it and make fun of the dubbing.) Heinrich grabbed for the package.

A woman's hand closed on it at the same time as his.

Annoyed, he looked up from the doll to see who else wanted it—only to discover Erika Dorsch, also annoyed, also looking up from the doll for what had to be the same reason. They stared at each other and started to laugh. "For my sister Leonore's girl," Erika said.

"For my goddaughter," Heinrich said. "Is there another one like it in the bin?"

"Let's see." Erika had to dig a little, but she found one. She handed it to him. "Here."

"Oh, good," he said. "Now we won't have to go to court, the way those two women did a few months ago when the craze was at its craziest. The judge should have played Solomon and cut the doll in half, if you ask me."

"*Ja*." Erika cocked her head to one side, studying him. "If we're not going to court, where *shall* we go?"

"I was going to pay for this and head back to the office," Heinrich answered. "It's been busy."

"It can't be *that* busy, if dear Willi takes Ilse out so often," Erika said. "And shouldn't you pay him back for the extra work you get stuck with when he does?"

Pay him back how? Heinrich wondered. He was afraid Erika would tell him—or show him. He had to be afraid of so many things. That this should be one of them struck him as most unfair. "It's not so bad," he said.

That didn't satisfy Erika, either. He might have known it wouldn't. "You're too easygoing for your own good," she said. "You let people push you around, do things to you—everybody but me."

"Ha," Heinrich said in a distinctly hollow voice. "Ha, ha. What would you do to me?"

She kissed him, right there in front of the bin of Vicki dolls. She made a good, thorough job of it, too. Behind Heinrich, somebody coughed. His ears felt ready to catch fire. But so did the rest of him, in a different way. The only way he could have kept from kissing her back and tightening his arms around her was to die on the spot.

"There," she said, breaking the kiss as abruptly as she'd started it. "See you later. Enjoy your work." She went off toward a cashier, that New Orleans Vicki still in her hand.

Heinrich stared after her. A man with a white Hitler mustache—probably a grandfather shopping for a granddaughter—winked at him. "You lucky dog. If Ulbricht's sold dolls like that, I'd buy myself one in a minute," he said, and cackled at his own wit like a laying hen.

"Lucky. Right," Heinrich said dazedly. The old man thought that was pretty funny, too. Still cackling, he went on toward a display of stuffed kittens.

Heinrich fumbled in his pocket for a handkerchief. He rubbed at his mouth. He could still taste the sweetness of Erika's lipstick—and of her lips. The handkerchief came away stained the same bright pink Erika had been wearing. To make sure he'd got it all, Heinrich went into a men's room and checked in the mirror. A good thing he did, too—he'd missed a large, incriminating spot. A few more dabs got rid of it.

He started out of the men's room, then stopped. The stained handkerchief went into the wastebin full of crumpled paper towels. Explaining how he'd lost it—a blank look and "I don't know"—would be easier than telling Lise how it had got those telltale stains on it. Anything would be easier than that.

He paid for the Vicki and went out onto the Kurfürstendamm to flag a cab for the ride back to *Oberkommando der Wehrmacht* headquarters. A taxi pulled up. The driver hopped out and opened the rear door for him. "Here you go, sir," he said.

"Thanks." Heinrich slid in. The cabby zoomed away from the curb. Heinrich looked down at the Ulbricht's sack on his knees. He'd paid for the doll, all right.

Alicia Gimpel peered out the window. "Here she comes," she hissed suddenly, and ducked back out of sight like a sniper who had to stay hidden to stay alive. She waved importantly to the other girls gathered in the living room. "Quiet, everybody!"

She needed to say it three times before they paid any attention to her. They finally did, just when Anna Stutzman and her mother came up the walk toward the front door. Anna's mother rang the bell. Alicia and her mother answered it. Francesca and Roxane stood behind them in the entrance hall. That was all right. Anna could see Alicia's little sisters. They lived here, after all. And it was quiet—pretty quiet, anyhow—in the living room.

"Hello, there," Alicia's mother said, opening the door. "How are you today? Heavens, Anna, you're getting so big!"

"I'm barely keeping up with Alicia," Anna said. That was true, but Alicia showed signs that she would be very tall when she grew up. Anna didn't.

"What does being twelve feel like?" Alicia asked after they hugged.

"Like being eleven, but one more," Anna answered. They both laughed. Alicia hadn't found out what being what eleven was like till a few weeks before.

"Come in, come in, come in," her mother said. Alicia thought Francesca and Roxane would ruin things then, because they made some of the most ridiculous faces she'd ever seen. But Anna didn't seem to notice anything wrong. Maybe she thought Alicia's sisters were always ridiculous. Alicia often did.

Francesca and Roxane raced back into the living room. That should have been a giveaway, too, but somehow it wasn't. Alicia and Anna and their mothers followed more slowly. Anna was saying, "Have you seen the new singers in the—"

"*Surprise!*" yelled a dozen girls. "Surprise!" Alicia echoed, grinning from ear to ear. It had worked! In spite of everything, it had worked.

The look on Anna's face was worth a hundred Reichsmarks. "You didn't!" she said to Alicia. "I'll get you for this."

"I did, too," Alicia answered, and the other didn't bother her one bit.

Anna rounded on her mother. "You must have known," she accused.

"Who, me?" *Frau* Stutzman said. That made everybody laugh again.

Before long, it stopped being a surprise party and just turned into a birthday party. Alicia didn't know all of Anna's friends very well. Some of them lived near Anna, while others were in her class at school. They seemed nice enough. They put up with Alicia's little sisters. Some of them would have little sisters or brothers of their own. Alicia would have got mad if they'd teased Francesca or Roxane. That was *her* job. As far as she could tell, none of the other girls shared the secret she and Anna did. That made the two of them special—or she thought it did, anyhow. How could she know for sure? She couldn't.

It also made Francesca and Roxane special. They didn't know it yet, though, and they wouldn't be too happy when they found out. Alicia shook her head. This whole business still seemed very strange.

But then, in the midst of games and songs and cake and ice cream and "genuine American hot dogs" from a stand that had opened up a few blocks away (they tasted like any other frankfurters to Alicia), she forgot all about the secret. When she'd first learned it, she hadn't thought she would ever be able to do that.

Anna unwrapped her presents. She squealed extra loud when she opened the New Orleans Vicki. Several of the other girls made envious noises. Alicia felt especially good because of that. She wanted to give Anna a really nice present.

More cake and ice cream followed. "You're going to make them sick," *Frau* Stutzman told Alicia's mom. She didn't sound as if she meant it, though. Not too much later, she went home, saying, "I'll see you in the morning, Anna. Happy birthday, sweetie."

The guests ran around and sang more songs and played games and fooled around with the Gimpel girls' dolls and toys. When it got late, they spread out sleeping bags on the floor of the front room. Nobody who'd ever gone on a *Bund deutscher Mädel* outing was without a sleeping bag. Francesca and Roxane had theirs, too, even though they weren't old enough to join the organization for German girls.

They might have got into the sleeping bags. The lights might have been out. They weren't going to fall asleep any time soon, though. Alicia's father made a brief appearance, coming halfway down the stairs. "Try to keep it down to a low roar, if you please," he said. He sounded as if he knew that was a lost hope.

They giggled. They gossiped. They told scary stories, which seemed even scarier in the dark. One of Anna's friends had read a translation of "The Telltale Heart." That was good for plenty of goose bumps.

Roxane started to doze. Every so often, she'd say, "I'm awake," in a small, faraway voice. She was still little, even if she would have indignantly denied it.

One by one, the girls did drop off to sleep. Snores replaced Roxane's protests. A couple of the girls Anna's age were snoring by the time Francesca gave in and slept. Alicia wasn't surprised. She knew how stubborn Francesca was.

By two in the morning, snores and deep breathing filled the Gimpels' living room. Alicia's sleeping bag lay next to Anna's. Not only were they best friends, but the party was in Alicia's house. She doubly had the right to be there. Her voice a tiny whisper, she asked, "Are you still awake?"

"No," Anna whispered back, and they both laughed.

"Did you have a happy birthday?" Alicia asked.

Anna nodded. Alicia could barely see the motion. "I'll say," Anna answered.

"Good. I'm glad," Alicia said, and then, "How are . . . things?"

"Things are all right with me." Anna poked her head up to make sure nobody else was awake and listening. Alicia did the same. She'd been sure Anna would know how she meant *things,* and she'd been right. Her friend even used the same word and the same little pause to ask, "How are . . . things with you?"

"They're not too bad, I guess." But Alicia couldn't leave it at that. She went on, "I think it's harder when other people in the house don't know." She stuck her head up and listened again. This would be a very bad time to find out Francesca was only pretending to sleep.

"I believe that," Anna said. Now she paused before continuing, "Gottlieb told me the same thing once. I was really little when he found out. I was younger than Roxane." She laughed at the follies of her youth. "He must have wanted to kick me a whole bunch of times."

Alicia had wanted to kick her sisters plenty of times. The trouble was, they kicked back. The other trouble was . . . "It's what you learn in school. It's what you see on the televisor. It's—it's just everything, that's all. I believed all that stuff till I found out." In a tinier voice yet, she added, "Part of me still wants to believe it."

"Oh, thank you!" Anna said. Alicia blinked. Anna explained: "I was afraid I was the only one who thought things like that." They both came halfway out of their sleeping bags so they could hug each other.

Not once, Alicia realized, had either one of them said the word *Jew.* Even if one of the other girls were listening, she wouldn't know what they were talking about. They were both so very careful. They had to be. If they weren't careful, they were dead. Alicia had known that was what happened to Jews long before she knew she was one.

Anna asked her, "What do you think of the new *Führer?*"

"I was going to ask you the same thing!" Alicia exclaimed. She liked it when she and Anna thought the same way. Nobody else thought like her, except her father every once in a while. Since Anna had asked the question first, she had to answer it: "He seems . . . better, anyhow."

"He does, doesn't he?" Anna said. "He talks about how there ought to be laws, not just . . . the triumph of the will." They'd both seen the film. Everybody saw it, in school and on the televisor. It was old. You could tell when you watched it. But it had a kick like a mule even so.

"You know the lady who made that movie?" Alicia asked. Anna nodded. Alicia said, "She died just a few years ago. She was over a hundred—even older than Kurt Haldweim." She shivered, remembering how she'd filed past the late *Führer*'s shrunken, wizened corpse as it lay in state in the Great Hall.

"That's scary," Anna said. Now Alicia nodded. Anna went on, "When your sisters . . . talk about things they don't know about, how do you stand it?"

"I don't know," Alicia answered. "Just after I first found out, it really used to drive me crazy. Now it doesn't, or not so much, anyway. They don't know any better, and they can't for a while. They're too little."

"That's funny," Anna said. Alicia made a soft, inquiring noise. Her friend went on, "Gottlieb said almost the same thing to me—almost the same thing about me—after I finally did find out what was what." The last few words came out muffled by a yawn.

Alicia yawned, too. They were both up long past their usual bedtime. Of course, that was what slumber parties were for. Alicia's head went down. "I think I am going to sleep now," she said. "Happy birthday again."

"It was the happiest!" Anna said. In a couple of minutes, both of them were snoring with the other girls.

Something peculiar was happening in Adolf Hitler Platz when Heinrich Gimpel and Willi Dorsch got off the bus from South Station. Heinrich asked, "What's going on?" He had trouble seeing, not only because of the mist and light drizzle themselves but because of the way they spattered his glasses.

"Looks like . . ." Willi brought up his hand. Heinrich wondered why. His friend didn't wear glasses. Maybe the hand helped the visor on his cap keep water out of his eyes. Maybe he just thought the gesture looked impressive. After peering, he said, "I will be damned. Looks like some Dutchmen are holding a demonstration over there."

"Dutchmen?" Heinrich echoed. Then, between raindrops, he too got a glimpse of the red, white, and blue flag with the stripes laid out horizontally, not vertically as in the French tricolor. A couple of dozen men and women huddled beneath the damp banner. A few of them carried signs. Distance and rain kept Heinrich from making out the words. He would have had to do some guessing, anyway; Dutch had a teasing almost-familiarity to someone who spoke German and English.

"*Vrijheid!*" the Dutch shouted. Heinrich didn't have to do much guessing to figure out what that meant. It was very close to *Freiheit,* the German word for freedom. "*Vrijheid!*"

Willi got it, too. "Where are the Security Police?" he demanded.

"Here they come." If Heinrich was dismayed—and he was—he didn't show it.

"About time," Willi said, which showed what he thought.

The men in black tunics and trousers trotted briskly across the square. They carried truncheons and pistols; a couple of them had assault rifles. Would it be arrests or a massacre? Lights blazing and sirens howling, police wagons followed the troopers. It turned out to be arrests. The Dutchmen and -women didn't try to flee. They kept calling, "*Vrijheit!*" as the Security Police herded them into the wagons, which screeched away. Adolf Hitler Platz was quiet again. The whole thing couldn't have taken more than three minutes.

"They must have been out of their minds," Willi said. "They don't have the faintest idea when they've got it good. Bunch of damned fools, like those Danes. Give 'em a little, treat 'em halfway decent because they're Aryans, and what do they do? Do they thank you? Hell, no! They grab with both hands, that's what."

"Maybe they're taking the new *Führer* seriously," Heinrich said as he and Willi went up the stairs to *Oberkommando der Wehrmacht* headquarters.

Willi gave him an odd look. "Maybe they're taking Buckliger *too* seriously," he said. "What'll we see next? Poles shouting for freedom? Russians? Jews?" He threw back his head and laughed.

So did Heinrich. The idea was, when you got down to it, pretty funny. He tried to imagine some of the handful of surviving Jews in Berlin getting out there in the middle of that enormous square and clamoring for their freedom. Would the Security Police even need to come? Or would ordinary people beat and stone them to death before the men in black uniforms got there? Everyone here, or as near as made no difference, had that same casual loathing for Jews.

"Do you think . . ." Willi sounded as if he'd decided to take Heinrich seriously after all instead of laughing at him. "Do you think Buckliger *intends* for things like this to happen?"

Heinrich didn't even try to answer that till the security guards had checked their identification cards and waved them through into the building. Then he said, "I doubt it. Who would? But how can you make changes in the way things work if you can't even talk about changes without getting arrested?"

"Oh, come on," Willi said. "These were Dutchmen. The others were a bunch of crazy Danes. You didn't see any real Germans out there, did you?"

"Not a one," Heinrich agreed. He wondered if he ever would. The Party had spent the last three generations teaching the Germans to be docile to their rulers, no matter how ferocious they were when they put on uniforms and marched off to war. Could they nerve themselves to speak their minds? After three generations of Nazi propaganda, did they have any minds to speak? He wasn't an optimist. On a question like that, he couldn't afford optimism. The cost of being wrong was too high.

"Coffee!" Willi exclaimed when they got to the room where they worked. He disappeared, presumably heading for the canteen, and came back five minutes later with a foam cup from which fragrant steam rose. He gulped it down, then sighed blissfully. "Ahhh!"

Heinrich wanted a cup, too. Even so, he said, "I've seen drunks who didn't cozy up to a bottle of cheap schnapps the way you did with that coffee."

"If you're going to enjoy something, you should *enjoy* it, shouldn't you?" Willi said. "Why only go halfway?"

"Because sometimes all the way is too far?" Heinrich suggested. Willi laughed at him again. It wasn't surprising that he should. National Socialist ideology scorned the idea of restraint. It always had. Heinrich wondered if Heinz Buckliger could change that, or if it had even occurred to the new *Führer* to try. He had his doubts.

He also had his work. He got some coffee for himself. With it unmelodramatically sitting there on the desk in front of him, he got down to business. Sure enough, with their assessments reduced, the Americans were paying even less than they had been. They were trying to see just how much the *Reich* would let them get away with before it clamped down. If he hadn't already been sure they would do that, it would have infuriated him.

The coffee hadn't had time to get cold before the telephone rang. He picked it up. "Analysis section, Heinrich Gimpel speaking."

"*Guten Morgen, Herr* Gimpel," an American-accented voice said. "Charlie Cox here. *Wie geht's mit Ihnen?*"

"I'm fine, thanks," Heinrich answered automatically. Then he blinked. "It's not morning where you are, *Herr* Cox. It's still the middle of last night. Are you up early or up late?"

"Late," Cox said easily. "I wanted to ask you something unofficial."

"Well, go ahead," Heinrich told him. "Of course, an answer to a question like that is worth its weight in gold."

"Aber natürlich," Cox said. He knew the answer wouldn't really be unofficial, then. By the nature of things, it couldn't be. That meant the "unofficial" question wasn't, either. Cox proceeded to ask it: "Just exactly how serious is *Herr* Buckliger about reforming the National Socialist system?"

"That's a good question," Heinrich said. He could see why the American and his leaders wanted to find out. A lot of other people in the Germanic Empire and in the Greater German *Reich* wanted to find out, too. Heinrich wouldn't have been surprised if Heinz Buckliger were one of them. He went on, "The only thing I can tell you, though, is that I don't know."

"Unofficially, dammit." Charlie Cox sounded annoyed.

You idiot. Don't you think there's a bug on this phone? Someone will be listening to you—and to me—if not right this second, then when he plays a tape. Aloud, Heinrich replied, "Official or unofficial, you'd get the same answer from me. Come on, Charlie. Use your head." *You'd better.* "I'm not at the level that makes policy. All I do is carry it out."

"The *Führer* talks to you," Cox said.

So that news had got across the Atlantic, had it? Either it had spread more widely than Heinrich thought or the Americans had better spies than Intelligence gave them credit for. That wasn't Heinrich's immediate worry, though. He said, "For heaven's sake, he just asked me for a few figures so *he* could set policy. That's what the *Führerprinzip* is all about."

"*Ja*," Cox agreed. "But if he likes the first edition as much as he says he does, how much does he care about the *Führerprinzip*?"

A lot of people in the Empire and in the *Reich* were also wondering about that. "I'm very sorry," Heinrich said, "but I still don't know. If you want advice—"

"I'll take whatever you give me," the American broke in. "You've always seemed like a decent fellow."

Are you naive enough to assume that about anyone in the Reich, *or do you think I'm naive enough to be flattered?* In a way, Heinrich *was* flattered, but not in a way that would do Cox any good. He said, "The only real advice I can give you is, wait and see. What the *Führer* does will show you exactly what he has in mind."

"I was hoping for a little advance warning." But he must have realized he wouldn't get it from Heinrich. With what might have been either a sigh or a yawn, he said, "All right. I'm going on home to bed. Thanks for your time, *Herr* Gimpel." He hung up.

So did Heinrich, with quite unnecessary force. Willi said, "Sounded like somebody was trying to get something out of you."

"An American," Heinrich said. "I think I'd better write up a report." If he did, the people surely monitoring the line would have less reason to read disloyalty into anything he'd said. As he began to type, though, he wondered how much good it would do. If the powers that be decided he was disloyal, they wouldn't worry about evidence. They'd invent some or do without and just get rid of him.

Will they, under this Führer? That Heinrich could wonder said how much things had changed—and how much they hadn't.

Walther Stutzman was a straight-thinking, rational man. He had to be, to make himself a success at the Zeiss computer works. Every so often, though, he found himself bemused by what he and a few others did—had to do—to keep themselves hidden from the all-too-nearly omniscient eye of the state.

Hitler had thundered that there was a Jewish conspiracy against the German *Volk*, against the *Reich*. At the time, he'd been talking through his hat. The Jews hadn't been plotting against Germany. Most of the Jews *in* Germany had thought of themselves as being as German as anybody else. Now, on the other hand . . .

Now the handful of Jews remaining in Berlin, in Germany as a whole, had to conspire against the *Reich* if they wanted to go on breathing. Hitler's extermination camps had had the ironic effect of calling into being what hadn't existed when he started making speeches. Even now, it wasn't the sort of conspiracy he meant. It didn't aim to take over the *Reich,* just to hide the few surviving Jews from it. But a conspiracy it undoubtedly was.

Here sat Walther, controlling computer codes that would have earned him a bullet in the back of the neck if anyone knew he had them. Some of the codes erased his tracks after he'd used others, which made discovering him harder. Over at *Oberkommando der Wehrmacht,* Heinrich Gimpel kept his ear to the ground. There was a Jew in a fairly high place in the Foreign Ministry. There were even three or four in the SS. Walther had helped create false pedigrees for a couple of them. The others he just knew about; he wasn't sure how they'd established their bona fides. His own work there still worried him. If it unraveled, so much was liable to unravel with it. Several other important ministries also held a Jew or two.

When a Jew in one place heard something that might be important, others soon found out about it. A chief undersecretary or a deputy assistant minister could meet with a friend at dinner or telephone a colleague in another ministry—sometimes not a Jew himself, but someone who could be expected to spread the news to the Jew who needed to know it. Heinrich said the American phrase was a grapevine. That fit well enough.

And that chief undersecretary or deputy assistant minister sometimes got to propose a policy that—purely by chance, of course (of course!)—made things a little easier, a little safer, for the Jews. Or, bureaucracy being what it was, one of those functionaries could sometimes ignore or soften a directive that might have hurt his people. Very often, one bad scheme blocked was worth three good ones started.

A Jewish conspiracy at the heart of the *Reich*. Hitler would have had kittens. He would have ordered all the Jews killed, and made horrible examples of the Germans who'd missed them. Walther thought of knives and piano-wire nooses. Himmler would have killed the Jews and made examples of some Germans, too, but he would have got rid of them more humanely. Kurt Haldweim would have got rid of the Jews and reprimanded, maybe demoted, the Germans.

Heinz Buckliger? Walther scratched his head. He didn't know. He didn't dare find out. Who would dare, when the consequences for being wrong were so irrevocable? For the first time in his life, though, he could think of the *Führer* without a shudder right afterwards.

"Hey, Walther! What are you doing in there?"

The booming voice jerked him out of his reverie. "Nothing much, boss," he answered honestly, hiding a start, too. "Just woolgathering, I'm afraid."

"You?" Gustav Priepke boomed laughter. "That'll be the day. Listen, something's come up, and I need you to take a shot at it."

Walther had told the truth, and Priepke hadn't believed him. That was what he got for having a reputation for working hard. If he'd had a name for doing nothing, he could have been working on six things at once and his boss wouldn't have believed that, either. He did his best to look bright and attentive, even if he didn't feel that way. "What is it?" he asked.

"The new operating system—what else?" Priepke answered. "We've got to make it work, or else." He didn't say or else what, but he didn't have to. The project was long overdue. That it was so long overdue made it harder, too.

"Well, there is one obvious answer we haven't tried yet," Walther said.

"What's that?" his boss asked. "I thought we'd done all the obvious things."

Walther shook his head. "No, there's one thing we haven't done that could save us a lot of time." Priepke let out an interrogative grunt. Walther said, "We could see how much Japanese code we can steal or adapt."

"*Donnerwetter!*" Gustav Priepke looked at him as if he'd suggested turning every *Ratskeller* in the *Reich* into a sushi bar. "What a bastardly idea! What the Japs know about real programming—"

"Is just what we need right now," Walther broke in.

"Jesus Christ!" Priepke said harshly. "You know what Hitler said about the Japs in *Mein Kampf*. If they didn't have Aryans to steal ideas from, their culture would freeze solid again like *that*." He snapped his fingers.

"Do you want to talk about politics or computers?" Walther asked. "I don't care about politics. I don't care at all. What I care about are computers. The Japanese have some ideas we can use, and I think we can extract them without too much trouble. Which counts for more, ideology or the operating system?"

"You wouldn't have dared talk like that in Himmler's time, let alone Hitler's."

"Oh, yes, I would," Walther said. "The Russians had a terrific panzer in the Second World War. The T-34 was better than anything we brought against it, but we had better crews, so we won. Our next panzer, the Panther, borrowed—stole—all sorts of ideas from the T-34. The designers didn't care who built it. All they cared about was that it was a good machine."

His boss grunted again, this time meditatively. Then he said, "What if the code's got traps in it?"

"If we can't find them, are we really smarter than the Japanese?" Walther asked.

One more grunt. Priepke said, "I can't decide that on my own. I don't want the Security Police landing on us with both feet half an hour after we start." He stormed away from Walther's cubicle.

Walther wondered whether he should have kept his mouth shut. Would the Security Police start asking him nasty questions now? All he'd wanted was to do the job the people set over him told him to do. Was that too much to hope for? Maybe it was. *No good deed goes unpunished,* he thought sourly.

Gustav Priepke didn't come back for more than an hour. That worried Walther, too. Had he got his boss in trouble? Or was the trouble waiting for *him* instead? He relaxed—a little—when Priepke did return. The big, burly man gave him a comic-opera Oriental bow. "Velly good. We tly that," he said in what he imagined was Japanese-accented German.

Walther made a face. "I wish I'd never suggested it," he said. Priepke laughed. He thought Walther was kidding, as he'd been. Walther knew too well he wasn't.

A chilly wind blew through Stahnsdorf. Rain was coming, but it hadn't got there yet. Inside the Gimpels' house, everything was warm and cozy. Heinrich moved at his wife's direction, putting this away and dusting that. He didn't move fast enough to suit her. "What's the matter?" she asked. "The Dorsches haven't been over in a while. Don't you feel like playing bridge?"

"It's not that," Heinrich said, and it wasn't. He was always ready to play bridge.

"What is it, then?" Before Lise went on, she looked around to make sure the girls were out of earshot. "Erika making you nervous?"

"Ha," he said in a hollow voice. Erika damn well did make him nervous. He hadn't said a word about running into her at Ulbricht's. He still didn't know what to think about that. The doorbell rang. He wasn't going to get a chance to decide now.

Lise was closer, so she opened the door. They all hugged and said hello and asked about children and said how glad they were to see one another. With a flourish, Willi handed Lise his usual offering of a bottle of wine. "Open it now," he said. "When we make mistakes at the bridge table, we always need something to blame them on."

Erika opened her mouth. Heinrich knew exactly what she was going to say. He didn't feel like having the sniping start before the Dorsches even got out of the front hall. Since he didn't, he forestalled her, asking, "How are—things?"

They could take that any way they wanted. Willi took it the way Heinrich had intended. He waggled his palm back and forth. "So-so," he said. "We have our ups and downs." Never one to leave a setup line alone, he finished, "Maybe not as often as when I was twenty-two, but we manage."

You'd manage more if it weren't for Ilse. Even you know that. Heinrich didn't say it. He did wonder whether Erika would, and how he could deflect her if she started to. Fortunately, she kept quiet. Heinrich wouldn't have wanted to be on the receiving end of the look she sent Willi, though.

"Let me go open the wine," Lise said. "Why doesn't everybody else sit down?"

Willi dealt the first hand. "And now to give myself thirteen diamonds," he said grandly.

"As long as you give me thirteen hearts, I don't mind," Heinrich said.

Reality returned as soon as he picked up his hand, which showed the usual mixture of suits and ten points. Willi opened with a club. Heinrich passed. Erika said, "Two clubs," which meant she had some support for Willi but not a great deal. He took it to three, after which everybody passed. And he made three clubs with no overtricks but without much trouble.

"A leg," he said as Erika wrote their sixty points under the line.

Heinrich gathered up the cards and started shuffling. "The only thing legs are good for is getting chopped off," he observed. He dealt out the next hand and opened with a spade. After a lively auction, he and Lise got to four spades. Willi doubled. If they made it, they would take the game and wipe out the Dorsches' partial score. If they went down, it would get expensive above the line.

Erika led a heart; Willi had been bidding them. When Lise laid out the dummy, Heinrich got an unpleasant surprise. He had the ace, queen, ten, and nine of spades, plus a little one. His wife had four little spades to the eight. That left the king and jack conspicuously missing, along with two little ones to protect them. Considering the other problems he had in the hand, it also left him in trouble.

Willi took the trick with the king of hearts, then led the ace. When that went through without getting trumped, he grinned at Heinrich and said, "Got you."

"Maybe." Heinrich shrugged. He thought Willi had him, too, but he was damned if he'd admit it.

"No maybes about it." Willi led a diamond. That wasn't the way to finish Heinrich off. He had to ace in his hand, while the king was on the board. He decided he would rather be in the dummy, so he took the trick with the king. Then he led a small spade from the dummy. Willi played another one. Heinrich hesitated, but only for a moment. He set down the ten. Behind the cards of the dummy, Lise blinked.

He felt like shouting when Erika sluffed a club. That meant Willi had all the opposition's spades. No wonder he'd doubled. But it also meant . . . Happily, Heinrich said, "I'm going to finesse you right out of your shoes."

Willi looked revolted. Heinrich didn't blame him a bit. Had he been sitting in that chair instead of this one, he would have been revolted, too. And he had plenty of board entries, so he could get back to the dummy whenever he needed to. He pulled Willi's trumps, one by one; Willi couldn't make any of them good. And he made the contract—doubled.

"A deep finesse," Willi said mournfully. "Who would have thought *you* would run a deep finesse? And who would have thought it would work?"

"I had to," Heinrich answered. "It was the only way I even had a chance to make four. So I thought, why not?"

"That's the way to do it," Erika said. "If you've got one chance—take it."

She looked right at him as she said that. He passed her the cards in a hurry. He knew too well she wasn't talking about bridge.

In spite of that hand, she and Willi won the rubber. They didn't win by as much as they would have if Willi hadn't doubled. Erika let Willi hear about that when it was over. He gave her a dirty look. "We won," he said. "Quit complaining."

If that wasn't calculated to annoy her, it certainly did the job. The only way Heinrich found to make them stop bickering was to bring out a fresh bottle of wine, a fancy burgundy. It made Willi wonder aloud whether he'd robbed a bank or started taking kickbacks from the Americans. Heinrich didn't care. If Willi was teasing him, he wasn't throwing darts at Erika. When he wasn't, he was good company—and so was she. Of course, the more they drank, the less they were liable to care what they said. Heinrich knew he might only be putting off trouble. If he didn't put it off, though, he already had it inside the door.

He and Lise won the next rubber. All the hands were cut and dried. Nobody could complain about anyone's play. That relieved Heinrich. How fast the bottle of burgundy emptied didn't, especially since Willi and Erika drank more of it than Lise and he did. He didn't begrudge them the wine. But he feared it wouldn't just be *in vino veritas. In vino calamitas* seemed much more likely.

The third rubber also went well enough. Erika and Willi won it as smoothly and as competently as he and Lise had taken the second. Heinrich's only bad moment came when Erika started loudly praising the first edition of *Mein Kampf*. But he could even cautiously agree with her. She couldn't be far wrong if the *Führer* was saying the same thing.

Because the first three rubbers had gone briskly, they decided to play another one. Lise, who drank the least of the four of them, broke out another bottle of wine. However much Heinrich wanted to, he couldn't yell, *My God, what are you doing?* Since he couldn't, he waited numbly—quite numbly, since he'd had a good bit himself—to see what happened next.

What happened next was that Willi went down three on a hand he should have been able to make with his eyes closed. Considering the way he played it, he might have had them closed all through it. When it was finally over, he looked at his tricks and the defenders' like a man contemplating a traffic accident he'd caused. "Well," he said in tones of rueful surprise, "*that* didn't work."

"I'll tell you why it didn't work, too," Erika said. "It didn't work because you're an idiot."

"I don't know what I could have—" Willi began.

She told him. She told him in great detail. And she was quite obviously right. Then she said, "If you can't hit the target any better with Ilse, she's got an—"

Heinrich and Lise both said something, anything, to keep Erika from finishing that sentence. Afterwards, Heinrich never could remember what had burst from his lips, or from his wife's. Erika *didn't* finish, either: a triumph of sorts. But only of sorts, for enough of the damage was already done. Willi went a hot crimson color; his skin might have belonged to a perfectly ripe apple.

"You've got a lot of damned nerve complaining about me," he said, his voice low and rough and furious. "You're the one who wants to—"

"Enough!" That wasn't Heinrich but Lise. She rarely raised her voice. When she did, as now, surprise made everyone pay attention to her. She went on, "There's a time and a place for everything, and this isn't the time and the place for that."

The Dorsches could easily have erupted. If they had, the friendship probably would have exploded right there at the bridge table. Heinrich waited. The shrapnel from that explosion would tear into him, not into his wife. But it didn't come. Erika and Willi kept on glaring at each other, but neither one of them said anything new and inflammatory.

After a long, long moment, Erika turned to Lise and said, "You make good sense. I see where Heinrich gets it."

"Oh, *Quatsch,*" Lise said. "Now I have to figure out which one of us you just insulted." She gathered up the cards. "In the meantime, can we play some bridge? Hitting each other over the head with rocks is a different game, and it shouldn't be a spectator sport."

"What do you know about it?" Willi asked, half blustering, half amused. "You and Heinrich never do it."

She and Heinrich both laughed raucously. Heinrich knew their marriage had its creaks and strains, as what marriage does not? He could put his finger on four or five without even thinking. No doubt Lise could do the same. And no doubt some of his wouldn't be the same as some of hers, which was in itself a strain. But none of that was anybody's business but his and Lise's.

That thought led him to the next one: "We just try not to do it when other people are watching."

"Oh, but having other people watch is half the fun," Willi said. Erika nodded. There, for once, she agreed with her husband.

Heinrich, on the other hand, did his best to hide a shudder. Little green men from Mars could have had no more alien an attitude. Put your life on display, as if you were characters on a daytime televisor drama? He couldn't imagine living like that. One of the reasons he and Lise got on so well was that she was as intensely private a person as he was.

"Whose deal is it, anyhow?" Willi asked, as easily as if he and Erika hadn't been shelling each other a couple of minutes before. "Let's see if I can butcher another one, eh?" Erika stirred. Suddenly, she jerked in surprise. Had Lise kicked her under the table? Heinrich had trouble imagining his wife doing such a thing. He also had trouble finding any other reason Erika would have jerked like that.

Willi did win the contract, at three diamonds. He made it. Heinrich hadn't been sure he would, but he did. If anything, that left Heinrich relieved. He wasn't used to rooting for the opposition. He didn't much like it. It took the competitive edge off the bridge.

The Dorsches won the rubber. Again, Heinrich wasn't sorry, and wished he were. Usually, they would have talked and drunk for a while after they set down the cards—or maybe they just would have played some more. Tonight, Willi and Erika got up and left with only the most perfunctory good-byes. Heinrich and Lise didn't ask them to stay longer, even in the most perfunctory way.

"Are we going to be able to have them over any more, or to go to their place?" Lise asked once they'd gone. "The bridge is all very well, but some things are more trouble than they're worth."

"Yes, I know," Heinrich said. He also feared he knew what Willi had been about to say when Lise forestalled him. After Erika jabbed him about Ilse, he would have jabbed her about making a play for Heinrich. If things had been bad, had been ugly, before then, how much worse and uglier would they have got afterwards?

Heinrich was a man who thought in quantitative terms. If he couldn't put numbers to something, it didn't feel real to him. He couldn't put numbers to this, but, for once, he didn't need to. It would have been about as bad as it could get.

Alicia Gimpel didn't like December. The sun rose late and set early, and clouds and fog were so thick you mostly couldn't see it when it did sneak into the sky. It rained a lot of the time. When it didn't rain, sometimes it snowed. Some people said they liked having seasons—it made them enjoy spring and summer more. Alicia couldn't fathom that. She wished she lived somewhere like Italy, where it was warm and nice almost all year round.

The only thing December had going for it was Christmas. She liked the tree and its spicy smell and the ornaments and gifts. She liked the fat roast goose her mother cooked every year. She liked the break from school she got at Christmas and New Year's. And, of course, she liked the presents.

This year, though, she looked at Christmas in a new way. Up till now, it had always been *her* holiday. If she was a Jew, though, it was someone else's holiday. Her family would still do the same things: she was sure of that. They would have to; if they didn't, people would wonder why not. But what they did wouldn't feel the same.

Then something else occurred to her. Jews had their own New Year's Day. They had other holidays of their own, too. She remembered Purim, when she'd found out she was a Jew. She asked her mother, "Do we have a holiday of our own that's like Christmas?"

Lise Gimpel was frying potato pancakes fragrant with onion in a big pan of hot oil. "Where are your sisters?" was the first thing she asked.

"They're upstairs," Alicia answered.

Her mother looked around to make sure Alicia was right. Then she answered. "We have a holiday at this time of year. It's called Chanukah." She told of Antiochus' war against the Jews more than 2,100 years before, and of the oil that burned for eight days instead of just one.

Alicia listened, entranced. Then, as was her way, she started thinking about what she'd heard. "The Persians wanted to get rid of us," she said. Her mother nodded. "And these Syrians or Greeks or whatever they were wanted to get rid of us." Mommy nodded again. Alicia went on, "And the Nazis wanted to get rid of us, too."

"You know that's true," her mother said. "They still do. Never forget it."

"I won't. I can't," Alicia said. "But what did we ever do to make so many people want to wipe us out?"

"I don't think we ever tried to do anything," her mother replied. "We just tried to live our own lives our own way."

"There has to be more than that," Alicia insisted. Her mother shook her head. She asked, "Well, why is it just us, then?"

"It's not *just* us," her mother answered. "The Turks did it to the Armenians; the Germans did it to the gypsies, too; the Americans did it to their blacks. I think it's happened to us so much because we're stubborn about being what we are. We didn't want to worship Antiochus' gods. We had our own God. We didn't think Jesus was anything special. People made us pay for that, too. We want to do what we do, that's all—do it and not be bothered. We don't bother anybody else."

"It seems like . . . an awful lot of trouble," Alicia said hesitantly.

"Well, yes." Her mother managed a smile. "But we think it's what God wants us to do, too, you know."

"I suppose so." Alicia frowned. "How do we know that's what God wants us to do, though?"

"I didn't say we knew. I said we thought so." Her mother sighed. "I could tell you that's what the Bible says, but if you look through the Bible and pick out this and that, you can make it say anything under the sun. So I'll just say this is what we've thought for all these years, all these generations, ever since before the Maccabees, before Esther and Mordechai. It's a long, long chain of people. The Nazis almost broke it, but they didn't quite. Do you want to let them?"

"No," Alicia said, "not when you put it like that." She had a child's conservatism: things that were should keep on going. And she also had her own strong sense of order, one much like her father's.

"When all you girls find out what you are, we'll be able to do a little more for Chanukah," her mother said. "You'll all get some Chanukah *gelt* for the eight nights. You're supposed to light candles, too: one the first night, two the second, and so on up to eight. I don't know if we'll ever be able to try that, though. If anybody caught us, it would be the end."

Hiding. Doing what you could. Remembering what you were supposed to do but couldn't. Maybe one day your descendants would be able to. If they ever could, those were things they would need to know. A long, long chain of people. That was what Alicia's mother had said. Suddenly, Alicia realized she wasn't the last link on the chain. Others would come after her. One day, in the far, far future, there would be as many ahead of her as behind her—if the chain didn't break here.

"I understand," she whispered. "I really do."

"Good." Her mother flipped potato pancakes with an iron spatula. "We make these at Chanukah, too. That's not part of the religion. It's just part of the celebration. And the nice thing is, it's safe, because people make potato pancakes all the time. Nobody particularly notices if you do."

"Nobody particularly notices if you do what?" Francesca asked from the doorway.

Alicia jumped. Her heart leaped into her throat. How much had her little sister overheard? Enough to send her running to the Security Police because she didn't know what was what? Maybe not, or she wouldn't have asked that particular question. She must have got there just before she spoke up.

Mommy never turned a hair. "Nobody particularly notices if you give somebody a potato pancake before supper," she said, and scooped out three—one for Alicia, one for Francesca, and one for Roxane. "Be careful with them. They're hot. And Francesca, go get your little sister, so she can have one, too. Yours will cool off in the meantime."

Away Francesca ran. Alicia shared a secret smile with her mother. They knew something the smaller girls didn't. And it would stay a secret for a while, and then get told. And the chain would go on.

X

As far as Susanna Weiss was concerned, faculty New Year's parties were as dismal as they sounded. People who often didn't much like one another gathered in a place where none of them particularly wanted to be. They talked too much. They drank too much. They made passes they would have known were hopeless or offensive if they hadn't drunk too much. And they had to show up and go through the ordeal every bloody year, because if they didn't they would hear about it from the department chairman. Franz Oppenhoff had a long memory for those who disdained his hospitality. Such mistakes had blighted careers.

To add insult to injury, he served cheap scotch.

Even if it was cheap, though, it—and the schnapps, and the brandy, and the wine, and the beer—did help loosen tongues. And even if people did talk too much, there was more to talk about than usual. It wasn't just who'd published what in which academic journal, who'd been promoted or passed over, and who was sleeping with which bright and/or beautiful student. This year, for the first time in Susanna's memory and probably for the first time in old man Oppenhoff's, too, people were talking politics.

"This system has grit in the gears, but I am of the opinion that we can clean it up, lubricate it, and make it run smoothly, the way it should," declared Helmut von Kupferstein, who was a Goethe scholar.

Susanna was of the opinion that von Kupferstein was a pompous ass.

He was also thirty centimeters taller than she was, and kept threatening to drop cigarette ashes in her drink without having any idea he was doing it. She also knew he would never have dared such a thing while Kurt Haldweim was *Führer*. Still, she could say, "I hope we can make things better," without fearing the Security Police would haul her away five seconds later, and so she did.

Von Kupferstein—he was the sort who insisted on the *von*—nodded ponderously. About a centimeter of ash from the cigarette went flying. Susanna jerked her glass aside just in time. The ash landed on the carpet. She stepped on it. He said, "All things are possible under Heinz Buckliger. 'He who wishes to uphold the truth and has but one tongue, he will uphold it indeed.' " He looked smug at working in a quotation from *Faust*.

But Susanna, here, couldn't quarrel with him—except about that damned cigarette. "This is a good attitude to have," she said. "We haven't always been perfectly truthful before. 'The great masses of the people will more easily fall victim to a big lie than to a small one.' " That was a quotation, too, from *Mein Kampf*. She couldn't very well go wrong there.

Helmut von Kupferstein nodded in recognition. "Oh, yes. But the National Socialists were up-and-comers then," he said. "Such things are beneath the dignity of those who actually rule."

"They haven't been," Susanna said, and walked away. If he thought indignity was the only thing wrong with lies . . . ! But even that wouldn't have occurred to him a year earlier (or, if it had, he wouldn't have had the nerve to say it). If Buckliger was making people look at the way things were and compare them to the way they ought to be, that was a step forward.

Near the liquor—no great surprise there—Franz Oppenhoff stood pontificating to several professors not clever enough to get away but clever enough to look fascinated at the department chairman's every word. Oppenhoff said, "Some remarkable things have happened this past year: not the least remarkable of which is that they have been allowed to happen."

"*Jawohl, Herr Doktor* Professor!" three members of the captive audience said at the same time.

"We have been ordered to be free, and so . . . free we shall be." Professor Oppenhoff stood there beaming, unconscious of any irony. The junior members of the faculty all but genuflected. That the department chairman didn't know he was being ironic frightened Susanna more than anything else.

And yet, was he so far wrong? All Heinz Buckliger had done was loosen the straps of the straitjacket a little. Susanna didn't think the *Führer* wanted anything more than to make it fit the *Reich* better. But if people started trying to wiggle out of the sleeves, how could he complain? He was the one who'd made it possible in the first place.

Would they really start wiggling? The English proverb was, *Give 'em an inch and they'll take a mile.* The *Reich* had taken both inches and miles from Britain, forcing the metric system on it. The point remained. If the *Führer* gave an inch . . .

Susanna shook her head and went over to the scotch again. If the *Führer* gave an inch, the SS was all too likely to take it away again—and to break your fingers because you'd tried to grab it.

Professor Oppenhoff fixed himself another drink, too. The old boy had to have a liver like a sponge; he could pour down a lot of sauce without showing it. Like an old-fashioned archduke, he inclined his head to Susanna. "A good New Year to you, Professor Weiss," he rumbled, and exhaled a cloud of cigar smoke almost as toxic as mustard gas.

"Thank you, sir. The same to you." Susanna wondered how she could get away.

"I daresay you approve of the radical changes we have seen lately," Oppenhoff observed.

There was a not-quite-question that dropped her right in the middle of a minefield. If she denied it, he'd know she was lying. She'd always been as radical as she could be in a police state. If she admitted it, that might come back to haunt her after a crackdown. The calculations you had to make, living in such a state . . .

"Hard not to approve of anything that lets us inquire more openly into all sorts of things," she said after no more than a second's silence. If she kept her answer strictly related to business, it was—she hoped—less likely to seem politically dangerous.

"Inquire more openly?" Professor Oppenhoff pondered that with a judicious puff on the cigar and another cloud of poisonous smoke. "We in the Department of Germanic Languages have never been greatly restricted in our scholarship."

"Well, no," Susanna said. Could he be as naive as he sounded? She had trouble believing it. True, the Nazis didn't interfere so much with a professor of Middle English or Gothic or Old High German. But why would they? Susanna's research touched the modern world almost nowhere. If she'd taught sociology or psychology or political science, it would have been a different story. Anthropology? Anthropology was so full of Aryan doctrine, it was hard to tell science—if there was any—from ideology there.

Franz Oppenhoff seemed oblivious to all that. "Inquiry is good," he said with the air of a man making a large concession. Then his gaze sharpened. "And I congratulate you on placing your recent articles in two most distinguished journals. This brings credit to the whole department."

"*Danke schön, Herr Doktor* Professor," Susanna said. "I hope you will agree it also brings credit to me?"

Did Oppenhoff turn red? With all the booze he carried, it was hard to tell. The cigar could have caused his cough. "No doubt it does," he said without conviction. "Your research is, ah, most original."

"Thank you again," Susanna said, though he hadn't meant it for a compliment. She'd undoubtedly written more about the roles of women in literature, for instance, than all the men in the department put together. *Herr Doktor* Professor Oppenhoff would have looked down his nose at that even more than he did—he was an unreconstructed *Küche, Kirche, Kinder* man—if she hadn't repeatedly placed her articles in some of the most prestigious academic publications in the Germanic Empire.

"Modern ideas," he muttered now. "Well, you are better suited to cope with them than I am. When they say they are going to change the ideology we have lived under for longer than I have been alive . . . Is it any wonder I have a hard time working up much enthusiasm?"

"If the change is for the better, we should make it," Susanna said. She made herself a fresh drink, wishing the scotch would change for the better.

"Yes. If," Oppenhoff said. "Who knows? Whatever happens, you are bound to see more of it than I do." With that cheery reflection, he went off to inflict himself on someone else. Susanna took a long pull at the new drink, even if it was nasty. If the Security Police ever found out what she was, the department chairman would outlive her by years.

"What's this?" Heinrich Gimpel asked as he and Willi Dorsch got off their bus and started toward *Oberkommando der Wehrmacht* headquarters. The trip in from Stahnsdorf hadn't been much fun. An icy dagger of a wind from off the Baltic—seemingly straight from the North Pole—brought flurries of snow and spatters of freezing rain with it, which made standing at the bus stop an ordeal. Then the bus had had to detour around a wreck the freezing rain had probably caused. And now black-uniformed Security Police stood alongside the usual *Wehrmacht* guards. The *Wehrmacht* men did not look delighted to have company.

"Have you forgotten?" Willi answered. "The *Gauleiter*'s going to tell us how *wunderbar* we are this morning."

"Oh, joy." Heinrich had no trouble containing his enthusiasm. Rolf Stolle, the Party leader who essentially ran Berlin, was a hard-drinking, womanizing bruiser. If this generation had anybody whose debauchery came close to the legendary Göring's, Stolle was the man. "What he knows about this place would fit on the head of a pin."

"Well, yes," Willi said. "But he'll be entertaining. Wouldn't you rather listen to him than stare at spreadsheets?"

The honest answer to that was no. If Heinrich said as much, Willi would laugh at him and call him a greasy grind. He shrugged instead. Willi laughed at him anyway, which meant he knew what Heinrich wasn't saying.

Up at the top of the stairs, the Berlin police scrutinized identification cards before giving them to the usual guards to run through the reader. The *Wehrmacht* men smirked slightly as they returned the cards to Heinrich and Willi. *These fellows think they're important,* they might have said. *They think so, but they're wrong.*

Signs taped to the walls said, HEAR ROLF STOLLE IN THE ASSEMBLY HALL! Heinrich sighed. He really would rather have worked. What did he need with one more tub-thumping Nazi blowhard? But he couldn't take the chance of antagonizing the Party. *If anybody wonders why one of my projects is late, I'll tell the truth, that's all.*

Televisor cameras were set up in the assembly hall. Whatever Stolle said would go out locally. It might even go out all over the *Reich,* all over the Empire. That did not rouse Heinrich's enthusiasm. Broadcast speeches were no more exciting than any other kind.

Rolf Stolle clumped around up on stage. He was a big bald bear of a man, with a wrestler's shoulders and an actor's large, graceful hands. Resignedly, Heinrich sat down in a plushy chair. He wondered if he could fall asleep without being noticed. He closed his eyes in an experimental way. But he was awake. If he hadn't had his morning coffee . . . He had, though. *Maybe Stolle will put me under*. There was a hopeful thought.

More analysts and officers and secretaries came in, till the front rows were full and the hall nearly so. It wouldn't do for the *Gauleiter* to make a televised speech in front of a lot of empty seats. Stolle took his place behind the lectern. More Security Police stood behind him as bodyguards. Heinrich tried to yawn without opening his mouth. By the way Willi snickered, he might have done better.

"Good morning, gentlemen—and all you pretty ladies, too," Stolle boomed. A couple of women giggled at his leer. Heinrich's guess was that the luck he enjoyed with them came from his rank, not from his person. *He* certainly wouldn't have wanted that big oaf pawing him. The *Gauleiter* went on, "We are where we are today because of what the *Wehrmacht* has done for the *Reich*. Without our armed forces, Germany would be weak and our enemies strong. With them, we are strong, and our enemies mostly dead."

Heinrich didn't bother keeping his mouth shut when he yawned this time. How often had he heard such boastful claptrap? More often than he wanted; he knew that. Next, Stolle would talk about how wonderful the National Socialists were.

And he did: "The *Wehrmacht* is the gun, and the Party is the man who aims it. We chose the targets for your might, and you knocked them down one by one. Wise leadership served us well."

It was all as predictable as the Mass. With fancy uniforms and swastika flags, the Nazis tried to make such ceremonials as majestic as the Mass, too. In Heinrich's private—very private—opinion, they were just bombastic. To most Party *Bonzen*, the two words might have been interchangeable.

But then, though Rolf Stolle kept right on hamming it up for all he was worth, he suddenly stopped boring Heinrich, for he went on, "Wise leadership is always important. And our beloved *Führer* is very wise in setting our affairs to rights. Some of the things we did in days gone by are no longer needed. And *some* of the things we did in days gone by, perhaps, we never should have done at all."

Heinrich looked at Willi. Willi was looking back at him. A low mutter of surprise ran through the hall. Whatever people had expected Stolle to say, this wasn't it.

"There are people who say, 'Let's not change this,' " he rolled on. "There are people who say, 'Let's not remember this.' There are people who say, 'Let's not remind the *Volk* that the Party was supposed to be democratic, that the first *Führer* said so right from the start.' These people, some of them, have lots of decorations. These people, some of them, have lots of power. These people, most of them, have got fat and comfortable and lazy with things just the way they are. And, *meine Damen und Herren,* that's a pile of crap!"

The mutter of astonishment that went through the hall wasn't low this time. Rolf Stolle beamed, as if he'd set eyes on a good-looking blonde. His bald bullet head gleamed under the televisor lights. "A pile of crap I said, *meine Damen und Herren,* and a pile of crap I meant. The *Führer* knows it, too, and he's trying to clean it up. But he needs help. And he needs something else, too.

"Trouble is, Heinz Buckliger is a gentleman. He wants to go slow. He wants to be polite. He doesn't want to hurt anybody's feelings, God forbid. But I am here to tell you, I don't think going slow and being polite will get the job done. I am here to tell you, when you see a pile of crap, you grab the biggest goddamn shovel you can find, you wade in, and you clean it up. No ifs, ands, or buts."

Stolle slammed his fist down on the lectern. "We have to move faster. We have to push harder. If it were up to me, I'd get rid of a lot of the lemon-faced naysayers who sit behind big desks and look important. Let 'em do something useful for a change, or else put 'em out to pasture. *And let the people speak.* As soon as we have real elections, you'll see what they think about folk like that. The sooner, the better. And let the chips fall where they may. They will, too. *Danke schön. Auf wiedersehen.*"

He made as much of a production of leaving the stage as most people did of coming to it. Only a thin spattering of applause followed him. Heinrich understood that. He hardly remembered to clap himself. What he'd heard, what Rolf Stolle had said, left him stunned. He couldn't possibly have been the only one, either.

Beside him, Willi said, "My God."

No, Heinrich couldn't have been, and he wasn't. He said, "Some people don't like the *Führer* because he's doing too much. I knew that. I never dreamt anybody would have the nerve to say he's not doing enough."

"Neither did I," Willi said. "Stolle's off the reservation—he has to be. And he'll be *on* the televisor. For all I know, that speech could have been broadcast live. What are people going to think? What's Buckliger going to think?"

"Beats me," Heinrich answered. "Maybe he's saying what Buckliger told him to."

"Fat chance! When was the last time anybody ever criticized a *Führer?*" Willi said. "And you were the fellow who didn't want to come," he added as they got up and started back to their office. "You were the fellow who didn't want to leave his precious desk. What do you think now?"

"I think I'd have felt like an idiot if I'd stayed away," Heinrich said honestly. "A speech like that will go in the history books." *If Stolle isn't taken out and shot in the next few days, anyhow.* By the look on Willi's face, he was thinking the same thing.

If Rolf Stolle thought his speech would land him in trouble, he gave no sign of it. He came into the office where the budget analysts worked. He wasn't after information, the way Heinz Buckliger had been. He just wanted to see and, especially, to be seen. Heinrich watched Ilse watching the *Gauleiter,* and watched Willi watching Ilse watching the *Gauleiter*. Ilse looked charmed, or perhaps calculating. Willi looked . . . *dyspeptic* was the word that came to mind.

And Stolle noticed Ilse, too. "Hello, sweetie," he said. "What do you do around here?"

"Why, whatever these gentlemen want me to do, *mein Herr,*" she answered in a breathy, little-girl voice.

"Do you, now?" the *Gauleiter* rumbled. His eyes lit up. "Maybe you could do that kind of work for me, too. Let me have your number. We'll see what we can find out." He didn't pretend to be anything but the predator he was. Ilse gave him her extension. Willi quietly steamed. Heinrich did his best to seem very, very busy.

Rolf Stolle swept away, flanked by his bodyguards. How many other phone numbers would he collect before he went back to his own office? More than a few, unless Heinrich was altogether mistaken. He missed some of the subtle human byplay that went on around him. He didn't think he was missing anything here. *Subtle* was not a word in Stolle's vocabulary.

But some of the words that were in his vocabulary . . . ! When this speech went out, a lot of Party *Bonzen* would hate him. But a lot of ordinary people would love him. Which counted for more? Till Heinz Buckliger took over, the answer would have been obvious. It wasn't any more.

And what *would* Buckliger himself think of Stolle's speech? That might be the most interesting question of them all.

Esther Stutzman looked up from the billing to see a woman and a little boy come into Dr. Dambach's waiting room. "Good morning, *Frau* Klein," she said. "Good morning, Eduard. How are you today?"

"*I'm* all right," said Eduard, who was just in for a checkup.

Maria Klein let out a long sigh. "I'm not so well, *Frau* Stutzman," she said. In public, they didn't let on how well they knew each other away from the pediatrician's office. But she didn't look good; makeup couldn't hide the dark circles under her eyes, and their whites were tracked with red. "Richard and I have decided to take Paul to a *Reichs* Mercy Center."

"I'm so sorry," Esther whispered.

"He'll be better," Eduard said. "He'll be happy after that. He's not happy now."

His mother winced and turned away for a moment. It wasn't that Eduard was wrong, for he wasn't. From everything Esther had unwillingly learned, Tay-Sachs disease was a slow descent into hell, made all the worse because the children who suffered from it were too little to understand what was happening to them. But that made it no easier for parents to let go of children who had it. How could you not love a child, even if—or maybe especially because—something was wrong with it?

"He was such a sweet baby," Maria whispered. "He still is, as much as he can be. But he—" She turned away again, and fished a tissue out of her purse. "I don't want Eduard to see me like this," she said, dabbing at her eyes.

"I see you, Mommy." To Eduard, none of this meant much. He was the lucky one. "And Paul will be all better. You and Daddy said so."

"Yes, sweetheart. He'll be just fine," Maria said. "Why don't you go sit down and look at a picture book till it's time to see the doctor?"

Eduard went. The book he picked up was *Trust No Fox in the Green Meadow and No Jew on His Oath*. It had been in the waiting room since before Esther started working for Dr. Dambach. The pediatrician took the book for granted. Why shouldn't he? It had been a children's favorite and a Party favorite for seventy-five years. Eduard opened it. He smiled as he swallowed a dose of cheerful, colorful poison.

Maria Klein saw what her son was looking at. The most she could do was exchange a rueful glance with Esther. If she'd come in for an afternoon appointment today, when Irma Ritter sat behind the counter, she couldn't even have done that.

So much Eduard will have to unlearn when he gets older, Esther thought sadly. Gottlieb and Anna were still battling that. So was Alicia Gimpel. Esther knew she was still battling it herself, and would be till the end of her days. When everyone around her thought she and all the people like her deserved to be dead, how could she help wondering whether what the Nazis taught wasn't right after all? Those were the black thoughts, the up-at-three-in-the-morning-and-can't-sleep thoughts. She knew they were nonsense. She knew, but they kept coming back anyway.

Maria sat down by Eduard. He held the book up to her. "Look, Mommy! It's funny!"

She made herself look. She had to know what was in there. When she was Eduard's age, she'd probably thought it was funny, too. With a visible effort, she nodded. "Yes, dear," she said. "It is."

A woman came out of one of the examination rooms carrying a wailing toddler who'd just had a tetanus shot. "She may be cranky and feverish for a day or two, and the injection site will be sore," Dr. Dambach told her. "A pain-relieving syrup will help. If the discomfort seems severe, bring her back in, and I'll look at her." How many times had he made that speech?

"Thank you, Doctor," the woman said. The toddler didn't seem grateful.

"*Frau* Klein, you can take your boy back in there now," Esther called. Poor Maria got no relief, for Eduard carried Streicher's book into the examining room with him. When he laughed at the anti-Semitic book, that had to be one more lash for her, especially since her other son was dying of a disease commonest among Jews.

Dr. Dambach had patients waiting in the other examining rooms. It was a while before he could get to Maria and Eduard. Once he went in there, he spent a good long while with the Kleins. Esther knew he was thorough. If he hadn't been, he wouldn't have noticed discrepancies in their genealogy. Usually, though, that thoroughness worked for him and for his patients.

When he came out with Maria and her son, he had one hand on the boy's shoulder and the other on hers. "This one here is in the best of health, *Frau* Klein," he said. "He'll drive you crazy for years to come."

"Crazy!" Eduard said enthusiastically. He crossed his eyes and stuck out his tongue.

The pediatrician ignored him, which wasn't easy. Dambach went on talking to Maria Klein: "And I think you are doing the right thing in the other case. The procedure is very fast. It is absolutely painless. And it does relieve needless suffering."

"Paul's, yes," she answered. "What about mine, and my husband's?"

"Things are not always as simple as we wish they would be," Dr. Dambach said with a sigh. "You have the suffering of doing this, yes, but you escape the suffering of watching his inevitable downhill course over the coming months, perhaps even over a couple of years. Which counts for more?"

"I don't know," Maria whispered. "Do you?"

The pediatrician shrugged. He was basically an honest man. Now that the Kleins had been released, he showed no antagonism toward them. He'd done what he thought he had to do in reporting the discrepancy in their pedigree to the authorities. If the authorities turned out not to care, he didn't seem to, either.

Maria went on, "And it's also hard knowing that there's a fifty-fifty chance Eduard carries this horrible—thing inside him."

"Don't let that worry you," Dr. Dambach said. "In most populations, this gene is very rare. Even if he does carry it, the odds that he will marry another carrier are also very slim. There is hardly any chance he would father another baby with this disease."

Maria Klein didn't answer. Like all surviving Jews, she was practiced in the art of deception, so she didn't even look towards Esther. Esther didn't look her way, either, but kept on with the billing as she and Eduard walked out. But she knew, and Maria knew, in fifteen or twenty years Eduard would probably marry a girl who was a Jew. And in how many of those girls did the Tay-Sachs gene lurk?

The Kleins left the waiting room. Esther called in the next patients. But she had trouble keeping her mind on her work. If Jews kept marrying Jews, would disease finish what the Nazis hadn't quite been able to? But if Jews didn't marry Jews, wouldn't the faith perish because they couldn't tell their partners what they were?

Was there a way out? For the life of her, Esther couldn't see one.

Susanna Weiss had been taking her students through Chaucer's *Troylus and Criseyde*. When she asked for questions, one of them asked, "This is the basis for Shakespeare's play, isn't it?"

"It's probably the most important source, yes, but it's far from the only one," she answered. Again, the question reminded her how Shakespeare was a more vital presence in modern Germany than in England. His *Troilus and Cressida* was rarely produced or even read in English.

A few more questions about the material followed. Students started drifting out the door. Others—not so many—came up to the lectern to ask questions of less general interest, to pump her on what the next essay topic would be, or to complain about the grades they'd got on the last one.

And then one of the students asked, "What did you think of Stolle's speech, Professor Weiss?"

"It was interesting," Susanna answered. "We haven't heard anything like it in a while." That was the truth. When had anyone ever publicly criticized the *Führer,* even for not pushing his own agenda far enough and fast enough? Had anyone ever done such a thing in all the days of the Third *Reich?* She didn't think so.

"But what did you *think* of it?" he persisted. "Isn't it wonderful to hear somebody come out and speak his mind like that?"

She didn't say anything for a moment. *Who are you?* she wondered. All she knew about this enthusiastic undergrad was that his name was Karl Stuckart and he was getting a medium B in the course. What did he do when he wasn't in her class? Did he report to the SS? Lothar Prützmann, who headed the blackshirts, undoubtedly had an opinion about Stolle's speech: a low opinion. And if Stuckart didn't report to the SS, did some of the other smiling students here? *The smiler with a knife*—a fine Chaucerian phrase.

One of those students, an auburn-haired girl named Mathilde Burchert, said, "I certainly think it's about time we get moving with reform. We've been in the doldrums forever, and the *Gauleiter*'s right. The *Führer*'s not going fast enough."

Several other students smiled and nodded. Susanna smiled, too, but she didn't nod. She didn't know much about Mathilde Burchert, either. Was she serious? Was she naive? Was she a provocateur, either working with Stuckart or independently? Were the young men and women who showed they agreed with her fools? Or did they sense a breeze Susanna couldn't, or wouldn't, feel?

She hated mistrusting everyone around her. She hated it, but she couldn't let it go. Were she worried about only her own safety, she thought she would have. But choices she would make for herself she wouldn't for other Jews she might endanger if she turned out to be wrong.

"What *do* you think, Professor?" another student asked her.

"I think the *Führer* will go at his own pace regardless of whether anyone tries to jog his elbow," she answered. Hard to go wrong—hard to land in trouble—for backing the *Führer*. It made her seem safely moderate: not a hard-liner who hated the very idea of change, but not a wild-eyed, bomb-throwing radical, either.

And what's a moderate? Someone who gets shot at from the right and *the left*. She wished she hadn't had that thought.

Karl didn't want to leave things alone. "I wasn't so much talking about what would happen. I was talking about what should happen."

No matter how Susanna seemed, her instincts were of the wild-eyed, bomb-throwing sort, and to a degree that made Rolf Stolle hopelessly stodgy. Like Buckliger, Stolle wanted to reform the *Reich*. Susanna wanted to see it fall to pieces, to ruin, to disaster unparalleled. She wished its foes would have smashed it in the Second World War, or the Third. Maybe then she could have lived openly as what she was.

I'll never do that now. Hiding is too ingrained in me. Even if I knew they wouldn't kill me, I couldn't reveal myself that way. Easier to walk up the middle of the Kurfürstendamm naked.

"I'd like to vote in an election where I had a real choice," Mathilde said. "I don't know who I'd vote for, but there sure are plenty of people I'd vote against."

Again, several of the youngsters up by the lectern showed they agreed with her. Only a couple of them frowned. But who was more likely to be a spy for the Security Police, someone who pretended to agree or someone who openly didn't?

Susanna sighed. That question had no answer. Anyone could spy for the Security Police, anyone at all.

Mathilde looked right at her. "How about you, Professor Weiss? Don't you think we'd be better off with real elections than with the ones where everybody just votes *ja* all the time? When Horst says all the *Reichstag* candidates got elected with 99.78 percent of the vote, don't you wonder how he keeps a straight face? It's such a farce! You must feel the same way, too. You're a sharp person. Anyone can tell from the way you lecture. Tell us!"

"Tell us!" the other students echoed. *Tell us you're with it. Tell us you're not a fuddy-duddy. Tell us we don't have to turn into fuddy-duddies when we're your age. Please tell us.*

Am I a sharp person? Susanna wondered. *Am I really? Am I sharp enough to keep my mouth shut when I really want to shout, to scream?* "I don't know anything about politics," she said. "As long as the politicians leave me alone, I'll leave them alone, too."

"But they *don't* leave us alone," Mathilde said fiercely. "If you say the wrong thing today, you're liable to get a noodle tomorrow." Camp slang permeated German these days. Often, people didn't even know where it came from. When you were talking about a bullet in the back of the neck, though, there wasn't much doubt.

"Well . . ." Susanna's conditioned caution warred with the fury and outrage she'd bottled up for so long. She surprised herself. What came out was a compromise, and she wasn't usually good at splitting the difference. All or nothing was more her style. But now she said, "I wasn't sorry when the *Führer* reminded the *Volk* about what the first edition of *Mein Kampf* says. In fact, I was in London for a conference last year when the British Union of Fascists reminded us all."

"You were in London for the BUF convention?" Was that awe or horror in Karl Stuckart's voice? Some of each, probably. Maybe he was wondering if *she* had SS connections.

"No, no, no." Susanna shook her head. "I was in London for the Medieval English Association conference. The BUF was meeting across the street." That she'd found some of the Fascist bruisers more interesting than her fellow professors was a secret she intended to keep.

"It's a shame the British had to remind us of what we should have remembered for ourselves—no, what we never should have forgotten," Mathilde Burchert said. Most of the other students nodded. They didn't seem to fear informers or provocateurs. Maybe they were too young to know better, although in the Greater German *Reich* you were never too young to learn such lessons. Or did they smell freedom on the wind?

Heinrich Gimpel pulled a copy of the *Völkischer Beobachter* out of the vending machine in the Stahnsdorf train station. A moment later, Willi Dorsch paid fifteen pfennigs for his own copy. On the front page was a color photo of Heinz Buckliger receiving an award in Oslo from the *Nasjonal Samling,* the Norwegian Fascist party. The *Führer* was a big blond man. The *Nasjonal Samling* officials in the photo were even bigger and even blonder, with long faces and granite cheekbones.

Willi saw the same thing at the same time. "Damned Scandinavians are the only ones who can racially embarrass us," he said. "Bastards look more Nordic than we do."

Was Willi kidding? Was he kidding on the square? Or did he really mean it? Heinrich had trouble telling. Willi loved to joke, but race, in the *Reich,* was as serious a business as Marxism had been in Russia before it fell. Even the *Führer* hadn't said anything more than that the Nazi founding fathers might not have understood race the right way. Heinrich gave back a grunt and a nod—a minimal answer.

They went up to the platform together, and got there just in time to catch the train to Berlin. Willi grabbed the window seat, then proceeded to unfold his paper and ignore the scenery rolling by. He'd seen it often enough, anyhow. So had Heinrich, who sat down beside him and also buried his nose in the *Beobachter*. Willi seemed to ignore his troubles with Erika, too, except that every once in a while he would come out with a remark that also left Heinrich wondering how to take it.

The two of them stiffened within thirty seconds of each other. They both pointed to the same article on page three. The headline above it said ENOUGH IS ENOUGH. The byline was Konrad Jahnke, not a name Heinrich had seen before. He soon found out why: the author declared himself to be a doctor from Breslau, not a reporter at all.

I am sick and tired, he wrote, *of inaccuracies that blacken the history of the* Reich *and the heroic deeds of our ancestors. Why men who were not there to see them now presume to cast judgment is beyond me. We should be grateful for what our ancestors accomplished. Without their heroism, Jewish Communists in Russia and Jewish capitalists in England and the United States would have swallowed up the whole world between them.*

"Well, well," Willi said. "Looks like the other shoe just dropped, doesn't it?"

"You might say that," Heinrich replied. "Yes, you just might say that. Someone didn't like Stolle's speech, did he?"

"Not very much," Willi said. They both spoke of the article elliptically and in understatements. That was the best way to play down how frightening it was.

Heinrich read on with a detached, horrified fascination: the sort of fascination he would have given to a really nasty traffic accident on the other side of the road. *The whole business of repression has been blown out of proportion in some younger men's heads,* Dr. Jahnke declared. *It overshadows any objective analysis of the past. Hitler may have made mistakes, but no one else could have readied the* Reich *for the great struggle against Bolshevism. Anyone who thinks he can deny this suffers from ideological confusion and has lost his political bearings.*

Jahnke wasn't afraid to name the *Gauleiter* of Berlin, saying, *Rolf Stolle, in his arrogance, departs substantially from the accepted principles of National Socialism. And,* he went on, *other leaders try to make us believe that the country's past was nothing but mistakes and crimes, keeping silent about the greatest achievements of the past and the present.* He didn't name Heinz Buckliger, but he came close.

There is an internal process in this country and abroad, the doctor from Breslau thundered, *that seeks to falsify the truths of National Socialism. Too many ignore the world-historical mission of the* Volk *and its role in the National Socialist movement. I, for one, can never forsake my ideals under any pretext.*

When Heinrich finished the piece, he let out a small, tuneless whistle. Beside him, Willi nodded heavily, as if he'd just done a good job of summing things up. "Who?" Heinrich said. "Who would have the nerve to publish such a thing?"

"Why, you see for yourself," Willi answered. "He's a doctor from Breslau. That gives him the right to say anything he pleases."

"*Quatsch,*" Heinrich said, and then several things a great deal more pungent than that. "Do you notice how carefully this was timed? Think it's an accident that it shows up in the *Beobachter* when Buckliger's out of the country?"

"Just a coincidence," Willi said airily. "What else could it possibly be? They got this letter, and an assistant editor liked it, and so. . . ." He couldn't go on, not with a straight face. He started to snort, and then to giggle. Any junior man who published an inflammatory—to say nothing of reactionary—piece like this without getting it cleared from on high would shortly thereafter wish he'd never been born.

"If you want to talk sense now, let's try it again." Heinrich unconsciously lowered his voice, as people did when they spoke of dangerous things. "Who?"

Willi leaned toward him and whispered in his ear: "Prützmann." Naming the SS chief was more dangerous, and so he did it more quietly. Still whispering, he went on, "Can't be anybody else. If Prützmann says to print it, who's going to tell him no? The *Führer* might make a no stick, but he's not here, like you say. Anybody else? Not a chance. No way in hell."

That made much more sense than Heinrich wished it did. If Lothar Prützmann disliked reform so much, did it have any hope of sticking? If Prützmann disliked Heinz Buckliger's policies so much, did Buckliger have any chance of staying *Führer* for very long? It seemed unlikely, to say the least.

"We'll see what happens when Buckliger comes home, that's all," Willi said. "If he lets this ride . . ." He didn't go on, or need to. If the *Führer* accepted a rebuke like this, any hope of change was dead, and things would go on as they always had. If Buckliger didn't accept it, though . . . If he didn't accept it, things were liable to get very interesting very fast.

The train pulled into South Station. Heinrich and Willi went up to catch the bus to *Oberkommando der Wehrmacht* headquarters. Whenever Heinrich saw somebody carrying a *Völkischer Beobachter,* he tried to eavesdrop. How were Berliners taking this? For that matter, how were people in

Breslau and Bonn and other second-rate towns taking it? This might not play out so neatly, or so quickly.

He heard only two snatches of conversation, both from people going down escalators as he was going up past them. One was "—damn fool—" and the other "—about time—" . . . and both could have meant anything or nothing. So much for eavesdropping.

Nobody on the bus out of South Station seemed to be talking about "Enough Is Enough." That might have been out of a sense of self-preservation; people on that bus were heading for the beating heart of the Greater German *Reich* and of the Germanic Empire. Or it might just have been to drive Heinrich crazy. He wouldn't have been surprised.

When he got off in front of *Oberkommando der Wehrmacht* headquarters, he looked across Adolf Hitler Platz to the *Führer*'s palace. Buckliger wasn't there now, of course. But if he didn't already have a copy of the *Völkischer Beobachter*, he would soon. What he did after that would say a lot about who ran the *Reich*.

As usual, Heinrich and Willi gave the guards at the top of the stairs their identification cards. One of the guards said, "We'll see if Stolle wants the blackshirts standing watch over him after what's in today's papers."

"Would you?" Willi asked. The guard waited till the card showed green on the machine reader, then shook his head.

That aspect of things hadn't occurred to Heinrich until then. If he were Rolf Stolle, would he want Prützmann's henchmen keeping him safe? He didn't think so. Who could arrange a tragic accident more easily than bodyguards? Nobody. Nobody in all the world.

Ilse was on the telephone when Heinrich and Willi walked into their big office. She hung up a moment later, her face flushed with excitement. "The *Gauleiter* is taking me out to lunch today! Me! Can you believe it? Isn't it amazing?"

Heinrich didn't say anything. Willi said, "Amazing," in tones suggesting the only thing along those lines to delight him more would have been an outbreak of bubonic plague. Ilse might not even have noticed his gloom. Next to Rolf Stolle, a budget analyst wasn't amazing at all.

How would Willi handle that? Heinrich sat down, got to work, and watched his friend from the corner of his eye. Willi sat there and fumed: so openly that Heinrich wondered if the office smoke detectors would start buzzing. If Stolle came to pick Ilse up, he might need protection against more than Lothar Prützmann and the SS.

But the *Gauleiter* of Berlin didn't come in person. And the men who did take Ilse off to whatever rendezvous Stolle had set up weren't the black-shirted guards who'd accompanied him on his last visit to *Oberkommando der Wehrmacht* headquarters. They wore the gray uniforms of ordinary Berlin policemen, men much more likely to follow Stolle than Prützmann. Willi noticed that, too. Heinrich could see it on his face. It didn't make him look any happier.

Willi's worries, of course, were personal. Heinrich's were more on the order of, *If the SS tries to assassinate Stolle, could those fellows keep him safe?* Only one answer sprang to mind—*how the devil do I know?*

Ilse came back from lunch very, very late, with a big bouquet of roses in her arms and schnapps on her breath. She giggled a lot and didn't do much work the rest of the afternoon. Somehow, Heinrich doubted Rolf Stolle had spent their time together talking about how to reform National Socialism.

Lise Gimpel got the last of the dishes in the sink as her husband called, "Hurry up, sweetheart. Horst is just coming on."

"Here I am." Lise sat down beside him on the sofa. She couldn't help adding, "I'd have been here sooner if you'd helped."

"Oh." Heinrich looked astonished, as if that hadn't occurred to him. It probably hadn't. She was just going to beat him about the head and shoulders for his male iniquity when he asked, "Why didn't you say something sooner, when I could have given you a hand?"

That hadn't occurred to her. "I thought you'd be tired from your day at the office."

"By now we're both tired. It's the tired time of day."

He was right about that. Before Lise could say so, Horst Witzleben's handsome, blond, ultra-Aryan features filled the screen. A moment later, after the newscaster's greeting, the scene cut away to a Junkers jet airliner—*Luftwaffe Alfa*, the code name was—landing at Tempelhof Airport. "Our beloved *Führer*, Heinz Buckliger, returned to the capital this afternoon after a highly successful tour of the Scandinavian countries," Witzleben said. "He spoke briefly to reporters before going on to his official residence."

The televisor showed Buckliger standing behind a lectern ornamented with the usual gilded Germanic eagle holding a swastika in its claws. Heinrich leaned forward intently. "This is important, really important," he said. "If he ignored the piece that Jahnke put out last week—"

"Why don't you just listen and find out what he said?" Lise asked. Her husband looked flabbergasted again, so much so that she almost laughed at him.

"I was pleased to visit our fellow-Aryan friends and neighbors to the north," the *Führer* said, "and particularly pleased to hear their leaders' expressions of support for the course upon which the *Reich* has embarked. Those leaders feel, as I do, that anyone who seeks to put the brakes on reform is suffering from a bad case of nostalgia for the dead days that will not and cannot return."

"Yes!" Heinrich exploded, as if the German team had scored the winning goal in overtime in the World Cup finals.

"It is proving harder than expected to get rid of old thoughts and habits, but we must not turn back," Buckliger went on. "Recently, some have claimed that we can justify everything that has happened in terms of world-historical necessity. But not all such deeds can be explained away. They are alien to the principles of National Socialism and only took place because of deviations from basic National Socialist ideals."

He went on from there, but that was the meat of it. When he finished, the picture cut back to Horst Witzleben. The newsreader said, "While certain uninformed persons have taken irresponsible positions in the papers, the *Führer* has made it unmistakably clear that a freer examination of the past and the lessons to be drawn from it is essential to strengthening and reforming National Socialist thought and practice."

Heinrich leaned over and kissed Lise. The kiss developed a life of its own. Suddenly, he didn't seem tired at all. On the screen, Horst kept on talking, but she had no idea what he was talking about. She didn't much care, either. When they finally broke apart, she said, "*Gott im Himmel!* If I'd known politics did *that* for you, I'd have got interested in it a long time ago."

He laughed. She might have been half kidding. On the other hand, she might not have. She wasn't sure herself. He said, "Up till last year, politics just made me want to get sick. But now they're . . . exciting, you know what I mean?"

"I certainly thought so," she said. She kissed him this time.

"What are the children doing?" he asked hoarsely when they came up for air again.

"Something in their bedrooms. Something too close to our bedroom. We ought to wait till they go to bed."

"Some things shouldn't wait." Her husband let his hand fall on her thigh. "Do you think we can get away with it if we're quick? The worst that can happen is, they embarrass us a little."

"They embarrass us a lot, you mean." But the thought of sneaking while the girls were awake and only a few meters away held a certain attraction of its own. Lise stood up and turned off the televisor. "Come on. We'd better hurry, though."

Hurry they did, behind a closed bedroom door. And they got away with it. "Here's to politics," Heinrich said, still panting a little.

"Never mind politics," Lise told him. "Put your trousers back on."

And that turned out to be good advice, too. No more than a minute and a half after they finished getting dressed, Francesca and Roxane started squabbling over a set of colored pencils. They both burst into the bedroom, each loudly pleading her case to the court of parental authority.

That court was primarily Lise. Because of what had just happened, and because of what might have happened had the girls stormed in a few minutes earlier, she was less concerned with fairness and more concerned with getting them out of there as fast as she could than she usually would have been. Neither one of them seemed too happy about her verdict. She took that as a sign she'd come somewhere close to justice, even if she hadn't hit it right on the nose.

Once they were gone, she sent Heinrich an accusing look. "You!"

"Me?" he yelped. "If I remember right, we were both here. And they didn't see anything. So what are you worrying about?"

"What might have been," Lise answered.

He took that to mean more than she'd intended: "For us, how could what might have been be worse than what really was?"

She thought about it for a long time, and couldn't find an answer.

Alicia Gimpel was talking with Emma Handrick and Trudi Krebs, waiting for the bus to take them home from school, when Francesca came up with steam pouring out of her ears. "What's the matter with you?" Alicia asked.

"The Beast, that's what." Francesca was so furious, she didn't even try to keep her voice down. Had a teacher heard her, she would have got in trouble, and not a little bit, either.

All the girls at the bus stop exclaimed in sympathy. Even some of the boys there did the same. The natural antipathy between *Frau* Koch and children overpowered the natural antipathy between girls and boys. Some of the other children had already had her. The ones who hadn't knew about her.

"What's she done now?" Alicia asked.

"You know that article that was in the paper a little while ago—that 'Enough Is Enough' thing?" her sister said. "Did your teacher talk about it, too?"

"Some," Alicia answered. Emma and Trudi nodded. Alicia went on, "*Herr* Peukert was pretty cagey about it, though." *Herr* Peukert, in fact, had treated the *Völkischer Beobachter* story as if it were a large, poisonous snake. He couldn't ignore it, but he didn't want much to do with it, either. Alicia said, "How come? What did the Beast tell you about it?"

"Oh, my God, you should have heard her!" Francesca said. "She thought it was the greatest thing since *Mein Kampf*. She went on and on about how Dr. Jahnke was a true patriot who really understood what National Socialism was all about, and how everybody who liked these stupid newfangled ideas ought to go straight to the showers. She said they sounded like a bunch of stinking, big-nosed Jews put them together."

"Even for the Beast, that's bad," Trudi said. Several people nodded.

"But that's not the worst of it," Francesca said. "She's been talking like this ever since 'Enough Is Enough' came out in the paper. And then yesterday the *Führer* made a speech, and *he* said the article wasn't any good, and we were going to go right on with the new stuff no matter what. And do you know what the Beast said?"

"Did she . . . say the *Führer* was wrong?" Alicia asked. A year earlier, the bare possibility wouldn't have occurred to her. All sorts of new possibilities had occurred to her in the past year.

Her sister shook her head. Her hair—straighter and a little lighter brown than Alicia's—flipped back and forth. "No. That would have been bad. What she did was even worse. She started going on about how we needed change and how good it was going to be. It was like she hadn't been talking about the other stuff at all. It was scary."

The bus came up then. Alicia and Francesca sat down together. Emma and Trudi sat on the seat in front of them so they could all keep talking. As the bus pulled away from the curb, Alicia said, "Didn't anybody ask her about that?"

"Werner Krupke did," Francesca answered. "She looked at him like he was something you had to scoop out of the cat box, and she didn't say a thing. Nobody asked any more questions after that."

"I wonder why," Alicia said. Trudi snorted.

Emma said, "Boy, I'm glad I never had the Beast."

Alicia was glad she'd never had *Frau* Koch, too. How could you call yourself a teacher if what you said on Wednesday didn't count on Thursday? The Beast probably still believed what she'd said before. You didn't say those things if you didn't believe them. When "Enough Is Enough" came out, she must have thought it was safe to say them out loud. How scared was she when she found out she was wrong? *Plenty, I hope,* Alicia thought.

Trudi had to wiggle past Emma to get out at her stop. "See you tomorrow," she called as she went up the aisle, down the rubber-matted steps, and out the door.

A few stops later, Emma got out with all three Gimpel girls—Roxane had been chattering with a couple of her friends toward the back of the bus. She'd got to the stop after Francesca, and hadn't even noticed how mad she was. Now she did. When she asked why, Francesca started ranting all over again.

"That doesn't sound very good," Roxane said when she could get a word in edgewise, which took a while.

"What does your teacher say about all this stuff?" Alicia asked her.

"She's said the *Führer* is making some changes in how things work, and they'll probably work better once everything's done," Roxane answered. That seemed sensible enough. And Roxane was only in the first grade. What more did she need to know?

"Has she said anything about 'Enough Is Enough'?" Francesca asked.

"She says that all the time—whenever we're too noisy." Roxane spoke with a certain amount of pride. If she wasn't one of the first-graders who made a lot of the noise, Alicia would have been surprised. But she'd plainly never heard of Dr. Jahnke's article.

Emma waved good-bye to the Gimpel girls when she came to her house. Alicia, Francesca, and Roxane walked on. Alicia said, "Maybe getting caught like this will make the Beast pull her horns in."

Francesca gave her a look. "Fat chance!" She was probably right. People like *Frau* Koch were the way they were, and that was all there was to it. The Beast wasn't about to change her mind or the way she acted. Alicia wouldn't have wanted to be Werner Krupke, who'd called her on her inconsistency. She'd likely make his life miserable for the rest of the school year.

"Home!" Roxane said with a theatrical sigh as they came to the front door.

Mommy let them in. Francesca told her horrible story for the third time. She'd no doubt tell it all over again when Daddy got home, too. Mommy never turned a hair. What was going on inside her? Did she feel the sting because her own daughter didn't know what she was? Of course she did. She had to . . . didn't she?

When Francesca was done, Mommy said, "The Beast sounds like she's living up to her name, all right. But you've only got her for this school year, and then you'll be done with her forever. And when you have children of your own, you can say, 'You think your teacher's mean? You should hear about the one I had. She was so bad, everybody called her the Beast.' "

Alicia smiled. Francesca didn't. She said, "That doesn't do me any good now!"

"Well, would cookies and milk do you some good now?" Mommy asked. Francesca nodded eagerly. Alicia and Roxane didn't complain, either—not a bit.

Susanna Weiss got back from a shopping run along the Kurfürstendamm a little past seven on a cold, snowy February evening. She set down her packages—three pairs of shoes, including some gloriously impractical high-heeled sandals—took off her foxskin hat, and got out of her overcoat. Then she dithered for a moment, wondering whether to make dinner right away or sit down and watch the rest of the news first.

She poured a knock of Glenfiddich over ice and turned on the televisor. That wasn't Horst Witzleben's face that appeared on the screen. It was Charlie Lynton's. The head of the British Union of Fascists spoke good, if accented, German. He was saying, "—intend here to bring the democratic principles of the first edition into effect as soon as possible. Most seats in the next Parliamentary elections will be contested. I particularly admire the *Führer* for looking on this course with favor, and for recognizing that he need not yield to the forces of reaction."

His image disappeared. Horst's replaced it. "Along with the Scandinavian leaders, Great Britain stands foursquare behind the Greater German *Reich*'s revitalization effort," the newscaster said. "We'll be back in a moment."

The picture cut away to an obviously German farm family somewhere in the conquered East—probably on the broad plains of the Ukraine. The advertisement was for Agfa color film. The smiling father took pictures of his wife and children. Relatives in a crowded German apartment admired then when they came in the mail. That not only promoted the film, it also urged Germans to go out and colonize. The Propaganda Ministry didn't miss a trick. Susanna smiled when that phrase went through her mind. It made her think of Heinrich and his passion for bridge.

Another advertisement followed, this one for Volkswagens. They still looked buggy, as they had for more than seventy years. But the lines were smoother, more rounded, now. The engine had moved to the front, the trunk to the rear. The engine was water-cooled these days, and didn't sound flatulent. The bumpers were actually good for something besides decoration. The VW still had a bud vase on the dashboard, though.

Horst Witzleben returned. "In St. Wenceslas Square in Prague, several hundred persons gathered near the statue of the saint to protest the incorporation of the Protectorate of Bohemia and Moravia into the *Reich,*" he said.

St. Wenceslas' equestrian statue was surrounded by figures of other Bohemian saints. Counting the large base, the statue stood seven or eight times as high as a man. It dwarfed the men and women at its base and the signs they carried. Some of those signs were in German. They said things like FREEDOM FOR THE CZECHS! and WE REMEMBER! Others, in Czech, presumably said the same thing.

And some of the demonstrators carried flags: the blue, white, and red banners of the long-vanished Republic of Czechoslovakia. A chill ran through Susanna when she recognized those flags. How many years had it been since anyone dared show them in public? Almost as amazing as the sight of the Czechoslovak flags was that of the policemen who stood watching the demonstration without storming in to break it up and throw everybody in sight into jail or a concentration camp.

"Because the protest was peaceful and orderly, no arrests were made," Horst Witzleben said, and he went on to a different story. He spoke as if that had been standard practice in the Third *Reich* from the beginning, not the next thing to a miracle.

A fat official pontificated about improvements to the harbor in Hamburg. Susanna hardly heard him. Though they'd vanished from the screen, she kept seeing those Czechoslovak flags fluttering in the long shadow St. Wenceslas cast. If those flags could come out of the dark backward and abysm of time—if they could come out and survive—what else might follow them? Susanna shivered with awe.

And then something else occurred to her. She shivered again, this time a lot less happily. Did even Heinz Buckliger know all that might follow if he let people say what they really thought? No one in the Greater German *Reich*, no one in the part of the Germanic Empire on this side of the Atlantic, had been able to do that for a lifetime. How much was bottled up? And how would it come out?

When the telephone on his desk rang, Heinrich jumped. That happened about a third of the time. When he was really concentrating, the outside world seemed to disappear. It seemed to, but it didn't. As if to prove as much, the phone rang again.

He picked it up. Willi was laughing at him. Ignoring his friend, he used his best professional tones: "Analysis Section, Heinrich Gimpel speaking."

"Hello, Heinrich." Had Willi heard the voice on the other end of the line, he would have stopped laughing, and in a hurry: it was Erika.

"Hello." Heinrich did his best to keep his own voice normal. It wasn't easy. "What . . . what can I do for you?"

"I'm at my sister's house. Leonore lives at 16 Burggrafen-Strasse, just south of the Tiergarten. Do you know where that is?"

"Yes, I think so," Heinrich said automatically. Then he wished he could deny everything. Too late, of course. For wishes like that, it always was.

"Good," Erika said: another questionable assumption. "Come over at lunchtime. We need to talk."

"You, me, and your sister?" Heinrich said in surprise. He hardly knew Erika's sister. Leonore, if he remembered right, was separated from a mid-ranking SS officer. She was a year or two younger than Erika and looked a lot like her, but wasn't quite so . . . *carnivorous* was the word that came to Heinrich's mind. He asked, "What about?"

"I'm not going to go into it on the phone," Erika said, which, considering that the lines into *Oberkommando der Wehrmacht* headquarters were monitored as closely as any in the *Reich,* was probably a good idea.

Heinrich thought it over. If Leonore were there, things couldn't get too far out of hand. And even if they did, all he had to do was walk out. "All right," he said. "I'll see you a little past twelve." Erika hung up without another word.

Willi looked up from whatever he was working on. "Going out to lunch with Lise and her sister, eh?" he said, proving he'd been snooping.

Thank God I didn't say Leonore's name, Heinrich thought. He managed a rather sickly answering smile. That avoided the lie direct, anyhow. Willi took it for agreement. He went back to the papers scattered across his desk. Heinrich, who kept his work area almost surgically neat, wondered how Willi ever found anything. But he did. Though he had his problems, that wasn't one of them.

When Heinrich wanted to do something at lunch, the time before he could leave crawled on hands and knees. Today, when he really didn't, hours flew by. Had he done anything more than blink once or twice before he got up from his desk? If he had, it didn't feel that way. At the same time, Willi headed out the door with Ilse. That had to mean Rolf Stolle never called her back. Willi was smirking. Seeing him with the secretary made Heinrich a little less uncomfortable about paying a call on his wife, but only a little.

Why didn't I say no? Heinrich wondered, waiting for the bus that would take him up to the park. He could have stood Erika and her sister up even after saying yes, but that never occurred to him. What he said he would do, he did.

Brakes squealing, the bus stopped in front of him. He climbed aboard, stuck his account card in the slot, and then put it back in his pocket. The bus wasn't too crowded. He sat down as it pulled out into traffic.

Ten minutes later, he got off at Wichmannstrasse, a little north of

Burggrafen-Strasse. When he looked across to the Tiergarten, he saw that it wasn't very crowded, either. Not surprising, on this cold, gray winter's day. A few stubborn people sat on the benches and fed the squirrels and the few stubborn birds that hadn't flown south.

Reluctantly, he turned his back on the park and walked south down Wichmannstrasse to where it branched, then turned right onto Burggrafen-Strasse. The neighborhood dated from the last years of the nineteenth century or the start of the twentieth. Time had mellowed the bricks on the housefronts. Here and there, gray or greenish or even orange lichen spread over the brickwork, as if it came not from the time of the Kaisers but from the Neolithic age.

Here was 20 Burggrafen-Strasse, here was 18 . . . and here, looking very little different from the houses on either side, was 16. With a sour half smile, Heinrich went up the slate walkway, climbed three red-brick steps, and stood in front of a door whose ornate carved floral border spoke of Victorian bourgeois respectability. Wishing he were somewhere, anywhere, else, Heinrich rang the bell.

"It's open," Erika called. "Come on in."

He did. The entry hall was narrow and cramped. It made a dogleg to the left, so he couldn't see any of the rest of the house from the doorway. A polished brass coat-and-hat rack by the door offered a mute hint. Heinrich took it, hanging his black leather greatcoat and high-crowned cap on two of the hooks. Then, with a shrug, he went into the front room—and stopped in his tracks.

He'd seen plenty of seduction scenes in films. He'd never expected to walk into one in real life, but he did now. It was almost too perfect. A pair of champagne flutes sat on a coffee table. Behind it, on a couch, lolled Erika Dorsch. She wore something white and lacy that didn't cover very much of her and didn't cover that very well. There were no perfumes in films, either. This one—Chanel?—was devastating. "Hello, Heinrich," Erika murmured.

If he wasn't going to go forward and do what she obviously wanted him to do, he should have turned on his heel and got out of there as fast as he could. He realized that later. At the moment, captivated if not quite captured, he simply stared. "Where's your sister?" he blurted.

Erika laughed musically. She sat up, which put even more of her on display as the lingerie gave ground. "You were the one who said she'd be here," she answered. "I never did."

Heinrich thought back. She was right. He'd assumed what he wanted to assume. Maybe she'd let him—no, she'd certainly let him—do that, but she hadn't lied. The collar of his uniform shirt felt much too tight. "I'd better go," he muttered—the first half-smart thing he'd said, and it wasn't any better than half-smart.

"Don't be silly. You just got here." Erika patted the couch by her. "Sit down. Make yourself at home. Have something to drink."

He didn't. "This is . . ." He cast about for a word. He didn't take long to find one. "This is ridiculous. What on earth do you want with me?"

"About what you'd expect," she answered. "Do I have to draw you a picture? I don't think so—you're smart. And you're *gemütlich*. You're . . . not bad-looking." He almost laughed. Even she couldn't push it any further than that. Then venom filled her voice as she went on, "And Willi's a two-timing asshole. So why not?"

She leaned forward to pick up one of the flutes. A pink nipple appeared for a moment as the lace shifted. Then it vanished again. Heinrich hadn't added a memory to the *things I'm glad I saw even if I wasn't supposed to* file since he was sixteen. He did now.

"Why not?" Erika repeated, this time making it a serious question. "Who'd know? Nobody but us, and I'd get some of my own back. Willi's probably out fucking that little whore right now."

So he was. Heinrich knew that, where Erika only suspected it. But she'd asked him why not, and he thought he owed her an answer. That was also, at best, half-smart. Again, he didn't realize it till later. His thinking, just then, was less sharp than it might have been. He said, "I love my wife. I don't want to do anything to hurt her."

Erika laughed at him. "You sound like a script from the Propaganda Ministry—except I happen to know that every Propaganda Minister from Goebbels on has screwed around on his wife whenever he got the chance. So where does that leave you?"

"Say whatever you want," he answered. "I don't think this is a good idea."

"No? Part of you does." Erika wasn't looking at his face.

Heinrich intended to have a good long talk with that part, too. The trouble was, it talked back. Unhappily, he said, "Find some other way to get even with Willi. Find some way to make him happy, if you can, and for him to make you happy, too. I know the two of you used to be."

Her eyes flashed. "You don't know as much as you think you do."

"Who ever does, when it's somebody else's marriage?" Heinrich said reasonably—he was reasonable most of the time, even when being reasonable wasn't. "But that's how it looked from the outside."

"I don't care how it looked," Erika said. "And I didn't ask you to come over here to tell you stories about my miserable marriage."

"No, you asked me to come over here so you could blow holes in it—and in mine," Heinrich said.

"Mine's already got holes in it," Erika said. Heinrich waited to see if she'd add anything about his. She didn't. Instead, she went on, "I asked you to come over so I could forget about mine for a little while."

She wouldn't forget hers. Heinrich was blind to many things that went on around him, but not to that. If this went forward, Willi would be in the back of her mind—or more likely the front of her mind—every second. She'd be gloating and laughing at him with every kiss, with every caress. Didn't she see as much herself?

He thought about asking her. While he thought, Erika lost patience. "Heinrich," she said in a voice more imperious than seductive, "are you going to make love to me or not?"

He had to fight the giggles. They wouldn't do just now. What she reminded him of was a *Hitler Jugend* physical-training instructor who'd always bawled out, "Well, are you going to push yourselves or not?"

"Well?" she said when he didn't answer right away. He bit down hard on the inside of his cheek. The giggles were very close.

He had to say something. What came out was, "I'm sorry, Erika."

"Sorry?" The heat that might have been passion turned to fury. One way or another, it *would* come out. "You think you're sorry now? *I'll* make you sorry, God damn you! Get out of here!" She grabbed the empty champagne flute and threw it at him. He ducked. It smashed against the wall behind him. He beat a hasty retreat as she reached for the full one. That got him in the seat of the pants. It didn't break till it hit the floor.

He had his greatcoat and cap on (the cap askew) and was out the door before he realized he had a wet spot back there. He shrugged. The coat would cover it till he got back to the office, and then he could sit on it till it dried. All things considered, he would rather have eaten lunch.

XI

Lise Gimpel knew something was wrong when Heinrich poured himself a healthy slug of schnapps as soon as he got home from the office. He didn't do that on days when things went well. Then he'd have a bottle of beer, if he had anything at all. But when she asked him what the trouble was, he jumped as if she'd poked him with a pin. "Nothing," he said quickly: much too quickly.

She paused, wondering where to go from there—wondering whether to go anywhere from there. But what he'd said and the way he'd said it were too blatant to ignore. She picked her words with care: "You don't lie to me much. When you do, you aren't very good at it."

"Oh," he said, and then, "*Scheisse.*" He knocked back the schnapps at a gulp. Lise blinked. That wasn't his style at all. As if to prove it, he coughed several times. His cheeks turned pink. Embarrassment or schnapps? Schnapps, Lise judged. Heinrich coughed again, this time as if he'd started to say something and swallowed it at the last moment.

"Well, are you going to tell me about it or not?" Lise asked.

For some reason, that set her husband off again, in a different way. If his laugh wasn't hysterical, it came close. Finally, he said, "I suppose I'd better. This is all by way of explaining how I managed to get a champagne stain on my ass this afternoon."

Now it was Lise's turn to say, "Oh." She didn't know what she'd been looking for. Whatever it was, that wasn't it. "I'm listening," she told him, which seemed safe.

He talked. It took about ten minutes and another drink, this one gulped down as fast as the first. Lise had seen and heard for herself some of what Heinrich was talking about. At the time, she hadn't realized it applied to him in particular; she'd thought Erika was venting her spleen at the world at large. ". . . and that's that," Heinrich finished. "That, as a matter of fact, is pretty definitely that. I don't think there will be any more bridge games with the Dorsches after this."

Bridge, just then, wasn't the first thing on Lise's mind. "How do you feel about all this?" she asked.

"Glad it's over." Heinrich reached for the schnapps bottle again.

That he did made Lise sure he wasn't saying everything on his mind. "Pour some for me, too," she told him. "If you've earned three, I think I'm entitled to one." After a sip, she went on, "You kept quiet about this for months."

"I kept hoping everything would just . . . settle down," Heinrich said.

"Is that what you were hoping for?" Lise said. Erika Dorsch made formidable competition. Those cool Aryan good looks, and the suggestion of raw heat underneath . . . Lise took another swallow of schnapps, larger than the first. Formidable indeed.

"If I'd hoped for the other, it would have been easy enough to get."

"Why didn't you?" she asked. "It might have been the easiest way out of the trouble."

Heinrich shook his head. "My life is complicated enough. It has to be, because of what I am—what we are. If you think I want any more complications on top of that, you're crazy. And besides, I love you."

She would have liked it better if he'd put those in the other order. Being who and what she was herself, though, she understood why he hadn't. She prodded a little, anyhow: "And you were enjoying yourself, weren't you, with a, a beautiful woman"—there, she'd said it—"falling all over you?"

"I might have enjoyed it a hell of a lot more if I hadn't been scared to death all the damn time," he said. "This is my *life* we're talking about, mine and lots of other people's. I hope I'm not stupid enough to put that on the line for a roll in the hay. If—" He drank instead of finishing.

"If what?" Lise asked. Her husband didn't answer. He peered out the kitchen window, resolutely pretending he hadn't heard. Lise almost repeated the question. But she could make a good guess at what he'd swallowed. It would have been something like, *If I weren't a Jew, or if she were . . .*

She supposed she could get angry at him for even that much. What was the point, though? Things were the way they were. There was no world where Heinrich was a *goy* or Erika a Jew. *A good thing, too,* Lise thought, and finished her schnapps with a gulp. She poured the glass full again.

"We're both going to go to sleep in the middle of supper," Heinrich said.

"That's all right. That's the least of my worries right now," Lise answered. "You turned her down. She's going to be angry—you said so yourself. What can she do to you? What can she do to us?"

"I thought about that," Heinrich said. "I can't see anything. Can you? She's not going to pour gasoline on the house and set it on fire, or anything like that."

"I suppose not," Lise admitted. She didn't stop worrying, though. How could any Jew in her right mind stop worrying? If you weren't worrying, you were likely to miss something that might kill you.

"Is it all right?" Heinrich asked anxiously.

"It could be better," Lise said, and he flinched. Considering all the things that might have happened, and all the different kinds of unpleasantness that might have sprung from them, she decided she had to relent, and she did: "It could be worse, too. So I guess it's all right. But if any more beautiful blondes make a play for you, you might want to let me know a little sooner."

"I promise," he said.

She snorted. "Or, of course, you might not want to let me know at all. But I hope you do." He had no answer for that, which was, in its own way, reassuring.

When Susanna Weiss watched Czechs demonstrating on the televisor without getting arrested, she was astonished. When she saw Frenchmen demonstrating, she was shocked. But there they were, marching by the Arc de Triomphe with signs that said, LIBERTY, EQUALITY, FRATERNITY! That slogan had been outlawed for seventy years. Ever since 1940, the motto of the French state had been *Work, Family, Country*. But, while the older phrase might have been forbidden, it hadn't been forgotten. Here it was, for all the world to see.

As in Prague, policemen stood around watching without doing anything. In their round, flat-crowned kepis, they looked even more French than the demonstrators. But they collaborated with the *Reich* more enthusiastically than the Czechs did—or they had up till now, anyhow.

For the French, collaboration had meant survival. To Germany, Czechoslovakia had been an annoyance. France had been the deadly foe. Crushed in 1870, avenged in 1918, she'd been crushed once more in 1940 and never allowed to get off her knees again. From that day till this, French Fascists had toed the German line. Anyone who didn't toe the line disappeared, mostly forever. When Germany spat, France swam. But while she swam, she breathed, if softly.

And now, with anyone who'd lived under liberty, equality, and fraternity a white-haired ancient, these Frenchmen—and a few Frenchwomen, too—showed they remembered them. And they got away with it. Susanna stared and stared.

Horst Witzleben said, "This peaceful demonstration was photographed by a German cameraman. No French televisor coverage was on the scene. The French regime would sooner not admit its citizens can find fault with it."

Susanna stuck a finger in her ear. "Did I really hear that?" she asked. No one was in the apartment with her but the cat, and Gawain, fat, lazy thing that he was, lay asleep on the sofa, his tail curled over the tip of his nose. But Susanna had to ask somebody. Germans had been making scornful gibes about Frenchmen since the very beginnings of the *Reich*, and no doubt long before. Still, Susanna had never heard one like this. It said, *We're going somewhere new, and you haven't got the nerve to follow us.*

The next story was about corruption in the Iron Guard, the Romanian Fascist party. Susanna had no trouble believing there was corruption in the Iron Guard. They'd held power for a long time, and corruption wasn't rare in the Balkans (or, come to that, anywhere else). Talking about it was. When a fat Iron Guard official who spoke German with a comic-opera accent spluttered out denials, he did his cause more harm than any accuser could have.

She wondered if the story after the St. Pauli Girl beer advertisement would be subversive, too, but it wasn't: it talked about the Brazilian football team, one of the favorites in the upcoming World Cup. Susanna almost switched it off; she had only slightly more interest in football than in suicide. But the longer she watched the piece, the more interesting it got. Here were some of the finest footballers in the world, footballers expected to give the mighty Germans a run for their money. Were they Aryans? Hardly. Oh, several of them obviously had some white blood. But Negro and American Indian ancestry predominated on the Brazilian team.

"Isn't that interesting?" Susanna murmured. The people at the Propaganda Ministry were working with a light hand. They weren't saying, *Look at these Brazilian mongrels. They're really quite impressive, aren't they?* Instead, the message was simply, *This is what the team that will challenge Germany looks like.* If watchers decided the Brazilian mongrels were impressive, they'd do it on their own. That they were getting the chance was remarkable enough.

Heinz Buckliger had said before that he had his doubts about the Nazis' racial doctrines. He and his people were practicing what he'd preached. Here they'd shown black and brown men as human beings.

Would they ever do the same with Jews? Susanna wasn't going to hold her breath. For one thing, in National Socialist dogma Jews and Aryans were natural enemies, like capitalists and proletarians in the dead lore of Communism. For another, Jews' craftiness made them all the more dangerous. And, for a third, Jews were thought to be extinct, so why bother rehabilitating them? Even the most radical reforms had limits.

Walther Stutzman used a couple of different portals to get into SS databases and see what the blackshirts were up to. He didn't like messing with them. Any time he poked around in there, he exposed himself to a certain risk of detection, even if he did have the proper passwords and some highly improper masking programs. Every so often, he went sniffing in spite of the risk. Not knowing what Lothar Prützmann and his cohorts were up to was also risky.

Today at lunch, he started in at one of the usual places, a weak spot that had been in the software ever since his father put it there. If and when the *Reich* finally did go over to the long-promised new operating system, it would have weak spots, too. Walther had put a few into the code himself. Out of so many millions of lines, who would find those few? One of these days, his son Gottlieb could exploit them.

That was what he was thinking as he started the electronic journey toward Lothar Prützmann's secrets. More from habit than for any other reason, he kept an eye on the monitor as the probe went through. When he saw an alphanumeric group that didn't look the way it was supposed to, he blinked. When he saw two, ice ran through him and he hit the ABORT key. If that wasn't a trap, he'd never seen one. Now he sat there wondering if it had caught him.

He didn't think so. He had programs that would muddy the trail, and he hadn't gone in far enough to be fully noosed . . . had he? He paused in indecision, something he didn't do very often. Then, reluctantly, he nodded to himself. Only one way to find out, and he badly needed to know.

He liked the second portal less than the first. It was closer to a busy stream of electronic traffic. If he made a mistake, he'd stick out like blood on the snow. *Just like that,* he thought unhappily. And if the bloodhounds were waiting for him here, too . . .

His finger stayed on the ABORT key all the way through the insertion process. If the hounds had been a little more subtle, they would have nabbed him the first time. He hated giving them another chance.

But, as far as he could tell, everything went fine now. He got inside the SS network without its being any the wiser. And, once he was inside, he could look at the other portal from the rear, so to speak. The trap pointed outward. He'd thought it would. People who designed traps like that were convinced of their own cleverness. They didn't think anyone could sneak up on them from behind.

And they had been very clever indeed, even if not quite clever enough. The more Walther studied their trap, the nastier it looked. If his probe had gone just a little farther through the portal, it would have been seized and traced back to its beginnings, and not one of his masking programs was likely to have done him much good. Oh, yes, the thing had teeth, sharp ones.

He wondered if he could draw those teeth, leave the trap seeming dangerous but in fact harmless. Shaking his head, he decided against it, at least for now. That wouldn't be something to ad-lib on a lunch hour. If he tried it, he would have to be perfect. The trapper would come back every so often to see what he'd caught. Everything would have to look fine to him.

Walther glanced down at his watch. Yes, it would have to be another time. People would start coming back from lunch pretty soon. He couldn't afford to take the chance of being seen doing that kind of work. And he was through the other portal. If he was going to look around inside Lothar Prützmann's domain, he had to do it now.

Too much information. Not enough time to sift through it. That protected SS secrets as well as any encryption algorithm, probably better. If Walther couldn't find what he was looking for, what difference if it stayed in plain sight? You couldn't read what you couldn't find.

He did find proof of Prützmann's hand behind the "Enough Is Enough" article in the *Völkischer Beobachter*. Under other circumstances, that would have delighted him. As things were, he shrugged. If Heinz Buckliger didn't already know who'd put Dr. Jahnke up to writing that piece, he was a fool. So far, he hadn't acted like one.

Still . . . A message revealing in which SS directory all the dirt on "Enough Is Enough" lurked wouldn't hurt. Walther had ways of bouncing such a message through the data system till it became impossible to trace. He used them.

And he was back to working on the new operating system by the time his boss lumbered back into the office. Gustav Priepke stuck his head into Walther's cubicle, saw what he was up to, and nodded approval. "That goddamn Japanese code really will save our asses, won't it?" he said.

"We've got a chance with it, anyhow," Walther answered.

"Good. Good. That was a hell of a good idea, using it," Priepke said. Walther started to thank him, but just nodded instead. Unless he misread the signs, his boss had forgotten whose idea it was in the first place. Because it was working so well, Priepke had decided it was his.

Had things been different, Walther wouldn't have let him get away with that. As they were . . . As they were, if Priepke was angling for fame and glory, he could have them. Walther didn't want them. They were no good to him. The less he was in the public eye, the better he liked it. And if his boss got a bonus and a raise, that was all right, too. The Stutzmans had plenty. They needed no more. No Jew dared be or even think like a moneygrubber these days.

"We'll do fine," Priepke said, as if Walther had denied it. "We'll do just fine."

"Of course we will," Walther said.

When Gottlieb Stutzman came home for a weekend's leave from his *Hitler Jugend* service, Esther was amazed at how brown and muscular he'd become. "They work us pretty hard," her son said, scratching at his mustache. That was thicker and more emphatically there than it had been a year before, too. He wasn't a boy any more. He was visibly turning into a man.

"How is it?" Esther fought to keep worry out of her voice. She'd been afraid ever since Gottlieb left the house. She hadn't feared he would be caught, or hadn't feared that any more than usual. He looked like an Aryan. He wasn't circumcised. He had the sense to keep his mouth shut about his dangerous secret.

But in a setting like that, suffused with the propaganda of the state and the *Volk,* what would have been easier than turning his back on the secret? It was a burden he didn't have to carry. Nobody did. If you chose to forget you were a Jew, who could make you remember?

Esther's fear swelled when Gottlieb shrugged and said, "It's not so bad." But then he went on, "Or it wouldn't be, if I weren't different." Esther let out a heartfelt sigh of relief. He accepted that difference, then. She'd thought he had, she'd thought he would, but you could never be sure. He gave her a quizzical look. "What was that for?"

"Just because—and don't you forget it," Esther answered.

"Sure." Gottlieb, plainly, was humoring his mother. Since he hadn't had much practice, he wasn't very good at it. The doorbell rang. "Who's that?" he asked as Esther started for the door.

"Alicia Gimpel," Esther answered. "She was going to visit Anna and sleep over tonight. They set it up before we knew you were coming home, and it was a little late to cancel by then. I hope you don't mind?"

"Why should I?" He laughed. "It's not like I'm going to pay any attention to Alicia one way or the other."

"All right," Esther said. Gottlieb no doubt admired one pretty *Fräulein* or another. Of course he did—at seventeen, what was he but a hormone with legs? No matter whom he admired, though, if he was as serious as he seemed to be about staying a Jew and passing it on, he would marry another Jew. Seventeen would pay no attention to eleven, but twenty-four might find eighteen very interesting. Seven years, right now, would feel like an eternity to Gottlieb. To Esther, they felt just around the corner.

She opened the door. There were Alicia and Lise. As Alicia came in festooned with sleeping bag, change of clothes, and the other impedimenta of a sleepover, Anna bounded down from upstairs to greet her. Through the squeals, Lise said, "It's a shame they don't like each other—tragic, in fact."

"It is, isn't it?" Esther said. They both smiled: here, for once, was irony that didn't hurt. Esther waved back toward the kitchen. "Come in and have a cup of coffee and say hello to Gottlieb. He got a free weekend and came home to visit."

Lise followed, but she said, "You should have called. Alicia could have come over some other time."

"Don't worry about it," Esther answered. "Gottlieb won't even notice she's here." Another smile from both of them. Some of the thoughts that had occurred to Esther had surely occurred to Lise, too. The Gimpels had three girls to marry off. They would have started thinking about possibilities a long time ago.

"My goodness, Gottlieb," Lise Gimpel said. "You're looking very . . . fit."

"I sort of have to be," he answered with a broad-shouldered shrug. "If you can't do what they throw at you, they make your life so nasty, you get into shape just so they'll leave you alone."

"What are they telling you now that we've got a new *Führer?*" Lise asked him.

He didn't shrug now. He leaned forward; this interested him. "When I first started, it was the same old stuff I'd always got in school," he said. "But it's changed since then."

"Well, what are they saying these days?"

"A lot more about what good exercise it is and how we'll make friends we'll keep for the rest of our lives," Gottlieb said. "A lot less about how it's getting us ready to be soldiers who'll go out and slaughter the *Reich*'s enemies. A lot less about our shovels, too."

Esther frowned. "Your shovels?"

Her son nodded. "In the *Wehrmacht,* it's your rifle. That's what people say, anyhow. In the *Hitler Jugend,* it's our shovels. We have to carry them with us everywhere. We have to keep them polished—the blade and the handle. If you let your shovel get rusty or you lose it, I don't know what they do to you. Something horrible—I know that. Nobody wants to find out what."

"Shovels," Esther repeated. It made sense, of a sort. The Hitler Youth was a dress rehearsal for the Army. Someone who knew how to take care of a shovel and had the discipline to do it—even if the act itself was fundamentally meaningless—would quickly learn how to take care of a rifle and gain the discipline to do it. And that would not be meaningless at all.

"The drillmasters don't yell at us as much as they used to, either," Gottlieb said. "Of course, we've been in for a while now, too. We know what we need to do. They don't have to yell at us all the time any more."

"What do you do for fun?" Esther asked.

"Polish our shovels," Gottlieb answered, deadpan. Esther made a face at him. He grinned. He'd got her, and he knew it. He went on, "A lot of the time, we just sleep when we get the chance. They do run us pretty ragged."

"You can't sleep all the time," Esther said, even if that was a risky assumption to make about teenagers.

But Gottlieb didn't deny it. He said, "We read. We listen to the radio—there's no televisor in the barracks. We play cards. We're not supposed to do it for money, but I'm about fifteen Reichsmarks ahead so far." He looked smug. Then he added, "And there's a *Bund deutscher Mädel* camp about half a kilometer from ours. Some of the guys sneak over there after lights-out."

There it was, the thing Esther feared. Lots of BdM camps were near those of the *Hitler Jugend*. Surprising numbers—or maybe numbers not so surprising—of BdM girls found themselves pregnant every year, too. "What about you?" she asked, her tone as light as she could make it. If some gentile girl won his heart, or a related piece of his anatomy . . .

"I haven't. I don't think I will," he said after due consideration very much like Walther's. "You get into real trouble if they catch you doing that—worse than losing your shovel. And besides, it's like I told Aunt Susanna the night Alicia found out what she is: it just wouldn't be a good idea for me."

Lise Gimpel smiled. Esther kissed him. She got lipstick on his cheek, but he didn't notice and she didn't care. She wanted to say something like, *You're a very good boy, and I'm prouder than I know how to tell you.* The only thing holding her back was the knowledge that the usual seventeen-year-old male, hearing something of that sort, would go disgrace himself just to take the jinx off.

On the other hand, Gottlieb was not your average seventeen-year-old male. Esther did say it. And Gottlieb proved his sterling qualities: he grinned.

Along with the New Orleans Vicki, which currently held pride of place, Anna's bedroom was full of hedgehogs: stuffed cuddly ones, smaller ones made of painted ceramics or bronze, a hedgehog lamp with the switch in his little black nose, even hedgehogs printed on her sheets. Alicia thought it was all a little too much, but she never would have said so. Besides, today she had something else on her mind.

"You're so lucky!" she burst out as soon as they were alone together. "*So* lucky!"

"How come?" Anna asked. "I'm just me, same as I always was." She never took herself too seriously.

But Alicia had an answer for her: "I'll tell you why—because everybody here knows what you are. You don't have to keep any secrets."

Her friend nodded, but then started to laugh. "Don't tell that to Gottlieb, that's all I've got to say. He knew for five years before they could tell me, and it was driving him crazy. Crazier."

"Oh." Alicia hadn't thought of that. "Well, everybody knows now, anyway. Some of the things Francesca and Roxane say make me want to smack 'em, and I can't, because they'd wonder why."

"Just pay no attention to them," Anna told her—easier said than done. She went on, "Gottlieb didn't pay attention to me when I said stupid stuff like that for all those years. Of course, he doesn't pay much attention to me now that I know better, either. I'm just a kid, he says." Her snort was intended to convey how little older brothers knew.

Alicia didn't know anything about older brothers—or younger brothers, for that matter. She wasn't much interested in learning more, either. The boys in her class were the worst sort of vermin: a poor recommendation for the male half of the species. When she said, "Gottlieb's not *so* bad," she was offering Anna an enormous concession. She'd known him all her life, after all.

But so had Anna, and at much closer quarters. If no man is a hero to his valet, no boy is to his little sister. "It's—peaceful now that he's off at the *Hitler Jugend* camp most of the time," Anna said.

"Peaceful," Alicia echoed. With Gottlieb gone, Anna had her parents all to herself. Alicia tried to imagine what that would be like. She couldn't. She hadn't even been two when Francesca was born. She didn't remember what being an only child was like, and she'd never know now. When she got bigger, she was the one who'd leave for a BdM camp. Her little sisters would get more attention from Mommy and Daddy, which hardly seemed fair.

"Here, let's do this," Anna said. The game that followed ended up involving the Vicki, several of the stuffed hedgehogs—including a big one who was bright red and had a devil's horns and pitchfork—an imaginary and magical snowstorm, and the willow tree that grew just outside Anna's window. In the summertime, when it had all its leaves, the willow was full of peeping finches and warblers; woodpeckers scuttled along the bigger branches and drummed as they drilled their way after caterpillars. Now the branches and twigs were bare. Still, a house sparrow perched on one and peered into the bedroom with beady black eyes.

"Look!" Alicia pointed at the sparrow. "It's an SS bird." It got incorporated into the game, which had been short of villains up till then.

They groaned when Anna's mother called them down to supper. *Frau* Stutzman put Alicia between Anna and Gottlieb at the table, the same way a nuclear engineer would put cadmium between two uranium bricks. "So," Gottlieb said, his voice very much a man's, "how do you like being one of us?"

That was a question Alicia couldn't have heard at the supper table at her house. "It's all right. I've kind of got used to it," she said. But then she decided something more was called for, and she added, "It is what I am, after all. I ought to know about it."

Gottlieb gave her a suddenly thoughtful look. "I said something like that, too. I took longer than you have to figure it out, though."

Alicia needed a little while to realize that was a compliment of sorts. Anna's surprised expression did more to help her figure it out than Gottlieb's words themselves. She had no idea what to do with praise from a seventeen-year-old boy, and so she didn't do anything but go on with supper. It was beef tongue with potatoes and carrots and onions, which she liked. *Frau* Stutzman spiced the tongue differently from the way her mother did, but it was still good.

Over dessert, *Herr* Stutzman started telling Gottlieb about something he called a software trap. He hadn't gone very far before he stopped speaking German, or at least any sort of German Alicia understood. Gottlieb followed well enough, and gave back some of the same gibberish. "You got through, though?" he said at last.

"Through the second portal, like I told you. That's how I got the backside look at the trap," his father answered.

"I hope that's not all you did," Gottlieb said.

"Well, I didn't have as much time as I wanted after the trouble at the first portal, and I did want to see what almost bit me," Walther Stutzman said. "But I got to look around a little. The *Reichsführer*-SS isn't very happy with the *Führer*."

Like Alicia's father, Gottlieb and Anna's had a way of saying things that were important as if they weren't. What sort of fireworks could go off if the leader of the SS didn't like what the leader of the *Reich* was doing? Before Alicia could do more than begin to wonder about that, Anna said, "Let's get back to the game."

"All right," Alicia said, though she wouldn't have minded sitting around and listening some more, either. The Stutzmans talked more openly than her own family did. Of course, they weren't keeping the secret around the house any more. They'd probably been a lot more careful before Anna knew.

It'll be years before we can tell Roxane, Alicia thought sadly. But Gottlieb had been thinking the same thing about Anna even longer. *We have something in common.* That was a pretty funny idea. It stayed in Alicia's mind for a little while. Then the vile deeds of the wicked SS bird made her forget all about it.

Susanna Weiss loathed faculty meetings. Nothing worthwhile ever got done in them, and they wasted inordinate amounts of time. But *Herr Doktor* Professor Oppenhoff loved them with a bureaucratic passion. Since he headed the Department of Germanic Languages, everyone else had to go along. Susanna eyed the conference room as if it were some especially nasty part of a concentration camp.

Part of her knew that was foolishness. The only poison gas in the room came from Oppenhoff's cigar. Two steam radiators kept the place comfortable, even toasty, despite the chill outside. Sweet rolls and coffee waited on a table next to the window; she didn't have to try to survive on camp swill. No SS guards prowled with guns and dogs. But she was stuck here when she didn't want to be, which gave the meeting the feel of imprisonment.

She listened with half an ear to a report congratulating the department for its impressive publication record. Three of the articles Professor Tennfelde mentioned were hers. She yawned even so. She'd learned to do it without opening her mouth, so it didn't show nearly so much. Tennfelde was dull, dull, dull. If he lectured this way, his students would be anesthetized.

The report finally ended. The spatter of applause the faculty gave seemed to signal relief that it was over. But Tennfelde knew who his primary audience was, and he'd pleased Franz Oppenhoff. "Very informative," the department chairman declared. "Very informative indeed."

Susanna drew a doodle of an alarm clock with a long white beard. And more reports were coming. None of them had anything to do with her. She could have gone her whole life long without knowing or caring what the interlibrary-loan committee had done lately, or whether discussions on merging the Flemish and Dutch subdepartments had progressed any further, especially since they hadn't.

She also yawned—open-mouthed this time—through a report on financial planning from a professor who specialized in the *Nibelungenlied* and dabbled in the stock market on the side. If he'd done well, he wouldn't have had to worry about his university salary. He plainly did worry about it, which meant he hadn't done well. Why anyone would want advice from a bungling amateur was beyond Susanna. She had a thoroughly professional accountant and broker, and no worries as far as money was concerned. Other things, yes. Money, no.

Again, though, Professor Oppenhoff seemed pleased. "I would like to thank *Herr Doktor* Professor Dahrendorf for that interesting and enlightening presentation. "He puffed on his Havana. Then he said, "And now *Fräulein Doktor* Professor Weiss will enlighten us on the current political situation and the changes we have seen in recent times."

Why, you miserable son of a bitch! Susanna thought. Oppenhoff hadn't warned her he was going to do any such thing. He sat there looking smug and pleased with himself. If she made an ass of herself, the rest of the department would assume she was incompetent, not that he'd set her up.

I'd better not make an ass of myself, then. "Thank you, Professor Oppenhoff," she said. She would sooner have substituted another verb for *thank*, but she gained a few seconds to gather herself even so. Some of these people couldn't get through a lecture even with the text on the lectern in front of them. She'd always prided herself on being able to think on her feet. *Well, here we go.*

First, the obvious. "Reform will continue. I believe it will intensify. The *Führer* has seen that we cannot stay strong by living on booty forever. That saps the fiber of the *Volk*." If Heinz Buckliger could use what sounded like Party doctrine for purposes that would have horrified an *alter Kämpfer*, so could she. She went on, "He has also seen that it is in the interest of the *Reich* to allow more expression of national consciousness within the Empire, especially among Germanic peoples." Czechs weren't Germanic, Frenchmen only marginally so. Susanna shrugged. That *especially* covered her.

"Also, the possibility of error in the past has been admitted," she said. "This appears to be a healthy development. If we know we have made mistakes, and we know which mistakes we have made, we are less likely to make similar ones in the future." *We won't murder millions of Jews again, because there aren't that many left. We might have a hard time murdering thousands of them.*

"Not everyone inside the Party is pleased with the direction reform is taking. I think the Jahnke letter in the *Beobachter* proves that. No one I know believes Jahnke could have published that letter without official, ah, encouragement. It's fairly obvious which officials encouraged him, too." She looked around at the language and literature professors. By their expressions, it wasn't obvious to a lot of them. They were safe. They were comfortable. Why should they get excited about politics?

"On the other hand, we've also seen that some reform has spurred a call for more reform," Susanna said. "Some people—people in high places, too—don't believe the *Führer* is moving fast enough. Like those who oppose any reform at all, they may grow harder to ignore as time goes on."

She looked Franz Oppenhoff in the eye. "And that, *Herr Doktor* Professor, about sums it up."

He'd wanted her to make a hash of it. She knew that. She'd had to suffer through a string of indignities no professor who pissed standing up would have had to endure. This was only the latest, and far from the worst. Now she wanted to see whether Oppenhoff would have the gall to claim she hadn't made a proper presentation. If he did, she intended to scorch him.

He scratched at the edge of his side-whiskers, coughed once or twice, and looked down at the papers in front of him. Still looking down at them, he mumbled, "I must thank you for your clear, concise report." People more than half a dozen seats from him undoubtedly didn't hear a word.

"*Danke schön,* Professor Oppenhoff. I'm glad you liked it," Susanna said loudly. She would get the message across, even if the department chairman didn't feel like doing it.

The meeting ground on. Oppenhoff didn't call on her any more. He did keep glancing over to her every so often. She smiled back sweetly, wishing she could display a shark's teeth instead of her own.

Heinrich Gimpel was finishing up a bowl of rather nasty cabbage stew in the *Oberkommando der Wehrmacht* canteen when a uniformed guard coming off his shift walked in and said, "Something juicy's going on out in the Adolf Hitler Platz."

"What now?" somebody asked him. "More damned Dutchmen yelling, 'Freedom!'? They probably won't even bother arresting them these days."

But the guard shook his head. "No, it's bigger than any of that piddling crap. They've got a podium and televisor cameras and all kinds of stuff."

That sounded interesting. Heinrich got up, threw out his trash, and put his tray on a moving belt that took it back to the dishwashers. By the clock, he should have gone straight to his desk. He decided to ignore the clock for once. Willi and Ilse had taken plenty of long lunches without ending the world. He figured he could get away with one, especially since he was only going out onto the square in front of headquarters.

As soon as he walked out of the building, he saw the guard was right. In fact, Adolf Hitler Platz held not one commotion but two. Proud banners flying ahead of it, an SS band full of tubas and thumping drums strutted through the square playing marches as loud as they could. If they weren't trying to drown out the man on the podium . . .

It was a bright spring day. It wasn't very warm—it couldn't have been above ten Celsius—but the sun shone down brightly. It gleamed off the speaker's head, which wasn't just bald but shaven. As soon as Heinrich recognized Rolf Stolle, he knew exactly why that band was blaring away.

He hurried down the steps and across the paving toward the podium from which the *Gauleiter* of Berlin was addressing a good-sized crowd. Stolle had a microphone. Even so, he was barely a match for the booming band.

He not only knew it, he took advantage of it, saying, "You see how it is, *Volk* of the *Reich*? Some of the powers that be don't want you to hear me. They don't want me reminding you that we need to go forward, not sit around with our thumbs up our. . . ." He stopped and grinned. "Well, you know what I mean. And I'll tell you something else I mean, too. These are the people in charge of protecting the *Führer*. He wants reform. He doesn't want enough of it. He doesn't want it quick enough. But he wants it. They don't. I've told Heinz and told him, 'Don't let these people get behind you so they can stab you in the back,' but he doesn't want to listen."

Stolle stuck out his chin and thrust his fist forward. The pose made him look like Mussolini. "Heinz Buckliger is a good man. Don't get me wrong," he said. "A good man, yes. But a little too trusting."

Whatever he said next, the thundering SS musicians drowned it out. Instead of getting angry about that, he laughed. He even sang a few bars of the march they were playing. People laughed and clapped their hands. Stolle grinned. He struck another pose, this time a silly one. When Heinrich thought of him as a clown, he hadn't been so far wrong. An appreciative audience made Stolle come alive.

The band moved a little farther away from the podium. The *Gauleiter* moved a little closer to the microphone. "If those noisy SS bastards will just go home, I'll get on with my speech," he said.

A man in the crowd shouted, "SS go home!" He shouted it again. Then three or four more people took up the call. Before long, everybody who'd come to Adolf Hitler Platz to hear Rolf Stolle was yelling, "SS go home!" The cry echoed from the long front wall of the *Führer*'s palace. Could Heinz Buckliger hear it in there? If he could, what did he think?

Heinrich wondered, but not for long. He was caught up in the thrill of shouting, "SS go home!" He never would have had the nerve to be first to yell such a thing. In the middle of thousands of others, his voice was only one, indistinguishable from the rest. *They'll have a hell of a time arresting all of us,* he thought, and yelled louder than ever. "SS go home! SS go home! *SS go home!*"

The chant swelled and swelled. Looking at the excited faces and sparkling eyes of the men and women all around him, Heinrich realized he wasn't the only one who'd wanted to say that for years. How many Germans did? How many would, if they got the chance? He smelled the acrid sweat of fear, but people kept shouting.

Rolf Stolle leaned toward the microphone again. "SS go home!" he called, leading the chorus. "SS go home!"

Heinrich watched the band. Would the musicians deign to take any notice of the people clamoring for them to leave? If they did, wasn't that a sign of weakness? If they didn't, how long before hotheads started throwing rocks and bottles and whatever else they could get their hands on at them? And what would the SS men do then? And what would the crowd—the mob?—do in reply?

Maybe those same questions were going through the band leader's head. Maybe he didn't like the answers that occurred to him, either. As if continuing a regular performance—which this was anything but—he led the musicians to the edge of the enormous square. They kept on playing, but they no longer interfered with Rolf Stolle's speech.

As the crowd roared in triumph, Stolle shouted, "Do you see, *Volk* of the *Reich*? Do you? Without you, they're nothing. And they aren't with you, are they?"

"No!" That was a great, pain-filled howl. Again, Heinrich yelled as loud as anyone. Had schnapps ever left him this giddy? He didn't think so.

"I was going to talk for a while longer, friends, but you just made my speech for me," the *Gauleiter* of Berlin boomed. The crowd cheered. Rolf Stolle went on, "And do you know what else? By this time tomorrow, the whole *Reich* will know what you've done!"

Ecstatic cheers drowned out the now-distant SS band. Heinrich joined them, but hesitantly. He thought Stolle was likely right. He wasn't so sure that delighted him. If this footage showed up on Horst Witzleben's newscast, would gimlet-eyed SS technicians pore over it, trying to identify every single person—every single subversive person—in the crowd? Could they identify *him*?

Most of the time, things like that would have left him scared to death. Today, he felt too much exultation, too much exaltation, to care very much. Germans—Germans!—had just told the SS (even if it was only a marching band) where to head in. He'd joined them. The SS (even if it was only a marching band) had retreated. And nobody had got shot.

If that all wasn't a reason to make a man feel three meters tall, Heinrich couldn't imagine what would be.

Something was going on. Lise Gimpel could tell as much by the way Heinrich acted when he came home from work. He had almost a mad scientist's gleam in his eye, an air of excitement, he didn't even try to hide. He wouldn't tell her what it was all about, though. That made her want to smack him.

The most he would say was, "We'll watch Horst after supper." Since he said that about three nights a week, it didn't give Lise much of a clue about why he wanted to see the evening news.

Dinner ran late, too. The chicken Lise was roasting took longer to get done than she'd thought it would. The family didn't finish eating till just before seven. Normally, Lise would have done the dishes while the news was on. If she missed the first couple of stories, well, the world wouldn't end. Tonight, she got the feeling it might. She left plates and silverware and glasses in the sink and sat down next to Heinrich to find out what Horst Witzleben had to say for himself—and why her husband had been looking wild-eyed ever since he walked through the front door.

"Our opening story," the newsreader said, "is the collision of two airliners on the runway at Gander, Newfoundland." A map flashed on the screen to show where Gander was. "More than 250 people are confirmed as fatalities. Only seventeen are known to have survived, many of them with severe burns." The televisor showed smoking wreckage, and then one of those survivors coming out of an ambulance on a stretcher.

Lise glanced over at Heinrich. Whatever he'd been waiting for, that wasn't it. She knew a certain amount of relief. She would have worried if he'd got that excited about a plane crash.

Then the picture shifted to Adolf Hitler Platz. Heinrich stiffened. This was it, all right. But why? There was Rolf Stolle, making one of his usual rabble-rousing speeches. And the rabble were indeed roused, as their cheers and shouts showed. But some oom-pah music kept coming close to drowning out the *Gauleiter* of Berlin. What was that all about?

Then Horst Witzleben said, "Despite attempted interference from an SS marching band, *Gauleiter* Rolf Stolle delivered another strong statement supporting the *Führer*'s reform program this afternoon in central Berlin. His large audience received him favorably, and showed their displeasure at the band's not at all coincidental presence in the square."

His voice cut off. Lise heard people shouting. For a moment, it was just rising and falling noise. Then she made out words: "SS go home! SS go home!"

Ice and fire rivered through her, both together. They'd said *that*? Nothing had happened to them? And now the authorities were showing the pictures on the evening news?

Heinrich grabbed her hand. His voice quivering with excitement, he said, "I was *there*, out in the platz. I was listening to Stolle. And I was shouting for the SS to leave along with everybody else. And they *did*!"

"You?" Lise said in amazement. Heinrich nodded. "Was that safe?" she asked.

"I don't know. I think so. I hope so," he answered. "So many people were there, I don't see how they can grab everybody." But he hesitated a little before he said that. Was he trying to convince her or himself or both of them?

"Well, it's done. I hope it turns out all right," she said, and then, "I didn't see you anywhere on the tape."

"Good. I didn't, either," Heinrich said. He'd been watching for himself, then, which meant he was more worried than he let on. Lise sent him a look half affectionate, half exasperated. He *would* try to play down whatever bothered him, because he didn't want her to worry. Once in a great while, that worked. The rest of the time, it only made her worry more.

An advertisement for a breakfast cereal tried to show that eating the stuff would make you rich, athletic, and beautiful. Lise remained unconvinced. "It tastes like library paste," she said.

"I wouldn't be surprised," Heinrich replied, "but how do you know what library paste tastes like?"

"How? I'm the one who helps the girls put school projects together, that's how," Lise said. "I eat the paste, I breathe it, I damn near bathe in it. Last week, *Frau* Koch wanted everybody in class to make a model of one of the forts the *Reich* uses to protect German farmers in the Ukraine from bandits. Do you have any idea how much fun it is to glue three strands of tinsel barbed wire to toothpick stakes?"

"As a matter of fact, no," Heinrich admitted. "Is that why you were in such a lousy mood last—when was it?—Wednesday night?"

"You bet it is," Lise said. "And there had to be *three* strands of barbed wire, too, by God, or Francesca would have lost points. *Frau* Koch said so. She really is a beast, if you ask me. Everything else about the project was like that, too: do it exactly this way, or else. How are they supposed to learn anything?"

"I'll tell you what they learn," Heinrich said. "They learn to obey."

Lise hadn't thought of that. But as soon as her husband pointed it out to her, she saw that he was right. School taught more than the multiplication tables and the capital of Manchukuo and how Bismarck unified the *Reich*. It taught children how to be good Germans, how to be good Nazis. One of the things they needed to know was how to blindly obey anyone set over them. The fortress needs to have three strands of tinsel barbed wire? *Jawohl, Frau* Koch! Three strands of tinsel barbed wire it shall have! And why does it need to have them? Because *Frau* Koch says so. No other reason needed.

But Germans—some of them Nazis, no doubt—had stood out there in Adolf Hitler Platz shouting, "SS go home!" They really had. And here was Horst Witzleben, showing them to the whole *Reich*, to much of the Germanic Empire, with every sign of approval. Would people be chanting the same thing in Oslo tomorrow? In London? Even in Omaha? What would happen if they did?

Horst Witzleben said, "Today, the *Führer* met with a delegation from the Protectorate of Bohemia and Moravia to discuss that region's future relationship with the Greater German *Reich*. At the close of the meeting, a spokesman for the *Führer* said that while Bohemia and Moravia, which have been part of the *Reich* since 1939, cannot reasonably expect to regain their former independence, a larger degree of autonomy within the German federal structure is not beyond the realm of possibility."

The picture cut to the delegation in the palace press room. Its leader, a white-haired man identified as—of all things—a playwright, spoke in Czech-accented German: "What we did here today marks a good beginning. I am not sure *Herr* Buckliger realizes it is only a beginning, but that is all right. If he doesn't, we will show him."

"They didn't arrest this fellow, either?" Lise said incredulously.

"Doesn't look that way." Heinrich sounded startled, too.

"This is all very strange," Lise said. Her husband nodded. She went on, "I'd almost rather Buckliger had left things alone. Then we'd know where we stood. This way, everything we've been sure of for so long is up in the air."

"What's that myth? Pandora? Is that it? The last thing that flew out was hope." Heinrich paused, frowning. "I think that's how it is."

"Yes, I think so, too," Lise said. "I don't know if I have any, not really. But even wondering if I could . . . It feels funny. It feels dizzy, like somebody spiked my drink when I wasn't looking."

"I thought so, too, this afternoon," Heinrich said. "But don't get too excited. For every scene like this, there's an 'Enough Is Enough' or something like it. The cards may have been dealt, but they haven't been played yet. And nobody's going to lay down a dummy. We won't get to see anything till it comes out during the hand."

"I suppose not." Lise sighed. "We're going to have to find some new bridge partners, you know."

"One of these days." Heinrich gestured toward the televisor. That Czech playwright was gone, but the memory of his calm assurance lingered. Heinrich said, "Plenty of interesting things happening right now. And pretty soon the kids will learn how to play."

"All sorts of things to pass on to the next generation," Lise said. They both started to laugh. Bridge wasn't even illegal.

SS men, some in black uniforms, others in camouflage smocks, swarmed near the campus of Friedrich Wilhelm University. Snipers with rifles with telescopic sights took positions on rooftops that had never known the footsteps of anyone but occasional repairmen and not-so-occasional pigeons. Susanna Weiss would have been more alarmed if she hadn't known that Heinz Buckliger was coming here to speak.

Along with the SS men, a horde of workmen and technicians had also invaded the university. Banging hammers and buzzing power tools disrupted the quiet that was supposed to foster academic contemplation. Since Susanna had never had any enormous use for quiet, she turned up the radio a little louder to try to drown out the racket of carpentry.

That did the job well enough, but curiosity accomplished what noise couldn't: it made her get up from her work and look out the window.

A platform for the *Führer*'s upcoming speech was rising in the open space between the two long wings that housed most of the university's classrooms and faculty offices. Rising with it were platforms for televisor cameras. Those would lift the cameramen above the level of the crowd and make sure no one's head got between Heinz Buckliger and his larger audience across the *Reich* and the Germanic Empire.

The crowd was already building. Susanna thought about going downstairs and joining it. Then she thought again. What was the point? She wasn't close to the platform here, but she could see it. If she went down there, she wouldn't be able to see a damned thing, because everybody around her would be taller than she was. Better to stay where she was. She'd hear Heinz Buckliger either way.

Curiosity satisfied and decision made, she went back to grading papers. Plenty of her students understood the scatology in "The Miller's Tale." Far fewer of them understood how the piece fit into *The Canterbury Tales* as a whole. They enjoyed gross jokes. Finding and defining structure in a work of literature was something else again.

Twenty minutes later, the telephone rang. She picked it up. "*Bitte?* This is Susanna Weiss."

"*Fräulein Doktor* Professor, this is Rosa." Professor Oppenhoff's secretary paused for a moment, then said, "The department chairman strongly advises against watching the *Führer*'s speech from your window."

"He does?" Susanna said indignantly. "Why?"

"Because the SS has told him they may shoot anyone they see appearing in a window. Whoever it is might be an assassin, they say."

"Oh." Now it was Susanna's turn to pause. "Well, I hope you get hold of everybody. Otherwise, we'll need to fill some vacancies next semester."

"I'll do my best," the secretary said, and hung up. Considering how badly they got along, Susanna knew a certain amount of relief that Rosa had called her. The other woman didn't seem to want to see her dead, anyhow. That was something.

Then she started to laugh. "God help anyone who's in the men's room when the phone rings!" she exclaimed.

Even if watching Buckliger's speech turned out not to be such a good idea, she could still listen to it. She opened her window a few centimeters so she could hear better. The *Führer* wasn't there yet, so none of the SS snipers took a shot at her.

Noise from down below swelled as the crowd built up. You could put a lot of people between the two main wings of the university buildings. From the excited buzz that rose, she knew to the minute when Heinz Buckliger came into sight.

"*Guten Tag*, students, faculty, and friends," Buckliger said. His amplified voice sounded a little tinny. Technicians would probably improve it for the radio and televisor. "I am glad to come to this great center of learning. Knowledge is at the heart of the *Reich*'s progress in war and peace. Without our talented scientists and engineers, we could not have won our great victories. Nor would the peace that followed have been so prosperous, so healthy, or so enjoyable."

He got a hand. Susanna might have known he would. She wouldn't have cheered that, not in a million years. Buckliger proved he was a German after all. The *Volk* might live prosperous, healthy, enjoyable lives. What about the Jews? The gypsies? Homosexuals? Poles? Russians? Ukrainians? Serbs? Arabs? Negroes? Feebleminded people? Did he think of them at all? Or only of his own comfort? From what he said, the answer seemed all too obvious.

"We need to know ourselves as well," the *Führer* said, after showing he didn't know himself so well even if he could sound like Marcus Aurelius. Would a Roman Emperor count as an Aryan? Probably not, not when he'd been fighting Germans along the Danube while he wrote the *Meditations*. Buckliger continued, "And the best way to know ourselves is to tell ourselves the truth.

"We cannot do that while the *Reichstag* is only a rubber stamp. It has been nothing more for much too long. As Hitler pointed out in the first edition of *Mein Kampf*, democratic elections are the best way to find representatives who will serve the people who chose them and not themselves alone." He paused for applause, and got it.

"This being so," he went on, "I am calling new elections to the *Reichstag*, voting to take place on Sunday, July 10. All seats are to be contested. Candidates need not be members of the Party, so long as they are of Aryan blood and good character. Ballots will be secret. There will be no penalty for voting one's conscience. I have not the slightest particle of doubt that the best will prevail. And the *Volk* and the *Reich* will be better for it."

The ovation this time was hesitant, as if the *Führer*'s audience was not sure whether it was allowed to cheer. That didn't surprise Susanna. What Heinz Buckliger had said did. But it was hardly surprising to be surprised in Berlin these days. That speech of Rolf Stolle's in the Adolf Hitler Platz where the crowd drove off the SS band . . . The SS had gone away, and not only did no one get arrested, the story made the evening news. Heinrich had been there. Up till today, Susanna had been sick with envy. Now she too had a moment of history to claim as her own.

"We National Socialists have ruled Germany wisely and well for many years," Buckliger said. "I have faith that the *Volk* will recognize our service and give us the large majority in the *Reichstag* we deserve."

Loud, confident applause rang out. Of course people knew they were safe clapping after the *Führer* praised the Nazis. Susanna thought Buckliger was probably right about the Party's winning most of the seats in the *Reichstag*. Even now, how many non-Nazis would be bold enough to run against Party *Bonzen?* How many who did run would win? Maybe some. Many? It seemed unlikely.

Did Buckliger really believe the Nazis had ruled Germany well and wisely? They'd won, thanks in no small measure to Hitler's demonic energy and Himmler's grim ruthlessness. But the blood of the people they'd murdered—the blood of the peoples they'd murdered—still cried out from the grave . . . and from the crematorium for those millions who'd never got a grave.

"I know reform, revitalization, cannot come overnight," the *Führer* said. "The *Reich* is large and complex. Those who call for everything to be perfect by tomorrow are naive. But those who say nothing needs repair are willfully blind. Change is part of life. It is here. It will go forward. And it will succeed."

He got another big hand. Susanna was intrigued by his methods. In back-to-back sentences, he'd skewered Rolf Stolle and Lothar Prützmann.

No doubt he meant to show himself as a moderate, as a man embarked on the only possible course. That could work. But she remembered the thought she'd had not so long before. A moderate was also somebody vulnerable from both the left and the right. Did Heinz Buckliger see that?

Most people would say, *What do you think you're doing, trying to guess along with the* Führer? Susanna cared very little about what most people said. If she had, she would have dropped her Judaism like a grenade with the fuse lit.

Besides, up till the time when Buckliger became *Führer,* politics in the *Reich* had been not only appalling but, worse yet, bloody dull. Some of the things that went on were still appalling. But only someone who was deaf and blind would have called them dull. And when things were interesting, how could you *not* try to guess what would happen next?

Outside, the applause went on and on, though the *Führer* didn't say anything more. Susanna concluded he was leaving the platform, leaving the university. Pretty soon, the coast would be clear. She could look out her window again without worrying about trigger-happy SS sharpshooters.

In the meantime . . . In the meantime, she still had her essays to grade. They would have been there even if Kurt Haldweim were still *Führer*. In a lot of ways, life went on in spite of politics.

And, in a lot of ways, it didn't. How many lives had the politics of the *Reich* snuffed out? Too many. Millions and millions too many. What did undergraduate essays matter, with that in the back of her mind?

But her life had to go on, no matter what the *Reich* had done. Shaking her head, she picked up a red pen and got back to work.

A day like any other day. That was how Heinrich Gimpel remembered it afterwards. It could have been any Tuesday. The kids were running around getting ready for school. Francesca was still grumbling about some new idiotic project *Frau* Koch had inflicted on the class. Roxane was spelling words out loud; she was going to have a test. And Alicia had her nose in a book. Lise had to yell at her to get her to put it down and do the things she needed to do. Yes, everything seemed normal as could be.

Blackbirds on lawns tugged at worms as Heinrich walked up the street toward the bus stop. The sun shone brightly. Spring was really here now. He couldn't recall any other spring that had seemed to hopeful, so cheerful. Was that Mother Nature's fault or Heinz Buckliger's? Heinrich didn't know. He didn't much care, either. He would enjoy the moment for as long as it lasted.

He waited at the bus stop for a few minutes, then got on the bus for the Stahnsdorf train station. Three stops later, Willi Dorsch got on, too. He sat down next to Heinrich. "*Guten Morgen,*" he said.

"Same to you," Heinrich answered. "*Wie geht's?*"

"It's been better," Willi said. "I have to tell you, though, it's been worse, too. Erika's been . . . kind of cheerful lately." He looked this way and that, a comic show of suspicion. "I wonder what she's up to."

"Heh," Heinrich said uneasily. As far as he could tell, Erika had never said anything to Willi about what had happened at her sister's house on Burggrafen-Strasse—or about any of the several things that might have happened there but hadn't. He supposed he should have been grateful. He *was* grateful. But he was also suspicious, and his suspicion had no comic edge to it.

When the bus got to the Stahnsdorf station, he and Willi bought their copies of the *Völkischer Beobachter* and carried them out to the platform. They climbed aboard the train up to Berlin, sat down together, and started reading the morning news. Almost as if they'd rehearsed it, they simultaneously pointed to the same story below the fold on the front page.

STOLLE ANNOUNCES CANDIDACY, the headline said. There was a small head shot of the *Gauleiter* of Berlin just below the line of big black type. The story, as bald as any Heinrich had ever seen in the *Beobachter,* announced that Rolf Stolle was indeed running for the *Reichstag.*

"Can he do that?" Heinrich said, and then, "How can he do that? He's already *Gauleiter.*" The puzzle offended his sense of order.

But Willi had the answer: "*Gauleiter*'s a Party office. *Reichstag* member would be a state office. He could hold both at once."

"You're right," Heinrich said wonderingly. The National Socialist Party and the *Reich* were as closely intertwined as a pair of lovers—or as a tree and a strangler fig. But they weren't quite one and the same.

"I wonder how the *Führer* will like that," Willi said.

"Stolle trying for a national forum?"

Willi nodded. "*Ja.* And Stolle trying for votes in general." He lowered his voice. "I mean, who ever voted for Buckliger for anything? Party *Bonzen* and *Wehrmacht* bigwigs, sure, but nobody else."

"You're right." Again, wonder filled Heinrich's voice. Till Buckliger's speech at Friedrich-Wilhelm University, that wouldn't have mattered. Who'd voted—really voted—for anyone who mattered in the *Reich*? No one. Elections had been afterthoughts, farces. This one felt different. Stolle must have sensed it, too. He might well have been a clown. Several of the moves he'd made lately convinced Heinrich he was anything but a fool.

And Willi, when it came to politics if not to women, was also anything but a fool. "I wonder *why* the *Führer*'s not running for a seat in the *Reichstag,*" he said thoughtfully.

That was an interesting question, too. Heinrich said, "Maybe he's worried he'd lose."

"Maybe," Willi said. "It's the only thing I thought of that made any sense at all, too. But it doesn't make a whole lot of sense, if you know what I mean. He can find a district full of Prussian cabbage farmers or Bavarian beer brewers that would elect him no matter what."

"You'd think so, wouldn't you?" Heinrich agreed. The more they talked about it, the more normal their tone became. The more freedom all the people of the *Reich* got, the more they seemed to take it for granted. The more they got, the more they craved? Was that true, too? Could that be true? Maybe it could. Maybe it really could. But who would have believed it a year before?

Willi suddenly looked sly. "The other side of the coin is what happens if Buckliger doesn't run for the *Reichstag.* If he doesn't, he's still *Führer.* He's still got all the *Führer*'s powers. He can tell it what to do."

"That's the way things work, all right," Heinrich said. But then he did a little more thinking of his own. "That's the way things work *now,* all right. If the *Volk* chooses the *Reichstag,* though, will it be so easy to ignore? What's the point to having a real election if right afterwards you go and pretend you never did?"

"You're right there," Willi admitted. "I don't see the point to that, either. Maybe Buckliger does."

"Who knows?" Heinrich said. "Who knows for sure about anything that's going on these days? We'll just have to wait and see."

"Sounds like traffic through Berlin, doesn't it?" Willi said as the commuter train came into South Station. "Of course, there's usually a lot more waiting than seeing with that."

"Maybe it won't be so bad," Heinrich said. Before Willi could say anything sardonic, he forestalled him: "Maybe it'll be worse."

As a matter of fact, they got to *Oberkommando der Wehrmacht* headquarters fifteen minutes early. Had they been fifteen minutes late, they both would have cursed and fumed. Early they took for granted. Heinrich looked out across Adolf Hitler Platz toward the *Führer*'s palace. Aside from a few joggers and a gaggle of early-rising Japanese tourists snapping photos, the vast square was echoingly empty. No *Gauleiter* growling out a speech this morning. No thumping, swaggering SS band trying to drown him out. No Dutch demonstrators, either.

Willi was looking across the square, too. "Almost gets boring to see it this quiet, doesn't it?" he remarked.

"It does," Heinrich said in bemusement. "It really does."

They went up the stairs and, after getting their identities confirmed, into the headquarters building. Heinrich sat down at his desk and immediately yawned. He got up and went to the canteen with Willi to fortify himself with a cup of coffee. He squirted some hot chocolate into the cup, too, from the machine next to the coffeemaker. "Viennese today, aren't we?" Willi said.

"Oh, but of course." Heinrich put on an Austrian accent. Willi laughed.

A Viennese aristocrat—even a Viennese headwaiter—would have turned up his nose at the concoction Heinrich had put together. But it was hot and it was sweet and it had plenty of caffeine. With all that going for it, Heinrich wasn't inclined to be fussy. After he finished it and tossed the cup in the trash, he thought about going back for another one. But his brains were moving a little faster, so he buckled down and got to work instead.

Ilse wandered over to Willi's desk and started playing with little ringlets of hair that hung down over the back of his collar. Without looking away from his computer screen, he swatted her on the fanny. She squeaked. She seemed to have recovered nicely from discovering that Rolf Stolle had had his fun with her and that his roving eye had then roved on.

She and Willi were all but molesting each other when they went off at noon. Heinrich had no doubt they would pick a restaurant somewhere close to a hotel. He walked back to the canteen. The lunch special there was roast pork. As he had all his life, he ate it without a second thought. He liked pork, though he'd had better than this.

When Willi and Ilse came in after a long, long lunch break, Willi mimed smoking a lazy cigarette. Ilse thought that was the funniest thing in the world.

Heinrich was plowing through an analysis of near-future American business activity when he looked up to discover three blackshirts standing around his desk. "*Was ist hier los?*" he asked in surprise but no real alarm.

"You are Heinrich Gimpel?" one of them asked.

He nodded. "That's me." He wondered if they wanted to take him to confer with Heinz Buckliger again.

They didn't. The two lower-ranking blackshirts grabbed him and hauled him out of his chair. The senior man said, "You are under arrest."

"Arrest?" Heinrich yelped in disbelief. "What for?"

"Suspicion of being a Jew."

XII

HERR PEUKERT WAS TALKING ABOUT NEGATIVE NUMBERS WHEN A CLERK FROM the office came into the room and took him aside to speak with him. Alicia was glad for the break. Her head was spinning. When you added negative numbers you really subtracted, and when you subtracted negative numbers you really added? It sounded crazy, to say nothing of confusing.

"What?" The teacher, who had been speaking quietly, exclaimed in surprise. The clerk nodded and muttered something else. *Herr* Peukert shook his head. The clerk nodded again. The teacher sighed and shrugged. "Alicia Gimpel!" he said.

Alicia jumped up to her feet. "*Ja, Herr* Peukert?"

"Please go to the office with *Fräulein* Knopp here. Something has come up."

"*Jawohl, Herr* Peukert." Alicia wondered what was going on. It sounded as if her mother needed to pull her out of class for some reason or other. Had Mommy forgotten to tell her about a dentist's appointment, or something like that? She was usually good about remembering all kinds of things, but she had forgotten once.

The way *Fräulein* Knopp kept looking at her all the way back to the office made her wonder. When they were almost there, the clerk asked, "Are you really?"

"Am I really what?" Alicia asked. But the clerk didn't answer.

When they got to the office, Alicia was surprised to find Francesca and Roxane already there. They looked surprised to see her. Roxane asked, "Are you in trouble, too?"

"I didn't think so," Alicia said.

"If they call you to the office, you're in trouble." Roxane spoke with experience born of more mischief than both her sisters together had got into.

Fräulein Knopp went into the inner office, the principal's office. Alicia heard her say, "They're all here now."

But the principal—a gray-haired, severe woman named *Frau* Fasold—didn't come out. Half a dozen large men in black uniforms did. One of them had a gray mustache that made him look like the boss. Sure enough, he was the one who spoke up: "You will come with us immediately, children, until this question is answered."

Roxane wasn't one to let anybody, even an enormous officer in an intimidating uniform, get the better of her. She tilted her head back so she could look him in the eye and said, "What question?" Alicia was suddenly, horribly, afraid she already knew.

And sure enough, the officer said the worst thing in the world: "The question of whether your father, Heinrich Gimpel, is a Jew, and of whether the three of you are first-degree *Mischlingen,* subject to the same penalties as full-blooded Jews." *Subject to being shot or gassed or anything else we feel like doing to you,* he meant.

A terrified scream bubbled up in Alicia's throat. But before she could let it out and give everything away, Francesca screamed first, and her shriek was pure fury: "*That's a lie!*" She went on, just about as loud, "We're no damned, stinking, big-nosed, big-lipped, lying, cheating, germy Jews! And neither is Daddy! And don't you say he is, either!" She kicked the Security Police officer in the shin.

"*Teufelsdreck!*" he shouted. He swung back his hand as if to slap Francesca. Roxane grabbed it and bit him. He roared in pain. "You idiots!" he yelled at his men. "Seize them!" He had to yell, because Roxane let go of him and started screeching it was all a lie, too.

That told Alicia what she had to do. She added her voice to the clamor, and did her best to fight and to get away before one of the big men grabbed her. "Christ, they sure don't act like a bunch of kikes," the man said, panting with the effort of hanging on to her.

Francesca and Roxane, of course, were convinced they were no such thing. Alicia realized she had to act as if she were, too. It was the only chance she and her sisters had . . . if they had any chance at all.

Frau Fasold finally did emerge from her office. She disapprovingly surveyed the chaos in the outer room. Shaking her head, she fixed the officer with the gray mustache with an icy blue glare. "Really, *mein Herr*," she said in a voice just as icy. "Is this disorder altogether necessary?"

Her manner could paralyze any student. It seemed to have the same effect on the Security Police man. "These are, uh, Jews, or, uh, *Mischlingen*, anyway," he said in a low voice. "We can't, uh, be too, uh, careful."

"These are children—and fine children, too, I might add," *Frau* Fasold said. Even in Alicia's terror, that astonished her. The principal never had a good word for anybody. *Frau* Fasold went on, "Why didn't you bring panzers and helicopters and flamethrowers, too? Then you could have been safe." She all but spat her contempt in the blackshirt's face.

He turned red. "We have our orders, ma'am," he said stonily. "We have to carry them out."

"Orders for murdering children?" *Frau* Fasold said. "Why?"

The Security Police officer turned redder. "It is our duty."

"God help you, in that case," the principal told him.

He turned his back on her, the way a petulant second-grader might have. Unlike a petulant second-grader, he didn't get a swat for being rude. Alicia wished he would have. He deserved one. But nobody was paying any attention to what she wished. The officer with the mustache nodded to his men. "Take them away."

They had their orders. They carried them out. It was their duty.

Lise Gimpel had just got back from the drugstore when the telephone rang. She muttered to herself. She'd been about to make a fresh pot of coffee. The ringing phone didn't magically shut up, the way she wished it would. She went over and picked it up. *"Bitte?"*

The first thing she heard was a car horn blaring. Was somebody playing a practical joke? Then, as traffic noises continued, she realized the call was from a pay phone on a busy street. "Lise, is that you?" a man asked.

"*Ja*. Willi?" she answered doubtfully.

"Dammit, I wish you hadn't said my name." Yes, that was Willi. But why was he calling from a pay phone and not from his desk? No sooner had the question formed in her mind than she found out, for he went on, "Listen, they've just arrested Heinrich for—for something completely ridiculous. I've got to go. 'Bye." He slammed the phone down in its cradle. The line went dead.

As if moving in a dream, Lise hung up, too. But it wasn't a dream. It was a nightmare, the worst nightmare she could have. *Something completely ridiculous* could mean only one thing, and it wasn't ridiculous, not to her. Like any Jew in Berlin, she'd rehearsed this disaster in her mind, hoping and hoping she would never have to use the plans she'd made. So much for that hope. She might not have long. They might be coming for her right now.

She reached for the telephone. It rang again before she could pick it up. She almost screamed. "*Bitte?*" she snapped. If it was some idiot salesman trying to get her to buy carpets . . .

"*Frau* Gimpel?" A woman's voice this, not a familiar one.

"Yes. What is it, please?"

"*Frau* Gimpel, this in Ingeborg Fasold, the principal at your daughters' school. I don't know how to tell you this, but . . . the Security Police have taken your daughters. They accuse them of being—forgive me for saying this—they accuse them of being part Jew. . . . Are you there, *Frau* Gimpel?"

"I'm here." In her own ears, Lise's voice sounded far away, eerily calm. "They've arrested my husband, too. It's all a lie, a mistake, of course." She had to say that. She remembered she had to say that. Somebody might be—probably was—listening.

"Of course." To her amazement, *Frau* Fasold sounded as if she meant it. She added, "I think it's a shame and a disgrace that they should take children, no matter what. How can a child have done anything bad to anyone? Even if the child *were* a *Mischling,* how could it? Nonsense. Pure *Quatsch.* Good luck to you."

"Thank you," Lise said in that same strange, calm voice. Her mind was racing a million kilometers a second. *Mischlingen.* They thought the girls were *Mischlingen.* She was pretty sure they'd arrested Heinrich as a Jew. That should mean they still believed she was an Aryan herself. If they kept on believing that, it might give her the chance to save everyone.

Or it might not help at all. She couldn't tell till she tried.

"If there's anything I can do, *Frau* Gimpel, please don't hesitate to ask," *Frau* Fasold said.

She really did sound as if she meant that. Lise's eyes filled with tears. "*Danke*," she whispered. "This is a false accusation. We will beat it."

"I hope so," the principal said. "Again, good luck." She hung up.

So did Lise. Maybe people were more decent than she'd ever dared dream. Willi, *Frau* Fasold . . . Neither had had to say a word. Both had taken a chance in picking up the phone. But they'd done it.

Lise had her own ideas about how and why Heinrich had been arrested. But finding out if she was right would have to wait. It didn't make any difference, not when she had no time to lose. The blackshirts were liable to come here next, to see what evidence they could dig up against her husband. Or they might not worry about evidence, and simply act. If they did that, Heinrich and the girls were lost.

So they won't do that. You have to think they won't. And if they come looking for evidence, they'd better not find any. There wasn't much to find: nothing printed in Hebrew, no Sabbath candlesticks, nothing like that. She had pork ribs in the freezer right now.

But there were those pictures, the ones that had come down from Heinrich's father. Lise had never looked at them, but she knew what they were. They recorded the murder of a people, first on this side of the Atlantic and then, a generation later, on the other. They would have been illegal any time. Now they were worse than illegal—they were incriminating. Heinrich had kept them to show the girls if the time ever came, to remind them what the Nazis did to Jews who revealed themselves.

Well, the girls wouldn't need that kind of reminder any more. Now they had a better one.

She knew which filing cabinet in the study held the photographs. She didn't know which drawer they were in, or which folder. Would the knock on the door come before she found them? That would be the cruelest cut of all.

Here they were! She started to carry the manila folder to the fireplace, then hesitated. They might wonder why she had a fire going, or find the remnants of photos in the ashes. Lise knew she wasn't thinking too clearly. She also knew she couldn't afford to take any chances at all.

She brought the folder into the downstairs bathroom instead. She started tearing the photos into little bits and flushing them down the commode. She couldn't help seeing some of what she destroyed. Here was the raw stuff of history, disappearing one flush at a time. Part of her thought that wasn't right—there should be some record of the Germans' crimes. The rest . . . She was shaking and in tears by the time the job was done. Heinrich would have shown *that* to little girls? The medicine was strong—too strong, she thought.

And she couldn't keep on shaking and crying. Even though this part of the job was done, she still had more to do. She went to the telephone and dialed. It rang six or seven times before a man said, "*Bitte?*" in a sleepy voice.

"Richard?" she said. "Richard, this is Lise Gimpel."

"What do you want? You woke me up," Richard Klein grumbled.

Woke you up? In the middle of the afternoon? Lise blinked at that. Then she remembered he was a trombone player. Musicians kept strange hours. "Richard, I need the name and number of that lawyer you used last year. You're not going to believe it, but Heinrich has the same problem you did."

"*Gott im Himmel!*" Klein exploded. He didn't sound sleepy any more. "Hang on. I'll get it for you." He came back on the line a minute later. "He's Klaus Menzel. Here's his phone number. Have you got something to write with?"

"Yes." Lise took down the number.

Richard said, "Good luck. Take care of yourself. Let us know what happens." Those were all things one friend could say to another without giving anything away to anyone tapping the line.

"Thanks," Lise said, and hung up. She could have made other calls: to her sister, to the Stutzmans, to Susanna Weiss, to a few—so few!—other people she knew. She could have, but she didn't. She had a plausible reason for calling the Kleins' house. She couldn't bring them under greater suspicion by doing so. That wasn't true of the others. She didn't want the Security Police wondering about her side of the family and her friends. Even if the worst happened to her, they could go on.

Besides, they would hear soon enough, one way or the other.

She called the lawyer and set up an appointment first thing in the morning—and got his promise to try to make sure nothing drastic happened before then. She'd just hung up the phone there when someone started banging on the front door.

She didn't need three guesses to know who that was. The banging went on and on. As she walked out to get the door, she wondered if she would be able to keep that appointment after all.

Susanna Weiss sat on her couch, a glass of Glenfiddich in her hand. The news was on, but she couldn't pay attention to Horst tonight. She took a long pull at the scotch. It wasn't the first one she'd had. It wouldn't be the last one she intended to have, either. If she felt like hell in the morning—and she probably would—well, that was why God made aspirin.

"Heinrich," she muttered, and shook her head in wonder mingled with despair. When Maria Klein asked her to meet for a drink, she'd known something was wrong. Something, yes, but *that*? She shook her head again.

Of them all, Heinrich Gimpel was the last one she'd expected to get caught. He was the one who never took chances, who never seemed to have the nerve to take chances. No Jew could afford to draw too much notice. But Heinrich often went out of his way to be not just solid and unexciting but downright boring. Susanna sometimes wondered what Lise, who was a good deal more lively, saw in him. She supposed something had to be there.

And now the Security Police had him. How hard were they leaning on him? How hard *could* they lean on him? The *Führer* had asked for information from him, after all. They had to know that. Even if he was a Jew, it should count for something . . . shouldn't it?

She finished her drink, got up, and poured herself another one. It all depended on how much they knew, or thought they knew. If they were sure Heinrich was what they said he was, they would go ahead and do whatever they wanted with—and to—him. The more doubts they had, the more careful they'd need to be. So it seemed to Susanna, anyway. They wouldn't want to tear answers out of a man who might be able to get his own back one day . . . would they?

They might not care. They might decide that, once they'd used him up, he wouldn't be able to do anything to them anyhow. Who in the *Reich* in the past seventy years had been able to do anything to the organization Lothar Prützmann now ran? Nobody. Nobody at all.

Horst went away. Susanna couldn't remember a single thing he'd talked about. A game show came on, with a wisecracking host and a statuesque blond sidekick. Susanna usually turned off the televisor the instant the news ended. Tonight, she left it on, more for the sake of background noise than for any other reason.

The questions were stupid. Some of the answers the contestants gave were even stupider. And the way the people jumped up and down and squealed—men as well as women—made Susanna cringe. *This* was the *Herrenvolk? This* was the material from which the Nazis had forged a *Reich* they said would last for a thousand years?

"If this is the master race, Lord help the rest of the world," Susanna said. But what had the Lord done for the rest of the world? Given most of it German overlords, that was what. How could you go on believing in a God Who went and did things like that?

Susanna looked down and discovered her glass was empty again. That, fortunately, was easy to fix. The book-crowded living room swayed a little when she got up. She made it to the kitchen and back without any trouble, though—and she didn't spill the fresh drink, either. As for how and why you could go on believing in a God Who did dreadful things—people had been wrestling with that at least since the time of Job. She wasn't going to settle it one drunken, frightened night in Berlin.

And if she drank enough, maybe she'd even stop worrying. She set about finding out.

Heinrich Gimpel sat in a cell that held a cot whose frame was immovably set in the concrete of the floor, a sink, a toilet, and damn all else. Whenever he stood, he had to hang on to his trousers. They'd taken away his belt—his shoelaces, too.

Of course, the first thing they'd done when they got him here was yank down his trousers and his underpants. They'd grunted when they saw he was made the same way they were. One of them said, "Is that all you've got?" He supposed that sort of insult was meant to tear him down so he'd be easier meat when they really started questioning him. He wondered why they bothered. He was already about as frightened as he could be. He was so frightened, he reckoned it a minor miracle he had anything at all to show down there.

They hadn't beaten him—not yet, anyway. They hadn't drugged him, either. They'd just tossed him in this cell and left him alone. He didn't know what that meant. Were they working up something particularly horrible? Or were they unsure he was what they thought he was?

Think, Heinrich, dammit, he told himself. If he could change the mess he was in to any degree, it would have to be with his brains. But what were the odds he *could* change it? Slim, and he knew as much. Still, he had to try.

If I were truly a goy, *how would I act?* He'd still be frightened. He was sure of that. If you weren't frightened after the Security Police grabbed you, you had to be crazy. But he would also be outraged. How *dared* they think him a dirty Jew? The anger he generated was ersatz, but after a while it started to feel real. He wondered if actors worked themselves into their roles this way.

For the time being, he had no one for whom to show off his fine synthetic fury. None of the cells close by had anyone in it. No guards tramped past. Why should they? He wasn't going anywhere.

"I want a lawyer!" he said loudly. "This is all a stupid frame-up! Get me a lawyer!" Maybe nobody was listening. He wouldn't have bet on it, though. A Security Police prison was bound to have microphones.

After what seemed a very long time—he didn't have his watch any more—two blackshirts came up the corridor. One pushed a food cart. The other carried an assault rifle. "Stand away from the bars," he ordered in a bored voice. Heinrich obeyed. The man pushing the cart shoved a tray into his cell.

"I want a lawyer," Heinrich said again. "You've got to get me out of here. The *Führer* himself has consulted me."

They ignored him. He might have known they would. How many prisoners had they seen? Thousands, without a doubt. How many had admitted they were guilty? Even one?

He ate what they gave him: cabbage stew with little bits of salt pork in it (did they think he would pick them out if he was a Jew?) and a chunk of brown bread. It wasn't as good as what he got at the canteen at work, but it wasn't a whole lot worse. He turned on the water in the sink and drank from the cupped palm of his hand till he'd had enough to cut his thirst.

Then he lay down on the cot on his back and stared up at the rough concrete of the ceiling. He hoped they hadn't grabbed Lise and the girls, too. He did his best to pray, but that didn't come easy. If God had let this happen to him, how reliable was He? But if you didn't believe, what point to staying a Jew?

Good question. He had no answer. He felt empty, useless. What happened to him now was out of his hands. He hoped it was in God's. He knew for certain it was in the Security Police's.

He fell asleep with his glasses on. He never heard the fellow with the cart retrieve his tray, which he'd left by the bars. He stayed asleep till a key clicked in the lock and half a dozen blackshirts burst in. "On your feet, you *Schweinehund,* you kike, you stinking sheeny!" they screamed.

Blearily, he obeyed. What time was it? Somewhere in the middle of the night, he thought. *I have to keep saying no. Whatever they do to me, I have to keep saying no.* If they killed him, they killed him. With a little luck—maybe a lot of luck—he could keep his family and friends alive.

The Security Police hustled him along the corridor. His pants fell down. They wouldn't let him pull them up again.

"I'm no Jew. I want a lawyer," he said.

"Shut up!" they shouted in unison. One of them stuck an elbow in his ribs. It hurt. He grunted. He'd never make a cinema hero, laughing at wounds that would kill the average hero. On the other hand, they could have done worse to him than they did.

INTERROGATION, said the sign over the door to the chamber where they took him. It wasn't quite, *All hope abandon, ye who enter here,* but it was, in the most literal sense of the words, close enough for government work.

They slammed him down into a hard chair and shackled him at wrists and ankles. They shone bright lights in his face. He'd seen this scene at the movies, too. The hero usually mocked his tormentors. Heinrich felt much more like screaming. He managed to keep quiet, which might have been the hardest thing he'd ever done.

"So, Jew . . ." said a voice from somewhere behind the glaring lights.

"I'm no Jew!" Heinrich exclaimed. "Jesus, are you people out of your minds?" The more offended and horrified he sounded, the better the chance he had . . . if he had any chance at all.

One of the blackshirts lifted his glasses off his nose. Another one slapped him in the face. His head snapped to the side. His ears rang. He blinked. It didn't do much good. Without glasses, the whole room was blurry.

"Don't spew your lies," the voice said. "You'll only make it worse for yourself."

How could I? he wondered bleakly. "But you've got the wrong man!" he wailed. "I've worked for *Oberkommando der Wehrmacht* for almost twenty years now, and—"

Another slap. This time, his head jerked the other way. "Tearing down everything the *Reich* builds up," the voice growled.

An opening! "*That's* a lie!" Heinrich said. "Look at my evaluations, if you don't believe me. I've served the *Reich*. I've never hurt it." That was true. He'd hated himself because it was true, too. Working for the regime might save him now, though. Quickly, desperately, he went on, "Ask the *Führer,* if you don't believe me."

Raucous laughter from the interrogator. "Tell me another one, Jewboy. As if the *Führer* cares about the likes of you."

One of the blackshirts who'd frog-marched him into the room muttered to the man behind the lamps. That man, whom Heinrich still hadn't seen, let out a scornful grunt. Then he shifted gears. He started hammering away at Heinrich's pedigree.

That pedigree was, of course, fictitious from top to bottom. The interrogator would have caught out a lot of Jews, grilling them about ancestors they didn't have. But Heinrich was a meticulous man. He knew the ancestors he didn't have as well as the ones he did—maybe better, since more about the fictitious ones had gone down on paper. He had to remind himself to throw in "I don't know"s every so often. How many people really could recite chapter and verse about great-great-grandparents off the tops of their heads? He didn't want the blackshirts to think he'd memorized a script, even if he had.

They slapped him a few more times. It stung, but he endured it. They weren't working anywhere near so hard as they might have to break him. Maybe they weren't sure what they had. Heinrich clung to that hope.

At last, after what could have been half an hour or three hours, the head man said, "Take the kike back to his cell. We'll have another go at him later."

Back Heinrich went. He could have done without that promise from the interrogator. But he hadn't told the Security Police anything. And they still hadn't roughed him up too badly. *It could be worse,* he thought. On his way out of an interrogation, that would do.

* * *

Alicia Gimpel envied her sisters. No matter what the Nazi matrons asked them, they couldn't give anything away. When they denied they were Jews, they believed those denials from the bottom of their hearts. Some of the blackshirts would remember taking them out of school for a long time.

The matrons called this place a foundlings' disciplinary home. The other children in here were ragged and scrawny, but very clean. The whole building reeked of disinfectant. They'd separated the Gimpel girls, maybe to keep them from coming up with a story together. For Francesca and Roxane, there wasn't any story to come up with. They were genuinely outraged at what was happening to them. Alicia had to pretend she was, too. If she could manage that, she had a chance. She might have a chance, anyway.

They'd put her in a room with a sharp-faced, stringy-haired blond girl named Paula. "What are you here for?" Paula asked.

"You won't believe it." Alicia assumed somebody was listening to everything she said.

"Try me." The other girl's smile showed pointed teeth. "I burned down my schoolroom." She spoke with nothing but pride.

"Wow!" Alicia wasn't sure she believed that. Maybe Paula was bragging. Or maybe she was trying to get Alicia to talk big, too, and hang herself. Could a ten-year-old be an informer? Of course she could.

"So what did you do?" Paula asked.

"They say I'm a Jew—or they say my father is, anyway," Alicia answered. That was the truth; admitting it couldn't hurt.

Paula's pale blue eyes widened. Now she was the one who said, "Wow!" and then, "That's so neat! I didn't think any of you people were left. The way the Nazis go on, they got rid of you. If you stayed ahead of 'em, more power to you."

She sounded as if she meant it. But then, if she was an informer, she *would* sound that way. *I can't trust her,* Alicia reminded herself. She said, "That's what they say, but it's a lie. I'm not, and Daddy isn't, either."

"Sure he's not." Paula's smile was knowing. "You've got to say that, don't you? If you say anything else, it's the showers or a noodle, right?"

That was what Alicia was afraid of. But she couldn't even show that the thought had crossed her mind. "They wouldn't do that to me!" she exclaimed. "I haven't done anything, and I'm not what they say I am!"

"Maybe you're not," Paula said. "What the hell—I don't know. But if they decide you are, you are, whether you are or not. You know what I mean?"

Whether she was an arsonist or not, she was a perfect cynic. How many brushes with the authorities had she had? How many of them had she won? More than a few, or Alicia would have been astonished. But not all, or she wouldn't be here. Alicia knew perfectly well what she meant, too. Here, though, she had to pretend she didn't. If she'd been seized for something she wasn't, none of these dire things would have occurred to her. She said, "They can't do that! It's *wrong!*" Maybe fear sounded like anger. She hoped so, anyhow.

All Paula said was, "When has that ever stopped them?"

Alicia had no answer, not at first. That had never stopped them. But then hope flared. "The new *Führer* won't let them do things like that."

"Buckliger?" Paula didn't try to hide her scorn. "You wait till the time comes. Lothar Prützmann will eat his lunch." She might have been handicapping a football match, not politics.

"Oh, I hope not!" Alicia said. Even that might have been too much, when Prützmann's Security Police had her. She said it anyway. She meant it. And she couldn't get in too much trouble for showing she was loyal to the *Führer* . . . could she?

Paula only laughed. "You just watch. You'll find out." In the hallway, a bell rang. Paula bounced to her feet. "That's supper. Come on."

It was a wretched excuse for a real supper: cabbage soup, boiled potatoes, and brown bread without butter. Alicia could see why Paula was so skinny. She looked around for her sisters. Each of them had a matron hovering close. When Alicia looked back over her shoulder, she saw one behind her, too. She decided not to get up and try to see Francesca or Roxane. Why give the matron the pleasure of telling her she couldn't? These women looked as if saying no was their chief pleasure in life.

She did ask her matron, "When will you let us go back to our mother and father?" She made sure she mentioned Daddy as well as Mommy. Nobody seemed to think Mommy was a Jew. She wondered how that had happened.

The matron frowned. She had a long, sour face, a face made for frowning. At last, after a pause for thought, she said, "Well, dear"—Alicia had never heard a more insincere *dear*—"that depends on what they decide to do with your father, you see."

Maybe she hoped Alicia wouldn't understand that. And maybe, if Alicia hadn't been a Jew, she wouldn't have. She was, and she did, but she had to pretend she didn't. *If they decide Daddy's an Aryan, you'll go home, too. But if they decide he's a Jew, he's dead, and your sisters are dead, and so are you.*

Lise Gimpel paused in cleaning up the house to take a pull from a glass of schnapps. The place was an astonishing mess. It might have suffered a visit from an earthquake or a hurricane, not the Security Police. They'd torn the place apart, looking for evidence that Heinrich was a Jew. If she hadn't flushed the photographs, they would have found it, too.

Her brain felt as badly disordered as the house. They'd roared questions at her while they were throwing everything on the floor. Why had she married a Jew? How long had she known he was a Jew? Why was she such a filthy whore? Did she think it was more fun sucking a circumcised cock?

Maybe they'd figured that one would horrify her into spilling secrets. All it did was make her furious. "You stupid fucking bastards!" she'd screamed. "You've got him! You know goddamn well he's not circumcised!"

They hadn't arrested her. They'd even been a little more polite after that—not much, but a little. They hadn't got anything out of her, or she didn't think they had. And they'd been in a rotten mood when they finally quit searching the house, so she didn't think they'd come up with anything there, either.

Now . . . Now all she could do was pick up the pieces. They hadn't smashed things on purpose, anyhow. All they'd done was toss them every which way. Getting them back where they belonged would take time, but she could do it. What else did she have to do, with Heinrich and the girls gone? Work helped hold worry at bay—again, not much, but a little.

The telephone rang. Lise jumped. "*Scheisse,*" she said crisply. The last thing she wanted to do was talk to anybody right now. But she knew she had to. It might be important. It might—literally—be life and death. Making her way through drifts of things on the floor, she went to the phone and picked it up. "*Bitte?*"

"Lise?" It was Willi. "How are you? Is there any news?"

"News? Well, yes. They've turned the house inside out. They've taken the children. Other than that, everything's jolly."

"Gott im Himmel!" Willi burst out. In the background, Erika asked what was wrong. He relayed what Lise had just told him.

"The children?" Erika said. "*Du lieber Gott!* I didn't even think about the children!"

"That's terrible," Willi said to Lise. "Is there anything I can do?"

"I've got Heinrich a lawyer. I hope it helps," Lise answered. "It should. He's innocent, so there's no way they can prove he's a Jew." She assumed more people than Willi Dorsch were listening to her telephone calls. She wouldn't have admitted what Heinrich was even to Willi alone. With the Security Police surely tapping the line, she wouldn't admit anything to anybody.

"There you go," Willi said. "Keep your chin up, and everything will turn out all right." He sounded like a man whistling past a graveyard.

Lise said, "Thanks," anyhow. Willi meant well. That probably wouldn't do Heinrich any good, but it was there. She went on, "I'm going to go. They left the house a hell of a mess."

"Oh. All right. Take care of yourself. We're thinking about you." Willi hung up.

So did Lise. *Thinking about me? Thinking what about me?* she wondered. *Thinking I may be a Jew myself?* But that wasn't fair. Willi had sounded the way a friend ought to sound. And Erika seemed genuinely horrified when he told her the Security Police had grabbed the girls, too.

They're good friends if they call, thinking Heinrich's not a Jew. They'd be better friends if they thought he was a Jew and called anyway. Maybe they did think so. But Lise would be a fool to ask them, and they would be fools to tell her.

Shaking her head, she got back to work.

"You! Gimpel!" a black-shirted jailer roared, and Heinrich sprang to his feet and stiffened to attention as if he were back in elementary school. Back then, he would have worried about a paddling. Now two more men from the Security Police leveled assault rifles at him. The jailer unlocked his cell and swung the door open. "Come with us."

"*Jawohl!*" Heinrich said. Another grilling? Another tentative thumping? Or were they really going to get down to business this time?

"Hands behind your back," the jailer told him when he'd stepped out into the corridor. Numbly, he obeyed. The man cuffed them behind him, then gave him a shove. "Get moving."

Feet light with fear, he obeyed. He couldn't do anything about his flopping trousers now. They didn't seem to care—they were hauling him along. They took him by a different route this time. He didn't know if that was good or bad. His heart thuttered. One way or the other, he'd find out.

They brought him to a room divided in half by a thick glass wall. A grill let someone on his side talk with someone on the other side. And someone did wait on the other side: a tall man, almost as tall as Heinrich, with an impressive mane of gray hair. The stranger wore a sharp pinstripe suit and carried a crocodile-leather attaché case with fittings that looked like real gold.

"Your mouthpiece." The jailer sounded disgusted. Neither he nor his gun-toting pals showed any sign of leaving the room. Whatever Heinrich said to the lawyer, he'd say in front of them.

He hardly cared. He shuffled to the grill. He had to stoop a little to put his mouth by it. He didn't care about that, either. "Who are you?" he asked. "Can you get me out of here? Did Lise hire you?"

"Your wife, you mean? *Ja*. My name's Klaus Menzel, and I don't have any idea whether I can spring you," answered the man on the other side of the grill. "I'll give it my best shot, though. All billable hours either way." He sounded cheerfully mercenary.

Somehow, that made Heinrich like him more, not less. He seemed less likely to be a Security Police plant, someone put in place to get Heinrich to spill his guts. Of course, if they'd wanted him to do that, they would have kept the guards out of the room.

"Do you know who falsely alleged you're a Jew?" Menzel asked. Again, the way he put things cheered Heinrich. He wasn't assuming his client was guilty. He wasn't acting as if he was assuming that, anyway.

Hearing him talk like that made Heinrich want to help him. Unfortunately, he couldn't. He tried to spread his hands. The cuffs wouldn't let him. He said, "I haven't the slightest idea. Will the Security Police tell you?"

Menzel shrugged. He had broad shoulders and a narrow waist, as if he were a retired soldier or—perhaps more likely—a football player who'd stayed in shape into his fifties. He said, "They're supposed to. Of course, they don't always do what they're supposed to." He raised his voice and called out to a blackshirt on Heinrich's side of the glass: "Isn't that right, Joachim?"

"Screw you, you damn fraud," answered one of the men with an assault rifle. "You had your way, the *Reich*'d be ass-deep in kikes. Then they'd study law and squeeze you out of business. Serve you right, too."

He sounded more amused than angry. For that matter, so did the lawyer. How often had they harassed each other? A good many times, plainly. Heinrich asked, "When will you know if you can get me out?"

"I'm not sure," Menzel said with another shrug. "When they hear somebody might be a Jew, they grab first and ask questions later. Depends on what they turn up next. Depends on how much of an uproar they want to get their bowels into, too. I can promise you the moon, but I don't know if I can deliver."

That wasn't what Heinrich wanted to hear. He would have loved to be promised the moon, all wrapped up in a pretty pink ribbon. But, again, Klaus Menzel seemed to work in the realm of the possible. Heinrich said, "What's your best guess?"

"I'll find out as fast as I can. A few days, most likely," the lawyer answered.

"Is Lise all right? The girls?"

"Your wife is fine. She's mad as hops because they made a mess of your house when they searched it. I like her. She's good people, and she doesn't scare easy." Menzel hesitated. As soon as he did, Heinrich feared he knew what was coming next. And he was right: "They've got your kids. If you were a Jew, they'd be first-degree *Mischlingen,* and subject to the same sanctions." That was a bloodless, legalistic way to put it. What Menzel meant was, *They'll kill them, too.*

Heinrich groaned. "They can't!" But they could. They'd been doing it for seventy years. Why should they stop now? He'd had a surge of panic when he heard the blackshirts searched his house. Lise must have managed to dispose of the photos before they got there. Otherwise, Menzel wouldn't have been able to do anything at all for him, probably wouldn't even have been allowed to see him. He would have been dead by now, and so would his children.

"Try not to worry too much," the lawyer said. "If you come out, the kids come out, too." *And if you don't, they don't.* That hung in the air. But if Heinrich didn't come out, he'd die. He wouldn't be able to worry then, either.

Will Alicia hold up? He didn't have to fret about the other two, not for that. They didn't know what they were. But if Alicia broke, if they broke her . . .

"You're out of time, Gimpel," said one of the men from the Security Police. "Back to your cell. And as for you, you lousy shyster . . ." He sent Klaus Menzel an obscene gesture. Laughing, Menzel returned it.

They marched Heinrich out of the room with the glass partition. *You're out of time, Gimpel.* The words tolled like a funeral bell inside his mind. And it wouldn't be his funeral alone. They had the girls, too.

No matter how grim tomorrow looked, you had to get on with today. So Esther Stutzman told herself, over and over and over again. But when a friend and his children were in the hands of the Security Police—and when, if they hurt him long enough and badly enough, he might cry out her name—it wasn't easy.

She tried to carry on as if nothing were wrong. When she went in to Dr. Dambach's office, she said not a word about Heinrich Gimpel. Dambach already knew she knew the Kleins. If he found out she was friends with someone else suspected of being a Jew, he might start wondering about her. The best way to stay safe was not to let anybody wonder.

"*Guten Morgen, Frau* Stutzman," the pediatrician said when she came in. "I was just about to start making coffee."

Those were words to alarm anybody. "Why don't you let me take care of that?" Esther said quickly. "Then you can do something, uh, useful instead."

"Well, all right," Dambach said. "As long as you're here, I'll start reviewing medical journals. With so much being published these days, it gets harder and harder to stay up to date."

"I'm sure it must," Esther said. "Yes, you get on with that, and I'll bring you some nice coffee just as soon as it's made."

"Thank you very much," he said, and went back into his private office. Esther let out a sigh of relief: one small catastrophe averted, anyhow. If only the big ones were so easy to get around.

The whole morning seemed one threatened small catastrophe after another. One by one, Esther managed and mastered them. She felt as if she were dancing between the raindrops without getting wet. Dr. Dambach had no idea most of them even turned up. Keeping him from needing to know about such things was part of her job.

When Irma Ritter came into the office at lunch, Esther did have to spend an extra five or ten minutes explaining some of the things that had gone on. "You had yourself a busy time, didn't you?" Irma said when she was through.

"One of those days," Esther answered. She made her escape and went down to the bus stop. She took a different bus from the usual; instead of going straight home, she rode up to the Kurfürstendamm to shop. Walther's birthday was coming up, and so was their anniversary.

She'd just got off the bus when a noisy parade came down the middle of Berlin's main shopping boulevard. At first, seeing the swastika placards some of the men on foot were carrying, she thought it was only another traffic-snarling Nazi procession. Then she realized she was wrong. It was a Nazi procession of sorts, but not one like any she'd ever seen. Along with the swastikas, the paraders carried placards with slogans like THROW THE RASCALS OUT! and REFORM CANDIDATES FOR THE *REICHSTAG*! and DOWN WITH THE PARTY *BONZEN*!

Men and women on the street stared. Everyone seemed as astonished as Esther was that the authorities would allow such a parade. But then people started to cheer, and to wave at the reform candidates. The politicians—many of whom were fairly prominent Party men themselves—waved back.

Esther spotted Rolf Stolle marching at the rear of the parade, and she began to understand. The *Gauleiter*'s bodyguards were gray-uniformed Berlin policemen, not the usual blackshirts. He carried a bullhorn. With his big, booming voice, he hardly seemed to need it.

"The *Führer* says you can be free!" he shouted. "That's good, because you've taken too many boots in the face for too long. If you don't believe me, ask Lothar Prützmann! The *Führer* says you *can* be free, yes. But I say you *ought* to be free! Do you see the difference?"

Raucous cheers said the crowd on the Kurfürstendamm sidewalks did. People were less restrained now than they had been while Kurt Haldweim was *Führer*. They'd begun to see that they could say some of the things that had been on their minds for years without worrying that the Security Police would bundle them into a car and haul them off to prison or to a camp.

But they aren't Jews, Esther thought, wondering how Heinrich was holding up—and whether he was still holding out. She wondered about Alicia, too. What would they do to a child? No one had come to bundle her into a car. That was all she knew. In an important way, that was all she needed to know.

"Things will look different once we elect a real *Reichstag*!" Rolf Stolle roared. "Too many have got away with too much for too long. We're going to show the world where the bodies are buried—and we all know there are lots of them."

More cheers. More shouts. People around Esther waved their fists in the air. She stared at Stolle. He couldn't be talking about Jews . . . could he? She grimaced. Odds were against it. Plenty of Germans—and others—had gone missing during the Third *Reich*. Who would get excited about millions of Jews now? Odds were, no one. After the First World War, who'd got excited about all the Armenians the Turks did in? Nobody. Hitler had seen as much, and noted it in *Mein Kampf*. And he'd been dead right. Yes, that was the word.

"Some people—some people with fancy jobs and even fancier uniforms—are going to have a lot of explaining to do," Stolle declared. "Will they be able to do it? Good question. Damn good question. We'll find out."

Then he broke out of the parade and away from his bodyguards and plunged into the crowd. Alarm on their faces, the Berlin cops rushed after the *Gauleiter*. He might have forgotten they existed. He'd spotted a tall, pretty blond woman on the sidewalk. She squeaked in surprise as he squeezed her, kissed her on both cheeks and then on the mouth, and very likely took a few other liberties Esther couldn't see.

"There!" he said, grinning enormously. "You're going to vote for your good old Uncle Rolf, aren't you, darling?" For good measure, he kissed her again.

"Uh, *ja*," she stammered, sounding as dazed as a hurricane survivor. Men whooped. Women laughed. Rolf Stolle not only had a reputation, he reveled in it.

He elbowed his way back through the crowd and into the procession down the Kurfürstendamm once more. "We *are* the *Volk*!" he roared through the bullhorn. "This is a *Volkisch* state. Everybody says that, but nobody says what it means. It means the state is ours, that's what. We *are* the *Volk*!"

"We are the *Volk*!" People picked up the rallying cry. "We *are* the *Volk*! *We are the* Volk!"

When Heinz Buckliger started calling for reform, had he expected *this*? As Esther ducked into a haberdasher's, she shook her head. She couldn't believe it. But, whether the *Führer* had expected this or not, this was what he had. And what would he do about it?

Now that Lise had the house straight again, she went through the motions of everyday life. With Heinrich and the girls gone, all she could do was go through the motions. Nothing she did seemed to mean anything. How could it, without the people who gave it meaning?

She fixed food for herself and ate it as if she were fueling a machine that needed to keep going. She had trouble figuring out *why* it needed to keep going: more in case her husband and daughters came back than for any independent reason.

Mechanically, she washed her few dishes. Once that was done, she kept having to find a way to get through the rest of the evening till it was time to try to sleep. She didn't want to watch the news. Horst Witzleben's half-hour suddenly seemed full of nothing but bright, shining lies. People all over the Germanic Empire were demanding their freedom or exulting in new freedom won. Up until a few days before, Lise had exulted with them. Now, with Heinrich in jail and the children stolen, other people's celebrations seemed a grim mockery.

She cleaned things that didn't need cleaning and read a novel where she knew she was missing one word in three. Every hour or two, she would look up at the clock on the mantel and discover another ten minutes had gone by. Most of her wished she were in captivity with the rest of her family. Staying free didn't make her feel safe—only guilty.

When the phone rang, she put down the novel without a trace of regret. It wasn't as if she were paying attention to it anyhow. Maybe it was her sister; Käthe owed her a call. Even if the line was bugged, the two of them could talk pretty openly. No snoop could penetrate their pauses and misdirections.

"*Bitte?*" Lise said.

"*Guten Abend,* Lise." It wasn't Käthe: it was a man. Lise just had time to shift gears and recognize Willi Dorsch's voice before he said, "I'm so sorry."

"Oh, my God!" Lise blurted. Those words, at this time, were the last thing, the very last thing, she wanted to hear. "What do you know, Willi? What have you heard? Tell me right this second, before I reach down the telephone line and pull it out of you with both hands!"

By what felt like a miracle, he understood her right away and didn't try to joke around. "Nothing about Heinrich—nothing, I swear," he said quickly. "But Erika's in the hospital. They think she'll be all right, but she's there."

"Wait," Lise said. Too many things were happening too fast—much too fast for her to follow. "If Erika's in the hospital, I'm the one who's supposed to be sorry, not you."

"I'm not so sure about that." Willi sounded most unhappy. He also sounded—embarrassed?

"Willi, please take this one step at a time. You're way, *way* ahead of me," Lise said. "First tell me why Erika's in the hospital."

"Well, she took too many pills. Took them on purpose."

"Why on earth would she do that?" Lise asked in honest amazement. "Not because you've been fooling around on her, for heaven's sake. That wouldn't do it. She'd get even instead."

A considerable silence followed. Mostly to himself, Willi muttered, "I might have known you'd know about that." Another silence, this one punctuated by a sigh. He gathered himself and went on: "You're not wrong. She did try to get even, only it didn't work out the way she wanted. That's . . . some of why she took the pills."

"You'd better tell me the rest of this." Lise thought she knew where he was going, but she wasn't sure, and she didn't want to guess, not here. Too much rode on whether she was right or wrong.

"Well . . ." Yet another long pause. "It seems she was trying to get even with me with, uh, with Heinrich, of all people."

Lise almost laughed at how surprised he sounded. He'd never dreamt of Heinrich as a rival. She thought her husband was pretty hot stuff. Why wouldn't another woman? But that was a question for a different time. All she said now was, "Go on."

"You know about that, too," Willi said in dismay. Lise didn't deny it. "Why doesn't anybody tell me these things?" he wondered aloud.

"Never mind that now," Lise said, as if there were reasons galore but she had no time to go into them. "Just get on with it, please."

"I guess Heinrich told her no?" Even though Willi put an audible question mark at the end of the sentence, he didn't really sound as if he doubted it. With a sigh, he continued, "Erika . . . doesn't like people telling her no. And so . . . and so she . . . God damn it, Lise, I'm *so* sorry." Willi's usually cheerful voice held something not far from a sob.

"She was the one who accused Heinrich of being a Jew?" Lise couldn't hear anything at all in her own voice. The words might have come from the throat of some machine. She'd been right, sure enough.

"I'm afraid she was," Willi answered miserably. "He said something about acting like Solomon and cutting a doll in half, and Solomon was King of the Jews, and that put the idea in her mind, I suppose. But she never thought about the children. When she found out about them, that was when she . . . did what she did."

"Wonderful." Lise's voice stayed flat, now choking back a scream. Erika hadn't cared if she killed Heinrich—hell, she'd wanted him dead. But she drew the line at the girls. *How generous of her.*

"When she's better, she'll go back to the Security Police and tell them it was all a lie. I swear she will," Willi said. "She wants to make things right if she can."

"Wonderful," Lise repeated, as flatly as before.

"It'll be all right. It really will." Willi was all but babbling. His laugh was nervous, but it was a laugh. "I know Heinrich's not a Jew—believe me, I know; don't get me wrong—but the way things are nowadays, Buckliger might not even care if he was." He laughed again.

Don't you have any sense in your head? Don't you know they're bound to be tapping my phone? Lise couldn't say that, because, of course, they *were* listening. Before she could say anything, someone knocked on the front door. "I've got to go," she told Willi, and hung up in a hurry. It didn't sound like the knock the Security Police used. It didn't declare, *We'll kick the door open if you don't let us in right this minute.* But you never could tell.

Guts knotting, Lise turned the knob and swung the door on its hinges. It wasn't the Security Police. It was Adela Handrick, Emma's mother, a rather squat blond woman who wore expensive clothes in loud colors that didn't suit her sallow skin.

Up till now, the neighbors had stayed away from the Gimpel house. The plague might have struck here. "Hello," Lise said hesitantly. "Uh—won't you come in?"

Frau Handrick shook her head. Lise got a whiff of some fancy cologne. "No, that's all right," the other woman answered. She sounded nervous, too, and licked her carefully reddened lips. "I just wanted to tell you that Stefan and I"—Stefan was her husband—"hope everything goes . . . as well as it can for you. Emma says she wants to see Alicia back in school, too."

Tears stung Lise's eyes. "Thank you," she whispered. "Thank you very much."

Seeming to take courage, Adela Handrick said, "You're all good people. Everybody in the neighborhood knows it. This is all nothing but a bunch of garbage. But"—an expressive shrug—"what can you do? You have to be careful. Maybe things will be better after the elections. But maybe they won't, too."

Even suggesting that they might be better was a wonder. Lise said, "All I want is for Heinrich and the girls to come home."

"What else?" *Frau* Handrick said. "Even if you were Jews, you'd probably want the same thing. Who could blame you?" She dipped her head. "Take care of yourself." Without another word, she started up the street toward her own house.

Lise stared after her. Willi'd said the one thing. Now she'd said the other. Maybe a lot of people paid as little attention to what they got taught in school about hating Jews as they did about geometry. But how could you afford to find out?

Alicia Gimpel had always been good at remembering her lessons. That helped her now. The Security Police were trying to get her to admit she knew her father was a Jew. They didn't have a real interrogation room at the foundlings' home. They had to make do with an office. A desk lamp glaring into her eyes was almost as bad as some of the fancy lights they would have had back at their own headquarters.

"You must have known!" one of them shouted. He slammed his fist down on the desk. Alicia jumped. So did the gooseneck lamp. He had to grab it to keep it from falling over. "How could you not know your own father is a stinking Jew?"

"He is not!" Alicia said shrilly. "That's a lie, and you know it!" She took her cue from her little sisters. They thought they were telling the truth, which gave them an edge on her. But she was acting for her life. And, while some people might not have learned their lessons, she knew what her teachers had drilled into her. "Jews are bloodsucking tyrants. They cheat people at business. They crawl around their betters with vilest flattery. They always try to steal credit where they don't deserve it. That's what *Mein Kampf* says! Does Daddy do any of those things? You know he doesn't!"

"Jesus!" said a blackshirt behind Alicia. "She's even worse than the other two brats. Maybe that son of a bitch really isn't a goddamn sheeny."

"Why'd they grab him, then?" asked the one at the desk. "If they grab you, you bet your ass you deserve it." He glowered at Alicia. He had a red, beefy face, with blackheads on his nose and between his eyebrows. His teeth were yellow; his breath stank of old cigars. "If you don't tell us the truth, you'll be sorry."

"I *am* telling the truth," Alicia lied. "Why don't you believe me? All I want to do is go home." She sure told the truth there. She wanted to cry, but held back her tears. When she did cry, it felt as if the Security Police had won something from her.

The blackshirts hadn't slapped her or hit her or done anything worse than that. As far as she knew, they hadn't hurt her sisters, either. Maybe even the Security Police didn't like the idea of torturing little girls. Alicia had her doubts about that. If you joined the Security Police, you had to want to hurt people, didn't you? More likely, they weren't sure enough about Daddy to have too much of that kind of fun.

They won't find anything out from me, Alicia vowed. *And they really won't find anything out from Francesca and Roxane.*

Scowling, the blackshirt who smelled like cigar butts said, "What do you know about"—he looked down at some notes on the desk—"Erika Dorsch?"

"*Frau* Dorsch?" Alicia said in surprise—this was a new tack. "The Dorsches are Daddy and Mommy's friends, that's all." This fellow couldn't think she was a Jew . . . could he?

With a leer, the man from the Security Police asked, "Is this Dorsch gal *real* good friends with your old man?" The other blackshirts laughed.

Most of that went over Alicia's head. "I don't know," she answered. "They all play bridge together and they talk till it's late."

"Bridge?" The blackshirt threw back his head and snorted in contempt. He needed to blow his nose. Alicia fought against revulsion. The man asked, "What *other* games do they play?" His pals laughed again.

Still out of her depth, Alicia only shrugged. "I don't know about any other games. I don't know what you're talking about."

"Forget it, Hans," said one of the fellows behind Alicia. "If this Gimpel bastard is fooling around with her, the kid doesn't know about it."

That was plain enough for Alicia to understand. She gasped at the very idea. "Daddy wouldn't do any such thing!" she exclaimed. "Not ever!"

All the blackshirts laughed at that. "No, eh?" said the one who was questioning her. "I sure as hell would. She's a piece and a half." He looked past her to his buddies. "You guys seen a picture of this broad? She's a blonde, good looking, built. . . ." His hands described an hourglass in the air. "Hell, I'd crawl through a thousand kilometers of broken glass just to let her piss on my toothbrush."

"Ewww!" Alicia's voice rose to a thin squeak. "That's disgusting!" The men from the Security Police thought her horror was funnier than their friend's joke.

The interrogator thought revolting her was pretty funny, too. He kept on asking her questions after that, but he didn't seem so mean and threatening any more. It wasn't much worse than getting grilled by *Herr* Kessler. *He taught me all kinds of things—including some he probably didn't intend to,* she thought.

Even so, she knew she'd never be able to look at *Frau* Dorsch the same way again.

Finally, the man from the Security Police turned off the desk lamp. "Well, kid, that's enough of that for a while," he said in oddly intimate tones, as if what they'd been doing together had somehow made them friends. Maybe he thought it had. He stepped back, straightened up, and stretched. Trying to get her to say things that would kill her father—and, incidentally, herself—was all in a day's work for him. "Go on, Ulf. Take her back with the rest of the snotnoses."

You should talk, Alicia thought. They'd made her miss supper. This wasn't the first time that had happened. She knew the staff at the foundlings' home wouldn't give her anything till breakfast. If you weren't there when they dished out a meal, that was your tough luck. They weren't actively cruel, but they had no give whatever in them.

She lay down on her cot. Even if the blackshirts hadn't beaten her, she felt trampled and miserable. For Hans and Ulf and the others, this was all just a game, a game they'd played hundreds or thousands of times before. Alicia's life was on the line, and her father's, and her sisters', and she knew it. And she didn't see how she could win.

Paula came into their room. In a practically inaudible whisper, she said, "Here. When I saw they weren't going to let you go, I swiped these for you." Like a magician pulling a rabbit out of a top hat, she produced two hard rolls from under her dress and tossed them to Alicia.

Alicia blinked. "If they caught you, you'd get in big trouble."

"Well, then, you'd better destroy the evidence, eh?" Paula wasn't especially smart, not in the way that got you good grades at school. Alicia could tell. But the other girl had a feel for what *needed* doing, one that Alicia couldn't begin to match. She took Paula's advice. The rolls quickly disappeared. They tasted like sawdust. Empty as Alicia was, she didn't care. "Better?" Paula asked when she was done.

"*Ja,*" Alicia said. "Thank you!"

"For what?" Paula waved it away. "Those shitheads are giving you a hard time. Anybody can see that. If they were giving a vulture a hard time, I'd try and get him some dead, smelly meat."

Springs squeaked as Alicia shifted on the cot. One of them poked at her, too, so she shifted again. She stuck her head out and flapped her arms as if she were a vulture. Paula thought that was so funny, she buried her face in her pillow to muffle her laughter. Alicia watched her out of the corner of her eye. The other girl acted like somebody who hated the *Reich* and the Nazis and everything they stood for. But if it was an act and Alicia fell for it, she'd ruin herself and her whole family. And so she wouldn't fall for it.

If Paula really did hate the *Reich* and the Nazis . . . then she did, that was all. Alicia couldn't afford to let on that she did, too, except for arresting her when they had no business to. And that, maybe, was the hardest, the saddest, thing of all.

* * *

Heinrich Gimpel sat in his cell, waiting for whatever happened next. That was all he could do. Boredom mixed with occasional terror—that was what his life in prison had been. He could see how the blend was in and of itself part of what broke prisoners down. As he sat on the cot, he could practically feel his mind slowing down, slowing down, slowing. . . .

And he was better equipped than most to fight boredom. He had a fine memory. He could call up books and plays and films in his mind, trying to squeeze out every last detail. He could set up complicated accounting problems and solve them in his head instead of with a calculator. He could remember the last time he'd made love with Lise, and the time before that, and the quickie they'd sneaked in, and. . . .

He could worry. He spent a lot of time worrying. That was part of leaving him here by himself, too. He knew as much, and tried to fight against it. There, he didn't have much luck.

He was brooding and wishing he weren't when guards clumped up the hallway toward his cell. One opened the door while two others pointed assault rifles at him. He couldn't understand why they thought he was so dangerous. Under different circumstances, it might have been flattering.

"Come on, you," growled the guard with the key. "Your mouthpiece is waiting."

As Heinrich rose, he got a whiff of himself. His nostrils curled. He'd done his best to stay clean, but his best wasn't very good. And he was still wearing the uniform in which he'd been arrested. It was ranker than he was.

Down the hall he went, holding up his trousers with one hand. At least they hadn't cuffed him this time. Never mind the assault rifles at his back. He couldn't very well make a break when his pants would fall down if he tried. Without laces, his shoes flopped on his feet, too.

Klaus Menzel stood waiting in the room with the glass partition. The lawyer had on another suit that would have cost Heinrich a month's pay. He stepped up to the grill and said, "I have some good news and some bad news for you. Which do you want first?"

"Give me the good news," Heinrich said at once. "I haven't heard any in so long. . . ."

"All right. Here it is." Menzel told him how the charges against him had come from Erika Dorsch, and how she'd tried to kill herself after she found out she'd got the girls seized along with Heinrich. Menzel added, "You should have just screwed the broad, Gimpel. No matter what your wife did to you afterwards, you wouldn't've landed in this kind of shit. And you'd've had the roll in the hay to remember."

"Heh," Heinrich said in a hollow voice. That had occurred to him, too. He went on, "You say Erika's going to be all right, and that's she's withdrawn these stupid charges." He needed to go on repeating that they were stupid, or the blackshirts were liable to think he believed them. "That's all wonderful! They have to let me out now, don't they?"

Gloomily, Klaus Menzel shook his head. "They don't *have* to do a goddamn thing, and you ought to know it by this time. Trouble is, they don't believe this Dorsch item. They figure she's got the hots for you, so she's lying to protect you."

"That's crazy!" Heinrich yelped.

"Tell me about it," Menzel said. "But the way things are now, they aren't about to let you go right this minute. They don't want to look soft." He wrinkled up his nose, as if at a bad smell.

"Is Prützmann—?" Heinrich began.

"I don't know anything about politics," his lawyer broke in. "If you're smart, you don't, either." That was undoubtedly good advice. With the guards in the room, with microphones bound to be picking up every word, saying anything bad—or anything at all—about the *Reichsführer*-SS couldn't be smart.

"Well, what are you doing about everything?" Heinrich demanded. That was a question he could legitimately ask, even here.

"Trying to get them to look at what's right in front of their noses," Menzel answered. "Maybe they will, maybe they won't. They haven't given you a noodle yet, anyhow. That's something, believe me. I don't remember the last time they arrested somebody here they thought was a fullblood, not just some kind of *Mischling*. Whoever the last bastard was, I bet he didn't come close to lasting as long as you have. So keep your pecker up, and we'll see what happens."

As soon as Menzel turned away from the grill, the Security Police jailers marched Heinrich back to his cell. There he sat, by the world forgot though he couldn't forget the world. They didn't take him out and shoot him or send him to a camp. That was his only consolation. No, he had one other: as long as they didn't do anything to him, they wouldn't do anything to the girls, either.

Three days later, a tall, blond man in the uniform of a Security Police major came to his cell along with the warder. The officer signed some papers on a clipboard and gave them to the warder, who read them, nodded, and opened the door. "He's all yours," he said.

"Good," the officer answered briskly. He pointed a leather-gloved finger at Heinrich. "You're Gimpel?" Heinrich nodded. The major gestured peremptorily. "Come with me."

Gulping, Heinrich came. He'd been here long enough to have learned to fear changes in routine. They were rarely changes for the better. He shuffled around, shoes loose on his feet, one hand holding up his pants. Behind him, the cell door clanged.

His fear grew when the officer took him down unfamiliar corridors. Would they give him the noodle right here, when he least expected it? He braced himself, not that that would do him any good. They left the cells and went into the prison's office block. The blackshirt opened a door. "In here."

The room was small and bare. The walls were whitewashed brick, the floor cheap linoleum. A bare bulb burned in a ceiling fixture. On a rickety wooden table lay Heinrich's greatcoat, his belt and shoelaces, his wallet, his keys, his comb, even his pocket change—the personal effects he'd had when he was arrested.

"Fix yourself up," the Security Police major said. Heinrich obeyed, though his hands shook so much, he had trouble putting the laces in his shoes. Would they shoot him "while attempting escape"? When he was dressed, the major took him to a bathroom across the hall. A scissors and a razor sat on the sink. "Shave." He did, trimming his beard with the scissors before attacking it with the blade. Shaving in cold water without soap was unpleasant, but he managed. The major nodded. "You'll do."

Heinrich was surprised when the blackshirt, after signing more papers, led him out of the prison. He was astonished when the man took him to a bus stop two blocks away, so astonished that he blurted, "What's going on?"

"You're free," the major said. "Charges quashed. Go home. This bus will take you right to South Station."

"My God," Heinrich whispered. "Menzel came through?" A few meters away, a wren scuttling through a flowerbed chirped shrilly. It was the sweetest music he'd ever heard.

"Your lawyer?" The Security Police officer threw back his head and laughed. "He thinks he did, anyhow." A bus came up. The wren flew away. The major winked at Heinrich. *Did I really see that?* he wondered. Casually, the fellow said, "You find us in the oddest places." The bus door opened. The major pushed Heinrich towards it. *Us? He couldn't mean*— He never got the chance to ask. The major had turned away, and the bus driver waited impatiently. Heinrich fed his card into the fare slot. The light flashed green. The bus rolled away.

XIII

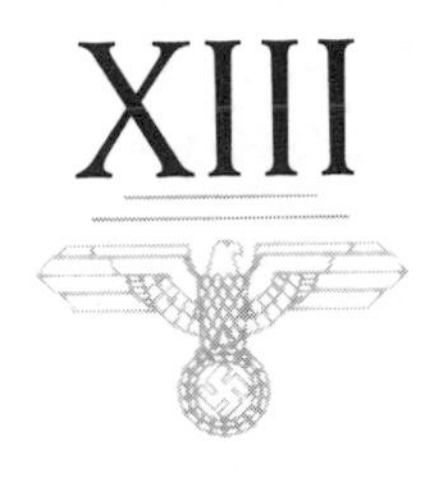

THE MATRON WHO RAN THE FOUNDLINGS' DISCIPLINARY HOME REMINDED ALICIA of *Frau* Koch. Like the Beast, she was perfectly Aryan: blond, blue-eyed, fair. And, also like the Beast, she had a face like a boot. She was tough and mean and ready to lash out at any moment. Alicia wondered why people like that had—or wanted—anything to do with children.

"Gimpel!" the matron said now, sticking her head into Alicia's room. "Come with me. This minute."

"*Jawohl!*" Alicia didn't know why the matron wanted her to come, or where she was going. Asking questions was not encouraged. Blind obedience was.

Alicia had to hurry to keep up with the matron, whose soldierly stride conceded nothing to smaller people. The woman always looked angry at the world. This morning, she seemed even angrier than usual. She kept glaring down at Alicia and muttering things the girl couldn't quite make out. *Maybe I'm lucky,* Alicia thought, and shivered.

"In here." The matron pulled open the door to her own office. Alicia hadn't been there since the day the Security Police pulled her sisters and her out of school. And there were Francesca and Roxane now. They sat on identical metal folding chairs and wore identical wary expressions. The matron pointed to another chair by theirs. "Sit down," she told Alicia. The next word seemed aimed at all three Gimpel girls: "Wait."

Still muttering, the matron stalked to another door and flung it open. In came . . . "*Daddy!*" Alicia shrieked, and ran to him. Her sisters' squeals might even have been higher and shriller, but couldn't have been any more delighted. The three of them put together almost knocked their father off his feet.

He bent down to kiss and squeeze all of them. Behind his glasses, tears gleamed in his eyes. "I've come to take you home," he said huskily. "The Security Police have seen that I'm not a Jew after all, and if I'm not a Jew, the three of you can't possibly be *Mischlingen*. And since you aren't, you don't have to stay here any more."

Francesca broke free of his arms and rounded on the matron. "I told you we weren't filthy, stinking Jews. I *told* you so, and you didn't want to listen. Well, now you see I knew what I was talking about." She had her hands on her hips. She might have been an irate housewife telling off a clerk who'd been rude to her. The matron turned bright red. Her formidable fists clenched. But she didn't say a thing.

Daddy was more polite. He asked the matron, "Is there paperwork I have to fill out so I can take my girls home?"

"Paperwork?" The woman nodded jerkily. Little by little, her angry flush faded. "*Ja,* there is paperwork. There is always paperwork, *Herr* Gimpel." She took forms from filing cabinets and out of her desk. Daddy signed and signed and signed. The matron studied everything. She finally nodded. "You may take them. Their behavior here has been . . . acceptable."

"I'm glad," Alicia's father said. "They should never have been brought here in the first place, but I'm glad." He gathered up the girls. "Come on, kids. Let's go."

Alicia had never left any place so gladly in all her life, not even the doctor's office after a shot. As Daddy led the three sisters towards a bus stop down the street from the foundlings' home, Roxane said, "They thought we were Jews! Ugly, smelly, yucky Jews!" She made a horrible face.

"They sure did. They're pretty dumb," Alicia chimed in. She and her father knew the truth, but her little sisters didn't. She had to hold up a mask in front of them. That wasn't any fun, but she'd just found out how needful it was.

"Well, they were wrong, weren't they?" Daddy said. Francesca and Roxane nodded emphatically. Half a heartbeat later, so did Alicia. Her father had to hold up a mask, too. Maybe the blackshirts had put a tiny microphone in his clothes. Maybe they were still listening. You never could tell. You never could be too careful, not where the Security Police were concerned.

Up came the bus. Daddy stuck his card in the slot four times. After a while, they got off and transferred to another bus. Then they did it again. The third bus took them into Stahnsdorf and, a little more than an hour after they'd set out, stopped at the corner up the street from their house.

Daddy herded Alicia and her sisters off the bus. "Let's go. Mommy's waiting."

When they got down onto the sidewalk, Francesca and Roxane raced up the street. Alicia hung back. She looked up at her father. "Is everything all right?" she asked. "Really all right?"

He smiled. "I know what you mean." As she had, he spoke cagily. "Everything is as good as it can be, sweetheart. We're out here. We're free, the way we should be, because they shouldn't have grabbed us in the first place." Yes, he too was playing to an invisible audience that might or might not be there. "I'm afraid we won't see some friends so much, and that's too bad, but. . . ." He shrugged. "There are worse things."

"The Dorsches?" Alicia asked.

Daddy stopped. "How do you know about the Dorsches?"

"The Security Police were asking me questions, just like they were with Francesca and Roxane." Alicia tried to remember just what the blackshirt had said. "Is *Frau* Dorsch really 'a piece and a half'?" She wasn't precisely sure what it meant, but it sounded impressive.

Her father turned red. He coughed a couple of times. After a long, long pause, he said, "Not . . . quite," in a small, strangled voice.

Alicia almost asked for more details. But the front door opened then. Her sisters ran into her mother's arms. "Mommy!" she shouted, and broke into a run herself.

Mommy had a hug for her, too, and kisses. "I know you were all brave girls," she said. Alicia's little sisters nodded eagerly. So did she, with a secret smile on her face. She'd had to be brave in a way Francesca and Roxane hadn't, because she'd known the truth and had to hide it, and they hadn't.

Their mother tousled her hair. She had a secret smile on her face, too. Yes, she'd meant that especially for Alicia. It went right over Francesca and

Roxane's heads. Alicia's smile got wider. She liked secrets . . . well, most secrets, anyway. The big one she carried? She still wasn't so sure about that. One thing she was sure of, though, and all the more so after this ordeal: like it or not, it was hers.

Daddy came up the steps. "Did you tell them about the surprise yet?"

"Of course not," Mommy answered. "If I told them, it wouldn't be a surprise any more, would it?" Naturally, that set all three Gimpel girls clamoring. Their mother looked innocent till she'd almost driven them crazy. Then she said, "If people look in the kitchen, they may find . . . something."

They ran in. Roxane's gleeful squeal rang out a split second ahead of her sisters'. The cake was enormous, and covered with gooey white icing. Big blue letters spelled out WELCOME HOME! When Mommy cut the cake, it proved to be dark, dark chocolate, with cherries and blueberries between the layers. She gave them huge slices, and when Francesca asked, "Can we have some more?" she didn't say anything about ruining their appetites. She just handed out seconds as big as the firsts.

Everything was so wonderful, it was almost worth getting grabbed by the Security Police. Almost.

Walther Stutzman muttered to himself. Threading his way past the electronic traps on the virtual road that led to Lothar Prützmann's domain wasn't his worry. He had their measure now. Sooner or later, an SS programmer would come up with some new ones, and Walther would need to spot them before they closed on him. Today, though, getting in had been easy enough. So was looking around once he'd got inside.

No, what made him mutter was not finding what he was looking for. Heinrich had given him a good description of the man who'd released him from prison: tall, blond, a major in the Security Police. By what the man had said, he was a Jew.

But Walther had been pretty sure he knew about all the handful of Jews in the SS. None of them, from what he recalled, matched this fellow. Looking through the records only confirmed that.

So who was the major, then? More to the point, *what* was he? Someone who'd tried a last trick to get a suspected Jew to reveal himself? That would have been Walther's guess, but it didn't fit the way Heinrich had described the scene a couple of days earlier. A joker? Or a real Jew, unknown to Walther and his circle of friends?

That would be good—the more who survived, the better. But it also raised doubts, frightening ones. Now somebody outside the circle, somebody no one in the circle knew, knew something about somebody in it. The last thing a Jew in the Third *Reich* wanted was for anybody to have a handle on him.

What can I do? Walther wondered. One thing that occurred to him was tracking down everybody on duty at the prison the day Heinrich was released. Not many majors would have been there. One of them should have been the man who turned his friend loose.

Before he could do that, though, his boss came back from lunch and bellowed, "Walther! You here, Walther?"

Three quick keystrokes, and everything incriminating vanished from his monitor. Three more made his electronic trail vanish. "I'm here," he called. "What's up?"

Gustav Priepke stuck his beefy face into Walther's cubicle. "You smart son of a bitch," he said fondly. "You goddamn know-it-all bastard."

"I love you, too," Walther said in his usual mild tones. His boss roared laughter. Still mildly, he asked, "Could you at least tell me why you're swearing at me today?"

"Delighted, by God," Priepke answered. "You're not only a smart son of a bitch, you're a thieving son of a bitch, too. You know that?"

Excitement tingled through Walther. Now he had a pretty good idea of what his foul-mouthed boss was talking about. "The code ran, did it?"

"Bet your sweet ass it did," Gustav Priepke said. "And backward compatibility looks as good as you said it would. We've got a real live modern operating system, or we will once we root out the usual forty jillion bugs. And we won't lose data, on account of it'll be able to read all our old files."

"That's—terrific," Walther said. Computer experts in the *Reich* had talked about modernizing the standard operating system for years. They'd talked about it, but they hadn't done it—till now. He was proud he'd had a part, and not such a small one, in turning talk into the beginning of reality.

And then he wondered *why* he was proud. A new operating system would only make German computers more efficient. It would help the government work better, and the government included the SS. It might make the search for hidden Jews more effective. This was a reason to be proud?

Yes, in spite of everything, it was. If he didn't take professional pride in his own skill, his own competence, life turned empty. Whatever he did, he wanted to do well.

As smoothly as only a man with no worries in the world could, his boss changed the subject: "You going to vote when the elections for the new *Reichstag* come up in a few weeks?"

"I suppose so," Walther answered. "You know I don't get very excited about politics." He didn't show that he got excited about politics, which wasn't the same thing at all. But Priepke—and the rest of the outside world—saw only the calm mask, not the turmoil behind it.

"Shit, I don't get excited about the usual politics, either," Gustav Priepke said. "But this isn't the usual garbage—or it had better not be, anyhow. If you've got a chance to make a real difference, grab with both hands." The gesture he used looked more nearly obscene than political, but got the message across.

"You really think it will make a difference?" Walther asked.

"It had better, by God," Priepke rumbled ominously. "You wait and see how many *Bonzen* go out on their ears when they run where people can vote against 'em. A lot of those stupid bastards really believe everybody loves them. I want to see the looks on their fat faces when they find out how wrong they are." Gloating anticipation filled his laugh.

Without answering in words, Walther pointed up to the ceiling with one index finger and cupped his other hand behind an ear. Had his boss forgotten he was bound to be overheard by someone from Lothar Prützmann's domain?

Priepke gestured again, this time with undoubted, unabashed obscenity. "Hell with 'em all," he said. "That's the point of this election—to teach the goddamn snoops we've got lives of our own. And if they don't like it, they can screw themselves."

He means it, Walther thought dizzily. *He doesn't care if they're listening. He doesn't think it matters.* He looked up to—no, past—the ceiling he'd just pointed at. *Please, God, let him be right.*

* * *

Another department staff meeting. Another dimly lit conference room foggy and stinking with Franz Oppenhoff's cigar smoke and innumerable cigarettes and pipes. Susanna Weiss drew a face hidden by a pig-snouted gas mask. Wishful thinking, unfortunately. She scratched out the sketch. As it vanished, she wondered why she bothered bringing a pad to these gatherings. Nothing worth noting ever got said.

At the head of the long table, the chairman stood up. Professor Oppenhoff waited till all eyes were on him. Then, after a couple of wet coughs, he said, "A change is coming. It is a change for which we must all prepare ourselves."

"The budget?" Half a dozen anxious voices said the same thing at the same time.

But Oppenhoff shook his head. "No, not the budget. The budget is as it should be, or close enough. I speak of a more fundamental change." If he'd been trying to get everyone's attention, he'd succeeded. Even Susanna looked his way. What could be more fundamental to a university department than its funding? Oppenhoff nodded portentously. "I speak of the changes that may come to pass in the *Reich* itself."

Two or three professors who cared about nothing more recent than the transition from Old High German to Middle High German leaned back in their leather-upholstered chairs and closed their eyes. One of them began to snore, and so quickly that he must have had a clear conscience. Susanna, by contrast, leaned forward. This was liable to be interesting after all.

And if the department chairman expected *her* to review the political situation again, she would, but he might not care for what she had to say. Like a lot of people in the Greater German *Reich*, she thought she could get away with much more than she had only a few months before.

But Professor Oppenhoff did not call on her. Instead, ponderously leaning forward, he spoke for himself: "Changes, I say again, may come to pass in the *Reich* itself. There has been much talk of openness and revitalization, some of it from those most highly placed in the state. And a certain amount of this is, no doubt, good and useful, as anyone will recognize."

He paused to draw on his cigar. *Now that he's shown he can say nice things about reform, what will he do next?* Susanna wondered, and promptly answered her own question. *He'll start flying his true colors, that's what.*

Just as promptly, Oppenhoff proved her right. "In all this rush toward change for the sake of change, we must not lose sight of what nearly eighty years of National Socialist rule have given the *Reich,*" he said. "When the first *Führer* came to power, we were weak and defeated. Now we rule the greatest empire the world has ever known. We were at the mercy of Jews and Communists. We have eliminated the problems they presented."

We've killed them all, is what you mean. Susanna's nails bit into the soft flesh of her palms. *Not quite all, you pompous son of a bitch.*

"All this being so," Oppenhoff continued, "some of you might perhaps do well to wonder why any fundamental changes in the structure of the government are deemed necessary. If you feel that way, as I must confess I do myself, you will also be able to find candidates who support a similar point of view."

Puff, puff, puff. "Change for the sake of change is no doubt very exciting, very dramatic. But when things are going well, change is also apt to be for the worst. Some of you are younger than I. Many of you, in fact, are younger than I." Oppenhoff chuckled rheumily. That was about as close to anything resembling real humor as he came. "You will, perhaps, be more enamored of change for the sake of change than I am. But I tell you this: when you have my years, you too will see the folly of change when the German state has gone through the grandest and most glorious period in its history."

With a wheeze and a grunt, he sat down. His chair creaked as his bulk settled into it. Susanna couldn't have said why she was so disappointed. She'd known Oppenhoff was a reactionary for years. Why should one more speech make her want to cry—or, better, to kick him where it would do the most good?

Maybe it was because, in spite of everything, she'd let herself get her hopes up. Heinz Buckliger had done more to open the *Reich* than his three predecessors put together. He seemed intent on doing more still—and if he didn't, Rolf Stolle might. Some of the folk the *Wehrmacht* had conquered were reminding Berlin that they still remembered who they were, and that they'd once been free—and they were getting away with it.

Yes, the Security Police had grabbed Heinrich Gimpel and his children, but they'd let them go. The accusation that he was a Jew hadn't come from anyone who really knew, but from, of all things, a woman scorned. Susanna had trouble imagining anyone chasing Heinrich hard enough to want him dead when she didn't get him. It only went to show, you never could tell.

The point was, though, that they *had* let him go. In a world where that could happen, what couldn't? Heinrich's release only made Franz Oppenhoff's comfortable, complacent words seem all the worse.

Susanna almost burst with the temptation of throwing that in Oppenhoff's face. She'd sometimes morbidly wondered which of the Jews she knew was likeliest to get caught. She'd thought she herself topped that list, just because she had the most trouble keeping her mouth shut when she ran into something wrong. Heinrich and Lise were almost stoic in the way they refused to let what went on around them bother them. Susanna was a great many things, but not a stoic. And yet here she sat, as safe and free as a Jew in the *Reich* could be. No, you never could tell.

"*Herr Doktor* Professor?" That was Konrad Lutze, who'd gone to the Medieval English Association meeting in London with Susanna—who'd almost gone instead of Susanna.

"Yes?" Oppenhoff smiled benignly. *Of course he does,* Susanna thought. *Lutze pisses standing up. How can he do anything wrong, with an advantage like that?*

And then Lutze said, "*Herr Doktor* Professor, shouldn't we return to the first principles of National Socialism and let the *Volk* have the greatest possible say in the government of the *Reich*? Please excuse me, but I don't see how this could do anything but improve the way the *Reich* is run."

Professor Oppenhoff looked as if he'd just taken a bite out of a hot South American pepper without expecting it. Susanna stared at Konrad Lutze, too, but with a different sort of astonishment. He was an indifferent scholar. Everyone in the department except possibly Oppenhoff knew that. She'd always figured him for more of a careerist than someone who truly loved knowledge. He was the last man she would have imagined sticking out his neck.

And he'd just thrown reform in the department chairman's face. What did that say? That Oppenhoff's politics were even more dinosaurian than Susanna had thought? What else *could* it say?

Back to work. Heinrich Gimpel climbed onto the bus that would take him to the Stahnsdorf train station. While he sat in prison, he'd wondered if he would have a job if he got out. It hadn't been his biggest worry. Next to a noodle or a shower, being alive and unemployed didn't look so bad.

But he still had his place. Nobody at *Oberkommando der Wehrmacht* headquarters had said so out loud when he called to inquire, but he got the feeling his superiors there enjoyed putting him back in that slot, because it gave the armed forces a point in their unending game against the SS.

Three stops later, Willi Dorsch got on the bus. His face brightened when he saw Heinrich. Then, almost as abruptly, it fell. The seat next to Heinrich was empty. Willi hesitantly approached. Heinrich patted the artificial leather to show he was welcome. (Back when Heinrich was a boy, people had called the stuff Jew's hide. You didn't hear that much any more. Till the reform movement started, Heinrich hadn't thought about it one way or the other. Now he dared hope it was a good sign.)

"It's damn good to see you," Willi said, shaking his hand. With a wry smile that twisted up one corner of his mouth, he added, "You'd probably sooner knock my block off than look at me."

"It's not your fault," Heinrich said, and then, cautiously, "How's Erika?"

"She's . . . better. She's glad the girls are all right. She's glad you're all right, too." That wry smile got wrier. "She wanted to find out just how good you could be, didn't she?"

"Well . . . yes." Dull embarrassment filled Heinrich's voice.

"I never would have figured that," Willi said. "And I really never would have figured that she'd go and call the Security Police. Sometimes I wonder if I know her at all. Now I suppose telling you I'm sorry is the least I can do."

Being sorry wouldn't have mattered if the blackshirts had got rid of Heinrich—and of Alicia, Francesca, and Roxane. Still . . . "It's over," Heinrich said. "I hope to God it's over, anyhow."

"Erika's sorry, too. If she weren't, she wouldn't have swallowed those stupid goddamn pills." Willi shook his head. "She swears up and down she didn't think they would go after you and the girls the way they did."

Heinrich only grunted. When she picked up the phone, what *had* Erika thought the Security Police would do? Invite him up for coffee and cakes? Plainly, she'd regretted what she did afterwards. At the time? At the time, she'd no doubt wanted him dead.

He asked a question of his own: "Are the two of you really going to patch things up now, or will you go on squabbling?" *And cheating on each other,* he added, but only to himself. He always tried to stay polite—maybe even too polite for his own good.

Willi answered with a shrug. "I don't know what the hell we're going to do. If it weren't for the kids . . . But they're there, and we can't very well pretend they're not." How much did he worry about his son and daughter when he took Ilse out for lunch and whatever else he could get away with? Maybe some. He did love them. Heinrich knew that. Love them or not, though, he went right on doing what *he* wanted to do.

At the train station, Heinrich shelled out fifteen pfennigs for a *Völkischer Beobachter*. So did Willi. As Heinrich carried the paper toward the platform, a sudden thought made him glance toward the other man. "When they grabbed me, did it make the news?" he asked.

"*Ja,*" Willi answered uncomfortably. "A Jew in Berlin—I mean, somebody they thought was a Jew in Berlin—*is* news."

"Did anybody say anything when they let me go?"

Now Willi looked at him as if he'd asked a very dumb question indeed. And so he had. "Don't be silly," Willi said. "When was the last time the SS admitted it made a mistake? The twelfth of Never, that's when."

The train rumbled up. Doors hissed open. Heinrich and Willi fed their cards into the fare slot, then sat down side by side and started reading their papers. The upcoming election dominated the headlines. Rolf Stolle had given another speech calling on the *Führer* to move harder and further on reforms. The *Völkischer Beobachter* covered it in detail, quoting some of the juiciest bits. A year earlier, even if the *Gauleiter* of Berlin had presumed to give such a speech, the *Beobachter* would have pretended he hadn't.

Out of the commuter train. Up the escalators. Onto the bus. Into downtown Berlin traffic. Willi looked out the window and shook his head. He said, "I'm glad I'm not driving in this."

"You'd have to be crazy to want to," Heinrich agreed. But the swarms of cars clogging every street argued that a hell of a lot of people *were* crazy.

Out of the bus. Up the steps to *Oberkommando der Wehrmacht* headquarters. Nods to the guards. Identification cards. One of the guards nudged his pal. "Hey, look, Adolf! Here's Gimpel back."

Adolf nodded. "Good. I didn't figure you were really a kike, *Herr* Gimpel. The Security Police couldn't grab their ass with both hands."

"I'm here." Heinrich pocketed his card once more. What would Adolf have said, knowing he was a Jew? That seemed only too obvious. But they'd decided he wasn't, or at least decided they couldn't show he was. There was an improvement in the way things worked. When Kurt Haldweim was *Führer,* suspicion alone would have earned him a trip to the shower.

He got to his desk late. Analysts and secretaries—and *Wehrmacht* officers, too—kept stopping him in the corridor to shake his hand and tell him they were glad to see him. He was slightly dazed by the time he finally did walk up to the familiar battleship-gray metal desk. He hadn't realized so many people cared.

He was just about to sit down in his squeaky swivel chair when Ilse spotted him. "Oh, *Herr* Gimpel, I'm so happy you're back!" she squealed, and ran up to him and gave him a hug and a kiss. Then she laughed. "Now I've got lipstick on you, the way I do with Willi."

Willi chose that moment to have a coughing fit. Heinrich would have, too. Ilse turned and made a face at her lunchtime lover. She pulled a tissue from her purse and rubbed at Heinrich's cheek. She drew back, looked him over, and rubbed a little more.

"There! All better," she said briskly.

"Is it?" Heinrich said. She nodded. He was almost as much an object to be dealt with for her as he had been for the Security Police. Her ministrations were a lot more enjoyable, though.

Off she went. Heinrich sat down. The chair did squeak. He tried to remember what he'd been doing when the blackshirts grabbed him. Before he could even come close, Willi stalked over and spoke in a mock-tough voice: "Trying to steal another woman of mine, are you?"

Heinrich hoped it was just mock-tough. He said, "The only thing I'm trying to do is mind my own business and have people leave me alone. Up till now, I never realized how hard that was."

Willi laughed and slapped him on the back. "All right. I can take a hint." Heinrich wasn't at all sure Willi could. But his friend—and in spite of everything, Willi did still seem to be his friend—went back to his desk and got to work. With real relief, Heinrich did the same. He knew he wouldn't accomplish much this morning. It would be like coming back from vacation: he'd need to figure out what had gone on while he was out before he could do anything useful.

Here, what had gone on while he was out couldn't have been more obvious if it had marched by with a brass band. The Americans were kicking up their heels. They took Heinz Buckliger's policy for weakness. Payments were lagging. Excuses were some of the plainest lies he'd ever seen. Over on the other side of the Atlantic, they were finding out how much they could get away with.

So far, they seemed to be doing exactly that. Panzers hadn't rolled out to plunder the countryside—or to surround the American legislature and bureaucrats in Omaha and make them cough up what was due the *Reich*. Haldweim would have arrested people. Himmler would have machine-gunned people. Up till now, Heinz Buckliger hadn't even squawked.

If I were running things . . . But Heinrich wasn't. He wondered if anyone was, or if the people above him were just letting everything drift till they got orders from the *Führer*. With worries closer to home, would Buckliger give orders about the USA?

"How about some lunch?" Willi asked. Heinrich looked up in astonishment. It couldn't be lunchtime yet. But his watch insisted it was ten to twelve. Willi went on, "How about Admiral Yamamoto's?"

"Sounds good to me." After cabbage stew in prison, any real food sounded good to Heinrich. Several big meals at home had only just begun to fill the hole inside him.

Shrimp tempura, teriyaki beef, and a plate of Berlin rolls enlivened with soy sauce and wasabi went some way toward hole-filling. Miso soup came with the meal. So did rice, which was to be expected, and potato salad, which never failed to leave him bemused. It was pretty good potato salad, but he didn't think the average Japanese came home to potato salad every night—or any night. But Admiral Yamamoto's wasn't the only Japanese place in Berlin that included potato salad in its meals, so maybe he was wrong. More likely, the restaurant owners just knew what their customers favored.

As usual, plenty of customers favored Admiral Yamamoto's. It drew people from every government agency within several kilometers, along with hotel clerks, shopgirls, and even the occasional Japanese tourist hungry for the tastes of home and discovering that the restaurant offered . . . some of them.

Heinrich ate, rather clumsily, with chopsticks. He sipped a good wheat beer, which went well with the spicy, salty lunch. And he listened to the people chatting at nearby tables. The tables were so close together, he couldn't help listening to his neighbors. One question he heard over and over was, "Who are you going to vote for?"

Once, to his astonishment, he heard one trooper from the *Waffen*-SS division *Leibstandarte Adolf Hitler* ask that of his pal. He was even more astonished when the second trooper answered, "Me? Stolle, who else?" The tough young Aryan warrior sounded as if no other choice besides the radical *Gauleiter* of Berlin were possible. And the first man nodded, plainly agreeing with him.

"I wasn't sure what I thought of this whole election business," Heinrich said. "Sounds like everybody's excited about it, though."

"Sure does," Willi agreed. "I'm as surprised as you are, maybe more so. And once the votes get counted, I can think of some other people who'll be more surprised yet." He mouthed Lothar Prützmann's name, but he didn't say it out loud, not in a restaurant full of strangers.

"Someone else might be surprised, too." Heinrich mouthed the *Führer*'s name, and Willi nodded. "I don't think he expected Rolf to get so popular so fast."

Willi nodded again, but he said, "Still, the two of them ought to be able to work together. They're going in the same direction. It's not like that other fellow, the one who wants to turn back the clock."

"No, I wouldn't think so. I sure hope not," Heinrich said. "The only thing that worries me is, what happens if the one of them gets jealous of the other?" Yes, not naming names was definitely a good idea. A few months earlier, Heinrich wouldn't have dared to talk about Party rivalries in a public place with or without names. Back in the days when Kurt Haldweim was *Führer,* he would have been leery about doing it even if private.

As usual, Willi Dorsch had more nerve than he did (of course, Willi hadn't been hauled away from his desk by the Security Police, either). "Buckliger should've run for the *Reichstag* himself," Willi said. "This way, Stolle will be able to say, 'The *Volk* chose me, but who chose you?' If elections really do stick, that could matter. It could matter a lot."

"You're right," Heinrich said. Willi might not notice something like his wife making a play for another man, but he missed very little when it came to politics.

And, when Heinrich tried to pay the tab, Willi wouldn't let him. "Next time, fine, but not right after the Security Police let you go. You don't need to show me you're no cheap Jew. I believe it."

"That's nice," Heinrich said. Willi laughed at the irony in his voice. But it held more irony than Willi knew. It was especially nice that Willi thought Heinrich wasn't a Jew when he really was. Had Willi—or anybody else—been truly convinced he was, he wouldn't be full of Japanese food right now. He would have been disposed of, and so would his children.

Willi got to his feet. "Shall we head back?" he said. "I know you're dying to, with all the catching up you've got to do."

Heinrich rose, too. "I don't mind," he said. Willi rolled his eyes and shook his head at such dedication. Heinrich meant it, though. He wasn't dying to get back to the office, but, as he'd thought a moment before, he would have been dying—or dead—if he couldn't go back. Given that stark choice, sitting at a desk and adding up long columns of figures didn't look bad at all.

Alicia Gimpel's class went out to eat their lunches and play on the schoolyard. She was about to walk out with the other boys and girls when her teacher called her name. She stopped. "What is it, *Herr* Peukert?" she asked.

"You've only been back in school for a couple of days, Alicia," he said. "You don't need to work so very hard to make up all the assignments you missed."

"But I want to get them out of the way!" Alicia exclaimed. "Then I won't have to worry about them any more."

"I'm not going to worry about them now, or not very much," *Herr* Peukert said. "You're a good student, and you've shown you can understand the material. That's what really matters." He hesitated, then went on, "And it's not as if you could help being absent, not with what happened to you. I'm glad you're back."

"Thank you, *Herr* Peukert. I'm glad I'm back, too," Alicia said. "Are you sure it's all right about the work? I don't mind doing it." Like her father, she was glad to have the chance to work.

"Yes, I'm sure." The teacher hesitated again. Finally, nodding to himself, he asked, "Has anyone given you a hard time about . . . about where you were, and why?"

"No, sir," Alicia answered, which wasn't strictly true. Wolf Priller and a couple of other boys had teased her, but it hadn't been too bad—certainly nothing where she felt she ought to tattle. "But . . ." Now she was the one who paused.

"But what?" *Herr* Peukert asked. "The charge made against you was serious, but it was false. Now that it's been shown to be false, people have no business—none—throwing it in your face. Do you understand?"

"*Ja, Herr* Peukert." Alicia would have let it go at that if her teacher hadn't sounded angry that anybody could still be bothering her. Since he did, though, she added, "It's not me, sir—it's my sister."

"Some of the students in your sister's class are giving her trouble?" Peukert sounded angrier still. "Who is your sister's teacher? We'll deal with this."

Alicia's heart sank. She wished she'd kept her mouth shut. "Francesca's in, uh, *Frau* Koch's class, sir." She'd almost said *the Beast's class,* but not quite. "The boys and girls aren't giving her any trouble, though. It's . . . it's *Frau* Koch." She waited to see if the sky would fall.

"Oh." The word seemed heavy as lead as it came from *Herr* Peukert's throat. "That's . . . very unfortunate, Alicia. I'm sorry. I don't know just what to do about that. I don't know if I can do anything about that. Some people . . . Some people can't be reasonable about some things. It's . . . too bad when those people get put in charge of others, but sometimes it happens."

"It's not fair. It's not right," Alicia said. "She shouldn't say those things. Daddy's *not* a Jew, and that means my sisters and me—and *I*—aren't *Mischlingen*." Part of that was true, anyhow. She and Francesca and Roxane weren't *Mischlingen.* They were full-blooded Jews. Alicia knew what she had to say, though.

Herr Peukert looked troubled. "If you like, Alicia, I will speak to the principal. But I have to tell you, I don't know how much good it will do, or if it will do any good at all. Inside their classrooms, teachers do as they see fit, as long as they teach what they are required to teach. And I know *Frau* Koch has been at this school a long time, much longer than the principal has."

He waited. Alicia needed a few seconds to understand what he was saying. If he talked to the principal, the principal might tell the Beast to go easy on Francesca. Because she told her, though, that didn't mean *Frau*

Koch would do it. She might act meaner than ever, to get even with Francesca for trying to land her in trouble. Knowing the Beast, that was just what she *would* do.

"Maybe you'd better let it alone, then," Alicia said reluctantly.

"I think you're being smart." Her teacher sounded relieved.

Alicia didn't feel smart. She felt shoddy. This was the same as not standing up to somebody on the playground even if you were right, because he'd beat the snot out of you if you tried. Sometimes you had to make choices like that. When you got to be a grownup, from what she'd seen, you had to make choices like that all the time. No matter what you ended up doing, you couldn't be sure it was the right thing. Sometimes there *was* no right thing.

Herr Peukert said, "Why don't you go out and play now, Alicia? This business with your sister will sort itself out sooner or later."

"Sooner or later," Alicia echoed in mournful tones. Whenever a grownup said that, he meant *sooner*. Whenever a child heard it, she heard *later*. As far as Alicia knew, there was no bridge across that chasm between the generations.

She went out. Emma Handrick and Trudi Krebs waved to her. She went over to them and started chatting. Everything was pretty much the way it would have been if the blackshirts hadn't taken her away. Pretty much . . .

Even while she was talking with her friends, though, part of her mind was chewing on something *Herr* Peukert had said about the Beast. *Some people can't be reasonable about some things. It's too bad when those people get put in charge of others, but sometimes it happens.*

He'd been talking about *Frau* Koch. He hadn't meant anything more. Alicia knew that. But she couldn't help thinking the words applied to the first *Führer* at least as well as they did to the Beast.

"Oh, thank you, *Frau* Stutzman," Dr. Dambach said when Esther set a foam cup of coffee on his desk. The pediatrician took a sip, then eyed her. "You're looking happy this morning."

"Am I?" Esther said. Her boss nodded. She shrugged and smiled. "Well, maybe I am. It's a beautiful day, isn't it?"

Dambach nodded again. "It certainly is. I saw more of it than I really wanted to, as a matter of fact."

"Did you?" Esther knew she was supposed to say something like that.

"I certainly did," Dambach answered. "I wanted to get here early so I could go through some of the medical journals that keep piling up"—sure enough, he had a stack of them on his desk, and a scalpel in place of a knife to open the pages of the numbers that didn't come cut from the printers—"but I got caught in a traffic jam, so I didn't come in more than five minutes earlier than usual."

"That's too bad," Esther said. "What happened? Was anyone badly hurt?"

Dr. Dambach shook his head. "It wasn't an accident. It was a political parade, if you can believe such a thing."

Up until very recently, Esther wouldn't have been able to believe it. The only parades allowed would have been those organized by the government, and they would have been publicized in advance. Someone efficient like Dambach would have known one was coming and would have chosen a route it didn't block. Things had changed, though. Esther asked, "Who was parading?"

"People who like that fat fraud of a Stolle," Dambach answered. "The man's out for himself first, last, and always. Anyone who can't see as much needs to go to an optometrist, if you ask me. Or do you think I'm wrong?" He tacked on the last question with the air of a man suddenly realizing the person he was talking to might disagree with him.

"I've told you before, I don't really pay a whole lot of attention to politics," Esther said. "I think everybody knows what our problems are. If the election could help get rid of some of them, that would be nice. And if it can't"—she shrugged—"then it can't, that's all."

"You have a sensible attitude," the pediatrician said. "Most people are fools. They expect the sun, the moon, and the little stars from this new *Reichstag*. Don't they see that most of the members will be the same old scoundrels who've been running things all along? They won't turn into angels just because people were able to write an X beside their names."

"I suppose not." Esther paid more attention to politics than she let on. She had more hope for the election than she let on, too. That hope was probably what made her add, "Isn't conscience supposed to be the still, small voice that says someone may be watching? Maybe the *Bonzen* will behave better when they knew people can vote them out if they don't."

"Maybe." Plainly, Dambach went that far only to be polite. "My guess is, they'll hold this election and maybe one more, and then they'll forget about them again—and we'll go back to sleep for another seventy or eighty years."

"Well, you could be right." Esther retreated to the receptionist's station in a hurry. Her boss's cynicism was like a harvester rolling over the fragile young shoots of her optimism and cutting them down. Maybe Dambach was right. The whole history of the *Reich* argued that he was. But Esther didn't—wouldn't—like it.

She got busy with the billing. As long as she was thinking about that, she didn't have to worry about anything else. Irma should have taken care of more of it than she had the evening before. Fuming at her also kept Esther from fretting about politics.

And then patients and their parents—as always, mostly mothers—started coming in. Nobody could get excited about Rolf Stolle or Heinz Buckliger or Lothar Prützmann with toddlers screaming in the background. Today, the racket seemed more a relief than a distraction. Telephone calls kept Esther busy, too. The busier she stayed, the less she had time to wonder if all of Buckliger's reforms were nothing but new makeup on the same old Party face.

Mothers talked in the waiting room, though thanks to their children she could hear them only fitfully. She did prick up her ears when Rolf Stolle's name came up. The woman who mentioned him wasn't talking about politics, though, or not exactly. If what she said was true, Stolle had made a pass at her sister. From everything Esther had heard, her sister was far from unique.

"That's not good," another mother said. Her toddler made a swipe for her glasses. She blocked the little arm with the practiced ease of someone who'd done it many times before. "That's not good, either, sweetheart," she told the boy, and then went back to politics: "Still, even if he does make passes at everything in a skirt, he won't send the blackshirts out to knock your door down in the middle of the night. Which counts for more?"

"Sometimes we need the Security Police," yet another woman said. "Look how they found a Jew a while ago. In this day and age, a Jew sneaking around in Berlin! If that doesn't scare you, I don't know what would."

All the women in the waiting room nodded. Esther had to nod, too. Someone might be watching her, wondering about her. Heinrich's arrest had made the papers and the radio and televisor. No one had said a public word about his release. As far as people knew, the blackshirts were doing their job, keeping Berlin and the *Reich Judenfrei* and safe from all sorts of *Untermenschen*. As far as people knew, that was an important job.

People didn't know as much as they thought they did. Esther wished she could tell them that. But they wouldn't listen, except for the ones who'd report her to Lothar Prützmann's henchmen. Too bad. Too bad, but true.

A woman came out of an examination room leading a blond four-year-old boy by the hand. Esther made arrangements for a follow-up visit in a week, then called to one of the women in the waiting room: "You can bring Sebastian in now, *Frau* Schreckengost."

"About time!" *Frau* Schreckengost sniffed. "My appointment was for fifteen minutes ago, after all."

"I'm so sorry," Esther lied—*Frau* Schreckengost, a doughy, discontented-looking woman, was the one who'd said Germany needed the Security Police. "Dr. Dambach has to give all his patients as much time as they require."

"And keep *me* waiting," *Frau* Schreckengost said. As far as she was concerned, the world revolved around her, with everyone else put in it merely to dance attendance upon her.

And if that didn't make her a typical German, Esther couldn't think of anything that would.

Susanna Weiss turned on the news. She'd timed it perfectly. The computer graphics of the opening credits were just dissolving into Horst Witzleben's face. "Good evening," the newsreader said. "The *Führer* today submitted an absentee ballot to the voting chairman of his precinct, as did his wife." The televisor showed Heinz Buckliger and his wife, a skinny blond woman named Erna, handing sealed envelopes to a uniformed official who looked slightly overwhelmed at having so much attention focused on him.

Witzleben went on, "The absentee ballots are necessary because the Buckligers will not be in Berlin for the election next week. They are going on holiday at the Croatian island of Hvar. Except for a ceremonial meeting with the *Poglavnik* of Croatia, they have no events scheduled for the time when they will be away, though it is expected that the *Führer* will offer some comment on the results of the upcoming election."

He disappeared again. This time, the shot cut to Tempelhof Airport, where the Buckligers were shown boarding *Luftwaffe Alfa*. The big, specially modified jet airliner taxied down the runway and lumbered into the air. As usual, fighters escorted it to its destination.

"In other news," Horst Witzleben said, "the *Gauleiter* of Berlin continued to call for accelerated reform." There was Rolf Stolle, shouting away from the second-floor balcony of the *Gauleiter*'s residence to a few hundred people in the small square below. The scene seemed to Susanna a parody of the *Führer* delivering an address to tens or hundreds of thousands of people in Adolf Hitler Platz.

But, as she realized when she'd watched a little more, it wasn't *just* a parody. It was also a comment, and a barbed one. Pounding his fist and bellowing up there on his little balcony with the old-fashioned iron railing (even rusty in places), Stolle made a genuine human connection with his audience. No *Führer* since Hitler had been able to do that. The *Reich* and the Germanic Empire had grown too overwhelmingly large. By the nature of his job, the *Führer* talked at people, talked down to them. Rolf Stolle reminded them what they were missing.

Of course, if he ever moved to the *Führer*'s palace, he would have to behave as Himmler and Haldweim and Buckliger had before him. Behaving that way was part of what being the *Führer* involved. Maybe Stolle didn't realize that yet. Maybe he did, but didn't want anyone else to know he did. Susanna wondered which would be more dangerous.

The *Gauleiter* got less air time than the *Führer*. Horst Witzleben soon cut away to dramatic footage of an industrial accident in Saarbrücken. A helicopter plucked a workman out of what looked like a sea of flames. More than a dozen other Germans hadn't been so lucky. "Along with the Aryans, an unknown number of *Untermenschen* also perished," Horst said, and went on to the next story.

Laborers from Poland or Russia or the Ukraine or Serbia or Egypt who'd been lucky enough to be chosen to stoke furnaces or clean chemical tanks or do some other work too hard or too nasty for Aryans and do it till they dropped instead of going to the showers right away . . . This was their epitaph: one sentence on the evening news. It was more than most of their kind would ever get, too.

With a shiver, Susanna turned off the televisor. If they'd decided Heinrich was a Jew, he would have needed a miracle to get sent to one of those man-killing jobs. The powers that be would probably have just given him a noodle and gone on about their business. And there was no doubt at all about what would have happened to his girls. They were too young to do any useful work, and so. . . .

"And so," Susanna muttered. She went into the kitchen and poured two fingers of Glenfiddich into a glass. She almost knocked it straight back, but that was a hell of a thing to do to a single-malt scotch. *Ice?* she wondered, and shook her head. She was chilly enough inside anyhow. She sipped the smoky, peat-flavored whiskey. Its warmth, dammit, couldn't reach where she was coldest.

That didn't stop her from topping up the drink a little later on. Put down enough and it would build a barrier against thought. She wasn't often tempted to get drunk, but that one dispassionate sentence on the news had gone a long way toward doing the trick. Heinz Buckliger talked about disclosing and ending abuses. Did he even begin to know what all the abuses in the *Reich* were? Susanna had begun to hope so. Now all her doubts came flooding back again.

The telephone rang. Her hand jerked—not enough, fortunately, to spill any scotch. "Who's that?" she asked God. God wasn't listening. When was the last time He'd ever listened to a Jew? It rang again. She walked over and picked it up. "*Bitte?*"

"Professor Weiss? Uh, Susanna?" A man on the other hand of the line, a nervous-sounding man.

"Yes? Who is this?" Not a student, whoever it was. No student would have had the nerve to call her by her first name, even hesitantly.

"This is Konrad Lutze, Susanna."

"Is it?" she said. "Well, this is a surprise. What can I do for you, uh, Konrad?" She had almost as much trouble using his first name as he'd had with hers.

She really did wonder what he wanted, too. Something to do with her work? With his work? With department politics? She tried to steer as clear of those as she could. With national politics? If he thought she was going to talk about those on the telephone, he had to be a little bit crazy, too. She wasn't anywhere near sure that was safe.

But after a couple of hesitant coughs, he said, "I was, uh, wondering if you would, uh, like to go to dinner and the cinema with me on Saturday night. That new thriller is supposed to be very good."

Susanna's mouth fell open. After her unfortunate experience with the drunk, she'd largely sworn off the male half of the human race. Because she was what she was, eligible bachelors were few and far between for her, and she hadn't thought he was eligible enough once she found out how he poured it down. (He, meanwhile, had married and was the father of a baby boy. Some people weren't so fussy as she was. From everything she'd heard, he still drank like a fish.)

How long had the silence stretched? Long enough for Konrad Lutze to say, "Hello? Are you still there?"

"I'm here," she answered. "You . . . startled me, that's all."

"What do you say?" he asked. "We would have things to talk about, anyhow. That is not so bad—do you know what I mean? If I go out with someone I just happened to meet, and she says, 'So, what do you do?' and I answer, 'I am a professor of medieval English at Friedrich Wilhelm University,' where do I go from there? Her eyes glaze over. I have never yet met a nurse or a librarian or a salesgirl who gave a damn about *Piers Plowman* or *Sir Gawain and the Green Knight*."

"I believe that." Giggling would have been rude, no matter how much Susanna wanted to. Being a Jew made her feel so alone in the world, it had hardly occurred to her that being a professor of medieval English literature could do the same thing. She did believe Konrad Lutze. Not many ordinary people would care about *Piers Plowman*.

"Will you, then?" Now he seemed almost pathetically eager.

Will I, then? Susanna asked herself. Every so often, Jews did fall in love with gentiles. Most of them stopped being Jews almost as completely as if the blackshirts had carted them away. Dinner and a film weren't falling in love, not by themselves. But, by the way Lutze talked, he hoped that was how things would work out. And Susanna wasn't interested in anything that didn't have a good chance of turning serious.

So . . . would she, then? Could she even imagine being serious about a gentile? (Whether she could imagine being serious about Konrad Lutze seemed an altogether different, and much smaller, question.)

"I—I'm sorry, Konrad," she heard herself say. "I'm afraid I've got other plans that evening."

"I see," he said heavily. "Well, I'm sorry I've taken up your time. I hope I wasn't too much of a bother. Good night." He hung up.

So did Susanna. Part of her felt as if she'd passed a test, maybe the hardest one she'd ever face. The rest . . . She filled her glass with Glenfiddich and poured it down the hatch as if it were so much rotgut. Then, two or three minutes later, she did it again.

Her head started to spin. She didn't care. Tonight, she would have been good company for the drunk she'd dumped. She'd feel like hell tomorrow. That was all right. She felt like hell right now, too.

Admiral Yamamoto's again. A big plate of Berlin rolls, herring and onion and seaweed and rice. Wasabi to heat them up. Wheat beer to wash them down. Imperfectly Japanese. Perfectly good.

The place was jammed, as usual. Heinrich and Willi sat at a tiny table wedged up against the wall. Bureaucrats and soldiers. SS men and Party *Bonzen*. Businessmen and tourists. Secretaries and shopgirls. A radio going in the background. Nobody paying any attention to it. Nobody able to pay any attention to it, because you couldn't hear anything but the din of people chattering.

After a bite of his shrimp tempura, Willi said, "Beats the hell out of what they were feeding you a little while ago, doesn't it?"

Heinrich eyed him. Try as he would, he couldn't find any irony. Reluctantly, fighting hard not to believe it, he decided Willi meant that as a simple comment, not as any sort of jab or gibe. Anyone else would have, anyone else at all. Heinrich nodded. "I thought of that the last time we were here. You might say so. Yes, you just might."

An SS *Hauptsturmführer* a couple of tables over laughed uproariously at something one of his underlings had said. He waved a seidel in the air for a refill. Willi raised an eyebrow. "Noisy bastard. Even for this joint, he's a noisy bastard."

"*Ja.*" Heinrich eyed the fellow. He'd seen him before. Even more to the point, he'd heard him before, right here. "Last time we were in this place at the same time as he was, he was pitching a fit about the first edition. I wonder what he thinks with the election just a few days away."

"Is it that same captain?" Willi tried not to be too obvious looking him over. "By God, I do believe you're right. All those SS *Schweinehunde* look the same to me." He said that very quietly. He might despise blackshirts, but he didn't want them knowing he did. Everyone who wasn't in it despised the SS. Hardly anybody dared to come right out and say so where anyone but trusted friends could hear.

Am I still Willi's trusted friend? Heinrich wondered. *When it comes to Lothar Prützmann's boys, I suppose I am—they threw me in the jug, after all. When it comes to Erika . . .* When it came to Erika, if he never set eyes on her again, that would suit him down to the ground.

The *Hauptsturmführer* poured down his fresh mug of beer. One of the noncoms with him said something Heinrich couldn't make out. The officer nodded. Putting on a comic-opera Japanese accent, he said, "They want an erection, ret them go to a borderro!" He made not the slightest effort to keep his voice down, and howled laughter right afterwards. His henchmen thought it was pretty funny, too.

"Charming people," Willi muttered—again, so softly only Heinrich could hear.

"Aren't they?" Heinrich agreed. "Shows they're good and serious about moving the *Führer*'s reforms ahead, too."

Neither his words nor Willi's seemed disrespectful to the SS. If anyone was secretly recording their conversation, he would have a hard time proving sardonic intent—unless he also recorded the *Hauptsturmführer*'s joke. Even then, he might think they approved of what the officer had said. Saying one thing and meaning another was an art people learned young in the Greater German *Reich*.

Not that SS men had to worry about such things. Of course, much of what they said amounted to, *I'm going to punch you in the nose, and you can't do a thing about it.* When that was the message, subtlety lost its point.

A pair of *Wehrmacht* officers got to their feet and stalked out. The looks they sent the *Hauptsturmführer* would have melted titanium. But not even they had the nerve to confront him directly.

He noticed. He laughed. He said something to the other SS men at the table with him. To Heinrich, they sounded like carrion crows cawing over the body of something that would soon be dead. Their black uniforms only emphasized the resemblance. And what sort of untimely demise would the blackshirts anticipate with so much glee? Only one thing occurred to Heinrich: the death of reform, the death of the chance to speak your mind, the death of the chance to remember the past as it really was, the death of the chance not to make the same mistake again.

He shivered, though it was a warm spring day and the crowded restaurant fairly radiated heat. He gulped what was left of his beer almost as fast as the *Hauptsturmführer* had drained his. Then he took out his wallet and laid down enough money to cover the bill. "Come on," he told Willi. "Let's get out of here."

Willi hadn't quite finished lunch. He started to say something—probably something pungent. But whatever he saw in Heinrich's face made him change his mind. "Give me half a minute," was as much protest as he offered. He devoured his last tempura shrimp in hardly more time than he'd promised. Still chewing, he got to his feet. "All right. I'm ready."

"Thanks," Heinrich said once they were out on the sidewalk.

"Don't worry about it." With an expansive wave, Willi brushed aside gratitude.

They walked toward the bus stop. After a few strides, Heinrich asked, "Why didn't you argue with me more?"

"Are you kidding?" Willi said. "You looked like a goose walked over your grave. You were going to get the hell out of there regardless of whether I came along. So I figured I might as well come." He made things sound simple. He usually did—whether they were or not.

"Thanks," Heinrich said again. After another few paces, he added, "It wasn't a goose—but you're close enough."

"Come on, Heinrich!" Lise said. "Do you want to be late for work?" She looked toward the stairway. Alicia, Francesca, and Roxane should have come down for their breakfast. They hadn't, not yet. Lise threw her hands in the air. "Does everybody want to be late this morning?"

"I'm going, I'm going," her husband said. He put down his coffee cup, gave her a quick, caffeinated kiss, grabbed his attaché case, and hurried out the front door, calling, "Good-bye, girls!" as he went.

Only silence from the second floor. Two minutes later, though . . . Lise decided that couldn't possibly be a herd of buffalo on the stairs, which meant it had to be her daughters. They swarmed into the kitchen. By the way they ate, she hadn't fed them for six or eight weeks. Eggs, bacon, sweet rolls—where were they putting it all?

"I ought to make you take off your shoes and see if you're hiding breakfast in there," Lise said. The girls made faces at her. The time they'd spent in that foundlings' home didn't seem to have done them any harm. Francesca and Roxane were still sure they'd gone there by mistake. Alicia knew better, even if she couldn't say so while her sisters were around. But even she was young enough to have a lot more resilience than most grownups would have. And she was young enough for death not to seem altogether real to her, which also helped.

Lise wished she could say the same. She'd died ten thousand times before her husband and children came home.

Then Roxane raced up the stairs with a wail of dismay: "I forgot to do my arithmetic homework!"

Unlike her sisters, she did such things every once in a while. This time, at least, she remembered she'd forgotten. "Work fast!" Lise called. "You still have to catch the bus."

"We could go on, Mommy," Francesca said.

"No, wait for your sister. You've got time." Lise looked at the clock on the range. "I hope you've got time. She'd better not take too long." Another glance at the clock. Why couldn't mornings ever run smoothly? *Because then they wouldn't be mornings, that's why.*

"She could do some of her homework *on* the bus," Alicia suggested.

"Let her do as much as she can upstairs," Lise said. Roxane liked to chat with friends when she rode to and from school. She was always talking about how they said this to that, or that about this. Once she was out of the house, even the threat of getting in trouble might not hold her to doing what she needed to do. "*Hurry up, Roxane!*"

"*I'm hurrying!*" That was a frantic screech.

Just when Lise was about to go upstairs and get her littlest daughter, Roxane came pounding down. "All right. I'm done." She was all smiles again.

"For heaven's sake, try to remember to do your homework when you're supposed to," Lise said. Roxane nodded solemnly. She'd be good now—till the next time she wasn't. Then they would go through this again. *Well, so what?* Lise thought. *Next to getting arrested and killed, forgotten arithmetic isn't so much of a much, now is it?*

Kisses all around. If Lise's were more heartfelt than they had been before the girls got taken away—well, then they were, that was all. Alicia, Francesca, and Roxane probably didn't even notice. Good-byes. Out the door the girls went. There was Emma Handrick, just coming out of her house up the street. If she wasn't late, they weren't, either. And she wasn't. So they weren't.

Lise closed the door. Sudden quiet inside the house. Not just quiet—peace. Time seemed to slow down after the frantic jangling of getting her family off to work and school. Now she could fix herself another cup of coffee, sit back, and listen to music for a little while. She could, and she would. After half an hour or so, her own batteries recharged, she could get on with the things she had to do today.

Plenty of cream and plenty of sugar in the coffee, a Strauss waltz coming from the radio, a couple of song thrushes and a blackbird hopping in the back yard hunting for worms . . . It wasn't bad. It would have been better if she hadn't gone through terror not long before, but it wasn't bad.

And then the waltz disappeared. It hadn't ended; it just stopped, halfway through. Close to a minute of dead air followed. *Somebody's going to catch it,* Lise thought. Foulups like that didn't happen very often.

Music began again. But this still wasn't the vanished waltz. It was "*Deutschland über Alles.*" The "Horst Wessel Song" came hard on its heels. Lise's brief sense of peace had shattered well before she heard the second national anthem. There hadn't been a mistake at the radio station. Something had gone wrong, badly wrong, somewhere in the wider world.

The "Horst Wessel Song" ended. After another stretch of silence, a man's voice came on the air: "The following important statement comes to you from the State Committee for the Salvation of the Greater German *Reich.*"

What the devil is the State Committee for the Salvation of the Greater German Reich*?* Lise wondered. She'd never heard of it. The government had nine million different committees and bureaus and commissions, so she didn't know how much that proved, but if it wasn't important, what was it doing on the air like this?

"The *Führer,* Heinz Buckliger, has been taken ill on the island of Hvar," the man said. "As a result of this illness, he no longer has the capacity to rule our beloved *Reich.* Under such emergency conditions, the State Committee will administer affairs."

Lise frowned. That sounded like . . . But it couldn't be. Nobody since the Night of the Long Knives, more than seventy-five years earlier, had tried to seize power like this.

The announcer went on, "We address you at a great and critical hour for the future of the *Vaterland* and of our *Volk.* A mortal danger now looms large over our great *Vaterland.* The policy of so-called reforms, launched at Heinz Buckliger's initiative and allegedly designed to ensure the *Reich*'s dynamic development, has in fact gone down a blind alley. This is the result of deliberate actions on the part of those who trample on the laws of the Greater German *Reich* so they can stage an unconstitutional *Putsch* and gather all personal power into their hands. Millions of people now demand stern measures against this gross illegality."

"*Du lieber Gott!*" Lise exclaimed. Whoever was on the State Committee for the Salvation of the Greater German *Reich,* they really meant it.

"By order of the State Committee, citizens of the *Reich* are to remain calm," the announcer said—and if that wasn't a command designed to spread panic, she didn't know what would be. The fellow continued, "The holding of meetings, street processions, demonstrations, and strikes is *verboten.* In case of need, a curfew and military patrols will be imposed. Important government and economic installations will be placed under guard by the SS, which remains loyal to the ideals of the state even in this time of corruption."

Aha! Lise thought. Now she could make a good guess about who was behind the Committee and the *Putsch.*

"Decisive measures will be taken to stop the spreading of subversive rumors, actions that threaten the disruption of law and order and the creation of tension, and disobedience to the authorities responsible for implementing the state of emergency." What did the announcer feel about the words in front of him? Was he for the *Putsch*? Did he hate it? He read like a machine, droning on mechanically: "Control will be established over all radio and televisor stations. Now serving as interim *Führer* of the *Reich* and of the Germanic Empire is Odilo Globocnik—"

"Who?" Lise had heard no more of him than she had of the State Committee for the Salvation of the Greater German *Reich*. His name hardly even sounded German.

"—who has previously served the state as High Commissioner for *Ostland* Affairs." He'd been in charge of slaughtering Slavs, in other words. And now they were bringing his talents to the *Reich* itself? Lise shivered. The difference between bad and worse was much bigger than the difference between good and better. Much, much bigger.

XIV

CEILING SPEAKERS IN *OBERKOMMANDO DER WEHRMACHT* HEADQUARTERS carried the announcement of Heinz Buckliger's incapacity moments after Heinrich and Willi sat down at their desks. "Decisive measures will be taken to stop the spreading of subversive rumors, actions that threaten the disruption of law and order and the creation of tension, and disobedience to the authorities responsible for implementing the state of emergency. Control will be established over all radio and televisor stations. Now serving as interim *Führer* of the *Reich* and of the Germanic Empire is Odilo Globocnik, who has previously served the state as High Commissioner for *Ostland* Affairs." After the announcement, "*Deutschland über Alles*" and the "Horst Wessel Song" rang out again.

Heinrich looked at Willi. Willi looked back at Heinrich. "It's an SS *Putsch*!" Heinrich said.

Willi nodded. "It sure as hell is," he agreed. And then he said, "Odilo fucking Globocnik?" in tones of absolute disbelief.

"Be careful, Willi!" Ilse exclaimed. "If you talk like that, who knows what kind of trouble you'll end up in?"

In times like these, that might have been excellent advice. But Willi only shook his head. "Odilo fucking Globocnik?" he repeated, even more amazed and disgusted than before.

Over the patriotic music blaring out of the intercom, Heinrich said, "He's Prützmann's puppet. He can't be anything else."

"Well, I should hope not," Willi said. "He's certainly nothing by himself. Didn't he get in trouble for driving drunk a while ago?"

"Beats me," Heinrich said. "I don't remember hearing that, but you could be right."

"I think so, but I'm not sure," Willi said. "Who the hell pays attention to the Odilo Globocniks of the world?"

Running feet in the corridor. Before Heinrich could respond to his friend's bon mot, someone—a soldier—stuck his head in the room and called, "Globocnik's on the televisor! They've got it on in the canteen!" The man didn't wait, but thudded down the hall in his jackboots and repeated his message for the next big office.

"Come on!" Half a dozen people said the same thing at the same time. Wheels squeaked as analysts pushed swivel chairs back from desks. A few stolid people went right on working. The rest, Heinrich and Willi among them, swarmed out of the room and toward the canteen.

So many men—and a few women—were going that way, something not far from a rugby scrum broke out in the corridor. Heinrich took an elbow or two and gave out a couple of his own. He squeezed into the canteen just in time to hear somebody yell, "Shut up!"—which made the clamor from the people already crowding the room drop a little.

Because Heinrich was ten or twelve centimeters taller than most people, he got a good look at the televisor screen even though he couldn't get close to it. Odilo Globocnik wasn't in the *Führer*'s office in the palace across the square from *Oberkommando der Wehrmacht* headquarters, or in the even more magnificent study in the *Reichskanzellerei*. He spoke from a studio that could have been anywhere.

And Globocnik himself was as unimpressive as his surroundings. He was in his fifties, and had the face of a street bruiser who'd gone to fat. His eyes and his short nose were both red-streaked. Heinrich would have bet that Willi was right and he did drink, probably a lot. He'd jammed his uniform cap down low on his forehead, perhaps to keep the bright studio lights out of those watery eyes.

He was reading from a text on a lectern in front of him, very obviously and not very well. "We will, uh, restore law and order. We will check anti-Party tendencies, at home and abroad. We will stamp out nationalist, uh, adventurism." His voice was a gravelly croak. His big, soft jowls wobbled as he spoke. When he reached up to turn a page on his speech, his plump, beringed hand shook. Was he stumbling over the speech because he was a stupid lout or because he'd had a snootful before he got in front of the camera—or maybe both?

How much did any of that matter, though? In the background, out of focus and only half visible but instantly recognizable all the same, sat Lothar Prützmann. The *Reichsführer*-SS might choose to rule through a puppet, but he was bound to be the power behind the *Putsch*. And what could anybody else do about it?

Nothing, was the only answer that occurred to Heinrich, who'd just got out of the clutches of the Security Police. But then someone in the crowded canteen said, "This is the national channel. What's on the Berlin channel?"

The buzz that rose from that made it hard to hear what Odilo Globocnik was saying—not that missing his speech meant missing much. "Will Stolle let them get away with this?" somebody asked.

"Can Stolle do anything to stop it?" somebody else came back.

"If he can't, nobody can." Two people said that.

A *Wehrmacht* colonel, no less, turned the dial on the televisor set. On the Berlin channel, a frightened-looking man sat on what looked like a quiz-show set. He was saying, "—not know how long you will be able to hear me, *meine Damen und Herren*. Armed men claiming to be from the Security Police have come to this studio. Our guards refusing to let them in, they opened fire. There have been casualties on both sides. We have asked for help from the Berlin city police, but we do not know if it will come or if it will be enough. We—"

The *Wehrmacht* colonel's voice rang out: "Sauer!"

"Ja, Herr Oberst?" someone—presumably Sauer—said.

"Get two companies of men to that studio on the double. They are to hold it at all costs. They will be reinforced if necessary. Do you understand me?"

"Jawohl, Herr Oberst!" Sauer started shoving his way out of the canteen. "Let me through!" The crowd parted for him like the Red Sea for Moses.

A telephone rang behind the man on the set. He didn't look like an announcer. He looked like a director suddenly in front of the camera instead of behind it. When the bell sounded, he jumped. He grabbed the phone, listened, said, *"Ja,"* a couple of times, and hung up. He started talking even before he turned back toward his audience: "*Meine Damen und Herren,* that was Rolf Stolle, the *Gauleiter* of Berlin. He calls the arrest—that is what he terms it, the arrest—of the *Führer* illegal, and says Globocnik and Prützmann and the forces of darkness—so he calls them—fear elections and the exposure of the truth and—"

He disappeared. There was Rolf Stolle himself, his shaved head gleaming as he glared out of the televisor set. "Am I on?" he rasped, and then, "*Volk* of the *Reich,* anyone who can hear me, listen and listen good. This is an SS *Putsch,* nothing else but. If you stand up against it, it will come to pieces right in front of your noses. If they don't shoot me, I'll kick 'em right in the teeth. Don't let the bastards pull the wool over your eyes, the way they've been doing for years. They—"

When his angry face vanished from the screen, everyone in the canteen groaned. But the feed didn't turn into predigested pap or a smiling SS announcer explaining that everything was fine. It went back to that harried-looking man in the Berlin station's studio. He said, "We've lost our transmission from the *Gauleiter*'s residence. I don't know whether it has just been cut off or they are under attack there. I—" The phone behind him rang again. He jumped again, too, and snatched the handset off the cradle. When he hung up this time, he looked relieved. "That was Rolf Stolle. He is still free. He—"

A cheer rang out, drowning his next few words. Heinrich joined it. He pumped his fist in the air. Willi Dorsch pounded him on the back.

"—wants you to come to the square in front of his residence," Stolle's amateur spokesman said when Heinrich could next hear him over the din. "How can the SS cut him down when all Berlin is watching? It maybe be dangerous, but—"

Heinrich waited to hear no more than that. He turned around and started swimming upstream against the throngs still battling to get into the cafeteria. "Where are you going?" Willi asked him.

"To Stolle's residence. Weren't you listening?" Heinrich answered. "After what Prützmann's bully boys just did to me, you think I'm going to let them screw the *Reich,* too, if I can do anything to stop 'em?" The *Reich* would be worse off with the SS in charge than with Heinz Buckliger, yes. Jews, he had no doubt, would be disastrously worse off. But his being a Jew played only a small part in this. As he'd said, it was personal.

He didn't look behind him. Suddenly, though, he had help breasting the crowd. "I'm with you," Willi said.

When Esther Stutzman turned the key to the outer door and walked into the waiting room, the radio in Dr. Dambach's office was blaring out patriotic marches. She scratched her head. The pediatrician didn't usually listen to that kind of music. He wanted something soft and calm in the office, something that might soothe both a crying baby and a worried mother.

"Dr. Dambach?" Esther called.

He must not have heard her over the thump of drums and the bronze clangor of bugles. Then the march ended and an announcer said, "Now, here is *Reichsführer*-SS Lothar Prützmann to explain the goals of the State Committee for the Salvation of the Greater German *Reich*."

"Dr. Dambach?" Esther called again, her voice this time rising in astonishment. What on earth had happened while she was coming to work?

Now her boss heard her. "Come in here and listen to this," he said. "I think they've gone right off the deep end."

It sounded that way to Esther, too. She hardly remembered to close the door behind her before hurrying into Dr. Dambach's inner office. In a surprisingly high, thin voice, Prützmann was saying, "—obvious symptoms of overwork and stress necessitated the *Führer*'s stepping down for reasons of health. Odilo Globocnik, our interim *Führer*, has already shown that he is fully up to the demands of the position."

"What the—?" Esther said. Dambach just pointed at the radio and mouthed, *Listen*.

"We have already outlined the prohibitions necessary for the success of the State Committee for the Salvation of the Greater German *Reich*." The *Reichsführer*-SS brought out the cumbersome name without a bobble. He might have been mulling it over in his mind for a long, long time before pronouncing it in public. He went on, "Now we must set forth the goals for which we struggle.

"First, we shall roll back the anti-Germanic, antistate measures *Herr* Buckliger was unwise enough to introduce. Aryan supremacy must always be the primary objective of the Greater German *Reich*. We struggle for the richness and variety of the Aryan's life in peacetime. We struggle for man's right to *Kultur*. This is the basis of the new social order in Europe. The capable individual must be able to occupy by his efforts the place for which he is fitted. And we struggle for the final solution to the question regarding the worker's standing. In the *Reich,* the path leading the worker to a secure existence has already been trodden. German workers are no longer proletarians. They have a legal claim to work, an adequate wage, medical care, and pensions. All this the so-called reforms of the Buckliger regime have threatened. But we, duty-bound to the highest concept of Aryan blood and honor, have rescued the state from his clutches. Order will soon be fully restored, so long as you obey. Thank you, and good morning. *Heil* Globocnik!"

The patriotic marches resumed, as loud and bombastic as before. With a gesture of disgust, Dr. Dambach turned the radio way down. "Isn't that a fine kettle of fish, *Frau* Stutzman?" he said. "They blather about law and order, but what's their blathering worth? I respect law and order. They don't. They throw such things over the side as soon as it's *their* ox being gored. Pah!" For a moment, Esther thought he would spit on the carpet.

"Everything was fine when I left the house this morning," Esther said, still dazed. "Or I thought it was, anyhow."

"Well, it isn't fine now," Dambach said. "Heaven only knows when it'll be fine again. Talk about your hypocrites and whited sepulchers!" He made as if to spit again, and again seemed barely able to check himself.

"What do you mean?" Esther asked.

"Don't you recall?" Dr. Dambach said in surprise. "The whole business with the Kleins and how they escaped the suspicion of being Jews after they had that poor baby with Tay-Sachs disease?"

"Of course I remember that they ended up being set free," Esther answered. "Didn't that nasty man from the *Reichs* Genealogical Office say they got away because Lothar Prützmann's niece had also had a Tay-Sachs baby?"

"Maximilian Ebert. A nasty man indeed." Dambach's round face was roundly disapproving. "But you seem to miss the point, or at least part of the point. What is the most likely explanation for the fact that Prützmann's niece had a baby with Tay-Sachs?"

"I'm very sorry, Doctor, but you're right—I think I am missing the point," Esther said.

The pediatrician clucked reproachfully. "The most likely explanation for the fact that Lothar Prützmann's niece had a baby with Tay-Sachs disease—not the only explanation, mind you, but the most likely one—is that there is in fact Jewish blood in Prützmann's family. Jews are the most common carriers of the disease—and who would have a better chance of concealing such an unfortunate pedigree than the *Reichsführer*-SS? . . . Yes, *Frau* Stutzman, you may well look horrified. I don't blame you a bit."

Esther hadn't known she looked horrified, but she supposed she might have. She remembered the hidden Jew, the practicing Jew, in the SS who'd helped Heinrich escape. He wasn't one of the little group of which she was a part. Walther hadn't been able to identify him for sure even after tapping into SS records. Whoever he was, though, he'd preserved his identity. Lothar Prützmann might have had Jewish ancestors, but he was no Jew.

Dr. Dambach rammed that point home: "Nothing but a damned hypocrite—excuse me, please—as I told you before. 'Duty-bound to the highest conception of Aryan blood and honor,' the *Reichsführer*-SS claimed, when the odds are he is not fully of Aryan blood himself. Tell me, *Frau* Stutzman, where is the honor in a lie?"

"I . . . don't see it, either," Esther said. Her boss nodded. Why not? She'd agreed with him. If that didn't make her a clear thinker, what would? She went on, "Do you mind if I call my husband from here, Dr. Dambach? I'd like to meet him for lunch."

"Go right ahead," Dambach answered. "But would you be kind enough to put the coffee on first? I really would like some, but I held off on making it till you got here. You always have better luck with the machine than I do."

It's not luck. It's following the bloody directions. But Esther said, "I'll take care of it right away." A *Putsch* might have overthrown the *Führer,* but Dr. Dambach messing with the coffee machine would have been a real catastrophe. . . .

Susanna Weiss' hand shook as she dialed the telephone. She had both the radio and the televisor going full blast. Lothar Prützmann talked about duty and Aryan blood on the radio. Odilo Globocnik was speaking on the televisor—rambling, rather, and not making a whole lot of sense. If he wasn't drunk, he could have made money doing impressions of someone who was.

The telephone rang—once, twice, three times. Then a woman picked it up. "Department of Germanic Languages."

"*Guten Morgen,* Rosa," Susanna said to Professor Oppenhoff's secretary. "This is Professor Weiss. Will you please post a notice in my classes that I won't be in today?"

"Yes, of course, *Fräulein Doktor* Professor," Rosa answered. "Now that we're finally rid of that stinking Buckliger, a lot of people are celebrating."

"I'm sure they are," Susanna said, and hung up in a hurry. Now she knew what sort of politics the department chairman's secretary had. She wished she didn't, though it wasn't really a surprise. Professor Oppenhoff himself was probably out in a *Bierstube* downing a couple of seidels and smoking one of his smelly cigars and singing along to the asinine lyrics of the "Horst Wessel Song."

She switched the televisor to the Berlin channel. There was Rolf Stolle staring out of the screen, sweaty and disheveled and furious. "If you can still see me, the thieving bastards in the SS haven't won yet," he growled. "They think they can get away with dirty deeds done in the dark of night, like they have for so long. *I* think they're full of shit. I think the *Reich* has seen enough of that to last it forever. I think it's seen too goddamn much. And I think the *Volk* are going to show Lothar Prützmann what they think of him, and of his lousy henchmen. If you think the same way, come and join me. *Deutschland erwache!*"

Ice ran down Susanna's spine. *Germany, awake!* had been a Nazi slogan years before the Party took power. To hear it thrown in the face of the *Reichsführer*-SS . . . to hear it thrown in Lothar Prützmann's face made Susanna's mind up for her. She turned off the televisor and hurried out of her flat.

It was a lovely day. Puffy white clouds floated across the blue sky. A blackbird chirped in a linden tree, yellow beak open wide to let out the music. The breeze, which came out of the west, brought the clean smell of grass and flowers and other growing things from the Tiergarten only a few blocks away.

Rolf Stolle's residence wasn't far, either: easy walking distance. The *Gauleiter* of Berlin had stayed in the same old downtown building long after the national government and Party apparatus took up their quarters in the grandiose structures Hitler had run up one after another to celebrate his triumphs. National officials might have been telling the Berliners, *You're not important enough to come along with us*. The Nazis had always distrusted and looked down on freethinking, left-leaning Berlin.

And now, at long, long last, the Berliners had a chance—a slim chance, maybe only a ghost of a chance, but a chance—to pay them back. On that slim chance, Susanna hurried toward the *Gauleiter*'s residence. Her heels clicked out a quick rhythm on the slates of the sidewalk.

She didn't see unusual numbers of soldiers or SS men or, for that matter, Berlin policemen on the streets. Most of the shops were open. A lot of them had televisors gabbling away. Some were tuned to the national channels. Others—a surprising number—showed Rolf Stolle, who went on bellowing defiance at the world.

"Deutschland erwache!" a young man shouted from a side street. Cheers answered him. Susanna wished Rosa could have heard them. *Maybe only a ghost of a chance, but a chance,* she thought, and walked faster. Her shoes started to pinch. She should have chosen a more comfortable pair. Her shoulders straightened. She wasn't going back now.

When she rounded a corner a couple of blocks from Stolle's residence, she stopped in her tracks. Ahead was nothing but a sea of people. No, not quite nothing but: they'd made barricades of trash cans and benches and planters and whatever else they could get their hands on. Men and women scrambled over them and shakily perched on top. How much good would they do against panzers? Susanna feared she knew the answer to that, but the very fact that the Berliners had dared to run them up heartened her.

Flags fluttered over the crowd. Most were the usual national banners: the black swastika on a white disk in a red field. But, just as she'd got chills seeing pictures of vanished Czechoslovakia's flag flying in Prague, so she did here once more. A few of the banners waving around Rolf Stolle's residence showed the black, red, and gold of the Weimar Republic, which had been extinct even longer than the Czechoslovak state. If people dared show *that* flag in public, maybe there really was hope.

She worked her way up the street and into the square that faced the residence. It took patience and the occasional shove. Everybody was trying to get closer to Rolf Stolle: to hear him if he came out, to protect him if the

SS came after him. Feeling like a chamois or some other nimble creature of the Alps, she scrambled over an overturned trash can. It shook only a little under her feet; instead of garbage, it held dirt and stones and chunks of concrete, to make it harder to move. They'd also give people ammunition of sorts if the SS did come. Rocks against panzers . . . The mere idea was enough to make her wobbly.

When she stumbled, a fellow in a bus driver's uniform steadied her. "Thanks," she said.

"You're welcome." His grin showed crooked teeth and vast excitement. "This is fun, isn't it, telling the *Bonzen* to go stuff themselves?"

"It's—" Susanna had been about to deliver a brilliant off-the-cuff lecture on how important this moment was for the future of the *Reich* and the *Volk*. She found herself grinning back instead. "Yes, by God. It *is* fun! We should have done it a long time ago." The bus driver's shiny-brimmed cap bobbed up and down as he nodded.

Televisor cameras on rooftops peered down at the crowd. Did they belong to the Berlin station, or was Lothar Prützmann gathering evidence for later revenge? For that matter, why hadn't the SS knocked the Berlin station off the air by now? Maybe the blackshirts weren't as efficient as they wanted everybody to believe.

Some people waved to the cameras. Others aimed obscene gestures at them. Somewhere not far away, a raucous shout rang out: "All the world is watching! All the world is watching!"

It rose like the tide. "All the world is watching! All the world is watching!" Susanna joined in, hardly even realizing she was doing it. She hoped it was true. It *could* be. Other stations, in the *Reich* and beyond it, could be picking up the Berlin broadcasts and retransmitting them. They could—if they had the nerve.

What was going on outside of Berlin? Susanna had no idea. Whatever it was, how much would it matter? Not much, she suspected. One way or the other, history would be made right here.

Someone stepped on her foot. He said, "Sorry, lady," so he probably hadn't done it on purpose. She pressed on. After a while, she got what would have been a pretty good view of Stolle's balcony . . . if a beanpole in a black leather trenchcoat hadn't been standing right in front of her.

She hadn't got as far as she had in life by being shy. She poked him in the small of the back and said, "Excuse me, please, but could you move to one side or the other?"

The beanpole turned around. He wore an irritated expression—which dissolved a moment later. "Susanna! What are you doing here?"

"Committing treason just like you, if things don't go our way."

Heinrich Gimpel grimaced. "Well, yes, there is that. But sometimes you have to try, eh?"

"I've always thought so." Susanna fit her words into pauses in the *All the world is watching!* chant. Heinrich, on the other hand, had always believed in staying under a flat rock. Amazing what even a short stretch in the hands of the blackshirts could do . . .

He patted the back of the man next to him, who was almost his height and wore an identical greatcoat. "You've met my friend Willi Dorsch, haven't you?"

"Oh, yes, I certainly have," Susanna said as Dorsch—who looked as Aryan as an overfed SS man—turned and nodded to her. She couldn't resist asking, "And how is your wife?"

By Heinrich's horrified expression, he wished she would have kept quiet. Well, too late now. She'd never been as cautious as he was. Willi Dorsch winced. "Dammit, I had nothing to do with that," he said, which, from everything Heinrich had told Susanna, was true. Willi went on, "I just wish it hadn't happened. We all wish it hadn't happened, even Erika."

From everything Heinrich had said, that was true, too. If Susanna did any more prodding, she might start more trouble than she wanted. No point to pushing anyhow, not when she'd got the needle under Willi's skin. And then, even if she'd wanted to, she lost the chance to add anything more, for a great roar from the crowd would have drowned out whatever she said.

"There's Stolle!" Heinrich shouted.

He could see over most of the people in front of him. Susanna couldn't even see over him and Willi Dorsch. She had to take his word for it that the *Gauleiter* of Berlin had come out onto his little balcony. Showing himself took nerve. The SS was bound to have assassins in the crowd.

"You are the *Volk*!" Rolf Stolle boomed through a microphone. "You are the Aryans! You are the people who would have chosen your own leaders if Loathsome Lothar Prützmann hadn't hijacked an election he didn't think his cronies could win. But do you know what?" A perfectly timed pause. "You're going to win anyway—*we're* going to win anyway—and there won't be enough lampposts to hang all those blackshirted pig-dogs on!"

"*Jaaaaaa!*" An enormous, ecstatic, almost orgasmic cry rose from the crowd. Susanna screamed her lungs out just like everybody around her, even staid Heinrich. Part of her thought they were all out of their minds. The rest, though, wondered whether Lothar Prützmann had even the faintest idea how big a monster he'd called into being.

The Tiergarten was quiet and peaceful. No one in the park seemed to know or care that the SS had staged a *Putsch* that morning. Esther Stutzman wondered whether such normality showed that nobody gave a damn or simply that it was a nice summer's day and strolling with an arm around your girlfriend's waist or lolling on the grass in the sun counted for more than whose fundament rested on the chair behind the desk in the main office of the *Führer*'s palace. Were the people in the park too apathetic to care about the *Putsch* or too sane?

Did the difference matter?

Here came Walther, hurrying past a juggler keeping a stream of brightly colored balls in the air and an upside-down hat on the ground in front of him for spare change, past a hooded crow and a red squirrel screeching at each other over a discarded crust of bread, and past a couple on the grass who'd almost forgotten anyone else was around.

Esther got up from her bench. Walther gave her a quick kiss. "Lord, I'm glad to have an excuse to get away!" he exclaimed. "The Zeiss works are going nuts."

"That bad?" she asked.

"Worse," he told her. "About one man in five is all for Prützmann and the SS. More, I think, are against them. But when the two sides start screaming at each other, there's another whole big lot who wish they'd both shut up and go away."

"I wouldn't be surprised if the whole country's like that," Esther said.

"Neither would I," Walther said. "So what's going on? I know something must be, from the way you sounded on the phone."

"Dr. Dambach was talking this morning, talking about Lothar Prützmann and his family. . . ." Esther went on to explain what the pediatrician had said. Then she asked, "Do you think we can do anything with that?"

"I don't know." Walther looked half intrigued, half appalled. "Do you think we *should* do anything with it?"

"I'm not sure. I was hoping you would be." Esther's hand folded into frustrated fists. "If we don't, and if the SS takes over . . ."

"But Prützmann's liable to win whether we do that or not," Walther said. "And if he does—or maybe even if he doesn't—using it's liable to put *us* in more danger."

Every word he said was true. Esther knew as much. Walther was nothing if not sensible. All the same, she said, "If we don't do anything, if we don't even try to do anything, what good are we? We might as well not be here. What difference would it make if they had wiped us out?"

"I haven't got a good answer for that," her husband said slowly. "About as close as I can come is, if we do try to do something, we'd better pick our spots with care, because we won't get many of them. Is this one? Is Buckliger that important? Are you sure?"

Before Esther could answer, the traffic noise around the Tiergarten changed. It was always there in the background, the only real reminder that the park lay in the middle of a great city. But suddenly it leaped from background to foreground. Esther had never heard such a deep-throated roar of diesel engines and rattling of treads, not even at a construction site.

She turned her head. Through the screen of bushes, she saw a column of panzers and armored personnel carriers purposefully pushing eastward, in the direction of Rolf Stolle's residence. The breeze shifted—or maybe the armored column made its own breeze. The harsh stink of diesel fumes suddenly clashed with the Tiergarten's green, growing smells.

The panzers rumbled past and were gone. Esther turned to Walther, raw terror on her face. To her surprise, he leaned forward and kissed her on the lips, almost as if he were one of the pair of lovers not far away who hadn't even looked up as the deadly machines went by.

"Well, sweetheart, you were right," he said. "Sometimes you have to try." He got to his feet and hurried away, off toward the Zeiss works, off toward trouble. Esther stared after him, hoping she'd done the right thing, fearing she'd just made the worst mistake of her life.

* * *

The crowd in the square outside Rolf Stolle's residence was for the most part orderly and well-mannered. Heinrich would have been surprised if it had been otherwise: it was a crowd full of Germans, after all. People shared cigarettes and whatever bits of food they happened to have. The *Gauleiter* threw the ground floor of the residence open to the throng. Two neat bathroom queues, one for men and one for women, formed seemingly of themselves.

Every so often, a chant of, "All the world is watching!" or, "We are the *Volk!*" would start up, last for a little while, and then die away. The rooftop cameras kept carrying pictures of the scene to the outside world. Heinrich hoped they did, anyhow. By the way the cameramen stayed with them, they were still working. He hoped so there, too. The more people who knew Berlin wasn't taking Lothar Prützmann's *Putsch* lying down, the better.

And then, instead of defiant chants, cries of alarm rang out from the distant fringes of the crowd: "Panzers! The panzers are coming!"

"*Scheisse,*" Willi Dorsch said, which summed up what ran through Heinrich's mind.

Some of the men and women who'd come to Stolle's residence decided they wanted no part of facing up to SS armor. They pressed away from the panzers and armored personnel carriers growling up the streets. Others as automatically advanced on the armored vehicles. *After all these years, Berlin still breeds street fighters?* Heinrich thought in amazement. He himself stood irresolute for a long moment.

Susanna surged toward the panzers without the slightest visible hesitation. The only thing that surprised Heinrich was that she didn't have a Molotov cocktail in one hand and a cigarette lighter in the other. After standing there for another few seconds, he went toward the armor, too. It didn't feel like bravery. Desperation was a much stronger part of the mix.

Willi grabbed his arm. "Are you nuts?"

"Probably." Heinrich shook free. "Go the other way, if you'd rather. I won't hold it against you."

"*Scheisse,*" Willi said again, in doleful tones. "You're going to get both of us shot, or more likely just run over." As Heinrich had waited before following Susanna, he waited before following Heinrich. But follow he did.

Berlin might still breed street fighters, but they were amateurs up against professionals. The panzers rolled over the barricades the crowd had run up as if they weren't there. As they crushed the second one, a horrible shriek rang out, for a moment rising above even the roar of their engines. After that, the lead panzer had blood on its left track.

The death might have broken the crowd. Instead, it infuriated the Berliners. They shook their fists at the black-coveralled panzer crewmen who rode with their heads and shoulders out of the vehicles. "Murderers!" they shouted. "Butchers! Assassins! *Schweinehunde!*"

Pulling a bullhorn out of the turret, the officer commanding the lead panzer aimed it at the crowd like a weapon. "Disperse!" he blared. "Disperse, in the name of the *Volk* of the Greater German *Reich*."

But that only roused fresh fury among his foes. "We are the *Volk*!" they shouted, over and over again. "We are the *Volk*!" Some of them added, "And who the hell are you?" They swarmed toward the armored vehicles. The driver of the lead machine stopped. He could only go forward by crushing scores of people under his treads—or by pulling out his personal weapon and opening fire on the crowd. He didn't. He was a fresh-faced young man, probably under twenty, and seemed astonished that people weren't listening to his superior's orders.

"Go home!" His superior seemed astonished, too, even with his voice electronically amplified. "Go home, and you will not be harmed!"

"We are the *Volk*! We *are* the *Volk*! *We are the* Volk*!*" The chant swelled and swelled. Through it, individuals shouted insults at Lothar Prützmann: "He's afraid of elections!" "He threw down the *Führer* because he wants the job himself!" "He wants you to murder Stolle the same way you just murdered that poor sap at the barricade!"

By then, Heinrich was up within ten or twelve meters of the lead panzer. He could see the frown on the driver's face, and the deeper one on the panzer commander's. Things were not going according to plan. The SS men didn't like that at all, and didn't seem to know what to do about it.

And Heinrich could also see the panzer's two machine guns, and the enormous yawning bore of the cannon. If the commander ordered a couple of rounds of high-explosive or, if he had it, grapeshot . . . He'd clear a path in front of him, all right. His panzer, and the vehicles behind it, would wade in gore all the way to Rolf Stolle's residence. *Some of that gore would be mine, too.* Heinrich wondered why he wasn't even more frightened. *Because it's too late now,* he decided. *If he does start shooting, I can't do any-*

thing about it. He looked around for Susanna. He could hear her, somewhere not far away, but he couldn't see her.

"Disperse!" the panzer commander shouted again through the bullhorn. "Go peacefully to your homes, and you will not be harmed. In the name of the *Volk* of the Greater German *Reich,* disperse!" That was what they'd told him to say before he set out from his barracks, and he stubbornly went right on saying it.

They didn't seem to have told him what to do if it didn't work. And it didn't. Instead of making the people around Stolle's residence leave, it just seemed to make them more stubborn, too. "We are the *Volk*!" they shouted back, ever louder. "We *are* the *Volk*! *We are the* Volk*!*"

The SS officer stared at them, his gray eyes wide. What was going on in his mind? Did he understand that what he'd been told and what he was seeing and hearing didn't add up? How could he *not* understand? Heinrich laughed at himself. SS men weren't trained to understand anything but the brute simplicity of orders.

But in that case, why hadn't this fellow already opened fire? Did he realize that *was* the *Volk* in front of him? Heinrich laughed again. Questions. Answering questions. What else was an analyst good for? When these questions got answered, it was all too likely to be with blood and iron. Bismarck could turn a phrase, all right.

Meanwhile, the tableau held. "We are the *Volk*!" Heinrich shouted again. Did the SS officer believe him, believe the others? He didn't start shooting, anyhow. "We *are* the *Volk*!"

Gustav Priepke plopped his fat bottom down on the corner of Walther's desk. "It's a goddamn crock, that's what it is," Walther's boss said. On a smaller scale, he reminded Walther a little of Rolf Stolle.

"It certainly is," Walther answered, hoping Priepke would go away if he didn't say much. He wasn't supposed to have access to the networks where he needed to plant rumors about Lothar Prützmann. How could he get at them with Priepke staring over his shoulder? He couldn't, and he knew it.

"Odilo Globocnik?" His boss shook his head. "Sounds like a goddamn skin disease. And Lothar Prützmann? Lothar Prützmann is a dose of the clap, and he aims to give it to the *Reich*."

"Uh-huh." Walther looked at the pictures of Esther and Gottlieb and

Anna on the gray, fuzzy wall of his cubicle. He looked up at the sound-absorbing tiles on the ceiling. He looked everywhere but at Gustav Priepke. He agreed with every word Priepke said. But the longer Priepke hung around saying it, the less chance he had to try to set things right.

"They say Buckliger's ill. My ass!" his boss said. "They're sick of him, that's what. I just hope to Christ they haven't given him a noodle, eh?"

"Uh-huh," Walther said again, and then, "You know, you'd better be careful. If you keep carrying on like that, people are liable to remember."

Gustav Priepke slid off the desk like a walrus sliding off an ice floe. He said, "If you're not going to show some balls now, goddammit, when will you ever? Or maybe you haven't got any to show?" When Walther didn't answer, Priepke lumbered off, shaking his head.

Walther swore softly. He'd just lost his boss's good opinion. But now, good opinion or not, maybe he could do more than grouse about what was going on. Maybe.

If anybody came into his cubicle while he was doing it, he was dead. That meant he had to work fast. If he made a mistake, though, he was just as dead. Sweat ran down his face and streamed from his armpits. He could smell his own fear. Just making his fingers hit the right keys was an effort.

He planted what Esther had given him about Lothar Prützmann's niece in more than a dozen places in the *Reich*'s computer network: places where SS officials, party big shots, and *Wehrmacht* officers were likely to find the news. What they would do with it when they found it . . . well, who could say? But Walther knew he'd done what he could.

Covering his tracks went faster than inserting the false data—or were they true data? Esther's boss seemed to think so. Walther hardly cared. Using reports of Jewish blood to try to bring down the *Reichsführer*-SS struck him as blackly delicious. Prützmann couldn't even start a pogrom if the move failed—against whom would he strike? And even if he got all the surviving Jews, there weren't enough left to make a decent pogrom. *See how you like it.*

One last keystroke . . . One last check . . . There. He was free. His swivel chair creaked as he leaned back in it. He'd earned the sigh of relief that burst from him. He'd not only done what he could do, he could relax. . . .

For about fifteen seconds. Then a programmer screamed, "Reactionary!" at the same time as another one yelled, "Radical!" One of them—Walther never knew which—shouted, "Asshole!" That cut across political lines. The meaty *thock!* of fist smacking flesh followed a heartbeat later.

"Fight! Fight!" The cry and the sound of people rushing toward the brawl took Walther back to the school playground and the fifth grade. He didn't get up. He would have gone running then. He hoped he was a grownup now.

Not so distant battle made the walls of Walther's cubicle shake. He stayed right where he was. He'd just taken worse chances than any of the hotheaded fools punching away at one another. If they wanted to waste time on black eyes and bloody noses, they could do that. But information packed a bigger wallop than even the hardest fist.

He hoped.

"We are the *Volk*!" chanted the crowd outside Rolf Stolle's residence, and, "Panzers go home!" and, "All the world is watching!" Heinrich sang with the rest. He was getting hoarse, but he kept on. He felt more real, more alive, while he was making noise. He also felt there was a better chance the SS armored vehicles wouldn't start shooting if the people in front of them stayed noisy.

A couple of hours had gone by now, and the officer in the lead panzer hadn't opened up yet. Every so often, he would raise the bullhorn to his mouth and order the crowd to disperse. No one paid any attention to him.

He'd ducked down into the panzer turret several times, probably to use the radio. What was he telling his superiors? What were they telling him? How much of what they were telling him was he heeding? Wouldn't they be yelling for him to murder everybody in sight?

"All the world is watching!" Heinrich called. "All the world is watching!" He hoped the world was watching. If it was, Prützmann's goons hadn't seized the Berlin televisor station. The cameras on the rooftops kept on panning over the crowd and the panzers. That was a good sign . . . wasn't it?

"Heinrich."

He jumped. He hadn't seen Susanna come back to him. He'd been watching the lead panzer and the officer standing head and shoulders out of the cupola. Good panzer officers were supposed to stand like that. They could see much more than if they stayed buttoned up inside. It also made them much more vulnerable to anything their foes did. He dragged his attention back to Susanna. "What is it?"

"You should go home," she told him. "You've got a family. One person here more or less won't make any difference."

She made good sense. After a moment, Heinrich shook his head anyway. "A lot of people here have families. If they all left . . ." He shook his head again. "Besides, now that I am here, I want to see how things play out."

"What would Lise say?" Susanna asked. That was a low blow. Before he could recover, she pointed to the panzer's cannon. "If the shooting starts, you won't see anything, or not for long."

"Neither will you," Heinrich pointed out. "I don't see you going anywhere."

She shrugged. "I'm a hothead. You're not. You're supposed to be too smart to do things like this." She sounded almost annoyed at him.

Before he could answer, there was a stir in the crowd behind them, back toward the doorway to Rolf Stolle's residence. The panzer commander was already looking that way. When his jaw dropped, Heinrich decided he'd better turn around. He did. His view wasn't as good as the SS man's, but after a moment he froze in astonishment, too.

"What is it?" Susanna demanded impatiently. "You tall people . . ."

"It's . . . It's Stolle." Heinrich had to work to bring forth the words. "He's coming out."

"What?" Susanna exclaimed in horror. "He's crazy. They'll kill him. For God's sake, somebody's got to stop him!" She was looking at Heinrich, as if she expected him to deliver a red-card tackle on the *Gauleiter* of Berlin.

More and more people spied Rolf Stolle and the squad of gray-clad Berlin policemen who surrounded him. Along with them came two photographers, one with a Leica, the other with a small televisor camera on his shoulder. Some of the people, like Susanna, called out for him to go back into the residence and stay safe. But there was a rising cry of, "Rolf! Rolf! Rolf!" as others cheered his courage. And there was another cry, one Heinrich had never dreamt he'd hear in Berlin and one he gladly joined, shouting it out with all his might: "Down with the SS! Down with the SS!"

Beside him, Willi Dorsch was yelling Stolle's name. He paused for a moment to shout into Heinrich's ear: "He's fucking out of his mind, but Christ! he's got balls."

"You ought to take Horst's place," Heinrich yelled back. "He couldn't have said it better." Willi's smirk said he wasn't sure whether Heinrich was joking. Heinrich nodded—he'd meant it, all right.

The noise of its hydraulics lost in the tumult, the turret of the lead panzer traversed a few degrees, so that that cannon and the machine gun beside it bore directly on the advancing Rolf Stolle. But the *Gauleiter* kept coming, and the panzer commander didn't open fire.

Instead, he raised the bullhorn to his lips: "*Herr* Stolle, you are at the center of an illegal and seditious rally, one outlawed by the State Committee for the Salvation of the Greater German *Reich*. Dismiss your followers and surrender to duly constituted authority at once."

Rolf Stolle didn't have a bullhorn. With his big bass voice, he hardly needed one. "Not likely, sonny boy! And if an illegal committee says we're illegal, that means we deserve a medal, far as I'm concerned."

A great cheer rose behind his words: "Rolf! Rolf! Rolf!" His name in the crowd's mouth sounded like the baying of a pack of hounds. Were they baying for freedom? Heinrich didn't know, but he shouted, "Rolf!" along with everybody else.

Stolle pushed through the crowd till he stood alongside the panzer. The officer in charge of it had to lean over awkwardly to keep an eye on him. The Berlin policemen got between the *Gauleiter* and the next panzer farther back. They might protect him against its machine guns. If its cannon spoke . . .

But Rolf Stolle wasn't thinking about getting shot. He aimed to cause the State Committee for the Salvation of the Greater German *Reich* as much trouble as he could. The still photographer and the televisor cameraman both captured his scornful kick at the panzer's iron road wheel.

"If those don't turn into famous photos—" Heinrich began.

"It'll be because Prützmann makes sure nobody ever sees them," Willi said. Heinrich bit his lip. His friend wasn't wrong.

Stolle shook his fist at the panzer officer leaning out of the cupola. "Go back to your barracks!" he bellowed. "Get the hell out of here! Using force now is intolerable—intolerable, I tell you. The *Volk* of the *Reich* will not let this illegal, tyrannical *Putsch* stand. The men who made it have no sense of shame and no sense of honor. All proper SS personnel, men loyal to the state and not just to the *Reichsführer*-SS, should show their high sense of racial courage and have nothing to do with this thievery."

"Rolf! Rolf! Rolf!" the crowd shouted, and, "Down with the SS!" Heinrich got a good look at the panzer officer's face. The man looked as stunned as if he'd just taken a right to the chin. Whatever he'd been looking for when his superiors sent him rolling toward the *Gauleiter*'s residence, this sure wasn't it. His orders were probably simple: go over there and arrest Stolle or kill him. They wouldn't have said anything about thousands of Germans (and even a couple of hidden Jews) furiously determined that he do no such thing.

Stolle and a couple of his biggest bodyguards had their heads together. The policemen raised him up onto their shoulders so the crowd could see him better. They staggered a little—he was a big man himself—but they held him. The cheers came louder and fiercer than ever. Stolle waved, not just to the crowd but also to the panzer commander.

"It doesn't look like they're going to shoot your *Gauleiter* right this minute," he called.

"Rolf! Rolf! Rolf!" The people shouted louder than ever. Heinrich's ears rang. He was yelling, too: "Down with the SS! Down with the SS!" And then both chants faded and a new one rose, driven straight into the face of the lead panzer commander: "Go home! Go home! Go home! Go home!"

If he'd looked stunned before, he seemed positively poleaxed now. He disappeared down into the turret. Jeers sped him on his way. "Go home! Go home!" The cry swelled and swelled.

Inside the panzer there, he was bound to be on the radio again. What were his distant superiors telling him? Kill! Strike! Destroy! Now! What else could they be saying? If they bagged both Buckliger and Stolle, the game was theirs. What was he telling them? That wasn't so obvious.

He came out again. He still looked as if he didn't know what hit him. Along with everyone else, Heinrich poured abuse down on his head. Then Rolf Stolle raised his right hand. Silence rippled outward, even to those who couldn't see the *Gauleiter*. Into it, Stolle spoke to the panzer officer: "You have taken your oath to the *Volk*. You cannot turn your guns against the *Volk*. The days of this *Putsch* are numbered. You must not cover the honor of the German soldier with the blood of the *Volk*. You must not, I tell you." His voice burned with terrible urgency. "You cannot blindly follow the men who made this *Putsch*. Here in Berlin, Lothar Prützmann's naked grab for power will not prevail. The *Volk* will. The first edition of *Mein Kampf* will. And we will stay in the streets till we bring those bandits to justice!"

An avalanche of cheers thundered down on him. He grinned and pumped his fist in the air. The lead panzer commander, or any other SS man whose gun bore on Stolle, could have ended things then and there. But no one opened fire. *Now they know what the people think of them,* Heinrich thought. *They don't want to be even more hated than they are.* And that the people could show what they thought, and that even SS men might believe it mattered, was not the smallest part of Heinz Buckliger's revitalization program all by itself.

Lise Gimpel dialed Heinrich's number. In her ear, the phone rang once, twice, three times. Someone picked it up. "*Oberkommando der Wehrmacht,* Analysis section." A woman's voice.

"Ilse? I want to talk to Heinrich. This is his wife," Lise said.

"I'm sorry, *Frau* Gimpel, but he's not here," the secretary answered.

"Do you know when he'll be back?"

"I'm sorry, but I have no idea. As soon as we heard . . . what had happened, he and *Herr* Dorsch and some other people, uh, left the building."

"Left the building? . . . Oh." Lise needed a moment, but she figured out what Ilse meant. They'd headed for Rolf Stolle's residence. That had to be it. Ilse wouldn't come right out and say so, though, not when the phones were bound to be monitored. She might have round heels, but she definitely had strong survival instincts. "Thank you," Lise said, both for the information and for the nonincriminating way the secretary had given it to her. She hung up.

Survival instincts, she thought, and shook her head. She'd always believed Heinrich had strong ones. But if he did, why had he gone running to stick his head in the lion's mouth? At first, she was inclined to blame Willi. A moment later, though, she shook her head again. Heinrich hadn't taken Willi all that seriously—not seriously enough to let Willi talk him into risking his life—even before the trouble with Erika.

The trouble with Erika . . . Lise saw, or thought she did. Before the blackshirts grabbed Heinrich and flung him into prison, he never would have done anything so crazy. Now, though, he'd lain in the hands of the SS. Maybe he thought anything that might help stop that committee with the silly name was worth doing.

It will happen just the same, with you there or without you. Lise couldn't shout that to Heinrich, no matter how much she wanted to. He'd had an attack of patriotism—and wasn't that a strange fit to come over a Jew at the beating heart of the Third *Reich?* Was the difference between Lothar Prützmann and Odilo Globocnik on the one hand and Heinz Buckliger and Rolf Stolle on the other really so enormous?

Lise wished she hadn't asked herself the question that way. The answer looked much too much like yes.

She turned on the televisor. Most of the stations were broadcasting reruns of daytime dramas or quiz shows or weepy advice shows. Every so often, words would glide across the bottom of the screen. *You are ordered to obey the decrees of the State Committee for the Salvation of the Greater German* Reich, the crawl said, over and over and over again.

The Berlin channel was different. It showed the crowd milling around Rolf Stolle's residence and, now, the stalled armored vehicles in front of it. "We are still here," a frightened-sounding announcer said over the noise of the crowd. "I don't know how long we can stay on the air, though. If we didn't have our own generator, we would have been shut down already. SS men have come here, but our guards turned them back. The guards have since been heavily reinforced by *Wehrmacht* troops."

Was that a warning to Prützmann and his henchmen? Or was it a bluff? The announcer seemed nervous enough to make the latter seem a real possibility. But then the picture switched to a tape of Stolle kicking at a panzer's iron tire and bellowing at the SS man leaning out of the turret. Seeing the *Gauleiter*'s nerve made Lise willing to forgive the announcer's nerves.

Her daughters got home from school just then. She thought that would distract her from what was going on downtown, but it didn't. They were more excited about it than she was. Francesca said, "*Frau* Koch says we have to do what the State Committee for the Salvation of the Greater German *Reich* tells us, and Odilo Globocnik is the new *Führer*."

"Odilo Globocnik!" Roxane echoed. "Teacher made us learn how to say it."

"Us, too," Francesca said. "The Beast made us memorize his name and State Committee for the Salvation of the Greater German *Reich,* and anybody who couldn't do it got a swat. I did it. She's not going to hit *me* again." She spoke with grim determination.

"What does your teacher say?" Lise asked Alicia, who hadn't spoken yet.

"He made us learn *Herr* Globocnik's name," her eldest answered. "He said there wasn't any law for a committee like this one, but that wouldn't matter if they held on to power. He said we'd just have to wait and see, pretty much."

"He'll get in trouble," Francesca said. "*Frau* Koch says the State Committee for the Salvation of the Greater German *Reich*"—since she'd memorized the name, she used it every chance she got—"is going to pay back everybody who ever liked what the old *Führer* was doing."

"Odilo Globocnik is the new *Führer*!" Roxane showed off what she'd learned, too.

"If that State Committee wins, they may do what *Frau* Koch says," Lise said carefully. "But Alicia's teacher has a point. They haven't won yet. *Gauleiter* Stolle and lots of people are protesting against what they've done." She didn't say that Heinrich was there. Even if things went sour in front of the *Gauleiter*'s residence, he might get away safe. *Well, he might,* she insisted to herself. Aloud, she went on, "They're on the televisor, too. Do you want to see?"

"Would you get us snacks first?" Roxane asked.

That seemed reasonable, so Lise did. Then they all went back to the living room. The Berlin channel was showing the tape of Stolle kicking at the panzer again. Francesca, in particular, watched wide-eyed. There was no room for dissent in *Frau* Koch's universe. Seeing that there was, or might be, in the real world seemed to hearten Lise's middle daughter. Alicia asked, "What are the other stations showing?"

"They were just putting on boring reruns, I suppose to make people think everything is normal," Lise answered. "But we can see what they're doing now."

She changed the channel. It wasn't a daytime drama any more. Horst Witzleben looked out of the screen at her and her children. "I have been given the following statement to read," he said. "And I quote. . . ." He looked down at a paper on his desk. " 'Rumors relating to the ancestry of the *Reichsführer*-SS are false, malicious, and despicable lies. He is of unblemished Aryan descent. This being so, anyone repeating or spreading the false rumors will be subject to the most severe penalties. By order of the State Committee for the Salvation of the Greater German *Reich*.' We now return you to your regularly scheduled programming."

Regularly scheduled programming turned out to be a nature film about the migration of storks. "What did that mean, Mommy?" Roxane asked.

"I'm not quite sure," Lise answered.

"He didn't look very happy about it, whatever it was," Alicia said. "He didn't sound very happy, either."

"You're right—he didn't," Lise said. Witzleben had been a cheerleader for Heinz Buckliger's reforms. If he'd actually been as enthusiastic a cheerleader as he'd seemed, what had Prützmann's bully boys done to persuade him to speak on their behalf? Held a gun to his head? Held a gun to his wife's head? There were, no doubt, all sorts of ways, and they'd be the ones to know them. She changed channels again. The Berlin station was still broadcasting. The crowd around Rolf Stolle's residence was still there. Lise shrugged. "We'll just have to see what happens, that's all."

"Let me through!" somebody with a big voice shouted behind Heinrich. "Get out of my way, dammit! Clear a path!"

"In your dreams, pal," Willi Dorsch said.

Even if they didn't clear a path, the man kept on coming, using his shoulders and his elbows to force his way forward. He was a Berlin police officer. People did try to move aside for him, but in the press of bodies it wasn't easy. "Let me through!" he yelled again. "I've got important news for the *Gauleiter*."

He pushed past Heinrich and Willi. A moment later, a woman spoke sharply: "You might say, 'Excuse me.' "

For a wonder, the policeman actually did say, "Sorry, lady." Then, as roughly as ever, he went on toward Rolf Stolle, who was still arguing with the commander of the lead panzer.

"Was that your friend who called him on his manners?" Willi asked, grinning.

"Susanna? I do believe it was," Heinrich answered.

"She's got nerve," Willi said admiringly.

"Oh, yes. That she does."

There was a stir when the police officer came up to the gray-uniformed men guarding the *Gauleiter* of Berlin. They must have recognized him, for they let him through. He spoke to Stolle for perhaps a minute and a half. Heinrich wasn't that far away, but couldn't hear a word he said. He could see Stolle's reaction, though. The *Gauleiter* stared. His eyes went wide with surprise. Then, to Heinrich's amazement, he threw back his head and bellowed Jovian laughter at the sky.

"What the hell?" Willi said.

"Beats me," Heinrich said.

That great bellow of mirth had made everybody within a hundred meters turn and look at Stolle. With a sense of timing an actor might have envied, the *Gauleiter* waited for people's attention to wing his way before shouting up to the panzer commander: "Hey, you! SS man!"

"What do you want?" the officer in the black coveralls asked warily.

"You know your boss? The high and mighty *Reichsführer*-SS? The chief Aryan of all time? Lothar goddamn Prützmann? You know who I'm talking about?" Rolf Stolle waited again. He looked as if he could afford to let the moment stretch. He also looked as if he was enjoying himself immensely.

The panzer commander saw that as clearly as Heinrich did. His nod was a small masterpiece of reluctance. "I know who you're talking about. What about him?" He didn't use the bullhorn now.

That was sensible. It was even smart. But when he went up against Rolf Stolle's leather lungs, it didn't do him much good. "What about him? I'll tell you what about him, you pickle-faced son of a bitch," Stolle boomed in a voice audible all across the square in front of his residence. "You know what your precious Aryan Prützmann is? He's a Jew, that's what—nothing but a lousy kike in a fancy uniform!"

"Why, you lying toad!" the panzer commander exclaimed, shocked out of his reticence as the crowd began to buzz.

Stolle shook his bullet head. "Not me, by God! What do you SS bastards use for a motto? 'My honor is loyalty,' that's it. Well, on my honor, it's the truth. It's all over the computers—and Prützmann's come out and said on the televisor that people aren't allowed to talk about it. If that doesn't make it true, what's likely to? Here." He shoved the newly arrived police officer forward. "Tell him, Norbert."

Norbert told the same story the *Gauleiter* had, in a higher, thinner voice but with more details. Beside Heinrich, Willi Dorsch listened with his eyes wide and his mouth hanging open. He had to shake himself to turn back to Heinrich. "That can't be true, can it? But if it's a lie, it's a lie that goes right for the throat. And if it's a lie, why would Prützmann deny it like that? Sounds like panic. And what would make him panic like the truth?"

"Beats me." Heinrich started to quote Hitler about the big lie, but checked himself. He remembered how the Kleins had got released after they were seized. One of Prützmann's relatives had had a baby with the same horrible disease as theirs. Maybe that was a coincidence. Or maybe the *Reichsführer*-SS really did have Jews in his woodpile, and his enemies were seizing on it.

Where was Susanna? There, only a few meters away. She was looking back toward him as he was looking for her. When their eyes met, he saw her thoughts were going in the same direction as his. Lothar Prützmann certainly wasn't a Jew in any meaningful sense of the word. But wouldn't it be luscious if the *Reichsführer*-SS came to grief because people thought he was?

The panzer commander disappeared down into the turret once more, no doubt to get on the radio yet again. Heinrich would have given a good deal to be a fly sitting on the breech of the cannon in there. No such luck. Whatever the officer said, no one else but his fellow panzer crewmen heard it.

He didn't emerge for some little while. When he did, his troubled features proclaimed that he didn't like much of what he'd heard. Even so, he raised the bullhorn to his lips once more. Gamely, he said, "*Achtung!* What the *Gauleiter* says is nothing but a pack of lies. Anyone saying such things about the *Reichsführer*-SS makes himself liable to severe punishment. You have been warned."

Rolf Stolle laughed again. "Yes, you have been warned, *Volk* of the *Reich*," he called, mockery dancing on his voice. "And what have you got to say about that?"

He waited. So did Heinrich. Would the people dare, after they'd been warned not to by men with guns?

They dared. "Prützmann is a kike!" somebody yelled, and in an instant the whole crowd was chanting it: "Prützmann is a kike! Prützmann is a kike!"

Heinrich shouted it, too, as loud as anybody. "Prützmann is a kike! Prützmann is a kike!" He looked over to Susanna again. She was shouting the same thing, her hands cupped in front of her mouth. When their eyes met this time, they both started to laugh. They went right on chanting, though. Heinrich had never imagined anti-Semitic slogans could be so much fun.

"Prützmann is a kike! Prützmann is a kike!" With her mother and sisters, Alicia watched the crowd in front of Rolf Stolle's residence from the safety of her suburban living room. The panzers in the televisor screen looked like toys, though she knew they were real.

"Kike! Kike!" Roxane chortled gleefully. The word was almost a joke to her. She didn't know that she'd ever seen a Jew, let alone that she was one.

Neither did Francesca. "I wonder what the Beast will tell us about *this*," she said. "She was going on and on about how wonderful the *Reichsführer*-SS was, and how brave, and how patriotic. If he's really a dirty Jew . . ."

"Dirty Jew! Dirty Jew!" Roxane didn't seem to care what she shouted, as long as she could make noise.

Alicia didn't say anything. She didn't know what to say. She sneaked a glance at Mommy, only to find her mother looking as confused as she was. Everything seemed not just upside down but dropped on its head. Alicia didn't know why Rolf Stolle and his followers thought Prützmann was a Jew. Why hardly seemed to matter. Of all the things they could call the head of the SS, none struck a harder blow against him. Alicia understood that. She also understood that the *Reichsführer*-SS was against all the changes the new *Führer* had made. Did that mean using this weapon against him was all right? She didn't know. That wasn't so easy to figure out.

Over the noise of the crowd, the announcer for the Berlin station spoke in a high, excited voice: "British Prime Minister Charles Lynton calls on the men who made the *Putsch* to end their lawless behavior at once and release the rightful *Führer*, Heinz Buckliger. He is joined in this call by the leaders of Norway, Denmark, Sweden, and Finland. The premier of France also agrees in principle."

"Can they do that?" Francesca asked in astonishment. The states that made up the Germanic Empire didn't talk back to the *Reich*. That was a law of nature. Neither did its little allies. Not talking back kept them from getting swallowed up.

"It means they think what's going on here is really, really wrong," Alicia said.

Mommy nodded. "That's what it means, all right. And they're braver than they used to be, because the new *Führer* made them freer than they used to be."

"Holland has joined in the call for the rightful *Führer*'s release. And"—even on this day of one astonishing surprise after another, the announcer's voice rose to a startled squeak—"in Prague, a Czech organization called Unity has declared the independence of the Protectorate of Bohemia and Moravia from what it terms the illegal, immoral, and illegitimate government of Odilo Globocnik and Lothar Prützmann."

"Oh, my," Mommy said. "That will mean more trouble after they get this trouble settled, if they do get it settled."

"When's Daddy coming home?" Roxane asked.

That question had also crossed Alicia's mind. She thought she'd got a glimpse of him—and maybe even of Aunt Susanna—near the panzer closest to Rolf Stolle's residence. But she hadn't been sure, and the camera had panned away before she could say anything.

"Pumpkin, I don't know," Mommy answered. "He went to the square there on the televisor this morning. Getting there was easy then. Getting away is liable to be harder. I'm not even sure they're letting people leave."

Alicia didn't like the sound of that. She tried not to show him how worried she was. She had to stay strong, to help Mommy keep her younger sisters from getting upset. All she could do was wait and watch the televisor.

"Nobody's done any shooting here," her mother said. "As long as it stays like that, everything's all right."

And then, suddenly, the Berlin station announcer's voice rose not in surprise but in anger and alarm and fear: "We are under attack! I say again, we are under attack! There are SS troops outside this building, and they are assaulting it as I speak! They want to cut the *Volk* off from the truth and—"

There were banging noises, and shouts, and what might have been gunshots. Then the screen went blank. Alicia and her mother exclaimed in dismay. Francesca and Roxane were too little to know what that static and those swirling grays meant. As far as Alicia was concerned, they meant the end of hope.

"Change the channel!" Francesca said.

"Wait," Mommy said. "I want to see what comes on next."

What came on next, after three or four minutes of hisses and scratchy noises that made Alicia wish Mommy would change the channel, was a test pattern. Francesca and Alicia groaned. The test pattern lasted longer than the static had. Alicia's patience was wearing very thin when it finally disappeared.

Horst Witzleben's grim face replaced it. The newscaster said, "The illegal and unauthorized broadcasts formerly coming from this station have now ceased. The public is urged and instructed to disregard them, and to ignore the slanderous insults aimed at the *Reichsführer*-SS. Regular programming will now resume here, and factual bulletins will be issued as necessary. Good evening."

Regular programming turned out to be a rerun of a game show. Alicia looked at her mother. Shaking her head, Mommy got up and turned off the televisor.

XV

HEINRICH GIMPEL HAD YELLED, "DOWN WITH THE SS!" AND "WE ARE THE *Volk*!" and "All the world is watching!" and "Prützmann is a kike!" all day long. He was tired and hungry. Some sandwiches and fruit had got to the crowd, but none had got to him. The SS's armored vehicles hadn't opened fire, but they hadn't left, either. They showed no sign of leaving. Nor was he sure they would let him—or anyone else—go.

The officer commanding the lead panzer had stayed down inside the turret for a while. Now he came out again, bullhorn in hand. "Yell as loud as you please!" he blared. "No one will hear you. No one will care. Your pirate televisor station is in the hands of the State Committee!"

"Liar!" people shouted. They shouted worse things than that, too. The panzer commander let the abuse wash over him as if it didn't matter. More than anything else, that convinced Heinrich he was probably telling the truth. If he'd got angry or defensive, he might have been bluffing. As things were, he seemed to think, *Sticks and stones can break my bones, but words will never hurt me*. And all the sticks and stones here were on his side. The crowd in front of the *Gauleiter*'s residence had only words.

Still stubborn, Rolf Stolle boomed, "You don't dare let what you do see the light of day. If you were honest, you would have started shooting while the cameras were rolling."

Beside Heinrich, Willi nervously shifted from foot to foot. "I wish he wouldn't say things like that, dammit. He'll give the bastard ideas."

"He's got ideas already. He has to," Heinrich answered. "Don't you think they've been screaming in his ear to open up for hours? He hasn't done it yet. Stolle's working on his conscience."

"Son of a bitch is an SS man," Willi said. "He had it surgically removed, just like the rest of them."

"Ha," Heinrich said: a mournful attempt at a laugh. Many a true word was spoken in jest. He wished Willi hadn't spoken these; they felt altogether too true.

Slowly, slowly, the sun sank toward the northwest. Berlin wasn't far enough north to get white nights in summer, nights where twilight never turned to real darkness, but sunset came late and darkness didn't last long. All the same, Heinrich feared it would last long enough to mask dark deeds.

He looked around for Susanna. When he spied her, their eyes met. She smiled and waved. "We've both chosen our spot," she said. "I think it's a good one."

A good one to get killed in, Heinrich thought. But maybe that was part of what Susanna had meant. She got passionately devoted to causes—and if you weren't passionately devoted to being a Jew these days, you weren't a Jew at all. Even so, Heinrich wanted to live. He had another generation at home to worry about. Susanna hadn't been lucky enough to hook up with anyone with whom she got along.

Looking for hope, he pointed up to the rooftop televisor cameras. "They're still filming, even if the signal isn't going out. The fear that people might see it one of these days may do for a conscience where nothing else will."

Susanna nodded. "Here's hoping."

Beside Heinrich, Willi said, "That should last us for another hour, maybe even another hour and a half. But what happens when it gets dark?"

Heinrich eyed the setting sun. He almost said something about Joshua and making the sun stand still. At the last minute, though, he didn't. Not too long after he said something Biblical to Erika, he'd ended up in one of Lothar Prützmann's prisons. He didn't think Willi would accuse him of being a Jew. All the same, prison would be one of the better things that might happen to him if things went wrong here.

Joshua he was not. In due course, the sun sank below the horizon. Twilight began to deepen. Shadows spread and lost their sharpness. Faces farther away grew dim and indistinct. Venus blazed low in the western sky. Above it, Saturn was dimmer and yellower . . . and that ruddy star between them had to be Mars. Heinrich almost wished he hadn't recognized it. Tonight, he wanted nothing to do with the god of war.

Lights on Rolf Stolle's residence were bright, but not bright enough to illuminate the square in front of it after the sun went down. The panzers and armored personnel carriers turned on their lights. That, though, Heinrich knew, was not for the benefit of the crowd confronting them. Their crews wouldn't want anybody to sneak up with a Molotov cocktail or a grenade in the dark.

And then, off in the distance but swelling rapidly, Heinrich heard one of the sounds he'd listened for and dreaded all day long: the rumbling snarl of more diesel engines heading toward the *Gauleiter*'s residence. He wasn't the only one who heard them. A low murmur of alarm ran through the crowd.

Willi Dorsch managed a creditable chuckle. "I don't know what we're worrying about," he said. "They've already got enough firepower here to massacre the lot of us."

"You always did know how to cheer me up when I was feeling low," Heinrich answered, and Willi laughed out loud.

The officer in charge of the lead panzer raised his bullhorn and aimed it at Rolf Stolle: "It's all over now. You can see it's all over. Surrender to me, and I'll make sure they don't shoot you 'by mistake.' "

"You can take your 'by mistake,' fold it till it's all corners, and shove it right on up your ass, sonny boy," the *Gauleiter* of Berlin shouted. "If you want me, if Prützmann wants me, you'll have to kill me, on account of I'm damned if you'll take me alive and give me a show trial. Buckliger let himself get caught, the poor, sorry son of a bitch. To hell with me if I intend to."

"He's got balls," Willi said admiringly.

"I know," Heinrich said. "But if they take him out, they'll take out everybody who's here with him."

He had to raise his voice to make himself heard over the engine noise and clanking, clattering treads of the approaching armored vehicles. Willi gave an airy shrug, as if to say, *Easy come, easy go*. Heinrich clapped him on the back. He regretted being here less than he'd thought he would. Susanna was right. This was a good place to stand.

Down the people-clogged street, farther away from the *Gauleiter*'s residence, jeers and hisses and derisive whistles rang out as the new contingent of armored fighting vehicles came into sight. If a hothead in the crowd had an assault rifle and opened up on the panzers from sheer frustration, that could touch off a massacre. Damn near anything could touch off a massacre now, and Heinrich knew it only too well.

"I *am* sorry about Erika," Willi said suddenly, as if he too was thinking this was the end, and some things should not go unspoken.

Tears stung Heinrich's eyes. He nodded. "It's all right," he said. "Don't worry about it."

And then the noises from down the street changed. As if by magic, boos and curses were transmuted into wild, even frantic, cheers. Heinrich's head, which had been hanging on his chest, came up like a dog's when it took an unexpected scent. So did Willi's. So did Susanna's. They all leaned toward the startling new noise. Heinrich willed words to come through the mad joy.

"It's the—!" More cheers drowned whatever the key word was. "It's not the—!" Frustrated again, Heinrich swore and kicked at the paving slates. But the third time was the charm. "It's not the goddamn *Waffen*-SS. It's the *Wehrmacht—and they're on our side!*"

Heinrich threw back his head and howled like a wolf. A crazy grin on his face, he grabbed Willi's hand and pumped his whole arm up and down as if he were jacking up a car. He shoved through the crowd toward Susanna. She was coming toward him, too. Laughing and crying at the same time, they squeezed each other. He was forty centimeters taller than she was. He had to bend down a long way to give her a kiss—and he did.

Susanna only half remembered actually clambering up onto this panzer. It hadn't been more than fifteen minutes earlier, but already it seemed like a mad fever dream. The panzer had handholds welded to the turret and the chassis so soldiers could cling to it and ride along. But the gray, capable engineers who'd designed it surely had never dreamt it would clatter through the neon nighttime streets of Berlin with as many people aboard as it carried.

The panzer commander seemed taken aback by the whole business himself. He rode head and shoulders out of the cupola, and couldn't have been as young as he looked—could he? "Be careful!" he shouted over and over again to his unexpected load of passengers. "If you fall off, you'll get squashed!"

He was bound to be right about that. This panzer was second in a long column rolling from Rolf Stolle's residence toward Lothar Prützmann's lair not far from the *Führer*'s palace. Susanna wondered where Heinrich had gone. He wasn't on this panzer. Was he riding another one, or had his usual prudence come back to life and persuaded him to stay away from places where guns were liable to go off?

Prudence? Susanna laughed. Nothing that had happened all this mad day had had even a nodding acquaintance with prudence. It wasn't even prudence that had kept the SS men from fighting it out when they found themselves outgunned by the *Wehrmacht*. They still could have killed Stolle then, as they could have killed him a hundred times earlier on. But their hearts hadn't been in their orders, and so they hadn't started shooting and had given up at the first excuse they got. SS men! Who would have imagined it?

Not Prützmann, Susanna thought, and chuckled evilly.

Here and there in the city, she did hear spatters of gunfire, but only a few. The panzer commander heard them, too. "What are you people going to do when we get where we're going?" he asked plaintively.

"Hang the *Reichsführer*-SS from a lamppost, that's what!" bawled a burly man near Susanna. She and the rest of the panzer-riders cheered.

"But we're liable to have to shoot some of those SS bastards, and they're liable to shoot back," the *Wehrmacht* man said. Whenever the panzer passed under a streetlight, the little silver *Totenkopf* on his black coveralls glittered for a moment.

"Give us guns!" that burly man said. "We'll shoot 'em ourselves!" Through more cheers, he went on to describe in vivid terms the personal and moral shortcomings of the SS. Then he nodded to Susanna. "Meaning no offense, ma'am."

"It doesn't bother me," she said. "They're much worse than that." The man blinked, then grinned enormously. Susanna grinned back.

SS men had barricaded the grounds around their brooding headquarters. What they'd run up looked much more formidable than the flimsy makeshifts the people of Berlin had erected in front of Rolf Stolle's residence. But there was no swarming mass of people behind these barricades: only Prützmann's alleged *Übermenschen*. And, as the first panzer stopped and turned its lights on them, the SS men looked quite humanly nervous, even if they did clutch assault rifles and a few antipanzer rocket launchers.

The commander of the lead panzer yelled, "You fuckers open up on us and we'll slaughter every goddamn one of you. We'll laugh while we're doing it, too. You shot our boys at the televisor station, and we owe you plenty. You got that?" He ducked down into the turret. The panzer's engine began to race and roar. The commander reemerged to issue a one-word order he surely hadn't learned in any training school: "Charge!"

His panzer thundered forward. It hit a parked truck head-on and hurled it out of the way. Susanna screamed with delight. Her panzer rumbled through the breach the lead machine had made. Others followed. So did trucks and armored personnel carriers full of *Wehrmacht* soldiers. The SS men didn't fire a shot. Troopers in *Wehrmacht* gray urban camouflage came down from their vehicles and began disarming the men who'd made careers of spreading fear and now suddenly discovered there were people who weren't afraid of them.

Fear is what they had, Susanna realized. *The* Wehrmacht *always had more muscle. Up till now, it never used what it had. Politics held it back. But tonight the gloves are off, and it's nobody's fault but Lothar Prützmann's.* She whooped again. The *Reichsführer*-SS hadn't known what he was getting into. He hadn't known, but he was finding out in a hurry.

Prützmann's office was on the third floor of the SS building, right above the monumental entryway. Anyone who paid attention to the news knew that much. The *Wehrmacht* panzer commanders evidently did. Half a dozen 120mm cannon rose and swung to point straight at the famous chamber.

One of the panzer commanders had a bullhorn, probably the same model as the SS panzer man had used outside of Rolf Stolle's residence. "Prützmann!" he shouted, his amplified voice echoing from the granite and concrete and glass. "Come out with your hands up, Prützmann! We won't kill you if you do. You'll get a trial."

And then we'll kill you, Susanna finished mentally. Hearing Lothar

Prützmann's unadorned surname blare from the bullhorn was a wonder in itself, a wonder and a portent. *How the mighty have fallen,* it said. Unadorned surnames blared at prisoners in interrogation cells. The *Reichsführer*-SS had surely never expected such indignities to be his lot. *Too bad for him.*

No answer came from the famous office. The lights were on in there, but closed venetian blinds kept Susanna from seeing inside. "Don't screw around with us, Prützmann!" the *Wehrmacht* commander shouted. "You have five minutes. If you don't come out, we'll come in after you. You'll like that a lot less, I promise."

Susanna looked at her watch, only to discover she'd somehow lost it. She shrugged. Five minutes wouldn't be hard to figure out. All the civilians on the panzer with her—and on the other *Wehrmacht* machines—shouted and cursed the *Reichsführer*-SS. Between their cries (including her own) and the rumble of the panzers' engines, whatever was happening more than a few meters away got drowned out.

The deadline had to be drawing near. The man commanding Susanna's panzer leaned down into the turret, presumably to give the gunner his orders. The commander had just straightened when a tall blond man in the uniform of a Security Police major came out with a handkerchief tied to a pointer to make a flag of truce. "Don't shoot!" he shouted.

"Why not?" said the commander of the lead panzer. "Why the hell not, you SS *Schweinehund?* Where's Prützmann? He's the one we want."

"He's dead," the blond Security Police major answered. "He stuck a pistol in his mouth and pulled the trigger. Didn't you hear the bang?"

A frantic tumult of cheering rose from the civilians. Through it, the lead panzer commander used the bullhorn to say, "Show me the body. Till I see the body, I figure this is some sort of scheme to buy time for him to get away." The blond major started to go back into the building. The panzer commander stopped him: "Hold it right there, buddy. If they don't bring Prützmann's body out, *you're* the one who's dead meat."

"Have it your way," the major said. "You will anyhow." He turned and shouted back into SS headquarters: "Hans-Joachim! Detlef! Bring him out! They want to see him."

Noxious diesel fumes from the idling panzer made Susanna cough. A dull headache pounded behind her eyes. It all put her in mind of Professor

Oppenhoff's cigars. She didn't care. To see Lothar Prützmann dead, she would have gone through worse than this.

Or so she thought, till two SS men—she supposed they were Hans-Joachim and Detlef—dragged out a corpse. Each had hold of a highly polished boot. The body wore the black dress uniform of a high-ranking SS official. In the glare of the panzers' lights, the blood that ran from the back of the head was shockingly scarlet. Susanna's stomach lurched. Death—anyone's death—was better contemplated at a distance than seen close up.

Again, so she thought. But the man who commanded her panzer said only, "It's a fresh corpse, anyhow. They don't drip that way very long." If that wasn't the voice of experience, she'd never heard it.

The commander of the lead panzer got down from his machine and bounded up the stairs to the entrance two at a time so he could get a good look at the body. He stooped beside it, then slowly straightened. With a fine flair for the dramatic, he spread his arms wide and waited till every eye was on him. Then and only then did he shout, "It's Prützmann!"

Susanna squealed. A great roar of joy rose from the crowd. That burly man on the panzer with her planted a big, smacking kiss on her cheek. He needed a shave. His beard rasped her skin. He smelled of schnapps and onions. She couldn't have cared less.

Where's Heinrich? she wondered again. *Is he seeing this, too?* That, she cared about. After a spell in Lothar Prützmann's prison, Heinrich of all people deserved to see his corpse.

"Where's that friend of yours, that Susanna?" Willi Dorsch bawled in Heinrich's ear.

"I don't know," Heinrich shouted back. "I haven't seen her in a while." The two of them had precarious perches on an armored personnel carrier full of *Wehrmacht* soldiers. As it rattled west through the streets of Berlin, one of the crew fired short machine-gun bursts into the air whenever he felt like it. The noise was shattering.

"If somebody starts shooting back at that trigger-happy maniac, we're all ground round." Willi sounded absurdly cheerful.

"This charming thought already occurred to me, thanks." Heinrich didn't.

Willi laughed. "So many crazy things have already happened today, I'm just not going to worry any more. One way or another, it'll all work out."

"Maybe it will." By then, Heinrich was past arguing. In fact, he couldn't very well argue, because a hell of a lot of crazy things *had* happened. The wind of their passage whipped around his glasses and made his eyes water. That wind was cool, but not especially clean; it was full of diesel exhaust from the other armored vehicles in this convoy. How many panzers and armored personnel carriers and self-propelled guns (to say nothing of soft-skinned trucks) were trundling around Berlin tonight? Even more to the point, how many different sides were they on? And what would happen when those on one side bumped up against those from another?

Rat-a-tat-tat! The machine gunner squeezed off another exuberant burst. A tracer round drew a hot red line across the night. Nobody returned fire. Heinrich approved of that. Somewhere, though, those bullets would be coming down. Even as falling lumps of lead, they could kill: they'd be falling from a long way up.

Treads growling and grinding, the armored personnel carrier turned left. Heinrich started to laugh. "What's funny?" Willi asked.

"Back where we started from," Heinrich answered. There on the left stood *Oberkommando der Wehrmacht* headquarters; on the right, across the wide expanse of Adolf Hitler Platz, the *Führer*'s palace and the vast, looming bulk of the Great Hall. Dead ahead towered the Arch of Triumph, as usual bathed in spotlights. Heinrich would have bet it had sharpshooters atop it. But were they wearing SS black or the *Wehrmacht*'s mottled *Feldgrau*?

The armored column of which the personnel carrier was a part turned right, rumbling toward the *Führer*'s palace. The panzers and APCs had to go slowly and carefully to keep from crushing people under their tracks. Adolf Hitler Platz wasn't jammed sardine-tight, the way the little square in front of Rolf Stolle's residence had been. It would hold more than a million people. At the moment, it held tens, perhaps hundreds, of thousands.

"*Wehrmacht* or SS?" somebody called nervously.

"Bugger the SS with a pine cone," the machine gunner answered, and fired another burst into the air. "We're the *real* soldiers, by God, and if those blackshirted pricks don't know it they'll find out pretty goddamn fast!"

The whoops that came from the crowd said that was what they wanted to hear. But SS men held the *Führer*'s palace. Sandbagged machine-gun nests outside the entrance were plenty to keep the people at a respectful distance. Panzers and armored personnel carriers laughed at machine guns—though Heinrich, on the outside of the armor plate, wouldn't laugh if they opened up. And if the SS had machine guns here, it probably had antipanzer rockets, too.

Heinrich didn't see any *Waffen*-SS armor. Maybe Lothar Prützmann had figured he wouldn't need it here once he'd got hold of Stolle. That only went to show he wasn't as smart as he thought he was.

Or does it show I'm not as smart as I think I am? Heinrich wondered. Would *Waffen*-SS panzers suddenly charge out of the night, their cleated steel tracks tearing up the pavement like those of the *Wehrmacht* machines? He shrugged. If the officer in charge of the *Wehrmacht* armor couldn't anticipate a threat like that, he didn't deserve his shoulder straps.

A blackshirt in front of the entrance stepped forward, his hands conspicuously empty. Try as he would to hold it steady, his voice quavered a little when he asked, "What do you want?"

"Globocnik!" Half a dozen *Wehrmacht* panzer commanders hurled the acting *Führer*'s name in his face. One of them added, "We know he's in there. We saw him come in this afternoon."

The crowd of angry civilians with the *Wehrmacht* men took up the cry: "Globocnik! Globocnik! We want Globocnik!" In a different tone of voice, those shouts would have warmed any politician's heart. As things were, if Heinrich had been Odilo Globocnik, he would have been looking for a place to hide.

Licking his lips, the SS man said, "You are speaking of the rightful *Führer* of the Greater German *Reich* and of the Germanic Empire. He orders you—he commands you—to disperse."

Maybe the panzer commanders answered. If they did, they couldn't make themselves heard even with bullhorns. The crowd's roars drowned them out. "Heinz Buckliger is the rightful *Führer*!" people shouted, and, "We won't take orders from Globocnik!" and, "Down with the SS!" Heinrich gleefully joined that last chant. He liked the others, but that one hit him where he lived.

"This is nothing but treason!" The SS man had got his nerve back. He sounded angry now, not frightened. "We will not surrender him!"

"Then you're going to be mighty sorry," one of the *Wehrmacht* panzer commanders said. The crowd bayed agreement.

"So will you, if you try to take him," the SS man answered.

He was used to making people afraid. He was good at it, too. After all, fear was his stock in trade. The German people had had almost eighty years in which to learn to fear the SS. But today, as Heinrich had seen in front of Rolf Stolle's residence, fear was failing. And intimidating men in panzers that carried big guns was a lot harder than scaring civilians who couldn't fight back.

Jeers and curses rained down on the SS man's head. More rained down on Odilo Globocnik's head. Was he listening, there inside the *Führer*'s palace? With a strange, snarling joy Heinrich had never known before, he hoped so. The SS man, in his own coldblooded way, had style. He clicked his heels. His arm shot out toward the crowd in a Party salute. He spun on his heel, executed an about-face of parade-ground perfection to turn his back on the *Wehrmacht* soldiers and the people, and marched away to his comrades.

And, to a certain extent, his intimidation worked even against his formidable foes. He might have been—Heinrich thought he was—bluffing when he warned that the SS could make the *Wehrmacht* sorry. But the panzers' cannons and machine guns waited tensely—waited for they knew not what. A nightjar swooped out of the darkness to snatch one of the moths dancing in the air around the palace lights. The sudden, unexpected streak of motion made men from the SS and the *Wehrmacht* turn their heads towards it. If it had startled one of them into tightening his finger on a trigger . . .

Heinrich never knew exactly how long the impasse lasted. Somewhere between half an hour and an hour was his best guess. What broke it was a high, clear sound that pierced both the yells from the crowd and the diesel rumble of the armored fighting vehicles: the sound of one man laughing.

The man was a *Wehrmacht* panzer commander. Like his fellows, he wore radio headphones. He laughed again, louder this time, and raised a bullhorn to his mouth. "Give it up, you sorry bastards!" he blared. "Prützmann's blown his brains out. The *Putsch* is falling down around your ears."

"Liar!" one of the SS men shouted, an odd desperation in his voice—it wasn't *I don't believe you* but *I don't dare believe you*.

"You've got your own radios," the *Wehrmacht* panzer commander answered through the bullhorn. "You can find out for yourselves. Go ahead. I'll wait." He theatrically folded his arms across his chest.

There in the glare of the panzers' lights, an SS radioman did call . . . whom? Somebody at Prützmann's headquarters, Heinrich supposed. He could tell when the radioman got his question answered. The fellow suddenly sagged, as if his skeleton had turned to rubber. He spoke to the officer who'd parleyed with the *Wehrmacht* soldiers. The officer clapped a hand to his forehead in an altogether human gesture of despair: the kind of gesture Heinrich had never imagined seeing from an SS man.

Little by little, the officer pulled himself together. He stepped forward again. "You seem to be right," he called bleakly to the *Wehrmacht* panzer commander. "What do you want from us?"

"Give us Globocnik," the *Wehrmacht* man said. "The rest of you lousy sons of bitches can go back to your barracks. We'll deal with you later if we decide you're worth the trouble."

The SS officer drew back to hash things out with his comrades. Heinrich couldn't hear a word they said through the growl of the armored fighting vehicles' engines and the shouting and oaths from the crowd. Those soon coalesced into a chant of, "Globocnik! Globocnik! Give us Globocnik!" Heinrich happily howled it along with everybody else.

When a squad of blackshirts with assault rifles turned and went purposefully into the *Führer*'s palace, he stopped chanting and thumped Willi on the shoulder. "They're going to get him!" he exclaimed. "They really are!"

"Either that or they're going to try to sneak him out of here," Willi said. "This place has got to have more secret escape routes than Brazil's got coffee beans."

"Their buddies will pay for it if they do that," Heinrich reminded him. "And besides, who'd want to rally behind Odilo Globocnik? Prützmann, maybe. Whatever else he was, he was sly. But Globocnik? He was never anything but a false front for other people to work behind."

Willi thought that over, then nodded. "Well, when you're right, you're right." He grinned at Heinrich. "You should try it more often." Heinrich snorted.

A shot rang out inside the *Führer*'s palace. Hearing it over the engine,

Heinrich jerked and almost fell off the armored personnel carrier. "Is that Globocnik taking Prützmann's way out?" he said. "Or was he 'shot while attempting to escape'?" The familiar SS euphemism for an execution had a fine ironic flavor here.

"We'll find out," Willi said. "What a man—the twenty-four-hour *Führer*!" He made as if to spit to show his contempt, but held back when he realized he was all too likely to spit on someone.

A few minutes later, the squad of SS men came out again. They half led, half dragged a lurching figure in their midst. Blood ran from their captive's head, but he seemed no worse than stunned. "Here's Globocnik!" one of the blackshirts shouted. "He tried to shoot himself, but he didn't have the balls to do it right. His hand twitched when he pulled the trigger, so all he did was crease his scalp. You want him, you're welcome to him."

They shoved Odilo Globocnik down the steps toward the waiting *Wehrmacht* men. He staggered as if drunk, his arms flailing wildly. But the soldiers never got him. Instead, the baying mob surged forward. Globocnik wailed once as they swarmed over him. The *Wehrmacht* men might have been able to stop it. They stayed in their panzers and APCs and did not a thing.

And when the people were through, they hanged the twenty-four-hour *Führer* by the heels from a lamppost. Heinrich looked once, then turned away, glad he hadn't eaten much since breakfast. What was left of Odilo Globocnik hardly looked like a human being at all.

Here was one morning where Esther Stutzman was glad she didn't have to go to work. She poured herself a second cup of coffee, turned on the televisor, and sat down in front of it. Horst Witzleben stared out at her. Behind him were the tarmac and buildings of Tempelhof Airport.

She'd caught him in the middle of a sentence: "—by Me-662 fighters, *Luftwaffe Alfa* is expected to land in about five minutes. The return of Heinz Buckliger from his confinement on the island of Hvar will, *hoffentlich*, bring to an end this bizarre episode in the history of the *Reich*. A *Führer* overthrown by *Putsch*, a man named *Führer* overthrown by the outraged *Volk*, the powerful *Reichsführer*-SS dead by his own hand . . ." Horst shook his head, as if to say the events of the past couple of days left him as baffled and bemused as anyone else.

Two of the escorting *Luftwaffe* fighters touched down side by side, smoke spurting from their tires as they hit the runway. Then the *Führer*'s personal jetliner landed. Two more sleek, deadly-looking Me-662s came in just behind it. *Wehrmacht* panzers rumbled forward to help form a protective cordon around *Luftwaffe Alfa*. If any diehard SS men tried to take out the *Führer*, they'd have their work cut out for them.

As soon as *Luftwaffe Alfa* had taxied to a stop near a terminal, airport workers wheeled a stairway to the plane's front door. In their wake strode Rolf Stolle, his shaved head gleaming in the summer sun. Bodyguards in Berlin police gray surrounded the *Gauleiter*. Seeing them reminded Esther how much things had changed. How many Nazi bigwigs had she seen on the televisor over the years? More than she wanted—she knew that. How many of them had had SS bodyguards in black? Every damned one. But no more. No more.

The door opened. A couple of alert-looking *Wehrmacht* men with assault rifles emerged first, making sure the coast was clear. Only after one of them nodded did Heinz Buckliger come out, Erna behind him. He waved awkwardly toward the televisor cameras broadcasting the scene across the Germanic Empire.

In a low voice, Horst said, "The signs of the *Führer*'s ordeal remain on his face."

Esther found herself nodding. Buckliger's features were pale and ravaged. He blinked against the sunshine as if he hadn't seen it in weeks, not days. Esther wondered what the SS had done to him while it had him in its clutches. He might have aged ten years in this small space of time.

Rolf Stolle, by contrast, fairly burst with youthful energy even though he was older than the *Führer*. He shook off his guards and bounded up the stairway toward Buckliger. The *Wehrmacht* men with the rifles looked uncertainly at each other for a moment. Then they both grinned and stepped aside to let him pass.

Still quietly, Horst Witzleben said, "Here is a meeting the world will long remember."

At the top of the stairs, Stolle stuck out his hand. Buckliger took it in a tentative way. One of them must have been wearing a microphone—maybe both of them were—for their words came clearly from the televisor set. "Welcome home, *mein Führer*," the *Gauleiter* of Berlin boomed. "We had a little bit of a mess here, but we cleaned it up for you just fine."

"Good. That's good." Heinz Buckliger sounded as worn and weary as he looked. He was the *Führer*, Stolle only the *Gauleiter*. Yet Rolf Stolle, by some mysterious reversal, was the one who seemed possessed of the greater authority. Or maybe the reversal was not so mysterious after all. Buckliger had had things done to him during the *Putsch*. Stolle had gone out and done things himself. How much of a difference that made Esther could see for herself as the two men confronted each other.

Stolle said, "Everything will proceed as you have ordered, *mein Führer*." He sounded deferential. No matter how he sounded, he wasn't. He promptly proved as much, too, for he went on, "After the elections, the *Reichstag* will be a different place, and we'll really be able to get something done. About time, too."

"*Ja*," Buckliger said. But his expression was that of a man who'd bitten into something sour. Stolle hadn't said, *You'll really be able to get something done*. He'd assumed power would lie with the *Reichstag*, not the *Führer*. And Heinz Buckliger, who'd been far away and under guard while Stolle led resistance against the SS *Putsch*, couldn't contradict him.

The *Gauleiter* of Berlin drove that home: "The *Volk* saved your regime, *mein Führer*." He was most subversive when he sounded most modest. "If they'd sat on their hams, you'd be a dead man, and so would I. But they liked the way the wind was blowing, and I maybe pointed them in the right direction once they got riled up. The first edition was right. Trust the *Volk* and they'll never let you down."

Adolf Hitler hadn't said any such thing, in the first edition of *Mein Kampf* or anywhere else. But Buckliger, again, was in no position to tell Stolle he was wrong. The *Führer* said, "Revitalization will continue." It was his first effort to get in a word for the program he'd pushed so hard.

And Rolf Stolle graciously granted him a nod. "Oh, *ja*, *ja*, revitalization." He might have been humoring a child. "But that's only the beginning. We've got to do something good and final about the SS, too, make goddamn sure the lousy blackshirts can't make trouble again. And we've got to give democratic rights back to some other Aryan peoples, too, not just to the *Volk* of the *Reich*."

Buckliger's eyes widened. He coughed in astonishment. "I am sure that this is not the place for such discussions," he said.

Stolle thumped him on the back—again, or so it seemed to Esther, indulgently. "Well, maybe you're right. You ought to get rested up, get ready to deal with the new *Reichstag* that'll be coming in after the elections."

The camera cut away from the scene at the top of the airplane steps. A few months before, it never would have lingered so long. During the time of the previous *Führer*, it never would have gone there at all. In tones full of wonder, Horst Witzleben said, "This is an extraordinary day in the history of the *Reich*. Let me repeat that: an extraordinary day. Heinz Buckliger returns to a state far different from the one he left when he went on holiday. Not all the differences are obvious yet. Some that seem obvious may not last. But surely some changes will be deep and far-reaching. Where the *Volk* once comes out into the streets against those who have proclaimed themselves to be the government . . . well, how can things possibly remain the same after that?"

Esther didn't know if things could stay the same after that. She also didn't know if their being different for the *Reich* as a whole would make them different for her. Buckliger and Stolle remained Nazis. She didn't expect any Nazi to have much use for Jews. But there were Nazis . . . and then there were Nazis. With a choice between this pair and the overthrown duo of Prützmann and Globocnik, she knew where she stood. And the German people stood with her. If that wasn't a miracle, what was?

Susanna Weiss got out of bed early on Sunday morning. If that didn't prove it was an unusual Sunday, she couldn't imagine what would; sleep, on weekends, was a pleasure she took seriously. So was coffee, any morning of the week. She said something unfortunate but memorable when she found she was out of cream. Then, discovering whipped cream in the refrigerator, she brightened. That would do. It would more than do, in fact. On reflection, she added a shot of brandy to the coffee. She had a sweet roll with it, which made her feel thoroughly Viennese.

But she left her apartment with Berlin briskness. This wasn't just any Sunday. This was the election day the late, unlamented Lothar Prützmann and his stooge of a Globocnik hadn't been able to hijack. She wanted to vote early. She really wanted to vote early and often, an American phrase that had been making the rounds in the *Reich* the last few days, but she didn't think she could get away with it.

Her polling place was around the corner, in a veterans' hall. She couldn't remember the last time she'd voted. What was the point, when the results were going to be reported as 99.64 percent *ja* regardless of what they really were—and when voting *nein* was liable to win you a visit from the Security Police?

As soon as she came out of her building, she stopped in surprise. However brisk she'd been, she hadn't been brisk enough. The line for the polling place already stretched around the block and came back toward her. Normally, she hated queuing up. Now she joined the line without a qualm. *Why is this night different from all other nights?* went through her head. The Passover question, the Jewish question, almost seemed to fit the *Reich* today. Germany really might be different after this election. It might. Or it might not. Life came with no guarantees. A Jew surviving in the Nazis' Berlin knew, had to know, as much.

A man in a battered fedora, a windbreaker, and a pair of faded dungarees got into line behind her. "*Guten Morgen,*" he said, scratching his chin. He needed a shave. "Now we get to tell the bastards where to head in."

He might be a provocateur. Susanna knew that, too. On this morning of all mornings, she couldn't make herself care. "You bet we do," she answered. "I've been waiting a long time."

"Who hasn't?" the whiskery man said. "They never wanted to listen before. Now, by God, they're gonna have to." He cursed the SS and the Party *Bonzen* without great imagination but with considerable gusto.

Up and down the line—which rapidly got longer behind Susanna—people were doing the same thing. They couldn't all be provocateurs . . . could they? Susanna didn't think so. The SS couldn't arrest everybody in the city. If they did, nothing would get done. And the blackshirts had their own worries at the moment. The *Wehrmacht* was gleefully cutting them down to size, with Heinz Buckliger and Rolf Stolle cheering the soldiers on.

Had Buckliger understood the animosity ordinary people felt toward the state when he ordered these elections? If he had, would he have ordered them? Susanna had trouble believing that. But order them he had, and now he'd be stuck with the results. Prützmann's failed *Putsch* might have been the best thing that could have happened to reform. It reminded people what they could be in for if they voted to keep the status quo.

The queue snaked forward. The closer to the polling place people got, the nastier the things they had to say about that status quo. Men and women who came out of the veterans' hall strutted and swaggered, proud grins on their faces. Nobody needed to ask how they'd voted.

The hall smelled of old cigars and spilled beer. Helmets were mounted on the wall: big, cumbersome ones with flaring brims from the First World War and the lighter and sleeker models German soldiers had worn during the Second and Third. The uniformed precinct leader stood around looking important. Clerks in mufti did the real work.

"Your name?" one of them said when Susanna came up to him. She gave it. He made sure she was on a list in front of him, then went on, "Your identity papers." She displayed the card; she would no more leave home without it than she would without a top. Once the clerk was satisfied, he used a ruler to line through her name and address in red. Then he handed her a ballot. "Choose any vacant booth. . . . Next!"

There were no vacant booths, not with the way people had swarmed to the polls. Susanna waited till a woman came out of one. She ducked into it herself, pulling the curtain closed behind her. She wasn't in Rolf Stolle's district, but she knew which candidate here supported reform and which was a Party hack. She knew which candidate for the Berlin city council was which, too. Voting for candidates had never mattered to her. Voting against them—being able to vote against them—carried a kick stronger than Glenfiddich straight up.

She put the ballot in its envelope, emerged from the booth (a tall man immediately took her place), and handed the envelope to the clerk. He put it in the ballot box, intoning, "*Frau* Weiss has voted."

"*Fräulein Doktor* Professor Weiss has voted," she corrected crisply. Every so often, the formidable academic title came in very handy. Half a dozen people in the veterans' hall looked her way. The clerk stared at her as she walked out.

She wanted to know right away how the election turned out. She couldn't, of course, because the polls were still open. Talking about results till they closed might have influenced those who hadn't voted yet, and so was *verboten*. That made most of Sunday pass in what felt like anticlimax.

She turned on the televisor a few minutes before eight that evening. Watching the end of an idiotic game show seemed a small price to pay for what would follow. At eight o'clock precisely, Horst Witzleben came on the screen in place of the Sunday night film that normally would have run.

"Today is a watershed day for the Greater German *Reich,*" the newscaster declared. "In Germany's first contested elections since 1933, candidates favoring the reform policies of Heinz Buckliger and Rolf Stolle appear to be sweeping to victory all across the country."

Hearing Stolle's name mentioned in the same breath as the *Führer*'s was new since the failed *Putsch.* The *Gauleiter*'s status had risen as Buckliger's fell. The one was a hero, the other a victim. Even in the *Reich,* it turned out, there was such a thing as moral authority.

A map of Germany appeared in gray on the screen. Here and there, it was measled with green spots. There were also red spots, but far fewer of them. "Green shows pro-reform candidates with substantial leads in their districts," Witzleben said. "Red shows candidates of the other sort who are in the lead. If we look more closely at Berlin"—the map changed as he spoke—"we see that every district but one in the capital of the *Reich* supports reform. Rolf Stolle himself is being sent to the *Reichstag* by a margin of better than six to one over his foe, building contractor Engelbert Hackmann."

"Good," Susanna murmured. That wasn't a surprise, but it was a relief.

The map went back to coverage of the whole *Reich.* More of it had turned green. Some more had turned red, too, but not nearly so much. Then it shifted again, this time to a detailed look at the Protectorate of Bohemia and Moravia. Most of that area was green, except for a few red patches in the former Sudetenland.

Horst Witzleben continued, "Along with electing delegates to the *Reichstag,* the people of the Protectorate are also voting on a nonbinding referendum concerning their relationship with the *Reich.* Latest returns show that seventy-seven percent favor the declaration of independence proclaimed by the Unity organization in the wake of the *Putsch,* while only twenty-three percent wish to continue as a *Reichs* protectorate—in effect, a province of the *Reich.* Most of the delegates elected are pledged to bring this issue to the attention of the new *Reichstag,* and to seek relief."

That was pretty dizzying, too. True, the referendum had no official weight, any more than the declaration had. But it wouldn't have been on the ballot if those things didn't count for something. And the Czechs had shown a lot of nerve in reminding the world they hadn't forgotten the freedom they'd known between the first two World Wars. How could a *Reichstag* chosen on the basis of self-determination ignore it once in office?

Maybe they'll say the Czechs are only Slavs, and too ignorant to know what they're talking about, Susanna thought cynically. But in that case, why give them the chance to speak their minds? Susanna had yet to hear anyone, no matter how radical a reformer, speak up for letting Poles or Ukrainians or Russians tell the world what they wanted. Their opinions didn't matter. Why else had God put them on earth except to be worked to death?

And no one had spoken up for keeping Heinrich Gimpel and his daughters alive when they were arrested. Had the authorities decided he was a Jew and they first-degree *Mischlingen,* they would have been killed, and that would have been that. The *Reich* had come further in the past year than in the previous lifetime. It still had a long way to go. Susanna suspected neither Buckliger nor Stolle realized how far.

Maybe Charlie Lynton did, over in London. He had the British Union of Fascists out several steps in front of the German National Socialists. That took special nerve in a subject ally. And the white-haired Czech playwright who led Unity seemed to have a good understanding of where the *Reich* needed to go. Whether it would go there was another question.

More and more of the map filled in. There were spots where red predominated over green: Bavaria, parts of Prussia, rural Austria (Vienna was a different story). But it looked as if reformers would have a solid majority. How solid would it have been had Prützmann not tried his *Putsch?* Susanna feared it would have been much less so, but nobody would ever know now.

Then the camera cut away from the map, away from the studio. There was Heinz Buckliger, walking through the little square in front of the *Gauleiter*'s residence with Rolf Stolle. Stolle was pointing to the makeshift memorials that had sprung up where SS panzers crushed Berliners: flowers, candles, notes to the dead, and one big sign that said, *FREIHEIT ÜBER ALLES!*

"The two chief architects of this remarkable day confer," Horst said quietly.

It didn't look like a conference to Susanna. It looked as if the *Gauleiter* was lecturing the *Führer*. And it looked as if Heinz Buckliger was taking it. He would nod whenever Stolle stuck out a finger and made a point. Once,

Stolle laughed at something and slapped him on the back, hard enough to stagger him. Buckliger took that, too, though it was anything but the gesture of a subordinate to a superior. Despite their titles, it didn't seem as if the *Gauleiter* were the *Führer*'s subordinate.

Stolle pointed to the FREIHEIT ÜBER ALLES! sign. Buckliger earnestly nodded again. Stolle didn't really understand what the sign meant, either. Susanna had already realized that. But if you said the words often enough, didn't you sooner or later have to go where they led you?

Didn't you? *We'll find out*, Susanna thought.

Francesca came bounding up to Alicia at lunchtime. "Guess what!" she cried.

"I don't know," Alicia said. "What?"

"*Frau* Koch is gone!" her sister caroled. "Gone, gone, gone! We've got a new teacher. His name is *Herr* Mistele. He smiles at people like he means it. Smiles! The Beast is gone. Gone, gone, gone!"

"That's wonderful. Too bad it didn't happen sooner," Alicia said, and Francesca's head bounced up and down in unreserved agreement. Alicia asked, "Did he say why the Beast left?" With *Frau* Koch not there, Alicia came out with the nickname without looking over her shoulder first to see whether any other teachers could hear.

Francesca frowned. "He said . . ." She paused, trying to make sure she got the words just right. "He said, with the political something the way it was—"

"The situation?" Alicia broke in.

"That's right. That's the word I couldn't come up with." Francesca started over: "He said, with the political sit-u-a-tion the way it was, it was better if *Frau* Koch did something else for a while. As far as I'm concerned, she can do something else forever."

"Maybe she will," Alicia said. "She liked Lothar Prützmann a lot, didn't she?" Francesca nodded again. Alicia continued, "Well, with Prützmann dead and gone and with the *Putsch* down the drain, naturally they're going to get rid of people like that. She's probably lucky she's not in jail. Or maybe she is."

"Ooh!" her sister said. "Ooh! I *hope* she is. She said Daddy deserved to be, back when they grabbed him and us. I hope she finds out what it's like." Francesca liked revenge.

"It could happen." Alicia didn't mind the idea of the Beast behind bars, either—far from it. And when one side won a political fight, the other side suffered. That had been true in the *Reich* ever since the Night of the Long Knives. Sooner or later, though, didn't revenge have to stop, or at least slow down? If it didn't, who'd be left after a while? That made more sense than Alicia wished it did. All the same, she couldn't help hoping vengeance wouldn't stop till *Frau* Koch got what was coming to her. She waved and called, "Hey, Trudi! Listen!"

"What's up?" Trudi Krebs called.

Alicia nudged her sister. "Tell her."

Francesca did. Trudi's eyes widened. "Really?" she whispered. Francesca crossed her heart. *I don't think Jews are supposed to do that*, went through Alicia's mind. *She* hadn't done it since she found out what she was. Then she stopped worrying about it. Trudi put one arm around her and the other around Francesca and started dancing both of them around in a circle, whooping while she danced.

"What's going on?" another girl called. Trudi and Francesca both shouted out the news. The other girl jumped straight up in the air. Then she ran over and started dancing, too. More girls heard the news, too, and joined the circle. It got bigger and bigger, spinning dizzily around the playground. A few boys even danced with them, mostly ones who'd had the Beast and knew what Francesca's class was escaping.

"*Was ist hier los?*" A man's voice—a teacher's voice—stopped the exuberance in its tracks where nothing else would have. "Alicia Gimpel, tell me at once."

"*Jawohl, Herr* Peukert." All panting and sweaty, Alicia paused. "It's nothing, *Herr* Peukert. We're just . . . happy, *Herr* Peukert."

Would he ask why they were happy? Would their being loud and disorderly count for more? It would have with a lot of teachers. *Herr* Peukert kept right on looking stern. But then, slowly and thoughtfully, he nodded. "Happy is not a bad thing for children to be. You may continue." He turned his back on the circle. He didn't turn around when the dancing started again.

"He knows why," Francesca whispered to Alicia. "He knows, but he doesn't care." Wonder filled her face.

"Nobody cares about what happened to the Beast." Alicia corrected herself: "Except that she's gone, I mean." She couldn't think of a better reason to dance.

When lunch ended and students went into their classrooms again, hers buzzed with the news. Nobody could hold still. Nobody could keep quiet. A lot of Alicia's classmates had suffered through a year with *Frau* Koch. Some of the ones who hadn't had a brother or sister who had, the way Alicia did. And all the boys and girls knew what the Beast was like.

Herr Peukert put up with it longer than Alicia thought he would. At last, though, he said, "Enough. If you want to dance at lunch or after school, that's your business. When you're here, though, we have work to do. You may not care about it now, but some of it will be important later on. Kindly buckle down and pay attention."

And they did, or most of them did. The bargain seemed fair to Alicia. The boys and girls—mostly boys—who kept on being noisy were the ones who were always noisy in class. *Herr* Peukert had a lot more patience than *Herr* Kessler had, but he didn't own an infinite supply. He gave the loudest, most obnoxious boy a swat. The whack of paddle on backside did an amazing job of calming the others down.

Nobody on the bus going home told the children to be quiet. They giggled and squealed and sang songs, most of them about the things a Beast did in the woods. They would have danced in the aisle, but that was too much for the long-suffering bus driver. "You got to stay in your seats," he shouted over the din in the bus. "You got to. Them's the rules, by God."

The children did sit down. Maybe that was simply fear about what would happen to them if they didn't, but maybe it was something more, too. In the *Reich*, few arguments carried more weight than *them's the rules*. The rules and good order went hand in hand, and German children learned to obey along with their other lessons.

But we wouldn't obey Lothar Prützmann, even if the Beast thought we ought to, Alicia thought. Then something else crossed her mind—*what do you mean, we?* She couldn't automatically think of herself as a German any more. That was what being a Jew did to her: it made her an outsider in her own country.

Part of her still wished for the feeling of belonging she'd had before she found out what she was. But, considering a lot of the things Germans had done, maybe being on the outside looking in was the better part of the bargain.

* * *

Had Lise Gimpel expected miracles from the new *Reichstag*, she would have been disappointed. Since she expected very little, she found herself pleasantly surprised every now and again. The delegates chose Rolf Stolle as their Speaker. The *Gauleiter* used his new bully pulpit to go right on slanging Heinz Buckliger for not doing enough, and for not doing it fast enough. That didn't surprise Lise at all.

Laws cutting back the powers of the SS did. So did the public hangings of a couple of Lothar Prützmann's chief henchmen. The dangling bodies—shown on the evening news—declared the new laws had teeth. The lesson was unsubtle and thoroughly Nazi, but no less effective for that.

Holland held elections, too, and chose a parliament with a non-Fascist majority. Panzers didn't roll. The German Foreign Ministry said not a word. Dutchmen didn't dance in the streets. They didn't seem to want to give the *Reich* any excuse to change its mind. Lise couldn't blame them.

As summer gave way to fall, Heinrich said the Americans were getting friskier than ever. "What will they do?" Lise asked him. "Will they try to rebel?"

"I don't think so. I hope not," her husband answered. "That would be just what . . . some people needed." He still spoke carefully. The house might be bugged.

"How hard would the government . . . the way it is now . . . try to stop them?"

"I don't know that, either," Heinrich said. "But if the government . . . the way it is now . . . didn't try to stop them, I don't think it would be the government for very long."

"But they really have put a boot on the SS's neck," Lise protested.

"I wasn't talking about the SS. I was talking about the *Wehrmacht,*" Heinrich said. "The Army won't put up with weakness here, and it won't want to let the Yankees get too strong. They aren't like the Dutch or the Czechs. They could be rivals. They could be worse rivals than the Empire of Japan, because they're more like us. The *Wehrmacht* wouldn't like that at all, and how can you blame it?"

Lise eyed her husband before answering. He'd tacked on the last half dozen words, she judged, to keep anyone on the other end of a bug happy. "Who possibly could?" she said in the same spirit. "After it broke up the *Putsch*, who could blame it for anything?"

Heinrich started to nod, then caught himself and wagged a finger at her, as if to say, *Naughty, naughty*. Lise stuck out her tongue. Maybe she'd meant you couldn't blame the *Wehrmacht* for anything because it hadn't done anything blameworthy. Or maybe she'd meant you didn't dare blame it for anything, because it was the greatest power in the land. Which? Her green eyes dancing, she shook her head. She was a woman. She was entitled to her mysteries. And she wasn't altogether sure herself.

"What about the Czechs?" she asked, changing the subject a little. "Will the *Reich* let them go?"

Her husband shrugged. "Beats me. They have the vote last summer to back up their declaration of independence. And if anybody can outfinagle the Foreign Ministry, it's the fellow they've got leading Unity. He can make you feel ashamed when you do something that isn't on the up-and-up, and how many people are able to do that? But . . ."

"Yes. But." Lise knew why Heinrich hesitated. The Czechs were Slavs, and Slavs, even Slavs like the Czechs who'd been entangled in German affairs since time out of mind, were in the National Socialist way of thinking *Untermenschen*. If you once started making concessions to *Untermenschen*, didn't you acknowledge they might not be so inferior after all? And if you acknowledged that, how did you justify the massacres and the slave labor that had filled the last seventy years?

Even more to the point, if you acknowledged that Slavs—or some Slavs—might not be *Untermenschen*, didn't you take a step towards acknowledging that Jews also might not be *Untermenschen*? *Could* a National Socialist government take a step in that direction?

"The *Führer* has said mistakes were made in years gone by," Heinrich said; if the *Führer* said it, it couldn't possibly be treasonous—as long as he stayed *Führer*. "If we decide to set some of those mistakes to rights, that wouldn't be so bad."

"No. Of course it wouldn't," Lise answered. Even though the Czechs were doing most of the agitating these days, they'd got off relatively easy. How could the *Reich* make amends to the relative handful of Poles and Russians and Ukrainians who still survived?

And, for that matter, how could the *Reich* make amends to the handful of Jews who, in spite of everything, still survived? Lise knew an impossibility when she saw one. Come to that, she didn't want a parade of blackshirts and Party *Bonzen* clicking their heels and apologizing to her. That sort of spectacle might appeal to Susanna, but then Susanna reveled in opera. All Lise wanted was to be left alone, to get on with her life regardless of what she happened to be.

"We're asking questions we couldn't even have imagined a couple of years ago," Heinrich said. "Next to the questions, the answers don't seem quite so important."

"Says who?" Lise inquired sarcastically. "If the Security Police had come up with a different answer to their question a few months ago, you wouldn't be here trying to come up with answers to yours." *And the girls wouldn't be here, either,* she thought, *and it wouldn't matter whether I was here or not because I'd be dead inside.*

After a brief pause, her husband nodded. "Well, you're right," he said. One of the reasons they'd stayed pretty happily married the past fifteen years was that they were both able to say that when they needed to.

"Politics!" Lise turned the word into a curse. "I wish politics never had anything to do with us. I wish we could just go on about our business."

"Part of our business is making the *Reich* better. That's part of everybody's business right now, I think," Heinrich said. "If we don't make it better, what'll happen? We saw before the election—other people will make it worse, that's what."

Lise wanted to quarrel with him. But she remembered too well the horror that had coursed through her when Lothar Prützmann's tame announcer started going on about the State Committee for the Salvation of the Greater German *Reich*. And, remembering, she too said those three little words almost as important as *I love you:* "Well, you're right."

Heinrich, Lise, and the girls closed their umbrellas when they came up onto the Stutzmans' front porch. The walk from the bus stop had been wet, but not too wet. Winter was thinking about making way for spring. It hadn't got around to doing it yet; still, the worst of the nasty weather was probably past. Heinrich dared hope so, anyway.

All three Gimpel girls raced for the doorbell. Francesca rang it a split second before Alicia or Roxane could. Heinrich and Lise smiled over the girls' heads. They would do that at elevators, too, which made their parents require that they take turns pressing those buttons. *Anyone would think they're children or something*, went through Heinrich's mind. He smiled again.

Esther Stutzman opened the door. "Come in! Come in! Welcome! Welcome!" she said, and stood aside. Delicious odors wafted out of the doorway: cooking meat, new-baked bread, and something else, something spicy, Heinrich couldn't quite place.

"Oh, good—you've got a mat out," Lise said. "We don't want to drip all over your front hall." She wagged a warning finger at the girls. "Don't you go running all over till you get out of your raincoats, do you hear me?" The warning came just in time. Alicia was trembling with eagerness to charge up to Anna's room.

"Is Susanna here?" Heinrich asked.

"She got here twenty minutes ago," Esther answered. Now she and Heinrich were the ones who smiled. Susanna always showed up early. Esther turned to Alicia, Francesca, and Roxane. "Why don't we hang those coats on the bar for the shower curtain in the downstairs bathroom here? That way, they won't get anything else wet." Heinrich and Lise followed so they could hang their coats in the bathroom, too.

Lise asked, "Did Gottlieb get leave from the *Hitler Jugend*?"

Esther shook her head. "I'm afraid not. He's stuck somewhere out in the provinces, communing with his shovel." Heinrich's laugh wasn't far from a giggle. He hadn't been ideal material for the *Hitler Jugend;* he was slow and ungainly and nearsighted and none too strong. But, by God, his spade had always gleamed, blade and handle both. He'd seen at once that survival lay in that direction, and he'd been right. He hadn't been an analyst yet, but he'd already thought like one. *Communing with his shovel.* He'd have to remember that. He could tell it at the office. Who hadn't gone through the *Hitler Jugend*?

"Come on," Anna said, appearing behind Esther as if by magic. The Gimpel girls were off like three brown-haired shots.

Esther nodded to Heinrich and Lise. "Here we are," she said.

"Yes." Heinrich nodded, too. "Here we are. There were times this past year when I wouldn't have given a pfennig for our chances, but here we are."

"What can I get you?" Esther asked.

"Beer will do," he answered.

"For me, too, please," Lise said.

They followed Esther toward the kitchen. Susanna sat on the sofa, scotch on the table in front of her. She got up to hug Heinrich and Lise. She and Heinrich each raised an eyebrow at the other. They were, in a way, veterans of the same campaign. It hadn't lasted long and there hadn't been many casualties, but it could have been much worse, and they both knew it.

"Did you ever find new bridge partners?" Susanna asked him.

"We play every now and then, but not regularly, not the way we used to," he replied. "Willi and I still get along fine at work, but. . . ."

"Yes. But," Lise said pointedly. "It's hard to play cards with somebody who tried to seduce your husband and then tried to kill him." Heinrich wondered which of Erika's transgressions his wife resented more. Since asking would have landed him in hotter water than knowing was worth, he expected he'd go right on wondering.

Esther came back with two steins of pale gold pilsner. "Here you are." She gave Heinrich one and Lise the other.

"Thanks." Heinrich sipped. He nodded appreciatively. "Is that—?"

"Pilsner Urquell?" Esther said it before he could. She nodded, too. "It's good beer. And besides, buying it sends the Czechs a little money. They deserve all the help we can give them." Her usually sunny face clouded for a moment. "Anyone who wants to get away from the *Reich* deserves all the help we can give them."

"*Omayn,*" Lise said softly. She and Heinrich and Esther and Susanna all smiled. That particular pronunciation of the word ordinary Germans said as *amen* was one Jews could only use among themselves, which meant it was one they couldn't use very often. Hearing it reminded Heinrich he was part of a small but very special club.

"Where's Walther?" he asked, at the same time as Lise was saying, "What smells so good?"

"I'm carving the goose," Walther called from the kitchen, answering both questions at the same time. He added, "It probably won't be the neatest job in the world, because the joints aren't quite in the same places as they are on a capon. But the taste won't change. Esther's responsible for that."

"The two of you cooked goose last summer, too," Susanna said. "Lothar Prützmann's, I mean."

Esther blushed like a schoolgirl. "Who can say for sure? The *Putsch* might have fallen apart anyhow. The SS had already started shooting at the *Wehrmacht* at the Berlin televisor station, and that would have started things rolling downhill on Prützmann all by itself."

Heinrich shook his head. "Don't sell yourselves short. You weren't in the square when Stolle shouted out that Prützmann was a Jew. It took the wind right out of the SS panzer troopers' sails, and it gave the crowd something new and juicy to yell at them." He sipped from his beer. "I was yelling it myself." That he'd yelled it embarrassed him now, though it hadn't then.

"So was I, as loud as I could." Susanna sounded proud and guilty at the same time.

Walther came out. He was wearing an apron, to guard against grease. He had a beer in one hand for himself and in the other a glass of liebfraumilch, which he gave to Esther. Heinrich raised his own seidel in salute. "Here's to getting that story out."

"I'm just glad it may have helped," Walther said. "At the time, I wasn't even close to sure I was doing the right thing."

"Who was?" Heinrich answered. "But it worked out—as well as anything could have, anyhow." If he'd had things exactly as he wanted them, everyone would have gathered at his house for supper, the way people had two years before. But he still had to assume the Security Police had planted bugs there, and that they were monitoring them. The blackshirts were down, but they weren't necessarily out.

Esther took his mind off his worries by saying, "Let's eat, shall we?" She went to the base of the stairs and hallooed for the children. Anna's bedroom door opened. She and the Gimpel girls reluctantly emerged. Whatever they'd been doing in there, they'd had a good time at it.

The table groaned with food. The goose was stuffed with sauerkraut and caraway seeds, and was done to perfection. There was liver dumpling soup, a purée of yellow peas, boiled potatoes with plenty of butter to slather on them, and a medley of green peas, carrots, asparagus, kohlrabi, and cauliflower garnished with more butter and salt and chopped parsley. There was home-baked bread with cinnamon and raisins and candied cherries—that accounted for the enticing spicy scent Heinrich had noticed when Esther opened the door. And there was a peach cobbler, if by some accident anyone had room for it.

Pilsner Urquell and liebfraumilch and Glenfiddich flowed freely for the grownups. For the children, as there had been two years earlier, there was wheat beer with raspberry syrup, not a treat they got every day. Anna and Alicia and Francesca were careful about how much they drank. Roxane wasn't. She put down a big glass of beer and turned almost as red as the syrup. She was yawning long before dessert, which didn't keep her from making a pretty good dent in the cobbler.

But that finished her off. Her eyes started to sag shut, no matter how she fought to keep them open. When she swayed in her chair, Heinrich went over and picked her up. "I'm not sleepy," she said indignantly, around a yawn that showed off her tonsils.

"I know, sweetheart," he said, "but I'm going to take you up to Anna's bedroom to rest for a little while anyway." She didn't argue with him, a telling measure of how worn she was. He carried her up the stairs. That was harder work than he'd expected; he'd put away a lot of food himself. When he laid her on the bed, she started to snore. He watched her for a minute or two to make sure she wasn't pretending, then smiled, shook his head once or twice, and went back down to the dining room.

He hadn't even sat down before Francesca said, "Something funny's going on." She pointed to Alicia. "When you turned ten like this, you got to stay up late, too, and Roxane and I had to go to bed. I remember."

Alicia looked at Heinrich. When he didn't say anything, she did: "*You're* ten now, so it's your turn."

"My turn for what?" Francesca asked, curiosity and suspicion warring in her voice.

Alicia looked at Heinrich again. This time, he knew he had to speak. Despite all he'd eaten and drunk, fear made his heart pound. The past two years had taught him more about danger than he ever wanted to know. But if this didn't go forward through time, what was the point to all that danger? None. None at all. He licked his lips. "Well, Francesca, we've got a secret to tell you. . . ."